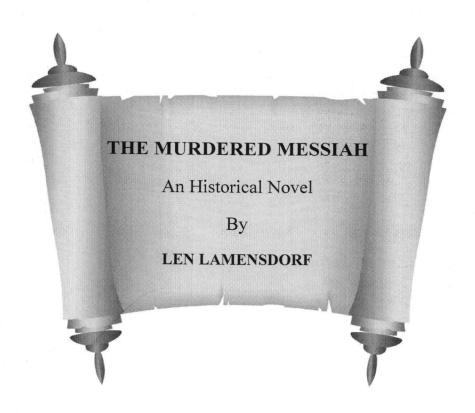

THE MURDERED MESSIAH

An Historical Novel

By

LEN LAMENSDORF

Foreword By Hal Taussig

SeaScape Press, Ltd.

Westlake Village, California

SeaScape Press™ 3835 E. Thousand Oaks Blvd., Suite 442
Westlake Village, CA 91362
Phone: 800-929-2906
Websites: www.lenlamensdorf.com
         www.murderedmessiah.com

SeaScape Press™ is a trademark of SeaScape Press, Ltd.

First Printing 2016

10 9 8 7 6 5 4 3 2 1

Printed in the United States of America
Cover by Mark Jacobsen

**Publisher's Cataloging-in-Publication
(Provided by Quality Books, Inc.)**
Lamensdorf, Leonard.
The Murdered Messiah: an historical novel / by Len Lamensdorf.
pages cm
Includes bibliographical references.
LCCN 2014908557
ISBN: 97809852381-0-0
Softcover ISBN: 97809852381-7-9
Ebook ISBN: 97809852381-1-7

1. Jesus Christ—Fiction.
2. Christianity—Origin—Fiction.
3. Historical fiction.   I. Title.

PS3562.A4635M87 2014   813'.54
QBI14-600089

FOREWORD

BY HAL TAUSSIG

Len Lamensdorf's novel, *The Murdered Messiah* places Jesus, as never before, within the crosshairs of the Roman Empire's massive violence. Long overdue, this fictional treatment gets at the character of daily life in Galilee under the Roman brutality of the first century. For the last two decades scholarship about the first century has revealed how crucial the endemic imperial violence is to an understanding of Jesus and the movements he inspired. Now this novel brings this central dimension of the life of Jesus to the fore in lucid prose, mapping it on his very character and surroundings that make Sunday School lessons look quaint and distorted by virtue of these major missing pieces.

The graphic title of *The Murdered Messiah* leads the way in laying bare how the collision of the social distress of an occupied country and peasant life in the eastern Mediterranean was inevitably combustible. Unmasking the way Christianity's traditional telling of Jesus's story and modern conventional piety have made the deep drama of Jesus enmeshed in the middle of roaring cruelty and loss into sentimental pabulum, this gripping new novel allows a whole set of meanings to emerge for the 21st century reader.

At the same time readers can take comfort in how close this story comes to a traditional portrait of the religious meaning of what a messianic character might look like in the first century. Thus, while this book opens extremely important historical perspectives, many readers will find much of the traditional character of Jesus still in place. To a great degree—and probably to the relief of many readers—the picture of Jesus as a miracle worker and Jewish religious teacher remains in full view. This does allow the valuable new historical picture of Jesus as a victim of murderous political intrigue by Roman tyrants to come into full view by affirming key religious tenets of a more traditional universe than would be comfortable for a *great* many historians.

Author Len Lamensdorf brings a broad and impressive background of fictional publications, film-making, and television direction to this major project. He has also done serious historical research, which far outshines the recent similar works of non-historians Anne Rice and Bill O'Reilly about Jesus. Not incidentally, Lamensdorf makes the most of his own Jewish background in thinking about the meaning of the life of Jesus for contemporary readers. Far more generous to conventional Christian meanings of the historical Jesus than I, Lamensdorf nevertheless contributes a significantly framed set of meanings from a Jewish perspective that have an important place in 21ˢᵗ century meditations on Jesus.

Author of 14 books, Hal Taussig teaches New Testament and Early Christianity at the Union Theological Seminary in New York and is Professor of Early Christianity at the Reconstructionist Rabbinical College. He is an ordained United Methodist minister. His books include A New New Testament: A Bible for the 21ˢᵗ Century Combining Traditional and Newly Discovered Texts; In the Beginning Was the Meal: Social Experimentation and Early Christianity Identity; and A New Spiritual Home: Progressive Christianity at the Grass Roots. His mediography includes the New York Times on-line edition, the Daily Show, Time Magazine and Newsweek opinion pages, the New York Times op-ed page, People Magazine, and Paula Zahn Now.

INTRODUCTION

From award-winning author, playwright and screenwriter, Len Lamensdorf, comes a thrilling new account of the life of Jesus (Joshua) of Nazareth, presented as an historical novel, based on original research and a profound understanding of the Gospels and centuries of relevant literature. Did Jesus believe he was the son of God? Of course, every Jewish male believed he was the son of God. Did Jesus consider himself to be divine? A very different question and one *The Murdered Messiah* seeks to answer. Did Jesus think he was the Messiah? Perhaps. Must the Messiah be a king? A warrior? A priest? A prophet? All of the above? Who did Jesus believe himself to be and how did he conceive his earthly mission? Why would a man whose entry into Jerusalem at Passover was a triumph, be suddenly and mysteriously murdered by the Romans?

The Gospels tell us nothing from the time Jesus spoke to the rabbis in the Temple when he was 12 until he began his ministry 18 years later. Some speculate that he traveled to Egypt, to Mesopotamia, even to India. Nonsense; Jesus never left Israel except to travel briefly to Tyre and Sidon and lands east of the Jordan. There is nothing in Christian scripture about his personal life. A young Jewish male of that era would almost certainly have been married. Was Jesus married? If so, what happened to his wife—to his children, if he had any?

If he were the Messiah, how could he be viciously murdered? Theologians have devised an explanation for the inexplicable: *He died for our sins.* Why is God so cruel that he demands this act of redemption? The Jewish people were the only true monotheists on the planet. Hundreds of thousands of Jews had congregated in Jerusalem to celebrate Passover, the feast of liberation. But if they were not miserable sinners, what was the reason for Jesus's terrible sacrifice?

Had he traveled throughout Israel, preaching the law and the love of God only to fall prey to the machinations of Pontius Pilate, one of the cruelest men in a very cruel empire?

The Murdered Messiah unravels these riddles and reveals the true nature of this remarkable man, with reverence for his extraordinary sacrifice and his passionate love for God.

Len Lamensdorf is the award-winning author of 9 novels, 3 full-length plays and one successful feature film. He is an honors graduate of the University Chicago College and Law School (editor, Law Review), and completed his post-graduate work at Harvard Law. For a more detailed biography see the Author's Biography following the Epilogue.

Opening Note

The man known to us as Jesus of Nazareth was almost certainly not known by that name during his lifetime. Jesus is the Greek translation of the Hebrew, *Yeshua* or *Yehoshua,* and since his mother, Miriam (Mary) and Joseph (Yosef) were observant Jews, they would have called him by his Hebrew name. If he had used the Greek, *Jesus,* he would have been treated with even greater suspicion than he actually suffered. The English equivalent is Joshua, which I have used so the reader can read these books without the automatic approval or disapproval that the Greek name, *Jesus,* brings with it. I have used Miriam instead of Mary for similar reasons.

There are many quotations from Jewish and Christian Scripture and other sources in these books. Many readers will immediately recognize them, but I have not included footnotes in the text so as not to interrupt the flow of the story. Most quotations are referenced in the Section of this book entitled *Notes and Citations.* The primary sources I have used are the King James Version, the Revised Standard Version and the New International Version, as published in the 1981 edition of the "New Layman's Parallel Bible." (See *Selected Bibliography* on the website). Errors and misquotations, if any, are mine alone.

Other Works by Len Lamensdorf

Novels:

Kane's World
In the Blood
The Will to Conquer Trilogy:
    The Crouching Dragon
    The Raging Dragon
    The Flying Dragon
Gino, the Countess & Chagall
The Ballad of Billy Lee:
    George Washington's Favorite Slave
The Mexican Gardener

Plays:

The Guest House
The Survival Game
The Ballad of Billy Lee

Film:

Cornbread, Earl & Me
    Executive Producer & Screenwriter
    Nominated for 5 NAACP *Image* Awards
Remake/Sequel in production

In Development

Angie & Little Marvin screenplay
Enamorada: Mom & the Movie Star (novel)
Caper (Film Treatment)
2 Untitled Novellas

CRITICAL PRAISE FOR LEN LAMENSDORF, whose novels have won Gold and Silver Benjamin Franklin Awards, three "Ippys," (Independent Publishers Award} and the

ForeWord Reviews Book-of-the-Year Award.

The Ballad of Billy Lee—George Washington's Favorite Slave
"One of the most poignant untold stories in American history"

— Joseph J. Ellis
Pulitzer Prize and National Book Award author

"I have always imagined [Billy Lee] much as you presented him: garrulous and funny, warm and achingly human ... perceptive about the momentous events he viewed from Washington's side...My congratulations."

— Ron Chernow
Pulitzer Prize winning author

Gino, the Countess & Chagall
"Lamensdorf presents a glowing tribute to the world of art through the life of a talented and charming painter who personifies a zest for life"

— *Publishers Weekly*

The Raging Dragon (Book 2-Will to Conquer Trilogy)
"Move over J.K. Rowling [this book] is a heart-stopping, history packed jaunt through Paris in the 1960s. From old airplanes to far older castles, from the Sorbonne to the eerie catacombs, readers will devour this tale to the exciting end."

— Gayle Lynds, *New York Times*best-selling author
***The Book of Spies* and many others**

The Mexican Gardener
"A true thriller—a pulse-pounding suspense-filled read!"

— **Fred Klein, Executive book editor and TV host.**
(Finalist for Book of the Year – *ForeWord)*

The Crouching Dragon (Book 1-Will to Conquer Trilogy)
"an unusual, intriguing adventure tale, with a touch of fantasy gaming...
suspense laden."

— **Sally Estes**
*Booklist (***American Library Association)**

The Flying Dragon (Book 3-Will to Conquer Trilogy}
"A fitting conclusion to this excellent trilogy, with a cutaway of the White
House, plus a map of D.C. and many fine illustrations.

— **Fran Halpern**
National Public Radio, author and host

"Lamensdorf has brilliantly mastered the subtle yet appealing way of teaching real history as a backdrop to his heroes' escapades...."

— *ForeWord Magazine*

The Raging Dragon (Book 2-Will to Conquer Trilogy) won the Children's
Choice Award, given by **The Children's Book Council** and **The International Reading Association**

Figure 1: Fishermen on the Sea of Galilee
Image believed to have been printed between 1890 and 1905

As always, for Erica

∞

"Love God and
   Love Thy Neighbor as Thyself
That is the Law,
   All the rest is commentary."
       — Rabbi Hillel
       1st Century, C.E.

You are not merely a drop in the ocean,
you are also the ocean in a drop
       — Rumi
          13th century Persian poet

Map 1

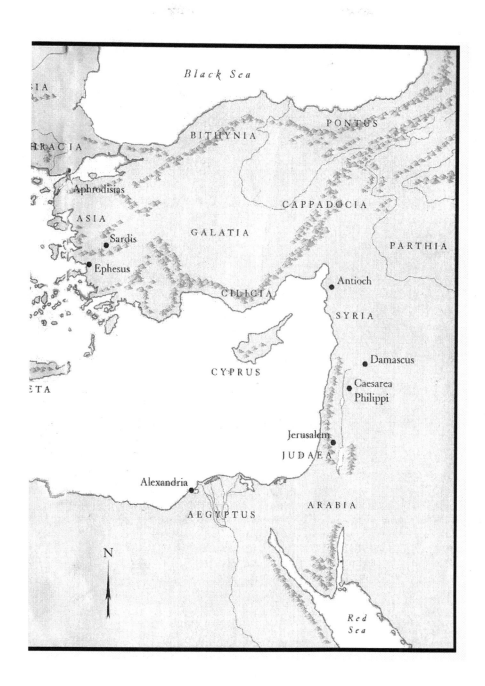

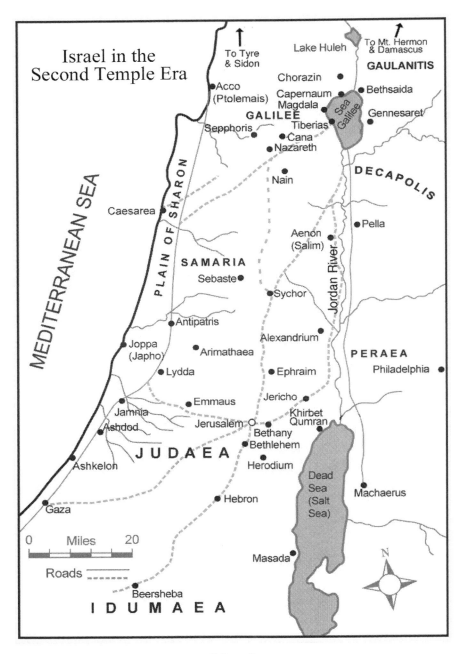

Map 2

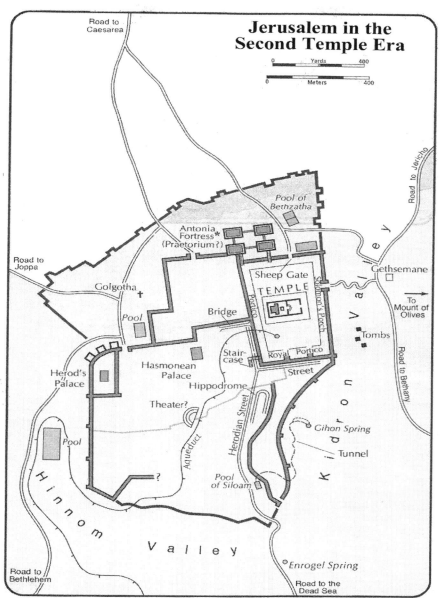

* This illustration shows the Antonia Fortress separated from the Temple, with 2 lines of steps providing direct access to the porticos, but this seems unlikely and the fortress is shown elsewhere as built into or against the North wall, with possible access onto the portico roofs.

Map 3

CONTENTS

BOOK ONE
MIRACLE IN GALILEE

BOOK TWO
MASSACRE OF THE INNOCENTS

BOOK THREE
RISING STORM

BOOK FOUR
WAGING PEACE

BOOK FIVE
DEATH AND TRANSFIGURATION
& EPILOGUE

EPILOGUE

Notes and Citations
Selected Bibliography
Attributions
Author Bio
Links

HISTORICAL TIME-LINE

BEFORE THE COMMON ERA (B.C.E.)

c. 1000   David makes Jerusalem the capital of his kingdom. Later, his son, Solomon,builds the First Temple.

920   Solomon dies; the kingdom is divided into Israel (North) and Judah (South).

722   Assyria under Sargon II conquers Jerusalem and deports the population.
Era of the prophet Isaiah, c. 745-665.

586   Babylon conquers Jerusalem, destroys the Temple and deports population toBabylon.
Jeremiah (died c. 570 B.C.E.)
Ezekial (final vision c. 571 B.C.E.)

c. 532   Persia conquers Babylon; Cyrus the Great permits exiles to return and to rebuild the Temple.
Prophet Daniel (Dating uncertain)

332   Alexander the Great conquers Judea. After his death in 323 B.C.E., Ptolemys in Egypt and Seleucids in Syria rule Judea for approximately 150 years.

167   Seleucid ruler Antiochus Epiphanes IV introduces pagan rites in Jerusalem,triggering the Maccabean revolt (Hebrew Festival: Hannukah).

141   Victorious, priestly Hasmonean family established as ruling dynasty of independent Jewish kingdom. Also origin of Dead Sea Scrolls community
(Essenes?)

63   Roman general Pompey conquers Jerusalem, violates the Temple. Hasmoneans thereafter reign as client kings of Rome.

37 Herod becomes sole ruler; builds the so-called Second Temple onmagnificent scale.

c. 4 Death of Herod. He has divided his kingdom between his sons Archelaus (Judea),
Antipas (Galilee and Perea); Philip (Transjordan).
Birth of Jesus (Joshua) of Nazareth

COMMON ERA (C.E.)

6 Augustus deposes Archelaus. Judea becomes a second-grade province under a Prefect (provincial governor), subordinate to the provincial legate of Syria.
A census promulgated by the new administration provokes a revolt led byJudas (Judah) the Galilean, which ends with the slaughter of thousands of Jews, many by crucifixion.

26 Pontius Pilate appointed Prefect of Judea; will rule until 36; see below.
Pilate raises Roman standards over Temple, precipitating protests at Caesarea.

28+/- Joshua (Jesus) baptized by John the Immerser (Baptist). John is later beheaded by Antipas at Machaerus.

28-30 Joshua (Jesus) begins his mission;

33-36 Joshua (Jesus) crucified in Jerusalem.

36 Pilate slaughters thousands of Samaritans on Mount Gerizim, and is recalled to Rome.
Caiaphas is deposed as High Priest.

Source: Paula Fredriksen: *Jesus of Nazareth: King of the Jews.* Vintage Books, 2000

Modern Jerusalem

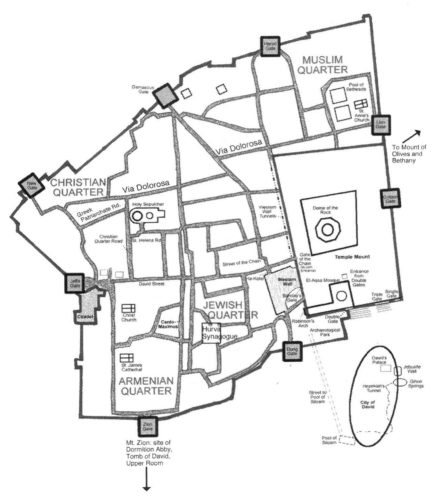

Map 4: Jerusalem, Old City: Modern Era

Figure 2: Western Wall Jerusalem
Israeli area in foreground. Viewed over wall: Dome of the Rock, left;
Al Aqsa Mosque, right; Mount of Olives and Bethany, beyond.

Figure 3: Church of the Holy Sepulchre, Jerusalem

PROLOGUE

The pounding on the door of my tiny apartment shocked me from sleep at 3 A.M. on a Saturday morning. I didn't immediately respond because I resented being awakened on the Sabbath, the one day I could sleep late. But I knew the voice yelling at me—Wajeeh Nuseibeh.

"Yossi, Yossi! Wake up! It's me, Wajeeh!"

I dragged myself out of bed, naked, the way I usually slept, slipped the locks and grudgingly opened the door a crack, but Wajeeh pushed his way in. Wajeeh is a nice middle-aged fellow with a balding head and a trim beard, always neatly dressed and usually quite calm. He's a thoroughly reliable sort, and that's why his family and another Muslim family, the Joudehs, have been entrusted with the only key to the most venerated shrine in Christendom, the Church of the Holy Sepulchre, in Jerusalem. According to tradition, their families have been performing this task for over one thousand years.

"You must come, Yossi!" Wajeeh cried, averting his eyes from my nakedness. "There is no time!"

"What's—"

"—Come, come! They will kill each other!"

I immediately knew who he meant, and I pulled on pants and a shirt without underclothes and jammed my feet into sandals, while Wajeeh virtually shoved me out the door. It was still dark, but the streets were filled with thousands of pilgrims dressed in thousands of different styles, some carrying flaming torches, some flashlights, all with unlit candles, and all hurrying to the same place. Wajeeh never let go of my arm, dragging me through the narrow streets of the Old City, not letting go even when we bumped into other people or bounced off walls. It wasn't easy running on the uneven streets, even though I was accustomed to this part of the city. I'd been a guide with the Government Tourist service for a dozen years and I knew every corner of Jerusalem well, but I lived in the Jewish Quarter of the Old City and loved it best of all.

"What's wrong now?"

Wajeeh was fit as well as trim, and even though he was running, he spoke without wheezing. "The church is filled to bursting with pilgrims waiting for the Holy Fire..."

I knew he meant the flame that miraculously appears within the chapel, and then is handed out by the Patriarch on a candle that is passed, hand to hand, candle to candle, by worshipers throughout the church. The entire building seems to explode in flame that races out into the streets, and according to some, across the world.

"...But the Patriarch has refused to enter the chapel. All of the priests and brothers, the Copts, Ethiopians, Armenians, Syriacs, Greek Orthodox, Roman Catholic, are blocking the way. Blows have been struck, pilgrims are screaming, Israeli soldiers can't get through the crowds."

"They're always battling--why is this different?"

Hearing this tale, I had unconsciously slowed my steps, but Wajeeh tightened his grip and pulled me along. I bounced off a priest with a long beard and a black robe, and I think he cursed me, but I didn't recognize the dialect.

The streets of the Old City are hundreds if not thousands of years old and they angle arbitrarily, the walls built with blocks and bricks of the peach-colored limestone that has been quarried in the area since the beginning. Even these narrow lanes are often fronted by shops, and a few of them were open despite the hour. As merchants placed their fruits and vegetables, trinkets and coins on display, the byways narrowed even more, and it wasn't long before we were jammed tightly with the pilgrims, virtually unable to move.

I marveled at Wajeeh, who didn't share religion or ethnicity with any of the sects that controlled the church, and yet he treated them as members of his family, or at least as his familial responsibility.

I knew the priests and monks in the church pretty well. I'd led many tours there during the dozen years I'd worked for the Israel Tourist Service, and I always urged the tourists to contribute generously to the various charities that supported the church. Not all of the priests were crazy about Jews, but they'd learned that I was a friendly, reliable sort of fellow, and a couple of years earlier I'd thrown myself down on Amos, the Armenian monk, when the holy fire had ignited his clothing and he was in danger of burning to death. They say I saved his life. Also, from time to time, I brought the holy fathers and brothers little gifts, Christian souvenirs from other places in Israel, and sometimes small packages of sweets; they didn't seem to mind that they were kosher. Another time, I'd talked the Israelis guarding the shrine out of arresting one of the Copts who had been attempting to punch an Ethiopian priest, but inadvertently slugged a soldier. I liked these fellows—not so much Father Paribas—he could be surly and irritating, but I was impressed with their devotion to the holy place, even if sometimes it was a bit extreme.

"Wajeeh!" I yelled, over the clamor of merchants and pilgrims—who should have been reverent and silent, but who jabbered at each other continually, "They're fighting again. So what?"

"Gregory is wielding a staff, and he struck the Copt, who is bleeding from the head, and Amos the Armenian is swinging a censer—solid bronze and twenty liters—while the others duck and scream. Constantinus, the Roman, is throwing punches at the air, but soon they will strike–they may already have struck!"

He yanked me harder, and by sheer willpower forced his way through the indignant crowd. When we reached the courtyard in front of the church there should have been more room, but it was jammed, too.

"What are they fighting about this time?" I yelled.

"The scrolls!" Wajeeh said.

That, too, was not a surprise. The leaders of the six sects had been arguing about the scrolls for as long as I could remember. It isn't well-known to the outside world, but archeologists and historians have been aware of the crypt beneath the Coptic Chapel for a very long time. No one knows what's in the crypt, if anything, but rumors of ancient scrolls have excited experts and the devout for a long time. Supposedly, there are six different locks to the crypt, and it can't be opened unless all of the keys are turned simultaneously. It makes for a good mystery, and I often told tour groups about it, even though—at the time--I didn't personally know if there was any truth to it.

Wajeeh yelled something more, but I didn't hear him. He turned and stared at me, even as he pulled me along.

"Didn't you hear me? The scrolls are missing!"

That *was* a shock. "Who took them?"

"No one knows—each one is accusing the others. They're all furious and frightened."

Ahead, close to the entrance, I glimpsed several Israeli soldiers. They carried no weapons that I could see, but they seldom did in this area, notwithstanding the suicide attacks. At least there was more light; the swinging lanterns threw a rosy glow on walls and faces. But there was only one entrance to the church; the authorities and the priests had been fighting over a second emergency entrance for years, but it had never been constructed. By now thousands of pilgrims and priests would be packed inside. If a fire started, thousands might die, from asphyxiation if not from flame.

As we continued to shove through the crowd of pilgrims, angering more and more of them, an Israeli sergeant yelled at us. He yelled in Arabic, which pleased me no end. I knew that with my bearded face and swarthy features, and my large, embroidered skullcap that could have been Muslim as easily as Jewish, I was often mistaken for an Arab.

"Shmuel!" I called. I knew the sergeant, a cheerful, burly fellow with a faint lisp.

"Yossi, why are you here? It's crazy inside, go home."

"I can't—Wajeeh says it's important—very important."

Shmuel shrugged. "I'll try to help you get in."

But he wasn't much help. The pilgrims weren't crazy about having Israeli soldiers enter the church. Some of them were Arab Christians, and that made them even more unhappy to see the military at the holy shrine. A few of them shoved back, but soon we were inside, working our way through the darkness. Every lamp and flashlight had been extinguished in anticipation of the Holy Fire.

We inched our way to the rotunda, mumbling apologies, and circled along the columns towards the Coptic chapel. It was dank and stuffy and the air was thick with incense and dirt and sweat and repressed ecstasy.

Then we heard them yelling at each other in their native dialects, while the pilgrims muttered with shock and outrage at their horrific threats and vile curses. That helped us get closer, for the pilgrims drew back in fear and confusion, while we were edging forward. Suddenly there were flashes of light.

There they were: six bearded men resplendent in robes and surplices, and the two patriarchs in tall gem-encrusted miters. Against tradition, Gregory, the Greek Orthodox priest, was swinging a lighted lamp that illuminated this strange gathering in slivers and shards and stripes. Amos, the Armenian, was swinging a censer that spilled a trail of smoke in circles like a puffed cigar. The pilgrims had backed away, clearing a space in front of the chapel, where the antagonists, circled and cursed, waved staffs, batons, censers and fists, yelling loudly. I heard an unexpected note of fear in their voices. They were blustering, filled with anger, and they might strike truly vicious blows at each other any second. But their rage didn't totally cover their doubts.

"It was you!" Gregory yelled, but he swung his lamp indiscriminately, not singling out just one.

"No!" said the Copt, a tiny man, holding his forehead where it was bleeding, just below a miter almost as tall as he was, and twirling a corded belt of some kind, screamed, "You, you, you!"

"You'll pay for this!"

"I'll kill you!!"

"You're going to Hell!"

Wajeeh shoved me and yelled, "Now—stop them!"

I stared at him, incredulous.

"Now," he yelled again, in a voice so loud that it startled everyone in the rotunda. "STOP THEM!"

For a brief moment there was a frozen tableau. Gregory with his lamp raised over his head, Amos with his arm held high and stiff, the censer swinging of its own inertia, Regulus the Copt, his corded belt unintentionally wrapping around his own neck.

"Wajeeh!" Gregory cried, "you've never been inside the crypt before!"

Again Wajeeh pushed me forward.

"Yossi," Amos said accusingly, "it's your Sabbath."

I straightened to my full, five feet and six inches. "You must stop fighting, my friends. It's almost Easter, and you cannot fail your people."

"The scrolls!" Gregory cried, anguish coloring his voice red and black. "They're gone!"

He advanced on me. We had only been a few feet apart to begin with, but now he was menacingly close. I had thought he liked me, but his eyes were crazed, and spittle shot from his lips with every word. He was trembling with anger and, I suspected, overwhelming fear.

"I'll help you find the scrolls!" I yelled. I don't why I said it, but I did. Perhaps to save myself from the huge priest bearing down on me.

Gregory stopped. "How?!" he demanded. "How will you find them?"

That struck a false note—as if Gregory knew where they were, and either believed I couldn't possibly know, or was fearful that I did. He looked like he might begin to move closer again.

"Don't hurt Yossi!" Wajeeh cried. "He's your friend!"

Gregory hesitated.

Amos, the Armenian, said, "He's right, Gregory. Smashing Yossi on the head won't help us find the scrolls."

Gregory wavered. I didn't know whether to run or stand fast. I had no idea what had prompted me to say I would find the scrolls.

Behind us, the crowd was beginning to murmur. "The Holy fire—where is the Holy Fire?" "Stop this fighting—send the holy father into the crypt." "Yes!" the pilgrims cried, "Now!" in twenty different languages.

The Patriarch suddenly broke from the group and headed towards the Sepulchre, with the crowd pressing behind him. In a moment the crowd was so thick, the priests and monks couldn't have struck each other without first clobbering the pilgrims.

Suddenly there was a flare of light—so bright that it blinded us. Then the Patriarch handed out a flaming candle, which he used to light candles for the other clergy, who each used his candle to light another candle, and then another and another and another. The church flared with light and the cheers of the crowd. The flaming light passed swiftly through the church and out into the streets. The pilgrims turned and tried to leave the church. Now was the time of greatest danger, with flames erupting everywhere and people rushing to reach the sacred fire and also to leave the church.

Gregory was still standing where he had been before. The crowd flowed around him, bounced off him, but did not move him. He stood staring at me, and now that there was light in the church, his eyes seemed black and he was even more ominous than before.

"What do you know?" he asked, his jaw tight, and the muscles trembling underneath the skin.

"You're sure the scrolls are gone?" I asked, temporizing.

Amos grabbed me by the collar and dragged me to the Coptic crypt.

"Look!" he said. "Empty! Empty!"

"Empty!" the others echoed, including Constantinus, who had been the first to have his candle lighted by the patriarch—beginning a remarkable ecumenical process.

"We'll form search parties," I said. "We'll scour every corner of the church. We'll find the scrolls."

"They're not in the church!" Gregory yelled, again raising my suspicions. "We've searched every corner."

"Every corner!" the others agreed.

But that didn't mean much. If one of the six groups had stolen the scrolls, they wouldn't have tried very hard to locate it.

"How can you be sure?" I asked. "None of you will allow the others into your own exclusive areas."

There was silence.

"You said you would find the scrolls," Gregory intoned. "How will you do it? When will you do it?"

"You've got to tell me why the scrolls are so important," I said, hoping to deflect Gregory's question until I had a decent answer—if ever.

The six men were silent again. But it was a strange kind of silence—a silence filled with energy. The Holy Land is a place that's dense with history and hatred, love and devotion. As you walk the streets of Jerusalem, you can feel the accumulated wisdom and conflict filling the air. The air is heavier, much heavier than anywhere else I've ever been, flooded with the words and deeds of thousands of years of cultures and civilizations, religions and cults, vying with each other. Voices seem to cry out from every corner of the land. There is no such thing as true silence in Jerusalem. The voices continually hum and chant and scream and sing, and you can hear them in your head, even during the night, even during a storm, even on the hottest day of the year.

I heard voices screaming and praying in that moment.

"If you don't tell me, I can't help you," I said, half hoping they would refuse and let me off the hook.

Regulus, the Coptic priest broke the silence. His voice was more a whisper, a vibration, an echo. "The scrolls challenge our faith—the faith of all of us. We don't know the exact words because we have all been forbidden to read them, sworn to secrecy."

"We would have destroyed the scrolls and solved the problem," Gregory said, "but we were also forbidden to do that."

"The sanctions go back to the Empress Helena, Constantine's wife," Constantinus said. "She discovered this site, the site of Golgotha, the crucifixion and the resurrection. She found the fragments of the true cross, and the relics that provide the basis for Christian faith, and ordered that a church be built here."

"The scrolls were given to her by persons unknown," Gregory said, speaking with more calm then I had expected. "St. Helena swore them to silence, and in each generation for nearly two thousand years, the keepers of the scrolls have given the same pledge."

"Why didn't she destroy them?" I asked.

"We don't really know," Amos, the Armenian, said, "but we're told that the giver of the scrolls was a descendent of the line of King David, and the scrolls were deemed too sacred to destroy."

"That's not all of it," Gregory said. "The legend is that he who destroyed the scrolls would himself be destroyed, and that this church would fall because of his actions, and the curse of his deeds would bring destruction on the world."

They were all nodding, a rare situation in itself, for they seldom agreed on anything. I began to feel a shiver of fear myself. What had I promised, and would the curse fall upon me?

They were all beginning to talk at once, and I barely heard the voice of Wajeeh behind me. A whisper. A single word. I turned to look at him, startled, but his face was blank, expressionless.

"Leila," he had said.

Leila. Leila Adjani. My ex-wife. Once Mrs. Yossi Granit, although she had never taken my name. The woman I still loved, but who had given up on me. An Israeli Arab who had abandoned me (I believed) to be with her people. I considered myself a peaceful, thoughtful Israeli, a Labor party man, who believed the Palestinians deserved their own homeland. But that was not enough for Leila.

Now, however, I began to understand. There were many men to whom Wajeeh might have turned when the priests battled. It was true that I knew them and they knew me, and we had a kind of friendship, but that was not all. Wajeeh knew that Leila was a noted archeologist and paleographer—an expert on the languages of the Middle East. I sometimes thought she had left me because I was not smart enough or well enough educated for her, which was true enough, but then, who would have been smart enough for this brilliant woman? I had been flattered that she liked me, astonished that she loved me, and profoundly grateful when she had married me. It was difficult to believe that she had divorced me over politics, but easier to accept than to think she considered me a fool.

Wajeeh was telling me that Leila was somehow involved in this mystery.

Gregory was yelling at me again. "Are you paying attention?" he asked. He looked as if he were considering shaking me.

"I'll take care of it!" I said, as forcefully as I dared, and while they stared at me I turned and stalked out of the church.

***

"Why didn't you tell me in the first place?"

"You had to see the holy men first," Wajeeh said, "to know how angry and frightened they are."

We were in Arab East Jerusalem, hurrying along the street called Salah ad-Din, named for the famous twelfth century sultan of Egypt and Syria, known in the west as Saladin. It wasn't safe for a Jew to be in this district, even in daylight, but Wajeeh was with me, and as I've said, I look generically Semitic—even Arabic, and I didn't stand out in this crowded neighborhood.

"Does she know I'm coming?" I asked.

"No," Wajeeh said.

"What makes you think she'll speak to me?"

Wajeeh looked surprised. "I thought you were on good terms."

"I mean, about the scrolls."

Wajeeh shrugged. "We'll see."

"Does she have them?"

"We'll see."

We passed the District Court building and turned into Abu Taleb and then into an even narrower street. I must say that East Jerusalem smells even more pungently than the Old City. Not bad smells, but sharp ones, and not all falafel. It has the smell of anxiety, of anger, of foreboding, but also of immense and repressed energy.

I had a pretty good idea where we were headed. Leila lived nearby, but I didn't think we were going to her apartment. She also had an office and workshop tucked behind and above a tobacconist, down an alley where the walls are so canted, you feel you have to walk leaning to one side or you'll crack your skull.

Just as we reached the turn-off, a burly figure came barreling out of Leila's alley. He wore Arab dress, kaffiyeh and all, but he wasn't an Arab, and despite his bent-over walk, and downcast eyes, I knew him: Avram Goren, the antiquities dealer. He was notorious for the items he bought and sold and the collection he claimed to own. The Israeli authorities hated him, for they said any item for sale on the open market was fraudulent. That was often true, but not always. They were trying to discourage the looting of tombs and other archeological sites, and if they could convince the world that all private dealers were phonies, supposedly the market would dry up and the thievery would end. That was ridiculous, but it was official policy.

I knew Goren pretty well. Leila had once taken me to his home on the Mount of Olives, an impressive old, limestone house, filled with objects that Goren claimed were authentic. It hardly mattered. Most of them were beautiful, and Avram had a marvelous story to go with each of them. If they were frauds, he had certainly done a good job of convincing wealthy collectors his finds were real; the sales of them accounted for his lavish style of living.

Goren didn't see us, and I had no intention of alerting him to our presence. In a moment, he had squeezed past us and was gone. I glanced at Wajeeh, but his expression was blank. Even so, I thought the corner of his mouth twitched very briefly.

We walked single file down the narrow alley, and indeed, Wajeeh was listing to the right. A few more feet, and there was a niche in the wall that revealed an extremely steep staircase. I followed Wajeeh up the stairs.

At the top was a heavy wooden door with a peephole in it. Wajeeh knocked several times, using a beat I'd have found difficult to copy. There was a long silence. He was about to knock again, when the door creaked in its tight frame and opened very slightly. The voice belonged to Leila.

"Salaam Aleikem, Wajeeh," she said, and the richness of her voice, the overtones and undertones gave the ancient greeting a vibrant, thrilling quality. Of course, I was still in love with her, but...

"Aleikem Salaam," Wajeeh said. "May we enter?"

There was a moment's hesitation, and then the door creaked open.

Leila. Tall, perhaps a tad taller than I am, with a slender figure. Eyes brown, almond-shaped, intense. Hair a very light brown, almost beige-blonde, unusual but not unheard of for an Arab girl. She wore a loose long-sleeved white cotton blouse, paint-stained jeans and worn sandals, very casual, but again, not rare in these times. Her hair was bound with a scarf, not a muslim-styled covering, just a plain, reddish scarf. There was a smudge of something on her forehead. Very endearing. She stepped aside and ushered us in.

"Shalom," I said, and she nodded briefly, but didn't respond.

Leila didn't offer us a seat, let alone something to drink. Her manners were atrocious for an Arab lady, but then, we had a history.

The room was large and indifferently furnished, with a couple of sloping drawing boards, a simple desk built of a large, heavily scored wooden door supported by concrete blocks. But the view through the outward and upward slanted windows was astonishing—the ancient city spread before us, stucco and stone houses, narrow twisting streets, the dun-colored crenellated Ottoman walls, and in the distance, the glinting tip of the golden Dome of the Rock. Within the room, books were piled everywhere—on the floor, on shelves, on desks. I didn't see any scrolls, but I wasn't expecting them to be lying around.

"He knows," Wajeeh said.

Leila didn't ask what I knew, didn't even respond.

"There is great danger," Wajeeh said, "that the holy fathers and their followers will begin a civil war."

"That's happened before," Leila said.

"Not like this," Wajeeh said. "They believe their most sacred duty has been breached. Not knowing who is to blame, they are ready to blame each other, even to martyr themselves to rectify the calumny."

"I've never seen them so angry," I said.

"Yossi prevented an immediate battle by promising the return of the scrolls."

A short, harsh laugh escaped Leila. "How will he do that?" She spoke as if I weren't even there.

Wajeeh temporized. "We saw Goren leaving here."

That wasn't precisely true—we had seen him exit the alley, but Leila's studio wasn't the only place that opened onto it. Still, Leila didn't deny Wajeeh's statement.

"What do you want of me?" Leila asked.

"To help us find and return the scrolls before it's too late."

"Perhaps it's already too late," Leila said. Her face was beginning to color, and the tone of her voice was rising.

Her words frightened me. "Have they been destroyed?" I asked. My voice was rising, too.

"For Christians," Leila said, her voice abruptly solemn but heavily charged, "it would have been better if they were destroyed."

I tried not to betray my astonishment, but at least, I thought, the scrolls are apparently still in existence.

Wajeeh sensed that Leila and I were on the verge of one of our famous quarrels—the repeated contretemps that had led to our breakup. I could never quite believe our marriage had foundered on religious matters.

Wajeeh was speaking. "In my experience, what is evil for Christians, is also evil for Muslims and Jews."

"Very pious," Leila said, and then she apparently realized how sarcastic her words sounded. Wajeeh was, by any standards, a very devout man, and she was fond of him. "If all men were like you, Wajeeh" she continued, "the world would be a far better place."

"Thank you," Wajeeh said, "but we're not thinking of the entire world, only this sacred city and those sacred scrolls."

"I've said too much," Leila said. "I'll take your concerns into account."

She unfolded her arms as if our meeting were over and she about to tell us to leave.

"You've not said enough," I told her. "It's clear you know the where-abouts of the scrolls and what's in them. The word will spread quickly. Avram Goren isn't known for his circumspection. He's probably shopped them already."

Suddenly there was a loud report, and one of Leila's tall windows exploded in a shower of glass shards. I grabbed Leila and pulled her down to the floor. Wajeeh, serene as ever, remained standing.

"Down, Wajeeh!" I yelled.

Another blast, and the wall opposite the windows erupted into shattered fragments of plaster, stone, and flying book pages. Wajeeh had flinched a bit, but remained standing.

I was aware of Leila under me, the softness of her skin, the smell of her hair. She sensed my reactions, shoved at me and slipped out from under my body. But she didn't stand up. I sat up and waited. I didn't have any idea what I was waiting for.

From the street, we heard the sounds of automatic weapons fire. Through the empty frames of the windows, clouds of smoke began to rise and drift.

Wajeeh strolled to the window and peered outside. "I don't think they're aiming at us," he said calmly. "The Israelis and militants are shoot-ing at each other."

"What does it matter where they're aiming," I said. "If they hit us we'll be just as dead."

Wajeeh actually smiled, but Leila surprised both of us.

"Get down!" she yelled, and Wajeeh instantly dropped to the floor.

Leila scrambled across the room, crouching low, opened a tall cabinet and pulled out an Uzi. That was the first time I had ever seen her with a weapon.

"Do you think," she said through tight lips, "they just happened to blow out my windows?"

She grabbed a handgun from the cabinet and slithered it across the floor to me.

"It's loaded," she said, her voice dropping to a near whisper. "Shoot anyone who comes through the door." Then, turning to Wajeeh, "Get behind the concrete blocks—they may protect you."

Wajeeh, for once, seemed rattled, but he followed instructions.

Leila sat cross-legged on the floor, the Uzi cradled loosely in her arms, but pointed towards the door.

A moment later, we heard the sound of footsteps racing up the staircase. Leila raised her weapon. Someone outside banged a fist against the door and yelled in Arabic, "Open up!"

Leila calmly fired the Uzi, raking the wooden door above the height of a man, and sending chips flying in every direction. There was a startled cry outside, a curse, and then footsteps retreated hurriedly down the stairs. A moment later there was a burst of gunfire outside and the rapid thud-thud of bullets hitting the door. They didn't penetrate, but the sound was unnerving. It was then I realized Leila's gunburst hadn't penetrated the door either. In fact I could see the shells embedded in the wood. Apparently the door was layered, with metal or some other material laminated between the wood panels.

Wajeeh was about to stand up again, but Leila, still staring at the door, raised a hand, and he sat down.

We waited. Minutes passed. Perhaps ten minutes, perhaps fifteen. I wanted to question Leila, but I didn't want to die with my mouth open, so I remained silent.

Finally, Leila stood up, walked to me and held out her hand. I thought it was a friendly gesture, and then I realized she wanted me to return the handgun. I gave it to her and she stored it and the Uzi in the cabinet.

"I suppose I'll have to explain," she said.

***

Leila was sitting on the floor again, almost in a lotus pose. When she spoke she was very composed, despite the could-have-been-deadly rain of bullets and the damage to her studio. "These documents are as important as the Dead Sea Scrolls, more important than the scrolls in the Geniza in Cairo, even the Nag Hammadi codices. Do you, does anyone, expect me to simply surrender such a find?"

"A find?" I couldn't help saying. "They were stolen."

Her eyes flashed. "The museums of the world are filled with works that you call stolen, from the Elgin Marbles in the British Museum to the jade in the Taiwan Museum taken from the mainland by Chiang Kai-shek. I don't believe anyone plans to give them back."

I was surprised—shocked, actually. I had always thought of Leila as profoundly honest. But now I knew that she had the scrolls. What could be in them that would change this honorable woman so drastically?

"If you knew," she said, understanding me as she always did, "you would feel the same way. Especially as an Israeli, as a Jew." She didn't speak contemptuously, but her voice was forceful and her stare implacable.

"Try me," I said.

There was another burst of gunfire, but it seemed to be farther away. I flinched, as usual, but not as much as before. Leila was watching me intently, and I was watching her. I don't think she flinched at all.

"First tell him how you acquired the scrolls," Wajeeh said.

My head was reeling. It seemed that Wajeeh knew much more about the scrolls than I had thought.

"They were stolen by Arabs connected to Hezbollah," Leila said, "the organization funded by Iran."

I noticed she didn't call them terrorists, only an "organization." That was worrisome. Even so, I couldn't believe that Leila had fallen so far that now she was affiliated with known terrorists.

"They disguised themselves as Christian pilgrims—monks in heavy robes with cowls," she said. "This past January, when the Orthodox were celebrating the date they believe was the birth date of Jesus, they joined the crowds at the Church of the Holy Sepulchre. Opening the crypt was no trick at all despite the six locks, which are almost identical, rotted and rusted, and could be opened with an ordinary pocket knife."

"No one noticed their action?" I asked.

"They were surrounded by real pilgrims who screened the view of them from the church fathers. The real pilgrims knew nothing about the scrolls and had no way of knowing the thieves weren't following some ancient ritual. It happened in a matter of minutes. They slipped the scrolls into their robes, replaced them with fakes and walked out of the church."

"You knew about this," I said to Wajeeh.

"A few days before the Christian Christmas last December, two well-dressed Arabs approached me as I left the church after opening the door. They said they were friends of my family from Nablus and they insisted on buying me tea at a local shop. They told me the scrolls had been stolen from the Arabs centuries ago and they asked me to help them regain possession of them. I was suspicious and I talked to my father who said he didn't know the men I described. When I met them again I said I wouldn't help them and urged them to abandon the idea. I thought they agreed with me, but I was so embarrassed by their actions, that I decided not to notify the Christian fathers at the church." He paused. "I feel I am responsible for the disappearance of the scrolls."

"You mustn't blame yourself, Wajeeh," Leila said.

"How did the Arabs know about the scrolls?" I asked.

Wajeeh sighed. "Stories about the scrolls have been told for centuries. But I believe that Father Paribas may have caused some of the trouble recently. He was very curious about the scrolls, and he talked to many people, from Avram Goren to the cultural attaché at the Eritrean embassy."

"Goren wanted to buy the scrolls from me," Leila said.

"How did he know you had them?" I asked.

"The Arabs who stole them went to Goren first," Leila said. "Avram told them he would buy them, but only if they were authenticated—and he gave them my name."

"Why didn't you return the scrolls to the church?" I asked.

Once again, the color was beginning to rise in Leila's cheeks.

"I didn't know where the scrolls came from or that they were stolen. The Arabs claimed they found them in a cave, just like the Dead Sea Scrolls."

"You believe they're authentic."

"I do."

"And now you know where they came from, but you still won't give them back."

"Not until the world knows what they say."

"All right," I said, "why don't you tell 'the world?'"

"The Arabs have split into two groups. One wants to sell the scrolls to Goren. The other wants to sell them to the Saudis who will use them to further their wahhabist teachings by discrediting the Christian gospels. I refused to deliver the scrolls to either of them."

"That's why they were shooting at you today."

"It's not the first time," Leila said. "I've been cooped up here with my Uzi and the Glock handgun for two weeks."

She walked rapidly to what remained of the cabinets on the west wall, and pointed to piles of canned goods and bottled water, some of it shattered by the gunfire.

"I'll get the Israeli military," I said. "They'll protect you."

She laughed harshly. "Yes, and then every Arab in the Middle East will want to kill me."

For the first time she looked truly frightened.

"I still don't understand. What's in the scrolls that could possibly harm anybody?"

She hesitated for a moment. "I'll let you read them. You'll soon learn why they're so dangerous."

I tried not to show my elation. "We should go somewhere that's safe. Surely the Arabs will return sooner or later. We should leave while there's still daylight."

"The scrolls aren't leaving here and neither am I," she said.

"May I go now?" Wajeeh said. He hadn't spoken a word for several minutes; I had almost forgotten he was there. "If the fathers and brothers don't see me they will be very concerned. I'll tell them that Yossi is working hard to solve their problems."

"Not a word of what you've seen and heard here," Leila said.

Wajeeh's back stiffened. "You need not have said that," he told her.

Leila nodded as if she agreed. Wajeeh rose to his feet and smiled at both of us.

"Be careful," I said.

The return look from Wajeeh told me I need not have said that, either.

***

We had not been alone together for many months. Once or twice we had passed in the streets of the Old City and exchanged pro forma greetings. Well, not exactly greetings; acknowledgements of the other's existence. There was a strange intimacy about this new situation. Even the weapons and broken glass and shattered shelves couldn't entirely eliminate the sense of closeness, of shared adventure.

"I must warn you," Leila said. "This was not a routine translation. We refer to the source materials as scrolls, but in fact they were fragments rolled together and not always in obvious chronological or even logical order. An ordinary, literal translation would have resulted in disjointed, perhaps even unintelligible sequences of words. Most of the material was apparently written down by a woman named Judith, who claimed to be the sister of Yeshua of Nazareth. She set down the words and ideas of many of the important religious and political figures of her time, as well as ordinary people whom we recognize from the Gospels, the Apocrypha and the Pseudepigrapha. Whether she faithfully recorded what she was told or invented some of it is not easy to verify, but the material is internally consistent and accords quite well with everything we know about that period and the people. For convenience, I've separated the text into what I believe are appropriate divisions—books and chapters."

Leila seemed to get more and more enthusiastic as she spoke. It was obvious the scrolls fascinated her, and also that she was proud of the work she had done.

"One day," she continued, "others will read the scrolls and my translation and reach their own conclusions. I'm confident that I've been faithful to the sources and to the truth."

"I'm not a scholar," I said, "but I have always admired your genius and never doubted your integrity."

She stared at me for a long moment, and then stood up abruptly. She moved to the bookshelves, checked the fallen and damaged books and slowly shook her head. Then she picked up a broom and began sweeping the shards of glass, stucco and wood into a pile in the center of the room.

I stood up, totally perplexed. Was the meeting over? Would Leila clean up her damaged office and dismiss me—by ignoring me?

"In the cabinet next to my drawing board," Leila said. "On the two top shelves you will find my translations divided into books and chapters for clarity."

THE MURDERED MESSIAH

BOOK 1

MIRACLE IN GALILEE

1.

MIRIAM
(5 B.C.E)

Swirls of spidery mist draped the green stone-studded hills where Miriam wandered. The town was behind her now, a random cluster of one-story gray stone houses of three or four rooms, perched in a grassy saddle of the Galilean hills. There were nearly three hundred families in Nazareth, enough to have built a small synagogue, of which the townspeople were very proud. Most of the people were farmers, tending small neat fields scalloped into the slopes, and herders husbanding their sheep in rock-strewn pastures. A few tradesmen and merchants served the town, but the people often traveled northwest to Sepphoris, southeast to Nain or all the way to the Sea of Galilee to find a sizeable market.

Miriam was walking beyond the last house, descending through sweetly scented trees to rolling meadows. She was a dreamy girl, a trait belied by her sturdy figure and warm-toned complexion. Her hair was long and black, deeply lustrous and wound into a tight roll that served to accent the smooth lines of her heart-shaped face. Miriam's eyes were wide-set, almond-shaped and deeper green than the hills. Her nose was narrow with a shallow inward curve and a slight flare that matched the fullness of her lips.

She was mercurial. Her eyes often changed from sparkling mischief to wistful self-absorption. To her mother, Hannah, it often seemed that Miriam wasn't there, and she would have to call her back to reality almost forcefully.

This spring morning, Miriam had risen before dark, dressed and hurried to the well, anxious to complete her chores and still have time for a stroll through the hills. She loved to walk through the mists, piercing them with her own footsteps, making them curl and dip and rise in mysterious patterns. Parting the fluttering strands would reveal saffron crocuses, pale pink gladioli, clumps of purple anemones and blood red tulips. Miriam seldom picked the flowers. She hated to kill anything, and besides, plucked flowers would wilt in the heavy heat of the day.

The sun was still a hazy blunt orange that would later pale into yellow. Shepherds grazed their flocks in the lower valleys. Above them, groves of olive trees marched down the hillsides, their silvery leaves whispering in the slight breeze. Later, as the heat increased, the shepherds would retreat to shadier levels. There they would linger, perhaps even sleep, under the trees or in cool shallow caves.

The flocks seemed far off this morning, and Miriam took the slanting path above them, feeling the zest of her life, exulting in her own breath, still trailing in the humid air. She broke into a slight run, but then she felt her breasts swaying and touching her arms. Miriam was aware of her body these days and not always happy with it. She felt bulky and all too obvious.

The breeze freshened, her spirits lifted and she quickened her pace. It was marvelous to be young and free, to enjoy the morning in glorious solitude. Then she remembered that her days of solitude were numbered. A few weeks, earlier, Miriam's parents had arranged a marriage for her. Somehow, the idea shocked her. She had chosen to believe her youth would go on forever. Miriam didn't mind the admiration of young men, but only when she wanted it, a flirting look, a shy smile, perhaps the touch of a hand. But not marriage, not children--Oh no, not that. However, Miriam was a dutiful girl and when they told her of the arrangements, she dipped her head and did not complain. If her father thought it was shy approval, he was mistaken

Miriam looked up to the sky. The filmy mists were parting, fading. She could see all the way to heaven. Is this my fate, she wondered, to be the wife of a tradesman, to bear a dozen children? I'm too young, I'm not ready.

The mists dropped suddenly, precipitously, and the sun seemed to pop upward, soaring into the blue. A few rays, still trapped in the shreds of the mists led her eyes to the highway and the line of figures winding slowly through the countryside.

***

Gaius Fabricius didn't sit his horse with the easy carriage of other centurions. Even after a year, he was not completely comfortable in his commission. For an ex-slave of dubious heritage, a freedman, his initial progress in the military was notable. Then, promises of advancement failed to materialize. Frustrated, he volunteered to join the eastern legions, never dreaming they would assign him to damnable Judaea—Athens perhaps, Alexandria, even Damascus, but not Judaea itself. In theory, Judaea was an independent Kingdom and Herod was its ruler, but the crown had been given to him by Roman emperors and the people had never accepted him. They treated his reign as just another form of Roman occupation, and Herod had requested the unofficial assignment of a Roman legion to help keep the peace, and especially to track down the most pernicious of the Galilean rebels. To Gaius's disgust, his legion was the one designated.

It would take a generous man to call the local people "unfriendly." At best they were sullen, at times they were angry and rebellious, and at worst they were murderous. Especially here in Galilee, famous for its rebels, where most people stared at him with frank hatred.

Gaius was trailing the most famous of those rebels, a man known as Judas of Galilee. He was the son of Hezekiah, a ruthless brigand whom King Herod had overcome many years earlier. But Herod was not satisfied with crucifying Hezekiah. Obsessive as always, Herod was determined to find and murder his family as well. The search had gone on for thirty years. Judas was now a brigand like his father, making occasional violent forays that usually ended with the death of Herodian or Roman soldiers. A few weeks earlier, Judas and his men had materialized at a customs house in this very district, but a troop of soldiers surprised them. The battle was brief and intense with many killed on both sides. Somehow Judas and a group of wounded men had managed to escape. It was Gaius's assignment to rid the district of this blight.

What made his mission all the more difficult was that he found it almost impossible to separate the brigands and rebels from the general population. Gaius had never known a people that hated the Romans more deeply than the Jews. In other parts of the Empire, the Romans were often welcomed or at least accepted because their rule was typically tolerant and they protected the natives from local outlaws or more terrible invaders. But tolerance was useless in the Syrian district, whether in Judaea or Galilee. There was no doubt in Gaius's mind that a major rebellion was in the offing. He would welcome the chance to slaughter some of these angry Israelites in open warfare. Looking for enemies behind every tree was disgusting and tiresome.

There were no friendly locals. Even the whores had to be imported from Egypt, Lebanon or Syria. Gaius Fabricius was personally insulted. He was a handsome man, tall and light-haired, with deep-set dark blue eyes.

His features were regular, almost perfect, except for a slight break in the line of his nose, where a slave owner had cracked him with a whip. In every other place he had been stationed, the local girls had found him attractive. Here, he was ignored—at best.

They were riding the main highway that morning, on one of their endless patrols, when Gaius noticed that his men were laughing, looking up towards a misty meadow above the highway.

"What is it?" he asked.

"A girl," one answered, "alone."

That in itself was unusual. The Galileans never allowed their women out in the countryside alone, day or night, even though Roman discipline was generally good and incidents were rare.

"Pretty," Septimus, a subaltern said.

Gaius laughed for the first time that day. "You can't tell from here."

Septimus was a well-built man of average height, with broad shoulders and a close-cropped head of unruly black hair. His complexion was uneven, with blotches and pimples, and he bore many scars from wars public and personal. His nose had been broken so many times that it looked like a round of stale bread and his brows were heavy and tangled together like blackened undergrowth across his forehead. He didn't like Gaius; the man was too handsome and his manners too…delicate.

Septimus found it difficult to keep the contempt out of his nasal voice. "The way I feel, every woman is pretty."

The others laughed; their tone struck Gaius as hard and artificial.

Then his eyes, too, were taken by the woman. She seemed unaware of them, stopping now and again to bend over the flowers. She appeared to be well-formed, even beneath the shapeless garments.

Finally, she caught sight of them and hesitated, perhaps thinking of running off.

"Never get away," one of the men mumbled.

The woman realized she couldn't escape. She bent to touch the flowers, ignoring the Romans

"I think," Septimus said, trying to look serious but with a smile curling the corners of his mouth, "we better question her, sir. She may know where to find that rebel."

"Perhaps," said Gaius. He was surprised that he had tacitly approved this foolishness.

Miriam watched them approach with growing concern. Be calm, she told herself, it's best not to show fear to these beasts. But her heart was pounding.

In a minute, the patrol surrounded her. The closeness and the heavy smell of the horses were overpowering. The men stank, too, and they were all grinning at her.

"Pretty," Septimus said.

"Very pretty," said another. "You can see her tits rising under her clothes."

Miriam didn't know the language, but she understood their looks. Her breath came faster and the color rose to her cheeks, which only made her look more desirable.

"I'd love to fuck her," Septimus said.

"Quiet." Gaius spoke firmly, but his body echoed the same wish. He spoke to the girl—she could not have been older than fourteen or fifteen—in Aramaic, the local dialect. "What's your name?"

Miriam didn't respond, so busy mastering her fear that she hardly recognized her own language.

"What's your name?"

This time she heard him. He was a large, handsome man with strong, clean features and straight teeth.

"Miriam," she said. Her voice was reasonably calm.

"Where do you live?"

"In Nazareth."

"What are you doing this far from town?"

"Walking. I like the hills and the flowers."

Her voice was breathy with fear, but clear and resonant. It was pleasant to listen to her.

Septimus was growing restless. He didn't want the centurion and the girl to become friends. "Ask her about Judas," he said

Gaius frowned, but didn't reprimand him. Septimus was outspoken, but he was a very good soldier and a superb horseman.

"Do you know Judas?" he asked Miriam.

Her look betrayed her. "Which Judas? There are many with that name."

"The son of Hezekiah the outlaw?"

Miriam hesitated only a second. To her family, Hezekiah was a hero, not an outlaw. "No, I don't know him."

Septimus glowered. "She's lying. He's probably hiding around here. I bet she's his woman."

Gaius was caught between the appealing beauty of Miriam, the agitation of Septimus and his own long unappeased lust.

"They think you are Judas's woman."

Miriam flushed darkly. "I am a virgin," she said, then realized she had made a mistake.

"You won't get the truth that way, Centurion. Let me have a chance with her."

Septimus slipped from his saddle and grabbed Miriam by both arms. Gaius sat frozen in his saddle, watching with fascination.

"Where is Judas?" Septimus asked in Greek, knowing the girl wouldn't understand.

Miriam said nothing, feeling the pain of the man's hands digging into her shoulders.

"Do you fuck Judas?" Septimus yelled. His hands moved to her breasts. Miriam twisted violently.

"Will you fuck me?" he demanded.

She spat in his face.

"Septimus," the Centurion said, but he spoke under his breath, and no one heard him.

Miriam's action enraged and inflamed Septimus. He ripped the front of her dress, exposing her fine, full breasts.

"Ah," the men said with one breath.

Miriam screamed and fought, tearing at Septimus's face with her nails. He held her away, half smiling, and stripped off the rest of her clothing. The others dismounted quickly.

Gaius Fabricius knew he should stop his men. His men knew it, too, and when he didn't act, they pressed closer to the girl, leering at her, touching her.

"To the woods," Septimus said, his voice high-pitched and giddy. Together, pawing her body, stifling her screams with their hands, they dragged her off.

Gaius slid down from his horse and followed.

One after another, they assaulted her, a Gaul and a Greek, a Spaniard and a Nubian, even an apostate Hebrew, and then, finally, Gaius Fabricius, who was ignorant of his heritage.

Miriam never stopped fighting, even under the weight of these power-ful men. Her body was numb with pain, smeared with her own blood.

Finally, it was over. Miriam lay on the ground, too sickened for tears.

Septimus leaned over her, a small knife in his hand.

"No," Gaius said.

"This way she won't be able to accuse us."

"No one will know," Gaius said. "Put away your weapon."

Reluctantly, Septimus sheathed his knife.

Quickly and in silence, the men mounted their horses. Perhaps they felt guilty. The girl had actually been a virgin and she had fought them fiercely.

Gaius stared at Miriam's face, trying to memorize her features. He brought the scraps of her clothing and gently draped them over her. Then he mounted his horse and led his men off at a crisp canter.

2.

JOSEPH

Miriam lay on the ground long after the soldiers were gone. Spasms of pain sliced up her legs and across her spine. Her whole body trembled with exhaustion and humiliation. Tendrils of blood streaked her skin. She didn't cry; the horror was too monstrous for that. Her lips moved as she silently prayed to God for deliverance. Her eyes slowly blinked while great white clouds cadenced across the sky. Birds sang and small animals scurried through the bushes, gnats and flies buzzed overhead and a gentle breeze bent the grass. To Miriam, dazed and fighting hysteria, it was incredible that the world could go on in its ordinary way.

Finally, she sat up, wincing at every movement. She stared at her torn clothes, then arranged the shreds to cover her nakedness. As if that matters now, she thought.

Overcoming great pain, she stood up, but could not keep her balance. A straight, thin tree branch lay nearby. Miriam staggered to it, and using the branch as a crook, dragged herself to the path home. The thought of what lay ahead was even more painful than the journey.

***

The Roman patrol galloped along the highway, raising a looping, swirling cloud of dust. The men laughed and joked, describing the girl and their use of her in rough detail. Gaius Fabricius rode with his head down, trying to blot out images of the girl. It was impossible. Her delicate features appeared again and again, forming an exquisite portrait of virginal beauty. But her eyes accused him—huge, deep green eyes that leaped up from the highway to impale him. The girl's lips moved, but she said nothing. She had struggled mightily but had not pleaded. Gaius Fabricius had fought in a dozen battles and never seen greater courage.

Septimus watched the centurion and smiled. I knew it, he thought, the bastard's no better than we are.

Gaius was beginning to feel the saddle, his horse, even the highway. The pounding was unbelievable, as if a hundred men with staves were beating at his feet, his back, his head. He clung to the saddle, almost losing consciousness.

Septimus leaned near. "Are you all right?" he asked, his crooked features cracked into a caricature of a smile. He held out a hand as if to help.

Gaius angrily brushed him away and forced himself erect. Septimus dropped back, covering his laughter. Weakling, he thought. He was pleased with himself; to have had the girl and the centurion in a single morning--that was true pleasure.

Gaius gripped the reins and rode on. His life would never be the same. He had surrendered to evil and he was beginning to pay the price

***

Hannah, Miriam's mother, sat in the doorway of her home, irritated that once again her daughter had managed to slip away unnoticed. Hannah was not a pretty woman, short and blocky, with a moon face, dark hair and uneven features, but she was sturdy and warmhearted. She had married Joachim at the "advanced" age of twenty-five and agonized for ten barren years until, finally, she had borne Miriam, now fifteen. The delivery had almost killed her, but the child was so beautiful that it was worth it.

Her vision was poor and at first she thought that the figure hobbling toward her was an elderly man. Then her heart told her it was Miriam. "Good God," she cried and ran toward her beloved only child.

Hannah's strong arms encircled her daughter. Miriam, feeling that first moment of safety, almost fainted. Somehow, she held on as Hannah half carried her home.

Neighbors came out of their houses, some to stare, others to help, but Hannah waved them off. "Miriam is all right," she said. In her heart, she knew better. The child was deadly pale, blood-streaked and bruised.

Hannah slowly eased Miriam down on her bed, whispering small, soothing sounds to her pain-wracked child. She hurried to get warm water and clear oils. Gently, gently, she removed the shreds of clothing and carefully cleaned her body. There was no need to ask what had happened.

Joachim hurried in, breathing heavily. He had been working in the fields a half mile away, when he was alerted by a neighbor. He was built like his wife, a short, bulky dark-haired man with blunt features and strong hands. It seemed a miracle that they had had a child as lovely as Miriam. Seeing his daughter bruised and wounded, Joachim screamed aloud.

"Quiet," Hannah said softly, rocking her child in her arms. "She needs quiet."

But Joachim could not remain silent. "What happened, Miriam, tell me what happened?" He took her hand and wept openly.

Miriam laboriously told her story while Hannah stroked her brow and Joachim ached with every word.

"I'll find them," he said in a low, trembling voice. "I'll kill them."

Hannah sighed and shook her head. "They're gone, Joachim."

"Did you see their faces?" he demanded of Miriam. "Would you recognize them?"

Miriam nodded slowly. "I'll never forget them," she said.

Hannah knew they would not find the Roman soldiers. A more important question nagged at her, cruel and unbidden: What will Joseph think?

He was a fine young man, with a good trade and he loved Miriam. Hannah unconsciously shook her head. Joseph would be sympathetic, but there would be no marriage, not to Joseph, not to anyone. Her daughter would never marry, never bear children. Hannah's anguished mind continued to struggle. Perhaps they could find a place where Miriam's ordeal would not be known. She was not a virgin, but....

Hannah grimaced. It was wrong to think this way. Silently, she asked the Lord to forgive her.

***

Everyone in Nazareth knew. They knew because of the silence from the house of Joachim and Hannah, because Joachim did not seek the opinion or the help of other men, not even of Ari, their ancient sage. They knew because the women who called to offer solace were turned away. Joachim continued to work in the fields and to pray in the synagogue, but he was tight-faced and close-mouthed.

Hannah, too, was remote and unresponsive. Miriam wasn't seen for days on end. The townspeople assumed the outrage was the work of Roman soldiers. If it had been outlaws, Joachim would have been heard from. The people guessed almost everything that had happened. They were simple, but they were quick and they were wise.

Joseph knew the facts even before he climbed down from the wall of the barn he was building for the widow Huldah, on the very day of the crime. Joseph was an humble, forthright youth with a thin face and strong regular features topped by unruly sandy-colored hair that would not lie flat on his head. He had large, expressive dark eyes, a shy smile and an easy friendliness. He often cocked his head when he talked, as if he were in his shop, examining a piece of wood. Joseph thought before he spoke and chose his words carefully. Sometimes his mind raced ahead and then he would stumble over his words. He struggled consciously to slow himself and avoid embarrassment. Joseph's voice was soft, almost whispery, but he held strong opinions.

He considered himself to be simple and plain and unattractive. Because his parents were dead, he had asked Bebai, his uncle, to find him a wife. Although Joseph had secretly been in love with Miriam since childhood, he had never even dared to hope that Bebai would approach Miriam's family. When Bebai brought him the news of their betrothal, Joseph's blood rushed to his head and he nearly fainted. Bebai had laughed and laughed and laughed.

It was Bebai who told him about Miriam's ordeal, yelling up to where Joseph was working. Bebai spoke bluntly, expecting anger and disgust. Joseph's pale features were quickly suffused with red and his eyes darkened. But he said nothing and Bebai was disappointed. Surely a man ought to react more strongly on hearing that his betrothed had been raped.

Joseph climbed slowly down from the wall and methodically gathered his tools. He said nothing to Bebai, who stood in the roadway, offended, blinking his eyes. Joseph walked slowly to his own house, the house he had planned to share with Miriam. He pulled the door shut and sat down on a low bench. He waited patiently, praying they would send for him. He doubted he would be allowed to marry her. Everyone would be against it, his own family and very likely hers. Joseph loved Miriam deeply and her pain must be overwhelming, but he knew he couldn't go to her.

After a while, Joseph began to blink his eyes rapidly and then, silently, his hands clutched together and his shoulders hunched forward, he began to cry.

Bebai came into the house, sputtering, but when he saw Joseph weeping, his heart was touched and he sat down on a chair, folded his hands and bowed his head.

***

Joachim dressed himself carefully in dark clothing and went to tell Joseph and Bebai that the marriage agreement was terminated. It was very difficult for Joachim, who was clumsy even in simple social matters and had never had to deal with anything as grave as this. He was fond of Joseph and had been looking forward to having him for a son-in-law.

Joseph listened without changing his expression, then took a deep breath. "I would like to speak to Miriam," he said in a voice so soft that Joachim had to lean close in order to hear him.

"That's not possible," Joachim said. "She isn't well enough to see anyone."

"I am not 'anyone.'"

"You're a good man," Joachim said, with considerable emotion, "but I hope you will respect our wishes."

***

The weeks passed with infinite slowness in the hard heat of summer. Joseph was very busy at a succession of various jobs. His work was competent, as always, but there was no longer any joy in it. He hammered and cut and fitted almost without seeing what he was doing. He worked and ate and slept and worked again. "I don't know what you want of me, God," he said.

***

It was not long before Miriam learned she was carrying a child, the spawn of some depraved Roman soldier. She stared at her belly with loathing, overwhelmed at how her body had betrayed her. Miriam didn't tell her mother. Something must be done, something to end this horror.

Both Joachim and Hannah were out of the house. Miriam felt sudden panic and a scream rose in her throat, but she choked it off. She must think. Carefully. Her eyes methodically scanned the room, stopping at a large knife hung on the wall above the baking oven. Miriam quickly looked away, frightened by her own thoughts. Then, as if someone had grabbed her chin and turned her head, her eyes went back to it. She took the knife from the wall and stared at it. Perspiration broke out on her forehead and she clutched the knife even tighter. Life meant nothing now. She would never have a husband, never. She would live alone with a hated child who would scorn and mock her.

She gripped the handle with both hands, pressed the blade against her breast, closed her eyes and took a deep breath.

12

She saw Joseph's face, pleading with her and she hesitated. Miriam opened her eyes to clear away the vision. She was trembling from head to foot, but she steeled herself, gripping the handle so tightly that it cut into her skin and once again closed her eyes. Once again she saw Joseph, shaking his head.

Miriam began to cry and to shake. The knife dropped from her hands and clattered to the floor.

I can't do it, she thought. I can't kill myself.

She began to sob more loudly, then covered her mouth with her hands to keep the sounds from escaping the house. The child, she thought. I'll kill the child.

Her strength returned. Why not? It was against the sacred beliefs of her religion to do such a thing, but surely, in these circumstances, she had justification. According to Jewish law the child would be a Jew, but not to Miriam. To call this pagan one of the "chosen people," was disgusting. Who knew what kind of hideous, deformed thing it would be?

Miriam looked around again. She would find something, long and narrow and place it inside her body and twist it until the evil creature was destroyed. She ran about the room, searching desperately. And then she found the metal prod used to stir the coals in the fire.

Miriam picked up the slender shaft and began to clean it carefully. She imagined it twisting inside her body, seeing the tiny blob of flesh being torn from her womb. Then, the blob became a child and the child began to cry.

Miriam screamed and flung the rod across the room.

***

"She's pregnant," Bebai told Joseph. "You're well out of it." He smiled.

Joseph stared at him soberly, then abruptly stalked from the house.

"Leave us in peace," Joachim said, barring the door with his blocky body.

"I want to speak to her."

Joachim shook his head, but Joseph gently pushed him aside and entered the house. "Forgive me," he said.

Hannah moved to shield her daughter while Miriam resisted the urge to cover her face with her fingers. She stared at Joseph with level, unblinking eyes. He looks very tired, she thought.

She's beautiful, Joseph thought, looking into her deep green eyes and seeing little flecks of white for the first time. He knew he was privileged to look beneath the surface of a great, wave-tossed sea, and he felt his heart crest within him.

"Shalom," he said to Miriam, speaking gently.

"Shalom," she responded, her voice clear and firm, her eyes level and holding on to his.

Joseph bent his head and seemed to be studying her very carefully before he spoke again. "I—I want to marry you," he said.

Hannah gasped and Joachim had to hold onto a chair to keep himself upright. Miriam felt a surge of hope in her heart, but stilled herself and spoke carefully.

"I am with child," she said.

This time Joseph didn't hesitate. "The child will be mine," he said, surprised only that he almost smiled as he spoke. Then, impulsively, he added, "We will have many children."

Miriam's heart lifted powerfully within her, so that she had no choice but to rise to her feet. She smiled a glorious smile and held out her arms.

3.

BETH LECHEM
(4 B.C.E.)

The long day of prayers, rituals and ceremonies was over. A quiet night had fallen on the Galilean hills and Miriam and Joseph were alone together in Joseph's house for the first time. Joseph was dressed in a fine white linen tunic, his hair brushed down and his skin deeply cleansed of the chips and dust of his trade. In the warm candlelight, his eyes glowed with a joy and intensity that Miriam had never seen before.

Modestly, she looked down at the bouquet of roses she held in her arms. Her fingers, moving nervously over the flowers, caught on a thorn and she cried out in surprise.

Joseph hurried to her, raised her hands and kissed the tiny wound. Looking down at the sandy hair carefully smoothed on his head, she felt the urge to touch him, to hold him to her breast. But her fear was great and she stiffened despite herself. Joseph was a good man, an affectionate man and she cared for him. He was entitled to a real wife, but the thought of lying with him frightened—even nauseated—her. Memories of the Roman soldiers falling on her, penetrating her, clawing at her body, obsessed and terrified her.

Joseph understood. He loved this vibrant, pretty girl and he wanted her badly, but he knew that she had been desperately wounded. Bringing her soft, pretty hands to his heart, Joseph looked into her eyes and whispered, "You needn't worry. There will be time enough for...love, in the days to come. I will ask nothing of you...until you're ready."

"Oh, Joseph," Miriam cried, her green eyes lighting up. Dropping the flowers, she embraced and held him to her for a long moment. Joseph closed his eyes and breathed in the fragrance of her hair and skin. It was he who gently pulled away. Then, looking at the speck of blood where the thorn had pricked her hand, he said, "We'll do...what we must to make our families believe our marriage is complete."

Tears of gratitude filled Miriam's eyes. She reached out and briefly touched his hair. "God bless you, Joseph. One day I'll make you a real wife. I promise."

He nodded, the corners of his eyes crinkled and his trembling lips parted in a shy smile.

Then his expression grew serious and he cocked his head when he spoke. "I think it'll be better if our child is born in another place, far from Nazareth. I have cousins in Beth Lechem. I can find work there until after our child is born."

Miriam was surprised, but she understood the good sense behind Joseph's words. "Of course," she said. "My husband is very wise."

***

Joachim understood, too, and although he was quite upset, he didn't want to anger his new son-in-law.

"It's a long way to Beth Lechem," he said, "and there are brigands everywhere."

Joseph smiled and spoke reassuringly, "We aren't traders laden with merchandise. No one will bother us."

"What about the Romans?" Joachim asked. It was a difficult question but he had to voice it.

"We'll travel by day, and only on the main roads."

It was obvious to Joachim that nothing he said would change Joseph's mind. The man was good-hearted, but immovable once his mind was made up. Joachim sighed and wished them well.

Hannah was not as easily persuaded. She questioned her daughter in private. "What will the family think if you leave town?" she asked. "After all, we are descended from the royal house of David."

Miriam laughed. "On which side? From a royal wife, a concubine or a whore?"

"Miriam," her mother cried, startled that marriage had changed her daughter so quickly. "It's an honor to be of the royal line."

"And small consolation to my child," Miriam said firmly, but with no bitterness.

Hannah was silent for a moment. Then she smiled a small and lopsided, but tender smile. "I'll miss you," she said, "and the royal prince."

"You're sure it's a boy," Miriam said.

Hannah folded her arms across her ample chest and cheerfully nodded her head.

***

They left Nazareth a few days later, riding on donkeys borrowed from Joachim. Joseph, usually the sober craftsman, surprised his bride by singing song after song along the road. Most were based on the psalms of David, but a few had earthier origins. Miriam blushed and laughed and then joined in. Together, they sang their way south.

From time to time, they passed Roman or Herodian patrols. At first, Miriam was frightened, but Joseph simply ignored the soldiers and gradually Miriam's fears subsided. Now and then, Joseph sighted riders in the distant hills who might have been brigands, but his heart told him that he and Miriam were in God's care. Not fearing violence, he didn't attract any.

Joseph had decided to follow the ancient highways from Galilee through Samaria and Judaea, instead of the road along the Jordan that his family had urged on him. They passed through the Jezreel valley, beautiful with its waving wheat, plump vineyards and gently sloping hills. One of these was Moreh, where Gideon with only three hundred men had somehow "surrounded" the army of the Midianites, "and the entire host ran, and cried, and fled."

In the heights was Megiddo, built by Solomon, the scene of many great battles. King Josiah had died there fighting an Egyptian Pharaoh. The vast ruins were still a place of pilgrimage, and some believed that even greater battles would yet be fought there.

Further south they entered Samaria, the highway passing between rolling, rocky hills, with row upon row of cultivated terraces rising above them. The Samaritans cherished their own form of Judaism. They looked upon the Jerusalem Temple with disdain and deemed the inhabitants of Judaea to be heretics and apostates.

Although Joseph felt little concern, he avoided entering the capital city, which had been the stronghold of the northern kingdom of Israel seven hundred years earlier. King Herod had recently renamed it Sebaste, the Greek name of the Emperor Augustus, and was engaged in a vast building program. The roads were clogged with carts and horses dragging huge stone blocks and transporting hundreds of workman from as far away as Lebanon.

Below the capital were Shechem and the famous twin mountains of Gerizim and Ebal. There, the Samaritans claimed to have received the law, as Moses had received the tablets at Sinai.

"This was one of the first cities visited by Abraham," Joseph told his wife. "Jacob owned ground here and Joseph was buried here."

"Your namesake," Miriam said, smiling. "You bear a heavy responsibility."

"My responsibility is to you," he responded.

The next morning they reached Shiloh, the ancient town where the Ark of the Covenant was kept from the days of Joshua until the time of Samuel and King David. Nestled below the mountains of Samaria, the town seemed quite humble. Only the rubble of ancient walls hinted of past glory.

"Joseph," Miriam said, "do you remember the story of Hannah, the wife of Elkanah?"

Joseph nodded. "Like your mother, she was barren for many years. But then she prayed to the Lord and promised that if she could have a child he would belong to God."

Miriam smiled. "Yes, and she was given a son, whom she called Samuel, meaning "promised to God.""

Joseph leaned close. "Shall we name our son Samuel?"

Miriam hesitated. "I don't favor that name, but I know the child will be promised to the Lord."

She touched her belly briefly and spoke to the child within. "Are you listening?" she asked. "You'll know the history of your people before you're born."

They left Samaria, not without a sense of relief, and passed through Bethel, another place where Abraham had camped, where Jacob had met God and built an altar, but also where Jeroboam had set up a golden calf.

Then they were close to Ramah, the hometown of Elkanah and Hannah and the place where Samuel had been born. It was there that Jeremiah said the voice of Rachel was heard, crying for her children who were no more because they had been taken to captivity in Babylonia.

Nearing the town they began to hear strange sounds. Could it indeed be wailing, could it be the cries of Rachel? Joseph and Miriam stared at each other. Should they go on?

Joseph refused to be intimidated. He slapped the flanks of his donkey and forced it into a trot.

The sounds grew louder. "Those are not wails," Joseph said. "People are laughing and cheering."

The road turned suddenly and they were in Bethel. The streets were filled with people, some dressed in their Sabbath best. It looked like a great feast, with huge crowds, laughing and talking. Many held wine goblets, and called out happy toasts.

Joseph grabbed the arm of a young man who was hurrying by. "What's going on here?" he asked.

The young man's face showed surprise. "Haven't you heard? Herod is dead."

"Yes!" cried a girl throwing her arms about the young man. "The monster is dead!"

"Drink to our king," said an older man, somewhat in his cups, "Israel will have a new king."

"No Edomite pretender," said another. "This time a real Jew."

They all laughed. The older man said, "Come with us," pulling at Joseph's arm. "Celebrate."

Joseph smiled, but didn't follow. The others laughed again and hurried away.

Miriam and Joseph couldn't move forward. It seemed that all of Judaea was out in the street, celebrating the death of the hated Herod. Joseph found a place off the road to camp and they waited patiently, hoping the crowds would clear with darkness.

But when night fell, the celebration grew even more intense, and the voices raised were even higher.

"We'll never get to Beth Lechem at this rate," Joseph said, but there was nothing he could do.

All through the night and into the morning, the crowd remained in the streets. But now there was fresh news to stir them. "They say the Romans have appointed Archelaus to be the king," a traveler told Joseph.

Another man refused to believe it. "He's no better than his father. There'll be war, you watch my word."

Miriam looked fearfully at Joseph. He shook his head. "Miriam," he said, "we'll have to try to get through, no matter how crowded the roads."

They quickly gathered their belongings and mounted the donkeys. Slowly, patiently, they made their way along the highway, moving only a few feet at a time.

On the steps of the synagogue, they saw a man haranguing the crowd. "I tell you," he cried, "we must act and quickly. It's not enough to be rid of Herod, we have to make certain we choose our own king."

"Careful," one of the elders said. "The word from the north is bad. Zealots attacked the garrison at Sepphoris. There's a battle going on at Nain."

The crowd cheered the news.

"Freedom!" a man cried. "Freedom!" others took up the cry.

"Death is what you'll get," the old man replied, but no one was listening. The younger men hurried off to find weapons.

Joseph tried not to betray his growing concern, but Miriam sensed his uneasiness. She rode close to him and pressed his arm reassuringly. "We'll be fine," she murmured. "The child is promised to the Lord and the Lord will protect us."

Ramah was only a few miles north of Jerusalem, but it took them most of the day to reach the Holy City. They had planned a brief visit to the Temple, but that was too dangerous. To the west they saw riders racing along the hilltops, whether Jews or Romans they couldn't tell.

Ahead, in the city itself, smoke was beginning to rise from many fires. The people on the road prayed for the peace of Jerusalem. Some of the younger men were angered and turned toward the city, ready to fight, but most of the travelers remained on the highway, moving as quickly as they could away from danger. They were joined by thousands of people leaving Jerusalem. Miriam and Joseph couldn't keep from staring at the city, its walls and towers shining in the setting sun, serenely rising above the struggle.

They became aware of terrifying activity near the northern gate. Great posts and crossbeams were rising, pulled upright by Roman soldiers, while troops stood by on watchful guard.

"My God," said a traveler in a strangled voice. "They're crucifying them."

One after another the crosses lurched skyward, carrying an agonized cargo of tormented human beings.

The travelers watched helplessly, as their countrymen were slowly murdered

"Don't look," Joseph said.

Miriam turned away, but the sight of those tortured souls would forever remain etched into her memory.

***

It was long after dark when they reached Beth Lechem. Meshullam, Joseph's cousin, a feisty little round-faced man, with a barrel of a body and an almost perpetual grin, greeted them warmly, joined by the members of his family. They all looked like Meshullam, even his wife and his daughters, cheerful little people with smiles that creased their faces and quick, agile movements that belied their chunky, round bodies.

"I feel like we've reached the Promised Land," Joseph said.

A smile brightened Miriam's face. She touched her belly. "And little Joshua has led us here."

Joseph's face glowed and he leaned across and kissed his wife.

For a moment, Meshullam lost his smile. "I wanted to give you the cottage on the hill," he said, "but there was an uprising in Gaza and my eldest son and his family returned home unexpectedly. I gave it to them."

Joseph's face fell.

"Don't worry, cousin," Meshullam hastily added. "There's a large storeroom beneath the main house and I promise you it's clean and dry the year round." Joseph glanced at Miriam. Had he brought her all this way to bear their child in a storeroom? Miriam didn't seem in the least distressed. She gave him a warm look that was expressly intended to reassure him. Gratefully, Joseph pressed her hand.

Fortunately, the storeroom wasn't as bad as it sounded. Although the air was pungent with the smell of animals, the room was large, the ceiling high, and the hillside insulated it from the extremes of heat and cold. Towards the east, the earth sloped away, framing an entrance only a few steps below ground. When Joseph propped open the large wooden door, fresh air flowed in and they could see a generous slice of the Judaean sky. He moved the troughs and bins out into the pasture and carried in the humble furniture that Meshullam gave them.

"Our new home," Miriam said, smiling and embracing her husband. "Help me find wine and bread so we can thank the Lord for all his blessings."

Tears of relief and gratitude came to Joseph's eyes.

By nightfall of the next day, Joseph had found his first job, rebuilding a plow for a neighbor. Within a week he had more orders than he could fill. Despite the unrest and violence in the land, the farmers of Judaea continued to plough and to plant. Joseph was doubly grateful; making agricultural tools made him feel close to the cycle of creation.

Beth Lechem was relatively peaceful, but every traveler brought word of violence somewhere.

21

"I hear they've brought in new troops from Damascus," Meshullam said. "They say thousands have been killed in Galilee and Samaria, Gaulanitis and Judaea. Over two thousand men were crucified in Jerusalem itself."

Miriam was almost sick with fear until Joachim managed to send word with a trader that the family was well and that Nazareth had seen little of the fighting.

Meanwhile, Miriam did her best to make the cave-like storeroom into a home, artfully dressing it with the humble household things her mother had given her. Ever alert for marauders, she cautiously roamed the fields, collecting gladioli and irises, anemones and roses. The flowers were colorful and they covered the homely scents of the former occupants.

Meshullam's wife, Mehetabel, happily shared the cooking fires in the main house with Miriam. It was a cheerful household despite the war and there was no rivalry among the women. Miriam learned a little of Judaean cooking and happily was able to teach a few spicy Galilean specialties to the others.

Unfortunately, there wasn't much light in the storeroom and it was too expensive to burn lamps continually. To keep up her spirits, Miriam stayed outdoors as long as she could. Her color grew ruddy, her face fuller and her eyes brighter. She had not cut her hair in a long time, and it swirled about her shoulders like a lustrous dark mantle. Gradually, her body grew larger, but she was young and healthy, with few pains and little discomfort.

Once past the original fear, the terrible loathing, she realized the child—her child—was as innocent as she had been. She grew impatient for the hour when she would hold him in her arms.

As her time drew nearer, Joseph managed to find work closer to home. He often appeared just as Miriam was going to the well, and carried the bucket for her.

"That's woman's work," Miriam would say, but secretly she was pleased.

4.

SEARCH

For months, the eyes of the girl tormented Gaius Fabricius. They would appear to him suddenly, asleep or awake, and their accusation never left him. He wanted to be rid of these terrifying visions and then—at the same time—he wanted to see her again.

Finally, his longings overwhelmed his reason and he led a patrol into the village of Nazareth. But not with Septimus. He didn't want the evil one with him. Gaius ordered a house to house search, puzzling his men, who wanted to know what they were looking for. He frowned authoritatively. "Follow me and keep your mouths closed," he growled.

House to house, farm to farm. Angry peasants and merchants glared at them. There were many girls, young and not so young, pretty and homely and plain. None of them was Miriam. The elders of Nazareth counseled together and reluctantly decided to approach the centurion. They were not obsequious. That's one thing about these Jews, Gaius thought, they don't grovel.

An old man with a head of long white hair and a full beard spoke in a surprisingly strong voice. "I am Ari Ben Avram," he said, his watery gray eyes staring directly into Gaius's cold, blue ones. "Tell us, Roman officer, what do you want?"

Gaius Fabricius stared at him imperiously. "I am inspecting the town."

"For what reason?"

Gaius hesitated. "There is to be a census."

It wasn't true, but the Jews looked stricken. A census meant taxes would be raised and taxes were already onerous. The Jews paid their own Temple tax and other taxes to support the late and much hated Herod's enormous building programs as well as the separate, Roman levies.

Ari was suspicious. "What has your inspection to do with this census?"

"It's not your business, old man." Gaius's tone was menacing.

Ari's eyes never wavered and the tone of his voice grew sharper. "What is the designation of your legion and where are you garrisoned?"

Gaius was surprised and intimidated. Was it possible that this unarmed old man could make trouble for him? Gaius angrily gave Ari the information and turned on his heel. Still the old men followed him.

Gaius tried to calm himself. Did they suspect he was the one who raped the girl? He felt that his guilt was written on his forehead and he began to perspire.

"Enough," he said angrily, "I can do my work without you."

Slowly the elders moved away, across the road and into the shade of a large Sycamore tree, but they never took their eyes off the Romans.

At the next house, a smiling, conniving face greeted Gaius. "Hail Caesar," the man whispered, "perhaps a cool drink on a hot day?"

Gaius guessed the man was a collaborator, a rare type among these Galileans.

"Hail Caesar," he responded. "A cool drink would be appreciated."

Gaius followed the man into his home. It was a pleasant enough place and the obsequious fellow quickly handed him a pitcher of lemon-tinted cool water. The centurion drank it gratefully. His host was short and bald and his entire face was focused in a simpering smile. Gaius thought briefly of smashing the pitcher into his groveling expression.

"My name is Mordecai and I would like to be of service."

Gaius spoke carefully. "We're preparing for a census. Can we use your home as a place of registry?"

Mordecai frowned briefly, then pulled a smile down over his face like a mask. Gaius preferred the frown.

"Of course," Mordecai said. "My humble home is at your disposal. Naturally, you'll tell the elders you forced me to let you use it."

Gaius nodded.

"Is there anything else?" Mordecai asked. He seemed eager to betray someone.

"You tell me," Gaius said. Mordecai seemed to be wracking his brain.

"Mordecai," Gaius said, "will many people try to avoid the census?"

His informant smiled, on surer ground now. "Of course, they don't want to be taxed."

"But you know everyone in Nazareth."

"Everyone."

"You'll tell us if anyone is missing."

Mordecai smiled his version of a benign smile.

"For example," Gaius said, "suppose I asked if anyone was missing today—what would you tell me?"

Mordecai launched into a listing of his neighbors who were away with the herds, or working in other towns, or who had died this week. He was very proud of himself. "And of course Joachim's daughter is in Beth Lechem with her husband, the carpenter, Joseph. They think we don't know she's pregnant."

A shock passed through Gaius, and he struggled not to betray his emotions. "Why are they concealing her pregnancy?"

"Because the child isn't Joseph's," Mordecai said smiling gleefully.

Gaius managed to return the smile. "These things happen," he said.

"Not to Joachim's daughter," Mordecai said petulantly. "He thinks he's better than we are, but we know all about Miriam."

At the sound of her name, Gaius found himself gripping the table. "Enough," he growled, anxious to cover his turmoil. Throwing down a coin to humiliate Mordecai, he stalked from the room.

Once Gaius was gone, Mordecai spat at the coin, then picked it up, cleaned it and put it in his pocket. Sometimes these Romans are as unpredictable as Jews, he thought. Mordecai laughed out loud. The Roman would believe he was a collaborator based on totally useless information. Often, such trivia led the Romans to trust him. That night he would find Judas of Galilee and tell him the Romans were searching the town and covering it with a silly story about a census.

In the street, Gaius Fabricius found his legs were weak and the sun seemed unaccountably bright. Miriam, he thought. The name seemed to vibrate in his head. A child, he thought.

Gaius vaulted into his saddle and rode swiftly off, while his men scurried to follow him. Sometimes, they thought, Roman centurions were as unpredictable as Jews.

***

Mordecai waited patiently for darkness, threw a heavy mantle over his narrow shoulders and strode off into the hills. An hour later, he reached a dense copse of wind-weathered pine. The needles crunched beneath his feet and the air was fragrant with their smell, but he hardly noticed. From this point forward he must follow the rules meticulously if he wanted to stay alive. Mordecai marched to the tallest pine, then walked exactly a hundred paces to a scrub oak and dropped his mantle.

"Shalom," a voice whispered.

"There is no peace," Mordecai responded.

A form materialized out of the dark forest and beckoned.

The small cooking fire was almost hidden in its pit, but even in the pale and flickering light, Mordecai saw sights that sickened him. On the floor of the forest, a dozen men huddled about the fire. Almost all were badly wounded, some had lost an arm or a leg and had bloody rags twisted at the stumps. Others were minus an eye or an ear.

Judas greeted him somberly. He was a tall, slope-shouldered man with scraggly black hair, gaunt features and deep black eyes. He and his family had been hunted for generations and he had the weary air of a man who has seen every disaster and somehow survived. Judas was the only one with no visible wounds, but Mordecai knew he carried the internal scars of a lifetime of struggle.

Mordecai was surprised to see a young child sitting cross-legged and shivering, staring into the fire. "Who is the boy?" he asked.

"My son Simon," Judas said with a weary smile. "The Romans would have killed him, too, if we hadn't hidden him in a well."

"I brought food," Mordecai said, and distributed strips of salted meat to the men. They accepted it in silence, too weary for thanks. Only the child refused the food.

"We're leaving tonight," Judas told Mordecai. "Now that that bastard Herod is dead, we're going south and join with other rebels." He raised a fist. "This is our best chance to get rid of both the Herodians and the Romans."

Mordecai listened in wonder and admiration. Even after a lifetime of being hunted, with his supporters limited to a handful of severely wounded men, Judas was still an optimist.

"You'll have to move carefully," Mordecai said. "A Roman patrol searched the town today. Said they were preparing for a census, but I think they were looking for you. I gave them some trivial information and now the centurion thinks I'm a collaborator."

Judas laughed.

"If I play this fellow right," Mordecai said, "I ought to get a lot out of him."

Judas clapped him on the shoulder, but then his son screamed as Roman soldiers erupted from the woods. The Jewish rebels leaped up and clutched their weapons, but the soldiers were upon them. Only a few were able to stand and fight.

Judas grabbed his son's hand and dragged him toward the forest. "Run!" Judas yelled, "Run for your life!"

A Roman soldier ran up with his sword drawn, determined to stop them. Mordecai threw himself onto the soldier and dragged him to the ground. They twisted on the earth until the soldier got hold of his knife and plunged it deep into Mordecai's chest.

"Get Judas and the boy!" Gaius Fabricius yelled, but they were already out of sight, running headlong through the woods.

Judas realized instinctively that Roman soldiers had surrounded the entire area and even now were closing in. He stopped abruptly and pushed his son up onto the lowest branch of an oak tree. "Climb as high as you can," he whispered, then pulled himself up into the tree. They scrambled upward in silence until the leaves became too thick, then Judas folded his body around his son and covered them both with leafy branches.

5

CROSSROADS
(4 B.C.E.)

Joseph and Miriam sat together in the pale light of a single candle. Earlier, Joseph had been reading from scripture, while Miriam was sewing clothing for her baby. Now they had put their work aside and sat in companionable silence.

They were surprised to hear someone running overhead and then suddenly, the door to the underground storeroom burst open and Meshullam rushed in. His usually smiling face was grim and he was dragging a young boy with him, a scrawny, dirty-faced lad whose eyes were clearly frightened.

"Forgive me," Meshullam said, "there's no time to explain." He shoved the boy under the bed.

"What are you—" Joseph began, but Meshullam wasn't listening.

"Miriam," Meshullam said, "get into the bed, now, at once!"

Miriam, bewildered but trusting, climbed into the bed. Meshullam piled the covers over her swollen belly. Mehetabel hurried in, carrying towels and a bucket of hot water.

"Heave," she told Miriam. "Moan, as if you are having the child. NOW!"

"This is ridiculous," Joseph said, "what kind of—"

But then the heavy beat of horses' hooves thundered overhead.

"Moan," Mehetabel whispered to Miriam, "for God's sake, moan!"

Slowly, Miriam began to murmur and then to moan. Joseph saw her fear, sat down beside her and took her hand.

Two burly Roman soldiers pushed open the door to the storeroom, ducked their helmeted heads and hurried in. They carried their swords unsheathed and their fierce faces were streaked with sweat.

"For God's sake!" Meshullam cried out. "My daughter's giving birth to her first child. Can't you leave us alone?"

Miriam's cries rose from the bed. Fear gave her moans the sound of reality. The soldiers hesitated, then moved toward her.

"Stay away!" Joseph said, rising from the bed, prepared to give his life for Miriam.

An officer hurried into the storeroom and pushed past the soldiers. Miriam stared at him—and screamed. It was the centurion—the one who led the patrol that raped her.

Miriam's scream startled everyone. Gaius peered at her in the flickering candlelight and was staggered. "Leave her alone!" he blurted out. "Search the rest of the room!"

The soldiers ripped down some cloth, kicked over a chair and a table, pretending to search although everything in the small room was in plain sight.

Gaius couldn't take his eyes off Miriam. Did she recognize him? Would she say anything?

Miriam watched him warily, her eyes wide, her body shaking. She realized the centurion had recognized her and that he knew she had recognized him. Would he kill her now—kill her and the baby?

Gaius tore his eyes away and watched his soldiers ineffectually ransacking the room. Exasperated, he swore an oath that included everyone in the room—everyone in the country. Then with a brusque gesture, he ordered his men to withdraw. Taking one last, agonized glance at Miriam, he followed them.

No one moved. Miriam gradually stopped trembling, but her heart was still pounding and there were tears in her eyes. She felt a strange kind of gratitude, of deliverance.

Joseph remained motionless, his heart beating harder than Miriam's, while the same sense of deliverance enfolded him. Meshullam's loud breathing was the only sound in the storeroom.

Overhead, hoof beats shook the earth. They echoed for a long time and then gradually faded.

Joseph embraced Miriam, reassuring her.

"I'm fine," Miriam said, brushing away the last of her tears.

Meshullam's face creased into a semblance of a smile. "You saved a life," he said. Meshullam reached under the bed and pulled the boy from underneath. "This is Simon," he said, "the son of Judas of Galilee."

Joseph gave in to the luxury of anger. "Tell us what this is all about!" he yelled.

"Forgive me, cousin," Meshullam answered, "The boy's father is the Galilean leader who defied the Herodians and Romans and led an uprising. Most of his men were killed, but Judas escaped to Gaulanitis. He sent his son to Beth Lechem, but a traitor gave him away. The boy escaped again and found his way here. You know the rest."

"Miriam and our child might have been killed," Joseph said, his eyes fixed on Simon ben Judas. The boy bravely returned Joseph's stern look.

"It's all right," Miriam said, putting an arm around Simon. "We all survived."

Joseph sighed deeply. "When will it end?" he asked.

"When the Messiah comes," Meshullam answered firmly.

"Pray he comes soon," Joseph said.

***

Simon ben Judas remained in the storeroom through the long night. He sat on the floor in the darkest corner with his back against the wall, his frail arms hugging his knees. He was painfully thin and obviously exhausted, but his large, luminous eyes, never closed for more than a few seconds. At the slightest movement, his lids would fly open and he would crush himself farther back into the corner.

Miriam brought him food, which he ate ravenously, but she could not get him to say more than a few words. His tension was palpable in the little storeroom, and it seemed to grow as dawn arrived, and then the long day passed with agonizing slowness and finally lengthened into evening.

Meshullam came for him. "We've found a safe house for you, lad. Come along."

Slowly, the boy got to his feet. He began to follow Meshullam, then turned suddenly back to Miriam. He gave her a quick and clumsy hug and would have pulled away, but she held him for a moment, then kissed him on his cheek.

"God be with you," she whispered.

He might have cried then, but he didn't dare. "Sholom Aleichem," he said, in a high-pitched voice, thin as a reed, and then hurried out.

***

Joseph and Miriam never forgot the time they sheltered Simon ben Judas, but as the days passed, their thoughts focused again on Miriam's child. One winter night, they were drawn outside by the spectacular clarity of the Judaean sky. Joseph held Miriam's arm, gently guiding her across the rocky ground. The sky was brilliant with stars and the moon so bright that it cast sharp shadows. Miriam looked especially lovely, her fine profile outlined by the luminous sky. Joseph was fiercely proud of her and just as fiercely protective. He drew his arm more tightly around her shoulder.

Miriam smiled up at him, noticing as if for the first time, how tall he was and how strong his features. It may be that I will actually learn to love this man, she thought.

High, high above them the sky suddenly grew even brighter, and a slim, fiery shape soared across the heavens. Joseph and Miriam stopped in their tracks. The brilliant light blazed overhead, a fiery arrow that seemed to point directly at them. Joseph gasped and Miriam held her breath. At that moment, she felt a stirring inside her.

***

A great grin covered Joseph's face: A boy—a beautiful boy, perfectly formed, larger than average, with astonishingly fair skin and strong, even features. As the child began to cry, his voice was remarkably resonant and the sound was more like a song than an infant's wailing.

Miriam, tired, but radiant, glowed with joy as she gave the child her breast. He took it greedily and she looked with soft love down on this beautiful gift. Her eyes beckoned to Joseph and he sat beside her, smiling again and again.

Mehetabel, who had supervised the delivery with cool, cheerful efficiency, called the rest of her family. They came bustling in, smiling and exclaiming over the child's beauty.

"Like an angel," Mehetabel said proudly, "and the birth was so easy. He popped out of the oven on his own."

"It's a miracle," Joseph said, his eyes fixed on the child.

Mehetabel smiled knowingly. "Of course," she said," every time."

"A boy," Joseph told them proudly, as if they hadn't noticed.

"He looks like you," Meshullam said and Joseph blushed. Tears of joy and gratitude streamed down his face.

THE MURDERED MESSIAH

BOOK 2

MASSACRE OF THE INNOCENTS

1.

JOSHUA

"Joshua," Joseph said, "take your time. You're working too quickly."

There was a frown on Joseph's face, but a smile in his heart and the boy knew it. He could feel his father's love wash over him, a sparkling sea of warmth and affection, of pride and approval. He nodded and slowed his strokes. It was not easy for him. Joseph had taught his son the rudiments of his trade at a very early age and Joshua had learned with astounding speed. But Joseph was a slow and cautious craftsman. Joshua was much quicker and although he, too, sought perfection, he found it difficult to adjust to his father's plodding pace.

Miriam recognized her child's cleverness very early. Joshua spoke in clear sentences when only a few months old. Often, when others tried to do things for him, he would grab something out of their hands and do it himself.

Joseph usually laughed, recalling that when he had circumcised Joshua on the eighth day after his birth, the child had wriggled so much that it seemed as if he were trying to do the work himself.

Miriam sensed a deeper issue. "My son, you must be patient with others, as the Lord our God is patient with us. Not all are as bright or quick as you, and you must love them as they are, as God loves them."

It was a difficult lesson and Joshua didn't learn it easily. At times he felt so impatient with his younger brother Jacob, that he would have to turn away, clench his fists and control himself.

On this day, once again, he had forgotten and was racing ahead. Joseph smiled and shrugged and tried to keep up with him.

Joshua. Even now, thinking or saying the name gave Joseph pleasure. His dead father's name was Jacob, which would have been a traditional choice for a first son, but Miriam had suggested Joshua, meaning, "salvation comes from God."

Joseph knew she had thought long and hard about naming the child. "He's going to be a great man," she told him, without a hint of doubt showing on her lovely face.

Joseph nodded. "Few men in all our history were greater than Joshua," he said. "He was much more than a warrior who led the Israelites into the Promised Land. He was a leader who built a nation, bringing together the new settlers with the old remnants of the Jewish community. Together, they pledged themselves freely to the great covenant offered by God."

Miriam's face had lighted up. "You understand," she said, "why I wanted to name him 'Joshua.'"

Joseph smiled. "We won't tell him what a heavy responsibility you have planned for him—at least not until he's nine or ten years old."

Miriam had laughed, but wasn't deterred. "We'll name the next boy, Jacob, if you agree," she said, her green eyes bright with hope that Joseph would approve her choice.

Joseph had hesitated only long enough to enjoy the moment, then smiled and assented. The embrace Miriam had given him was well worth it.

Out of the corner of his eye, Joseph watched the boy's golden head bent over his work. There was a glow about him—there always had been, even as an infant. A thousand times, he had heard people exclaim over the child's beauty. Working day after day in the bright sun on the house of Ari the Wise, Joseph's skin had become very dark, but Joshua's was still remarkably fair. Joseph had long since ceased to notice such differences. Even here in Nazareth, the people had slowly, grudgingly, accepted them as father and son.

In the intervening seven years, Miriam had borne six more children, four boys: Jacob, Joseph, Simeon and Judah, and two girls: Sarah and Judith. Joshua was the brightest, the most beautiful, but they were one family, cheerful, healthy, prosperous and loving.

Once again, Joshua quickened his strokes. Joseph laughed. "I can't keep up with you," he said. But the boy saw he was smiling and he answered with a smile of his own, a bright happy smile that illuminated his already glowing face.

Joshua loved his father for many reasons, not the least of which was that Joseph had taught him the mysteries of wood.

"Every tree is unique," Joseph said, his head cocked in that special way. "Each has both strengths and weaknesses. Oak is sturdy, good for roof beams and furniture, but not so good for small tools. Pine is supple and suitable for rafters or ties, but shouldn't be used for columns or pilasters."

"If you look carefully," Joseph said, "you'll see the piece of work that lives inside each branch and log and stump. The wood was once alive and God made it in a certain way, just as he made men, all individual and each with a purpose. It's our duty to see that the wood fulfills its purpose."

It astonished Joshua that his father, usually so quiet, often tongue-tied, could speak with such eloquence when he talked about his trade. It was a lesson he would not forget.

That day, Joseph and his son were working on the house of Ari the sage, framing a new roof to replace the ancient one that had buckled under the onslaughts of a powerful spring wind. Despite the heat, Ari came outside to watch them. He was wiry and slender, sixty-five years old, with a froth of thinning white hair and a flowing beard. His skin was almost as white as his hair, for he spent most of his time in the small synagogue of Nazareth, studying Torah—the law—praying over it and discussing it.

Ari's gray eyes were soft and his mouth quick to smile. Often, a line in the Torah conjured up a personal vision, and his expression became otherworldly. When Ari walked the narrow, sloping streets of Nazareth, his neighbors watched carefully, fearful that in his reverie he might slip or stumble. But he never lost his way. "God guides his footsteps," they said.

Ari's wife had died long ago and his children were in Lebanon, but he was kindly as well as wise and his door was always open. Even small children wandered in, hoping to hear a lively tale drawn from scripture. Because of his vast knowledge and good heart, many sought his counsel. Some said that he was a prophet, but Ari denied it.

"God speaks to me, but not through me. I am the parchment, not the pen."

Nevertheless, his neighbors called him "the wise one," "the sage," sometimes the "seer." Ari hated to be called a "seer" because that implied conjuration, and he detested magicians.

When the wind ripped open Ari's roof, he interpreted that as a sign from the Lord that he should lift his eyes to the heavens. Therefore, he didn't plan to have it repaired, and besides, he couldn't afford it. Joseph, knowing Ari's slender means, offered to repair the roof for a few shekels. Ari thanked him, but explained that the hole in the roof was the Lord's way of keeping his thoughts on higher things.

Joseph smiled and said, "Your thoughts are always on higher things. Anyway, if you want to look at the sky, you can step outside."

Ari laughed, and realizing that Joseph's generous offer was another gift from God, he gratefully accepted.

Despite the heat, Ari found it was pleasant to watch the man and the boy together. They worked at varying speeds but there was a harmony in their work that transcended strength and skill. It seemed to the sage to be a ritual, almost a sacrament. Ari watched, fascinated, as they mortised a corner. The sun beat on his balding, sparsely covered head. He felt a whisper of giddiness, but he was reluctant to go in.

The whisper became a tremor, then a throbbing that spread from his head to his heart. His lips opened to call Joseph, but he uttered no sound. Then, slowly, like an empty sack, Ari sank to the ground.

"Ari!" Joseph cried, but even as he began to climb down, Joshua leaped to the ground, a leap that exceeded his own height by twice, and yet he landed as gracefully as a dancer. With remarkable strength, he pulled the old man into the shade and lifted his head into his lap.

While Joseph ran into the house to get water, Joshua passed his gentle hands across the old man's face and prayed fervently, "O God, bring Ari back to us." He stared intently into Ari's watery eyes, glazed and wobbly. Joshua's expression grew stern. "Ari," the boy whispered, "come back." As his hands caressed the ancient sage, the blood returned to Ari's face. He blinked his eyes and the glazed expression disappeared.

Joseph raced up carrying a pitcher, preparing to splash water on Ari, when he saw the old man's eyes were open.

Ari sat up suddenly, fully alert, his eyes fixed on Joshua. He spoke strongly. "I was dying," he said. "My heart stopped beating. I saw a heavenly chariot."

He reached out and took Joshua's smooth hand in his withered and gnarled fist. "I felt myself leaving the earth. I said the sacred words—the 'Shema,' but then you touched me. It was like being in the hands of God. My vision cleared and my heart began to throb as in my youth." He brought Joshua's fingers to his lips and kissed them.

Joshua blushed and tried to pull his hands away, but Ari held on tightly. "We must pray," Ari said.

***

Word of Ari's stroke and his recovery spread through the village. Ari became exasperated with the repeated questions. "The boy saved me, I tell you. I was a dead man."

The elders hurried to the house of Joseph. They found Joshua sitting cross-legged on the floor, looking at them with clear eyes. One of the elders grabbed Joshua's hands and studied them intently. "They're ordinary hands— a bit smooth for a carpenter, but otherwise ordinary."

"Leave him alone," Miriam said, her hands clasped firmly in front of her, doubt and anger mixed in her expression.

Jacob and Judith giggled.

"Hush," she said and cuffed Jacob on the arm. "Go outside." The two children hurried out of the house.

"How did you heal Ari?" one of the elders asked.

Joshua spoke sharply. "Only GOD heals," he said. Something in Joshua's eyes intimidated them. They stepped back, confused. The boy was only eight years old. Why did they feel fear?

Joseph's expression darkened and he waved a hand, pointing to the door. The elders sighed, took a last, apprehensive look at Joshua and turned to leave. Ari the Sage, looking fit and strong, pushed past them, carrying a large object cradled in his arms. The elders paused, curious.

Ari held out his gift. Joshua smiled and took it gently into his hands. Slowly, carefully he unwound the bindings.

One of the elders whispered, "Torah."

"The law," Ari said, looking steadfastly at Joshua. Their eyes held in a moment of shared love and understanding. Even in the dim lamplight, the parchment of the scroll was luminous. The curved oak handles, polished by the repeated, loving touch of Ari's hands seemed to gleam.

"It's too valuable *not* to give," Ari said.

Joshua pressed the scroll to his heart and kissed Ari. The old man embraced him with surprising strength. They both cried and their tears fell like blessings on the sacred writings.

2.

THE STUDENT

Joshua and a few of the other children of the town, rich and poor, had begun attending synagogue school at age five. They learned Hebrew directly from scripture, poring over scrolls written in long, unbroken rows of letters, all of the same size, without any indication of where a word began or ended.

The teacher was the Hazzan, the guardian of the sacred books. His lessons were limited almost entirely to rote learning and he had little time for individual training. Joshua could quote an amazing amount of scripture from memory, but his questions often went unanswered.

Therefore, when Ari made his gift of the precious scrolls he also offered to instruct Joshua, who enthusiastically accepted. Sometimes Ari taught Joshua in his home or in the synagogue, but usually he led him to a sheltered spot on a hillside under the pines. There, overlooking the rolling hills and valleys and under a blue sky crowded with clouds in rapidly moving patterns, Ari knew they were much closer to God than in any building, no matter how sacred.

Joshua constantly questioned the meanings and purposes of scripture. "Why is this story in Torah?" he would ask. Or, "Why is this story so long and this one so short?"

Ari had spent much of his life studying the commentaries, the Halakhah and Aggadot, but he did not wish to confuse Joshua with the serpentine logic of the scribes or the esoteric reasoning of the rabbis. He gave the boy the plain and simple truths as he understood them.

"The sacred writings are much more than a history of our people. Each story is included because it teaches us how God wants us to live."

"Why are there evil stories as well as good ones?" Joshua asked, his clear blue eyes fixed on the cloudy gray ones of his teacher.

"Because man is both good and evil, and we are required to choose between the two. It is very easy to be confused."

Joshua nodded his head. Even in his brief sojourn on earth he had learned that choices must be made—especially when one has mischievous younger brothers.

"Where is God now?" Joshua asked.

"Where he has always been—everywhere?"

"But my father often complains that we're like slaves in our own country. Why doesn't God do something now that we need him so much?"

It was a difficult question. "We must not only need God, we must be worthy of his help. Many cry out for God to save them, but they don't honor God or obey his law."

"Is that a sin?"

"To be separated from God," Ari said, "that is the greatest sin."

"Are we better than they are?" Joshua asked.

"Better than who?"

"The gentiles."

Ari shook his head vigorously "The Lord told us:

'Are not you Israelites,

the same to me as the Ethiopians?

Did I not bring Israel up from Egypt,

The Philistines from Crete

and the Syrians from Kir?' We are all the children of God. Why do you think we're better?"

"Because we're not 'separated' from God. We have the Law."

"Yes and it is one of God's greatest gifts, but it is not ours alone."

"We are the chosen people."

"That," said Ari, "is a matter of God's grace and not our special worth. But God has not merely selected us—he has given us our great task."

Excited, Joshua broke in. "It says in Exodus that we are to be a kingdom of priests and a holy nation."

Ari smiled. "In the words of God to Isaiah:

'I will give you as a light to the Gentiles,

that my salvation may reach to the end of the earth."

"Then why," Joshua asked, "do we stay apart from the gentiles? Why does my father refuse to take any meals with them?"

Ari looked down at his gnarled hands, crossed with a network of veins, appearing and disappearing beneath the wrinkled skin. So many paths, he thought, so many paths. "We believe that it is our duty to remain clean, and that if we dine with gentiles who eat forbidden foods and do not wash before eating, that we will be unclean, too."

Joshua shook his head scornfully. "I've watched Ezra, the Philistine goat-herd, bathe himself in a freezing cold stream in winter. He's as clean as any Jew."

Ari sighed. "Of course," he said, "and we cannot hope to teach the gentiles if we remain apart from them."

Joshua was perplexed. "Sometimes gentiles come to the synagogue to listen to our teaching. No one turns them away."

"It seems strange, doesn't it," Ari said, "that a man who would not sit down with a gentile in his home will welcome him into the synagogue? Sometimes we draw the line too finely—even forgetting why it's there. But there is still hope. You see, my son, even now there are Jews everywhere in the Roman Empire, most of them converts from pagan religions. A learned traveler once told me that one in ten Roman citizens is a Jew."

"We'll get the other nine," Joshua said, his eyes alive with excitement. "That way they'd only be oppressing themselves."

Ari almost laughed, watching his student with wonder.

But Joshua wasn't finished. "If they're not careful, we'll conquer them with love."

***

Joshua happily accompanied his father to the synagogue on the Sabbath. He loved to chant the prayers and sing hymns in his high, sweet voice. He listened carefully when the elders expounded scripture and discussed political and religious issues. The women of Nazareth also attended the holy ceremonies, but did not recite from scripture, nor participate in discussions.

"Why don't you speak up?" Joshua asked his mother. "You're as clever as any man."

Miriam flicked her eyes quickly at Joseph, who pretended not to be listening, then said, "The men argue and argue, but never seem to decide anything. We women have more important tasks."

"What can be more important than God?" Joshua asked, but Miriam only smiled and went on with her work.

To Joshua's surprise, he found there were sharp divisions in the congregation.

"It seems to me that a Jew is a Jew," he told Ari. "We have but one holy scripture not two or three or ten."

Ari tried to explain. "We are only human," he said, "and each of us finds something different in Torah. Here in Galilee, there is only a handful who follow the priestly party, the Sadducees. They believe truth is limited to the literal words of scripture which was divinely inspired and is complete in itself.

"Many of the people hereabouts, including your father, follow the Pharisees. They're less rigid though no less pious. They accept the teachings of the rabbis and the scribes and have developed more recent traditions. While the Sadducees believe only in the present life, the Pharisees believe in resurrection—that men may die, but one day they will live again in God's holy kingdom."

That satisfied Joshua for a while, but the very next day, he stopped his father and questioned him on the same subject. "How can a man be dead and buried and come to life?"

Joseph smiled. "Surely God who gave us life in the first place can bring us back to life if and when he chooses."

"In the same body?" the boy asked.

"God is wise. Let's trust him to do it the best way"

Joshua wasn't completely satisfied with his father's answer. "I like the idea of rebirth," he said. "When I read the book of Job I couldn't believe God would permit such evil things to happen. But if there's another life, there's still time to make everything right."

Joseph smiled at his son. "You understand better than many of your elders," he said.

Miriam was proud of Joshua, but in her heart she sometimes wished he was as simple as the other children. Like any mother, she wanted her child's life to be happy and serene.

Joshua had his private side, too. Much as he loved his family, at times he had his fill of the noise and the laughter, the tears and the bickering. Then he wandered off by himself, as Miriam had done when she was a girl. Joshua would climb the rocky hills near his home until he found a sheltered place where he could sit and think. He watched the clouds drifting overhead and the breeze bending the trees

"Why, Lord, why am I here?"

The breeze freshened and it seemed to Joshua that he heard a whisper, but he couldn't follow the words. Overhead, the towering cumulus clouds formed into a great flowing shape that seemed both powerful and friendly.

"Is that you, Lord?" the boy asked.

"No, it's me," a squeaky voice called.

Startled, Joshua turned to see Jacob, laughing and running down the hill. He leapt up and followed his younger brother.

"Never catch me," Jacob cried, but at that moment, Joshua left his feet, soared through the air and threw his arms about Jacob. They crashed to the ground together and Jacob began to wail. His knee was bruised and his finger was cut.

"I'm gonna tell Momma," Jacob cried, sucking on his bloody finger and holding his knee."

Joshua took the corner of his tunic and tried to dry the bloody finger, but Jacob pulled away.

Joshua grabbed it firmly and dried it, holding off the squirming Jacob.

"I'm sorry," Joshua said. "I didn't mean to hurt you." He looked earnestly into his brother's eyes. "Please believe me," he continued, still ministering to the injured knee and bloody finger.

"All right," Jacob said, his love for Joseph overcoming his pain, "I believe you." In a moment, the wounds had healed.

"How did you do that?" Jacob asked. He forgot to cry as he stared at the place his wounds had been.

"Do what?" Joshua asked.

Jacob was staring at the finger; he saw no cut. He glanced at his knee; the bruise was gone.

"You did that so Momma won't see how you hurt me," he said petulantly.

Joshua burst out laughing. Then Jacob began laughing, too. Joshua pulled him to his feet and they walked back into Nazareth, arm in arm.

Thereafter, whenever Jacob was hurt, he would go to Joshua for help. In time, the other children did the same. They took it for granted that Joshua would heal them. Miriam watched and marveled and then, almost in the same instant, worried what it might mean. She was afraid to ask anyone, unwilling to raise new questions about Joshua's uniqueness.

On rare occasions, Joshua was able to escape from his family, sit on his hilltop and talk to God without being interrupted. He had spoken aloud to the Lord since he was a small child. He didn't expect an answer to his questions, but he enjoyed these one-sided conversations, knowing that God was near and caring even if he didn't always respond.

The day after the incident with Jacob, Joshua managed to return to the hilltop towards sunset, when his work was done. He sprawled on the crisp grass, pulled out a long blade and chewed it thoughtfully. "You didn't answer me, yesterday," he said. The wind rose as before and in the rush of air he thought he heard a voice saying "Yes, I did."

Joshua was astonished. The voice surely wasn't Jacob's. He looked about him, but saw no one. The wind rose again, and Joshua saw the clouds forming and reforming, into what looked like a face of great and noble proportions. The lips seemed to be moving and as the wind rose, he again thought he heard a voice saying, "I spoke but you listened to Jacob and did not hear. That is the way of man. He listens to his brother and not to God."

Joshua nodded. "I'll listen, Lord, I promise."

He heard no response and the face in the clouds grew hazy and disappeared. Joshua waited patiently on the hilltop, but the sun set and the evening grew cold and he heard nothing more that day.

***

As the months passed, Joshua became an ever more capable craftsman. Joseph entrusted to him even the most difficult and painstaking projects and his handiwork became prized in Nazareth.

Meanwhile, his studies continued and his vision broadened. Joshua was fascinated by the story of Abraham. "Ari," he said, "When Abraham prepared to sacrifice Isaac, he must have a very old man and Isaac about the age of my father."

"True."

"An old man couldn't have held down his grown son unless the son was willing."

Ari nodded, his eyes glistening.

"Then Isaac's faith was as great as Abraham's," the lad said. "Each one trusted his father."

Ari nearly wept.

The events of scripture became more alive to Joshua with every passing day. It was as if the entire history of his people were taking place in his own lifetime. He groaned over his people's bondage in Egypt and rejoiced over their liberation. He puzzled over the history of King David, a man of such glaring contrasts, yet always ready to admit his weaknesses and the Lord always ready to grant forgiveness.

Joshua cried over the destruction of the Temple by Nebuchadnezzar and cheered the rebuilding. He drew no line between the stories of scripture and the events of the day. To Joshua, the current sufferings of his people were but another event in scriptural history. Once it had been the Babylonians, then the Greeks. Now it was the Romans. Hardly a week passed without word of an uprising provoked by Roman brutality or abuse of Jewish traditions.

"We've lived under foreign occupation for a long time," Ari told him. "We've been subjugated, but we have never submitted."

"Tell me about King Herod. They say he was a Jew, but no one speaks well of him."

"He was an Edomite who followed our religion in name only, thinking an outward show of piety would keep the people loyal to him. Herod was a strange, erratic man who spent huge sums on building the Temple but even more on glorifying himself. He was a sick man and a dangerous one. His spies were everywhere. In Herod's time, a man couldn't speak his mind without fear of being betrayed.

"He didn't even trust his own family, especially those descended from the Maccabees. He murdered his wife Mariamne, a woman he claimed to love dearly. He murdered his own children, believing they were plotting against him. When he died, the people erupted, believing they were casting off over thirty years of oppression, but Herod's rule was replaced by even harsher rule. Once again, our people are growing desperate. Some pray for another Judas Maccabee."

"His story isn't part of our scriptures," Joshua said.

"No," Ari answered, "but it should be." Then he told Joshua how two hundred years earlier, the Greek Seleucid ruler, Antiochus Epiphanes had decreed the abolition of the Jewish religion and converted the Temple at Jerusalem into a shrine to Zeus.

"The people rose up under an ancient priest, Mattathias. One of his sons, Judas called Maccabeus, 'The Hammer,' led the revolt. After many remarkable victories, he and his army recaptured, cleansed and rededicated the Temple.

"The Book of Daniel was written hundreds of years before the Maccabees, but based on that book the people began to renew their hopes for the Messiah, the Anointed of God. Daniel had a dream in which he saw four great beasts, and the fourth was the most terrible. In Daniel's time, the Jews believed the fourth was the Greek Kingdom, but now the sages say it is the Roman Empire.

"In Daniel's words,

'The one that was ancient of days took his seat;

and his raiment was white as snow, and the hair of his head like pure wool;

his throne was fiery flames,
its wheels were burning fire.'

"Then, as Daniel watched, the beast was destroyed.

'and behold, with the clouds of heaven
there came one like a Son of Man,
and he came to the Ancient of Days
and was presented before him.
and to him was given dominion
and glory and kingdom,
that all peoples, nations, and languages should serve him;
his dominion is an everlasting dominion,
which shall not pass away,
and his kingdom one
that shall not be destroyed.'"

Ari's eyes blinked with tears as he finished. When he spoke again, his voice was a whisper.

"The Son of Man," he said, "is the anointed one, the Messiah."

"When will the Messiah come?" Joshua asked.

Ari smiled. "Perhaps he's already among us. It is written that he will come in the 'Last Times,' and that in those times the forces of good and evil will struggle with each other—a time of great suffering for the Elect of Israel, to be followed by an age of righteousness and bliss, the age of the Kingdom of God.

"Many believe we are now in the Last Times. But when—on what exact date, the Messiah will reveal himself—of that no man can be certain."

Ari watched his young student, avidly committing these testimonies to memory.

"Dear Joshua," he said. "The Messiah could be someone from Galilee, someone from this town, someone even now a child." He took a deep breath, placed his hand on Joshua's slim shoulder and spoke words he had held in his heart for a long time: "The Messiah could be you."

3.

MOTHER

I remember the joy of having him—the joy and the fear. Joseph did everything he could to reassure me, but what if the child were brown or yellow, or had strange features or even a combination of oddities? Thank God that didn't happen. He came from my womb fresh and pink and lusty and beautiful and the first time he took my breast I knew that he would be wonderful. He was blonde and blue-eyed; that was glorious, but hard to explain. My eyes were green and Joseph's brown. My hair was black and Joseph's sandy. We didn't explain, didn't try to explain. We simply loved and enjoyed the child.

Joseph was good about the name: Joshua. He might have insisted we follow tradition and name him after his own dead father, but he cheerfully agreed to the name I had chosen, the one that had occurred to me suddenly on the road to Beth Lechem. Later, I wondered at the choice and feared it might have been better to choose another, but I believe the name came to me from the Lord.

Joshua was a good baby, a very good baby. He soon slept through the night without waking us. He was alert, cheerful and his eyes always had a certain something in them, something knowing, warm and special. I gained strength from being near him, from watching him grow and eat and sleep. Yes, he spoke very early and walked very early and was more agile than any child I ever saw. But none of that startled me. I was very proud of him, but not amazed, although others were surprised at 'how quickly he learned.

The first sign that he was truly different was the cut. He fell and cut his hand on a rock. He began to cry, but not loudly, more or less in surprise. I picked him up and comforted him. "It's all right, Joshua," I murmured, "it's all right. God will heal your little cut."

I carried him swiftly toward the house where there was clean water and a cloth to wipe the cut. He looked at the wound, spewing blood and with his other hand slowly traced his finger along the jagged line of the tear.

I wanted to say 'No, don't touch that,' but I saw that each time he drew his finger over the cut, the flow of blood diminished.

I stopped moving—I couldn't help it—and I watched. The next time his finger passed over it, the cut began to close. Another touch and it was closed. Then the angry redness disappeared, and finally, where there had been a cut, there was only a line, now red, now pink, now brown, now hard to see.

Joshua touched it one last time, then turned his face to me and smiled. I didn't know what to do. I smiled back, but I was amazed. Should I tell Joseph? Should I discuss it with my mother, or with the president of the congregation, or with the rabbi or with Ari?

I did none of those things. I was afraid they would laugh at me. Or if they believed me, they might think there was something dangerous about my child. They would remember how he had been conceived, and they might fear the evil eye or some form of magic. We Jews detest magic and magicians.

I kept silent. I saw it happen again some months later with a bruise on his knee and then with a cut on his forehead, the usual childhood injuries. Each time a touch of his hands and the damage would disappear. Later, others saw him heal himself. I ignored it if I could and denied it if I couldn't. But people saw and they began to realize what I already knew: this child was different.

Perhaps, in the early years, I protected him too much, carried him about more than I should have. I wasn't afraid he would be injured, only that others might see him heal himself.

He yearned to be free. He was weaned early, earlier than I would have liked it, for I needed him at my breast more than he needed me. But soon there were other children—every year for several years another child at my breast, all beautiful, all wonderful. I loved them all—even bearing them, which came easier every time. But none were like Joshua. Perhaps it's always that way with your first child.

He wandered away time and again. I never could keep track of him, neither could Hannah, my mother, who was such a help when the children were young. Suddenly Joshua would be gone. We would scurry around and finally find him, examining a plant or a butterfly (but he would never pull off the wings) or maybe a toad or a tree. Often we found him sitting alone, staring into the distance.

He liked to be alone. That was difficult in a small house with many children. Not that Joseph didn't do well for us. He did. He was a builder, not merely a carpenter, and his jobs were very large sometimes and he hired other men to help. But later, when the children grew up, Joseph taught the boys his trade. First among them was Joshua who was better than Joseph with tools, better at drawing plans, even better at talking to people and learning precisely what they wanted to build.

Oh, it's hard to believe how quickly he grew, how quickly he learned. At times, he was impatient with me.

"Mother," he would say, "why don't you know about Shadrach, Meshach and Abednego—they're in the book of Daniel?"

I would smile and tell him I didn't have time to read the book of Daniel and he would frown and say I ought to make the time, and then I would be angry, what with cooking all the meals and caring for all the children and I would say so. "You take care of the children," I would say, "and I'll read your Daniel," and then he would laugh and embrace me.

"No," he said "I think I'll keep to carpentering."

But in fact, I knew he wouldn't keep to carpentering. I knew that God had more in store for him. I suppose every mother feels that way, that I'm not really unusual. Still, the signs were many with Joshua. Even when we had him circumcised, the president of the congregation in Beth Lechem said he would be an important man in Israel. That alarmed me, because we were not from Israel, but from Galilee and in fact, there was no Israel on that day, at least not an Israel that belonged to the Jews.

Then there was the miracle of saving Ari, which puzzled and frightened the elders of Nazareth.

But it wasn't those external events that caused me the most concern. After all, every child has his good times and his bad, the times you're proud of him and the times when you fear for him. But with Joshua I always had a sense of destiny. I had no idea what that destiny was and yet I feared it. I was ashamed of fearing it, concerned that my very doubts would somehow bring unhappiness to my beloved son. I prayed to God to free me of my doubts.

No matter how fervently I prayed, my fears were never lifted, never eased. As the years went by without event, I thought my doubts might be put aside. My son would live to a ripe old age, be honored and go to his grave as our ancestors had done. But I knew better. Time was passing, but the crisis was coming closer. Sometimes I looked into Joshua's eyes and

I believed that for a fleeting second we shared that knowledge. Then the moment would pass and we would act like any other mother and son in Galilee. For a while.

I never believed I could change his fate or affect it in any way. In a sense, I didn't even want to know what it was, although, instinctively, I did know. But there was no one to share it with. Except the Lord. And He had warned me, told me to be brave, but never told me how.

Now, looking back, what do I think? That isn't fair. When Joshua, full of love for his people and zeal for God, told us his plans at the Passover, I was distraught. I would have preferred he had stayed away from Jerusalem altogether But I knew he wouldn't listen to me.

I couldn't help thinking of earlier festivals we shared with Rebecca and the children in Beth Sholem. I recalled, with a pang, the happier times when the whole family was together, everyone laughing and talking at the same time. Given the choice, would I wish for my son a long and simple life, a life warmed by a good wife and fine children, a life of good health and quiet pleasures? Forgive me, Lord, but yes I would. Many say that Joshua was a hero, one of our greatest heroes. Others say he was clearly the anointed of God and that the last of the story is yet to be told. Many come to me and tell me of the lives he saved and the sick he brought back to health and they tell me I should be very proud. I am. But I love my son more than my pride and I wish he were with me now.

4.

FESTIVAL
(APRIL, 7 C.E.)

They were up long before dawn, feeding the animals, packing their belongings and eating a hurried meal. The trip to the Holy City would take several days, and they wanted to arrive at least a few days before sunset on the fourteenth of Nissan, the eve of the Passover and the vernal equinox as measured by the priests. They regretted they would not have a full week to perform the complete rituals of purity, but they would do the best they could.

The three younger boys, Joses, Simeon and Judah, and the girls, Sarah and Judith would remain home with their grandparents. Miriam was radiant. The very idea of the trip was exciting and it would truly be a festival to be responsible only for Joshua and Jacob. She bustled about the house, singing.

Joseph observed his wife with deep delight. She was even more beautiful than when he had first seen her, a lovely, laughing, green-eyed girl, running to the well. With the birth of each child she had grown more beautiful to him, warmer and happier. Joseph smiled again when he thought of Joshua. He was their favorite, though neither of them would have said so. Already, he was almost as tall as Joseph, with a flowing head of blonde air, broad shoulders and powerful hands.

Joshua was thrilled at the thought of his first trip to Jerusalem. He knew of the scriptural obligation of all Jews to attend the great festivals in the Holy City. Soon, he would be thirteen, legal age among his people, Joseph had decided it was time to begin fulfilling that responsibility.

Jacob would be coming, too, even though he was a year younger. But Joshua loved his younger brother and was pleased to have his company.

"You must do what I tell you," Joshua said trying not to smile, "when we're in Jerusalem."

Jacob smiled. He was much shorter than Joshua, with curly black hair and dark eyes that often crinkled in mischief. "Of course," he said, "seeing as how you're such an expert."

Joshua laughed. Jacob had a way of deflating him when he was taking himself too seriously.

It seemed that all of Nazareth was in the street, beginning the pilgrimage. Asses were braying, heifers lowing and goats bleating. Men piled their belongings on carts and called to their loved ones.

"Shaloms" filled the air, together with the plaintive cries of children left behind and the gentle weeping of elders, too old for the journey. Neighbors greeted neighbors, families grouped and re-grouped. Young ones scurried back for forgotten things and angry fathers called after them.

But most of all, the scene was one of joy. Already, pilgrims were passing through from the north, rocking and swaying on their animals, or marching steadily on their own feet. In the excitement of the festival, the people had chosen to forget their problems. Drought had struck the usually fertile valleys of Galilee the past year. Then, Quirinius, the ruthless new Roman legate in Syria, proclaimed a census would be taken. The people knew what that meant: new taxes. The burden would be especially hard to bear after a season when the crops had failed. There were sporadic incidents of confrontation between the census takers and angry farmers. Then the revolt spread through the country, led by Judas, the Galilean. It was crushed and thousands of rebels were crucified, although Judas had escaped.

But this morning, such concerns were forgotten. Even in the misty dawn, dust rose from the highway. Joshua saw the spiraling dust as long swirling ropes stretching from all the ends of Israel down to Jerusalem where the strands were bound together, even as the tribes joined together for the feast. Perhaps this would be the season when the liberation of Israel would be more than an ancient symbol.

A pretty girl, swathed in a new black robe, came swaying by on a mule. Her eyes glowed at the sight of Joshua with his blonde flowing hair and piercing blue eyes.

"Shalom," she called to him. "See you in Jerusalem."

"Shalom," he called back and watched until she disappeared.

"Was that Rebecca, Bochar's daughter," Miriam asked.

"Yes."

"A beautiful girl," Miriam said

Joshua nodded.

***

Now they were on the main highway to Jerusalem, they and thousands like them. Laughter and singing rippled along the column. Faces lifted to the sun and voices soared upward, while the plodding animals and plodding pilgrims accentuated the rhythms.

"Blessed are those whose way is blameless,
Who walk in the Law of the Lord."
Others responded, "Blessed are those who keep his testimonies,
Who seek him with their whole heart."

Many musicians, carrying lyres and psalterys, accompanied the singing pilgrims, plucking out the rhythms alone or in groups.

The feeling of fellowship was universal. Joshua felt he was caressed in the bosom of Abraham. He smiled at his own family and at the family of Israel.

"Look," Jacob said, grabbing his arm. Joshua followed his brother's pointing finger, to another swirling cloud of dust approaching from the west.

Soon all the pilgrims saw it. The singing voices faded slowly, the instruments stopped playing. Here and there a child cried, but otherwise, the pilgrims advanced in silence, their eyes on the swirling cloud.

Miriam took Joseph's hand and held it tightly, as the cloud became men on horseback, Roman cavalry bearing down on the pilgrims. Fear tightened Miriam's heart strings. The horses' hooves rang on the hard, rocky soil, singing a song of steel and violence.

"Make way!" someone screamed, but there was no time. The column bore straight down on them, the soldiers yelling and swinging their swords.

The pilgrims broke and ran. Women and children screamed and asses, roughly pulled, brayed angrily. For a moment all was confusion, as the horsemen sliced through the column. Joseph's anger growled in his throat. He reached for the short knife in his belt, but Miriam held his arm tightly.

The last of the Romans thundered through the fleeing pilgrims, knocking down those who were not agile enough to avoid them, maiming animals and breaking pottery. Fortunately, no one was killed, but several people suffered cuts and broken bones.

At first, the men were dazed by the onslaught, but then they began to mumble in anger. "Damn Romans."

"Did that on purpose."

"Just to frighten us."

"Some day…"

"Maybe today."

"When the King Messiah comes, we won't have to take this."

"We don't have to take it now."

The murmurs grew louder. The anger increased.

"Pray for the peace of Jerusalem." Joshua began to sing the phrase from the hundred and twenty-second psalm in a quiet voice, then sang with increasing strength. "They shall prosper who love thee." He sang in a clear, strong voice, with rising volume, inventing a simple melody to match the familiar words.

"Peace be within thy walls, and prosperity in thy palaces."

The mumbling quieted as the pilgrims listened. The words were familiar, the melody serene and the voice as clear as a mountain brook. Others picked up the song, joining Joshua.

"Pray for the peace of Jerusalem,
They shall prosper who love thee…"

The prayer and the music spread along the column. Angry grimaces smoothed, racing blood slowed. The paean to peace spread over the column like a warm mantle, drawing the pilgrims together under the protection of God.

Miriam looked at her son with wonderment. He was singing now in full voice, his eyes heavenward. He did not seem to see or hear the others.

***

"You sing very well," the man said. He was short and fat and his jowls rolled as he rode in a litter, carried by two stern-faced household servants.

"It's easy," Joshua said, "when the psalm is so beautiful."

The fat gentleman smiled and his pink face was as wrinkled as a fresh fig, but his eyes sparkled. "You're from Galilee," the man said, "what town?"

Joshua was surprised. "Nazareth. How did you know I'm from Galilee?"

"Your voice has a special music to it."

Thus Joshua learned his speech was distinctive, somewhat sharper than the smooth tones of this gentleman. He realized that not everyone would find it "musical."

"Nice town," the fat gentleman said. "The hills are very pretty, but the people are…excitable."

Joshua smiled. "Are you from Jerusalem?"

"Yes, I am a Priest," He tapped his leg. "My ailments prevent me from serving my regular course. I heard your parents call you 'Joshua.' I am Nicodemus."

***

"Mother, father," Joshua came running along the line of pilgrims. "Good news—a priest, his name is Nicodemus—has invited us to share the Passover in his home in Jerusalem."

Joseph and Miriam couldn't believe their good fortune. They had expected to pitch their tent outside the walls, sacrifice the lamb they had brought and celebrate the Passover with thousands of other pilgrims in the open air.

Joseph smiled broadly. "Come, lead me to this Nicodemus. I want to thank him myself."

***

Towards evening on the fourth day, a horseman came cantering slowly along the column. His face was drawn with fatigue and he was covered from head to foot with dust and grime. Even his horse gave off little clouds of dust each time his hooves struck the earth. The rider wearily reined to a halt near Nicodemus and slipped, almost fell, from his horse. He leaned on the shoulder of one of Nicodemus's servants and spoke in whispery tones to the former priest.

Other pilgrims, worried and curious, crowded close to Nicodemus's litter while the rider spoke.

"Another uprising," he gasped, "east of the sea. Judas of Galilee raided the customhouse and killed the collectors."

"You must rest," Nicodemus gently told the tired rider.

The man shook his head. "Judas is rallying the people, telling them not to pay the taxes. 'No ruler but God,' he says."

"No ruler but God," Nicodemus repeated, moved by the words in spite of himself. But then he shook his head and returned to reality. "What are the Romans doing?" he asked.

"More soldiers from Syria," the rider said. "Attacks in Gaulanitis, skirmishes in the mountain country. Some dead, many wounded."

Nicodemus put his hand on the man's shoulder. "Is there a true rebellion—is it spreading?"

"Hard to say. Some men have gone into the hills. Roman patrols everywhere. You'll come on them yourselves."

"We already have," Nicodemus said. "They rode through the column. Now we know why they were angry."

Word of the uprising spread quickly among the pilgrims.

"'No ruler but God,'" a man said, "I like that."

"You like it?" his wife said. "You have small children."

Everywhere the debate went on.

"We should go back," some of the younger ones said, "and fight with Judas."

"Don't be foolish," the elders responded. "The Romans will wipe out the rebels."

"God will help us," the young ones said angrily. Several of them pulled out of the column and turned north, while their wives and friends pleaded with them to remain.

All along the column, the pilgrims were moved by word of the uprising. Ultimately, only a handful turned back, although most of the men yearned in their hearts to join them.

"The Festival," they told each other. "We must go to Jerusalem for the Festival. God will tell us what to do."

Joshua listened to the arguments with avid interest. He could feel the anguish of his people deep in his bones. Jacob poked a hand in his back. "We going back?" he asked.

Joshua shook his head.

"Why not?" Jacob asked. ."Aren't we going to fight for God?"

Joshua smiled at him. "Only if the Lord tells us to."

"How will we know?"

"We won't talk," Joshua said, "we'll listen."

Jacob glared at him, but held his tongue.

Joseph patted Joshua on the back. "Well spoken, my boy. Now, let's get back on the road."

***

They had left the main road and swung over to the Jericho road, hoping the crowds would be smaller, but they were mistaken. The long columns of pilgrims stretched up in flowing lines from the floor of the valley, past Bethany to the top of the Mount of Olives.

Jacob was in trouble again—he had poked a lamb and sent it screaming down the hillside and Joshua was forced to chase it. He had just returned it to its owners when the column halted suddenly and he heard a collective sigh from the pilgrims.

Ahead, the sky was streaked with orange and scarlet, white and pink, saffron and blue. The sun had dipped below the horizon, but its rays still scaled the heavens and cascaded down on the Holy City. The walls were in shadow, except at the south, where they glowed a deep pink. Towers and battlements marched in a stern pattern from north to south and then bent around the city.

"The Temple," Nicodemus sighed"

"The Temple," others echoed. Limestone walls and colonnades were edged with fire. Celestial sparks struck off the gold parapets and pinnacles, the gem-encrusted roofs and pilasters. In the fiery glow of the sunset, the images of the city and the Temple were thrown forward, floating above the Kidron Valley. From the inner court of the Temple, flames could be seen, flickering and dancing while columns of thick smoke curled into the air.

"They're sacrificing the paschal lamb," Nicodemus said softly to Joshua. "Hundreds of thousands of pilgrims, tens of thousands of lambs. We must hurry."

But Joshua didn't seem to hear. His eyes were huge, as he stared at the Temple. To Nicodemus, the blonde halo of his hair echoed the glow of the gold-tinged sanctuary.

Among the pilgrims, voices began to rise. A trumpet sounded from the Temple and echoed across the Kidron to the Mount of Olives. Lyres and pslaterys were struck in response and the voices began to swell.

"Pray for the peace of Jerusalem," sang one group.

"Blessed are those whose way is blameless, who walk in the law of the Lord," sang another.

Still others sang, "I will lift mine eyes unto the hills, from whence comes my help.

My help comes from the Lord, who made heaven and earth."

The hymns varied in melody and words, but they blended in the longing of the pilgrims, and rose triumphantly into the crystalline sky.

Nicodemus watched Joshua and Joshua watched Jerusalem.

***

As they approached the city, the crowds grew thicker and the pace slowed. Joshua was fascinated by the bewildering variety of pilgrims. They came in every size and shape, bearded and clean-shaven, blonde and brown and black and red haired, swarthy and fair, sturdy and slender. For the first time he was aware of the infinite variety of his countrymen—and women. He was accustomed to the simple, ruddy and healthy-looking girls of Nazareth. Now he saw women with complexions as white as the linens they wore and others whose skins were very dark. Some walked with the plain, almost masculine pace he was accustomed to, but others rode donkeys as if they were royal carriages or walked with such a dainty tread, it was hard to believe they were not being carried.

"See a pretty one for yourself?" Miriam teased.

He blushed and didn't answer, but his thoughts went to Rebecca.

Miriam smiled and tousled his blonde hair. As she touched the glowing, silken softness, a tremor went through her, a memory she thought she had forgotten. She pulled her hand away abruptly, surprising Joshua. She tried to smile, but he had seen her fear and wondered at it.

The sounds of the city clanged in their ears. On the road, the noises had been free to roam. Within the walls they were confined and they echoed back and re-echoed again. Joshua saw that his mother was frightened again—this time as Roman soldiers tried to direct the crowd. They were not brutal, only brusque, plainly irritated by the unending crush of pilgrims. But they stood fast, splitting the column that entered through the Hinnom valley gate and sending it into different streets.

Joshua was pressed between the donkey that bore his mother and the litter that carried Nicodemus. The smell of incense and burnt offerings filled the sky with a heavy, suffocating odor. He wrinkled his nose, but could not avoid the smell.

Jacob, almost choking, made a vulgar sound and Joseph cuffed him on the ear. "That's a holy smell," he said, but then he, too, almost gagged.

They made their way slowly through the easternmost open triple polished-bronze Huldah gate, twice as tall as a man, gleaming with carved flowers and vines. Then they entered the courtyard of the gentiles, thronged with pilgrims and their animals. The great marble columns soared upward into graceful porticoes and the gold leaf glittered on the capitals and the roofs.

Joshua uttered a brief prayer, awed that he was now within the bounds of the Temple enclosure. All around him, masses of people were chanting and praying, singing and calling to their friends. Merchants were changing money for the pilgrims and selling animals for the sacrifice. Joshua was staggered by what seemed to him a violation of the shrine.

Then, he had another shock. On the roofs of the colonnades, spaced at brief intervals, stood Roman soldiers in full armor, carrying weapons. The pilgrims and priests tried to ignore them, but every time they moved, they cast a shadow on the proceedings.

Farther off rose the gray hulk of the four-towered Antonia Palace, cut into the northwest corner of the Temple, with porches and towers that loomed over the courtyard. There, too, Roman soldiers grimly surveyed the crowd, their very presence an obscene violation.

Joshua carried a lamb, bleating and twisting in his arms as if it understood its fate. Soon they reached the entrance of the Court of Priests, climbing the curved steps, passing through the gold covered Nicanor gate. The glow of marble and polished gold was dazzling. The Levites assigned to the sacrifice were young, muscular men, wearing bloodstained garments and weary expressions. With skill and precision, they slaughtered thousands of lambs in an endless chain, threw the entrails and fat onto the fire and returned the butchered animals to their owners. Burning flesh sizzled in the roaring fires, smoke billowed in dense clouds and bleating animals screamed to the heavens.

As Joshua watched in dismay, a Levite reached for his lamb. Joshua held back. The young man understood. "It's all right," he said. "The little fellow will soon be with God." He pulled the lamb from Joshua's arms. Joshua watched numbly as a priest slit the lamb's throat, collected its blood and poured it before the altar.

A horn kept sounding insistently to mark each sacrifice, blaring in counterpoint to the bleating of the slaughtered animals. Blood spilled through the gutters and rolled toward the Kidron Valley. The stench was overpowering and the noise unbearable. Joshua would have stopped his ears but he thought it might be an offense to the Lord.

They handed him back the remains of the lamb and he stared at it, unbelievingly. He tried to speak to his father, but Joseph couldn't hear him over the clamor. Joshua spoke louder and louder, until even the priests could hear his question:

"How much blood does God require?"

5.

NICODEMUS

The home of Nicodemus was in the upper city, near the palace of the High Priest, but somehow remote from the Temple. The streets were broader and far quieter than in the lower city, which was a bleak but boisterous warren of small box-like houses, all colored a monotonous pale desert tone, flanked only by shadows. In the upper city, trees and shrubs flourished in trim enclosed gardens and lush vines cascaded over the walls. Nicodemus's villa was two stories high and built of stone and plaster surrounding a pleasant courtyard, with date palms and lemon trees, banks of flowers and a splashing fountain. From shaded balconies, one could see the city, but the sounds were muted and fragrant flowers covered the acrid smells.

"Some believe that King David is buried here, beneath these very stones," Nicodemus told them, "but I think it's only a charming myth."

He showed them where to stable their animals and gave them pleasant, whitewashed rooms to sleep in.

"We could sleep under the stars," Joseph said.

Nicodemus smiled. "It's a privilege to house a pilgrim—you mustn't deny that to me."

When they were alone, Jacob whispered in Joshua's ear. "He must be the richest man in Jerusalem. Wouldn't it be great to have him for a father?"

Joshua shook his head and smiled. "If you didn't have the father you do have, you wouldn't be here at all."

That was too complicated for Jacob to understand. He shrugged, pushed a chest against the wall and climbed up to see what was visible from the high window. Joshua had to pull him free when he got stuck in the grating.

***

"Praise the Lord.
Praise, O servants of the Lord,
Praise the name of the Lord."

61

Even Jacob could repeat from memory the One Hundred and thirteenth Psalm that Nicodemus had asked him to sing. Jacob obliged in a high piping voice that rose above the tables. The others smiled and joined with him.

"Blessed is the name of the Lord

from this time forth and forevermore.

From the rising of the sun to its setting

The name of the LORD is to be praised!

The LORD is high above all nations,

and his glory above the heavens!"

Joshua's eyes caressed the room, its many tables covered with costly cloths and adorned with heavy, carved silver and delicate, painted and glazed pottery. The families of Nicodemus and Joseph gathered beneath the flickering lamps and among the fragrant flowers. All were dressed in white, plain or edged with gold.

"He raises the poor from the dust,

and lifts the needy from the ash heap,

to make them sit with princes...

He gives the barren woman a home,

making her the joyous mother of children.

Praise the LORD."

Truly, Joshua believed he was seated with the princes of his people. Nicodemus led the service, his wrinkled, pink face and benign gray eyes aglow as they lighted on each of his own children and then on the family of Joseph.

Together the families drank the diluted wine and chanted the ancient prayers. They washed their hands and partook of lettuce dipped in tart liquid. They ate the lambs which had been sacrificed, together with *matzo*, the unleavened bread, and bitter herbs, dipped in *charoset,* a mixture of nuts and fruit in wine. It was Passover, the feast of liberation. God had smitten the Egyptians and led the Jews out from bondage. Joshua felt a yearning for liberation, strongly and personally for the first time in his life.

Johannon, the youngest son of Nicodemus, a wiry lad a year younger than Jacob, rose to ask his father the traditional question: "Why is this night different from all other nights?"

Nicodemus responded with great seriousness. "Remember," he said, "each of us personally came out of Egypt, for it is written, 'This is what the Lord did for me when I left Egypt.' The Holy One, blessed be his Name, redeemed not only our ancestors—He redeemed us as well."

Nicodemus paused and leaned forward. "The Lord redeems each of us again and again. No one knows when or how our liberation will come, but we know it will come."

Joseph looked fondly at his family and silently prayed that the liberation of which Nicodemus spoke would come, if not in his generation, at least in the generation of his children.

The stories and commentaries continued:

"...The congregation of Israel shall kill their lambs in the evening. Then they shall take some of the blood, and put it on the two doorposts and the lintel of the houses in which they eat them. They shall eat the flesh that night, roasted; with unleavened bread and bitter herbs they shall eat it."

Following the traditions of the holiday, Nicodemus explained that the bitter herbs represented the bitter life in Egypt and the unleavened bread, the haste with which they had left. It was the bread of freedom. The paschal lamb was the most important, for the Lord had instructed the Israelites to smear it on their doorways. "It is the Lord's Passover...The blood shall be a sign for you, upon the houses where you are; and when I see the blood I will pass over you and no plague shall fall upon you."

As he listened to the familiar ritual and sang the ancient hymns, Joshua almost forgot the sickening sacrifices in the Temple. At that moment he felt free, liberated, as his ancestors had been. But his eyes clouded and he was startled by a powerful image of the doorway of his own home. A man was carefully smearing blood on the lintel. His back was turned and Joshua was unable to identify him. He felt a pang of pain, like the one he had felt when the lamb was sacrificed in the Temple that afternoon. The vision faded.

"The Lord has promised us freedom," Nicodemus was saying, "and He will give us—"

There was harsh pounding on the doors below and then the bellow of rude voices. The families gathered in the upper room of Nicodemus's house were silent, holding their wine cups upraised.

"Open this door!" a coarse voice yelled, and immediately thereafter there was a rending sound and a great crash.

Nicodemus jumped to his feet and the others rose, too. Joshua hurried to his mother. He had seen the flash of fear again in her eyes and he wanted to protect her. Booted feet ascended the staircase. A servant hurried in, fear stretching his face, but before he could speak, he was pushed to the floor and heavily armed soldiers rushed into the room.

A centurion grabbed Nicodemus roughly by his tunic and yelled at him, while the women screamed.

"Where is he?"

"I don't know what—"

The centurion shook him to silence. "Judas—the Galilean—he's hiding here."

"No," Nicodemus said, his face red with fear and anger. "I don't even know him."

Meanwhile, soldiers battered the other men, pushed over the tables, and smashed pottery.

"Why?" Joseph asked, but before he could say more, he was knocked to the floor. Miriam and Joshua ran to him. He was shaken, but unharmed.

Other soldiers raced through the house, beating servants, kicking over furniture.

"This is an outrage," Nicodemus yelled, "on the holy holiday. The governor will hear of this!"

"The governor ordered it!" the centurion yelled and slammed Nicodemus against the wall. Stunned, he sank slowly to the floor.

"Nothing here!" a soldier yelled.

"No-one!" another called out.

The centurion gave the room one last, contemptuous look. "Go back to praising your God," he laughed and left the room.

In a moment, they were gone. There was a brief silence, broken only by the sound of running feet. A moment later, muffled by distance, they heard pounding again. Another neighbor was being assaulted on his holy day.

Joseph helped carry Nicodemus to a sofa, while the rest of his family anxiously gathered around him. Johannon, his son, stared at his father with frightened eyes. Joshua placed a comforting arm around his shoulder. The servants, still frightened, began to right the tables and sweep up the pottery, glancing nervously at their master.

Color returned to Nicodemus's bruised face and he sat up. He spoke haltingly, quoting the psalm:

"'Though I walk in the midst of trouble,

Thou dost preserve my life;

Thou dost stretch out thy hand against the wrath of my enemies,

And thy right hand delivers me.

The Lord will fulfill his purpose for me;

Thy steadfast love, O Lord, endures forever.

Do not forsake the work of thy hands.'"

Nicodemus looked around the room. "We've been taught that before the Messiah comes, Jerusalem will groan under the weight of her oppressors and blood will run in the streets." His expression was grim, but he held his head high. "We shall be ready," he said.

Then Nicodemus's expression brightened. "Look," he said, "there's still wine in the pitcher, Praise the Lord!"

Nicodemus masked his pain, rose to his feet and walked from guest to guest, filling their cups. He raised his own cup: "Blessed art Thou, O Lord our God, Ruler of the Universe, who has given us the fruit of the vine."

"Amen," they responded and all sipped slowly from their cups.

Joshua watched with admiration, his eyes brimming with tears. He raised his own cup and in a strong voice said, "Blessed art Thou, O Lord our God who has given us the Passover, to remind us of our freedom, now and forever."

Nicodemus placed an arm around Joshua's shoulders. "Amen," he said strongly and drained his cup.

6.

THE BOND

The sky was clear and the air cold. Stars sparkled in the heavens and a full moon floated above the city, silhouetting the awesome arches of the Temple, the blocks of the Antonia Fortress and the sloping roofs of Herod's palace. On a typical Passover in Jerusalem, crowds would have strolled through the streets until late at night and congregated in the courtyards and porticoes of the Temple. But on this festival, word of the rebellion led by Judas of Galilee had reached the city. The Governor, Coponius, had ordered patrols of Roman soldiers to search Jerusalem. It was doubtful that Coponius truly believed Judas had entered Jerusalem, but he was determined to quell any rebellious thoughts as soon as possible. The patrols had driven the people indoors and they were intensely aware they were less free on this Passover than they had ever been during the period of the Roman occupation.

Joshua lay awake long after the others had gone to bed. His heart was pounding. Perhaps, he thought, it was the wine. But he knew that it was the brutal Roman action on this holy festival. He was deeply moved by the message of freedom in the Passover texts, but perplexed that the Lord had permitted the continued oppression of his chosen people.

It isn't right, Joshua thought, it isn't fair. He realized he was angry at God, but he couldn't control his feelings. What is our sin, Lord? he wondered silently in the darkness. What must we do to be worthy of your deliverance? When there was no response, he grew even more agitated. But then, a breeze drifted through the window and caressed his brow. It soothed and calmed him. I must be patient, he thought, the Lord will tell us when the hour is right. Again the breeze touched him, a light, warm stroke that closed his eyes.

He dozed off, then awakened suddenly and instinctively glanced toward Jacob's bed. Even in the semi-darkness, he realized that the shape on the pallet was too lumpy to be his slender brother. Joshua sighed, dressed wearily and climbed to the roof.

There he found Jacob and Johannon, the son of Nicodemus, huddled against the parapet, shivering in thin clothes and staring out at the city. Jacob smiled when he saw his brother, but Johannon jumped to his feet, feeling guilty.

"It's all right, Johannon," Joshua said.

The boy smiled. "My friends call me 'Nico'—like a small Nicodemus,"

"Look, Joshua, how beautiful it is," Jacob said, his gesture including the entire city. For a few moments they looked out over Jerusalem, edged in silver by the brilliant moonlight.

"What is the sky like in Nazareth?" Nico asked.

"It's much bigger," Jacob said.

Joshua smiled. "I don't think the sky can ever be bigger than it is over the Holy City."

The younger boys nodded solemnly, finding Joshua's words especially wise.

Joshua knew he should send his brother back to bed, but he sensed there was something important about this night and the companionship. "We must speak softly," he said.

They sat together on the roof, sharing country and city tales. Nico told the brothers about Jerusalem, with its multitude of festivals and religious occasions, the races and mock battles staged by the Romans in their theatres and hippodrome, the comings and goings of foreign kings and international traders, the entries and departures of Roman armies.

Jacob and Joshua told Nico about the hills and valleys of Galilee, of farmers and herdsman and the craftsmen of the towns, including their father. Their stories were not nearly as exciting, but Nico assured them that the open countryside sounded fascinating.

A Roman sentry called out the watch and another answered.

Nico frowned. "When I grow up I'm going to be a soldier and drive the Romans from our city."

"But yours is a family of priests," Joshua said.

Nico hesitated. "Many priests have been warriors. The Maccabees were both. Even Judas of Galilee is from a priestly family."

"Strange," Joshua said. "That seems to be a contradiction."

"It's true," Nico said, a bit irritated.

"Yes, it's true, but I'm not sure it's right."

"Are you saying I can't fight for my country?" Nico asked. His eyes glowed brightly, and his back stiffened, as if anticipating an attack.

Joshua smiled. "You must do what you think is right. I hope there's a way to save the Holy Land without slaughter."

"I don't know," Jacob piped up. "Being a soldier doesn't sound bad to me."

"You do enough damage without a sword," Joshua said.

"But you have a soldier's name," Nico said to Joshua.

"And a prophet's," replied Joshua. "I'd rather be a prophet."

"Prophets get killed, too," Jacob said, "and most of them don't even get to carry swords."

The boys laughed together, then hushed each other, for fear they would be heard in the house below.

Nico looked thoughtfully at Joshua. "Maybe my father is right. Maybe you are the Messiah."

Joshua flushed in the darkness. "That's not what your father said. He said the Messiah would be a son of Israel—*like* me."

Nico ignored the distinction. "Think about it, Joshua. Maybe you can be the Messiah if you work hard at it."

Joshua and Jacob both laughed, and then Nico was laughing, too.

***

As the Passover ended, the pilgrims reluctantly packed their belongings. In the valleys surrounding the city walls, thousands of tents were struck, falling to earth like grain before the scythe. Within hours, the population of Jerusalem would be hardly more than a fifth its size during the festival.

Nicodemus urged Joseph to stay an extra day and avoid the crowded roads, but Joseph declined.

"You have become family to us," Nicodemus said, "you must return next year."

While his parents prepared for the return trip, Joshua felt drawn out of the courtyard and into the busy streets. As if in a dream, he followed the now familiar path to the Temple. Inside the Court of the Gentiles, most of the stalls were shuttered and the booths empty. One lone merchant hawked a stringy pair of doves in a sing-song voice, but with little enthusiasm. A fresh west wind had risen in the night and the heavy, oppressive smell of dead animals had drifted away. The smoke, too, had floated off with the wind and spread over the land.

In a columned loggia, a teacher spoke to a huddled group of students. He was a small, very thin man with a trim beard and lively brown eyes. His expression was gentle, but his voice rippled out with surprising resonance. "The Passover must never be taken for granted, my sons," he said. "The day of liberation is more than a symbol. It is the very essence of Jewish belief: freedom under God." He glanced up toward the Roman guards on the roofs.

The students seemed listless in the aftermath of the Festival. It was warm in the sun, and the colonnade was protected from the wind, so they remained serene and relaxed, eyes half closed, ears half open.

"The Law stands above all," the teacher said. "We follow the rules and the rituals, not merely for their own sake, but to indicate our acceptance of the sovereign reign of the Lord God. That is why we perform the ancient sacrifices of the Passover in the Holy City, year after year."

Joshua couldn't resist the urge to speak. "'Will the Lord be pleased with thousands of rams, with ten thousand rivers of oil?'"

The students turned, startled by Joshua's unexpected words and surprised by his youth.

The teacher smiled benignly. "The words of the Prophet Micah. Very good, my son. However, Deuteronomy says 'You shall not sacrifice to the Lord your God an ox or a sheep in which there is a blemish, nor any defect whatsoever; for that is an abomination to your Lord.' Surely this must mean that the sacrifice of a perfect animal, one without blemish, is pleasing to God."

Joshua didn't smile; the smell of the entrails and fat of lambs was still in his nostrils. "Perhaps, Rabbi, enough is enough."

The teacher scanned the group, as if to say, "Are you listening?" and then fixed his eyes on Joshua. "The feasts of Israel are ordained forever," he said.

Joshua felt his excitement grow. "'What to me is the multitude of your sacrifices? says the Lord; I have had enough of burnt offerings...'"

Captured by Joshua's boldness, another youth also quoted Isaiah: "I do not delight in the blood of bulls, or of lambs, or of he-goats."

Still another student spoke: "I cannot endure iniquity and solemn assembly. Your new moons and your appointed feasts my soul hates."

The boys smiled at Joshua and Joshua pleased by this companionship of the spirit, smiled back.

The teacher clapped his hands. "Perhaps," he suggested, "we have a new student."

Joshua shook his head. "I'm from Galilee."

"Your speech told us that," the teacher offered mildly, his eyes twinkling, "but that doesn't prevent you from studying with us."

"I'm sorry, Rabbi, but I'm returning home today with my family."

Joshua turned to go, but the teacher wasn't ready to release him. "The lines you quoted from Micah—do you know the ones that follow?"

Joshua nodded: "And what does the Lord require of you but to do justice and to love kindness, and to walk humbly with your God."

"Amen," the teacher said and the students repeated, "Amen."

"Isn't that more important than any festival?" Joshua asked.

The rabbi didn't give an immediate answer. He paced a few steps before he spoke again. "Once I was accosted by a Roman sailor who said, 'Rabbi, I hear you Jews argue about your religion day and night. Can't you make it simple for a simple man? Tell me as much about your faith as you can while standing on one foot. If I like what I hear, I swear you'll convert me.'

"'My friend,' I said, 'I'm too old to hop around on one foot, but I'll make it as simple as I can: Love God and do unto others as you would have them do unto you—that is the Law—all the rest is commentary.'"

The rabbi smiled and clapped Joshua on the shoulder. "My name is Hillel," he said. "When you come again to Jerusalem, look for me. We'll plant both feet and talk about Torah."

"Joshua!" voices cried out across the courtyard and Jacob and Nico came hurrying up. "Everyone is searching for you," Nico said.

"They're very angry," Jacob added, his face creased in a grown-up frown. "Father says he has important business in Nazareth."

"But I have been on my Father's business," Joshua replied.

Hillel and his students nodded in agreement.

7.

JACOB

It wasn't easy being his younger brother. He was so much smarter and stronger than I was and it didn't take a scholar to realize our parents loved him more than me. I couldn't blame them. He was such an unusual person, not plain and ordinary like me. I suppose I could have been jealous, but that was impossible because he was so kind. He told me stories sometimes—wonderful stories that I guess he made up out of his head because I never heard them anywhere else.

"Where did you get that story?" I would ask and he would smile and say, "God told it to me."

That was scary, but I believed it. I never doubted he could talk straight to the Lord any time he wanted. We all knew he had a special relationship with God. It showed in everything he did and said. Well, almost everything.

Once I borrowed his favorite hammer without asking and sure enough I broke it. He came running after me and knocked me down and picked me up and knocked me down again. His face was red with anger and I could only stare at him and cry.

He saw my look and he stopped.

I couldn't believe it was Joshua and he knew that was exactly what I was thinking. He grabbed me and pulled me to him and held me against him. "I'm sorry, Jacob," he said, "I didn't mean to hurt you. I got so mad—I didn't know I could get so mad."

I forgave him, but I didn't exactly trust him for a while and he knew that and felt real bad about it. But it was impossible to stay mad at Joshua—he was so good a person—and after a while we were friends again.

It was strange seeing him with other kids. Our family was used to him, with all his smart talk and quick moves. But kids who didn't know him might be surprised. When he started talking about the scriptures like he owned them, bigger kids would shut him up or just walk away—that is some of them. Others would be impressed and listen.

The thing with the healing was the hardest. He used to heal himself. We all saw that and took it for granted. We also knew he could heal us if we needed and plenty of times he did. When Judith was about six or seven, we were out by the well when she scraped her finger on the iron wheel. It began to bleed and Joshua matter-of-factly took her hand in his and stroked it until the bleeding stopped.

There was a girl who had been walking with Judith whose name was Tamar, and when she saw what Joshua did her eyes got real wide and she ran off and came back with her older brother. He was Jason, maybe fifteen and kind of a bully.

"What did you do?" he asked Joshua.

Joshua didn't know what Jason was talking about and just shrugged his shoulders. Jason grabbed him by the neck and said, "I asked you what you did to your sister?"

Joshua looked up at him fearlessly—he was about half the size of this fellow—and said, "I helped her. She cut herself on the wheel, if that's what you mean?"

Jason shoved Joshua aside and grabbed Judith's hand and looked at it.

"Take your hands off my sister," Joshua said.

"No cut I can see," Jason said. He pushed Judith away.

"I tell you," Tamar said, "she had a cut on her thumb and he put his hand on it and it went away."

Other people, grownups, were gathering near the well, listening.

I was getting nervous. "Come on, Joshua," I said. "Let's go home."

"No you don't," Jason said. He stood in my path and when I tried to get past him, he knocked me to the ground. Jason laughed as he hit me, but not for long. Joshua was on him in a second, swinging his right hand and slapping Jason across the face. The blow must have been pretty hard, because Jason staggered back two steps and fell to his knees, looking at Joshua with big eyes. Joshua was after him, closing on him, when Jason threw up his hands.

"No!" he screamed. "Not again."

Joshua's face was very red. The sight was comical, really, this young boy, big for his age, but much smaller than Jason, glaring at Jason, and Jason shaking and unable to look him in the eye.

"Get out of here," Joshua said, and I saw that he was trembling with anger.

Jason scrambled to his feet, turned and ran.

Both Judith and I ran to Joshua.

Somehow, he had calmed down. "It's all right," he said, putting a hand on each of our shoulders. "We can go home, now."

The grownups had watched without saying anything. Now they were talking to each other, gesturing and pointing, as we went home.

Jason remembered that day and so did I. For a long time, I didn't say anything, but then I couldn't help it. "Joshua," I asked, "how were you able to heal Judith's hurt?"

He frowned. "God does the healing."

"Yes," I said, "but I can't get God to help me that way."

He looked confused for a minute. "For a long time, I thought it was natural, that everyone could do it," he said. "But now I see that's not true, people don't know how to heal themselves."

"How did you learn?" I asked.

He seemed unable to answer. His blue eyes fixed on me with a look I'd never seen before.

"I'm trying to understand, Jacob. I want to do what's right. I know that no one can be healed without God's help, but I guess that he has given me a calling. Like some men are good carpenters, you know?"

"Yes, but you're also a good carpenter."

He was silent and he seemed a little upset.

"I didn't ask for this," he said.

"What about Jason?"

His expression darkened again. "That was evil of me. I let my temper control me. I have to stop that."

"It wasn't wrong, Joshua. You were protecting me."

He tousled my hair. I was only a year younger, but he always treated me like he was much older, maybe like an uncle.

"If I was really good at things, I'd be able to protect you without hurting anybody else."

Like I said, it wasn't easy being his brother. He was bigger, stronger, smarter and a lot better with his hands as well as his tongue. It was hard knowing that no matter how hard I tried I would never be as good as he was. Never. But he loved me. I knew that. And I loved him. Once in a while he would get real angry and I would be afraid, but after a while he seemed to have learned to control that anger, because he never struck me again. And sometimes, I deserved it.

8.

CONFESSION
(16 C.E., AUTUMN)

"You must tell him." Ari's expression was stern. His lips were pressed so tightly together that they made a slit of his mouth and for once he didn't seem kindly.

Joseph marveled at his old friend's grim demeanor, but he was not prepared to yield. His own jaws were clamped together so tightly that it was difficult to speak. "I can't," he said.

Ari slapped a brown dappled hand on the table and the sound echoed sharply.

"The boy loves me," Joseph said.

"Of course," Ari said.

"He would hate me, if I told him."

Ari shook his head only once. "I've never met anyone, regardless of age, more understanding than Joshua."

Joseph's resolve was unchanged, but his voice shook. "I know he would hate me."

"What have you done, that he should hate you? Marrying his mother was an act of kindness."

"Love," Joseph said, quite offended, "not kindness."

"Forgive me—an act of love. Surely the boy wouldn't hate you for an act of love."

Joseph was silent for a while. "I can't take the chance," he said.

Ari rose to his feet. He had recovered from his stroke at Joshua's touch, healed in body and spirit, younger than when the blow had fallen. But more than a dozen years had passed and age was gaining on him. He limped rather than paced the room.

"For all these years, you've lived in fear. It's a miracle that he hasn't heard rumors already."

Joseph was frightened. "Do you think...?" he couldn't complete the thought.

"I don't know," Ari said. "The lad is very sensitive—sometimes I think he already knows, but is waiting to hear from you."

Again there was a brief silence.

"What about Miriam?" Ari asked.

Joseph looked down. "She's as frightened as I am, but she agrees with you."

"Aha."

"I can't do it!" Joseph's face was lined with worry, pale with doubt and concern. "Perhaps," he said, "when I'm gone."

Ari looked at him sharply. "You're still a young man, Joseph. "What does that mean?"

"What I said."

"Don't smooth your face, Joseph. What are you telling me?"

"The pain has come again." Now it was Joseph's turn to pace the room. Ari realized that Joseph had grown thin and his complexion was disturbingly gray for a man who spent so many hours outdoors.

"Most of my family died young. That's why I wanted to marry young and have many children."

"Tell me about the pain," Ari said.

Joseph stopped pacing. "Here," he said, pointing to his chest. "Sometimes, it comes sharply and I can hardly breathe—like a fist is squeezing my heart."

"Does Miriam know?"

"No one knows. Fortunately, each time I had an attack I was alone, and I recovered before anyone found out."

"Secrets, Joseph, always secrets."

"What is a man to do?" Joseph's expression was one of bewilderment.

"Share the truth with those who love you, Joseph. Why should your family suffer a bitter surprise?

"Why should they worry over something they can't change? I don't want to be treated like a cripple."

There was color in his face now, but it was an unhealthy color and Ari was afraid. He put an arm around Joseph. "Don't be agitated, my friend. God will show us the way."

**

Joseph and Joshua worked together on the watchtower perched on the highest hilltop in Nazareth. The uprising by Judas of Galilee had been ruthlessly suppressed years earlier and Judas and most of his followers had been crucified. But Galilee was still a hotbed of civil unrest and the authorities continued to build fortifications and watchtowers throughout the district. Nazareth's tower had been commissioned by the elders, although part of the funds came from Herod Antipas, which provoked a bitter debate in the synagogue.

Menasseh, the president of the congregation, a youngish, fiery man, whom some suspected of being a secret member of the Zealot party, spoke out against the project. "We'll build it and sooner or later the Herodians or the Romans will use it to kill our own people."

"Why should we protect your friends, the Zealots?" Joachim, the father of Miriam asked. "They'll provoke a civil war and we'll all die."

Menasseh was furious. "Are you content with your life of slavery, Joachim? The Zealots would set you free."

"They're ruthless," Joachim said, "almost as dangerous as the Romans."

"That's a lie!" Menasseh said and many of the younger men agreed.

Zechariah, an ancient, wizened man responded. "I don't know much about these political matters. I don't think I've ever met a Zealot in my life. But this I know: thieves and brigands roam the hills—no respecters of law-abiding folk. Why, my son-in-law Ephraim was telling me—"

"—Please, Zechariah," Joachim said, "make your point."

"My point is, we've been pillaged by thieves and brigands more than Herodians, Romans or Zealots—whoever they are. The tower will help us protect ourselves."

The argument went on for hours and Ari waited to speak until the rival parties were exhausted. "My friends," he said, "the watchtower will be built, whether we like it or not. Either the Herodians will build it and tax us to pay for it, or we'll build it ourselves and then we can properly claim that we should have the right to use it for our own protection. Antipas believes he's getting the best of us, but I tell you, we're getting the best of him."

No one could fault Ari's logic. The men voted and the building of the tower was approved

***

Now, the tower had risen above the rooftops of the town. Joshua and Joseph were working on the wooden scaffolding, erecting a railing that would edge the top level. Joshua was humming as he worked, fitting the wood, already cut and measured on the ground, into the slots prepared for them.

Joseph couldn't help glancing at his son. At age twenty, the lad was now taller than Joseph, taller than most men. His hair was still burnished gold and his eyes piercing blue, but his skin no longer held the pale, pale hue of his childhood. Joshua's skin was almost as dark as an Ethiopian's and with his topping of long, bright golden hair, he was an arresting sight.

But joy in his son's vigorous appearance was not what moved Joseph. It was the way Joshua worked and sang. His gestures had always been quick and graceful. Now, in the fullness of young manhood and the maturity of his skill, Joshua moved more like a dancer than a carpenter. Even when he stopped to fit a rod into the railing, it was like a musical pause.

Joseph smiled when he saw that Joshua canted his head to one side as he studied his work, a gesture he had unconsciously learned from his father. Joseph glanced down toward the town, across the cluster of flat roofs to the square where the synagogue stood in its solemn copse of oaks and poplars. A mother and child played on the ground before the steps of the building. The child held a small polished object, perhaps his mother's mirror. It caught the sun, and the delighted child flashed the light first on the synagogue and then towards the watchtower. The light flickered in Joseph's eyes and as it did, he felt a twinge in his side. He knew that now was the time.

"Joshua," he called softly. Joshua turned and saw that his father's look was strained, that his eyes were shining.

"Are you all right, father?" he asked, hurrying along the lightly swaying framework.

Joseph thought of climbing down the scaffold, but it seemed appropriate that they were together on the watchtower. "I'm all right, Joshua, I...I just want to talk to you."

Joshua smiled. "Fine," he said.

Joseph struggled to still his throbbing heart. "You must be strong, Joshua, very strong... when you listen to what I say. I wanted to tell you for many years...but I was afraid."

"I've never seen you afraid, father."

Joseph forced a smile. "I've been afraid many times, but that doesn't matter now. You're a man, young but mature. A good son, a fine craftsman. Soon you'll be married to Rebecca, a lovely girl." Joseph found he had to pause between phrases. "But as you prepare...to begin your own life, to move to a home of your own...to raise a family, you must know the truth."

Joshua wanted to tell his father he loved him, that there was nothing that couldn't be said between them, but out of respect, he listened in silence.

Joseph had imagined this moment many times and had never been able to think of anything that would soften the blow. "When your mother was a girl"—he had to take deep breath—"she got up early one morning, did her chores and went for a walk in the hills."

Joseph felt another, sharper, twinge and although he masked his reaction, Joshua saw that he was perspiring heavily. "Father," he said, "it's too hot here in the sun."

Joseph's strength was fading, but not his determination. "Listen," he whispered. "Just, listen."

Joshua, distracted by Joseph's frightening appearance, tried to focus on his words. When Joseph described the approach of the Roman soldiers, he felt fear and apprehension. When Joseph haltingly told of the rape of his mother, Joshua felt desperate pangs of pain as if he himself were being assaulted. Perspiration broke out on his forehead and he struggled to keep from shaking. Unconsciously, his hands went to the railing for support. Again and again he felt the twisting, burning pain, reliving his mother's struggle.

Joshua was so blinded by tears he could hardly see his father. He was not aware that Joseph's face had grown gray and pinched. Feeling his mother's pain, he did not realize it was also Joseph's agony. Joseph was in the throes of the most powerful attack he had ever suffered. This time two hands had grabbed his heart and were squeezing together. His breath came in short gulps and he, too, had to hold onto the scaffolding.

Joseph gathered his strength one final time. "You see, dear Joshua, I'm not your father."

The words were a hammer, smashing Joshua in the gut. He bent over suddenly as if he had been physically struck, understanding for the first time what the story meant for him. He stared at Joseph, open-mouthed. "No!" he said. "NO!"

Joseph gritted his teeth and continued. "I love you like a father—as much as any of the children—even more. You're...a great blessing to me, Joshua. You're my soul."

Joseph let loose of the railing and reached out for Joshua.

But the shock was too great for Joshua. He staggered back, out of reach. "No," he said. "It isn't true."

Joseph bowed his head. There was nothing more to say. The pain came in quick insistent blows. He grew dizzy and his vision blurred.

Joshua was crying so freely that he did not see Joseph's suffering. Shaking with pain and despair, he turned his back and began to climb down the scaffolding, recklessly, missing handholds.

"Joshua," Joseph cried. "Come back—please come back." He sagged to the floor of the scaffolding as Joshua leaped to the ground and began to run.

"For God's sake!" Joseph cried. He reached out, with both hands, slipped between the restraining strips of wood, and with a scream, fell towards the earth.

The scream stopped Joshua in his tracks. He turned to see Joseph plummeting toward the ground.

"Father!" he yelled and began to run, but despite his strength and speed, he was too late. Joseph struck the ground, spread-eagled on his back, at his very feet.

Joshua fell to his knees, and threw his arms around Joseph. "Father," he whispered.

Joseph's body was broken in a dozen places and blood streamed from his mouth and ears. But through the pain and the deepening haze he could make out Joshua's face and feel his arms holding him. "Forgive me," Joseph mumbled.

"Forgive *me*," Joshua cried, tears streaming down his face. "I love you, Father."

Joseph's bruised and broken lips curved in a brief smile. Then he died.

***

Wind and rain swept the town of Nazareth, bending the wheat and barley and turning the unpaved streets to mud. The sun had not been seen for days and the farmers remained in town, mending their tools and patiently waiting for the skies to clear. Singly and in groups, hunched and huddled together against the stinging rain, the townspeople made their way to Joseph's home.

A few candles made feeble pools of light in the room where Miriam and her children sat together receiving the condolences of their friends and family. Miriam sat very erect, her face pale and pinched. She wore her hair pulled back severely—she would never let it loose again. Her naturally pink lips were as pale as her skin and her deep green eyes were rimmed with red. She folded her hands and carefully held them together so that she would not twist and pull at them. She did not cry before the visitors, but only privately in the room she and Joseph had shared.

Once Miriam realized, with wrenching agony, that Joseph was truly gone, her thoughts focused on her children. Jacob and Joses, Simeon and Judah, Sarah and Judith sat together on benches close to their mother. The boys, especially the older ones, tried bravely not to cry. The girls also tried to mask their sadness, but their strength would fail and they would begin to cry again. The boys tried to hush them, gently. Then they, too, gave way to tears. The children leaned on each other and rocked together in each other's arms. Miriam did not interfere with their expressions of suffering. From time to time she embraced them and held them close until their weeping eased.

Joshua sat apart. He was pale beneath his deeply-tanned skin, weak beneath the strength of his muscled body. He had not cried since Joseph died—he didn't believe he was entitled to cry. He had prayed fervently in the synagogue and at the gravesite—prayed for the soul of Joseph, but not for his own. His heart had closed around his pain like the fists of pain that had closed around Joseph's heart.

He repeatedly recalled Joseph reaching out toward him and saw himself drawing back. He heard Joseph crying his name and felt the shame and guilt of not responding. He fought the urge to leave his home, to climb the tower and step off into emptiness.

Miriam was profoundly disturbed to see the malaise that had overcome her eldest son. The other children were also troubled by Joshua's obvious torment. Jacob was the most deeply affected. "Can I help?" he asked anxiously, but Joshua only shook his head.

Even Rebecca was shut out by Joshua's suffering. She was a pretty girl, a few years younger than Joshua, with a slender, proud figure, dark hair and a lovely smooth, olive complexion. Her eyes were wide-set, her nose flaring and her cheekbones high and prominent. She faintly resembled Miriam, but her step was quicker and she laughed more easily.

Joshua had been fond of her since childhood. Despite her playful nature, they had often spent long hours discussing scripture. Joshua was pleased at her ability to match him with apt quotations from difficult writings. Most of all, Joshua appreciated her exuberant joy in life, her love of beauty and her sweet, even temper.

Joseph had been keenly aware of Joshua's affection for Rebecca and had asked if he wanted him to speak to her parents about arranging a marriage.

"Let me speak to her first," Joshua said.

"But that's not proper," Joseph had said, astonished.

"I promise I won't embarrass you, father."

Joseph had reluctantly agreed.

The very next day, Joshua had managed to intercept Rebecca on her way to market. "I want to speak to you about something very personal," he said.

"People are watching," Rebecca said, but in fact, she seemed not to care.

"We've been friends since childhood," Joshua said.

"Yes."

"More than friends."

"Yes."

"I've never thought of spending the rest of my life without you," Joshua said.

For the first time, Rebecca didn't respond. Her expression became very serious and he saw that she was swallowing rapidly. He himself felt unaccountably shy, but determined to go on. "My father asked me if I wanted him to try to arrange a marriage with you."

She was staring directly into his eyes. Her expression was fixed, almost as if she hadn't heard, but he knew she had. He waited to see if she would say anything. It soon became clear she wasn't going to help him.

"I told my father I would talk to you, myself, first."

Still, she said nothing.

"Rebecca, are you listening to me?" He felt his face getting red.

"Of course."

"Then why don't you answer me?"

"You haven't asked me anything."

He realized that in fact, he hadn't.

"Do you want my father to speak to your father?"

"Is that what you wanted to tell me?"

"Now you're asking the questions."

"Is that forbidden?"

He felt frustrated by her responses and yet he realized she wasn't trying to confuse him.

"That's right," she said, correctly reading his mind. "I want to know what you want."

"I love you," he said.

She blushed, and her blush touched him deeply, enriching his feelings for her.

"Have your father talk to my father," she said and ducked around him and ran towards the market.

He shook his head, then smiled.

Within the month, they were engaged to be married. Still, not even Rebecca could reach Joshua after Joseph's death. She came to the house again and again, and although Joshua was courteous and respectful, he seldom smiled, never took her hand.

The townspeople came to the house in erratic waves that surged and receded. During one of the cherished quiet moments when the family was alone, Ari entered the house. His years showed more heavily than ever and his stride was so slow that Jacob leaped to his feet to help.

Ari waved him off. "If I accept help, I may never be able to walk by myself again."

Slowly, slowly, Ari made his way to Miriam and sat down heavily beside her. She gave him a wan smile and accepted his brief embrace.

"There was no finer man in Nazareth," Ari said.

Miriam smiled again and touched his hand.

"Everything Joseph did was touched by the grace of God," he continued. His voice lifted momentarily. "He loved his family more than life, and you are a family worthy of his love."

The children bent their heads in thanks, all except Joshua, who seemed to shrink even further into himself.

Startled, Ari glanced at Miriam. "Don't worry," he said. He forced himself to stand and made his way to Joshua, who sat hunched forward, looking down at the floor. Ari took Joshua's chin in his hand and raised his head. He stared into Joshua's lifeless eyes for a long moment.

"Joseph told you everything," Ari said. It was a statement, not a question. "And you hate him for what he told you."

Joshua shook his head once, abruptly, pulling free of Ari's feeble grasp. "No," he whispered.

Miriam hurried to her eldest son, frightened that his response might be an accusation. Joshua saw her fear and reached out to embrace her. "I love you, mother," he said.

"Do you forgive me?" Miriam asked.

"What is there to forgive?"

"Not telling you."

"I realize now I wasn't ready. I'm barely ready now. But there's nothing, nothing to forgive."

"Yes there is," Ari said.

Joshua and Miriam, clinging to each other, looked at Ari.

"You must forgive yourself," Ari said.

Joshua released his mother and dropped his arms. His voice was rough, strained and broken. "I killed him," he said.

"No," Miriam said, reaching out to comfort him, but he was unable to accept her embrace.

"No," Ari said. His voice was stronger now and his eyes flashed. "You are arrogant to think so. Life and death are in the hands of God."

"If I had stayed on the scaffold, he would be alive today."

Ari grabbed Joshua's arms and with surprising strength drew him towards him. "Did you look at him closely? Did you see how gray his skin was, how feeble his grasp? He was sick, Joshua, sick unto death. That's why he told you when he did—because he knew he was dying. Joseph had suffered many attacks before, but he hid them from all of us."

Joshua shook his head in disbelief.

"It's true," Miriam said. "I knew even though he never told me, even though, when I asked, he always denied it. Joseph's father and his father before him died the same way."

"Do you think he would have fallen from the scaffold," Ari said, "if he wasn't ill—your father, who could climb like a cat?"

Joshua looked from Ari to his mother and back again. The truth was there, in their eyes, and he could no longer refuse to hear it. Slowly he began to cry. Ari and Miriam held him while he sobbed and trembled and the evil which had invaded his body slipped slowly away.

9.

CAESAREA
(18 C.E., SUMMER)

They had neither a horse nor a donkey, so they walked, carrying their belongings slung across their shoulders and using long crooks to ease the way. They were bundled up in flowing burnooses so that on first glance they looked like two men. Their path took them across the Jezreel valley, lush now with ripening crops. The spring rains had been unusually generous for this fickle climate. The grain was rich and tall and flowers were plentiful. Rippling ribbons of blood-red poppies edged odd-shaped fields of waving wheat and barley. The farmers were cheerful and friendly; a successful season had loosened their tightly knit souls.

The road to Megiddo and the sea was busy but not clogged. Farmers bringing crops to market rocked along on strong pack animals, alongside merchants with their swaying loads of cloth and pottery, trinkets and magical wares. Everyone seemed ready and willing to smile.

Especially Joshua and Rebecca. Both families had expected them to settle down at once to domestic life, but Joshua had other ideas. After his father's death, two years earlier, Joshua had patiently arranged matters for his bereaved mother, helped his brothers to set up a workshop and learn their trade, and his sister Sarah to find a husband. Only then was he ready to follow his own desires and marry Rebecca.

At first, she had been angry over the delay, but she was quickly forgiving and then very patient. Her parents had urged her to break the long engagement. She was a pretty girl and many men wanted her, some far wealthier and more important in the community than Joshua.

"You'll end up without a husband," her mother said, "and without children to care for you in your old age."

"If that's what you believe," Rebecca said, "why don't you understand Joshua caring for his own family?"

"He's a strange one," her father said. "A young man should have natural urges. What's wrong with him?"

Rebecca didn't listen. She waited in her parents' home, saw Joshua when she could, learned to cook, sew and be patient.

"I promise we'll be married," Joshua said. "There's no one else for me."

He kept his word and the nuptials were especially joyous because they were so long delayed. "You deserve the best," his mother told him. "God will grant you a happy marriage and fine children."

It was Joshua's idea that he and Rebecca should postpone making their home until after they had taken a trip. "I've never seen the Great Sea," he said, "although once, west of Megiddo, I thought I heard it in the night."

"Too far away," Ari said, dressed in his finest for the wedding, "you must have dreamed it." Ari seemed much older now. He spoke slowly but clearly and there was still a hint of a sparkle in his eyes. He drew the young man aside, took his hands and stared at them, then, looked into his eyes.

"When, my son?"

Joshua shook his head.

Ari peered more intently. "You won't, or you don't know?"

"I don't know," Joshua said.

"God needs these hands, Joshua. Israel needs these hands."

"Indeed Israel has them," Joshua said.

Now it was Ari's turn to shake his head. "God needs no carpenters and Israel has more than enough."

"I'm a good carpenter," Joshua said, knowing he was evading the question.

"With these hands," Ari said, "you can fashion more than houses, more than ploughs, more even than synagogues and watchtowers. You can help to build the Kingdom of God."

Joshua smiled. "Tell me how?"

"You must find the way, not I. You must pray, Joshua, pray to the living God. And when he speaks to you—and he will—you must follow his every word."

Ari gazed long and hard into Joshua's eyes, before he finally loosened his grip. Then his head sagged a bit and he looked like he was dozing off. Joshua leaned forward and kissed Ari on the top of his head. But Ari was not asleep, he was praying, and he didn't notice Joshua's kiss.

It was a long and happy night, filled with song and dance, good wine and good wishes. Finally, Ari did doze off and Joshua and Joses carried him home, snoring gently. They laid him in his bed and covered him and turned to leave.

"When, Joshua?" he whispered, startling them. A moment later he was snoring again.

***

Rebecca and Joshua reached the sea at sunset. The tide was rising and great waves came crashing onto the long, sandy beaches. The sun was a fiery orb blazing beneath a single row of fish scale clouds. Streaks of pink and purple, red and yellow scored the heavens, and the sea was the color of fine wine, sparkling as if poured from a bottle. Joshua's voice caught in his throat and he fell to his knees, staring out at this magnificent sight. Rebecca knelt beside him, holding an arm about him.

"Blessed are thou, O Lord our God, ruler of the Universe," Joshua whispered, "Who has given us the Universe."

"Amen," Rebecca said softly. They embraced on the beach, clinging to each other, while they watched the sun sink below the horizon and the sky blaze forth in ever changing colors. They lingered as long as the light, then Joshua found a comfortable spot under the great Roman aqueduct that arched for miles along the coast. There they spread their belongings.

Joshua built a small fire and they cooked their meal. Rebecca found pomegranates in a small oasis and Joshua poured wine from a wineskin straight into his throat. Rebecca wanted to do the same thing, but she missed and the wine squirted onto her face. She screamed and Joshua laughed. Then she giggled and they fell into each other's arms.

Even though the sun was down, the night was still mild, and luminous cascades of stars poured across the sky. The clouds had drifted away and the heavens were clear.

"Where do the stars come from?" Rebecca asked.

"Ask God," Joshua said.

"You're my teacher," she said. "I expect you to know these things. Tell me, how many stars are there?"

"Exactly as many as God made, less the ones he discarded."

She pinched his nose. "You mean you don't know."

He shook his head. "I gave you an accurate answer. It's too bad you don't appreciate it."

She wrinkled her nose. "Are you going to be a tyrant of a husband?"

"Probably," he said.

"That's good," Rebecca answered. "Then I won't have to make a lot of decisions." She settled into his arms.

He had never felt the closeness of her quite like this. The star-filled sky, the still-warm sand and the gentle, flickering breeze only served to focus his senses on the softness of Rebecca's lips, the smoothness of her hands, the supple warmth of her body. He held her to him gently and then fiercely and she yielded gladly. They clung together in the night, sharing their love, whispering and singing. From time to time, they prayed, prayers of thanks and dedication. Their spirits and their bodies were one, even as God had first made them.

In the morning, the rising tide slapped at their toes, wakening them. Joshua pulled Rebecca to her feet and dragged her into the water.

"No," she cried, "it's cold."

But Joshua wouldn't let go. He pulled her into the waves, screaming and giggling. Rebecca splashed water in his face and he was so surprised he let go of her hand. When he reached again, she had plunged into the sea and was swimming away.

"Where did you learn that?" he called.

"A secret," she said, laughing as she swam. "A woman must have some secrets."

Joshua watched the way she moved her arms, then plunged in after her. The water was buoyant and the flailing of his arms seemed to work. With a few powerful strokes he was beside her.

"You're amazing," she said. But then he lifted her out of the sea and into his arms. Her body was shaking a little from the cold, but it felt very good to him, even through the garment she wore. Her lips, tart from the sea water, were delicious.

They lay on their backs in the sun until their clothing was almost dry and then strolled along the beach. Now and then they saw vessels following the coastline, small fishing boats and larger merchant ships. They came upon a fisherman casting into the foam. He smiled amiably and greeted them.

"Can you really catch fish that way?" Rebecca asked.

The fisherman pointed to a small woven basket floating in the sea and tethered to a post driven in the sand. Rebecca waded out and to her delight found it filled with Sea Bass.

"Take one," the fisherman said. "A wedding present."

"How did you know?" she asked.

The fisherman smiled.

They thanked him and returned to their nest below the aqueduct, where Joshua cleaned the fish and Rebecca cooked it on a stick.

"Delicious," Joshua said. "You're going to be a perfect wife."

Rebecca glowed.

Later, they followed the great stone aqueduct into Caesarea, a surprising new city with great stone palaces, a huge Amphitheatre and a Hippodrome where horses were raced. The streets were straight and well-paved, the trees recently planted and the people well dressed. Roman standards and banners lined the streets marking a festival.

"They're honoring us," Joshua said.

They reached the harbor with its great stone jetties and breakwaters. Ships of every size rocked in the man-made bay and slaves of every hue unloaded endless streams of produce and merchandise.

Joshua was thoughtful. He knew that his beloved country was a small place, great only in her ideas and aspirations. Now he had a sudden glimpse of the world outside, a vast realm the rabbis taught him was filled with pagans. And yet, they, too, were God's children. How could they enter the Kingdom of God?

"You look sad," Rebecca said.

"I'm thinking about the Great Sea and the Great World around it and the Greater World around that."

She huddled close to him. "It's much too big to think about," Rebecca said.

"God is even bigger," Joshua said, "and there's nothing else to think about."

They sat together for a long time on the jetty, silently, while Joshua tried to fit together his ideas of God and man and Israel and Joshua.

Rebecca tried to share his thoughts. "When Moses led the Israelites out of Egypt," she said, "God parted the Red Sea, and when Joshua led the Israelites into the Promised Land, He piled up the Jordan. Do you think God could part the Great Sea for you, Joshua?"

Startled, he looked into the trusting eyes of his new bride. He put his arm around her shoulders and held her close. It wasn't cold, but Joshua was trembling.

Then the wind rose and the sea crashed against the jetty and they huddled closer together. In the harbor, men were lowering sails and lashing down cargo. But the wind rose even higher until the sound of it was a howling chorus. In the roaring sea and the rising wind, Joshua heard a voice calling "When?" and then again "When?" until with every surge, the question became a drum beat in his ears.

10.

REBECCA

I remember him from childhood, all bright and light and yellow-haired with those huge eyes that sometimes didn't even blink. When they did, his long ashes would sweep across his face and my heart would leap. I guess I loved him even when I was a little girl. His house was close to mine and I would see him outdoors playing with his brothers and sisters. They seemed to have a lot of fun and sometimes Joshua would tell them stories. Occasionally, the stories were serious and the children all looked solemn, but other times he made them laugh.

One day I heard Joshua telling them why they had to be grown up before they could do some of the things they wanted to do. He pointed to old man Haran's barn, the one with the twisted roof. "Haran was so impatient," he said, "that he built the barn with green wood and the wood warped and pulled the roof off to one side. You, too, are green and if you try things before you're ready, you'll get warped like Haran's roof, and your heads will be bent over to one side".

He cocked his head to show them. They laughed a lot and for a few days, all any of them had to do was bend his head over his shoulder to make the others laugh.

Another time the story had to do with a jealous man who was trying to keep his eyes on his wife while he took a trip into town, so he got onto his donkey facing backwards. When he slapped the donkey on its rump to get it going, the donkey leaped forward and the man fell off the back.

"You can't go two ways at once," he told them, "so you better make sure you're aiming in the right direction."

I knew about him healing the children and knocking down great big Jason with a single slap and none of that seemed strange to me. I always thought that Joshua could do whatever he wanted, if and when he wanted to do it. But he told me that wasn't so. He couldn't do anything unless God wanted him to.

When he got a little older and I got a little older, it was pretty obvious how good-looking he was and how interested all the girls were in him. We'd all talk together and wonder whose father would make a match. About then, he'd walk by, tall and handsome, and smile at us and we'd just about faint. We giggled a lot and hoped he'd notice. I always thought he liked me especially, but there were so many pretty girls in Nazareth. Some were the daughters of Jews from faraway places with exotic looks that I thought he might find more interesting. I was just an ordinary girl with ordinary Galilean features. I knew some people thought I was pretty, but I wasn't unusual.

It was hard for me to talk about Joshua to the girls and to giggle like they did, because it wasn't really funny to me. I wanted him very badly. I wanted him to be the father of my children. I wanted to kiss those long lashes and feel those strong, supple carpenter's hands carry me into our own home. But I didn't flirt with him like the others. I talked to him a lot, especially about scripture, which he knew better than anybody except maybe Ari the sage, or Menasseh, the president of the congregation. I was lucky my father had scrolls of scripture in our house and I read them all the time, because I wanted to know what interested Joshua so much.

He often told me bible stories and I would ask him questions. He was very good at answering the questions, but he didn't pretend to know what he didn't know.

"I'll have to ask my Father," he said. He called the Lord, "Abba," Father, as if he were as close to God as he was to Joseph.

I knew that sometimes he walked far out of town and sat on a hillside. I have to confess that I followed him more than once, just to watch. He would sit and fold his hands and look up to the sky with his lips moving. I never did hear what he said, at least not until we were married. I figured out that he was talking to God and that made me feel comfortable. I also knew that if I wasn't supposed to be there, God would have let me know somehow.

Finally, the miracle happened and Joshua's father and my father made the match. We had to wait a long time because of Joseph's sudden death. My parents became very anxious, but I wasn't really worried. I trusted God and I trusted Joshua. I didn't think the Lord would have me love this man for so long, if it wasn't right.

Joshua was a wonderful husband, a wonderful father. He was a very good carpenter, a good builder and we lived well, but he had problems that

I hadn't expected. Galilee is a very political place and men were always asking Joshua what he thought of this or that. He was a prominent young member of the community because he was prosperous and a skilled crafts-man and also because he was so knowledgeable about scripture. Sometimes the discussions in the synagogue would get very angry. Our people have been oppressed for so long, that many were tired of hearing that there was nothing to be done, that God would take care of our enemies. Some, especially the younger men believed it was time for action.

"The action will be taken—but it will be taken by God," Menasseh would say, patiently. He was neither old nor young, not a pacifist, but certainly not one to advocate violence.

"God will help us," young Aaron Ben Israel said, "if we help ourselves. The Lord is disgusted with us for putting up with the Romans."

"When the time is ripe," Ari said, and everyone loved Ari, "God will send the Messiah to lead us."

"Of course," said Aaron, "that's the way of old men and cowards. Always wait for somebody else to help us—that way we can put it off. Until the Messiah comes, whoever that is, we have no responsibility."

"Ari is not a coward," said Joshua rising to his feet. "And you have no right to insult him in the house of God."

"Good," said Aaron smiling grimly, "then I'll insult you. You're not old, but you're a coward—you spout the same mischief about the Messiah. You give yourself the same excuses as the old people, when the truth is you're too afraid to do anything yourself."

"A man who throws water into the river is not likely to drown the river, but a man who spits into the wind may find it blown back into his eyes."

"What does that mean?" Aaron asked.

"If you're so brave," Joshua said, "why quarrel with us, we're not your enemies. Go join the rebels and fight the Romans."

Aaron stared at him for a moment, his jaw working and the veins showing in his neck. "Very well," he said hoarsely, "I'll go," and he began to walk from the synagogue while the women in his family screamed from the aisles.

But Joshua moved quickly to block his way. "I didn't mean to shame you into battle," he said. "I take back what I said."

Aaron would have none of it. He pushed Joshua aside and continued on his way. Joshua reached out to take his arm, but Aaron shoved him, trying to get loose. When he could not, he struck Joshua in the face with his free hand. Joshua stared at him, and many were afraid that he would attack Aaron, there in the synagogue, before God and man. But Joshua dropped Aaron's arm and stepped back.

"Forgive me, Lord, for transgressing against you. Forgive me, Lord, for transgressing against Aaron who is also your child. Persuade him, Lord, that valor lies not in violence but in love and patience. Teach him, in the words of Isaiah, 'to wait upon the Lord.'"

Aaron's look softened for a moment, but then his jaw stiffened again and he left the synagogue.

From that day forward, there were those who hated Joshua for driving Aaron from the town and those who thought him right for counseling patience. Joshua didn't want to take sides at all, but the politics of Nazareth put him in the middle and he was deeply saddened. No longer could he walk the streets and smile and know that everyone was his friend. Some wouldn't speak to him and others wanted him to lead the peaceful faction. He didn't want to lead anyone. The ones who supported his gestures of peace began to be angry because he would no longer speak out.

"Every time I speak I make an enemy," he told me. "I'll hold my peace and try to retain my friends."

"It won't work," I said.

He looked at me sadly. "I know," he responded, "but I have to try."

Joshua was strong, so I think he would have been able to deal with those who opposed him politically or disagreed with his interpretation of scripture. But there was something else that made our life difficult. Since childhood, we all knew that Joshua could heal. Joshua himself didn't claim any special powers and made no show of the healing that he did, and the town respected that. Then came the incident with the little girl who had seemed to drown in the River Nir. Perhaps it was the uncertainty of the times, or the drama of the rescue, but the people responded as they never had before.

Old people began to ask Joshua to have their lives extended and their ailments cured.

'I don't hear so well anymore," an old man said.

"Don't you believe that is God's will?" Joshua asked him.

"I tell you I can't hear and I want to hear and you can help me." The old man spoke as if he had the right to be healed.

Joshua shook his head. "I'm a carpenter," he said.

"You saved the little girl. You have to help me."

Joshua felt respect for the aged, but this man offended him. "I'm sorry," he said. "I don't believe the Lord wants me to do anything."

The old man was infuriated, and left cursing Joshua. So did a woman suffering from a dimming of her eyesight, who also demanded his help. Again he made an enemy.

But there were many he helped: a young girl with a terrible limp from a withered leg, a small child, who couldn't see, an old man who didn't ask his help but instead asked Joshua what he could do to help those who suffered and who himself had had terrible pains in his head for years.

Joshua pleased those that he helped and offended those he didn't.

"I can't take much more of this," he told me. "The people won't let me do my work. Even when I'm building a roof, they climb up to demand help. If I go off into the woods, they follow me. In the synagogue, they interrupt my prayers. If I tell them to ask God for help, many of them say, "Never mind God, you help me.'"

"Don't you think the Lord is working through you for His own purpose?" I asked.

"Of course, but I don't know what that purpose is?"

He decided to speak to Ari, ancient now, confined to his home, but still revered. Ari took Joshua's hands as he often did and stared into his eyes. "When, will you accept your calling? Rebecca has asked the right questions, why don't you give the right answers?"

"What do you believe God's purpose is in sending you these messages and granting you such powers?"

"Ari, there are others who can heal and that doesn't make any of them the Messiah. Besides, we're told that the Elijah will first return and tell us of his coming."

"Some believe that," Ari said," some do not."

"I believe it," Joshua said.

"Because you want to wait, because you don't want to follow the Lord's instructions."

Joshua was startled. "Forgive me, dear friend, but I don't believe I've received such instructions. If I had, I would surely follow them. I'm not worthy, Ari, not worthy to be called 'Messiah.'"

Joshua told me of his meeting with Ari. He was very concerned, but still convinced of the rightness of his path. "Rebecca, I have no doubt the call to the Messiah will be very clear. It's blasphemy for me to think that I am the anointed of God."

What could I tell him? Only that I loved him. How was I to know whether he was the anointed of God?

One thing was certain. We couldn't continue to live in Nazareth. Joshua and a few others decided to begin a new town several miles away. The others simply wanted a quieter life. Joshua hoped to avoid those who demanded his healing powers as well as those who hated his beliefs.

It was difficult for me to leave my aging parents, but it was more important that I follow my husband. I hoped we would be very happy in Beth Sholem and thus far I've not been disappointed. I hope Joshua will find the answer here and that he will learn what is wanted of him by God. If he knows, he hasn't told me.

11.

GAIUS
(26 C.E., SPRING)

Gaius Fabricius busied himself at his desk in the Government Palace, reading official documents, signing and sealing and sending them on. Giulio, his secretary, a pudgy, young bureaucratic type with a bulbous nose and vast ambitions, hurried in and out, rustling papers and officiously dispatching couriers. He was noisy but harmless and Gaius ignored him.

The office was huge, with high ceilings and tall windows, impressive and ornate, like most of the city Herod had built at Caesarea. Gaius found it a fine symbol of the Empire: vast and impressive, but overbuilt and a bit drafty.

Gaius's windows commanded a splendid view of the bustling harbor and the coast road to the north. At any time, the new governor and his retinue would be coming down that road, and Gaius would be able to see them a long way off. It was a bright, sunny morning and the sea was calm and deep blue, gently washing the harbor and wafting soft breezes into the room. Still he was irritable. The entire Roman community had been anticipating the new governor for weeks. The old one, Valerius Gratus, had been an aging esthete with somewhat questionable tastes. During his eleven year administration, government had gradually sunk into a somnolent state, totally unsuited to the agitated, rebellious population of the province. Now he was being replaced with a man reputed to be energetic and decisive by his patrons and a brutal tyrant by his detractors—of whom there were many.

Gaius was confident that he would get along with the new governor; he was a deputy, with no thought of advancement and good at his work, hardly a threat to anyone. That was why he couldn't account for his nervousness. It was true he hadn't slept well, but then he seldom did, not since he had served as a soldier.

Gaius had left the service a dozen years earlier. He was nearing fifty-seven years old, but he had aged well. His features were still strong, his skin firm and his blonde air thick and full. A sprinkling of white hairs blended with the blonde and most men thought he was at least ten years younger. Still, Gaius was surprised when people told him he looked well. His life had changed irrevocably with the rape of Miriam, the Jewish girl from Nazareth and he thought his appearance had, too. In fact, he often wondered why he had been permitted to live.

Thoughts of Miriam and her child had obsessed him for thirty years. Again and again, he recalled following the son of the Jewish renegade, Judas of Galilee, to Beth Lechem, where he was startled to find himself close to Miriam. Gaius had known instinctively that the boy they were hunting was hiding under the bed where Miriam lay moaning with birth pangs. But if the boy had been found, Gaius would have had to arrest everyone in the room. He had decided, on the instant, to avoid that terrible prospect.

Thereafter, Gaius had little enthusiasm for military service. But he had no personal means beyond his army pay and he was determined not to return to Rome, far from Miriam and her child. Nevertheless, he promised himself that he would stay away from Miriam and thus save both of them further distress. But as the years passed his curiosity continued to grow and he finally resolved to search her out.

One day, years earlier, he had ridden into Nazareth, disguised as a trader. His accented Aramaic marked him as a foreigner, but the people were accustomed to dealing with itinerant traders. He had been prepared to stay as long as necessary to find Miriam, but on the very first day, he saw her shopping at the stall of a local peddler. Gaius watched from the shadows, hiding his face with the edge of his burnoose.

Miriam was even lovelier than he had remembered. Her face was fuller, but her complexion was still flawless and her eyes glowed with great warmth. Miriam glanced his way and her eyes lingered, briefly. She sensed something both dangerous and yet familiar. Puzzled, she turned back to the peddler's wares.

A child came running up between the stalls, a golden-haired boy of six or seven. Miriam called him Joshua and the name became engraved on Gaius's heart even as he watched the child laughing and talking to his mother. Joshua's fair skin, blonde hair and blue eyes startled Gaius. The lad had his coloring, there was no doubt of it. He scanned Joshua's face as boldly as he dared and he found in the thin, faintly curving, high-bridged nose, an echo of his own. The cleft in Joshua's chin was deeper but still quite reminiscent.

His breath caught in his throat and he felt dizzy as an idea leapt into his head: "That child may be my son?"

Later, far from Nazareth, Gaius searched his memory, trying to remember all of the men who had raped Miriam. It was a painful exercise, and in fact he barely recalled most of them. He examined those half-remembered faces for resemblances to Joshua. Some, the darker skinned ones, he eliminated quickly. Then, gradually, he eliminated each of the others. It was an unfair contest but he wouldn't admit it. He finally convinced himself that he was the only one who could possibly be the father of Miriam's child.

Gaius felt a surge of strength, almost of ecstasy. "I am the father of a beautiful boy," he told himself. "Joshua. Not a bad name...Joshua. My son."

Thus, Gaius Fabricius dreamed through the long nights, his feelings of guilt and fatherhood growing together. He never married, feeling sullied by his crime. He was celibate, except when extreme need drove him to prostitutes, and then he felt guiltier than ever.

Gaius began to read Hebrew scripture. He told himself that he was doing it to better acquaint himself with the "enemy." He was fascinated by what he read. Here was a religion unlike any he had known. These strange people worshipped only one all-powerful and invisible god. This remarkable deity was not territorial but universal, not limited to dealing with one aspect of the world or another, but all-powerful, all-knowing and present everywhere. Gaius had to admire the imagination of the Jews: For a tiny nation, they were capable of vast and marvelous visions.

He was further astonished to learn that this enormously powerful GOD was a God of forgiveness. He might rail at sinners, lash them with terrible punishments, but he remained always open and forgiving. The sinner had but to repent and to turn to God. The more he learned, the more Gaius's fascination grew. He had always been skeptical of the religious teachings of his childhood. His mother had been pious, faithfully attending the shrines of a number of gods, but Gaius had been perplexed by the often contradictory claims, and rituals, sometimes obscene. When the Emperor Augustus announced that he, too, was a deity and must be worshipped, Gaius had laughed—privately, of course. Only moments before, this slender unprepossessing fellow had been a frail human being, but instantaneously, by his own decree he was equal to, if not greater than Mars and Jupiter. For Gaius, it had somehow seemed more appropriate to worship a bronze statue than a flesh and blood human being.

Then Gaius read in Isaiah, words that he never forgot:

"The carpenter...cuts down cedars...Half he burns in the fire; over the half he...roasts meat and...warms himself...the rest...he makes into a god, his idol...He prays to it and says, 'Deliver me, for thou art my God1'

"No one says...'Half of it I burned in the fire, I also baked bread on its coals, I roasted flesh and have eaten. Shall I make the rest of it an abomination? Shall I fall down before a block of wood?'"

Gaius laughed again; the Jews were right to condemn such foolish practices. The basic concept of the Hebrew scripture struck him forcibly. A god—No, not a god, but THE ONE AND ONLY GOD, invisible, all wise and powerful and ever present. A God of all men, not only of the Romans or Egyptians or Jews.

After great study and much thought, Gaius decided that he wanted to become a Jew. The idea terrified him, but he was also exalted by it. He made quiet inquiries and learned there was a saintly and highly revered man in Jerusalem known for his teachings and his own exemplary behavior.

Gaius used his next military leave to travel to Jerusalem. Late at night he knocked on the door of this sage, the rabbi called Hillel. Awakened from sleep, Hillel was startled to find a Roman soldier, standing at his door. Gaius amazed Hillel by speaking in fluent Hebrew and the rabbi, delighted, welcomed Gaius into his home.

Gaius was so obviously excited, almost hysterical, that Hillel brought him a cup of wine and tried to calm him down.

"I've studied your holy books, Rabbi, and I've mastered them." He quoted a long section from Deuteronomy, to Hillel's astonishment and pleasure.

"Wonderful," the Rabbi said. "Such scholarship is rare."

"I'm not a scholar," Gaius responded, his brow furrowed over his deep-set eyes, his jaw working even when he was not speaking. "I'm a believer."

"Praise God," Hillel said.

Gaius took a deep breath, but still his voice trembled. "I want to confess all my sins. I want to repent and to be a Jew."

Hillel looked at him with compassion. "My son," he said, "whatever your sins, If you truly repent, I know God will forgive you. But it's not necessary to become a Jew to have God's forgiveness."

Gaius was touched, but he wanted Hillel to know that he was moved by more than guilt. "I believe in your scripture," Gaius said. "I truly want to be a Jew."

"You understand," said Hillel, "that you must not only believe in One God and follow our moral law, but you would also have to be circumcised and observe our dietary laws."

Gaius smiled briefly. "I know circumcision will be painful, but I'm prepared. However, if the others find out it could be very dangerous for me. As for the dietary laws, I want to follow them, too, but that will be very difficult for a soldier. I couldn't let the Romans know."

Hillel nodded, but dropped his eyes for a moment. "You wish to become a Jew, but you want to do it in secret."

"I can be of great help to the Jews in my position."

Hillel took Gaius's hands in his own. "My son," he said, "I don't believe God wants you to do anything you cannot freely profess to the world."

Gaius paled. "Surely you understand why," he said.

"Of course. But if you want to become a Jew, you must do so openly, before God and man, or not at all."

Gaius was shattered. The light went out of his eyes and his body sagged. Hillel was afraid to let go of his hands.

Gaius gathered his strength and spoke in desperation. "But how can I have forgiveness, how can I find salvation if I'm not a Jew?"

Hillel smiled. "God doesn't limit the gift of His salvation solely to the Jews. He is more gracious, more forgiving than that. Any man may find salvation if he will accept the Covenant of Noah."

Hope stirred in Gaius. "What is that?"

"After the great flood, God promised Noah that never again would He curse the earth, or destroy all living creatures or change the sequence of the seasons, provided that Noah, representing mankind, would fulfill certain obligations. These obligations, you too, may fulfill."

The rabbi looked deeply into Gaius's eyes. "First, you must accept and believe in the one, the only God.

"Second, you must not commit fornication, and

"Third, you must not murder, for as the Lord told Noah, 'Whoever sheds the blood of man, by man shall his blood be shed; for God made man in his own image.'

"Do these things," the rabbi said, "repent your sins and you will be as certain as any man to enter the Kingdom of Heaven."

The light came back into Gaius's eyes. He slipped to his knees. "I accept the Covenant of Noah and I do repent with all my heart. Thank you, Rabbi," he said.

Hillel smiled and shook his head. "Thank the Lord." Then, together they began to pray.

***

Thereafter, Gaius found it increasingly difficult to remain in the military. He sought a position that would not require mortal combat, but found none open. Then suddenly, his Legion was called back to Rome. He applied for reassignment to Judaea, but this was denied. Desperate to remain near Miriam and Joshua, Gaius resigned his commission and sought a position in the Civil Administration.

Gaius had every qualification for eastern service: Long experience, knowledge of several languages, and great desire. But those in authority seemed suspicious of his enthusiasm—who would want to be assigned to Judaea? But he was persistent and eventually a menial position opened up in the Syrian Department. He was assigned to Damascus and then to Tyre. He worked as a clerk and a secretary. Gradually, based on his many skills and hard work, he moved up the ladder. At last, during the governorship of Valerius, he was assigned to Judaea, stationed alternately in Jerusalem and Caesarea.

At the first opportunity, Gaius visited Nazareth. By discreet inquiry he learned that Joshua and his brothers carried on a thriving business. He found their workshop, gathered his courage and pretended to be looking for a contractor for some government construction.

Joshua was not there, but a younger brother, Jacob, spoke amiably. "We do fine work," Jacob told him, "although, frankly, the governor usually brings in Greeks from Lebanon."

"Perhaps we can change that," Gaius said.

Jacob was a plain-looking fellow of average height, but with a playful smile and sparkling eyes. He seemed not in the least surprised to be discussing business with a Roman official.

Gaius drew him out, on personal as well as business matters. He learned that Miriam had been recently widowed and that Joshua was married but had no children.

As Gaius was leaving, a tall handsome blonde man with a trim beard entered the shop. Joshua. Gaius's heart stood still.

"Brother," Jacob said, "this is Gaius Fabricius, deputy to the governor. He's thinking of giving us some work."

Joshua smiled and put out his hand. Gaius took it eagerly—for the first time, he had touched his son.

"Good," Joshua said.

Gaius was speechless. He nodded vigorously and hurried out of the shop.

"Quiet fellow," Joshua said.

Jacob laughed. "Not with me," he said.

Out on the street, Gaius vaulted onto his horse as if he were once again a young centurion. He spurred the horse into a gallop and raced out of town, feeling the wind in his face and great joy in his heart. His son was beautiful—kind and bright and beautiful. It had been worth the struggle just to see him this one time.

12.

THE GOVERNOR

It was late in the afternoon when Giulio came bustling into Gaius's office. "The lookouts have seen the prefect's party." He waved a hand towards the window, where a column could be seen moving parallel to the Aqueduct, some miles north of town.

Gaius looked up briefly. "Good," he said and resumed working on his papers.

Giulio was aghast. He couldn't resist clasping his pink, pudgy hands as he asked, "Aren't you going to meet them?"

Gaius smiled. "They've been traveling for days. I don't think they'll want us leaping all over them."

Giulio's face twisted in a prissy frown. "I wasn't planning to 'leap all over them' —sir."

But Gaius was absorbed in his work. Giulio threw up his hands and hurried out of the room.

When Gaius looked up again, he was so surprised that he rose and walked to the window. No doubt of it. The column stretched all the way from the outskirts of Caesarea to the horizon. The new governor was apparently bringing an entire legion with him. Why hadn't that been noted in the dispatches? Gaius shook his head. He had better go down to the courtyard and greet him.

***

To Gaius's amusement there was a flourish of trumpets as the retinue entered the gates of the palace. Guards lined the courtyard and Nubian slaves rushed in. Gaius felt himself to be the object of hostile inspection and he would not have dared make a quick movement.

The governor and his wife were carried on two huge litters, each supported by so many Nubians that their brown flesh was like an undulating segmented creature. The litters glided forward with only the slightest sway, gloriously decorated in elegant silks and satins and edged with gold and gems.

The litters came to halt at some silent order, at the foot of the palace steps. There, they were lowered, but only to a level where the perspiring slaves created a comfortable step.

The governor's wife was a thin, almost haggard woman with a great blonde wig, dressed in silvery silks. Her face was as lined as a leather purse and her features so sunken that she seemed like a corpse in lavish burial dress.

Gaius stepped forward with a ceremonial bow, but she ignored him. Her eyes were fixed on a mirror held by a slave and she frowned at what she saw.

Then the governor alighted. For a moment, he, too, ignored Gaius as his eye took in the courtyard. The governor was also slender but his whitish hair was full and wavy, and as it arched from a high forehead, it seemed to be his own. He was of average height, but his carriage was extremely erect, and he seemed taller than he was.

At close range, his pale skin was streaked with spidery webs of faint pink and purple as if his face was encased in a loose skein of thread. His eyes were pale and the whites were hatched with pink like his skin. Gaius had seen the same signs in people who had led dissolute lives, but never in one who stood so straight or viewed the world with such hauteur.

A former associate in Rome had sent Gaius a warning letter about the new prefect: "Pontius Pilate is considered vain and unpredictable. He comes from the merchant class, not the nobility, and tries to obscure his background with a great show of wealth and luxury. He was not pleased to be sent to a border province, least of all, Judaea. You'll have to deal carefully with him."

Gaius spoke in modulated tones, being cautious not to stare into the eyes of such a man as this. "Greetings, Prefect. I have the privilege of being your deputy, Gaius Fabricius. I trust you have had a pleasant journey."

Pontius Pilate looked at him with disdain. His voice was pitched a notch too high and the tones were faintly lisping. "The country is bleak," he said, "and the season too warm. The food is appalling and the natives surly. Only to indulge my beloved Emperor, would I travel at such a time to such a place."

His wife laughed once, a rude cackle that echoed her husband's charm.

Gaius bowed his head even lower. "Your quarters are ready, sire. I hope you find them more pleasant than your travels. If there is anything you require, please call on me."

Gaius's obsequious words did little to mollify the governor. "I'll speak to you in the morning, uh, what is your name?" It was a calculated insult.

"Gaius Fabricius"

"The son of the Senator?"

"No, sire."

"Hmmm," the governor said and marched slowly up the steps, with his wife following, one step below and to the left.

***

"Forgive me, Governor, but I believe it is a great mistake."

"A great mistake?" Pilate's voice rang with incredulity, as if he were giving Gaius the chance to retract an inexcusable remark.

Gaius gathered himself and continued. "Surely, in the first days of your administration, you would prefer not to have a...disturbance."

Pilate's face purpled and his colorless eyes seemed red. "These swine must be taught a lesson. How can they possibly object if the imperial standards bear the embossed face of Tiberius Caesar?"

"The Jews have religious laws that prohibit making a graven image of any god—even the Emperor. To plant such standards in their holy city will be regarded as a serious provocation."

The response came from behind Gaius. "Good," the voice said. "We'll show them who runs this province."

Gaius spun about. "Septimus," he said.

He was much older now and the lines in his face had narrowed, multiplied and deepened. His hair had grayed, but without giving him dignity. He still had the face of a ferret and every look was a sneer.

"You know each other," Pilate said.

"Septimus was my subordinate when I was an officer."

"Now, he is the captain of my guard," Pilate said.

Septimus put out a hand and clasped Gaius's arm as if they were old friends. Gaius could not avoid the contact, but when he looked into Septimus eyes, he saw echoes of the old hatred.

"We'll be waiting," Septimus said. "If the Jews give us even the slightest opportunity, we'll fall on them with everything we have."

Gaius turned to Pilate. "I believe our orders are to avoid an uprising."

"Of course," Pilate smiled. "But surely we're not to stand by while rebels attack Roman troops?"

Septimus laughed and Pilate smiled.

Gaius spoke doggedly. "All previous governors have kept their standards out of Jerusalem."

"I am not a 'previous governor,' Pilate said. "When I am a 'previous governor,' I, too, will keep my standards out of Jerusalem."

He and Septimus laughed together.

***

In the dusky dawn light, the Levites prepared for morning prayers and sacrifices. The rain had washed the multi-colored marble floor of the Temple courtyard, but puddles still glistened here and there.

One of the younger men glanced up toward the hated Antonia fortress. He grabbed the arm of another priest and they both stared.

Joseph Caiaphas, the High Priest was entering the Temple, through the vast, stone-arched tunnels that gave direct access to the sanctuary. He had walked alone from his large and elaborate palace in the Upper city, a comfortable distance from the residences of the lesser courses of priests. Their modest homes were perched on the Ophel in the Lower City, the original part of Jerusalem, the City of David.

Caiaphas was an unusually tall man with a full head of tightly curled iron gray hair and a beard of the same even color. His eyes were also iron gray, large, deep-set and forbidding. His family had held the position of High Priest for generations and Caiaphas believed their reign was ordained by God. Of course, the family also made substantial contributions to the Romans to assure the continuance of the dynasty, but that was a necessary evil required to fulfill God's will. Caiaphas had held the position for less than a year, but he had been training for it all his life. He walked with a measured tread and spoke in a measured voice. He had no doubt that he was beloved of God and directed by Him to save his people, these willful and emotional Jews, from their own destruction.

Caiaphas did not hate the Romans as much as he despised them. At a private meeting of the Sanhedrin, the Ruling Council, he expressed his views with calm assurance: "Perhaps a handful of these Romans are educated, civilized men, but on the whole, they are ignorant superstitious and grasping. However, only a fool would ignore their vast military and political power.

"There are some among us who counsel opposition. Such men are well-meaning but deluded. If we attempt to thwart the Romans they will grind us ever harder and our suffering will intensify."

Caiaphas went on. "Opposition is dangerous, but there are some—I trust none in this council—who urge outright rebellion, holy war." His cold gray eyes scanned the chamber. "Such men are not fools, they are traitors—traitors to the nation and to God."

Some in the Council were offended and began to voice their protests. Caiaphas ignored them. "We are a small, a pitifully small nation. If we are so sinfully stupid as to rise up against the Romans, we will plunge our people into the greatest disaster we have ever known. The Assyrian conquest of Israel will be recalled as a pleasure-outing in comparison. The removal to Babylon would seem an afternoon's entertainment.

"There are those who believe that if we fight, God will descend from on high and that His hand will weigh in the balance. They assure us that with the Lord's assistance, a few thousand Jewish soldiers will overcome hundreds of thousands of Roman and mercenary troops. These self-appointed patriots are not followers of God—they are insane zealots, and it is our duty to stamp them out."

Gamaliel, leader of the Pharisees, rose to his feet. "I counsel neither war nor rebellion," he said, "but surely, the High Priest does not believe that Rome will rule us forever. One day the hand of God will be raised in our behalf. In the meantime, I refuse to condemn any of our brothers."

"You won't have to condemn them," Caiaphas said. "The Romans will nail them to wooden crosspieces and then they can appeal for help directly to God."

On this morning, as Caiaphas mounted the steps to the main level, a young priest came hurrying toward him. Caiaphas tried to stop him with a look, but the boy was too agitated.

"Eminence," he cried. "The Romans have desecrated the Temple."

Caiaphas's eyes followed the young priest's frightened gesture, pointing to the gold and blue standards of the Tenth Legion draped over the crenellated parapet of the Antonia Fortress. Each carried a medallion with the carved face of the emperor and the Latin words naming him deity. Caiaphas tried not to show his surprise.

Another group of young priests had entered the Temple through the Huldah gates and hurried to the Court of Israel.

"Eminence," they cried. "The Romans have raised standards visible from the Temple with the face of the Emperor on them."

Caiaphas stared them into uncomfortable silence.

"We have a new governor," he said, speaking in cold, precise tones. "Perhaps he is unaware of our laws. I will send a delegation to speak to him."

"Some of the people are already on the way to Caesarea," a priest offered hesitantly.

Caiaphas turned angry eyes on the young priest. "Who is leading them?" he asked.

"No one," the priest said. "They saw the standards and a crowd of them just started walking to Caesarea."

Another spoke up. "On the Cheesemakers street, they met Nico, the priest, the son of Nicodemus and asked him to speak for them."

Caiaphas frowned and spoke to Reuben, his deputy, a middle-aged man with burly shoulders and a blunt manner. "That's the problem with these simple peasants. They're easily stirred up and ready to follow anyone in any cause."

"This time," Reuben said, "their cause is just."

Caiaphas responded imperiously, "We can't allow ignorant and inexperienced people to bring our grievances to the governor. I want you to go to Caesarea, at the head of those farmers and peasants, if necessary and speak to the governor. You may say that you represent the High Priest."

13.

STANDARDS

Their numbers gradually grew as they traveled along the road, most on foot, a few on donkeys, even fewer on horseback. Some carried a pack with a little food, but even though it would take at least three days to reach Caesarea, most did not seem to care where they would camp or what they would eat. Many had simply dropped their tools and joined the protestors.

Reuben mounted an ass and by hard riding reached the column by early afternoon. He was perspiring heavily and puffing mightily, when he found the young priest, Nico, humbly dressed and walking cheerfully at the head of the protestors. Nico was fairly tall and well-built with straight cut brown hair and undistinguished features. It was difficult to believe that he came from an important priestly family.

Reuben spoke bluntly, in part because he was short of breath. "The High Priest has assigned me to speak for the delegation."

Nico looked up at him, burly and puffing hard, his face red with exertion. "Can I help you my friend?" he asked.

"Did you hear me?" Reuben said.

"Yes, of course. We're pleased to have the High Priest on our side."

The word passed down the column and was greeted generally with approval, though not without suspicion. The people often found themselves at odds with the priestly hierarchy. Reuben, despite his peasant appearance, was a Sadducee and therefore assumed to be an apologist for the Romans.

"There will be no violence," Reuben said.

Those who heard him were angered.

"We're going to protest," a man cried out, "not to start a war."

"We come in peace," said another.

Reuben frowned. "Good, then let me do the talking."

"Agreed," Nico said.

The crowd continued to grow, as many along the road heard of the desecration and spontaneously joined the marchers. They were now several thousand strong, strung out for miles along the highway.

They were fervent in their mission, but hopeful the matter could be resolved peacefully. "Perhaps the Romans just made a mistake," some men were saying.

"Yes, the legion is newly posted here. Maybe their officers don't know our laws."

"Surely the governor will order the standards removed."

They marched in relative quiet along the coast road. At dark, they made camp beside the highway, shared what food they had and slept on the ground.

***

Joshua had been sitting by the river Nir, looking up at the clouds when he saw the strange form in the sky. He could not make out the exact shape of it, but he saw a face, a face that seemed arrogant to him and dangerous.

For a moment the shape that bore it seemed to flutter and the face dissolved. Then it returned, brighter and more menacing than before. He knew he had to follow it as it drifted towards the west, towards the Great Sea.

"Will you be all right?" Joshua asked his wife, anxiously.

"Of course," Rebecca said, kissing him on the cheek. "We've been alone before."

"I can't say that I really know why I'm doing this," he said, with a crooked smile.

"Because you have to," Rebecca said softly.

They embraced, Joshua kissed the children and left the house. At the far edge of the meadow, he turned and waved a final goodbye. Rebecca and the children watched him until he disappeared into the forest.

***

The marchers were sighted by Roman outposts half a day's travel from Caesarea. Pilate and Gaius were in the governor's quarters when a courier brought word of their approach.

Pilate bristled with anger. "Rebellion? Already? Call Septimus."

Septimus already knew about the marchers, "War is it?" he said, a great smile splitting his rocky face and animating his gravelly voice.

110

"No," Gaius said, "according to the courier they have no weapons and merely want to present a petition to the governor."

Septimus frowned. "Gaius always sees the good side of the Jews."

Pilate looked at him quizzically. "Is that true, Deputy?"

Gaius shook his head. "I have no more taste for sedition than you, sire. But I don't believe the Emperor will be pleased to learn that only a few days after you arrived, the country is at war."

Pilate sniffed and stared out the window for a moment. "He's right, you know, Captain. Let's wait and see what these pigs want."

As they neared the Governor's Palace, Reuben slowed the column and gathered the marchers into a tighter formation. "Good," said Reuben, proud of his work. "That's more dignified." Nico, aware they were being shadowed by Roman cohorts, knew the closeness was dangerous, but he said nothing.

As they approached, guards appeared on the walls. Reuben signaled a halt. "Stay here, while I speak to the governor."

"We didn't walk sixty miles to wait outside," a voice yelled.

"That's right," another called out.

"Yes," the men cried. "We want to talk to the governor."

Nico raised his hand. "Obviously, the soldiers are not going to let all of us into the palace. Twenty of us will go into the courtyard—the rest will remain outside." There was some grumbling, and it wasn't easy to select the twenty, but finally it was done.

Pilate watched from the shadows of a high window. "What a grimy, noisy group," he said. "Roman citizens would never act in such a disgusting manner."

Septimus agreed. Gaius could have given the governor some famous examples of Roman mob action, but he thought it unwise.

Pilate gestured suddenly, and the guards quickly closed the great iron gates right in the faces of the delegation.

"Why?" Gaius asked.

"These Jews will learn not to trifle with their leaders." Pilate said smugly.

Reuben spoke to the centurion who stood stern-faced behind the gates. "We have come to peacefully petition the governor," he said. "We respectfully request an audience."

The centurion stared at Reuben, then stalked off without replying. He marched up the staircase and disappeared into the palace.

"Sire," the centurion began, "The Jews want—"

"—I know what the Jews want," Pilate said. "Tell them I'm not available. I'll speak to them when I have time."

The centurion saluted and hurried out.

"When will you see them?" Gaius asked.

"When the mood strikes me," Pilate said.

***

Reuben smiled confidently at the approaching centurion, expecting to be admitted promptly.

"The governor is busy," the centurion said brusquely. "He'll call you when he has time." Then he turned abruptly, muttering something to the guards. They laughed, looked at the Jews and laughed again.

Reuben tried to cover his disappointment. "Understandable," he said to the delegates. "He didn't know we were coming."

After a while Reuben began to pace. When an hour had passed, the others sat on the ground, but Reuben stubbornly remained on his feet.

After two hours, Reuben asked the guards to call the centurion, but they did not respond.

The sun began to sink in the west and still no one had come for them. Once more, Reuben spoke to the guards, trying a smattering of all the languages he knew. Sometimes they smiled, but they never responded. He tried again, at nightfall, when the guard changed, but still there was no response. Behind him, the twenty delegates were silent, waiting patiently. But the great mass of protestors was getting restless and their voices rose.

"What are we waiting for?"

"Why don't they come for us?"

"We're being ignored."

Reuben, perspiring now, even though the sun had fallen, decided he had better calm them.

"My friends," he said, "we've spent three days traveling here. Surely we can wait a while to speak to the governor."

"You can wait. I have work to do."

Others agreed.

"What do you say?" many asked Nico.

"They are testing us," he said. "If we are noisy and unruly they'll believe we're common troublemakers, rebels or worse. They'll have an excuse for not listening to us. And, since, we can't tolerate the standards, we'll have a terrible confrontation. We must avoid that if possible."

"He's right," one of the protestors said.

"Yes," another agreed. "That centurion looked like he'd enjoy nothing more than running a sword through us."

Reuben regarded Nico with new respect. "Good," he whispered. "You spoke well."

No one came for them that evening. Disappointed but not yet rebellious, they withdrew a ways and camped out in the fields below the palace. The word had spread in Caesarea and men and women from the Jewish community brought them food and other necessities.

In the morning, they assembled again before the gates. The same centurion was on duty and Reuben tried to be ingratiating. "Centurion," he smiled, "We are still waiting. Can you please inform the governor we are available at any time convenient to him?"

The centurion stalked off without answering.

The hours passed. Other people arrived and were allowed to enter and leave through the gates, but not the Jewish delegation. They grew more restless.

"They'll never let us in," some said,

"We should go back and tear down the standards," others said.

"Or get rid of Reuben—it's him they won't talk to."

"Don't be silly," Nico said. "The Romans want us to quarrel among ourselves. They hope we'll give up or turn violent. We must be patient."

The day stretched on, without word from the governor. From time to time, someone would claim to see him in a window. In fact, they were right. Pontius Pilate watched the crowd with growing pleasure. "They're close to erupting," he said cheerfully. "Septimus and I are hoping for that."

"They're a patient people, Sire," Gaius said mildly. "And they love their God."

Pilate raised a hand and smoothed his carefully waved hair. He had a way of arching his back and looking down his nose when he spoke, especially to inferiors. And in Judaea, everyone was his inferior. "You do like these Jews, don't you?" he asked.

"It's not a matter of liking," Gaius observed. "I'm sure you'll agree it's important to understand your adversary."

"Understand them?" Pilate said. "If they remain out there much longer, we'll be able to smell them."

The others in the room, serving men and slaves, secretaries and lackeys, laughed appreciatively. Pilate allowed himself a slight smirk.

***

In the late afternoon of the second day, Joshua reached Caesarea. He had met many travelers and learned about the standards flying over the Temple. Now he understood what he had seen in the clouds and why he was called to Caesarea and the Great Sea. Still, he was surprised by the great number of protestors. It's a good sign, he thought. The people do care about their God.

When he reached the palace, he found a huge crowd of his countrymen standing or sitting on the great lawn before the walls. Armed guards paced the battlements, but it was clear the Jews were unarmed.

"Joshua, Joshua," a familiar voice cried out.

Joshua recognized Nico and they embraced happily. But then Nico frowned. "I'm worried," he said. "The governor has kept us waiting for days. The people are angry and there are rumors of armies forming in the hills."

Joshua shook his head. "The Romans have a full legion here. We would be slaughtered."

Nico nodded grimly. "You can help me keep the people calm."

Together, they walked among the protestors, speaking to everyone who would listen, counseling patience. No one could doubt Nico's sincerity, and many from Jerusalem told others that he was reliable. A few from Galilee knew Joshua and respected him.

***

The second day stretched on without word from Pontius Pilate and became a third. Fortunately, the autumn weather remained warm and it was not difficult to sleep out at night. The Jews of Caesarea took some of the older men into their homes. Reuben would have liked to join them. He wished fervently the High Priest had given the honor of this mission to someone else.

In Jerusalem, Caiaphas convened the Sanhedrin, but he could only report Reuben's mission. Anxiety spread through the city and into the countryside. Travelers and merchants carried the story throughout Judaea,

Samaria and Galilee. Other men began the march to Caesarea, swelling the ranks of the protestors.

In the hills, bands of rebels began to prepare for battle, hoping this was the event that would trigger a major uprising. Perhaps the Romans had done the very deed that would bring God's wrath down on their heads. Had not the Lord responded when Antiochus sullied the Temple and when Pompey had entered the sacred place? They sent word to all their allies, to that loose confederation of people known as "Zealots". But although they were known by one name, their views were widely different and each leader had his own idea of how to accelerate the coming of Messiah.

The third day became a fourth and the fourth a fifth. The band outside the palace had grown to five thousand men and the Jews of Caesarea were hard put to feed them. The people were hungry, angry and dirty. The supply of water had been cut off and they could only bathe in the sea, but they were unwilling to leave the field before the Palace. The gentiles of Caesarea were growing angry at this large and ragged group on their doorsteps. They, too, appealed to Pilate.

Septimus repeatedly asked the governor's permission to drive the protestors into the sea. Gaius felt growing anxiety, but spoke with great restraint. Pilate listened to both and for the moment gave no orders, but he clearly enjoyed the impasse.

Neither Nico nor Joshua had slept in two days, passing from group to group, calming the protestors, assuring them that quiet waiting was the right response. But the people were very short-tempered and almost any action might have incited a riot.

On the morning of the sixth day, the centurion appeared at the gate, and beckoned to Reuben. Reuben was clean-shaven when his trials began, but now he had a small gray beard.

"Bring your people to the Hippodrome. The governor will speak to you there."

Reuben thanked the centurion and delightedly reported the news to the delegates. They in turn spread the word among the rest of the protestors. Their spirits lifted and it was a happy group that trooped to the Hippodrome.

At the gates, they were met by Roman soldiers, who instructed them to gather on the grass, within the great oval of the track where the horses raced. It was a vast area, and despite their numbers, they did not fill it.

Then, suddenly, a trumpet sounded, and to their astonishment, thousands of Roman soldiers rushed into the Hippodrome from every gate until they were surrounded by armed men, three rows deep.

"What is this?" the men cried to each other.

"Are they going to kill us?"

Nico and Joshua joined Reuben in raising their arms and calling for quiet. "Don't move," Nico yelled. "Don't give them reason to harm you."

While the crowd sullenly settled down, the governor and his retinue entered the Hippodrome. Brawny soldiers placed a tribunal at the Imperial box and Pilate took his seat, arms folded, his legs crossed beneath his toga. He surveyed the Jews with disdain.

Reuben was petrified with fear. The time had come for him to act, but he didn't know what to do. "Nico," he whispered. "You speak to him."

Nico glanced at Joshua, who nodded, and they walked forward together. However, when Nico reached the front rank of the protestors, an officer pulled his short sword and held it to his chest. "One more step and you're a dead man."

Gradually, the great stadium quieted. Still, Pilate was silent. If he expected the crowd to lose patience, he was disappointed. Finally he rose and spoke in a loud, lisping voice that carried to every man in the Hippodrome.

"I am your Governor, sent by the Emperor to rule in his name. I have brought the emblems of Empire, among them the Royal standards of the Tenth Legion, bearing the portraits of Tiberius Caesar," he paused, "Emperor and GOD." The crowd began to murmur, but he spoke above them. "Those standards are carried by every Roman Legion from East Anglia to Parthia, from the German marches to Carthage."

His voice was a notch higher and much louder. His eyes, previously cold, flashed with determination.

"And those standards will fly over every Roman Army, every fortress, every palace in all of the Syrian Department, including your beloved Jerusalem."

"No," the people cried, angered and astonished. "No." They moved slightly toward the tribunal.

Pilate looked at them with surprise. His face purpled, as the little nets that held his face together filled with angry color.

His arm swept high. "Roman soldiers draw your swords."

Two thousand men drew their weapons.

116

Pilate rose on his toes as he spoke. "You will receive the emblems of The Emperor's divine authority with honor, or you will be cut down without mercy." His final words were almost a scream: "Submit or die."

The last word rang in the Hippodrome and ricocheted from the rows of ranked seats.

The Jews stared at Pilate and then at each other.

Reuben was trembling. Perhaps he could somehow convince someone that he wasn't here to make trouble, only to ask questions.

Nico did not know what to do. This he had never expected. But even as he hesitated, Joshua stepped forward onto the track. He took the collar of his tunic and ripped it from his neck. Then he put one knee down on the gravel and bowed his head.

Nico watched for a moment, understood, tore his own tunic and followed Joshua in kneeling on the floor of the Hippodrome.

Other Jews watching did the same. A wave moved through the crowd, as one after another, the Jews, thousands of them, tore their tunics, knelt and lowered their heads.

Pilate was startled. "What—what are they doing?" he asked Gaius.

"They're taking you at your word. They've bared their necks to make it easy for your soldiers. They would rather die than transgress their laws."

Pilate turned on him. "You're mad—utterly mad."

The look in Pilate's eyes was so filled with hate that Gaius was frightened. "You can see for yourself."

Pilate turned his eyes on the Jews. He was trembling with anger. "I'm warning you. One more minute of this defiance, and you'll all die."

In the field below there was only silence.

"You're mad!" Pilate screamed. "You Jews are all madmen!" Again, the last word echoed in the Stadium.

Below, Septimus looked up expectantly. His mouth was dry with anticipation.

Pilate stood uncertainly, filled with loathing for these disgusting Jews. How could he explain slaughtering five thousand citizens over those damn flags? He turned abruptly and strode out of the box.

Septimus blinked. Was that the signal he had been waiting for? He saw that Gaius was shaking his head. Damn that man, Septimus thought.

Gaius spoke mildly, but his voice carried. "The governor has instructed me to tell you that the standards will be removed from Jerusalem."

The Jews wanted to cheer, but they knew better. Slowly, dazedly, they raised themselves. It was over. Their ordeal was over.

Pilate heard Gaius's words as he left the Hippodrome. Gaius had said what he, himself, could not bear to say. Well, it was done. The Jews had won. But they would pay for this humiliation. He swore they would rue this day.

14.

QUIET MORNING

Gaius Fabricius could feel morning in the air, although the sky was still dark. The villa he was staying in was almost new, a long, low house nestled in the hills high above Tiberias, surrounded by pines and junipers. A gust of wind from the Sea of Galilee ruffled the curtains, bringing with it the fresh smells of the lake. Gaius welcomed the coming of day even as he dreaded it. The night was terrible, filled with evil dreams and premonitions, but the day might be even worse.

Pilate had sent him to Tiberias, ostensibly to reorganize a lax Roman customs system. Actually, there were disturbing rumors of growing Galilean unrest and Pilate wanted a first-hand account. Technically, Galilee was under the rule of an Ethnarch, Herod Antipas, son of the former King. That was why Gaius's assignment was informal and why he was staying in a lavish villa.

To complicate matters, Pilate had sent Septimus and a contingent of troops. They had every right to be in Galilee, at least temporarily, but their presence was certain to arouse the volatile Galileans. Gaius understood full well that it was not Pilate's intention to soothe the disaffected, but rather first to arouse and then to ruthlessly suppress them.

Ominously, in the past several months, Septimus had grown restless. He had come to hate the Syrian Department, Judaea, Galilee and Gaius Fabricius in ascending order. He asked Pilate to reassign him to a district where he would have more "military opportunities."

Pilate laughed when Septimus, of all people, used such a euphemism, but he refused the request. When he finally unleashed Septimus, the man would be foaming at the mouth.

In fact, Pilate was just as bored as Septimus. His own hopes for reassignment to a more prestigious post were dashed time and again. The only good thing about Judaea was that it was so far from Rome that his harsh administration was not seriously criticized.

But now the people's anger at Roman rule was growing, in Judaea and Galilee. For the Galileans, Jerusalem, although in Judaea, was the center of their religion, and therefore offenses against the Judaeans were offenses against them as well. With any luck, Pilate thought, this would boil over into open rebellion and he would have an opportunity to indulge his innate cruelty, even while gaining a reputation for stern and effective control. Then, he might gain an assignment more congenial than this benighted post.

Gaius stirred in his bed. The curtains were open so that he could catch sight of the first rays of the sun. In the light breeze, the candles guttered but did not go out. A parchment scroll lay beside him—a copy of the Scriptures of the Jews. It was dangerous reading, but perhaps justifiable for an official in the Syrian Department.

The fact that Gaius had learned to read not only the Hebrew text, but also the Aramaic Targum—a kind of interpretive translation—could be explained because Aramaic was the every- day language of the people and even more valuable to a local official than Hebrew.

That night Gaius had not touched the scroll as he lay in his bed, worrying about his mission in Tiberias. But as the hours passed, Gaius's practical concerns were replaced by familiar visions. As on a thousand previous nights, he was tormented by the girl. The "girl." He laughed soundlessly. Miriam was no longer a girl, any more than he was a young centurion. If she were still alive, she would be middle-aged.

He relived the scene of her violation, an image he could not escape, even with the passage of over thirty years. Then he saw the boy, his son Joshua, and for a moment his spirits lifted. A beautiful child, a handsome young man, and now in his maturity, an upright citizen with a wife and children. Gaius had not seen Joshua in years. Still, Joshua was his life, his immortality.

But then, unbidden, the tormenting pictures of the rape of Miriam returned, a bitter accusation of an unconscionable crime. His body shook with guilt, his forehead gleamed with perspiration. Gaius cursed himself for the millionth time. The rabbi, Hillel, had promised God's forgiveness. But Gaius could not forgive himself.

Once again, the breeze off the lake ruffled the curtains. Exhausted, Gaius dozed off. But then, hard steps echoed in the corridor and a strong hand pounded on his door.

Without waiting for permission, Septimus rudely entered his bedroom. Gaius almost smiled. He believed that Septimus was a particularly fitting part of his well-deserved punishment—a mark of divine retribution that might occasionally be lightened, but would never disappear.

Septimus spoke in a strangled rage, his face purple, the veins standing out in his neck, his voice darkened with hatred. "Night patrol—filthy rebels slaughtered our boys—eight bodies in the draw."

"How did it—"

But Septimus would not be interrupted. "Ambush—surprised our men—outnumbered them ten to one."

Gaius could hear the story developing even as Septimus told it. He would turn the Romans into heroes, one way or another.

Septimus went on, detailing the gore, as if he had never seen dead men before. Gaius noted that the story was taking a new turn. Septimus was trying to goad him into action, by describing the killings as even more horrible than they were.

Gaius spoke mildly. "That's not like the rebel Jews. They seldom strike at night and we've broken up all the large bands."

Septimus's eyes bulged. "You're defending the Jews—is that it? Dogs that murdered our soldiers?"

Gaius realized he had made a mistake. "Of course I'm not defending the Jews. Killing Roman soldiers is a foul deed that must be punished. But we're here to keep the peace, not provoke a war."

As Gaius spoke, Septimus's hands were working, as if he needed to use them on something or somebody, perhaps Gaius Fabricius. His mouth was working, too, muttering curses under his breath, so that he hardly heard Gaius. "Fool," he was thinking. "The man is a fool."

Gaius was on his feet, his hand on Septimus's shoulder. "Calm yourself, Captain. We'll report this to Antipas—"

"—He moves too slowly."

"But this is his territory. We're obliged to let him know, before we take military action."

"Not in an emergency." Septimus leaned closer until his face was only inches from Gaius. "I know where they are," Septimus said. It was a lie and he hadn't known what he was going to say when the words leaped from his mouth. A plan, a wonderful plan was working in his mind.

Gaius was suspicious. "Where?"

"A few leagues from here. A settlement they call Beth Sholem."

"A whole army is hiding there?"

"The leaders."

Septimus was very proud of himself. The story was developing easily in his mind. "I'll take a patrol, scout the town, and confirm the reports."

The man was obsessed—that was clear. "What then?" Gaius asked

"We'll capture the lot of them—quietly of course. Don't want to stir up the countryside. Then we'll turn them over to Antipas."

"I'd better come with you."

Septimus laughed— if you could call it that. "This is a military matter. I followed the rules and informed you. I don't need a nursemaid."

"You're under my direction."

Septimus leveled a look at Gaius that was remarkable for its undisguised hatred. "While you're quibbling over regulations, the killers will escape." He turned on his heel. "Follow me if you like—but stay out of the way." The door slammed behind him.

For a moment Gaius was puzzled by Septimus's behavior. "What have I unwittingly authorized?" Gaius asked himself.

He shook his head and called for his servant. A shivering black slave boy hurried in carrying a bowl of steaming water, which scalded his hands as he carried it. Gaius cautiously dipped a towel into the steaming brew and gingerly wiped his face. Then, startled by a flash of understanding, he jumped, spilling the water. "Beth Sholem, that's where—." He shoved the boy aside and ran out of the room, naked and yelling Septimus's name. But it was too late. Only a cloud of bitter, gray dust marked the patrol's departure.

***

Joshua settled comfortably in a corner of the room, a blanket over his shoulders, his back against the wall and a brass oil lamp spreading warm, even light. Rebecca and the children were asleep, but he would stay awake most of the night reading from his precious scrolls. In addition to the holy writ, he had collected other writings which lacked official sanction, but which he felt were inspired. He kept them clean and safe in a fine small cabinet he had built. He thought of it privately as his own small "ark of the covenant."

Joshua and Rebecca had been married for almost fifteen years, but Rebecca still retained her slim, youthful figure and there was no gray in her dark, smooth hair. Her eyes still sparkled when they lighted on Joshua. She was a plain-spoken cheerful woman, happy with her lot, but vaguely distrustful of Joshua's infatuation with the Law. "You read all night and work all day. You'll make yourself ill."

"I'm fine," he answered. "Reading the holy words renews my strength."

Rebecca knew that was true. Although it seemed he never slept, his energy grew rather than diminished. In his mid-thirties, he had the strength and agility, the enthusiasm and purpose of a far younger man. His blonde hair and beard had darkened a fraction, and there were a few lines in his brow, but otherwise he was as youthful as the day he had first loved her, on the beach at Caesarea.

They had two children: David, a blonde boy very like Joshua in appearance, and a dark-haired girl, Rachel, very like Rebecca. Both doted on their father and his way with them was magical. If they were injured, he knew how to heal their hurts, and when they were troubled, he found the ways to heal their emotional wounds.

It was the same for Rebecca. In the beginning, she had been attracted by his physical beauty—the glow of his coloring, the evenness of his features, the perfection of his limbs. But in time she learned that he was as beautiful inside as out—a man of good heart and fine intentions, a wonderful husband and father, a good provider. Best of all, he brought joy into the house—joy and the love of God.

Rebecca was profoundly grateful to have children. She did not conceive for nearly three years after they were married and in despair had urged Joshua to divorce her and take a wife who would bear him children. Joshua listened quietly, smiled and held her to him.

"We waited years to be married. Can't we wait to have children? He quoted from Isaiah,

'They who wait for the Lord shall renew their strength,

They shall mount up with wings like eagles,

They shall run and not be weary,

They shall walk and not faint.'

When God decides it is time, we'll have children."

Joshua as always, proved right. First Rachel and then David arrived There were no more, but Joshua and Rebecca were content.

After an hour, Joshua rose from his scrolls and checked on his family. The children slept close to each other on small mats, resting with their arms flung out, the covers kicked off their bodies. Joshua gently kissed them and pulled the covers back up.

Rebecca's pose was similar. She lay on their bed with the blanket pushed aside and her arms open, breathing easily. She slept well, did Rebecca, knowing Joshua was awake and reading his scriptures and protecting his home.

Joshua looked about him fondly, then returned to his corner and reopened the scroll. He had been reading in Isaiah, his favorite text, which never failed to refresh and replenish his soul. He smiled and decided that when he returned for his midday meal, he would show David and Rebecca the quotation from Isaiah, the one that went...

"The wolf shall dwell with the lamb,
and the leopard shall lie down with the kid,
and the calf and the lion and the fatling together,
and a little child shall lead them."

There could be no more important passage than that and he wanted eleven year old Rachel and ten year old David to think about it and discuss it with him.

He was happy in Beth Sholem, a tiny settlement close to the Jordan. It had been difficult to leave his mother and brothers, but once his sister Sarah was married and his brothers firmly established in their trade, there was no longer a pressing need for his support.

In Beth Sholem he found the freedom and the privacy denied him in Nazareth where he had been the center of attention ever since Ari the Sage had given him credit for saving his life.

When Joshua was ten, no older than his son David, he had come upon a little girl floating face down in the Nir, a river that flowed into the Jordan. Joshua waded into the stream and cradled her cold body to him. He planned to take her to shore and force the water from her body, but even as he held her, the child opened her eyes her and smiled. "God," she said.

From the other side of the river, her parents came splashing through the cold water. They had been picking berries on a distant hill when they saw her wander into the fast-flowing stream. As they ran, they watched in despair as their daughter struggled, lost the struggle and was swept downstream by the current. They saw Joshua pick up her apparently lifeless body. Moments later, she was awake and clinging to Joshua, calling aloud "God" and then "God" and then "God," again.

Joshua smiled and stroked her head. "Yes, thank God for his goodness and your life."

Still smiling, he handed the little girl to her parents. They took their child and embraced her, but she saw only Joshua. "God," she said, again and again.

The parents tried to thank Joshua, but he refused to acknowledge having any part in what had happened. "Please," he said, "give your thanks to the Lord." Feeling embarrassed, he ran home.

The story of the rescue spread through Nazareth and a crowd of people came to the house of Joseph and Miriam, clamoring to see Joshua and to be helped. Joseph refused to talk to them and he kept Joshua home until the clamor had died down.

But that was not the last such event. As he grew into young manhood, the experiences intensified. Time and again, Joshua found he could help the sick back to health, and the crippled to regain the use of their limbs. People looked into his eyes and trusted him. He looked into theirs with a natural affection and a desire to help. When his hands touched them, he could feel them relax and at the same time, their blood quicken.

Joshua believed fervently that healing came only from God and he took no credit for himself. Thus he was surprised, even shocked, when others treated him as if he held a mysterious kind of supernatural power. Joshua had seen magicians and soothsayers who preyed upon the helpless and the gullible. He did not want to be ranked with these tricksters and charlatans.

But the people of Nazareth were not put off by his humility. They came to his shop and interrupted his work. They descended upon his home, to plead for and even to demand that he cure them.

He was dismayed. "I'm not a physician," he said.

"You're better than that," a woman said, who wanted him to remove a tumor from the back of her neck, "you have holy gifts."

"No," he said. "That's blasphemy. May God forgive you." Feeling both angry and disturbed he closed the door to his home.

The woman was furious and remained on his doorstep for hours, cursing him. Joshua was saddened by her pain and her anger, but her faith was in him rather than in God, and he knew he would not be able to help her.

Joshua could no longer bring his problems to Ari. His dear friend and teacher had died when he was an even ninety years old. Joshua searched his memory, trying to recall anything that Ari had said which might bring him solace. But the words he remembered were not reassuring.

"You have great spiritual gifts," Ari had told him.

"It's not true. I'm an ordinary man."

Ari smiled. "An ordinary man with extraordinary powers."

"Please, Ari, not you."

"You must not turn your back on the blessings that God bestows."

"I'm not turning my back. People are healed because they yearn to be healed, because they believe they will be healed, because God wants them to be healed."

"All true," Ari said, "but you must not deny that you are the instrument of God's will."

"We're all the instruments of God's will," Joshua responded stubbornly, his jaw set.

"Also true, my boy, but you are different from the rest of us."

Joshua was silent. He did not want to believe he was different. One woman might be blonde and another dark-haired; one man might be a good carpenter and another a better shepherd. That only showed the diversity in God's kingdom. Surely no one was better than his neighbor.

In time, however, the strain of living in Nazareth grew too great. Joshua couldn't leave his house without being accosted by the ill and infirm. Many came to him for his blessing, as if he were a holy man. "My small help, I can give when God approves," he said. "Blessings come directly from the Lord." But they didn't believe him and some behaved as if he were a god, which angered and appalled him.

Joshua had felt compelled to move to move to Beth Sholem, where the settlers respected his privacy and did not seek miraculous cures. At times, he felt guilty that he was not available to any who might need him, but he firmly believed that was not his purpose in life. He didn't know what that purpose might be, but he was certain that if he watched carefully and listened for the word of God, he would be told.

15.

JUDAS

As Joshua read Isaiah, he unconsciously responded to the drama in the text, nodding his head at a wise saying, smiling at a brilliant insight, frowning over the tragic mistakes of Israel.

The lamp flickered in a strange way and his senses were alerted. Joshua set aside the scroll, rose and, wrapping the blanket about his shoulders, quietly opened the door of his home.

It was a bright, moonlit night and the small homes of Beth Sholem stood out clearly against the pale silver sky. There was no breeze and nothing moved, but Joshua heard a sound that drew him to a small gully a few rods below his home. He looked over the edge and was not surprised to see a man lying there, resting on his back and breathing jaggedly. Joshua slipped over the side of the gully and slid down in the loose sand. At the sound, the man sat up suddenly and raised a dagger.

Joshua didn't blink or retreat. "Easy, brother," he said. "I won't harm you."

The man staggered to his feet and stared at Joshua, trying to determine whether he could believe what he heard. He gripped the dagger tightly and looked about wildly.

"There's no one else," Joshua said softly.

The man moved toward Joshua, holding the dagger pointed directly at his chest. He walked with great difficulty, moving his feet without lifting them. Joshua remained motionless, waiting. The man moved closer, until his weapon was touching Joshua's tunic. Then he fainted and the dagger fell to the ground.

Joshua grimaced as he picked up the dagger and shoved the distasteful thing into his belt. He lifted the man—he was blocky and heavy but Joshua was very strong—and carried him up the sloping side of the gully, across the road and into his home.

Rebecca and the children still slept peacefully. In the brighter light of the house, Joshua saw that the man had suffered a terrible wound in his chest and that a rag, black with blood, had been stuffed in it. Even as Joshua watched, a red line of fresh blood slipped through and spilled to the floor.

Joshua quickly placed the man down on a mat, then stoked the coals of the fire into life beneath a pot of water, still simmering above it. He found clean cloths and taking a deep breath, he removed the filthy rag stuffed in the wound. Immediately, fresh blood spurted forth and Joshua forced a clean cloth down against the flow. He pressed hard against the wound, praying fervently to God as he worked. The man's face turned pale and feverish and great beads of perspiration stood out on his face. He moaned, but did not waken.

He was a hard-muscled man of medium height, with an uneven hairline of brown unruly hair clipped short and a broad flat nose. He didn't have a full beard but obviously hadn't shaved for days. Above his lip, a long thin scar curved from below his nose up into his left cheek, so that at first glance it looked like half a narrow mustache. He was swarthy, with heavily pock-marked skin, mottled with many brown spots.

After several minutes, the first cloth was soaked and seeping. Sweat stood out on Joshua's brow as he gently pulled the bloody binding away and pressed down with another. He held it there, applying all his strength, redoubling the pressure and his prayers.

The man began to stir. Once again he moaned, and this time the sound brought Rebecca in from the other room. She was startled to see Joshua bending over a wounded man and her hands went to her lips stifling a cry. Joshua gestured for help and she quickly brought him fresh cloths. It seemed to Joshua that the flow was decreasing, but he did not release the pressure on the wound. He stopped praying only long enough to give his wife a brief account of what had happened.

"Do you know him?" she whispered.

Joshua shook his head. "Perhaps a bandit, perhaps a Zealot."

"What about the Romans?" Rebecca asked.

Joshua shrugged. "Dampen a cloth and wipe his face and chest," he told her.

They worked together for over an hour, applying fresh cloths, cleaning the old ones, praying together.

After a while, the man stopped writhing and perspiration ceased to bathe his body. He began to breathe more regularly. This time, when Joshua removed the cloth, it was almost dry and the wound seemed to be smaller.

The man's eyes popped open. He looked into Joshua's eyes for a long startled moment, then jumped up, pushing Joshua onto his back. Rebecca screamed and backed away. The man leaped to his feet and reached for his dagger. He was dismayed to find it was missing.

Joshua stood up slowly and stood between Rebecca and the wounded man. He drew the dagger from his belt and held it out, hilt first. "Do you want this?" he asked.

The man hesitated, staring at Joshua and Rebecca. Then a strange look passed over his face and his hands and eyes went involuntarily to the wound on his chest. He was so surprised that he staggered and only the wall kept him from falling.

"We've been taking care of you," Joshua said quietly. "I believe we stopped the flow of blood."

The man blinked and tried to speak. At first the words wouldn't come. Finally, he steeled himself and spoke in a rasping voice, like the scrape of metal on metal. "The wound—it's almost gone." Once again, he rubbed his hands across his chest, astonished.

"Blessings be to God," Joshua said. "Rebecca, we have a guest, please bring us some wine."

Rebecca, assured by Joshua's calm words, hurriedly brought a wine-skin and cups. The bewildered man took a cup but did not drink.

Joshua took his cup, blessed the wine, and waited courteously for his guest. The man didn't move.

"Perhaps you feel uncomfortable drinking with a stranger," Joshua said evenly. "My name is Joshua ben Joseph," he said. "This is my wife, Rebecca. What's your name?"

For a long time, the man only stared at him. "Judas," he said.

"Well, Judas, let us drink to your health."

Slowly, his lips peering over the rim, Judas sipped from the cup.

The wine brought new color to his face, but still there was suspicion in his eyes. Once again he touched his chest. "This was a terrible wound," he said. "Are you a healer? What did you do?"

Joshua laughed. "Nothing magical. Only God is the healer. You may thank Him for stanching the blood."

It was evident now, even to a man as suspicious as Judas, that these people were not dangerous. "Thank you for your help," he said. "I must go."

"It's dark," Joshua said. "Why not wait until morning?"

"It's safer for me to travel at night."

"Yes, but you have several hours until daylight, and you're still weak from loss of blood. You could rest a while and still travel a long way before dawn."

As Joshua spoke, a wave of dizziness passed over Judas. Joshua hurried to his side and helped him to a chair.

"Thank you," Judas said, "you're very kind." Then, for the first time, his face opened up and he smiled. It was a full smile, marked by fine, straight teeth that were in marked contrast to the jagged, irregular quality of the rest of his face. When he smiled, one could feel drawn to him.

Joshua sensed the change and was warmed by it. "Can you tell us what happened to you?" he asked.

"It's better you don't know," Judas said. But Joshua felt strongly that it was important to know and the strength of his belief reached Judas who looked at him with a curious smile. This man, this Joshua, was a strange one. Gentle, yet somehow powerful.

As he spoke, Judas's smile faded. His expression became stern and impassioned and his words sounded hard in the dark night.

"My friends and I, perhaps twenty of us, were ambushed in the hills by a cohort of Roman horseman. We fought as well as we could—killed many Romans—but most of my men were killed. A few of us escaped in the darkness. I found my way here."

Joshua waited, knowing there was more. Judas stared at him, feeling the invitation, perhaps the demand, for more of an explanation.

"They won't stop us although losing so many men is a terrible blow. I blame myself for not being better prepared. But there are still hundreds like me hidden in the hills. When the time is ripe, the Romans will hear from us again."

Even that was not enough for Joshua. Unaccountably, Judas felt the need to justify himself, to explain why he did what he did. "My friends and I believe it's wrong—that it's sinful to patiently bow our heads and accept the rule of these Roman dogs. God doesn't want us to follow the ways of pagan animals.

"We won't obey their laws, we refuse to pay their taxes. We attack their soldiers and their customs houses whenever and wherever we can. We've abandoned our homes and we live off the countryside. We trust no-one. Sometimes we've been betrayed by people we believed were our friends. Their fate is worse than that of a Roman soldier."

Judas jutted his chin and spoke with anger. His eyes flashed and his face was red. "They call us 'Zealots,' although I hate the name. If it means we insist on freedom, that we recognize no ruler but the Almighty, then I come from three generations of 'Zealots.' My grandfather, Hezekiah, was called a Hasid, a 'pious one,' and he believed what I now believe. When he put it into action they called him a brigand, a common thief. Roman soldiers, commanded by Herod before he was king, killed my grandfather."

Judas's voice rose even higher. Joshua and Rebecca listened, fascinated.

"My father lived by the same rules and he, too, was killed. He suffered the most terrible death possible—crucifixion. Only Roman swine would kill human beings in such a manner.

"But no matter how many generations it takes, they won't stop us. No matter how many they kill, we won't give in. We are 'Soldiers of the Lord.'"

A chord of remembrance sounded in Joshua's mind. "Was your father also named Judas? The man whose rallying cry was, 'No Ruler but God?'"

Judas nodded. "I was born Simon ben Judas, but I am now called merely 'Judas.'"

Joshua smiled. "We were this close once before," he said. "I was born in Beth Lechem, in the house of Meshullam, my father's cousin. A few days before my birth, the Romans slaughtered a band led by your father, but you and he escaped. Your father went into Gaulanitis while friends brought you to Judaea and finally to Meshullam's house. Ah, I see you remember, of course. The Romans tracked you there, but Meshullam hid you under my mother's bed while she pretended to be giving birth to me. The Romans were fooled and you escaped. You see, we are old friends."

A great smile split Judas's face. He came to Joshua and embraced him. But when he stepped back, there were tears in his eyes. "Once again you have saved me. Thank God you are one of us."

Joshua sighed. "I believe, as you do, there is 'no ruler but God.'"

Judas's intense eyes never left Joshua's face, but he was smiling again. Joshua realized that emotions passed over this man like waves on the sea. Beneath these mercurial changes there was strength that Joshua had sensed from the beginning.

"Join us," Judas said.

Rebecca gasped, but Joshua shook his head. "I don't think so."

"There's no hope unless we fight," Judas said. "The Romans will never leave our country voluntarily."

"God will send help," Joshua said.

"The Messiah?" Judas asked, his eyes searching Joshua's.

Joshua nodded.

Judas did not look away. "I, too, believe in the Messiah, the anointed of God. I pray for his coming every night and every day. Some men thought my father was the Messiah. Others are so foolish as to believe it's me. I know better. If I were the Messiah, God would tell me and God would strengthen me. He hasn't told me—and as for my strength, without your help I would probably have died. Still, I'm strong enough to be a soldier in the Messiah's army. Until he comes, I'll struggle to prepare the way."

"By killing Romans?"

"Before they slaughter us. They pretend they want to govern us in peace, but they can't be trusted. A man who forces another man into slavery never does it for the sake of the slave. One day an Emperor will come to power who will slaughter us for the pure joy of it. We would be fools to wait patiently for that to happen."

Joshua was silent. Judas picked up the wine cup, drained it and reached out his hand. Joshua handed him his dagger. "I pray," Joshua said, "you will never need to use it again."

Judas smiled, thinking to himself that this man was strong, yes, but very naive.

"I, too, hope I've pulled it from my belt in anger for the last time—but in my heart, I know better."

He nodded to both Joshua and Rebecca, touched his chest unbelievingly once more and hurried out into the night.

They waited, breath bated, for several minutes, hoping that Roman soldiers were not outside waiting to pounce on Judas. It was a long time before they were confident he had escaped.

"Do you think there will be war?" Rebecca asked, her eyes large and almost pleading.

"Of one kind or another," Joshua said, "until the Lord reigns supreme."

Rebecca sighed. "Come to bed," she said.

"Perhaps in a while," he said, kissing her gently. He sat quietly in the room, thinking about Judas and the anger in the land. Then, when dawn cracked open the gray sky, scattering slivers of mauve and pink and red, he gathered his tools and set off for work.

16.

SIMON BEN JUDAS

I never had as strong feelings about anyone in my life. I owed him so much—in fact everything. I know there are those who doubt my story, but I tell you I was bleeding to death from a terrible wound and he healed me. I don't know how. I was unconscious most of the time. I don't really care. All I know is that if he hadn't come upon me, hadn't carried me to his home, hadn't ministered to me, I would have died. I'm certain of that, believe me.

There's something else. I know that soon after I left his home, terrible things happened. Again, I don't know exactly what went on, but I couldn't help thinking that t somehow the Romans had learned that Joshua had sheltered me in Beth Sholem, and they had searched him out and did those evil deeds as punishment for his "crime" against the state. Joshua said it wasn't so, that it had nothing whatsoever to do with me. I wanted to believe that, but I was never completely certain.

My feelings were certainly mixed. Beyond what he did for me that day in that little town, there was the time I heard him speak to the Maskil at Qumran and to Johannon and me. His speech was so passionate and his delivery so compelling, that I was never the same again. Immediately I realized this was the man, the one who could unite us all. It didn't take any special skill to recognize that. Anyone who ever heard him preach knew how he could overwhelm your senses. It was partly physical: his good looks and fine voice, his flashing eyes and powerful gestures. You felt that when he swung his arms, he might be able to knock down a mountain. His eyes, blue, on the edge of black were impossible to avoid. If you looked into them, you couldn't look away and he had a way of resting his eyes on one person after another in a crowd that made you believe he was talking to you alone.

Lord knows we needed a leader. My own family had been fighting the invaders of our land for hundreds of years. Some of my ancestors fought alongside Judas Maccabee. After a while, we fell away from the

Hasmoneans; we thought they had become power-hungry, but we always respected their energy and the great good they had done for the nation in the earlier years. We were a family of priests, although after a while, few practiced the profession. My grandfather was Hezekiah, murdered by Herod after a long hunt and a terrible battle. That was before Herod was king and surely we didn't like him any better when he pretended to be a Jewish king than when he was a Roman lackey.

We were always on the run, always being hunted. My father was Judas of Galilee, a big raw-boned fellow who looked like a blacksmith and fought like a bear. But he was gentle to me and protected me as best he could. He never thought he was the Messiah, although when he led the uprising in the year of the census, many called him by that title. My father laughed; it was one of the few times I remember him laughing. "If I am," he said, "I wish the Lord would tell me, too."

But don't misunderstand what I'm saying. My father was a devout man, who wouldn't fight on the Sabbath or any festival and more than once it cost him dearly. He knew scripture from one end to the other and could quote it in synagogue or on the battlefield.

The Romans killed him, too. That's a tradition in our family, dying at the hands of the authorities. I suppose that will be my fate, as well.

They hung my father on the tree—that's the way we Jews refer to crucifixion. It's such a terrible and humiliating death that we don't use a direct description. Yes, they hung him on a tree and I'm thankful I didn't have to watch. He was such a fine, strong man. I wouldn't have been able to see him die like that.

Afterwards, the family and their supporters expected a lot of me. Everyone knew that when I was old enough I would take up where my father had left off. I never thought any different myself. They called me Simon ben Judas and then ben Judas, and finally, just Judas. They wanted to remind me of my heritage and my obligation, although that wasn't necessary. I never forgot it.

I traveled the land from the time I was a boy, and I met most of the leaders of the ones who were called Zealots. I think you should understand that didn't mean we were fanatical killers, but rather that we were zealous for the law. We couldn't abide the rule of heathens, the desecration of holy places, the worship of foreign gods. Not within our boundaries and not forced upon our people.

I traveled the land and I fought many battles and people accepted me as a leader. You hear? As *a* leader, not *the* leader. I knew I was one of many and didn't ask for more. But I also knew all the petty differences that kept us apart. There were some who would only fight in Galilee and some who wouldn't leave Judaea. There were those who thought we had to wait for Elijah and those who thought we needed the Messiah immediately—at that very instant. There were other differences, large and small, and I knew of no one man who was strong enough to have the support of all of the groups.

I thought Joshua was the one. I can't really explain it. I just knew it, believed it and acted on it.

In a way, I was relieved. My family had been engaged in the struggle for so long, that many expected too much of me. Much more than I had to give. I knew the countryside and I could direct men, but I didn't want to be responsible for the decisions that affected all of Israel. When my father led the protests in Galilee, he didn't believe he spoke for the nation. He hoped that what he did might spread throughout the country and that a national leader might arise, but he never thought he was that leader.

Part of the problem for both of us was that we were from Galilee. Galilee of the gentiles, some said. Although my own family had been believers for hundreds of years, that wasn't true of all the people of our area. Many were recent converts. Few could claim descent from the House of David.

That was the curious thing about Joshua. He was from Galilee, but also from the royal family. There were some who said he was the bastard son of a Roman soldier. I didn't believe it, but some did and could never have followed him just for that reason. They were stupid. There never was a man more Jewish than Joshua ben Joseph. He was as fervent a believer as any man I've ever known, priest or Levite or otherwise. And he knew his scripture. Knew it so well that he understood what was important and what was not. Knew it so well that he realized it wasn't essential for every man and every woman to be a religious fanatic.

He had a vision, a vision different than any I had heard or known of

Bar Abbas, one of the most dedicated men I knew, couldn't stand him. "He's a fool," he said. "All he has to do is stand on the steps of the Temple and declare a holy war. Tens of thousands will rise all over the land and we'll drive the Romans into the sea. But he can't bring himself to do it. He buries his head in his bible and comes up with all these weak and ridiculous plans. Yes, he's a fool and probably a coward in the bargain."

I didn't agree with Bar Abbas, but he was a single-minded man who gave no quarter and expected none. He had never accomplished any of his goals without killing Romans. He thought that was the only way. It was no use arguing with him, or anyone like him. Surely Joshua was neither stupid nor a coward. I thought he could carry it off. I thought he was the only one who could. But we differed as to the means and ultimately, we disappointed each other. And yet, we would come very close.

17.

STRANGE HAVEN

Judas made an effort to get as far away from the tiny village as possible in the shortest time. If his pursuers were in the area, he did not want to attract them to Joshua and Beth Sholem.

He ran easily over the uneven ground, helped by his exceptional night vision. As he ran, his thoughts were of Joshua. Here was an altogether remarkable human being, handsome, strong, intelligent and kind. And a true healer in the bargain.

Judas knew full well that the wound he had suffered would have proved fatal without attention. Judas doubted that any ordinary physician could possibly have saved him. Yet Joshua had not only saved his life, but he had somehow healed the wound itself. When Judas examined his chest, he could find only a hint of a scar where a deep slash had been. Even the wound on his face, a far shallower sword cut, had left more of a record on his skin.

Was the man some kind of sorcerer—a magician? He neither looked nor behaved like one. In fact, Judas was now able to recall that even in his delirium, he was aware of the simple, traditional Jewish prayers that Joshua had pronounced over him.

He had memorized Joshua's face. It had a purity and goodness he had never seen before in his life. The man was a saint—a pious one, that was certain.

Judas felt himself drawn to this man as he had never been drawn to anyone. He had felt the power of the man's mind. Without words, Joshua had asked questions that Judas felt compelled to answer. He had astonished himself by explaining and defending his actions. He had never done anything like that before. And yet he was not embarrassed.

Gratitude. That must be it, and yet, instinctively, Judas knew better. His response went far beyond gratitude; He felt love.

Judas suppressed a laugh. He, Judas, the rough chief of hardy warriors, feeling love for a man—a man he had never seen before? It was ludicrous. And yet it was true.

He stumbled against a bush in the dark. "See," he told himself. "You're still weak—you're not yourself. That's why you're having these crazy thoughts."

He forced himself to focus on the narrow trail he was following up into the hills. He must concentrate or he would lose his way.

A few miles from Beth Sholem, his instincts took command and he dropped to the ground and rolled into the brush, holding his breath. Moments later, horsemen came crashing through the woods, Roman soldiers, riding hard and calling to each other. They thrashed about noisily, but did not see him. In a few minutes they were gone.

Judas smiled grimly, picked himself up and continued on his way.

"Messiah." The word came at him from nowhere. He shook his head and continued to lope along the pathway. But then the word formed in his head again: "Messiah."

Could this be the Messiah? Joshua, a carpenter from Galilee? How could this simple man be a king? It was the most ridiculous idea he had yet had. Judas forced a silent laugh and continued on his way.

But Judas knew his scriptures well, knew that the Lord did not consult the judgment of men when He poured the sacred oil on the head of the chosen one. David was only a shepherd.

The word, the idea became a drumbeat in his head. Judas had traveled from town to town, searching out the Zealots, but despite repeated shows of good will and the avowed sharing of goals, there was no common leadership. Each group went its own way, harassed the Romans by its own means.

What if the Messiah had come? What if God had led Judas to Joshua? Surely, in the days of the Messiah, the people would be united under the banner of the King. He felt a sense of exaltation. This night, which had begun so disastrously, might be the omen for a great triumph of his people.

Then he sensed another drumbeat—a throbbing that he had ignored in his excitement. Judas dropped to the ground and pressed his ear to it. Horsemen, distant and he could not be certain of their direction.

He peered through the forest with his keen and practiced eyes. The night was seamless, but the moon was still high and light was dangerous. Something drove him on.

He saw the glow of light and climbed cautiously to the top of a hill and looked down into a natural bowl. Flaming torches circled a clearing and in the center he saw a group of people facing a small building, a temple or a shrine. Judas dropped to the ground and peered through the bushes.

The group was larger than he had first imagined. Some were sitting on the ground, drinking wine and singing. Others were dancing and swaying before them. A few were playing stringed instruments in strange, unpleasant melodies. All of them—men and women—were naked.

Before his astonished eyes, the dancers paired off and began a series of ritualized embraces. They kissed and stroked each other's bodies, then dropped to the ground and embraced again. They held each other tightly and writhed in complex poses. Then, at a sound from the musicians, the women broke free and stood up, cupping their breasts with their hands and offering them to the men.

The men reached up and pulled them to the ground again. After a sequences of gestures and sounds, accentuated by strange music and the chants of the watchers, the men began to penetrate the women.

The others continued to watch and sing, moving in a sensual, rhythmic pattern. But soon, they were aroused by what they saw and began to embrace each other. The musicians abandoned their instruments and sought partners. There were more women than men, and those who could not find male mates began to embrace each other.

There was no longer any singing, but some moaning and a few ecstatic outcries as the entire group writhed on the floor of the clearing, engaged in wild sexual gyrations.

Judas realized the group must be the followers of a fertility cult, not uncommon among the non-Jewish population of the land. He had heard of such rites, but never seen them. Ever since his people had come to the Promised Land, they had been warned against the wanton sexual practices of the inhabitants. Time and again, Jews were drawn into these vile cults and time and again God had punished them.

Of one thing Judas was certain—the rituals would eventually attract the Roman horsemen. He listened to the ground again, and now the sound of the hoof-beats was closer. He decided to circle the clearing and continue on his way.

Judas began to move along the hills that edged the bowl, trying to keep trees between him and the light. When he reached the opposite hilltop he was startled to see lights flickering in the distance. Romans with torches, obviously on horseback. To his horror, the torches were approaching the clearing in a wide arc. Judas turned back, but now, looking toward the place he had come from, he saw another line of torches.

And then another. No matter what direction he looked, lights were moving. What a fool he was. He had penetrated the ring of soldiers and now the ones who had passed him by earlier had doubled back. He was surrounded.

Judas was too experienced to panic, but he felt fear for one of the few times in his life. He knew what the Romans would do to him. Perhaps a little torture out here in the woods, and then he would be dutifully brought in to Tiberias or Caesarea to be crucified.

The rise on which he stood was too exposed, so he climbed down towards the shrine and the Canaanite rites. Perhaps the Romans would leave these wild fools alone. He doubted it, but their nakedness and lewd behavior might distract the Romans' attention from the Jewish patriot hiding in the trees.

The revelers didn't notice the approach of the Romans. They were all drunk or drugged and aware of little besides the writhing bodies they were attached to. They murmured and chanted obscure words while coupling on the ground in every variation of perversity.

One man pulled free of his sexual partner, and to Judas's amazement, caught his semen in his hands even as it spurted from him. Then another and another did the same. The women took spices and ointments and mixed it with the semen and then all of them, men and women alike, began to spread the mixture on their bodies.

They laughed and chanted and sang and covered themselves with a gleaming mixture of oils and semen, then raised their hands to the heavens where the full moon floated. They chanted in Aramaic, praising the god of the moon and the god of the sun, and the juice of men and women and the rebirth of Tammuz. Some mixed the semen with grain, stuffed it in their mouths and ate it.

Judas knew that his survival demanded he concentrate on the Romans, but his eyes were drawn to the fantastic spectacle before him. He recalled he had been told that such worshipers sometimes ate female menses as part of their rites, and until now that had seemed incredible.

The religious revelers were chanting loudly, invoking Baal and El and Tammuz and Ishtar—a whole panoply of gods.

Instinct took over for Judas. He dropped his dagger and ripped his clothes from his back. He ran into the circle, smeared his body with oils and grabbed the nearest woman. She didn't recognize him, but she was too far gone to complain. At that moment, Roman torches rose over the hills surrounding the clearing, lighting the scene like a sudden burst of sunlight. Even so, the revelers hardly noticed. It was as if the light were part of their ritual.

Judas held onto the woman. She was young and well-constructed, but she smelled of oil and semen and sweat. Still, he clung to her as if she were the most desirable woman in the world. Her eyes were glazed and her hand was working in his groin, but he paid no attention. He was looking over her shoulder at the Roman cavalry. They sat their horses in a tight ring around the clearing and they were as stunned as he had been.

The woman Judas was holding wriggled in his arms, but he knew that if she slipped away, the soldiers might see he was circumcised and then he would be a dead man. He held her to him with an iron grip while she mumbled approvingly.

An officer yelled at the revelers. "Roman Army—Tenth Legion—we want your help."

A few women looked idly over, but they only smiled vaguely.

"Do you hear me?" the officer yelled. "I want your attention."

A few more women and some of the men looked again. They giggled and waved at the horsemen. A few of the soldiers laughed aloud.

"Stop that," the officer cried.

He spurred his horse into the clearing, a subaltern behind him. "I want you to listen to me," he said, reaching down and grabbing the arm of one of the men. But the man's body was so greasy, that he slipped from the officer's grasp and dropped to the ground. The officer looked at his hand in disbelief.

A woman staggered over to the officer and grabbed his hand. "Come down and join us," she murmured. Angrily, he pushed her away, and she, too, fell to the ground, but the drugs had dulled her senses and she did not feel the fall.

"This is disgusting," the subordinate Roman officer said, but Judas noticed that his eyes never stopped flickering over the naked women.

"We won't find the Jew here," the officer said. "Let's get away before the men lose interest in the chase."

He spurred his horse up the hill and signaled his men to follow. Many lingered for a moment, gaping at the naked women.

Finally, they were gone. The woman holding Judas became more insistent. She dropped to her knees and was pressing her mouth to his body. Judas gently pushed her away. "Thanks," he said, "perhaps some other time." He picked up his dagger and his clothing and melted into the forest.

18.

JOHANNON

Joshua walked on the higher ground overlooking the banks of the Jordan. The river was at full flood and the waters raced toward the south, splashing over rocks and sweeping small growth before it. Joshua loved the river, especially in the spring, but even in the fall, when heavy rains once again swelled the river. The scents of late harvests were in the air, freshened by the waters of the river and deepened by the sun, rapidly climbing in the sky.

A new day. What would it bring? Joshua did not even stop to wonder. All would be revealed in due time. He smiled when he thought of his family, rising as usual with the sun.

A small crest rose before him, tangled with brush and autumn flowers, small roses, asters and oxeye daisies, pushing through the piled up debris of the season. Joshua heard laughter and then voices. He was surprised because this stretch of the river was uninhabited and it was early in the day.

As he mounted the crest, he saw below him a group of men and women, gathered on the west bank of the Jordan, many standing in the shallows.

Their eyes were fixed on a very tall, very broad-shouldered man with a full head of unkempt gray-streaked brown hair that burst from his head and merged with a flowing beard that reached almost to his waist. His face was craggy with a broad brow, a large broken nose and a powerful jutting chin set on a neck like twisted cords of rope. His skin was bronzed and burned by the sun, so that it was peeling in patches, but his light-colored eyes were large, bright and commanding. He wore a shaggy hair garment bound with an ancient leather girdle and he stood with his feet planted in the stream, the waters swirling about his knees.

"Come closer," he called to the people on the shore. His voice leaped across the water, skipped on the banks and bounded up to where Joshua stood. "The Lord won't drown you and neither will I."

But the people huddled closer together and watched, silently.

The huge man shifted in the stream and hit the water with the flat of his hand. The bantering tone left his voice. "Beware, my friends, beware. God in his heaven is watching you. The day of retribution will soon be upon us." His voice no longer skipped—it boomed. The tones struck fierce blows against the air and the water and beat upon the ground.

"Repent, children of God, repent before it's too late. Save yourselves from the Wrath to Come." He flung his arms above his head and spoke to the heavens. His tone changed; there was a plea in the powerful voice. "Time, Lord, give them a little time. They are a foolish people and they have stupidly turned away from you. But one day they will understand Thy ways and know Thy goodness."

He looked again toward the shore and his expression grew fierce. "Come now, evil and depraved though you be—come, repent your vile sins and then purify your bodies in the Jordan. THE KINGDOM OF GOD IS AT HAND."

The people stepped back, frightened by his powerful voice and fierce expression. The giant laughed, a booming laugh that rattled in Joshua's ears. "Are you more afraid of me than of God Almighty?" He took a step toward the shore. "I tell you there is no time to waste. Save your souls or be damned to death everlasting."

Hesitantly, an old woman moved into the stream, stumbled and seemed about to fall, but the giant was at her side in one quick movement. His voice was gentle. "Are you ready to be saved?" he asked. She nodded and he put his hands under her arms and lifted her up as easily as if she were a flower.

The old woman stopped shaking as she stared into his eyes. "Do you repent?" he asked. She nodded and the giant looked up to heaven.

"Forgive her, Lord. She is old, but she is thy child." He plunged her under water for only a brief moment, then held her aloft, as she shook her head and coughed.

Again he laughed. "You see, grandma, your sins are washed away. God forgives you."

The old woman was weeping now and trying to hug him, but his chest was so vast that her outstretched hands barely reached his arms.

"Enough," he cried and swiftly carried her to shore, where she happily rushed into the arms of her friends.

"You," the huge man said, taking a young man by the arm. "You're next."

The youth was tall and well-made, but he was slim as a sapling next to the giant. He was awed by the powerful expression fixed upon him and he felt powerless to resist. Effortlessly, the giant lifted him off his feet. "Do you repent?" the giant asked, his face almost touching the young man's.

The young man trembled. "I do," he whispered.

"I can't hear you!" the giant yelled.

The young man spoke louder, but his voice cracked. "I repent," he called out.

The giant shook his head and yelled even louder, "The LORD can't hear you."

The young man threw back his head and yelled, "I REPENT MY SINS."

"Praise God," the giant boomed and plunged the young man into the icy waters of the river.

"Another sinner saved for you, Lord," the giant cried, as the youth came up sputtering, but laughing, his face alive with excitement.

Delighted, the huge man laughed, too. "It's great to be saved, isn't it? Yes, the ways of the Lord are good."

"Now, go defend the poor, help the weak and do righteously before your God." He slapped the young man on his bottom and pushed him toward shore. He ran up on the bank, shaking his head like a wet puppy.

While Joshua watched, another man, and another, a young woman, and then another struggled into the water.

"Forgive me, Lord," "Forgive my sins," "God save me," they cried individually and in chorus, raising arms to heavens and splashing in the water.

"Do you repent?" the giant boomed out and they all nodded vigorously and yelled aloud. "Yes, Yes, YES."

One after another he plunged them into the spring-swollen Jordan, sometimes praying, sometimes laughing, sometimes singing.

"Do you think he's really Elijah?" a man whispered.

"I don't doubt it," his friend answered.

"You're changed," the giant told the people he had immersed in the Jordan. "You've found new life—you can't go back to the old ways. God loves you—God forgives you. Go home and live righteously, for the Kingdom is at hand. Hallelujah." He laughed aloud, a rippling, roaring laugh that included the whole world.

Joshua watched, fascinated. This huge man was using the Jordan River as a miqveh, the ritual bath used by the Jews to cleanse themselves from impurities, after menstruation, or intercourse and before entering the Temple, and for a variety of other reasons. Impurity did not mean sin, but this fellow was taking care of repentance and cleansing and using the living water to do it. Here was a man doing the Lord's work whose devotion was mixed of equal parts of reverence and joy. Joshua, pleased, laughed to himself.

"Come down here and laugh with us." Joshua realized the man was talking to him, beckoning with his huge arms.

Startled, Joshua stood motionless.

"Frightened are you, lad? Don't be. I'll hold you tight as I dip you in the healing waters of the Jordan. God's never lost a sinner, yet."

He laughed but Joshua still didn't respond. The people on the shore watched him curiously.

"Can't talk, eh? Come down here and the Good Lord will heal your throat. You'll cry his blessings to the heavens."

Joshua smiled. Then he waved a friendly goodbye and continued on his way to work.

"Don't give up, my boy," the giant boomed after him. "The Lord God loves us all—especially the quiet ones."

19.

BETH SHOLEM

"Where are they?" Septimus held the thin, bald man's throat in his hands, squeezing as he pushed him down to the ground. All of the people of Beth Sholem, roughly gathered by the soldiers, stood in a circle, watching in fear.

In Septimus's unrelenting grasp, the man choked and purpled. "Tell me!" Septimus screamed at him. The man opened and closed his mouth, desperately trying to speak, but no sound could escape Septimus's tightening grip.

"Protecting murderers. We'll find them with your help or not." He released his grip for a second, then hit the shaking, coughing man a powerful blow on the side of his head that knocked him unconscious. Septimus stood erect, then coldly kicked the man viciously in the head. His neck snapped and his wife screamed.

Septimus's eyes bulged as he spoke to his men. "Find the killers," he said. "I don't care what you have to do—find them."

The soldiers hesitated, uncertain how to carry out their orders. Septimus grinned a hideous grin, and grabbed casually at the first person he could reach, a slender, dark-haired young woman. "Will you tell me where they are?"

The woman shook her head. "I don't know," she said, terrified.

Septimus removed his short dagger from its sheath and plunged it into her heart. The woman's cry was short, the blood spurted from her chest and she sank to the ground, as others cried out and shrank back. Even the soldiers were startled.

Septimus glared at a young Roman armor-carrier who was staring at the woman, strangling in her own blood as she writhed in her death throes. The armor-carrier was pale and about to be sick. Septimus cuffed the young man's head. "They would kill you just as easily if they could," he told him.

Septimus advanced on an elderly man.

"God help me, honored sir," the old man quavered, his mouth trembling and death in his eyes. "I don't know the men you are seeking."

Once again, Septimus plunged his dagger in to the hilt, then yanked it out. The crowd screamed and broke, trying to run away. They knocked down some of the soldiers as they struggled to escape.

"They're attacking you!" Septimus yelled at his soldiers, "Don't let them get away."

The soldiers began to chase the people of Beth Sholem and to corner them. Some struggled, some fell to the ground, some pleaded.

"They're murderers!" Septimus cried. "Kill the killers!"

Goaded by his words, confused by the screaming and struggling people, the Roman soldiers struck more heavily, slashing and hacking at the helpless people, while the dying and the wounded cried to the heavens.

***

Gaius Fabricius rode grimly across the countryside at a full gallop. Sometimes, when the road twisted, he briefly left the highway and cut through the brush, shortening his route, while punishing himself and his horse.

Gaius prayed as he had never prayed before. "Please, Lord, let me get there in time," he begged. "God of the Jews, God of the Romans, God by any name and of any people, save them."

His horse stumbled and Gaius pulled him roughly upright, and then galloped on. He ducked to avoid low branches, felt needles scar his legs as he bulled his way through dense brush and over steep slopes. Even as he struggled, Gaius prayed without cease, while blood sprang from cuts on his body and his sweat mingled with the sweat of his horse.

"Please," he prayed. "Please."

***

Joshua turned inland from the Jordan and reached another tiny settlement, a place without a name, where he was building a house for Elia the tanner. The image of the giant man at the Jordan was clear in his mind, his flowing beard and fierce eyes—the man's anger and humor, his strength and gentleness.

Perhaps, Joshua thought, I should have accepted the invitation to repent. Somehow, he felt that he wasn't ready. The hour had not yet come.

Still, the man had claimed that time was short, that the wrath of the Lord would soon be upon them.

Joshua did not doubt the words. He had watched his people groaning under the oppression of the Roman occupiers. He knew first hand of Roman crimes against his people, of murder, rape and robbery. He had seen them desecrate the holy places and defile even the Temple with their armed presence. No people who loved God as fiercely as his countrymen could abide such treatment forever.

To make matters worse, the people were oppressed with heavy taxes. Happily they paid the half shekel levied to support the Temple, but in addition they were required to pay customs wherever they went and tribute to support the Roman Empire, perhaps even to support pagan gods.

Some of the most important people in the land, the High Priest and his party, had become subservient to their Roman masters, claiming it was better to accommodate than to be destroyed. Even in Galilee, known for its fierce independence, Joshua had seen elders of the synagogue bending their heads before the Romans.

Some, mostly younger men, had left the towns for the back country, to live lives free of Roman domination. They were stern, even ruthless, convinced their mission came straight from God, and that it was God's will the Romans be driven from the Holy Land. Visions of the Maccabees and the Hasmonean kingdom inspired them to believe that even though they were overwhelmingly outnumbered by the Roman armies, the Lord would lead them and they would triumph in His name.

But despite great hopes, their victories were as limited as their numbers. Meanwhile, the Romans were determined not to let the flame of rebellion spread and they treated rebels with unspeakable cruelty.

Among the elders were those who inveighed against the Zealots and pleaded with them not to plunge the land into a holocaust of war and death. The rebels were caught between their hatred of Roman oppression and fears of destroying the very people they were trying to liberate. But their faith in the rightness of their cause sustained them.

Joshua sighed. A few weeks earlier, he had been approached by Efrem, a young man from Nazareth, who was a member of yet another band of Galilean revolutionaries. Efrem was only a boy, less than sixteen years old and he was blunt. "Will you join us and fight for your freedom?" he asked Joshua.

Joshua shook his head. "I don't believe that violence is the answer," he said.

Efrem was angry. His pimply face was flushed as he spoke. "Violence? We didn't start it, the Romans did. Haven't they murdered our people, time and again, without just cause?"

Joshua nodded. "True, but must we kill them in return? Is that the teaching of God?"

"Your face is always in the holy scrolls," Efrem said. "Aren't the scrolls filled with war? Haven't we always had to fight for our homeland?"

Joshua put his hand on Efrem's shoulder. "Yes, so it seems. But the battles in scripture are not merely the battles of soldiers, they are the battles of the spirit, seeking for the higher way."

Efrem was infuriated. "You doubt the holy word—the history of your own people?"

"I believe," said Joshua, "that God has placed us here for a purpose and that purpose is not to kill or to maim, but to love one another and live in righteousness."

"While you're living in righteousness," Efrem answered, "the Romans will kill our families and destroy our homeland. Don't deceive yourself, Joshua—you're a coward."

He shoved Joshua aside and hurried away.

The experience saddened Joshua. He liked Efrem and didn't doubt his love for the land and its people. He wondered if Efrem and Judas were right. Was he afraid to fight? How would he defend himself, his own family, if the time came? How would he know what God wanted?

These questions nagged at Joshua as he built the house of Elia the tanner. He worked alone as he preferred except when the character of the work made it impossible to do so. That gave him an opportunity to think about the Lord and to review in his mind the Holy Scriptures. After years of diligent study, he had committed most of them to memory. Still, he obeyed the teaching of the rabbis, that it was necessary to read directly from the scrolls whenever possible, to avoid making errors and to protect against the arrogant assumption that one was the "owner" of the scriptures rather than the recipient of a priceless gift from God almighty.

The sun climbed higher in the sky as Joshua cut and mortised the wood and pounded with his mallet. He had stripped to the waist and perspiration drenched his body. It was good to work, to build a home for men, while he built his own spiritual home in his head.

A vague but oppressive feeling prodded him. At first he thought it might have been the words of the bearded giant at the river. Had he missed an opportunity to honor the Lord by seeking forgiveness?

Was it Judas—Judas and Efrem and their words of war? As much as he might disagree with their methods, he found it difficult to blame them. Judas, especially, had suffered at the hands of the Romans. Both his grandfather and father had been killed by them.

Nevertheless, Joshua didn't believe it was the thought of these men that was perturbing him. There was a hint of evil in the air, even though as far as he could see, the land was good, flowers were in bloom, the sky was clear and the sun without blemish.

He felt a whiff of something in his nostrils, then tasted it on his tongue: smoke perhaps, and yet it was more like blood than smoke. Could one smell blood—at a distance? He shook his head and continued his work. He tried to concentrate on a passage in Isaiah. But the sensation came to him again, of smoke mixed with blood—of a sacrifice, one not intended for the glorification of God, but a sacrifice nonetheless.

The impulse to return home gripped him, but he could think of no reason for it. His obligation was here, to the tanner, to build his home.

Meanwhile, words from Ezekiel leaped into his mind unbidden: "Sigh, but not aloud; make no mourning for the dead. Bind on your turban, and put your shoes on your feet; do not cover your lips or eat the bread of mourners."

Then the face of Rebecca appeared to him, a plea on her lips. He could bear it no longer. Joshua dropped his tools and began to run.

20.

THE CHOICE

Even from a distance, Gaius could see the plumes of smoke—slender, spiraling tendrils straight ahead, in the direction of Beth Sholem. It might mean nothing, have nothing whatsoever to do with Septimus and his troop.

There seemed to be a scent, rather a stench in the air. It was vague and indefinable, but it made him think of a battlefield. Gaius groaned and urged his horse on again.

***

Joshua was a man given to the strong and even stride, but now he ran as never before, straight across country, uphill and down, ignoring the footpath, leaping over small ravines and scrambling through the brush. He did not allow his fears to capture him. Soon enough he would know.

***

Gaius slowed his horse to a canter and then to a walk. Beth Sholem consisted only of a handful of houses, some of them little more than huts, and all of them were aflame. A hock of hay was burning, too, clumps of it drifting off in the light breeze.

A dead horse lay in the road, its throat cut and blood still pouring from the wound.

Then Gaius came upon the body of a very old man holding his throat, but it, too, had been cut. The man lay on his back, his life drained from him, hands clenched to the wound, trying vainly to staunch the flow.

Gaius slipped down from his horse and dropped the reins. As he walked, eyes on the ground, he saw body after body. Men, women, children, their throats cut, stab wounds in their chests. Some were in pleading postures, others with heads down, turned away from their killers.

Gaius's blood ran cold, the horror of it gagged in his throat. Dead bodies on every side, husbands clutching wives, mothers clinging to children. Dead, all dead. And not a weapon among them.

Gaius wrenched his eyes upward. Septimus stood in the middle of the dusty street, his back straight, a short sword dripping blood in his hand, his body splashed with the blood and guts of the townspeople.

Septimus stared at Gaius, his eyes bulging from his head, his lips twisted together in a knot of hatred that included the whole world. Behind him stood his men, holding their own bloody weapons, staring about them, beginning to see what they had done.

From the opposite end of the hamlet, Joshua ran out of a copse of trees. He stopped as if he had run face first into a wall. He rocked and staggered, but did not fall.

Bodies of dead friends, lying in their own blood, confronted him. His head began to spin, but he willed himself to remain upright. Fearfully he took a step, then another. His home was only a few feet away, but he didn't have to enter it. Rebecca lay in the doorway. David and Rachel clung to her fiercely. Dead, the three of them were dead. Their blood had flowed together, covering them all. Rebecca's hands shielded Rachel's face, but the child's eyes were open and they reflected horror. David's face was pressed to his mother's breast.

Joshua dropped to his knees, like a tall tree falling slowly to earth. He embraced the three of them, clutching their bodies to him, his body wracked with sobs, tears falling freely, mingling with the blood of his loved ones. God had commanded Ezekiel not to cry for his dead wife, but He had not mentioned children.

Small strangled cries came from Joshua's lips as great sobs shuddered through his body.

The Romans heard the cries. Septimus, his eyes still glazed with his triumph, turned toward him. Gaius bolted forward and grabbed the centurion's arm.

"Will you kill him, too?"

"Murderers," Septimus said thickly, through cracked and bloodied lips. "Got to kill them all."

Gaius spun Septimus around, grabbed the sword from his hands and slapped him sharply across his mouth.

Septimus hardly blinked. His cracked lips opened in a cruel caricature of a smile. "Told you I'd get the killers—got 'em all."

"Killers?" Gaius said. His voice was high and harsh. "These women were killers? The children, too? The babies in their mother's arms?"

The loud voice pierced Joshua's pain and suffering. He turned his head and saw the Romans, heard their quarrel, but it meant nothing to him. He clutched his dead family even tighter, crying and moaning, mumbling words of love and despair, talking to each of them as if they were alive. "Rebecca, my dearest, David my boy, dear, dear Rachel."

His eyes searched upward. "Why, dear God? Tell me why?" But no answer came from the heavens.

Gaius Fabricius held Septimus in an iron grip. "You're mad, Septimus, totally mad. There are no killers here, except for you."

Septimus regained a measure of control. His bloodlust was satisfied and he recovered enough to be able to respond. "I did what you ordered, sir, I tracked down the killers of our soldiers."

"Liar!" Gaius screamed. "You came here for cold-blooded murder. You knew that they had nothing to do with the ambush."

"My report will say otherwise. My soldiers will support me."

The men shifted restlessly. They could not look at Gaius or Septimus, least of all at the dead littering the street. Their fears were beginning to grow. Here was a conflict of authority—they would have to be careful.

Gaius didn't care for authority or rules or responsibility. His mind, his heart, his eyes were filled with the slaughter of these innocents. He did not loosen his grip on Septimus and he dragged the officer with him, along the dusty road. The soldiers parted to make way for them. Gaius pulled the stumbling Septimus to where he had seen a man crouching in a doorway. The man's face was turned away, but it was obvious he was holding the bodies of his family.

For a moment, Gaius could not speak. The sight of this poor man cradling his dead family almost overwhelmed him. But then his anger strengthened him. Straining to control himself, he spoke softly. "A word, Sir, please."

Joshua did not hear and therefore did not answer. Gaius had to repeat his words while Septimus stood by sullenly, enjoying the misery of the Jew.

"Will you please speak to me?" Gaius cried out. At that Joshua turned and looked at him. Gaius was startled. It was Joshua, his son. Gaius stared, speechless for the moment, loosening his grip on Septimus who pulled away.

"Is it really you?" Gaius asked Joshua, who looked at him evenly, but did not understand. The Roman's face was familiar, but what did that matter, now?

With great effort, Gaius forced himself under control but then the realization struck him that Septimus had killed the family of his son. These dead children were his grandchildren. Enraged, he grabbed Septimus's arm and dragged him in front of Joshua. "Do you see—this is the man who killed your family."

Joshua said nothing, staring into the evil face of Septimus.

Gaius thought he had not understood. "This man, a Roman officer, is the one who murdered your wife and children."

Joshua finally understood. Slowly, gently, he rested his family on the threshold of his home and stood up. A million thoughts were going through his head. This man, with the evil face and the terrible eyes—this man was the killer. Great waves of emotion swept over Joshua. He began to tremble, awed by the passion that roared inside him. Anger, hatred, disgust filled his very soul. These were emotions with which he was unfamiliar. He felt a harsh, stabbing pain in his chest, as if his heart was being ripped from him. The pain spread through his body until it seemed larger than he was, enclosing and crushing him. He opened his mouth, but could not speak. He stared at Septimus with a look of such great loathing that Septimus flinched. But he could not look away. The Jew held his eyes with strength that was more than mortal.

Gaius suffered with Joshua, echoing the pain that Joshua felt. He took Septimus's sword and pressed it into Joshua's hand. "This is his sword—the sword he murdered your family with. Kill him. Avenge your wife and children. KILL HIM NOW."

Septimus looked about him wildly, but Gaius stood only a step away, his own sword aimed at Septimus. It was impossible to flee.

The Jew stared at Septimus fiercely, powerfully, shaking now with anger that distorted his face. He seemed to grow in size to match his anger. Septimus had never seen such strength or such hatred in human eyes.

Joshua held the sword so tightly that the hilt cut into his hands. Slowly, deliberately, he raised it above his head. Septimus, unnerved, sank to his knees.

Gaius watched with righteous anger. Now the beast would die, the foul beast who had defiled his life again and again.

Joshua shuddered from the anger inside him, the hatred and the knowledge of life and death. Here was evil—as he had never seen it in a human being. The murderer of his innocent family, a killer with a warped and vicious soul. The man cowered before him, twitching now, blood drained from his face. Joshua raised his arms higher. This was the moment of his revenge. His eyes bulged, his jaw worked, the muscles in his arms were knotted like tree trunks.

The trembling was greater now, as Joshua drew breath after labored breath, deeper and deeper, reaching into reserves of emotion he had never plumbed before. He braced himself to pull the sword down, to crush the evil cowering before him.

A scream, a scream of pain and agony seared Joshua's lips, a scream so fearful that it froze the blood of all who heard it.

Then, with all his strength focused into this one point of pain, seeing so clearly that the light of his vision almost blinded him, Joshua flung the sword away. It soared through the air with a whistling sound and dug into the earth, quivering.

For a moment, no one moved. Joshua stood, weaponless, with arms upraised, a bitter triumph in his heart. Septimus would have fainted with relief, but Gaius still stood nearby, blood in his eyes and his own sword still gripped firmly.

"What—what are you doing?" Gaius asked. He moved toward Septimus, ready to give the final blow himself, but Joshua stepped between them. Gaius stared into Joshua's eyes and wavered. Slowly, he lowered his arm.

Joshua was still trembling. He had triumphed over himself, but the wounds of the battle remained. The Roman killer was hateful to him. "Vengeance," he whispered to Gaius, "belongs to the Lord."

Then, because he was not totally free of the hatred that had possessed him, he deliberately turned from Septimus and forced himself to walk away, toward the edge of the hamlet.

Gaius and Septimus and the other Roman soldiers watched, murmuring in amazement.

Slowly, Joshua forced his steps before him, willing his feet to move in a ragged, stiff-legged pattern. After a while, he disappeared over the hill.

In the village, no one moved.

THE MURDERED MESSIAH

BOOK 3

RISING STORM

1.

THE JOURNEY

Gaius watched Joshua until he disappeared from sight. The urge to follow him was great. But if he did follow him, what then? Should he embrace Joshua, comfort him in his time of loss, like a true father? Or should he fall on his knees before Joshua and beg his forgiveness? But a force greater than Gaius restrained him. Joshua must be left alone, to follow his own course. That was the least Gaius Fabricius could do for his son.

Wrenching his eyes from the empty distance, Gaius turned to the soldiers. "Bind this man," he said pointing to Septimus "Then we will bury the dead."

He looked toward the threshold of Joshua's house, realizing once more that the slaughtered children lying there were his own grandchildren. A cry escaped his lips and the soldiers stared at him. Gaius quickly masked his look and growled at the men "Bind him, I say." They hurried to do his bidding. Septimus, recovered from his brush with death had resumed his usual arrogance. A thin smile curled his lips as the soldiers lashed his arms.

Gaius glared at him, his anger aroused again, but the agony of his suffering was greater. He forced the pain down and turned away from Septimus, shuddering with a sense of loss and deep pity for the slaughtered children. "This is my punishment," he thought. "Surely I have earned it."

***

Joshua walked along the shore of the Jordan, his eyes straight ahead, but fixed on nothing. At times, he stumbled or tripped over the underbrush. Once, at a bend in the river, he stepped into the water. But he hardly noticed. He continued walking until his feet touched the shore again and he walked once more on dry land.

The sky clouded over suddenly, hiding the sun, but Joshua didn't notice. A few soft drops fell, touching his face, as if to renew the tears that streaked his face. He didn't feel them. The rain gradually increased, drenching him, soaking his clothes, matting his hair to his head. He blinked now and then, but he willed himself to go on.

Joshua walked erectly, holding his body together, barely swinging his arms, not looking from side to side. A wind came up, driving the rain against him, pelting his face, stinging his eyelids. It was a cold rain after the hot sun, but he didn't feel the cold any more than he had felt the heat.

He passed the small cove where the gigantic man had dipped his followers into the stream. They were gone. Joshua was vaguely aware they were gone. He almost hoped the man would be there, to help him, to plunge him into the water. But it was too late for that now—or perhaps too early. As Joshua passed the place of the earlier ritual, he startled a flock of doves hidden in the grass. They rose into the sky, brushing against him. One seemed to caress his cheek as it mounted into the heavens. But Joshua walked on, his eyes fixed on the distance, his feet marching in a steady pattern, his eyes blinking with tears that no longer fell, while the rain washed over him.

Joshua walked on and on, ignoring the rain and the wind, unaware of the passing hours. The day darkened and became night. Still he walked along the Jordan, as if it were a highway that he must follow. At times, unbidden thoughts stirred his mind. Deep inside was a fragment of fear—that he would turn about and seek out the killer of his family—that the anger would come again and this time he would not control it.

Time and again he saw the faces of Rebecca, David and Sarah. The faces were smiling, unblemished, unmarked by pain or death. They smiled at him steadily and then faded. These visions staggered him. He saw no hint of pain, no hint of accusation. Yet the visions were an accusation. Had he betrayed his own family? Had God wanted him to avenge their deaths? He shuddered, more from pain than cold and rain.

"Oh God," he prayed. "Not my will, but thy will."

The wind roared as he spoke, thunder tore the heavens and lightning split the sky. The force of the rain doubled. Joshua trod doggedly onward, leaving his dead family ever farther behind him.

Even in the night, the great rain continued, lashing Joshua, sometimes staggering him, sometimes blinding him. As the night wore on, his steps slowed. He still followed the margin of the river, but his pace became uneven. He slowed even more, then stopped. For several minutes, he stood swaying as the wind whipped about him. Then, his expression unchanged, he fell forward onto the soggy bank.

First light wakened Joshua. He lay where he had fallen, face down in the mud. He rolled over slowly and sat up, wiping clods of mud from his hair, his brows and even his mouth. The rain had stopped, but a great north wind was driving the clouds before it. As Joshua watched, the clouds seemed to roll up and disappear, revealing a brilliant sun. Joshua washed his face in the Jordan, straightened his tunic. He hesitated only for an instant, before turning his face away from Beth Sholem.

He had not eaten since early on the day before, but he did not even think of food. This day, the sun was hot on his back and face, which meant no more to him than the rain of the previous day. His pace was slow but steady, although he took little note of the places he passed. From time to time, he came upon fishermen, their nets spread in the river. He ignored them. They glanced at him and saw a man deeply absorbed in thought—a blonde man with blue eyes, unshaven and dirty, with bare feet and a torn tunic. He posed no danger and he seemed not to see them, so they ignored him in return.

At intervals he reached small settlements. There the sounds were louder. Men worked and women called to each other, children played and cried and ran. Each child's voice was a dagger to Joshua—a knife of conscience, and of loss. The blows touched him, but only spurred him on. He stepped into the Jordan to avoid people and objects, or veered inland when necessary, but spoke to no one.

Occasionally someone spoke to him, but he didn't hear and he neither answered nor slowed his pace.

As the day wore on, the sun rose and the heat became oppressive. Perspiration accumulated on Joshua's brow and dripped into his eyes. He blinked it away, but that brought visions of his family. Again, he saw the smiling faces of his wife and children, like flickering images on a shimmering banner that waved before him and then disappeared. The sense of torment returned, an internal struggle that almost tore him apart. He reeled before the visions, gestured in front of his face as if to brush the images away. Always, he staggered onward, forcing his feet to move in the direction he had chosen.

Joshua didn't eat that day. He splashed water on his face when he was dusty and gulped some of it directly from the river, but that was all. He strode along the river, following it wherever it turned, through marsh and meadow, across salt-fields and dusty beaches. He walked erect as always, his face forward, looking neither right nor left and even if he tripped or stumbled, his focus never changed.

The sun went down and the wind died. White stars glittered in the sky and the waning moon curved across the horizon. Once again, fatigue sent him to the ground. Once again, he slept where he fell.

Joshua walked along the Jordan for four days, seldom resting. His body was covered with dust and dirt. The dirt hardened on his face, forming creases in the smooth skin where none had been before. He looked thinner and older. His blonde hair whitened and his blue eyes faded in the sun. His skin became red and burned and scarred by the sun. He did not feel the burns.

Joshua's sandals wore down to strips of leather, which then fell off his feet. His clothes were torn by the brush and bleached by the sun.

Joshua didn't realize it, but his strength was being worn away in the glare of the unending sun. His progress slowed; the march became painful. His feet, at first strong, were torn and bloodied. He had open sores that festered and began to ooze yellow secretions. Joshua ignored the sores and the pain and was unaware that his steps were faltering.

Vegetation thinned out and then disappeared. The cliffs on his right hand grew higher and more jagged. He walked in the Arabah, the bleak Judaean desert, where the sun was hotter and there was no shade whatsoever.

Ultimately, the Jordan itself slowed. Then it moved, sluggishly and heavily into the Salt Sea.

The sun's rays glinted up from the dense water and glared in Joshua's eyes. A strange bitter smell offended his nostrils. There was no longer any water to drink and Joshua had not eaten for days. He remained close to the shore of the Salt Sea, but he was wavering now, almost delirious from lack of food and water. Joshua wanted to go on, although he did not know where he was going. The banners with his family painted on them became fainter and then fluttered away. He turned his head for the first time, trying to follow the banner with Rebecca's face on it, but it curled up and disappeared. He found himself looking into the eyes of a young man, with short brown hair and a trim beard, of very short stature, wrapped in a shapeless, colorless garment, leaning on a stick and smiling at him.

"Good morning, old fellow," the young man said to Joshua.

***

The young man's face was so friendly and his voice so gentle, that Joshua smiled. He realized vaguely that he had been mistaken for an old man, but that neither surprised nor annoyed him. He felt old, very old, so old that age had ceased to have meaning.

"I am called Baruch," the young man said. He took Joshua's arm as if they were old friends and led him away from the water's edge. The path was narrow, but well-worn and it wound its way to a hodge-podge collection of stone buildings, plastered and bleached so colorless by the all-pervasive sun that they seemed to be the same tone as the ground itself.

The buildings were surrounded by a low stone wall, pierced by a few arched gates. Outside the walls were clusters of less permanent structures, tents and small huts.

As Joshua and Baruch approached the main gate, which stood open, a group of men materialized from the shadows. They were of various ages, all bearded and all wearing the same shapeless garment wound about them. Seeing Joshua, they halted and talked among themselves.

Baruch anticipated their reactions. "A wanderer," he said, "walking along the lake shore. Harmless, I'm sure."

He looked at Joshua with the same natural, guileless smile. "There's no harm in you, is there?" Baruch didn't wait for an answer and Joshua didn't offer one. It seemed appropriate to him that he was leaning on the arm of this pleasant young fellow and that he had arrived at this colorless place.

The other men were not convinced and drew Baruch aside to speak to him privately. He gave Joshua his crook to lean on and went off to talk to them.

"He's filthy and he smells," one of the older men said to Baruch.

"The Master says we are to judge men by their souls, not their appearances," Baruch answered.

"Does he wish to join us?" another asked.

"I don't know. I just found him a few minutes ago. I think he's ill and we should care for him."

"You're taking a great deal of authority for one who's only recently been admitted to our Community."

"I have no authority," Baruch said, "and I don't wish to take any. I want to help this poor fellow."

The others grudgingly agreed. Baruch returned to Joshua, the same beneficent smile on his face. "The brothers are suspicious of strangers, but I've promised them you're not dangerous," he said. Despite Baruch's assurances, the "brothers" studied Joshua warily as he passed. Joshua looked from face to face. In other times he might have smiled, to reassure these men, but a smile did not come easily to him now.

Within the gates was a bleak courtyard and then a warren of buildings of varying shapes and sizes with walls that angled here and there, edging narrow winding lanes.

Surprisingly, within the courtyard, a stream of fresh water gushed though a stone channel and disappeared into one of the buildings. Seeing Joshua's reaction, Baruch explained that the water was collected during the rainy season in great natural depressions in the Judean hills to the west and then flowed through aqueducts into the settlement where it was held in a system of cisterns.

But Joshua hardly heard the explanation. He was busy examining his surroundings, with a heightening sense of anticipation. Next to the gate was a watchtower, with no one watching. The jumble of buildings, or perhaps it might better be described as one, large rambling structure, was of uneven height, but only one section was of more than one story.

Joshua felt himself drawn to that structure. The increase in his energy was so great that Baruch sensed it, too. "No," he said, "strangers are not allowed there." But Joshua was pulling against his arm, almost dragging the little fellow with him. Baruch shrugged. "So be it," he said.

They passed a shop where smoke was rising from a metal smelter and one could hear workman pounding metal, but Joshua did not pause. He made directly for the door of the two story building. Once inside, Joshua found a staircase and mounted it quickly, Baruch hurrying behind him. It was difficult to see after being in the blinding sun, but Joshua blinked and narrowed his eyes.

On the upper floor, a group of men sat at low tables, goose quills in hand, laboriously copying from scrolls onto other scrolls. They did not look up when Baruch and Joshua entered, but concentrated on their work with passion and all-consuming intensity.

Joshua's eyes adjusted to the new, lesser light with remarkable swiftness. He bent over the table where one of the men was working and studied the scroll. The words flickered and danced before his eyes, then formed into shapes that were recognizable.

"Torah," he said. It was the first word he had spoken in days. He was surprised at how strong his voice sounded. All the scribes looked up, startled.

"Torah," Joshua said, this time more softly. And this time he smiled.

2.

THE HEALERS

As they came out of the Scriptorium, Baruch studied Joshua, wrinkling his nose. "I think a bath may be in order."

He led Joshua through a bewildering combination of corridors into a large, neat room with steps leading down to pools of water. Baruch removed his own tunic and helped Joshua remove his and then led him down into the first pool, flowing with water pleasantly heated by the sun.

Baruch gently bathed Joshua, washing away the grime of many days.

"My goodness," Baruch said, "You're much younger than I thought."

Joshua smiled again.

"What's your name?" Baruch asked

"Joshua ben Joseph."

"What an appropriate name," Baruch said. He realized that Joshua's body, though clean, was peeling severely, in fact bleeding in some places. Even Baruch's gentle touch, sometimes made Joshua wince.

Baruch helped Joshua out of the pool into another one, rinsing away the residue of his journey.

When they were dry and dressed, Joshua felt dizzy. Baruch saw that he was wobbly and his expression was glazed, the pupils dilated. He reached out to support Joshua. "I think we better bring you to Omriel," he said. Then, half leading and half-supporting Joshua he brought him to another structure. Inside was a scrupulously clean dispensary, with rows of beds and shelves stocked with neatly marked jars.

Omriel, the physician, a mite of a man, with a shaved head and pink skin hurried up. One look at Joshua told him enough to defer his questions until he had helped Baruch carry him to a bed. They stripped away his tunic and laid him down gently.

Joshua found it pleasant lying on the clean white bedding in the clean white room. His smile was hazy, but at least the world had stopped spinning.

Omriel examined him quickly, looking into his eyes, gently opening his mouth and manipulating his limbs. "Little to drink and less to eat. Much exposure to the sun. Otherwise looks healthy. What would induce a man to treat his body this way?"

Baruch shook his head and told Omriel he had found "Joshua" wandering along the Salt Sea. He had no idea where he came from or where he had been.

Omriel wanted to question Joshua, but he had dozed off. "Good," the physician said. "We'll let him rest—obviously he needs it. In the morning, we'll start feeding him -- fluids at first and bring his strength back."

Baruch smiled. "Thank you, Omriel," he said.

Omriel's pink lips pursed in his pink face. "Don't thank me yet. Let's see what kind of creature you've found lurking out there."

***

In the morning, Joshua came awake slowly. Before he could orient himself, Omriel was at his side, bringing a cup of hot broth. Joshua accepted it gratefully.

"Slowly, my friend," Omriel said. "Very slowly."

As Joshua sipped the broth, he looked about and remembered vaguely coming into dispensary. A few of the other beds were occupied, all by men, and all much older than he was.

He saw that the physician was working at a table, grinding leaves into a bowl. Omriel saw that Joshua was watching. "Myrtle," he said. "Wonderful for healing." After he had ground the leaves into a powder, he poured some oil into the bowl. "Myrrh," he said, "blended with other oils that we have been entrusted with knowledge of." He was a cheerful, little fellow and proud of his profession. "God taught Noah and Noah taught Shem. The wisdom was passed down through Abraham and Jacob to Levi and thus to the Priests." He laid a finger alongside his nose and smiled. "But only the elect know the true secrets—in the hands of the wicked it would be very dangerous."

Within minutes he had completed his work and brought the mixture to Joshua. "Lie back and I'll apply it." Joshua did as he was told. The fluid felt cool and pleasant on his tortured skin. The fragrance was mild and natural and soothing.

Omriel's touch was light, and as he worked he observed Joshua closely. "Tell me your name."

"Joshua ben Joseph."

"Where are you from?"

"Galilee, near Nazareth."

"Your trade?"

"Carpenter."

"Family?"

Joshua's body tightened briefly, then he shook his head. All the while, Omriel was peering at him, watching his eyes closely, sensing his responses from his hands, gently smoothing on the oily substance.

Baruch had entered the dispensary and was standing by.

Omriel smiled at Joshua. "Healing is more than a physical process—it is spiritual as well. I have the feeling you understand that. Our practice is to find and name the demon that possesses a man. When we have done that, we can force it to leave and thus to clear the way for God's grace and healing power."

He glanced at Baruch before he spoke again to Joshua. "No demon possesses you, Joshua ben Joseph. Your soul is clear and clean and belongs only to God. Some day you'll tell us about your family."

He patted Joshua once on the shoulder and turned to his other patients. He worked quietly and efficiently, using varying unguents for each patient and frequently laying his hands on affected and diseased areas. The patients obviously trusted him. Some were very old and very ill, but they were calm and their spirits good. There was an atmosphere of good will and hope in the dispensary.

Baruch smiled at Joshua. "Omriel is a marvel. You'll be up and around soon."

It had occurred to Joshua, somewhat vaguely, that he might be able to help cure himself, but he decided not to try. It was best to leave matters to Omriel and see what he could learn from him. But he did make certain that his mind and body were receptive.

Within three days, the sores on Joshua's body had healed almost entirely. He had progressed from broth to well-cooked vegetables and he was growing restless.

Omriel smiled. "I'm returning you to Baruch," he said. "You don't need me any longer." Joshua smiled his thanks and walked out into the hot clear air of the settlement. Baruch was waiting. He clapped his hands with pleasure and led Joshua across the level ground on which the settlement was clustered and out through a gate.

The people of the community did not live in the permanent structures, but rather in tents or huts on the plateau and in natural caves that dotted the cliffs overlooking the settlement. Baruch lived in one of the caves, of modest dimensions, but not an unpleasant protection from the extremes of temperature that assailed this ragged stretch of the Rift Valley adjacent to the Salt Sea.

Baruch brought Joshua to his cave and gave him a pallet to rest on. Then he went down to the fresh water spring, some distance south of the settlement and filled a bucket with drinking water. When he returned, Joshua had dozed off.

For several days, Baruch was the only one who spoke to Joshua. Joshua asked few questions, and Baruch did not want to overwhelm him with information, but he told him a little about the community from time to time. "There are about one hundred and twenty of us here, all men. Once there were a few women, aged widows and the like, but none now. We are not the only ones—there are others of our people who live in the cities. But there they can't follow our strict rules."

And then, at another time, "There are many places along the Salt Sea where water bubbles up in hot springs. The source of these springs is said to be on the eastern side of the Sea. There, on God's orders, the archangel Raphael bound Azalel and other devils and imprisoned them deep in the earth, writhing in a fiery underworld from which the heated waters escape. The water though, is supposed to be healthy—except for evil men. King Herod came here for the springs and when they lowered him into them, he almost died."

Later, Baruch said, "Do you know what happened a short distance north of here, on the Jordan close to Gilgal?"

"Yes," Joshua said, "that's where the Israelites crossed into the Promised Land."

"Good," Baruch said, "led by your namesake, Joshua, the son of Nun." The idea seemed to delight Baruch. "It was Joshua who chose the 'cities of the wilderness,' and built fortresses there. Our community is on the very site of one of those cities. Some call this place Mesad Hasidim, the Fortress of the Pious, others name it Qumran, but in Joshua's time it was called Secacah or Sukkah, like the desert booth of boughs and branches we build for the feast of tabernacles.

"In its way, our home is a 'desert booth,' and we use the myrtle, part of the Sukkah, for healing. In Aramaic, the word for healer and myrtle are alike, Assayya, and from that some call us Essenes or 'healers.'"

Each morning at dawn, the Community gathered on the plateau for morning prayers, led by a man whom Baruch told Joshua was their High Priest and another whom he called the "Master." Joshua understood that he was not to join the group in their devotions. He remained apart and offered his own prayers. For the first time, he prayed for the souls of his murdered family. It was a painful prayer and he faltered more than once.

After prayers and blessings, the community ate a brief meal and then divided in accordance with an established pattern. Some moved toward the south, to tend their fields and a small herd of undersized cattle. They ate no meat, but used the milk of the animals, in part, as a medicine.

Others entered the permanent buildings to continue their work as scribes and copyists, healers and physicians. Still others had tasks that Joshua did not understand, but did not question, either. It was obvious that this was a tightly knit and exclusive group and that they did not readily accept outsiders. Joshua realized it had not been easy for Baruch to persuade them to permit Joshua to remain among them.

Baruch's work was in the fields and Joshua accompanied him there. Baruch offered him a small hoe, and Joshua happily weeded between the rows of vegetables. It was pleasant to have something—something simple and useful—to keep him busy. In the early part of the day, before the sun began to bake the plain, it was cool and comfortable. Baruch smiled in approval. The others noted Joshua's presence, but did not speak to him. In fact, they seldom spoke to each other, dutifully fulfilling their tasks in silence.

They did not eat at midday, but rested from the heat of the sun. Baruch led Joshua back to his cave, believing a morning's work was enough for him. He brought forth a napkin from under his tunic and handed it to Joshua. Joshua opened it and found it filled with greens, nuts and dried fruits. Joshua shook his head.

"Omriel says you must eat," Baruch told him and pushed the napkin at him.

Joshua shrugged and smiled. At first, the raw food was strange in his mouth. He ate carefully and sparingly, but even the small portion helped restore his energy.

Later, when it was time to return to the fields, Baruch suggested Joshua remain in the cave. However, feeling restored, Joshua said he wanted to work. Baruch reluctantly agreed. But then, from the height of the cave, Joshua's eye was caught by a group of men raising roof beams on a small structure attached to the Scriptorium.

"The library," Baruch informed him. "We can go look at it, if you like."

As they approached, Joshua observed the work with the practiced eye of a carpenter. He saw at once that the beams were insufficiently braced and would not hold. Even as he watched, one of the supports began to slip and the roof with it. Joshua ran to the wall and raised his arms to hold the beam. He was too weak to do it alone, but others quickly understood what was happening and hurried to help.

When the beam was secured, they looked at Joshua with appreciation. Meanwhile, he was searching the ground. Finding a piece of wood that suited him, he picked up a mallet and deftly nudged it into place. "That will hold it," he said.

The men looked at each other and smiled. "The Lord ALWAYS provides," one said. The others looked heavenward and uttered silent thanks.

Baruch smiled at Joshua. "You're needed here," he said, and went off to work in the fields alone.

***

The men of the community, "the brothers," as Baruch called them, accepted Joshua's help in building the library, but otherwise left him to his own devices. Joshua was not offended. He was not ready for communication.

At dusk, Baruch brought Joshua a simple meal. Then he joined his brothers for evening prayers. They bathed carefully in the bath house, purifying themselves, after which they dressed in clean linen clothes and shared a meal in the Hall of Congregation.

Baruch explained that the meals were a religious sacrament, including many prayers and succeeded by important discussions of scripture and community affairs. The brothers were seated in the Hall according to a strictly defined hierarchy and comments and questions followed a rigid set of rules.

Later, from the cave, Joshua heard them singing hymns that concluded the evening. At those moments, Joshua felt a sense of loneliness. It would be pleasant to join the brothers, to listen to their discussions, to join with them in singing holy hymns.

It was usually quite late when Baruch returned to the cave, but regardless of the hour, he was always warm and friendly, full of enthusiasm over the teachings of the evening. His pudgy face formed a veritable basket of smiles as he happily shared everything he had learned with Joshua. In return, he would have welcomed any confidence Joshua might have offered, but he understood that Joshua had suffered a great loss and that he was not ready to share it with anyone.

Joshua's sleep was tormented with dreams. Again and again he saw his murdered wife and children. Each time his heart would rise, as they smiled encouragingly at him. Then, when he was about to embrace them, the cruel face of Septimus would appear. Joshua would raise a sword over his head and feel anger suffusing his body. At that instant he would waken, startled and sitting bolt upright on his pallet, sweating and shaking.

Night after night, Joshua found himself poised to strike Septimus. An earthquake of anger would send tremors through his body. He would feel all of his energy, his very being focused in this one instant—this one gesture. He never struck the blow and yet he never rested. He would be nervous when he awoke, trembling from the exertion—the struggle to keep himself from killing Septimus. And then he would feel the doubts return. Vengeance indeed belonged to the Lord and yet the Lord had often designated men to take vengeance. Had Joshua imposed his will, instead of God's will?

He nearly wept with confusion and doubt. It was wrong to kill—always wrong. God would not want him to repay murder with murder.

Baruch sometimes awakened briefly in the night to see Joshua turning in his sleep and often to hear him moaning. He yearned to help Joshua but he didn't want to pry into private matters.

One morning, finding Joshua awake as usual, Baruch felt bold enough to ask a question. "Have you a family?" he asked.

Joshua blinked and steeled himself for the reply. "My wife and children were killed by Roman soldiers," he said.

Baruch stared at him with huge, sympathetic eyes. For a moment, he couldn't speak, then tears appeared in his eyes. "I'm sorry," he said. He put out a hand and touched Joshua's shoulder. Joshua felt the young man's compassion spread through his fingers and he in turn put his own hand on Baruch's hand. Together, spontaneously, they began to pray a traditional mourner's prayer.

***

Day after day, the men of the community followed their rigid schedule, rising in the darkness, praying before dawn, working all day at their assigned tasks and even into the night by candles and lamps over their precious scrolls.

Joshua continued working with the building crew. It was obvious that they were painfully inexperienced. By necessity, Joshua became their leader. Fortunately, they were willing learners and energetic workers. With each passing day, Joshua was able to work harder. Except for his calm face and quiet voice, the others would have thought he was possessed.

In a way, he was. Joshua's dead family was never far from his thoughts. He hoped that if he became deeply totally absorbed in his work, thoughts of his family would disappear, or at least fade. He prayed almost continuously, even as he worked. The men he worked with realized that although he was physically engaged in building the library, his mind was focused elsewhere.

3.

COVENANT

Baruch told Joshua more and more about the community.

"We love our families and cherish our friends as much as other men, but we have left them behind because we could not live in their world. It says in our sacred book, our manual:

'And when these things shall come to pass in the Community of Israel... they shall separate themselves from the midst of the habitation of perverse men to take to the wilderness to prepare there the Way of Him as was written: "Prepare ye in the wilderness the Way of the Lord: make straight to the desert a highway for our God." This Way is the study of the Law...so as to act according to all that was revealed time after time, and according to what the Prophets revealed by His Holy Spirit.'

"We followed these words in building our community here. While others give in to the urges of the flesh—we obey the laws of the spirit." Baruch's childlike face had become very serious.

"Jews must repent or be destroyed. We trust in the word of God. Jeremiah told us: 'Behold, the days are coming, says the Lord, when I will make a new covenant with the House of Israel and the House of Judah...I will put my law within them, and I will write it upon their hearts; and I will be their God, and they shall be my people. And no longer shall each man teach his neighbor and each his brother, saying, `Know the Lord,' for they shall all know me, from the least of them to the greatest, says the Lord; for I will forgive their iniquity, and I will remember their sin no more.'"

Baruch spoke with rising passion. "We believe," he said, "that only by divine intervention can we be saved. In the cities, even in holy Jerusalem, there are many who profess to follow the Lord, but are only liars and hypocrites. Even as they pray piously for Justice and Wisdom and the Way of the Lord, they live evil, unrepentant lives. Their prayers are in their mouths but not in their hearts.

"We have withdrawn from the contamination of the cities, to form our own community—to sanctify our lives and wait for the Lord."

Joshua nodded. "Behold," he quoted from scripture, "the days are coming, says the Lord, when I will fulfill the promise I made to the house of Israel and the house of Judah. In those days and at that time I will cause a righteous Branch to spring forth for David; and he shall execute justice and righteousness in the land."

Baruch smiled, delighted. "Yes, those too are the words of Jeremiah."

"The words of the Lord," Joshua said.

"Of course." Baruch spoke to Joshua with delight and anticipation. "Then you, too, are waiting for the coming of the Messiah?"

Joshua hesitated before he spoke. "Would we know him if he stood before us?"

***

"Baruch tells me that you know scripture—from beginning to end."

"There is no end," Joshua said.

"Indeed."

Joshua sat in the scrupulously clean, but small room, opposite a slender, vigorous looking man with thick black hair that came down to a sharp point on his forehead, a trim gray beard that contrasted startlingly with his hair, and alert brown eyes.

His skin was almost as light as the bleached linen tunic he wore. Joshua knew he was close to fifty years old, but his complexion was clear and unmarked. He was quite tall and his bearing was noble, his expression benign, but his eyes penetrating. When he spoke, his voice rumbled in his chest, even before it issued from his lips. There were long pauses between phrases, some times between words. The man was more learned than Joshua's father had been, but his manner of speaking reminded him of Joseph.

This was the man whom Baruch called "the Guardian" and more often, "the Master."

"Baruch also tells me that you are... a fine craftsman...We are indebted to you for your work on our new library."

"There is no debt," Joshua said, "only duty."

"Indeed."

They sat facing each other for a long time, both erect and unblinking. It was not a contest, but rather a mutual, though amiable, evaluation.

"We don't ask where our people come from—only where they are going."

Because the Master had not demanded to hear his history, Joshua felt free to tell it. He spoke briefly and as unemotionally as he could, telling of the terrible death of his family.

Joshua felt the Master's compassion, even before he spoke. "You have suffered a great loss," the Master said. "You bear it with dignity."

Joshua was silent.

"Perhaps we can help you."

"You've helped greatly by providing a sanctuary for me and a place where I can practice my trade. I won't abuse your kindness. Please tell me when it's time for me to leave. 'There is a time to every purpose under heaven.'"

The Master smiled. "Do you wish to join us?"

As the Master asked the question, Joshua felt a rush of feeling, of release from doubt and confusion, of warmth at being wanted. Surely, the Lord had purpose in guiding his feet to this place. When Baruch had found him, he had been delirious with his pain and suffering. Joshua had learned that the outside world was one of great shocks and bitter disappointments, of terrible surprises and heavy blows.

Now he was without wife and children, without responsibility or even purpose. Within this community he had found a severe but pleasant existence, free of strife. He had no responsibilities other than to perform his trade with other quiet men. He was free to study scripture to his heart's content. At the moment, he could not imagine returning to the world he had known.

"Yes," Joshua said with great assurance. "I would be honored to join you."

"We have strict rules. No one can remain in Secacah who has not been initiated into the covenant."

"Aren't we all sons of the covenant?"

"The old covenant has been sullied...We pledge ourselves to a new covenant with God—by a binding oath to return with all our hearts and souls to every commandment of the Law of Moses...in accordance with all that has been revealed to the Teacher of Righteousness, the Keepers of the Covenant, and the Seekers of God's will."

Joshua waited.

"To become a full member of the community takes two years...Only then would you be admitted to the food and drink of the congregation...We give up all worldly things and contribute all we have to the common fund... Until you are admitted, you would be able to do the work of our group and to listen to our teachings."

"Are you the Teacher of Righteousness?"

The Master smiled. "No. You are speaking of Zadok, whose very name means 'righteous.' We deem ourselves the 'sons of Zadok.' He founded our community, over a hundred and thirty years ago...based on renunciation of the world and its evil ways...and return to the holy word of the Almighty. For this he was hated, reviled and persecuted...Finally, about one hundred and fifteen years ago, he was crucified by Alexander Jannaeus, a Jewish king who had usurped the position of High Priest—an evil man our Teacher condemned for his ungodly ways...Zadok was crucified on the oak known as the Teacher's Oak, close to the town of Gilgal, a few miles from here."

The Master leaned forward and spoke intently. "Perhaps that is why you are here. We believe this is the place to wait for the Messiah—near the crossing where Joshua, your namesake, led the Israelites into the Promised Land, close to Gilgal where he built an altar and directed the people to rededicate themselves to their Covenant with God. We wait for another Joshua, who will triumph again in the name of the Most High."

Joshua was surprised at the sudden burst of passion from the usually serene Master. When Joshua responded, he spoke softly and watched the Master's reactions carefully. "Some of your brothers," Joshua said, "believe you are the Messiah."

The Master frowned, but Joshua sensed that he was flattered. It seemed to Joshua that one would not be able to flatter the Messiah. Still, the Master spoke firmly and with evident sincerity. "I don't encourage such thoughts. If I have been righteous, that is my duty. If I have suffered for my devotion to the Lord, that is God's will.

"We believe that the Teacher of Righteousness has been translated straight to heaven, as were Moses, Enoch and Elijah...We believe our Teacher is now at the right hand of God, mediating on our behalf. He will return to us as the Messiah, the anointed of God, but we know not when or in what form."

Joshua did not speak and the Master looked at him with deepened curiosity. "Are you sent here to test me?"

"Not I," said Joshua.

But the Master was not satisfied with Joshua's answer.

"Who sent you?" he asked.

"You know the answer," Joshua said.

The Master sat back abruptly, pondering this response.

***

Baruch was ecstatic that Joshua had chosen to join the community and that the Guardian had accepted him. After a ritual bath, Baruch brought him a clean tunic and new sandals, replacing the worn clothes he had been wearing. Then, together, they walked to the Hall of Congregation. The room was filled with brothers, dressed in their white tunics, waiting for the Master and the High Priest. They did not look towards him but Joshua felt warmth radiating from the group.

The Master entered and then the High Priest. The latter wore a long robe and a prayer shawl edged with blue and gold striping. On his head was a conical crown, also laced with gold threads.

He was older than the Master, a wispy man of average height, with a heavily lined face and an expression of other-worldly preoccupation. He walked slowly and laboriously to the front of the room, mounted the simple platform and gestured for Joshua to come forward.

Joshua looked into the eyes of the High Priest and found concentration but not warmth, depth but not individual concern. Still, the priest's expression was not unkindly, and his eyes were on a vision far beyond the Hall of Congregation.

"Blessed art thou, O Lord, our God, ruler of the Universe, who has given us the blessings of Torah and the gift of Thy divine covenant. Look down on this assembly with loving-kindness and teach us thy ways in peace."

"Amen," the brothers responded and Joshua joined with them.

The High Priest then looked down at Joshua and placed his hands gently on his shoulders.

"Are you here freely, and are you prepared to join this congregation and to accept the responsibilities of the covenant?"

"I am," Joshua said, his eyes clear and direct, gazing without fear into the eyes of the High Priest.

"Then, state for me, the words you have been taught." Joshua's eyes never wavered as he said, "I swear a binding oath to return with all my heart and soul to every commandment of the Law of Moses in accordance with all that has been revealed to the sons of Zadok, the Keepers of the Covenant and Seekers of His will."

The High Priest nodded, his expression grew more kindly and his eyes seemed briefly alive with personal feeling for Joshua. He placed his hands on Joshua's head.

"We thank thee, O Lord, for bringing us this new son of the Covenant and we ask your blessings upon him."

Then, it was done. The High Priest was gone, retiring into a world of his own. But the Master congratulated Joshua and embraced him and other brothers clustered about, smiling and nodding, welcoming him. It was a warm and pleasant moment and it gave Joshua respite from the ever present loss he had suffered.

They offered him a glass of wine and he blessed and drank it. He smiled at his new brothers.

***

In the community of Essenes, "The Healers," the days passed quietly. Joshua "belonged," but he was only a proselyte, not a full member, He was still not permitted to eat the meal of Purity, nor to attend the meetings of the brothers where more important matters were discussed. He was allowed to sit in the Hall of Congregation when the Master was teaching from the Torah and the writings of the community.

The weather grew warmer and the crops ripened in the community's tiny fields. Joshua continued to work in the library, building tables and shelving and containers for the precious scrolls. Some of the scrolls were wrapped in linen and sealed in tall earthen jars made in the community's pottery shop. The Master told Joshua that this fulfilled a sacred writing, known as "The Assumption of Moses," according to which Moses directed Joshua to protect the holy scriptures in a place where they might be stored until "the day of repentance," where the "Lord will visit them in the consummation of the End of Days." This was confirmed also by Isaiah, who had written, "Bind up the testimony, seal the teaching among my disciples." When the Messiah came and the Holy Temple was purified again, these scrolls would be brought to Jerusalem in triumph. Meanwhile, the great jars were stored in underground chambers and in the caves in the cliffs above Qumran.

After some weeks, the Master approached Joshua "You have moved from the fields to the construction of our library, to the building of shelves. Perhaps it's time for you to be involved with the books themselves."

Joshua smiled.

"I have need of a secretary—one who would not only handle the routine papers of our work here—but someone I could trust to search in the sacred texts for the words that I need in my studies —someone to compile my writings and the sacred writings entrusted to us. Are you interested, Joshua?"

"Would I be permitted to study the sacred texts on my own—on my own time?"

"Of course," the Master said.

They both smiled to seal the agreement.

The Master was as good as his word, allowing Joshua many hours for his own studies of scripture. In addition, The Master often took time to discuss the sacred writings with his secretary. He also showed Joshua the text of "The Assumption of Moses," and other writings Joshua had never seen before, including a book called "Jubilees," and another about the patriarch, "Enoch." These were strange and wonderful books and Joshua was fascinated to read them, though uncertain of their authority. He knew that the Healers, the sons of Zadok, treated them as sacred and oracular.

Despite his doubts, Joshua listened to the Master expounding these texts with great interest and total concentration. He found the Master to be as erudite as Ari the Sage—perhaps even more.

"The Jews have lost their way," the Master told him. "That is why God has visited the Roman plague upon us...We are being tested, and thus far we have fallen short."

"When do you believe this 'plague' will end?" Joshua asked.

"When the people...are ready to bend their will to that of GOD in heaven. When they understand that it is not their will, but the divine will that must be understood and followed.... "

"God will show us the way."

The Master paused and looked upward, "The Lord has shown us again and again....but the people refuse to see, refuse to listen. His patience is at an end...They will soon know his wrath."

"All the people?"

"All stubborn sinners."

"Won't the Messiah save the people?"

"What do you think, Joshua?"

"Baruch says the Messiah will be a great warrior, a King who will rally the Jews to a great victory in which the Romans will be totally destroyed."

The Master frowned. "Baruch is well-intentioned, but like many others, he does not seem to understand...the Romans were sent here as a sign, a warning of greater suffering to come."

His voice rose. "It is the people of Israel who should be frightened, not the Romans. The Messiah will indeed come...and with him the wrath of God. The Jews mistake the Romans for the evil that afflicts them...They are their own affliction...When the Messiah comes, all corruption will be swept away. That is why we are here. God must know that we are the righteous remnant...We have no part of the evil that contaminates this land."

"Is there no hope for others?"

"It is too late. They worship foreign idols instead of the Lord...They are vile sinners and there is no escape from their wrongdoing."

Joshua felt a chill as he listened to the Master's angry judgment of the people. He thought of the Twenty–fifth psalm and he could not resist quoting from it:

"'Look upon mine affliction and my pain;' David said to the Lord, 'and forgive all my sins...keep my soul and deliver me; let me not be ashamed; for I put my trust in thee. Redeem Israel, O God, out of all his troubles."

Joshua waited for the Master to respond but he was silent. Joshua spoke quietly. "The Lord God is forgiving," he said.

The Master smiled. "God is forgiving, but God is not a fool."

***

"You're wrong, Joshua," Baruch said, his voice trembling with agitation. "The Master himself won't say so, but we believe he IS the Messiah."

"The reborn Teacher of Righteousness?"

Baruch hesitated, unsure of Joshua's meaning. "The Master is good, he is pure, he has been afflicted for his righteousness."

"I agree that he is a wise and righteous man, but if he is the Messiah why does he remain here, away from the children of the Lord?"

"WE are the children of the Lord."

"The ONLY children?"

Baruch fought for words. "Not everyone has earned God's blessings."

"God offers his blessings to all."

"Yes, of course. But the others—they aren't pure. They turn their faces from God. The Master will show them."

"Will he destroy them?"

"Yes—No. I don't know, but he will do what God wants him to do."

"When will he do these things?"

Baruch did not enjoy the questioning, but he liked Joshua and wanted to be patient. "When he is ready."

Baruch's devotion to the Master was great, so great that Joshua thought it might be blinding him. He shook his head sadly. It seemed to him that the Messiah would be openly anointed by God— that all would know him. He smiled encouragingly at Baruch. "The Messiah will recognize your goodness," he said.

***

Despite the Community's self-chosen isolation and ascetic life, many travelers reached Qumran and were welcomed there.

Late one afternoon, as Joshua left the workshop where he was building shelving for the library, he was surprised to see the Master standing before the entrance to the Scriptorium, in conversation with a huge, but familiar figure. It was the giant whom Joshua had seen at the Jordan, calling upon people to repent and immersing them in the river.

He could not resist approaching this strange but compelling figure. The Master smiled at him. "Come here, Joshua. This is our great friend, Johannon."

At this proximity, Johannon was even larger than Joshua remembered. His hair was still wild, his skin torn and burnt by the sun, but his great eyes were beacons that could not be ignored.

Johannon squinted at him. "We have met before," he said.

"You know Joshua?" the Master said.

Johannon smiled. "Joshua, exactly the right name for this place," he said. "Perhaps it's a sign. Although, he chose not to let me immerse him," Johannon said.

"You do remember," Joshua said.

"More the ones I lose than those I gain." And he laughed heartily, although the expression in his eyes was still intent. He leaned down so that his eyes were almost level with Joshua's. "Is it time?" he asked.

Joshua smiled. "Perhaps. I'm sure the Lord will tell us."

"Well said," Johannon affirmed and clapped Joshua on the back with such strength that he almost staggered him.

When he had regained his breath, Joshua asked, "Are you joining the community?"

"We share the same ideals," Johannon said, "but the brothers and I disagree as to the means. The Master believes it's right to remain here and wait for the Messiah, accepting those who truly wish to abandon a life of sin. I believe God wants me to go out among the people and seek for those who may be saved, to turn as many from sin as I can before the Day of Judgment."

The Master smiled. "You're always welcome among us," he told Johannon. The great man smiled and Joshua, looking into his eyes could not help but share the smile. Yet he sensed in Johannon a deep tension and a fearful anxiety.

**

A few days later, Joshua believed he had seen yet another familiar figure. It was after dark and he was strolling at the edge of the plateau when he literally bumped into a man hurrying from the settlement. Joshua grabbed the man's arms to keep from falling, and that gave him a glimpse of his face. Both were startled, and the man pushed away and hurried into the night.

Joshua remained standing where he was, trying to reconstruct this face and to recall where he had seen it. Then the one unique feature tripped his memory—a curious curving scar that looked like a mustache. Judas. The Zealot he had cared for in Beth Sholem, just before his family was slaughtered. He winced at the memory, recalling painful thoughts he had been trying to overcome. But his faith told him there was a reason for this and he would try to find that reason.

When Joshua questioned Baruch, he was evasive; the first time that Joshua had seen him behave in this fashion. "We are not Zealots here."

"I didn't say that you were," Joshua responded. "I thought I saw a man I know to be a Zealot, coming from the Hall of Congregation."

"I don't know who you saw."

Realizing that he could learn nothing from Baruch, he went to the Master. He responded to Joshua's question with narrowed eyes. "Why do you ask?"

Joshua told him about the wounded man he had cared for. "His name was Judas."

The Master sighed. "You're right, of course. Judas was here. We are not Zealots—we do not fight against the Romans with swords and daggers. But these men, whatever the means they use, also love God. They claim to be pious men and they believe that they, too, are fulfilling scripture. We may sometimes shelter them, but their doctrines trouble us."

The Master shook his head. "They take inspiration from the Maccabees, who drove the Seleucid Greeks from the land, purified the Temple and built a new Kingdom of Israel. In the end, however, they fell prey to their own greed and wickedness. They fell away from God, until the days when they were even guilty of profaning the temple and of slaughtering their own countrymen—even our own Teacher of Righteousness. The Zealots believe they can be the Maccabees of today, but more pious and reverent. Perhaps, but the Romans are more powerful than the Greeks, and Israel is more helpless. Unless the Lord intervenes, we are lost. And when the Lord intervenes, it will be his might and not swords and spears that will save us."

4.

THE FAMILY

Gaius Fabricius had recognized at once that Joshua would not return home; he seemed to be heading south along the Jordan River. Gaius had felt a powerful urge to follow him, to help and comfort his son. But he knew he could not. Joshua would neither understand nor appreciate his help, and if he was called upon to explain his interest, Gaius was not ready to confess that he had raped Joshua's mother.

Therefore, he watched Joshua disappear with great pain and a profound sense of helplessness. He would have directed his anger against Septimus, but if his son was strong enough not to kill the man in a blind rage, how could he be the instrument of Septimus's punishment?

Fiercely controlling his disgust and anger, Gaius personally trussed the centurion from head to foot and threw him over a horse. "Take the bastard back to Caesarea and throw him into a cell," he told the Decurion. "And watch your own step, or you'll follow him."

The Decurion, already shaken by the slaughter he had taken part in, nodded stiffly and ordered his men out of town.

Gaius had thought of burying the dead, but he knew the Jews would not thank him for that. He ordered the men to carry the bodies into the ruins of the buildings that had not been completely destroyed and to cover them so that they would be protected from weather and vermin.

A terrible task remained. If Joshua was not going to bury his wife and children, the family must be informed. He could not bring himself to tell Miriam that her daughter-in-law and grandchildren were dead. He would have to tell Joshua's brothers.

The ride to Nazareth was a slow and heavy one. Time and again, Gaius thought of turning about and heading to Tiberias, sending a messenger with a letter to the brothers, but that was too insensitive.

He reached Nazareth and once more traced his way to the carpentry workshop.

"Welcome." Jacob, the open-faced one, greeted him cheerfully. "Have you brought us a contract?"

Gaius swallowed hard and began his story. "There was a Roman raid on Beth Sholem," he said. "It was unauthorized—the work of a mad centurion. The man was sent back to Caesarea to be punished."

The smile on Jacob's face had faded. Even as Gaius spoke, Jacob watched in wonderment. He knew this man was over fifty years old, but he had previously seemed much younger—an intelligent man with a surprisingly open face for a Roman official, a friendly smile and a casual manner. But no longer.

As Gaius told Jacob of the terrible fate of his loved ones, Jacob's face shriveled before his eyes. Wide, sun-bronzed cheeks became pinched and gray. Lively brown eyes dulled and died. Jacob's shoulders sagged, his hands dropped to his sides. He swayed, so that Gaius stepped forward and took hold of him.

Jacob moved away, very slightly from Gaius's touch. Gaius understood. But he saw that Jacob put a hand against a wooden counter to support himself. Gaius watched to see if Jacob turned his anger against him, but Jacob understood that Gaius would not have brought him this message if he were a criminal, too.

Gaius held back tears, and so did Jacob. He stood stock still, then called, in a broken, wavering voice, "Joses, Simeon, Judas."

The brothers came up to the front of the shop, hearing the strange quality in Jacob's voice. They were wiping their hands and laughing, but then they were surprised to see the Roman official and Jacob standing together, both looking like death. And then they understood the message was one of death and they grew silent.

"Tell them," Jacob said in a half-whisper. "Tell them what you told me."

***

Miriam screamed once and collapsed. Judith, the eldest girl caught her as she fell. The brothers helped carry her to a bed. But, even as they laid her carefully down, Miriam had awakened. The one scream was all she allowed herself. In that moment, she had understood everything, suffered all of the pain she was able to sustain and had found the rock depth of her strength.

"I'll be all right," she said, sitting up and pushing away the helping hands. "Judith, you must tell your sister what has happened. Jacob, you and your brothers must bring the family home."

The brothers took strength from their mother. They steeled themselves, brought carts and lashed them to donkeys and set out for Beth Sholem. Jacob led them on the way. He was the oldest after Joshua, but he had never been a leader. None of the others was a leader, either, nor would they have thought of Jacob as a forceful and decisive person.

Miriam had instinctively sensed the change in him and the other brothers had understood the rightness of her judgment. The boyish playfulness was gone from Jacob. The man had taken charge.

***

By the time Gaius returned to Caesarea, it was too late. Septimus had indeed been thrown into prison and the Decurion had dutifully reported to Pilate.

Pilate was fascinated by the story and immediately insisted that Septimus be brought to him.

"You actually slaughtered an entire village without having the foggiest notion where the true criminals were?"

Septimus grudgingly nodded his head. He had had high hopes for Pilate but apparently this governor would be like the others—more anxious to protect his own ass than tame the damned Jews.

"Delicious," Pilate said, smiling. "What a clever way to deal with sedition. This way the slimy wretches will know that somehow they'll pay the price—probably innocent family members in the bargain. They'll never again think they can get away with murder just because we don't know the actual criminals."

Septimus looked up uncertainly. Pilate was smiling at him.

"Brilliant, Centurion," Pilate said. He lofted a wineglass which just happened to be at his elbow. "I salute you." He downed the wine while Septimus blinked in astonishment.

"Unfortunately," Pilate said, "not everyone will appreciate your bold stroke. Some, like that pious deputy, Gaius Fabricius, will tell me that you have violated all the rules of human decency and the ordinances of the empire." He paused. "Probably true, but a brilliant tactic just the same."

Septimus's head was reeling. Was he going to be flogged, hanged or decorated?

"I think," Pilate said, "that a few weeks in Damascus are called for. Leave this hour, Centurion, or I may be forced to follow the approved procedures."

Septimus held out his hands and in a moment the chains were struck off. He saluted Pilate and literally ran from the room.

Pilate laughed heartily and raised his cup.

***

In the weeks after the funeral, Jacob and his brothers had gone back to work with aching hearts. Jacob had wanted to follow Joshua at once, worrying that some evil might have befallen him. Miriam would not hear of it. "We have no idea where he might be. I have no sign that evil has come to him. I know he is grieving, but I sense that otherwise, he's well. We must be patient. In a few days we'll hear from him."

But they did not hear from him. And after several weeks of growing concern in the family, Miriam finally gave in to Jacob's urgent requests to set out and look for him. She knew that, even if she had not approved, Jacob would have gone anyway.

"I'm coming with you," she said.

"No," Jacob said. "The roads are dangerous—can't we learn from what happened to Rebecca and the children?"

"Our lives are in God's hands," Miriam said. "I'm going with you."

The brothers rigged a cart that would provide comfortable passage for their mother. Miriam smiled. When she smiled, they could see her great inner beauty. "The Jordan bends time and again," she said. "A cart will make me dizzy and drive the donkey crazy. I'll ride an animal, just like Jacob."

"Good," Judith said. "So will I." And thus, when Jacob left Nazareth, he was accompanied by his mother and eldest sister. While he protested and complained, in his heart, he was pleased.

They passed through Beth Sholem on the way. The town had been swept clean by the families of the fallen, but the shells of empty houses were a painful reminded of the abominations committed there. Miriam and her family rode through silently, looking only ahead, crying in their hearts but not otherwise.

They reached the copse of trees where the Roman official had last seen Joshua and turned south along the Jordan.

"Jericho," Miriam said. "Below Jericho, we will find him." She had no idea where the thought had come from, but she was certain it was correct.

Jacob smiled at her words. He sensed immediately that his mother was right. That would make their task much easier. They would not have to stop at every small village along the Jordan to ask after Joshua.

Along the way, they passed the town of Gilgal on the Jordan and were surprised to find a huge crowd of people surrounding a shallow ford at the river's edge. At first the crowd was too large for them to see what was happening. Jacob wanted to go on, but Miriam followed her instinct and turned her donkey towards the river.

She dismounted and tethered it to a tree and patiently made her way through the crowd. Jacob and Judith shrugged and did the same.

The people were singing hymns and praying, many of them raising their hands to the sky and calling out the name of the Lord. Others seemed entranced, unaware of what went on around them. Still others were obviously sightseers, grinning youngsters and offended older people.

A little boy sitting on his father's shoulders was telling what he saw. "Now he's got them in the water. They're praying or something. Now he's got his hands up in the sky and he's yelling. He's pushing them under water."

A kind of a cheer went up from the crowd.

A well-dressed man was whispering to another. "Disgusting. These people think because they take the first bath in their lives that God will perform miracles for them."

His neighbor laughed, but another man called out, "Watch your tongue. That man is the messenger of the Lord."

Miriam, Jacob and Judith listened and wondered and made their way slowly to the banks of the river.

Finally they saw a very large, very tall man dipping people in the Jordan.

"Who is he?" Jacob asked.

"Johannon," a young girl told him, smiling at Jacob's simple, attractive face.

"They call him the 'Baptizer,' or the 'Immerser,'" another girl said. She, too, was attracted to Jacob.

Miriam noticed their interest in her son. Jacob had never married and that had long worried her. Now she saw that he had no interest even in very pretty women. But she was no longer worried. Her mother's instinct told her that Jacob was about to devote himself to more important matters.

Judith was another problem altogether. She was tall and wiry, very like her brothers in her strength and unusual agility. She was plain, but not unattractive, with an open, freckled face, green eyes and reddish hair, reminiscent of Miriam's father, Joachim. Miriam openly complained that Judith had not married. She had used Cleophas, Joseph's brother as a go-between. Cleophas had proposed a match or two, but Judith's disapproval had been so great that Cleophas had grown discouraged.

"I can't get her a rich man or a scholar," Cleophas said, "and she thinks she's too good for a farmer or tradesman."

Judith had laughed. "I'm not too good—I just don't care. There are enough men in my life— my five brothers."

Judith was in her thirties and the possibility of marriage seemed remote. Still, Miriam had not given up. Watching her daughter at the river bank, Miriam decided that when they returned, she would undertake this marriage business herself.

"Why is he pushing them under water?" Judith asked, watching the proceedings with wonder.

"First, they are repenting their sins," a young man said, smiling at Judith, "and then he is immersing them, to cleanse and purify them."

Judith shook her head. "That doesn't make any sense," she said. "A Jew should confess his sins to God, on the day of Atonement if not sooner. God will grant his forgiveness. You don't need some big, half-dressed man to plunge you into the water."

Others were angered by her words and tried to hush her up. "If you don't want to be saved from sin, what are you doing here?"

"From the sound of your voices, you're not from these parts."

"Galilee," a voice said. "You can tell 'em by their voices."

"They always think they know better," another called out.

People in the crowd were beginning to grow angry, some who had not even heard what had been said. Jacob pushed close to his mother and sister, ready to protect them.

"What's going on here?" A great voice boomed in their ears. Judith spun around to look into the eyes of Johannon, looming above her. She was astonished, struck dumb by the power and the closeness of him. He smelled of water and bee's-honey and other man smells.

"She's been making fun of you," an old lady whined.

"She did not," Jacob said, intimidated by the large man, but determined to defend Judith.

"Did so."

"Did not."

The voices began to sound like a children's quarrel.

"SILENCE," Johannon yelled. And immediately there was silence.

"What do you say?" Johannon asked Judith, staring at her fiercely, but with the corner of his mouth twitching. "Have you come to poke fun at God Almighty, the very God who made you?"

She shook her head.

"Do you know that the Kingdom of God is at hand—that the Day of Judgment is nearing—that the wrath of the Lord will fall on those who have not repented their sins?"

Again Judith shook her head.

The Baptizer threw back his head. "Forgive her Lord, for she does not know that the hour is nigh. Don't turn away from her, Lord. She is thy child and she will do thy will."

As he spoke, it was as if a dam had breached within Judith's heart, and the pent-up longing of her thirty years was released. She began to cry, but her eyes were gleaming and she stood very tall. "Forgive me, Lord," she cried out, "for I have sinned."

Johannon held out his hand and Judith took it. He held out his other hand to Jacob, who took it as well.

Johannon spoke mildly to Miriam. "Come with us, Mother, and help us find the Lord."

Johannon led the three of them down into the water. He raised his arms high, still holding the hands of Judith and Jacob, and then Miriam walked beneath his arms. When he lowered them, they were locked together, Miriam and her children and the Baptizer.

"Forgive them, Lord, repair their wounded hearts and cleanse their spirits. They are good and they love you and they pray for your forgiveness."

Then he plunged them all, together, into the stream. They came up exhilarated, cleansed and purified. Judith was still crying and Jacob had begun to cry, but Miriam wore a glorious smile.

***

Joshua's joy exploded inside him. Mouth helplessly open, he stared and stared and finally reached out.

Miriam, Jacob and Judith surrounded and embraced him. Still speechless, he hugged and kissed each of them in turn, then hugged and kissed them again. Baruch, who had brought them in, slipped away, smiling.

Last of all, Joshua embraced his mother once more, rocking her in his strong arms. "Mother," he sighed, "how good, how good you are." Tears sluiced from her eyes, but she was smiling, almost laughing. She pushed him away.

"Thinner? Yes, a bit thinner. But your eyes are clear. Why are you so pale?"

He laughed. "Inside work. Many books and papers."

"You've not been sick?" she asked suspiciously.

He laughed again. "Believe me, mother, I'm fine. But how did you find me?"

"The giant, Johannon," Jacob said. "He told us."

"We said we were looking for a tall, blonde and handsome man," Judith said. "He knew just who we meant, at once."

"Flatterer," Joshua said, kissing her full on the mouth. She clung to him and he swung her off her feet. "Skinny—too skinny."

"Johannon didn't think so," Jacob said, a semblance of his old crooked grin on his face.

Judith blushed, but said nothing.

Miriam frowned at Jacob and he caught the frown and changed the subject.

"He immersed us—almost drowned us in the Jordan," Jacob said.

"The three of you?" Joshua was amazed.

"We repented all our sins and he said God forgave us."

"My mother is not a sinner," Joshua said righteously.

Miriam smiled.

Judith pouted. "Does that mean Jacob and I *are* sinners?" she asked.

"Not any longer," Miriam said, smiling again. "We've all been forgiven—even Jacob—"she teased. "Now, of course, we have to live righteously and love God."

Joshua's expression had grown serious. "I'm glad of it," he said. "Glad you chose to do what you did. The hour is near. There's little doubt of it. These are the times that the prophets foretold, the times of tribulation and suffering—the Last Days."

They were all silent for a moment. Judith grinned and touched his cheek. "You're too serious, Joshua."

"You're not serious enough," and he slapped her bottom.

"Tell us," Miriam said, "how did you get here?"

Once again, Joshua's expression changed. But the subject had to be dealt with. "When I reached Beth Sholem, Rebecca and the children were dead. A Roman official showed me the killer and gave me his sword. He told me to kill the killer. I tried, but the Lord wouldn't let me do it. I left Beth Sholem immediately, fearful I might be tempted to return and kill the Roman. I walked here along the Jordan. I think it took me four days, but I'm not certain. I didn't eat or drink and didn't sleep much either. I just walked. The brothers took me in, healed my sores, allowed me to join their community. There's not much more to tell."

They listened to his simple story of the death of his family and felt like crying again. But Joshua didn't cry and they didn't want to burden him with any more pain. They sat and listened with love and pain in their hearts, nodding and yearning to help him.

"They must be very kind, the brothers, to have taken you in and cared for you."

"It's pleasant here," Joshua said. "I've worked a little in fields and helped with the construction. Now I assist the Master with his administrative work and the research for his writings. I spend a lot of time with the scriptures, which you know that I love."

They were silent for a moment, waiting. Jacob wanted to ask, but he deferred to his mother.

"Will you come home with us?" Miriam asked.

Joshua shook his head.

"Perhaps in a month or two—or in the spring?"

He shook his head again. "I don't think I can go back. I had a family and tried to live the life of a tradesman, but God did not want me to have a family or live such a life. I'm trying to find out what God wants me to do. For the moment, it seems he wants me here with the brothers."

"You're young, Joshua," Judith said. "Too young to hide yourself behind walls in the desert."

"I'm not hiding, Judith. Anyway, one can't hide from God. Jonah learned that."

"He was a prophet," Jacob said. "Are you a prophet?"

He smiled. "I won't know that unless God tells me."

They sat silently, not knowing what to say. Finally, Judith rushed to him and threw her arms around his neck. "Come home, brother, come home with us."

She clung to him and cried. And he cried.

Jacob approached shyly, too, and touched Joshua's arm. "We miss you, all of us."

Joshua nodded and looked at his mother. She did not come to him. She loved him and wanted him home, but she understood that he was different from her other children—different from anyone she had ever known. "I love you," she said. Nothing more and nothing less. Joshua was deeply touched that she understood.

5.

INITIATION

It was difficult for Joshua to say goodbye to his mother, sister and brother. Perhaps it was more difficult for them. Joshua sensed that he had a mission. His family feared that his mission would not include them.

Joshua turned his face resolutely from the world he had known and plunged with even greater dedication into the life of the community. The Master noted his renewed and redoubled efforts and appreciated them. He knew that Joshua was searching for and fighting with his commitment and he respected that struggle. The Master had lived through it himself.

A steady stream of visitors arrived from "camps" in all parts of Israel—that is, communities who accepted the teachings of the Essenes but who still lived in the cities. Their lives were governed by rules less ascetic than those of the community at Qumran, but they too considered themselves part of the "faithful remnant" of Israel that would be saved in the Last Days.

Some came to be healed by the physicians of the community. The physicians gave their services generously, but guarded their secrets zealously. Baruch said that the various herbs and drugs were compounded from formulas handed down from generation to generation back to the days when God had given the secrets to Noah so that men would not be at a disadvantage when dealing with evil ones.

The cures of the community were more than physical. The Healers identified illness with possession by devils and demons and thought it part of their art to restore the suffering one by driving out the demons that possessed him. Thus they attempted to heal the "whole man," treating both body and soul, and for their work they were widely known.

Joshua was impressed by their dedication and their sincerity. He saw men enter the compound crippled by infirmity, and he saw them leave, upright and well. Since the "Healers" were so pious in their way of life, he did not doubt that their work was blessed by God.

The people of Qumran lived by a different calendar than the "false calendar" used at the Temple in Jerusalem and in the rest of the country. They celebrated the Feast of the First Fruits of the wheat harvest, Shavuot, the Pentecost, at a later time. As that day approached, Qumran was thronged with pilgrims from the "camps," coming "home" for the Annual Assembly at which they would celebrate the Renewal of the Covenant.

Individuals and families raised tents in rings around the plateau. Only males attended the actual Assembly, but the cries of children brought life to the usually somber scene.

Baruch was delighted. "You see, there is hope," he told Joshua. "Israel will be redeemed."

The Hall of Congregation was too small to contain the pilgrims, and the meetings of the Assembly were held on level ground between the plateau and the Salt Sea. Women and children and strangers were excluded, but the voices of the celebrants carried in the clear desert air. The families and Joshua could both see and hear the ceremonies. Joshua watched and listened carefully. One day, he would participate in this very same ceremony when he became a full member of the covenant.

A trumpet was blown just before first light, while the Morning Star was still bright and the faithful assembled, all wearing the white linen garments favored by the brothers. A gentle breeze riffled the waters of the Salt Sea, carrying the briny smell inland.

The High Priest and twelve other priests, representing the tribes of Israel stood before the congregants. The High Priest wore a tall cloth crown embroidered with precious stones. A long gold chain looped around his neck and hung to his waist. He began with a prayer directed to the Morning Star. He spoke of the light that preceded light, of the light that was the wisdom of the world, which protected the Sons of Light from Satan. He spoke of the days of Moses and the Exodus, when a pillar of smoke had accompanied them by day and a pillar of fire by night. Thus light was the protection of the pure and the enemy of sinners.

The High Priest said that as the Morning Star heralded the Sun, so Elijah would precede the Messiah, the lesser light in advance of the greater light and the greater light shining with goodness and wisdom of the Almighty. Then, as the sun began to rise above the palms on the eastern shore, the High Priest raised his hands high, so that his tall figure was silhouetted against the many-hued dawn.

"We thank thee, O Lord, who has created heaven and earth, the sun, the moon, the stars and all living things. We thank thee for giving us this day and renewing the gift of life. We ask your blessings on this congregation, and pray that we may do thy will with all our hearts, all our souls and all our might."

While the congregation murmured "Amen," the High Priest turned to them and spoke again.

"O people of the Congregation, you must seek God with a whole heart and a purified soul, and do as He has commanded, as revealed to us through Moses and the Prophets. You must love all that God has chosen and hate all that He has rejected. You must abstain from evil and hold fast to good, practice truth and righteousness on earth, and no longer stubbornly follow a sinful heart and lustful eyes."

His voice rose even higher. "To be admitted to the Covenant of Grace, you must live perfectly before God in accordance with all that has been revealed, and you must love all the Sons of Light, each according to his lot in God's design, and hate all the Sons of Darkness, each according to his guilt in God's vengeance."

The High Priest paused and looked over the congregation, gathering himself before he spoke again. "This year, as every year we must renew our commitment to the Covenant, and we shall do so every year, as long as the dominion of Satan endures."

At a sign from the High Priest, the new communicants stepped forward. "Do you agree to freely devote yourselves and all of your possessions to the Community of God, to purify your knowledge in the truth of His holy precepts? Do you promise to obey all His commandments and not to abandon Him, during the dominion of Satan because of fear, terror or affliction?"

"We promise," the communicants cried.

"Then," said the High Priest, "Together we ask the blessings of the God of Salvation and Faithfulness on all the sons of the Covenant assembled here today."

"Amen," sang the Levite Priests. "Amen, Amen," echoed the congregants.

Once again the voice of the High Priest boomed forth. "Who can measure the goodness and mercy of the Lord? His blessings have been granted unto us in generation after generation from Abraham to our time."

The Levite Priests responded, "But Israel has failed thee, O Lord. The people have fallen away from thy teaching. They have followed idols and false prophets and done iniquity. They have rebelled against thee, O Lord and followed the way of Satan."

Then, those entering the covenant cried aloud, "We have strayed! We have disobeyed! We and our fathers have sinned and done wickedly. God has judged us, but He has bestowed His bountiful mercy from everlasting to everlasting."

The High Priest raised his arms in benediction over the Community. "May God bless you with all good and preserve you from all evil. May he lighten your heart with life-giving wisdom. May he raise his face toward you for everlasting bliss."

The voices of the Levite Priests were then raised in chorus, their faces turned from the sun and towards the hills, still dark, and beyond the hills, the city and people of Jerusalem. "A curse on ye men of Satan. May He deliver you up for torture at the hands of the Avengers. May God not heed you when you call on Him, nor pardon you by blotting out your sin."

"Amen, Amen," the voices of the Congregation cried.

The priests then cursed those who pretended to join the Covenant but retained the love of Satan in their hearts.

Joshua did not hear them. He could no longer listen to the fearful curses of the priests.

6.

MESSIAH

When the Pentecost was over and the pilgrims had returned home, Qumran returned to its normal quiet existence. Now that he was employed as secretary to the Master, Joshua had full access to the library of the community. He found this a special blessing because he was seldom able to sleep anyway. It was better to read holy writ than to lie awake on his pallet and wrestle with visions of his slaughtered family.

Thus, whenever Baruch wakened in the night and found his companion gone, he smiled, knowing that Joshua was in the library, poring over manuscripts.

Joshua now read in scripture with a special purpose. For most of his life, he had heard people, ordinary people, saints and seers talk endlessly of the Messiah. Few seemed to have any real idea what this catchword meant.

Some "Messiah-seekers" seemed to envision a warrior king, a man like Saul or David, or Judas Maccabee, who would drive the heathen from the holy land.

Others conceived of the Messiah as a Priest, a holy man of the order of Melchizedek. Ari had told him that the priestly party in Jerusalem, the Sadducees, followed Deuteronomy, and expected the Messiah to be like Moses. For hadn't Moses said to the Israelites that in their time of need, "The Lord your God will raise up for you a prophet like me from among you...him you shall heed."

The "Healers," the brothers of Qumran, anticipated the coming of two Messiahs, a King and a Priest. They envisioned a war of the Sons of Light against the Sons of Darkness, but it was not clear to Joshua whether this was to be a literal, physical conflict on an earthly battlefield or a spiritual struggle of the soul. Even the Master was not clear in his explication on this issue, although the High Priest of Qumran surely had an otherworldly view.

In the synagogue at Nazareth, Joshua had absorbed the teachings of the Pharisees. These men had a broader world view than the Sadducees who would not consider a word not found in authorized scripture. Ideas propounded in other literature or hallowed by oral tradition were without merit in their fundamentalist view.

But the Pharisees believed it was of vital importance to learn from history—and not only the history recorded in the Torah, but that which had happened since. Dismayed by the struggles between priests and kings and priestly kings that had marred their nation's recent history, the Pharisees preferred to expect a powerful royal king of the line of David. They conceded that he would have a priestly forerunner, in the form of a reborn prophet Elijah. The Healers, too, had a place for Elijah, as a sign of the imminent coming of God's kingdom.

Joshua had found in the writings of the prophet Malachi, the words:

"Behold, I send my messenger to prepare the way before me, and the Lord whom you seek will suddenly come to his temple..."

And more specifically: "Behold, I will send you Elijah the prophet before the great and terrible day of the Lord comes. And he will turn the hearts of the fathers to their children and the hearts of children to their fathers...."

The masses of the people were not as particular as the brothers in the desert, or the scholars of any sect or persuasion. They wanted a Messiah—regardless of kind or type or persuasion—a man sent from God to lift the burden of their oppression and usher in the heavenly kingdom.

Joshua, himself, was all too aware of the increasing harshness of Roman rule. Time and again, the Romans had threatened to affront the people by defiling their holiest shrines. Time and again, they had imposed heavy taxes, even in years of drought and natural disasters.

Every change in government, whether in the Holy land or in Rome, was time for fresh concerns—would the new governor or emperor respect the Jews, or persecute them? Pilate, the present governor, was renowned for his hatred of the Jews. He was an irritable man, quick to anger, swift and vicious in his retribution.

Joshua knew, better than most, how capricious and cruel the Roman administration could be. He also knew that what had happened to his family was not an isolated incident. Families all over the Holy Land had suffered grievous losses at the hands of the Romans. And there was no end in sight. The Roman Emperor, Tiberius, was noted for his own personal debauched life and his cruel tastes. He was a dying man, but in his decline, he had grown even more depraved.

Little wonder that Jewish patriots had abandoned reason and negotiation and taken to the back country, there to attack the Romans when they could and make them suffer as much as they could. These Zealots hoped that, at the least, they would make the Romans pay for their atrocities. Perhaps, even, that their attacks would make the occupation so painful, the Romans would give up and withdraw. Their greatest hope was that God would intervene on their behalf and with his hand in the balance, overthrow the Roman oppressors.

To add to the pain and suffering of the Holy Land, had come a succession of disasters— great earthquakes that had shaken the land from one end to another, toppling large structures and killing men. Long, desperate droughts that stripped and eroded the land, followed by great storms, all combining to cause hunger, even starvation.

It was evident to all the people that the Last Days were at hand. The time of tribulations, spoken of by Daniel and the prophets was upon them. Could the Lord's judgment be far behind? Driven by personal suffering, the people were in a high state of agitation. Any incident was likely to arouse a disturbance and a disturbance could erupt into full-fledged conflict.

Joshua had seen all this first hand, living in Galilee, traveling to Jerusalem and Caesarea. He had heard the talk in the streets and the synagogues, seen the desecrations. Personally, he had suffered the greatest possible personal losses.

But while he had seen these signs, a part of him had denied them. He had worked at his trade, raised his family, prayed to his God and waited for outside help to save the Holy Land. Then, the blow had fallen. All that was meaningful to him had been senselessly destroyed.

He had retreated to Qumran, finding a haven from the bitterness of life. But that had given him time to think—to understand that the people, in their natural good sense, were right. All the signs were there. The evil days were reaching a climax. The hand of God was raised, ready to strike.

The hour of the Messiah could not be far behind. Now, in the brief time left, Joshua would study holy writ. He would learn to understand the Messiah. Surely, in God's holy words he would find what to expect. Then he would be ready—wherever he might be, to do his share.

That is what sent him back to the scrolls. But this was no mere intellectual exercise. Joshua felt a stirring in his soul. He had recovered his physical strength during his stay in Qumran. Now his spiritual resources must be replenished.

"I will find out who I am and what I am required to do. When I understand the Messiah, I will understand myself."

Joshua decided to put aside all he had learned from sage and seer, rabbi and teacher, friend and relative. He would read holy writ himself—that and the books of Qumran, Jubilees and Enoch, The Testaments of the Twelve Patriarchs, Baruch, and many others. He would form his image of the Messiah from these works, inspired by God. He began his search with a high sense of anticipation.

***

If some, particularly ordinary people, the farmers and shepherds, expected a warrior, Joshua thought they were misguided. From Isaiah he had learned of the Messiah, that:

"With righteousness he shall judge the poor, and decide with equity for the meek of the earth; and he shall smite the earth with the rod of his mouth, and with the breath of his lips he shall slay the wicked."

That didn't sound like a warrior to Joshua. He was reminded that Ari the sage had shown him a book called the Psalms of Solomon, from which he had learned that the King Messiah would be a righteous king who would not

"...put his trust in horse and rider and bow, nor shall he multiply unto himself gold and silver for war...For he shall smite the earth with the word of his mouth."

Ari had told him the Messiah would be free from sin and would be powerful not because he led a great army but because he "leaned upon his God."

Joshua painstakingly copied out of the books he read, all of the words and phrases, the psalms and proverbs that he thought were important. Gradually he built a picture in his mind of the Messiah. He treasured these testimonies of the Messiah that he gathered while at Qumran, and he carried them with him for the rest of his life. When times were difficult and he was overcome with despair, he would refresh his memories of the great times to come by referring to this small book he had compiled.

It did not take Joshua long to realize that the Messiah would be hated and rejected,

"Kings of the earth set themselves, and the rulers take counsel together, against the Lord and his anointed..."

"He was despised and rejected by men; a man of sorrows, and acquainted with grief; and as one from whom men hide their faces he was despised, and we esteemed him not."

"The stone which the builders rejected has become the head of the corner."

"My enemies say of me in malice: When will he die, and his name perish?... All who hate me whisper together about me;... Even my bosom friend in whom I trusted, who ate of my bread, has lifted his heel against me."

"And if one asks him, 'What are these wounds on your body?' he will say, 'The wounds I received in the house of my friends.' Awake, O sword, against my shepherd... Strike the shepherd, that the sheep may be scattered."

"For wicked and deceitful mouths are opened against me, speaking against me with lying tongues. They beset me with words of hate, and attack me without cause. In return for my love they accuse me, even as I make prayer for them. So they reward me evil for good, and hatred for my love."

The words moved Joshua greatly. As he read he felt the isolation of the Messiah, and his deep sadness. While all of Israel seemed to be crying for the Messiah, he saw that the Messiah would not be everywhere greeted with love and joy. Some would deny him, others would revile him for their own ends. The Messiah would have to be strong to withstand the hatred of his enemies. He would have to be able to bear this suffering alone, for he would not always recognize his enemy. Joshua had never been denied by friends and family, but he instinctively understood how difficult that would be. Joshua had lost his father, his wife and children. These losses were grievous, yet he still held the affection of his mother, brothers and sisters. Would he be able to go on if they turned against him?

He imagined such a loss with deep pain and he wondered if he would be strong enough to be totally alone.

Joshua continued his study, copying out the words that he found, as painful as they might be. The words began to build a pattern—a pattern of persecution, even of death.

"I gave my back to the smiters, and my cheeks to those who pulled out the beard; I hid not my face from shame and spitting."

"He was oppressed and he was afflicted, yet he opened not his mouth; like a lamb is led to the slaughter, and like a sheep that before its shearers is dumb, so he opened not his mouth. By oppression and judgment he was taken away... stricken for the transgressions of my people."

"My God, my God, why hast thou forsaken me? Why art thou so far from helping me, from the words of my groaning? O my God, I cry by day, but thou dost not answer; and by night, but find no rest... Scorned by men, and despised by the people, all who see me mock at me, saying... He committed his cause to the Lord; let him deliver him. Let him rescue him, for he delights in him... I am poured out like water, and all my bones are out of joint; my heart is like wax, it is melted within my breast... Thou dost lay me in the dust of death... Yea dogs are round me; a company of evildoers encircle me; They have pierced my hands and feet— I can count all my bones—they stare and gloat over me; they divide my garments among them, and for my raiment they cast lots."

"Insults have broken my heart, so that I am in despair. I looked for pity, but there was none, and for comforters, but I found none. They gave me poison for food, and for my thirst they gave me vinegar.

"When they look on him whom they have pierced, they shall mourn for him, as one mourns for an only child, and weep bitterly, as one weeps for a first-born."

When Joshua had compiled these testimonies, he was distressed and shaken. Tears filled his eyes. He felt the lash himself as if he personally had suffered such pain and degradation. No longer could Joshua share the naive notion that Messiah would simply appear and evil would melt away, and that thereafter Messiah would rule in God's name and that God's kingdom would be forever and ever.

The path of the Messiah would be dangerous. He would be abused and tormented. He might even have to die for his cause. And his death might prove to be humiliating, not glorious.

Joshua read and reread these testimonies, but he could see no way to escape them. The agony he felt was deeply personal, as if he, himself had suffered these things.

"Why," Joshua asked himself, "would any man choose to be the Messiah?" Then he realized it might not be a matter of choice, but of designation. The Messiah would not choose himself—God would choose the Messiah. Perhaps he would act through a man—as Samuel had anointed Saul and then David. Perhaps in Joshua's time, too, a prophet would anoint the Messiah.

Joshua recalled the story of Jonah, who had been chosen as a prophet and had fled from the Lord's election. But there was no escape. The Lord had brought Jonah back to witness to the Ninevites and, in the end, to save them. But Jonah had escaped with his life. The Messiah could not be assured of earthly deliverance.

Joshua thought about this in the silence of the night, in the library of the Community of the Healers. He was deeply touched, so sorrowful that to even think about the Messiah moved him to tears. But he could not turn away from his investigation. Joshua returned to his studies, humbled, but steadfastly searching his mind as well as scripture for the cause and course of the Anointed one of God.

Surely God would not forsake the Messiah. Though his life might be painful and could end in agony, there must be consolation.

"Though I walk in the midst of trouble, thou dost preserve my life; Thou dost stretch out thy hand against the wrath of my enemies, and thy right hand delivers me. The Lord will fulfill his promise for me; Thy steadfast love, O Lord endures forever. Do not forsake the work of thy hands."

"The cords of death encompassed me, the torrents of perdition assailed me, the cords of Sheol entangled me, the snares of death confronted me. In my distress I called upon the Lord; to my God I called for help. From his temple he heard my voice, and my cry reached his ears. Then the earth reeled and rocked; the foundations also of the mountains trembled and quaked because he was angry... The Lord also thundered in the heavens and the Most High uttered his voice, hailstones and coals of fire... Then the channels of the sea were seen, and the foundations of the world were laid bare... He reached from on high, he took me, he drew me out of many waters. He delivered me from my strong enemy, and from those that hated me."

"Come, let us return to the Lord, for he has torn, that he may heal us; he has stricken, and he will bind us up. After two days he will revive us; on the third day he will raise us up, that we may live before him."

"I keep the Lord always before me; Because he is at my right hand, I shall not be moved. Therefore my heart is glad, and my soul rejoices; my body also dwells secure. For thou dost not give me up to Sheol, or let thy godly one see the pit. Thou dost show me the path of life; in thy presence there is fullness of joy, in thy right hand are pleasures for evermore."

"For God will ransom my soul from the power of Sheol, For he will receive me."

"In thy strength the king rejoices, O Lord, and in thy help how greatly he exults! Thou hast given him his heart's desire, and has not withheld the request of his lips. Selah... For thou dost meet him with goodly blessings; thou dost set a crown of fine gold upon his head, He asked life of thee; thou gavest to him length of days for ever and ever. His glory is great through thy help; splendor and majesty thou dost bestow upon him."

Joshua's pain was released. From the depths of despair, he felt himself rise to elation, even to ecstasy. The Lord would not abandon his anointed. The Messiah would be abused, tormented, viciously tortured, perhaps even killed. But God would give him triumph over death. That was the Baptizer consolation.

Joshua wept again, but this time with tears of joy. The way of the Messiah would be painful, but God would not let his anointed go into the pit. The Lord would redeem him and He would rule for ever and ever.

Joshua smiled at his small book of prophecy. It was not a tale of defeat, but of victory; not of death but of life everlasting. He clutched the pages tightly in his hands and prayed to God:

"Thank you Lord, for your wisdom and strength, for the blessings of your word and the triumph of your love."

"I will be ready," he told himself. But then a voice within asked, "When will the Messiah come?"

Joshua could not find the answer in his book of testimonies. There was no doubt that the agony of Israel was great and the suffering of her people cried out for release. Surely God would not long continue the torment of his Chosen People. It was true that some had fallen away from God, but many more, especially the ordinary peasants and farmers, the shepherds and craftsmen, were God-fearing and law-abiding.

When Pilate had sought to raise the ensigns on the Temple proclaiming Caesar as Emperor and God, thousands had spontaneously marched to Caesarea to seek their removal.

When Pilate had scorned the people as a mob and threatened to punish them, they had offered their throats to the sword, choosing to be slaughtered rather than disobey the word of God. Surely a people as devout as the Jews, deserved the healing grace of divine intervention.

Yes, Joshua felt deep in his bones that the Messiah would soon come, that even now his goodness and justice must be on the way.

A thought struck him: Elijah must come before the Messiah. Baruch had said to him—with a laugh—that some said the giant preacher, Johannon, was Elijah reborn. Miriam, Jacob and Judith had been so moved they had accepted remission of sins and cleansing from him. Their action was spontaneous—was he, Joshua, guilty of too much reflection?

He ought to have spoken to Johannon at greater length, questioned him more closely. Was it significant that Johannon preached and immersed the repentants along the Jordan, from the very place where Elijah had been translated to heaven? He would have to ponder these things.

Setting aside his testimonies, Joshua felt he had completed a difficult but necessary work. Looking back over the texts, he had laboriously copied out, he felt as though he had suffered with the Messiah himself, but then had been lifted up and shared in his glory.

That night he returned to his cave lodging and slept better than he had on any night since he had reached Qumran.

7.

CHALLENGE

Joshua had returned to the office of the Master late one evening to file some documents and copy a manuscript when he heard the voices.

"I tell you there's no other way."

"I don't agree. I think you're making a grave error."

Joshua hesitated, but by then the Master had seen him and gestured that he should come forward.

The Master sat at his worktable, hands flat on the surface, as if he were keeping it from leaping up into his face—or preparing himself for a vault into the future.

On the other side, two familiar men faced each other. One was Johannon, wearing his usual skins and sandals, flowing hair and beard and peeling, sun-baked skin. He stood hands on hips, feet spread widely, facing Judas, the Galilean.

Judas's appearance had changed. He had allowed his hair to grow and brushed it forward so that it spilled over his forehead. Also, he had grown a rough beard and untrimmed mustache that almost completely covered the tell-tale scar on his cheek.

Judas was trying to poke a finger into Johannon's face, merely to make a point. But he was too short and the Baptizer too tall. Johannon could have enclosed Judas's head within one hairy hand.

Neither man paid any attention to Joshua, who picked up the documents from the edge of the desk and began sorting them on the shelves that lined the room.

"It's no good, Johannon," Judas was saying. "You can stand in your damn Jordan until judgment day and you can dip them from morning till night, but you'll never free the Jews."

"I do what the Lord tells me," Johannon said. He spoke rather mildly, but the room wasn't built for his size and scale, and even at low key, the words bounded and echoed in circles. "The Lord says the end is near—save who you can. I'm doing that, my friend, and I'll continue to do it as long as the Lord wants me to."

"Did the Lord tell you to attack the Ethnarch, Herod Antipas?" The Master had spoken, but his hands still rested on the table.

Johannon looked at him as if he had been betrayed. "The man had no right to marry Herodias—she was his brother Philip's wife. You know that as well as I do, Master. You're a better student of scripture than I am."

The Master shook his head. "It's a technical question," he said.

"God's law is not technical," Johannon boomed.

"Nor is Herod's anger," Judas said. "Aretas, the Arabian King, is angry enough that Herod discarded his daughter—let HIM punish Herod. Why do you mix yourself in this business?"

"I do what I must," Johannon answered. "To turn your face from evil is to be guilty of it."

"And when the Arabians march north and drag us all into war, what will you say then?" The Master rose to his feet as he spoke.

"I see," Johannon said. "You're not concerned for God's word. You're worried the Arabs may march through here and upset your daily schedule."

"I am responsible for one hundred and twenty men—at festivals, hundreds more—the faithful remnant of Israel."

"Of course," Judas said, "I, too, am responsible for many men. I understand your position and support you. Johannon is responsible only for himself."

Joshua could not complete his work with three men circling the Master's desk. He would have retired from the room, gracefully, if he could, but now his path to the door was blocked.

Johannon was about to respond to Judas in righteous anger when the Master raised his hands. "What's done, Johannon, is done. There is nothing we can do to change it. Frankly, I believe the dangers to you from Herod may equal the dangers to Qumran from Aretas."

Johannon smiled and shrugged his shoulders. He knew nothing of fear and would never have considered tempering his words for any man.

Judas returned to the matter which had brought him to Qumran. "The danger to all of us from Roman domination is far greater than Herod or Aretas. I must have your help, Master."

The Master began to pace in the brief strip behind his desk. There were lines in his brow that Joshua had never seen before. "I'm sorry, Judas, but I can't permit you to store arms in all the camps of the brothers—especially, I can't permit you to store them here."

"Face the truth," Judas said. "The Last Times are upon us. The enemy grows more evil every day. Violence against the Jews is a commonplace occurrence. Only I and others like me, who are armed and ready, can save the nation."

The Master stopped pacing. "Roman spies are everywhere. Herod's spies are almost as numerous."

"We'll bring the weapons at night."

"We store the word of God here, not swords and spears."

"That's why Qumran is perfect. No one will believe that you keep weapons out here in the desert."

"If the weapons are found, they'll slaughter us—Romans, Herodians, all of them."

"You're going to be slaughtered if you don't protect yourself."

"God will protect us," Johannon cried.

"Amen," said the Master.

Judas bit his lip and calmed himself. "There are hundreds of us, thousands of us, all over the land. Like the Maccabees, we wait for the right moment. We'll arise in every city and when we do, God will help us. Better to die as freemen than be butchered as slaves."

"Do you believe God wants the people to be butchered?" Joshua asked. He had listened in silence as long as he could. Then, the bickering had gotten to him.

The others looked at him, surprised that he had spoken. Judas, who had hardly looked in his direction, now realized this was the man who had saved his life. He wanted to say something, but Joshua, flushed with anger was still talking.

"The people of Israel are not depraved or evil. They are simple, kind and good. And it is the people who will die in any war. Does God want that? NO, God doesn't want the people to die. He wants them to live. Is it the people who have failed? NO, it's their leaders. Do I hear you offer to sacrifice yourselves for the people? NO, you want them to sacrifice themselves for you."

"That's not true—" Judas was saying.

But Joshua wasn't finished. "Do you think the Lord has his favorites? That you or I are to be saved, but the mass of mankind is to die? Is that what the Lord created us for? NO, the Lord God wants us all to live. The

Lord God wants to save us all. The Lord God wants us all to share in His heavenly kingdom.

"It's not a righteous few, or a 'precious remnant' who are to be saved. It is all of mankind. And it is the sacred responsibility of the Jews to be a priestly nation, to witness to the world and to make certain that all—Jews and Gentiles alike, will share in the heavenly kingdom."

Joshua's words rang in the room. The Master, The Zealot and the Immerser were all silent. They had heard the truth and they did not doubt it.

Joshua's passion still ran high. "The Messiah will come. Even now he treads the Holy soil of Holy Israel. God will fulfill his promise and we will have the Messiah, not because we deserve it, not because we have earned it, but only when we are ready to accept it.

"God not only chose Israel—ISRAEL CHOSE GOD.

"That is our secret. God offered his word to all the world, and only the Jews accepted. We are righteous and holy only if we choose to be righteous and holy.

"I tell you that God not only chooses the prophets, but the PROPHETS CHOOSE GOD. Isaiah heard the voice of the Lord saying 'Whom shall I send, and who will go for us?' And then Isaiah said, 'Here am I! Send me.'

"So it must be with the Messiah. We will have the Messiah only when we choose to be the Messiah."

Joshua's voice filled the small room and vibrated in the heads of the men assembled there. They saw him as they had not seen him before. They listened in awe and they knew they had heard words they had not heard before. He was taller now and his back was straighter. His jaw was firmer and his eyes commanding.

Joshua knew that he was changed as well. He no longer saw the Master, Johannon or Judas. He had begun to see his destiny. When he walked from the room, Johannon and Judas stepped aside to let him pass.

8.

VISITORS

They came on foot in the middle of the night, a band of perhaps thirty men, women and children. Joshua became aware of them when they were still far off. He had been awake, thinking of his encounter with the Master, Johannon and Judas. He was waiting only for dawn, when he would gather his few belongings, say his goodbyes and depart. But then, knowing of the travelers, he wakened Baruch.

"How do you know?" Baruch asked, irritated at being awakened and straining his ears, but hearing nothing.

"You must trust me," Joshua said.

Reluctantly, Baruch got to his feet. "Enemies?"

"No," Joshua said.

Baruch was so tired he didn't think to ask how Joshua could be certain. But he awakened some of the brothers—and after deciding not to disturb the Master over so questionable an enterprise—they set a watch at the northern end of the settlement.

In a few minutes, Joshua's words proved true, as a group of weary travelers arrived at the outpost. They carried no food, little water and were without weapons except for the typical small knives most men carried.

"What do you want?" one of the brothers asked.

The leader, a bulky, muscular bald man called Aaron spoke in blunt words. "Food, water, rest."

"We're not an inn."

"Some call you the 'pious ones.'" Aaron said. "Surely you won't turn away your starving brothers and sisters."

The men of the community hesitated.

Aaron's voice broke. "The children haven't eaten in days."

"Of course we'll feed you," Joshua said, unable to accept the hesitation of the others. He gestured firmly and the band followed him into the dining hall.

Baruch was agitated. "Joshua," he said, "I don't think the Master—"

But Joshua wasn't paying any attention. Some of the brothers hurried to the storeroom to find bread and vegetables, wine and water. Others milled about, frightened and confused.

Joyfully, the travelers seated themselves at the plain wooden tables, eagerly tearing the bread and stuffing it into their mouths, tilting the water-skins and sending the cool water pouring down their throats. Aaron, speaking between gulps of food, told how an outbreak of violence between Zealots and Roman soldiers near Jericho had driven them from their homes. They had heard that the Essenes of Qumran might help them.

The children were laughing and giggling, the mothers smiling, the fathers busily and methodically eating.

"WOMEN!" A powerful voice boomed through the room. Immediately, the room was silent. Even the children stopped laughing.

The Master stood before them, his pale face darkened with anger, his hands shaking as he spoke. "Out," he said. "Out of here at once!"

The travelers looked uncertainly from the Master to Joshua and the other brothers.

"Master," said Baruch, his face showing pain and confusion. "They are hungry and we are feeding them."

The Master turned on Baruch, his eyes flashing with anger. "You know that women are not allowed within these walls—not here in the Hall of Congregation. We came here to avoid the world of corruption and evil."

"Man is born of woman," Joshua said stolidly, trying to keep his rising anger under control.

"In pain and in sin!" The Master thundered.

Aaron rose to his feet. "Don't quarrel over us. We thank you for the food and drink. We'll leave at once." He beckoned to his followers, who rose reluctantly, some still pushing food into their mouths.

"I can't believe you will send them away," Joshua said.

"They are leaving of their own free will," the Master responded. He stared at Joshua, unblinking, confident of his own righteousness.

But Joshua did not waver. He stared fixedly at the Master, who spoke again, in softer tones." Give them food to carry with them," he said.

Baruch and the brothers helped the travelers carry quantities of bread and vegetables with them as they filed out of the room.

Soon the travelers had left the building and moved away from the grounds of the settlement. Joshua and Baruch walked with them for a short distance, directing them to nearby caves where they could rest, out of the night cold and dew.

"Forgive him," Joshua told Aaron.

Aaron smiled. "Perhaps we'll be safe farther south."

***

At first light, Joshua put away his pallet and gathered his few possessions.

"Don't leave, Joshua," Baruch said, his usually jolly face buried in a wrinkled frown. "You're needed here."

Joshua smiled. "A good carpenter can always find work."

"The Master respects you. I'm sure he wants you to stay."

"For a long time, I was tempted. It seemed pleasant to hide here and be spared human pain and affliction. But that was a foolish and unworthy desire. I'm rid of it now."

"I, too, was troubled by what the Master did last night. But he has great wisdom. The Master—He knows things we don't know."

"What the Master did tonight is not the only reason I'm leaving. I have a mission to fulfill. The Master has only proven what I had already learned: that my mission cannot be fulfilled here." He laid a fond hand on the shoulder of Baruch. "You love and trust the Master, Baruch. But it's more important to love and trust God."

"The Master is the chosen of God."

Joshua was silent.

"Why?" asked Baruch. "Why don't you believe it?"

"God doesn't limit his blessings only to men or only to women. He is not the property of the Jews and therefore inaccessible to the Romans. He is the Master of all, whether we acknowledge him or not."

"But some people are good and some evil."

"All are the children of the one God. The brothers are righteous men and claim to love the Lord, but they wish to exclude others from His mercy. God is the God of all creation."

Impulsively, Baruch grabbed Joshua's arm. "Bless me, Joshua."

"Only the Lord can bless you."

"Bless me in the name of the Lord."

Joshua looked into his earnest eyes and felt the need to satisfy Baruch's request. "May the blessings of the Lord be upon you, now and forever."

"Amen," said Baruch and then, surprising both of them, he fell on his knees before Joshua.

Joshua quickly pulled him to his feet, something close to anger in his eyes. "Man must kneel only before God."

"I understand," Baruch said, his eyes fixed on Joshua's.

9.

BAPTISM

The Joshua who walked purposefully north along the Jordan gave the outward appearance of having regained his youth. During the months he had spent with The Healers, his skin had grown taut again and color had returned to his hair and eyes. He walked with a firm tread, confident that his way would soon be revealed to him.

The inner man had aged considerably and changed greatly. Joshua had faithfully lived the life of the solitary carpenter and then of the family man. The rewards had been many and he had enjoyed them, but disaster had overtaken him, had shown him he was not an ordinary man and that he could not live an ordinary life. He loved his wife and children. Even now he could not think of them without feeling a terrible twisting in his heart. They had played a part in his life that could not be erased, that would not be forgotten. He had gained, through joy and bitterness, an understanding of the frailty of life and the fragile blessings of human companionship. These lessons would remain with him.

In the night, he still saw the faces of Rebecca, Sarah and David, still felt the spasms of pain and loss. His consolation, the object of desperate prayer, was that his loved ones were with the Father. He believed that, passionately. He could not have gone on living if he had not believed it.

The evil face of Septimus had begun to fade, and with it, the urge to kill. Sometimes, in darkness, he questioned his own courage—his sense of justice in sparing the man.

"Oh, God," he prayed fervently, "tell me if I have done your will."

There was no direct answer, and yet there was no condemnation. He would wrestle with the question, as Jacob had wrestled with the angel, and like Jacob he would not give up. Septimus would be punished, of that he was certain, but punishment belonged to the Lord.

Even though he had been cut off from his family, his stay with the Healers had taught him a seemingly contradictory lesson: he must reject a life totally apart from his fellow creatures. That was not the answer, human or spiritual. He was saddened that a man as enlightened as the Master failed to understand the teachings of God. Joshua prayed he would not forget the lesson either—if it is difficult to lead a spiritual life among men, it is impossible to do so without them.

As Joshua strode along the river bank, he became increasingly aware of the sights and sounds around him. It was near harvest time and the waters of the Jordan were at their lowest. Joshua walked on ground that had been covered by the torrent months earlier. The meaning of this was not lost on him.

He heard a rumbling sound, almost like thunder, but the sky was clear. Again, he heard the same sound, but this time it was even louder. His path along the Jordan led directly towards the reverberating echoes.

"It's a voice," he realized suddenly and just as suddenly he knew whose voice it must be. He smiled and quickened his pace.

The sun was falling rapidly and the Judaean hills were silhouetted clearly against the sky. Ahead, on a gentle rise of land above the Jordan, stood a tall man with arms outstretched, surrounded by a group of listeners: Johannon, called as Joshua had learned, "The Baptizer." Johannon's voice rose and fell, sending waves of sound pulsing into the ether. The rumbles were like thunder, but as Joshua drew closer, the rumbles defined themselves and became words and phrases.

"There is but one God and ye have pretended there are many. You think the sun is a god and the moon. You pray to trees and animals—even dogs and swine.

"You ask the Lord's blessing from carved sticks and lumps of clay, from modeled marble and sculptured stone.

"GOD IS NOT A STICK OR A STONE. You cannot be blessed by dead trees or slaughtered animals. Only the Living God has the power to bless you and save your souls.

"God has watched you in your fornication with false gods. He has been patient with your abominations. BUT HIS PATIENCE IS AT AN END. THE WRATH OF GOD IS COMING.

Not one of you will be spared. REPENT. REPENT NOW WHILE THERE IS STILL TIME."

Johannon leaped suddenly into the crowd and grabbed a young man by the front of his tunic. "You cannot hide from the Living God. He knows your every thought.

"Come, Lad, into the river. ASK GOD FOR FORGIVENESS. NOW, this very moment. Together, we'll wash away your sins."

But the young man twisted out of the giant's grasp and scrambled away, falling down the hill, head over heels, then jumping up and running off.

"You cannot escape the Lord!" Johannon cried after him, and the hills echoed back, "You cannot escape the Lord!"

A group of men in rich robes and barbered beards snickered at the sight of the young man hurrying off.

Johannon turned on them, and his eyes were deep and cold. "Why do you laugh, you generation of vipers."

The well-dressed men stopped laughing, affronted by Johannon's words.

"Do you know who you are talking to?" one man said, a man of considerable size himself, not intimidated by the huge form of "The Baptizer."

"Do I know—" Johannon broke off and stepped closer. He took the tunic of the speaker in his hand and pulled the man toward him as if he were a bag of dirty clothes. He raised his head and bellowed into the sky, "Son of Man, prophesy against the shepherds of Israel."

He looked into the face of the man whose tunic he held and said, "You are a shepherd, you and those like you. As God told Ezekiel, God tells me, 'Speak against the shepherds.'" He shoved the man back until he fell against his friends. They supported him, but they fell back, even more frightened, as Johannon advanced toward them.

"Shepherds of Israel, you have been feeding yourselves instead of the sheep. You eat the fat, you clothe yourselves in wool, you slaughter the fatlings, BUT YOU DO NOT FEED THE SHEEP."

Johannon advanced again, and again the men fell back, startled, frightened, wanting to run, but caught between their dignity and their fear.

"The weak you have not strengthened," Johannon said, "the sick you have not healed, the crippled you have not bound up, the strayed you have not brought back, the lost you have not sought."

He paused and his look swept across the crowd. "As I live, says the Lord God, I AM AGAINST THE SHEPHERDS!"

It was too much for the well-dressed men. They broke and ran, scurrying over the hill even faster than the young man, while the people who remained, laughed aloud.

Johannon was not finished. He turned to the crowd that had laughed, enjoying the fear of the wealthy ones who had run away.

LEN LAMENSDORF

"As for you my flock...I will judge between sheep and sheep." They were silent, waiting, watching to see if his wrath had turned on them.

Johannon spoke intensely, but with less anger. Joshua watched and listened, marveling as the man picked and chose his words from scripture, words that Joshua himself had committed to memory.

"Is it not enough for you to feed on the good pasture, that you tread down with your feet the rest of your pasture; and to drink of clear water, that you must foul the rest with your feet?"

They sighed and looked at one another. Could he mean them? But they were humble men, how could it be?

Johannon rumbled on. "Because you push with side and shoulder, and thrust at all the weak with your horns..."

No, the crowd thought, shaking their heads, no.

"Yes," Johannon cried. "I mean you. You live in your iniquity and you do not see it. But God sees it."

Joshua was moved by Johannon's sincerity and touched by his passion. He lingered, feeling a stirring within.

Johannon looked up and saw Joshua and a great smile creased his face. He lifted his hands toward Joshua. "I knew you would come."

Joshua walked down the hill and the Baptizer came splashing out of the water. They embraced on the shore. "They tell me we're related," Johannon said, "but I don't know if it's true."

"Who told you that?"

"Your friend, Ari the Sage, years ago. He told me to watch you—that you would do wonderful deeds."

Joshua smiled. "Ari was a good and kind man and he taught me a great deal about scripture."

The crowd on the hill had drifted down to where Johannon stood talking with Joshua. The Baptizer seemed to have forgotten them, just when many were about to follow him into the Jordan. They were curious as to what he found so interesting about Joshua.

"I'm sorry about your family," Johannon said.

Joshua stiffened and his expression changed. Johannon touched his arm gently. "That won't do, my friend. Today, you're going to put that behind you."

Joshua hesitated. "How did you know I would come?"

"I knew you would leave the Essenes, just as I did, years ago. They're a good-hearted bunch, but too full of themselves. The old boy especially. He

218

loves it when they whisper loudly that he's the Messiah." Johannon roared with laughter and Joshua couldn't help joining him.

Johannon's look grew serious. "You're the one I've been waiting for."

"Are you certain?"

Johannon nodded. "Come with me to the river."

Joshua smiled. "I'm ready," he said, holding out his hand to Johannon.

Johannon turned, leading Joshua with him. The giant's grip was strong, but Joshua could have pulled away if he had wanted to. The crowd parted to let them pass. It was getting darker every minute as the sun plunged behind the hills in the west. The people in the crowd had to peer closely to make out the fine features and fair hair of Johannon's friend.

Joshua's heart beat faster with every step. They walked into the Jordan, side by side. The bottom was soggy and slippery and they had to be careful of their footing. When they were knee deep, Johannon stopped and raised his head to the heavens, eyes closed.

"God, I come before you humbly, leading this man who is far more important to you than I am. I have not the right to absolve him from sin—that right belongs to you alone. I believe that his spirit is pure—as pure as any I have ever known. Yet, even so, he must repent and be cleansed in the river. That is required by your law and his need. I am but your instrument.

"I do not know your sins," Johannon said. "That is between you and God Almighty. But YOU know your sins. Do you repent them—here and now, before the living God?"

Many images rushed through Joshua's mind. He nodded vigorously. "I do," He said. "With all my heart I repent my sins!"

With that Johannon gripped Joshua by both shoulders and peered deeply into his eyes. What he saw startled and nearly staggered him. Then he dug deep in himself for all his resources of strength and love and plunged Joshua into the cold waters.

For an instant, it was like death. Joshua felt the Jordan close above his head and he stared blindly into the murky darkness. Johannon held him there until his lungs were bursting, until his life seemed to tremble within him. The faces of his family raced past him and disappeared. They were gone—dead and gone. Now, he too was dead.

A silent cry came from his heart to God to help him, to save him. But Johannon still held him firmly below the water and the world went black. Then he was released and Johannon lifted him from the Jordan. Joshua's eyes flew open and he gasped gratefully for breath. A dove, white and soft, fluttered down out of the darkness, lighted on his shoulder for a brief moment and then seemed to melt into the sky. A fresh wind came up. The touch of the dove sent a rush of love deep into Joshua's heart and he inhaled deeply of the divine wind.

The sun, angling between the hills found an opening that sent a blazing shaft of light into the sky, illuminating the heavens with bright glowing beams more like dawn than sunset. The light struck Joshua as forcefully as a physical blow, and he felt his illusions drop away, and the light of God's wisdom search and fill his heart and mind.

The people on the shore stared in awe at this celestial demonstration and at the dove, a white shadow that soared across the heavens. Johannon didn't see the unearthly display. His eyes were fixed on Joshua's eyes. They opened suddenly, bright and clear as the sun's rays they reflected. The film of death was gone. "I'm free," he whispered. "In the image of God, I am."

"You are reborn," Johannon responded. And indeed, he knew that he himself, had been reborn as well.

10.

ZEALOTS

Judas left Qumran is a state of high excitement. His men were waiting at the edge of the Judaean hills, but he scarcely greeted them. That was unlike Judas. Despite his prodigious anger and unpredictable humors, he was careful—no, suspicious—and he seldom met a man or group of men without inspecting them carefully. Even in the case of men he had known his whole life, he would not assume that a brief absence was unlikely to create a change. Instead, he would peer cautiously into the eyes of the other, note his nervousness or lack of it, the manner of his dress and the words he used. As far as Judas could tell, it would only take a man an instant to change from a friend to an enemy.

But this time he was distracted. His men saw it at once and were concerned. But he quickly climbed into the saddle of the horse they had waiting for him and led them at high speed across the bleak Judaean Hills. This was a wasteland of undulating, round-topped hills, studded with rocks and unrelieved by vegetation. The sound of the ground beneath the horses' hooves was metallic, guttural, ominous. They had passed this way a hundred times, and there never was any relief. The terrain was harsh, but also dangerous. From any direction, crossing any wadi, they might find Roman cavalry hidden, waiting and ready. There was no place to hide, no protected route through this region, nor any friendly village or way station.

Occasionally they saw Arab sheepherders, grazing their animals on—nothing, or so it seemed. But the Arabs had committed the land to memory. They could quote it as easily as a scribe could quote Torah. They knew where there was water, where there was no water—where there was grass and where there was no grass. They knew when grass would break through the earth and when it would dry up.

The Arabs were not dangerous. They had no politics and wanted none. They heard Judas and his troop miles off and could tell they were not a risk. They didn't even look up when the horses thundered past.

Judas smiled for the first time that day. The feel of the horse beneath him was good, especially because the horse had been stolen from a Roman officer and it was a splendid animal. Trained and toughened, it bore him easily over long distances and though it might break a pouring sweat, it would recover quickly. For years, he had walked this land, making fifteen or twenty hard miles in a day. Now he could travel three times as far and be better rested.

The men riding with Judas were much like him, tough, hard-bitten men of strong faith. They had been farmers or artisans, independent men who could not stand to have others tell them what to do. They would have had problems even in ordinary times, getting along with any administration, even a Jewish one. To be under the rule of Jews was bad enough, but to be ordered about by heathen Romans, swine eaters, drunkards and whoremongers was impossible. Their vision was narrow, but clear. Their patience was limited, but their tolerance for pain and deprivation extraordinary. They could ride all day and fight all night, then ride again and fight again. They knew how to live off the land and how to build and make the things they needed to live. They were hardy and self-sufficient—and God-fearing. Their days began and ended with prayer. Every meal was an occasion for prayer. They observed the Sabbath, except when Roman soldiers kept them from it and they observed every festival with devotion.

They were naturally as suspicious as Judas. Most farmers are suspicious. They learn that God gives and takes away and that one can never know how or when. The land that yields gladly one year will turn bitter the next. The river that flows freely this spring is dry by fall and gone thereafter. The sun is both friend and enemy. Only God endures. And the land, if God wills it.

Still, they trusted Judas. His father and grandfather before him had been rebels. Both had died for the cause, and Judas had come close to death himself, many times. He never complained. He asked nothing of his men he would not do himself. He played no favorites. He never tired.

Judas rode like a farmer, not a soldier, slouched instead of erect, reins low instead of high. His eyes checked the terrain with a practiced eye, but his true vision was elsewhere.

"Joshua," he heard in his head. And again, "Joshua." The horses' hooves seemed to sound the word, every time they struck ground.

***

"I tell you he's our man," Judas said. He spat the coarse bread particle into his hand, then shoved it back in his mouth and fought it again.

Amos stared at him, disliking Judas for his coarse ways, liking him for his truthfulness. Amos was a merchant. He sold cloth on the street of the cloth-makers in the lower city of Jerusalem. That was his worldly business. He had another. He was a rebel. Amos was one of several who controlled Zealot bands based in the city. Today, Josiah the fuller and Benjamin the tanner were in his house. An unlikely meeting place and an unlikely meeting. Amos and Josiah, Benjamin and Judas agreed on one thing—the Romans must be driven from the land. They all believed this passionately, so passionately they would have given their lives, if necessary, to accomplish it. But they could not agree on how or when this was to be done.

Their lives were more dangerous even than the bands that roamed the countryside with the same goal. Amos, Josiah and Benjamin operated in the Holy City itself, liable always to surprise, to betrayal and to death. Even Jews could not always be trusted. The Sadducees—mostly higher priests, rich merchants and the aristocracy, were doing well under Roman rule and they feared any who might interfere with their wealth and power. On the road, the rebels could attack a Roman column, rob a customs-house and disappear into the forests. In Jerusalem, so many were watching, it was difficult to know who was a friend and who an enemy. Thus, for a variety of reasons, their activities were far more dangerous, not only for them, but for the city itself and the mass of its peaceful inhabitants. A wrong step by the rebel leaders and innocent people might suffer. They had to curb their anger and use more subtle tactics. Roman provisions might be tainted or spoiled, Roman functionaries might be hurt or killed in apparent "accidents." Roman rules might be frustrated or thwarted, but not so as to cause undue suffering to their countrymen.

On all of these matters, Amos, Josiah and Benjamin were in agreement. They also were in full agreement that the Jews must rise, not just in small groups, but as a nation, simultaneously, all over the land. Then God would help them, then the Romans would be driven out.

"We agree," Amos had said, "but we have no strategy. My men are so strong-minded, it is difficult to get them to arrive at the same place at the same time—how can we organize a rebellion?"

All of them said the same thing more or less. They had fought stubbornly but with little effect. They lived on determination not hope, on scriptural assurance, not day-dreams.

Amos said nothing, nor did the others. Judas surveyed them again, thinking, "Lord, why have you given me these men to work with? Why this addition to my penance?" But he said no such thing. "I tell you," he said again, "he's our man."

"A carpenter?" Amos said.

"From Galilee?" Benjamin said. He was beginning to wonder about Judas.

"He's tall and strong and very imposing in appearance—blonde hair and blue eyes—"

"—A Jew?" Josiah asked. "He sounds like a foreigner."

"A Jew," Judas said. "Devout, and he knows scripture with the perfection of the High Priest."

"What was he doing in Qumran?" Josiah asked.

"Recovering. The Romans killed his wife and children at Beth Sholem."

The men were moved. Tough though they were, all had families, all loved their families. This was the kind of atrocity they aimed to root out.

"You must hear him speak," Judas said. "He has the power of Johannon, the Baptizer, and the grace of old Nicodemus, the former priest."

"We need soldiers," Benjamin said, "not talkers."

"You're wrong, Benjamin. Very wrong," Judas said. "We need a man who is brave enough to be a soldier, learned enough to be a priest, strong enough to suffer any loss and powerful enough to lead the people—We need the Messiah."

Amos laughed. "This blonde man from Nazareth—this is the Messiah?"

But even as he laughed, Amos saw Judas's brows gather over his eyes, like storm clouds over a heavy sea, and the smile left his face.

"Do you think I'm a fool? Do you believe this is easy to say? I tell you there is something about this Joshua, different from any man I have ever met. When he spoke, I was rooted to the ground—I could hardly blink my eyes. When I listened to him, I heard the truth."

The others exchanged glances. Whatever their thoughts about Judas, his rudeness and occasional fits of anger, he was not an easy man to fool.

"He saved my life," Judas said. "He found me bleeding to death and he healed my wounds. My life was pouring out of me"—he touched his chest where only a thin line remained—"and I was healed. Almost instantly."

Amos didn't like such talk. "The highways are clogged with healers—magicians, charlatans, frauds."

"This was no trick," Judas said, rising up and advancing on Amos. He ripped open his shirt and grabbed Amos's hand, running it along the thin scar. "A Roman broadsword—here—deep as a hand— blood spurting— and then it was gone—GONE! You see, a thin line, enough so I'll remember. He took no credit, mumbled no strange incantations. He fell on his knees and thanked God."

"On his knees?" Josiah asked.

"I said he was the Messiah," Judas said. "Not God."

"Who has anointed him?" Benjamin asked. He wasn't convinced, but it was an exciting thought. The Messiah. Surely, it was time.

Judas looked about the room. "Johannon immersed him—but God, the Living God has anointed him."

11.

THE BROTHERS

Johannon sat on a rock by a small fire along the banks of the Jordan. Since he ate only raw foods, the fire was not for cooking and it was too small to give much warmth. But that meant little to the Baptizer. He usually slept in the open, regardless of the season. Occasionally, if it wasn't too far out of his way, he might stay in a cave, but generally he preferred the open sky. It made him feel closer to God. He liked the light of the fire, the flicker of it in the dark sky. He saw visions in the flames and he liked the visions.

Two men sat on the ground watching Johannon in companionable silence. The eldest was Simon, a young man with very broad shoulders and heavily muscled arms. His waist was very small compared to his chest and his legs were almost thin, but very powerful.

Compared to any man but Johannon, Simon would have seemed large and powerful, but standing next to the Baptizer he was dwarfed. It was in part Johannon's size that attracted Simon to him—the same affinity that large men often feel for each other. For such men, people of average size don't seem to be worthy opponents. There's little profit and no glory in challenging them. Therefore, the large man welcomes and values a sizeable opponent—as his natural friend.

Simon was far from handsome. His head was large and his face heavily lined despite his youth. His jaw jutted alarmingly behind a short black beard. His brows were a heavy black rope wound over far-seeing brown eyes that might turn black at any moment. Simon's nose was prominent and broken in the middle and his hair curled like iron around his head. He was not a man to trifle with.

Netzer, sometimes called Andrew, Simon's younger brother, looked like him, but was smaller and slimmer. He was wiry where Simon was wide, and his actions and movements were almost bird-like. He often moved his head sharply, hearing sounds or sensing movements about him. But he was very strong for his size and his energy was exceptional.

The brothers spoke in one of the more common Galilean dialects. Simon was the more articulate of the two and there was a rich sing-song quality to his voice that others found compelling. Simon was not a man to use his voice as a weapon, knowingly. He didn't always realize how often his melodious speech had spared him from violence.

There was a great closeness, a harmony between the brothers. When they fished the Sea of Galilee, they worked in silence, anticipating and understanding the other's needs. Simon, with his powerful arms could sling a net as far and as gracefully as any man. Andrew could repair their nets and sails with the skills of a woman.

They knew the lake completely and perfectly—the warm spots where fish would gather in winter, the cool shadows where they hid in summer. Simon and Andrew worked in harmony with the lake and the seasons. They never fought the elements, but yielded to them and lived within them. They had no fear, even when unexpected storms stirred the waters into a raging sea and clouds and fog dropped to the very surface. They sailed with skill and ease and they swam like the catfish they both prized.

They first heard the Baptizer speaking at a shallow ford not far from the narrow funnel where the lake emptied into the Jordan, at a place known as Bethabara. Johannon boomed his message of repentance and forgiveness and the end of the world. He spoke plainly and he lived plainly and he was full of the love of God.

The two fishermen could sense that in their bones. They were simple and that was their strength. Hearing his voice rippling over the lake on a calm day, projecting from the place where he stood downriver, they had poled into shore and beached their boat. They followed his voice and hunkered down on the bank a distance from the crowd. The voice they heard was wise and compelling. They ignored the screams and cries from the people who watched and listened and were immersed in the water.

Simon and Andrew didn't talk to each other, didn't discuss the wisdom or purpose of what they had heard. Andrew was all too aware that he had been involved with a Perean girl from the other side of the lake. His mother, had she known, would never have approved. He was feeling a little guilty about that, especially since the girl had shown him the little wooden god she worshipped, one she claimed looked like Andrew. It had a large member and Andrew had blushed at the sight. The girl hadn't blushed at all and when she drew Andrew into her house, he found that his own member did indeed resemble the wooden one.

Simon was married and he was faithful to his wife. But he had other matters on his mind. His mother's eldest brother, his favorite uncle, had been killed by Roman soldiers for no apparent reason. Simon had learned of the killing weeks after the event and after exploding in a rage of pain and anger, he had wanted to find the villains and avenge his uncle. He didn't know where to start and after a while he had given up the thought. He felt guilty even though he didn't know precisely who had murdered his relative.

Now, listening to Johannon, he sensed there was another way.

The brothers waited until dozens had been baptized, darkness had fallen and the crowd had returned to town. The Baptizer waded to shore and flung himself on his back, his skin a bit crinkled from exposure to the water.

Andrew, smiling, shyly handed Johannon a plump catfish.

Johannon sat up and smiled. He saw at once they were brothers and fishermen and sincere.

"Thanks, my friend, but I don't eat the stuff."

Andrew blinked. "You don't like catfish? We can get you some—"

Johannon laughed. "—Don't eat fish or fowl or meat. Only moving thing are locusts and nobody seems to miss them. Most of the time, just nuts and berries and honey, if the bees are agreeable."

Simon stared at him, wondering how he stayed so large on such a small diet.

"Don't worry," the Baptizer said. "I'm strong as a bull."

They hunkered down near him, looking at him and not knowing what to say. Johannon knew enough to keep quiet.

After a while, Simon spoke for the two of them. "We want to repent and then be purified by you. Can we come back at dawn?"

Johannon smiled. "No need," he said. "It works in the night just as well as the day."

He stood up and took their hands and led them into the water. He thought he'd have to say something, but Simon spoke out, loudly. "We're poor sinners, Father. Just a pair of fisherman and we repent all the evil things we've done."

"Me, too," Andrew said, moving his head about sharply.

"That's good enough for me—and the Lord," Johannon said. He took both their heads, one in each huge hand and plunged them under the water. They both were good swimmers and knew how to hold their breaths for a long time, but they knew that wouldn't be right and so they left their mouths open and choked and swallowed like ordinary folk.

They came up sputtering and smiling and feeling very good.

Johannon liked them immensely. He was used to people coming out to be immersed for all kinds of reasons, but these two were different. He sensed they didn't have any terrible secrets and they wouldn't know how to be self-righteous.

"The Lord forgives you," he said, "and He loves you."

They nodded their thanks and got into their beached sailboat and poled away. "A few more like that," Johannon thought, "and the Kingdom of God is going to be a mighty fine place."

When he woke in the morning, Johannon was startled to see the two of them sitting on the ground, waiting for him. They didn't tell him the catch had been very good that season, and they had taken care of their families. Simon didn't explain he had told his mother and wife he had to do this thing. He didn't mention they had cried a lot, but he had promised to return and anyway, they had known he was not a man easily swayed.

Andrew didn't explain that he had no wife and he had completely wiped the Perean girl and her wooden god out of his mind. His mother had hollered a lot about him, too, but she was no fool and not about to scream her lungs out in a lost cause.

Johannon knew the brothers were going with him and he was not unappreciative of the company. What he did was a lonely kind of business. These two were strong and dependable and when the crowds got too big they could probably help out. Anyway, he hoped the crowds would get too big.

Along the way, Johannon taught them a lot of scripture. "I'm not the one," he said. "I hope you realize that. I'm just called upon to open the door. After me the real one will come, and it's up to us to recognize him. It's a matter of the heart," he said, "not the mind. When he comes, we'll know him."

They had worked their way down the river, with Johannon drawing great crowds and baptizing and preaching repentance before the End of Days. Once in a while someone would come out who looked important and Andrew, especially, would think he might be the one. But Johannon and Simon always shook their heads.

Then one day, when they were at a place on the west side of the river close to Jericho, Johannon's keen eyes had lifted over the crowd and he had smiled. It was a wonderful smile, partly because it was such a big one. Johannon's mouth was huge and his teeth were white despite all the berries, and when he opened that mouth and smiled, the glow seemed to Simon like Mount Hermon capped with snow in the winter.

Yes, Johannon had smiled and caught Simon's eye and then Andrew's. "There he is," Johannon said, "and I tell you brother, we're not worthy to tie the laces on his shoes."

The brothers, who were tall, but not as tall as the Baptizer, had climbed out of the water, where they were helping Johannon and stood on the shore. In the distance, striding toward them, they saw Joshua.

They had watched when Johannon had immersed Joshua and they had seen the wondrous experience of that event. They had looked at Joshua's face and caught their breaths in surprise, looked into his eyes and realized he saw things they had never known.

Now they sat with Johannon at a small fire on the riverbank, waiting, watching and listening. Joshua sat apart from them, on a small, steep hill above the shoreline, in the silence of the night. The brothers wanted to look at him, again and again, but they were too polite. They kept their eyes on Johannon and he looked into the fire. His eyes glowed and he smiled often but he said nothing.

12.

PARTING

The cresting Jordan broke the moonlight into fragments that flickered on the surface like millions of white flowers. Beyond, on the far side of the river, in the land of Moab, rose the shadow of Mount Nebo, where Moses had gazed on the Promised Land he was forbidden to enter.

Joshua sat on the shore that Moses had never reached, understanding the Promised Land was not a physical place but a spiritual one and knowing he had been blessed and permitted to enter.

Overhead, a brilliant canopy of stars flickered in the heavens like the moonlight on the water. Joshua sat alone on his hilltop, with millions of flowers below and above him.

The excitement of the day had not faded. The moment of his spiritual death and rebirth were brilliantly clear in his mind, the light from the light- that had pierced him. He recalled the members of the Qumran community declaiming the war of the sons of light against the sons of darkness, and he realized that what they had said had its kernel of truth, but they had withdrawn from the "real" world, and had failed to recognize that all people had the spark of divine life in them—every man, woman and child, all born in the image of the divine. But each had to recognize this divine light and bring it forth—within and without.

Again, Joshua heard the inner voice from God, telling him he had been chosen. No more would he see visions of his wife and children. He knew they were at peace in God's kingdom, and that he need not fear for them any longer. God had taken Joseph that Joshua might learn he had but one Father and that was the Lord. God had taken Joshua's wife and children that he might know that He was both companion and creator.

Now, free of all responsibility and earthly burdens, the Lord had asked who would go and Joshua had shouted his acceptance of the mission.

He felt strength and power he had never known. Joshua understood that with this power there was nothing he could not accomplish. But even as he understood this, a cloud crossed the moon and a shadow crossed his heart. A low voice, evil and ominous, whispered in his ear, "If you will say the word, the people will rise in war and rebellion. You will be a warrior king and the people will revel in your triumph."

Joshua shuddered. He remembered Isaiah's words:

"Woe to those who go down to Egypt for help and rely on horses, who trust in chariots because they are many and in the horsemen because they are very strong, but do not look to the Holy One of Israel or consult the Lord."

God was the God of the living. He demanded peace not war, love not hate, life not death.

A vision appeared to Joshua. He saw himself standing on the very pinnacle of the Temple, with the people below, prostrate, worshipping him. He was a priest, the High Priest and his vestments glowed with gold. Again, he shook his head. He did not seek adoration that was for God. Man should fear the Lord and serve him only. Joshua did not want to preside over great rituals and solemn feasts. Least of all did he want the people to abase themselves before him. He wanted to lift them up, not set them down, to recognize the godliness within them.

The image changed. A voice whispered in his ear, while a hand pointed at the rocks before him. "You have but to touch these rocks and they will change into bread, or gold, or precious jewels. Whatever you decide, that is what will be. And the people will love you for you will give them great wealth."

Joshua raised his hand in a sweeping gesture that wiped this shadow from before his face. "Man lives not by bread alone," he whispered, "and surely not by gold or precious gems. Man lives by the precious word of the Lord."

Again, words came to him from Isaiah:

"'Woe to the rebellious children,' says the Lord, 'who carry out a plan, but not mine.'"

No, the plan must be God's plan, and that was neither war nor wealth nor unrepentant ritual. Joshua knew it was the way of love and peace and he had been chosen to accomplish it.

***

Johannon sighed and rose and mounted the little hill where Joshua sat. Joshua smiled as the Baptizer approached.

"I must tell you something," Johannon said. Joshua waved him to sit down.

"As you know, Herod Antipas is furious because I condemned him for violating scripture and marrying Herodias, the wife of his brother. Ordinarily, Herod would only growl and threaten—he tries to ignore preachers and so-called holy men. But now Aretas, the Arabian king is angry because Herod put aside his sister in order to marry Herodias. Aretas is forming an army and Herod is preparing to defend his territory. He's afraid that while he's fighting Aretas, I may spark a rebellion. The brothers, Simon and Andrew, tell me they have heard rumors that Herod plans to arrest me."

"Would you lead such a rebellion?"

Johannon smiled. "I'm a man of peace."

"Perhaps it would be prudent for you to travel to a safer place."

The Baptizer laughed. "What place is 'safe' for me? The Herods are all related and Pilate is worse than any of them. Besides, I have no taste for hiding, and even if I did, I'm the wrong size for it."

Joshua smiled. "What will you do?"

"It's not myself that I'm worried about. If they come to arrest me, they may kill anyone who is with me. You're the one who needs to find a safer place."

"I've no more taste for hiding than you have," Joshua said.

Johannon sighed. Joshua's answer had not surprised him.

***

The troop loped along the bank of the Jordan. They were Parthian mercenaries, chosen by Herod for their toughness and cruelty. The Herods employed many nations, Gauls and Germans, Greeks and Syrians, but they preferred the Parthians for their total lack of compassion and total commitment to their paymaster.

Ekenias, their leader, was a Greek—most of the Parthian units had Greek officers—but he was a weak and venal man, with his own strain of viciousness.

"You'll know Johannon, the one they call 'The Baptizer,' when you see him," Ekenias told his men. "He's a giant in size, but carries no weapons and wouldn't step on an ant. Antipas wants him alive—do you hear me—Alive."

The men growled. They had grouched through weeks of inactivity and were delighted to have something to do. But they had hoped for more action. Arresting some Jewish preacher, even a giant of a man, didn't seem like much fun.

"There may be others with the Baptizer," Ekenias said. "I have no orders about them, so if you have the urge to cut a few throats—I won't stop you."

The men perked up and began, unconsciously to ride faster. A little throat-slitting would certainly make the evening more entertaining. Especially if the victims were Jewish. The Parthians hated this country and the self-righteous Jews who populated it. Now, if there were only some women, the night could be very satisfying.

***

By the river's edge, Simon and Andrew were hurriedly stamping out the fire. They ran up the hillside to Johannon and Joshua.

"Riders," Simon said, "soldiers I think and very close."

He pointed to the river's edge, where a troop of riders was galloping along.

"There they are!" Ekenias yelled.

The Parthians could see them easily in the bright moonlight, four men outlined against the sky on a hilltop. They seemed to be standing there, waiting for the Parthians. Ekenias grinned, thinking of the greeting he and his men were going to deliver.

He drew his sword and the others followed. They turned inland where the fire had been and started up the hill.

"My God," Simon said, "they have their swords drawn."

"Are you afraid?" Johannon asked.

Simon nodded, his eyes large.

Andrew nodded in agreement, but he saw that Simon made no move to escape.

"Leave us," Joshua said, "there's still time." But Simon, although he was frightened out of his wits, would not allow the others to see it. He would wait here and take his fate as it might come. If this fellow was truly the Messiah....

The Parthians were at full gallop now. Some of them were salivating at the prospect of cutting up these Jews. They loved war and slaughter, rape and rapine, especially when there was no one fighting back. It was obvious these fools would not fight back.

"Cut out the big one!" Ekenias yelled. "Don't kill him no matter what he does."

The Parthians noted he said nothing about maiming the giant. The troopers at the rear pulled even with their fellows, fearful the slaughter would be completed by the front ranks. The Parthians were spread in a single line now, urging their mounts up the hill, swords swinging in the sky, yelling fierce cries—which was why they didn't hear the horses coming over the hilltop above their left flank until the last moment. The appearance of these unexpected enemies startled the Parthians. They saw the horsemen bearing down on them at full gallop, silent and relentless, a line as wide as theirs.

"Turn!" Ekenias yelled, "turn and repel!"

The Parthians swung their horses and their attention to the oncoming horsemen, but they had lost momentum and they were frightened. This was supposed to be a simple slaughter, a massacre not a battle. How many were there? Who were they?

The line of horsemen swept down upon them from above, riding faster than the Parthians who were still urging their horses uphill. The attackers swept across the line of Parthian horsemen before it had fully turned, stabbing, lopping heads, shoving riders from their horses. Men and animals screamed.

Judas, standing in his saddle, called out. "Save the horses, kill the men!"

Johannon and Joshua, Simon and Andrew recognized their rescuer.

"No!" Johannon was yelling. "Don't kill them! Stop—stop now, in the name of the Lord!"

But it was too late. Nineteen of the twenty lay dead. Judas leaped from his horse and held the last, Ekenias, their officer, at sword's point on the ground, debating only whether to question him before he ran him through.

Johannon grabbed Judas's arm and pulled him away.

"Are you mad?" Judas said. "He would have killed you."

Johannon helped Ekenias stand up and held him easily in his powerful hands. Ekenias could hardly believe that he was still alive, but he didn't trust any of these strange people. He spoke quickly, stammering over the words, in a high-pitched voice. "Didn'...Didn' come to kkkkkill you—sent by, by, by Herod to bbbbring you in—alive."

Judas spat in the dust. "He's a liar."

"I'll go with you," Johannon said to Ekenias. "My friends won't harm you."

Judas grabbed Johannon's arm and turned him around. "They'll butcher you," he said.

Johannon smiled grimly. "I'm harmless," he said. "Even this man can swear to it?" He looked encouragingly at Ekenias.

"Yyyyyes," Ekenias said. "I'llll ssswear to it."

Joshua knew instinctively that Ekenias could not be trusted. "He can't speak for his superiors, Johannon. Come with me."

Johannon shook his head. "I've done what I was sent to do," he said. "Now that you're here, my work is complete. It's in your hands now."

Judas's men were growing restless, listening to these holy men dispute. "We've got to get out of here," one of them muttered, circling his horse anxiously.

Joshua was staring hard at Johannon. "The work is only beginning," he said. "I need your help." He had grown fond of the Baptizer in the short time he had known him, and he realized there were few men in Israel—or anywhere, for that matter, who were as strong for the Lord. He felt a pang at the thought of losing him.

Johannon was deeply touched by Joshua's concern for him and the affection that was evident in his eyes. "No," he said, reluctantly, "if I don't surrender now, they'll keep hunting until they find me. They'll keep killing as long as I'm free—that's how they think. Once they have me, the killing may stop." He smiled suddenly. "Always wanted to meet Herod. Maybe he wants to repent. Maybe I can save another soul." He roared with laughter while Ekenias stared at him with horror and disbelief.

Simon and Andrew had listened to this exchange with doubt and confusion. They, too, had become fiercely attached to the Baptizer. The thought of him willingly giving up to Herod's murderous troops dismayed them. But they also felt drawn to Joshua. He was not as imposing physically as Johannon, but his strength was even deeper.

Joshua understood their doubts. "Well," he asked them, "what will you do?"

"Don't know," Simon said, "we're just fishermen."

"Come with me," Joshua said, "and be fishers of men."

"You're all crazy," Judas said, but he loved and admired them. Here were men as brave as any zealots, and without weapons.

Johannon lifted Ekenias into the saddle of his horse and handed him his helmet and his sword. "Want you to look proper," he said, "when you bring me in."

"Hhhhow will I explain tttthis?" he asked, pointing to the bodies of the Parthians.

Johannon shrugged. "It will take a lot of imagination," he said. "You want to tie a rope around me? I'd rather not, if you don't mind."

"No rope," Ekenias said, throwing a quick look at Judas, then turning to Johannon. "Aren't you going to ride?"

"No," Johannon said. "I'm afraid of horses."

Judas laughed. "I didn't think you were afraid of anything," he said.

"God and horses," Johannon said. He slapped Ekenias's horse on the rump and it started walking. He followed, a step behind. The Baptizer neither spoke nor waved his hand toward his friends. He was preparing himself for the ordeal ahead.

13.

THE PLAN.

They rode along the Jordan at a fast canter. Simon and Andrew had never been on horseback before and they clung to the saddles with desperation. On the sea, they would have been able to keep their balance in the heaviest storm, but the movements of horses were a mystery to them.

Joshua had ridden both mules and horses and he was reasonably comfortable. He would have preferred to walk, but Judas had warned him that other troops would soon follow the Parthians and it was best to get as much distance as possible between them and their pursuers. East of Archelais, they crossed the Jordan into Perea. That was Philip the tetrarch's territory and he was more relaxed in his administration. Besides, it was his brother who was seeking the Baptizer and his followers. Philip had no quarrel with Aretas.

They huddled together in a wadi west of Pella: Joshua, Judas, Simon and Andrew. At Judas's insistence, his men had gone back into Samaria, to wait for him at a camp near Sychar. Judas himself was anxious to talk to Joshua. He was convinced that he had finally found the way to unite the Zealots of Israel and root out the Romans.

The moon was down and a cold wind had come up. Judas forbade them to start a fire for fear of hostile patrols, and although the wadi was safer than open ground, it formed a channel that increased the pressure of the wind.

Judas was shaking his head. "I don't see how you're going to do it," he said.

"I don't plan to do it," Joshua said. "God will."

Judas paused. One had to be careful with Joshua, not because he was easily offended personally, but because he was quick to note any insult to God. "Rabbi," Judas said, not knowing he was the first to call Joshua by this name, "I'm only trying to understand. I trust you and I trust God. But I'm not inspired as you are. Things have to be explained to me."

Joshua smiled. "Don't be humble, Judas," he said. "It doesn't become you."

Judas smiled. This man was his match every time. He held out his hands in a gesture of submission.

"I believe as you do," Joshua said, "that the people cannot long continue under Roman domination. Their rule is evil—and against the word of God. But if the people rise in armed rebellion, they will be slaughtered. Not because they are weak, although Roman armies are strong, but because the Lord will not be with them."

"Why would the Lord abandon Israel in her hour of deepest need?"

"The Lord will not abandon Israel if she follows God's will. The ways of war are not God's will. The lessons of scripture are clear. We must 'beat our swords into plowshares and our spears into pruning hooks.'"

"Then the Romans will surely slaughter us," Judas said.

Simon was nodding, listening to Judas. In his experience, the Romans weren't gentle when they found weakness.

"Not weakness," Joshua said, reading Simon's mind and astonishing him. "Strength—the strength of a nation united, not a group or a remnant, not Zealots or Sadducees or Pharisees, surely not Essenes sealing themselves off from the world in the desert."

Joshua could no longer sit as he spoke. He rose to his feet and paced, his shoulders thrown back, his voice rising, his fine, strong hands slicing through the air. The others hoped that in the wind, he wouldn't be heard by their enemies, but they didn't think of stopping him.

"Everywhere the word is that the 'End Times' are upon us—the Lord, our God, will intervene to save us from destruction by the Romans and begin a blessed new era of the Kingdom of God. But when, what time will this occur? Today, tomorrow, a month from now, a year? In the meantime danger surrounds us. The Romans are more vicious than ever. People are frightened, but also angered. At any moment an act of brutality, greed by a tax collector, a ruthless soldier, may light the spark and the whole nation will be on fire. Rome's legions will pour down on us, thousands will be slaughtered, villages burned, even the Temple may be pillaged."

Judas leapt to his feet. "Then we must attack the Romans at once!"

Joshua raised a hand to calm Judas, who slowly sat back down on the ground, but his eyes still blazed.

"Yes, my friends, we must act—we must confront the Romans, but not with weapons of war. In such a war we are doomed. The Roman armies will overwhelm us. Many, many will die, but we will not be free. The end time will not be the Lord's time it will be the end of Israel.

"We must all rise at the same time—not in war, but in peace. We must refuse to pay the Roman taxes, refuse to submit to their customs. We must not obey any Roman law. Even more important, we must stop planting and harvesting crops, breeding and slaughtering our herds. Yes, Simon, we must stop even drawing fish from the lakes, the rivers and the seas. We must declare a new and total Sabbath year—a year of devotion only to the Lord. If we grow no crops, fish no fish and herd no herds, there is no way they can exact tribute from us. We will make it unprofitable for the Romans to rule us."

Judas was amazed. "The coming Sabbath year does not begin until the month of Tishri, after the Day of Atonement."

"True, but we must declare a new and different Sabbath year."

Simon did not like to be the one who questioned Joshua, but he felt befuddled. "When will this 'new' year begin?"

Joshua smiled. "At the coming Passover. And then from this Passover until the next Passover—as long as it may take!"

Judas was amazed. "What will the people do—how will they live?"

"They will have finished the barley harvest and stored it by the Passover," Joshua said. "They will also have planted the wheat, but on Shavuot they won't harvest it—because the new Sabbath year will be in effect."

Simon, even more confused, ventured another question. "Just leave it in the fields, where strangers can take it, animals feed on it?"

"Of course," Joshua said. "Isn't that what always happens in a Sabbath year?"

"But, Rabbi, that's not the timing of the Sabbath year set forth in scripture."

"No, but we will honor scripture by extending the time of observance, not making it shorter. We will do more than is asked of us, not less. God will take account of our sacrifice, He always does."

Judas was not convinced. "The people may suffer."

"They are already suffering, and without purpose. We will give them a reason for their sacrifice—freedom, the very reason we celebrate Passover and the liberation of our people."

Joshua saw that he was beginning to reach them. "Yes, there will be costs for this, but that is the risk the Jews have always been willing to take. Besides, for a while they will be able to eat from the crops already stored after the barley harvest. But primarily they will live off the land, like their fathers did—as nomads as their fathers were. They must rely on the Lord to provide for them, just as he provided the manna in the desert."

"Some may die," Simon said.

"They're dying now," Joshua said. "The Romans slaughter us at will—without reason. We ask Rome for a new governor or king and we rely on that king or governor to be good to us. But they're men and they rule like men. They are capricious—sometimes generous, other times vicious. We are slaves—asking only for a change of slave-masters. We must rise together, and throw off our chains. As your father and grandfather said, Judas, 'NO RULER BUT GOD.'"

In the silence, the wind howled down the wadi. Simon and Andrew were shaking from the cold, Joshua from inspiration and Judas with anticipation. When Joshua spoke, his voice sent fire through Judas's blood. He wanted to leap to his feet and do his bidding, whatever that might be. But then, the old Judas took hold of him, calmed him down. The experienced and cynical Judas who had seen destruction and betrayal could not easily accept these idealistic words, these messianic delusions.

Judas could not reject the plan entirely. The idea was naive, but it was brilliant. It had never been done and the risks were great, but it might work. Most important, here was a leader, a man inspired by God, a man whom the others could rally around. Perhaps it wouldn't work out precisely as Joshua saw it, but in the meantime, it was a way of unifying the rebellion, of uniting fierce and powerfully individual groups around one man. If Joshua succeeded on his own terms—all well and good, and if not, Maybe Judas could still use his power in his own way.

"This is indeed madness, Joshua," Judas said, "but I believe it is divine madness. If we throw ourselves on the mercy of the Lord, how can He abandon us?"

"Exactly," Joshua said. He was delighted that Judas had expressed agreement with him, but he also sensed the man's reservations. It was not easy for a man of war to throw down his weapons—not after three generations of fighting. Joshua would have to watch him closely, to keep reassuring him, to make certain he didn't fall into old ways. "You can help me spread the word," Joshua told Judas. "If you tell your men to put down their arms, they will listen. Then, other Zealots will do the same. Soon, we will all be following the words of Isaiah."

A warning sound went off in Judas's head. "If I tell the men to put aside their arms before others are ready to do the same, before the nation is ready to join with you, the people are with you, they won't trust me. They'll think I'm a fool or a traitor."

"You?"

"Even me. These men are zealous for God, but they are tough and they are practical."

Joshua frowned. "We must trust God," he said. "If we hold back, we are demonstrating our doubt of his word."

"If we act hastily, we surely won't be following God," Judas said

"Of course," Joshua replied. "You must have the trust of your men. If even one speaks or acts too soon the Romans will use the excuse to come down on all of us. You must proceed as you know best, and you must swear your men to silence."

Judas nodded. "What of the rest of the nation?" he asked.

"We will continue our ministry as before. I will speak to them in parables so that the wise will understand, and be prepared, but no one will have cause to use violence on them before all is prepared."

"What about the Romans?" Simon asked. "Who says they'll throw down their arms?"

Joshua smiled. "Even the Romans won't want to slaughter an entire people. When they see we mean them no harm, but have no intention of submitting to them, they'll understand the depth of our devotion to our God—they will realize there is no profit to be had here. Then we shall have the opportunity to follow God's will—to be a nation of priests and a holy people. We'll witness to the Romans here and then to the rest of the empire. We will teach Love of God to the entire world."

Joshua's arms were flung out and he was clearly visible, even against the moonless sky. He seemed especially vulnerable to Judas, Simon and Andrew, but the force of his beliefs surrounded and protected all of them.

Judas masked a frown. It was one thing to free Israel, another to convert the entire world into believing in the one God. He knew that was the Lord's ultimate plan, but he found it hard to believe that it was to be organized by this little group of Jews huddled in a wadi in the desert.

Joshua smiled and looked intently at him. "If you don't believe, who will?" Joshua paused, letting the words sink in before he spoke again. "They tell me that Hillel said, 'If I am not for myself, who will be for me. If I am only for myself, what am I? If not now, when?'"

They were all silent, thinking about the Hillel's words.

"The Lord has chosen me," Joshua said, "to carry this message, and I have agreed to do it, with all my heart, all my soul and all my might."

"You are the Messiah," Andrew said, "the anointed of God."

"Those are but words, Andrew," Joshua said gently. "God is not interested in the honors or titles we use on earth. He wants us to do his will. Then each of us will be the Messiah."

"But the people," Simon said. "They need a leader—you know that. If we can tell them you're the Messiah, they'll rise up around you."

"And the Romans will kill you the next morning," Judas said. "They appoint the rulers here, and a rival King means sedition against the state."

"Oh, ye of little faith," Joshua said, smiling sadly at Judas. "I will die when God wants me to die, not when the Romans decide.

"But there is something the people must decide, if they are to be saved from destruction. They must know what the choices are and they must accept the word of God. The Messiah cannot lead a people that is not ready to be led, that does not know where it is being led.

"God has told me that I must speak to the people, that I must make them understand that freedom or slavery is their choice—they must choose the way of the Lord, freely and without reservation."

"You'll have to be careful" Judas said stubbornly. "If you go from town to town teaching and the Romans understand your true message they will treat you as a rebel—they'll throw you in jail or worse."

"You're a practical man," Joshua said. "That must be why God has brought us together. I will tell the people, but in a way that won't arouse the Romans. I'll have to prepare the people so that when we're ready, we can all rise up and speak for God."

"We'll do our best to help you," Judas said. "We have friends and safe places all over the country. You can stay with us and we'll help you organize."

"Can you speak for all your friends?" Joshua asked.

"No—not without your help. You'll have to speak to them yourself—convince them that your way is best."

"The only way—God's way," Joshua said. "Any other way will lead to slaughter. That's what the Lord is telling us—these are the last days—the last chance for Israel to do the Lord's will and be saved. Otherwise, Roman rule will spark the nation into war and that will be the death of Israel."

They talked for most of the night. Simon and Andrew only listened. They were impressed with this joining of a holy man with a hard-nosed soldier. Joshua's plan sounded difficult, maybe even far-fetched. How could you oppose a violent nation with peace, how could you reward cruelty with kindness? But they didn't doubt his sincerity and his power. They knew of his life and the sacrifices he had made. This was not some inexperienced visionary who knew nothing of the world, but a practical man like themselves—a carpenter, a strong man, a man who had lost his entire family to the Romans and still counseled peace.

Most important of all, there was the glow of the man. A rabbi had once told Simon about the "Shekinah," the special aura of the heavenly presence. Simon felt and saw that Shekinah when he looked at Joshua. "If I am to be a follower," he thought, "Surely there is no better man to follow."

Judas never slept that night. What had he committed himself to? Why was it that whenever he listened to this man, some of his good sense seemed to disappear? For three generations his family had been soldiers, bitter, hard soldiers, dealing with the Romans as ruthlessly as the Romans dealt with them. Now, he had joined a counsel of peace—an attempt to solve the problems of the nation by means never used before. Could a man make himself defenseless and still triumph?

But Judas believed in the word of God, in the message that Joshua wove so skillfully out of the law and the prophets. Perhaps it was the very boldness of it that startled and moved him. Three generations of warfare had resulted only in death and more death. Could he really claim that war and violence were the answer? If they were, why hadn't God helped his grandfather and his father?

In a crazy way, Joshua made sense. And, in a crazy way, Judas believed that he was, indeed, the anointed of God. Surely the man himself believed it, even as he shied away from the name. He was humble but confident. And without such a leader, there was no hope whatsoever.

Still, Judas would try to keep all his options open. He would help present this man as the leader, the future king of Israel. He would help plan the "uprising" that would not be an uprising. But he would keep his lines of communication open. He would bury his arms, but he would remember where they were buried. He would try it Joshua's way, but if it didn't work, he would be ready to change course.

Joshua lay awake, thinking, too. He knew that God had given him the answers to his questions. He was the man and peace was the way. God would help him persuade his countrymen. He would offer them God's salvation on God's terms. Surely they would not turn away. The people had fallen away from God from time to time in the past, but God had always left the path to redemption open. The people would understand that and they would follow God's word. As terrible as conditions were in Israel, those were the very conditions that would make the people ready. They must understand that the burdens of their present lives were, as the Master of Qumran had said, a warning from God. Salvation lay with their own actions, their own choices. It was not the Romans who must change—at least not first. It was the people of Israel.

14.

RENEWAL

Simon and Andrew insisted on waiting at the foot of the hill below the house.

"I assure you that you're welcome," Joshua said. But they both shook their heads.

"Have a little time with them alone," Simon said. "We'll be waiting here."

Joshua shrugged his shoulders and traveled the last few steps. He smiled and pounded vigorously on the door. It was opened by Jacob, who stared at him blankly for a fraction of a second. "Joshua," he yelled and grabbed his larger and heavier brother around the waist and lifted him off his feet.

The rest of them came running up, Joses and Simeon and Judah, Sarah and Judith. Then the wives of Joses and Simeon and the husband of Sarah. Jacob and Judith were as yet unmarried. They were all exclaiming and hugging him, until his sides began to ache.

It was Erev Shabbat, the eve of the Sabbath and the clan was gathered at the house of Miriam.

Joshua was laughing and greeting his brothers and sisters and looking over their heads for his mother. Then she was there, lovely as ever, her hair carefully wound about her head for the Sabbath, her smile as serene and lovely as ever.

"Mother," he said, and the others let him go. He opened his arms and embraced Miriam, gently but firmly. She kissed his face and held him tightly, while tears streamed from her eyes.

"We heard such terrible thing—Roman patrols attacking helpless people again—we didn't know what to think."

"Sit down," Jacob said, wiping away his own tears. "The Sabbath meal is almost ready."

Joshua hesitated. "I have two friends," he said.

Miriam smiled. "There's always room in a Sabbath household for friends."

Joshua stepped outside and called. The brothers came loping up the hillside. Joshua could see they had washed the dust off at the well and plastered their hair flat on their heads. They both looked a little damp and rather embarrassed.

"This is Simon and this is Andrew. They are brothers, and they are very good friends and very loyal."

"Shalom," Miriam said, smiling and holding out her hands to them and the others echoed her greeting.

"Come," Miriam said. "It's time to kindle the lights."

***

"When will you come back to work with us?" Jacob asked.

"We miss you," Judah said.

"Of course," Sarah said. "Now he has to do all the hard jobs."

They laughed and questioned Joshua, but he put them off until the Sabbath meal was finished, until they had shared the beauty of the ceremonies and the fullness of Miriam's and the girls' cooking, and they were all relaxed and seated about the room.

Then, with his beloved family gathered around him, he told them briefly of his stay with the Essenes.

"They're good men and pious," he said. "But I fear they misunderstand God's law. They think of themselves as set apart, predestined by God himself, to be the sole remnant that participates in God's kingdom. They don't have any room for anyone who doesn't believe as they do."

"Is that anything new?" his brother Joses asked. "Most of these sects believe they know the only way."

"Most priests and scribes," Jacob laughed.

Joshua's face grew serious. "There's no time and no place for such divisions. We are all God's children, made in his image, with a spark of the divine light in each of us, and the Kingdom of God within and all around us. If we look down on our brother or our sister, God will look down on us."

He told them about Johannon and his own immersion by the Baptizer— just as Jacob and Judith and Miriam has been immersed by him.

"It's not easy to describe, but I felt that the light from above had joined with the light inside me. I understood there was work I must undertake, and now Andrew and Simon have joined me—and Judas. You recall him,

247

Mother, the grown-up version of the child you hid beneath your bed in Bethlehem a little before I was born."

"Yes," said Miriam, and she ventured a smile, but it was difficult because she knew the history of that man and his family and she worried for her eldest son.

There was a moment of silence, uneasy silence, as they all struggled to make sense of what Joshua was telling them.

"So serious," Sarah said, playfully.

She was the youngest and prettiest and therefore the most spoiled. Joshua couldn't help smiling for a moment. "Is there any choice, but to be serious? Everywhere one goes the Roman oppression is heavier and heavier. Everywhere the people are angrier. The Romans have killed many, ruined the homes of some, imprisoned others. They have changed the laws of the land, the rules of trade so that many have lost their farms and their homes. Others are barely eking out a living.

"The Romans have garrisons over the Temple itself—they scorn our religion. They hold the very vestments of the High Priest, who must have permission of the governor to remove them from the Antonia Fortress to wear them on Feast days. The people are angrier every day. And an angry people is likely to do angry things. I fear for the Jews."

There was a moment of silence in the room. Joshua took a deep breath. "I won't be coming back to work here," he said.

"Where *will* you work?" Jacob asked. He had been watching Joshua closely and had seen that he was a changed man, changed even from the one who had surprised him at Qumran. Jacob had responded to the change in his brother. He had ceased to be as carefree and playful as before. Now Jacob understood that Joshua's meeting with Johannon had caused further change and he felt so close to his brother that he shared in this change even without a word being spoken between them.

"Simon's family has a house in Capernaum. He has kindly offered to take me in and that's where I'm going."

"Is business better in Capernaum?" Judith asked.

"I don't expect to do much carpentering," Joshua said. "I have another calling."

The look that came over his face stopped their questions.

"I can't watch my countrymen die in fruitless war and rebellion. I want to help them—to teach them the message of scripture as God has revealed it to me. I want to share this message and help my people to live in peace and freedom."

Still, they were silent. Joshua had always been different and they all knew it. What he was saying struck a new but harmonious note, as if he were telling them something they had long suspected.

Miriam, knew this as well or better than any of them, yet she was the most distressed. She tried not to show it, but she knew that the course he was choosing was fraught with danger. And she also knew that Joshua would never shrink from danger. Her heart went out to her son, knowing the travails he would undergo, the disappointments he would endure, the misery he might suffer. She cried within herself, masking the pain, steeling herself so that none would know.

Joshua moved to his mother, kneeled before her and took her face in his hands. "It would be useless of me to tell you not to worry, but the Lord is watching over me. Tell yourself this, hold on to it, and you need never fear for me."

She took his head in her hands and stared into his eyes. How she loved this son of hers, conceived in agony and to die—in agony? Suddenly she knew it, as certainly as she had ever known anything. She could not help herself. She wept.

15.

CAPERNAUM

The synagogue sat on level ground only a few steps from the water at the northern end of the Sea of Galilee. The houses of the town surrounded it in every direction except toward the lake which was south and thus pointed toward Jerusalem and the holy Temple. The ground between the synagogue and the water was an open plaza where the people gathered for political and social functions. It was paved unevenly with flat stones; weeds and flowers grew between them.

The sea was calm in the early morning sun and the boats of the fishermen, unused on the Sabbath, were as motionless at their moorings as the ones pulled up on the shore. Toward the east, the sun was rising over the heights of Gaulanitis, a bleak and barren area that led toward Damascus.

To the southwest, the houses of Tiberias, rising on the hillsides were still shrouded in mists.

The synagogue was a pleasant limestone building with a columned portico across the front and a wide entrance that led to a simple rectangular room, divided by three rows of columns. The center space was the widest and held the *bema*, or platform with rows of wooden benches surrounding it. In the aisles, on each side, the women would gather

When they prayed, the people would face towards the Temple and therefore the wall containing the niche and the scrolls should have been south instead of north, but the builders had not been willing to leave a wall facing the sea and so they had oriented the structure with its entrance toward the beautiful lake. That complicated the services, but the congregation was pleased with the plan.

Joshua, Simon and Andrew had arrived early, when the keeper of the building had just been opening the doors. They wore their phylacteries, the little wooden boxes with excerpts from the Torah on their foreheads and forearms, and the talliths, their prayer shawls over their heads and shoulders. Simon's wife and mother had not come. His mother was ill and his wife had stayed home to tend her.

Simon had spoken to Jairus, the leader of the congregation, and had told him that after the service, Joshua wanted to speak to the congregation. Jairus knew Simon well and had quickly agreed.

Soon the synagogue was filled with worshipers, dressed in their Sabbath best, the men all wearing their phylacteries and prayer shawls. They greeted Simon and Andrew whom they knew, but viewed Joshua with some concern. He looked rather foreign, with his blonde hair and blue eyes. They were accustomed to non-Jewish believers in the one God attending their services—the God-fearers, but this one wore his phylacteries and tallith and must be a Jew.

The services were conducted by Jairus and other members of the small congregation. Prayers, blessings and benedictions echoed in the plain stone room with its pointed wooden roof. Then Jairus stood on the platform and spoke the most important prayer, the *Shema*, together with the congregation all standing as they recited these word:

"HEAR, O ISRAEL, THE LORD OUR GOD, THE LORD IS ONE."

"Blessed be His Name and His glorious kingdom forever and ever."

The worshipers spoke fervently these ancient words from scripture that Moses had brought them from God.

"Thou shalt love the Lord thy God with all thy heart, and with all thy soul, and with all thy might. And these words which I command thee this day shall be upon thy heart. Thou shalt teach them diligently to thy children, speaking of them when thou sittest in thy house and when thou walkest by the way, when thou liest down and when thou risest up. Thou shalt bind them for a sign on thy hand, and they shall be for frontlets between thine eyes. And thou shalt write them upon the doorposts of thy house and upon thy gates."

In the cool morning, the service continued with the *Amidah*, the benedictions, also part of the designated service. Joshua knew the *Shemoneh Esrei*, the eighteen blessings, well—taught to him by Ari the Sage, but this day, certain phrases stood out in his mind.

"Lord, open my lips that my mouth may declare Thy Praise...Master of all...mindful of the loving piety of our fathers...He will lovingly bring a Redeemer to their children's children...

"With great love Thou revivest the dead, Thou upholdest the fallen, Thou healest the sick...

"Blessed art Thou, Lord who revives the dead....

"Our God, God of our fathers...Gratify us with Thy goodness and gladden us with salvation...."

Then they read the *Kedushah*:

"Let us hallow Thy name in this world below, even as in the prophet's vision the Seraphim hallowing it in the heavenly heights call to one another:

'Holy, holy, holy is the Lord of Hosts; his glory fills the whole earth...

"The Lord shall reign forever, Your God, O Zion, through all generations. Hallelujah. Praise the Lord.'"

The service continued, with Joshua listening as if the words were new to him.

"Thou art the Rock of our life and Shield of our deliverance...Thy miracles are forever with us...Thou are goodness, Thy compassion never fails... Thy loving-kindness never ceases...

"For all this, our King, be Thy name blessed and exalted evermore."

Two men brought forth the scrolls and circled the congregation as psalms were sung and then Jairus beckoned to Joshua. He was offering him a high honor—an opportunity to read from the cycle of the scriptures.

Joshua was thrilled to have the opportunity. He rose and walked to the wooden platform where the scrolls were spread on a table, held open by two men who smiled at him encouragingly. They were very old, but their eyes were lively and encouraging.

The Sabbath portion was from Isaiah. In his heart, Joshua knew that God had chosen this appropriate moment in this appropriate place and this appropriate text.

He spoke in a clear, rich voice that was neither too loud nor too soft, that carried with passion and meaning to all the corners of the room. Following the biblical injunction, he read from the text itself, rather than from memory, but his command of the verses was so great that he could emphasize the words that he chose to emphasize. This would be no bland reading by a mumbler or one who had to struggle for the words. As he read, the men of the congregation leaned forward, intently, captured by his resonant tones and his sincerity. The women were even more taken by him. Joshua was a strikingly handsome man, but he had none of the arrogance of such a man. His eyes were warm and his voice, though powerful, was gentle and caressing.

When the service was ended and it was time to discuss scripture, Joshua gazed about the congregation with a compelling look that said, Listen my friends, I have something important to share with you.

"I am pleased," Joshua said aloud, "that the Sabbath text is Isaiah. I confess that Isaiah is my favorite. My father, blessed be his memory, read Isaiah to me and I read the prophet to my children, may they rest in peace."

As he said these words, and the congregation understood what he had said, there was a sigh of sympathy for Joshua. To the women, especially, he was even more appealing than he already seemed to them. Some were wondering if his wife were alive.

"Isaiah speaks so clearly, in images that even a child can understand. He talks of beating swords into plowshares and spears into pruning hooks. Can anyone forget such an image? I could not.

"He gives us a vision of peace, where

'The wolf shall dwell with the lamb and the leopard shall lie down with the kid, and the calf and the lion and the fatling together, and a little child shall lead them.'

"How the eyes of my children shone when I read them those lines. They could see it all very clearly and they could imagine themselves as the bringers of peace.

"Did that mean that Isaiah was a tale only for children, something to lull them to sleep with on a wintry night?"

Joshua paused. His voice deepened. "I don't think so—Isaiah's voice speaks just as clearly when he speaks of God's wrath kindled against those who

'Call evil good and good evil, who put darkness for light and light for darkness, who put bitter for sweet and sweet for bitter!'

"Then, as Isaiah tells us, 'the anger of the Lord will be kindled. He will stretch out his hand and smite them. The mountains will quake and their corpses will be as refuse in the streets.'

"Isaiah can speak harshly—God can speak harshly, if He must. If we turn away from him; if we scorn his laws and his revelation.

"And yet, the vision he has for us is a beautiful one, a vision free of war and struggle, where weapons of war become tools of the harvest, where hostile creatures mingle together in love and harmony.

"What does this mean to us, today? The land, our beloved Israel groans under the Roman heel. Our laws are scorned, our people abused. Brigands roam the highways and often soldiers are worse than brigands."

As his voice boomed out, Jairus looked nervously toward the door. Neither the Herodians nor the Romans had ever violated his sanctuary, but there was a first time for everything.

"Is Isaiah's dream dead? No, not dead, not even asleep. It is with us today. If we will follow the ways of the Lord, the peace and freedom He has promised will be ours."

Joshua paused and dropped his voice. "Remember, I said peace, not war. The answer to our prayers is not an army—is not the slaughter of children, it is peace. The Lord has promised us that his anointed will come. Can we doubt that the time of his coming is soon? I doubt it not. I know it in my heart and in my soul.

"'For to us a child is born, to us a son is given, and the government will be upon his shoulders, and his name will be called 'Wonderful,' 'Counselor,' 'Mighty in the Lord.' 'Everlasting father,' 'Prince of Peace.'

"Do you hear that, good people of Capernaum. Not warrior king, but 'Prince of Peace.' For that is the promise. And the promise is that the reign of peace and justice will never end.

"That is our promised Messiah. Before Isaiah tells us of the lion lying down with the lamb he explains precisely how it shall happen.

"There shall come forth a shoot from the stump of Jesse, and a branch shall grow out of his roots. And the spirit of the Lord shall rest upon him, the spirit of wisdom and understanding... with righteousness he shall judge the poor, and decide with equity for the meek of the earth; and he shall smite the earth with the rod of his mouth, and with the breath of his lips he shall slay the wicked.'"

Joshua raised his hands to the heavens. "I trust that the Lord will send the Messiah—that he has sent the Messiah—that even now he walks the earth.

"People of Capernaum, you must be ready. The hour is nigh. Trust not in those who carry swords or ride fierce horses. Believe not in those who would murder in the name of justice, slaughter in the name of wisdom and destroy in the name of peace. The Messiah shall smite the earth 'WITH THE ROD OF HIS MOUTH AND WITH THE BREATH OF HIS LIPS HE SHALL SLAY THE WICKED.'"

Joshua's voice became a whisper. "Cleanse yourselves, my people, purify and prepare yourselves. Repent of the evil you have done and live righteously. The time of the Messiah is nigh. That is not my promise—it is the promise of the Lord Almighty."

Joshua kissed the scroll and strode from the *bema*. He sat down next to Simon and Andrew.

There was silence in the synagogue for a long time—a dynamic silence filled with awe and love and hope. Still, there were a few who questioned Joshua's selections from Isaiah, the order in which he had spoken them and the paraphrases he had used. But they did not speak out.

***

The people gathered about him outside, including Jairus and other elders. They wanted to know his name and his family and who he thought the Messiah might be.

He smiled. "In the hour that is chosen, the name of the chosen one shall be given. And the hour is not far off."

"Tell us, Rabbi?" a pretty woman said. "Have you yourself seen this Messiah?"

"Look within and look without," Joshua said. "Search you heart and you, too, will see him."

Joshua was pleased by the response of the people, but he knew that what he had done was enough for that day. He thanked the elders for permitting him to speak and hurried off to the house of Simon.

16.

SIMON'S FAMILY

Some of the women followed Joshua as far as Simon's house, questioning him about scripture and many other matters, not all of them relating to what he had said, but trying to hold his attention. He wanted to be pleasant and patient, especially since this was his first experience at speaking before strangers in a synagogue. However, he sighed with relief when Simon closed the door to the house, leaving several jabbering women still talking outside.

To Joshua's surprise, Jacob and Judith were waiting. He embraced them happily, asking, "When did you come?"

"We've been here since before the eve of the Sabbath, yesterday," Judith said, "staying at the house of a friend. We met Simon and he told us you were going to speak at the synagogue, so we didn't tell you we were here—we didn't want to make you nervous."

"You knew they were here," Joshua said to Simon. Simon blushed and then he and his wife, Ruth went in to see his mother, who was lying abed, ill.

"You heard me speak?" Joshua asked.

"Yes," Jacob said, "you were so intent on your message, we didn't think you would notice."

"What did you think of what I said?"

Jacob and Judith glanced nervously at each other. "We were very impressed," Jacob said.

Joshua laughed. "That's a careful answer. What does it mean?"

"We listened," Judith said, "and we were moved by what we heard. We know you want something of us—of all the Jews, but we aren't sure what that is."

Joshua smiled. "Good—you're excellent students."

"You taught me how to saw a straight line and mortise a clean corner," Jacob said, "but this is different."

Joshua shook his head. "No," he said. "It's exactly the same."

Simon came out of the sickroom, his blunt face creased with worry. "Her fever is higher. I don't know what to do."

Joshua pressed his shoulder and entered the room. Simon's mother lay on the bed, moaning and shivering. She was very pale and perspiration poured from her body, dampening the bedcovers. Ruth, Simon's wife was wiping her face and arms, but to no avail.

Joshua sat on the bed and gazed into the eyes of the sick woman. Her eyes were red and unfocused, and she murmured sounds of pain and discomfort, words of despair. He continued to look at her, staring into her eyes, until gradually she stopped turning her head, and looked at Joshua. After a moment, she blinked hard and focused on him.

"Hannah," he said, "that's also the name of my grandmother, a name beloved to me."

She looked at him, blinked again and almost smiled.

Joshua took the cloth from Ruth's hands and wiped Hannah's face. She gazed at him as he did so. "The Lord God loves you," he said, "and does not want you to be ill."

She nodded faintly, but the pain was great and she winced, even as she nodded.

"Pray with me, Hannah, to God, to relieve your pain and your illness." He spoke very quietly. "O Lord," he said, "please spare Hannah this suffering. Give her the grace of your healing and your loving care."

Hannah's lips followed Joshua's, mouthing the words in silence, as he spoke. Joshua laid the cloth aside and touched her cheeks gently, then stroked her brow. As he touched her febrile features, the dampness seemed to dry. As he continued to stroke her face, the color came back into her cheeks, while at the same time, the redness grew fainter in her eyes.

Joshua smiled. "I see that you're feeling better, already."

Hannah blinked with wonder, raised her own hands to her cheeks, feeling the heat was gone and the perspiration had disappeared. She took Joshua's hands in her own and gazed into his eyes. She breathed deeply, shuddered once, and suddenly sat up. She looked around the room at her sons and her daughter-in-law, at Jacob, Judith and last of all, Joshua.

"I'm better," she said in a clear voice. "I'm better. God bless you."

Joshua leaned close and kissed her brow. "God has blessed us both," he said. Then he stood up.

The others were staring at him in wonder. Judith was clutching Jacob's hand and Jacob was feeling a surge of love and admiration for his brother.

"What," Ruth asked. "What did you do?" She was a practical woman and she wanted to know what methods of healing Joshua used. They might be useful with her children.

Joshua looked sharply at her. "I did nothing," he said. "God healed your mother-in-law. How? That is not for you to know."

Hannah pushed the covers to one side and leaped from the bed. "If you'll let me dress," she said. "There is challah I baked before the Sabbath that you must taste."

***

They sat together in the evening, after the Sabbath, eating Hannah's fine dinner. Hannah bustled about, smiling and heaping Joshua's plate with food. "You're too thin," she said. "We have to fatten you up."

"Am I to be your next sacrifice?" Joshua asked. They all laughed, except Jacob, who waited until after dinner to take his brother outside and speak to him privately.

They strolled along the water's edge at the stone quay, while boats gently rocked in the water. The sliver of moon was reflected in the lake and it seemed to be an arrow, pointing to the two of them.

"We're worried, Judith and I," Jacob said. "We know you have undertaken a great task and we're afraid that you may suffer because of it."

"All of life is a risk," Joshua said. "Those who seek the smooth way are often disappointed."

"You know I love you," Jacob said. "There's always been a closeness between us— sometimes I think I hear your words in my head before you speak them."

Joshua smiled. "What a mischievous little fellow you were."

"Yes, but I knew you would protect me. Now, I can't protect you, but I can help. I want to be with you."

Joshua stopped strolling, turned and looked at his brother. "I'm grateful, Jacob, but you have a family."

"None of us will have a family unless the Roman burden is soon lifted."

Joshua nodded. "That's true, but I already have Simon and Andrew."

"Would you take them and deny your own flesh and blood? If you're going to do what I think you're planning, you can't have too much help."

Joshua smiled. "I don't want to have to worry about you."

"We'll take care of ourselves—and you. Please, Joshua, don't turn us away."

Joshua drew his brother to the water's edge and looked closely at him. "Who do you think I am?" he asked.

Jacob blinked, bewildered. "My brother, Joshua Ben Joseph."

Joshua smiled. "Good," he said. "You have it right." He turned and walked back towards Simon's house, smiling to himself.

Jacob scratched his head, then hurried after his brother. He had a feeling he had given the right answer and the wrong one at the same time. Well, life with Joshua would never be dull.

In the house of Simon, the families were laughing and singing psalms. Hannah, radiant with joy, was dancing as she had not danced since she was a girl.

17.

JUDITH

He was a good brother, a very good brother. So, too, was Jacob. Even Joses. Simeon and Judah were all right, but Joshua was different. Everyone thought he was remarkable. Perhaps not even he realized how much he was respected, even by those who disagreed with him. Later, feeling the pressure of people who sought to take advantage of his special abilities, Joshua moved out of town. I thought that was too bad, that he would have done better to remain.

But once Joshua made his mind up, it was not easy to change it.

It was difficult for him, too, for he had to leave the workshop. He enjoyed working side by side with his brothers and after he moved he would be unable to do so. Sometimes he came into town for the Sabbath, sometimes not, but when he did, there were the same old pressures. Except he was stronger because he wasn't subjected to them every day. He smiled even when the lame and the halt were pressing him to help them, and he tried to do his best to help as many as he could. But sometimes, the people were rude or offensive and then he would turn away.

My memories are clearest of the early years and the late ones. When I was a child, Joshua was pure magic to me. I knew that our people distrust magicians, but how could I distrust Joshua? His skills were extraordinary and his strength matched his skills. When it was necessary to raise the rafters for a roof over a building, Joseph would often call on Joshua to help and even as a boy he had the strength of a grown man—perhaps two grown men.

Everyone knew of his healing powers, and frankly, I took those for granted. I had seen him heal the sick and cure the wounded ever since I was a little girl and thought little of it.

Joshua was in every way the older brother, the hero that every young girl dreams of. Before he married Rebecca, he was the most sought after young man in Nazareth. Many pretty girls wanted to be my friend because they thought being nice to me might help with Joshua. I understood that, but I didn't mind. I agreed with the girls; he was worth the effort.

He was good to me, very good. He told me stories when I wasn't old enough to read myself. They were bible stories and I thought he was quoting straight from scripture until I got older and learned he had simplified the stories just for me. He made a point of telling me about Judith, my namesake, and other women who did heroic deeds. He wanted me to be proud to be a woman, and I was.

I guess I was jealous of Rebecca early on. He treated her like a sister, and more, even when they were children. I was close enough to Rebecca's age to notice. But of course, Joshua had so much love that no-one was ever slighted. The more people there were, the more love he had to spread around.

I never told Joshua, but in a way he's responsible for the fact I didn't get married. What man would seem exciting or handsome or interesting after my brother? I'm sure he would have felt badly if I had told him that, but it was true. He didn't affect Sarah that way—she married young, but that's the way that I felt about it. I also thought that he needed me, not as a wife, of course, nor as a mother. He had a perfectly fine wife and a wonderful mother. But after he took up his work, he needed people to follow him and to help and care for him. Not at first, but later. I knew I would be needed, even if I didn't know when. I thought I better be free to go with him when he called me. If I had a family I couldn't do that.

Maybe I'm just making excuses. I surely wasn't the best-looking person in the family, not as flawlessly lovely as our mother, or as round and exuberant as Sarah. Still I think I could have had a husband if I wanted one. Joshua would have found me a husband if I wanted him to.

Later, there was a time when I felt something for Johannon, the one they called the Immerser or the Baptizer. He was big and rough and frankly, although he was often in the water, he didn't smell that good. His language was sometimes coarse, too, but he was a powerful man and he loved Joshua as much as anyone, perhaps as much as I did. But that was not to be. I really knew it all along, but when we lost Johannon, especially in such a terrible way, I felt very bad—for a long time.

Among many other things, Joshua taught me to write our language. Sarah could read pretty well, but she couldn't write more than her name. Joshua taught me how to copy the characters in scripture, how to make the letters firm and clear. I knew there was a reason for that, and when he later asked me to write things down, to keep the record of what had happened to him, I knew why he had taught me what he did and I understood that he had indeed needed my help. He said I had a good way of describing things, just the way they happened—that I didn't make them pretty or ugly, but just the way they truly were.

"I want the truth," he said, "the real truth, not the way people elaborate on a story just to make it sound good. I want you to write down the words I say, the very words, not ones you might invent to make me sound good. And I want you to write down what people say of me, the good and the bad, the ones who agree with me and the ones who think I'm working for the devil. You're the one, Judith. The one I can trust."

I liked that from Joshua. I loved him and admired him so. But I did what he asked of me, even writing down the words of those who hated him. Sometimes I had to rely on others, for example, Baruch, who was a postulant at Qumran. I believed him to be honest and accurate, but there were others I wasn't so sure of.

Most important, I knew my brother was restless and unhappy. He saw the suffering in our country and he felt it deeply himself.

"I don't know why I should have it so easy," he said to me while he was building his home in Beth Sholem. "Many are dying for love of God, and others are suffering for lack of food and decent places to live. All I have to do is build a house for myself and live here peacefully with my wife and children. It is a great blessing, and I'm not sure I deserve it."

"It may not always be so easy," I said. "You may remember these days with longing."

He looked at me sharply.

"I don't know anything," I said. "Don't look so concerned."

He smiled then and gave me a hug, but I felt I did know something and the time would come when all would be made clear. Joshua wasn't the only one in the family who got messages.

Even so, I wondered about his life, buried as it were, in little Beth Sholem. I told him that more than once, until he got annoyed.

"I'm not running away and even if I were, surely God knows where to find me."

"You told me the story of Jonah when I was a child, Joshua, and for a long time all I could think about was being swallowed by that big fish. But now I understand that the message is when God tells you what to do, it's no use running in the other direction. God brought Noah back and when he wants to, he'll bring you back, too."

That time I got a glare instead of a hug, but I knew it was because I was close to the truth. If I wasn't, Joshua would have just laughed.

Later, of course, God did "find" him, and then it was an entirely different matter. Now, it seemed there never was enough time for what he wanted to do. He realized that time was short, that things were happening in our land that might result in disaster. Joshua thought it was his mission to avoid that disaster. It was a terrible burden for one man to bear, and Joshua was certain the Lord hadn't intended for the job to be his alone. But it was an enormous struggle moving the people.

"They follow me, but often for the wrong reasons," he told me. "Many are moved because they feel that I can heal them, even though it is the Lord who heals them. I may be the instrument of that healing, but nothing more. Still, they don't see that, and what's worse, they don't see the reason they are being healed—they don't see it's clearing the way to share in God's kingdom. No, they want the healing, and that's enough. Then they fall away, go back to their old way of life. Sometimes, it breaks my heart."

I looked at him with compassion, hardly knowing what to say. "Joshua, you're doing the Lord's work. What more can a man do?"

"I'm not good enough, or fast enough or strong enough. The final battle may be close and my struggle may be only a pebble tossed into the sea."

"The people love you," I said.

"Sometimes, for the wrong reasons," he said, his voice touched with pain. "There are women who love me because they find me handsome, and men who love me because they think I speak well. There are even some who follow me because they think I'm a god. Can you imagine that? Jews, believers in the one, the invisible, the all-mighty Lord of Hosts, and yet they think that a mere man is the eternal God? It sickens me."

I was surprised. "But, Joshua, you know how weak we humans are. Is it any surprise that some find what they want to find, anything that gives them hope. Why worry if they misunderstand a little?"

His face, his beautiful well-formed face seemed to grow in size and turn purple in anger. That was his weakness; his temper. Sometimes it led him astray.

"MISUNDERSTAND A LITTLE? THEY MISUNDERSTAND EVERYTHING."

Then he heard his voice echoing off the walls of the room and he was startled at his own anger. He lowered his voice. "God wants our love and our faith, unconditionally, but founded on true understanding. It is easy enough to worship an idol, or fall on your knees to an earthly king, but that is precisely what The Lord tells us we must not do. A man who worships a stone or a carved piece of wood, or even worships another man, that man is closing his mind, locking the door that might lead him to heaven. Such a man is lost and until he finds himself, he will never enter the Kingdom of Heaven."

18.

SARAI AND NAHUM

On Tuesday, which was a market day, they walked to Chorazin. There were many fishing boats on the lake and they could see that the catch was good. Still, there were many unused boats on the shore, some of them rotting. Where were these fishermen? Had they given up their trade? Had they been killed or injured in the many wars and raids that had afflicted these areas?

Along the road were many beggars, more than Joshua had ever seen before. Perhaps they had been there, but he hadn't noticed. Now, his eyes were clear and he saw the fields that were tended and those that were not, the rich harvests next to waste. He saw the homes of peasant farmers abandoned and the boats on the shore, untended. He saw many along the road who seemed to be wandering, unaware of where they were. Some mumbled and talked to themselves, others accosted other wayfarers and were usually rebuffed. These were lost souls and Joshua longed to regain them.

Joshua realized that he had seen these scenes repeated throughout Galilee and Judaea, each year with increasing intensity, but his thoughts had been elsewhere. Very moved by this realization, Joshua spoke to Simon and Andrew, Judith and Jacob of what he had seen.

"The land is groaning, and the people with it."

"It's the rich landowners," Andrew said.

"Perhaps," Joshua replied. "But even more, it's the Roman occupation."

"They say," Judith said, "that tens of thousands have been killed since Herod's time."

"And many more made homeless," Simon said.

A ragged, sightless man was tapping his way towards them. He was painfully thin, his face streaked with dirt, his blank eyes fixed on the heavens. Yet he smiled.

Joshua smiled back. "Bless you," he said, stopping the man and pressing a round of bread into his hands.

The blind man's smile broadened and he thanked Joshua. Then Joshua scooped up some dirt from the roadway, spat into it and made it into a poultice that he gently pressed on the blind man's eyes.

"It's very cool," the man said. "Thank you."

Joshua held the poultice for a moment, and then slowly removed it. The man blinked and stared at the crust of bread. He looked up and stared at Joshua and blinked again. He was truly smiling now. His lips opened, but he could not speak. His lips moved in thanks, but no sound came out. He dropped the bread, grabbed Joshua's hand and tried to kiss it.

Joshua pulled his hand away, picked up the bread and handed it back.

"Thank you, Master," the blind man was finally able to say, as tears washed his eyes.

"Thank God," Joshua said.

A traveler was passing, and the blind man started to call him, to tell him what had happened, but Joshua pressed his fingers to the blind man's lips. "Tell no one," he said "but go to the synagogue and bless the Lord."

Joshua hurried away, with his followers close behind.

"How?" Jacob asked. "What?" But then words failed him.

Judith was pulling on his arm. "Was he truly blind? Or just pretending?"

"What do you think?" Joshua asked, but he would not discuss it further.

They reached Chorazin at midday. To Joshua it seemed shabbier than it had before. The ruts in the road were deeper and the buildings less cared for. There were more beggars than ever. Joshua's heart went out to his people. The time must surely be nigh.

Andrew went off to find some friends who would put them up for the night. Joshua had planned to enter the synagogue, but the poor people, the beggars in the street, stopped him. He would wait until the Sabbath to go to the synagogue.

He entered the street of the merchants, clogged with hawkers and peddlers and people simply wandering. Simon and Judith and Jacob stood apart, waiting. They did not know what Joshua would do.

Joshua went up to the stall of a man selling birds. They were hung from poles in cages woven of dried cane. The merchant said little, letting his birds sing for him.

Joshua smiled at the merchant. "Shalom," he said. "your birds are very nice."

"The doves are special," the merchant said. He was an elderly man with a cast to one eye. His own gray, somewhat dirty clothing contrasted sharply with the cleanliness of the birds.

"They say the dove is a bird of peace," Joshua said.

"True," the merchant said, "a very lucky bird to own."

"I say we need more than luck, friend," Joshua told him, "if we are to have peace."

"But there is no war," the merchant said. "Hasn't been a battle fought in these parts for years."

Joshua shook his head. "I can't agree with you. People are struggling with hunger and poverty. Many battles are being fought—but they are inner battles—battles of the soul."

"I wouldn't know about that," the merchant said. He didn't like the way the conversation was going. As far as he could tell Joshua carried no purse and there was nothing strapped about his waist. He didn't look like a buyer—though he surely didn't seem dangerous.

"You're at peace then," Joshua said. "Good, that means your heart must be pure. You must be one of the righteous."

A woman who was tending the next stall, a fishmonger, began to laugh. "Righteous indeed, old Pekah here, that's a good one."

Pekah frowned. "What kind of talk is that? Mind your own business."

"It's everyone's business," Joshua said. "Because it's God's business."

"I thought so," Pekah said. "A holy man. We're wasting our time talking to his kind."

"I dunno," the fishmonger said. "He's kind of nice-looking." She smiled winningly at Joshua. "I'm Sarai," she said.

"Joshua—Joshua Ben Joseph."

She looked at him closely. "You the one who preached in the synagogue at Capernaum on the Sabbath—friend of Simon, the fisherman?"

"The same," Joshua said.

"My husband, Nahum is a fisherman, too—knows Simon. Nahum was in the synagogue. Said you spoke well. People were moved by your words."

"God wants the people to do more than be moved. He wants them to change."

"How?" the lady fishmonger asked.

"To repent their sins and turn to the Lord. To follow his way only, and unlock the goodness within their hearts, the light of holiness, that the Lord provides."

The bird-seller spat in the dust. "We're law-abiding folk here. We give honest weights and keep the Sabbath."

"What of your brothers who are starving?" Joshua said. "What of that beggar lying against your stall?"

"Didn't see him," the merchant said. "Get out of here!" he yelled to the beggar. "You're bad for business."

The beggar scrambled off, but only a few feet, then he settled against a wall and held his hands out again.

"I didn't want you to drive him off," Joshua said. "I thought you would feed him."

"You care so much," the merchant said, "YOU feed him."

Joshua glanced toward Jacob, who sighed and brought out the remaining bread he had with him. But the fishmonger was out of her stall carrying a good-sized catfish. "Here," she said, "this should help." She handed the fish to the beggar, who stared at her in surprise.

"Thank you," he whispered and scurried off to eat his meal in private.

Joshua smiled at the woman. "God will bless you, Sarai."

"I hope so," she said. "Here come all the other beggars." They came, limping and running, yelling and pleading, the beggars of the town, to the stall of Sarai the fishmonger.

"Please," "Help us," "Sarai, Sarai."

The woman looked at them with bewilderment. "I'm a poor woman," she called. "I can't feed you all." But they were pleading and pushing against the stall. Jacob and Judith came running over, planning to help Sarai against this mob, but Joshua waved them off.

She looked at Joshua who stared back at her and smiled.

"All right, holy man, this day I'll be my brother's keeper." She pulled the covers off the trays of fish and let the beggars at them. They yelled joyfully and in moments they had emptied the stall.

The other merchants had come out of their stalls to watch. They were frightened.

"You shouldn't have done that," the bird-seller said. "You've lost a day's business and now we'll never be rid of them."

The others agreed. "What will you do now, Sarai?" a woman asked. "When your husband comes back from fishing, he'll be very angry."

"That was stupid," said another.

"Stupid indeed," called yet another.

Sarai was blinking, near tears at the jibes and taunts from her neighbors. Joshua put his arm around her shoulder to comfort her.

The crowd parted before a wiry little man dragging a cart.

"Sarai," he called out, "what's happening?"

Sarai, big as she was, folded herself into the arms of the little fellow.

"It's Nahum, her husband", the bird-seller said. "He'll give her what for."

"Nahum," she was crying, "there were beggars, many of them. I—don't know what came over me—I gave them all the fish."

Nahum smiled. "Look," he said, pointing to his cart. "The biggest catch I've ever had. The fish were leaping into the nets as if by magic. I never saw anything like it. We couldn't possibly sell it all before it turned rancid. I was going to bring it to the synagogue, so they could give it to the poor. Sarai—you beat me to it."

They were both laughing and crying now. The other merchants looked on in surprise, then drifted back to their stalls.

"Nahum," Sarai said, "I want you to meet a true holy man."

19.

CHORAZIN

The synagogue at Chorazin was much smaller than at Capernaum, a simple box-like structure with a flat wooden roof. Many of the townspeople had crowded in, having heard that a stranger was to speak. The blind man had told the leader of the synagogue how Joshua had healed him, but the leader had never believed the man was truly blind, so he disregarded the story. Still, the former blind man had made a gift of several denarii to the synagogue and that had made the leader wonder.

The blind man had also told some of his friends, and a small group of them, crippled and blinded, had come to the synagogue.

Sarai had told the story of how she had given away all her fish and had been given double in return.

"That had nothing to do with the holy man," her friends said. "Nahum is just a good fisherman."

But Sarai knew better. "The gift is from God," Sarai said. "Never forget that."

Even those who did not believe the Godly connection were waiting anxiously in the synagogue. Those who did believe, and they were many, were very hopeful. This might be one of the signs they had been waiting for.

Again, that week, the reading was from Isaiah, but this time Joshua chose another text for his commentary.

One of the elders frowned. "You should be talking on Isaiah," he said to Joshua.

"I go where the Lord leads me," Joshua said, but he spoke mildly. The man was aged and Joshua showed him respect.

Joshua knew that he should be reading from the scroll, but he felt compelled to quote from memory, speaking in a rich, clear voice that echoed in the small sanctuary:

"'Refrain from anger, and forsake wrath!

Fret not yourself; it tends only to evil.
For the wicked shall be cut off;
But those who wait for the Lord shall inherit the earth.
Yet a little while, and the wicked shall be no more;
though you look well at his place, he will not be there.
But the meek shall inherit the earth;
and shall delight themselves in the abundance of peace.'

"What David tells us in this psalm," Joshua said, "is coming nigh. The mild and the gentle, the honest and the God-fearing shall indeed inherit the earth—and in peace."

He looked about him at the crowded congregation. He could sense their yearning and their doubts. "I know that it is difficult to believe these things, after wars and pestilence, earthquakes and drought, after years of occupation by the soldiers of other lands. And yet—that is the promise of the Lord, and it will be fulfilled if we will but follow the Lord's way.

"God told us through the prophet Jeremiah, 'I set before you the way of life and the way of death.' He told our forefathers that they who fought would die, but that those who surrendered would have their lives as a prize. But our forefathers would not listen. They fought and they died and their Temple was burned to the ground.

"That will be our fate, too, if we do not listen to the Lord.

"What does God mean by surrender? Must we bow and bend the knee to the oppressor? No, we must bend the knee to God. We must follow the way of the Lord—wherever it may lead us. Then, indeed, in meekness we shall inherit the earth and the Lord God will protect us from our enemies."

The people of Chorazin shifted uncomfortably. The words confused them. Was Joshua telling them to oppose the Romans—or not? And if they were to oppose them, in what way?

"In the Book of Exodus, God enjoins us that if we come upon our enemy's ox or ass going astray, we should bring it back to him. If the Lord wants us to return our enemy's beast of burden, how much more must it be our duty to lead our enemy himself back when he has gone astray?

"A proverb also warns us that we should not rejoice when our enemy falls or be glad when he stumbles.

"If the Lord our God tells us to help our enemy when he goes astray and not to rejoice when he falls, if our God tells us not to fight our enemy but to seek peace—can those who counsel war be right?"

He waited for a moment before he spoke again. "The words of God are clear. It is in Him that we must trust. It is the Almighty who will defend us from our enemies, who will lift the burden of our oppression. God will do this, in God's time—and I tell you that time is nigh—if we will but prepare ourselves. If we will turn away from evil and turn back to God. If we will purify our very souls and bend the knee before the Lord. He has given us every sign. If we will but listen, we will be saved. If we turn away, then we will surely die.

"Let us follow the counsel of the Lord—let us choose life."

The people stirred, moved by his powerful voice and the urgency of his words.

One of the elders, a powerful looking old man, spoke out. "What if the Romans will not let us 'choose life.'?"

"The Romans can't stop you," Joshua said. "Your life is in God's hands."

"Why has he permitted our land to suffer?"

"The Lord has tested you, but the time of testing will soon end. You must turn to the Lord; you must repent all your sins—for the Kingdom of God is at hand."

Someone called out, "Where, when, how?"

"Are you not made in the image of God?" Joshua responded. "Is not the light of God's truth and love within you? It's time to live in the light that only the Lord can provide, the light we all share, that lives within us, struggling to break free."

The blind man spoke from the back of the crowd. "I trust him," he said. "He healed my blindness."

"It's not true," someone whispered. "He was never blind."

"It is true," someone called, "I've known him since birth."

The argument spread through the congregation. Joshua raised his arms and closed his eyes.

"Oh, Lord," he said, "in whose great name all blessings come. Let these people know that all healing comes from Thee alone—that all goodness comes from Thee in thy divine mercy. Save us Lord, save us from the wicked and the evil, from the slayer of men and the slayer of good thoughts. Give us thy love and the blessings of thy salvation."

"Amen," said the leader of the congregation, and the elders echoed amen and so the affirmation spread through the congregation.

Joshua strode from the *bema*, made his way through the crowd and out onto the open space before the synagogue. The congregation spilled from the building.

"Heal me, Master!" cried a child with a crippled leg.

"Heal me," called another with blind eyes. The cries rose all around him, while the healthy ones in the congregation watched. Joshua knew that God had used him to heal many times, but he was always reluctant to heal before a crowd, not wishing to flaunt the privilege the Lord had given him. But he was touched by the weak and the wounded, pleading with him, and he saw, too, that in this congregation, if he refused to heal, that many would be turned from the Lord.

"Come," he said, "down to the lake."

The crowd followed, many walking and trying to gain his attention, some singing psalms of David.

"Simon," Joshua said, "you and Judith will help me."

"How?" they asked.

"The Lord tells me we must persuade these people to repent their sins, and then immerse them in the lake, to purify them. We must do as Johannon did on the banks of the Jordan. And then we must prepare them for what is to come."

He turned abruptly before Jacob and Judith could ask him what he meant by those words. They hurried after him.

When they reached the shore of the lake, Joshua stood on a small rise of ground and raised his arms for silence.

"Blessed art thou, O Lord, our God, ruler of the universe, who ransoms the captive and heals the sick, who brings peace and joy to the righteous."

"Now," he said, "first you must repent your sins and then into the lake with you."

Simon and Judith led the crippled ones into the shallows. Some resisted and turned away, but others waded in, their faces radiant with hope.

"God, these are your creatures, your sons and your daughters. They have come to repent their sins and to give their lives only to you."

He waded into the water, touching each of the cripples with his hands as he moved.

"Pray, my friends, pray. Repent your sins and pray that the Lord will hear your prayer and forgive you."

"Forgive me, Lord," one cried, and then another, until a hymn of repentance rose from the lake to the very heavens.

"Now," Joshua said. Judith and Simon began to immerse the cripples in the lake, one after another, while Joshua raised his face to the heavens and prayed fervently. Others of the congregation, on the shore, moved by what they saw, also began to pray.

"My arm," a boy cried out. "I can move it."

A cheer from the shore, and then a blind woman screamed. "Lord, God, thank you. I can see! "

"Let them see," Joshua called. "Those whose eyes are covered by wounds and those whose eyes are covered by sin. Let thy healing love bless them all, Lord."

Those in the water were calling to God, jumping up and down and laughing. Several had taken hands and were circling in the lake.

Others on the shore—those who were not crippled or blinded physically, but whose hearts were troubled by their misdeeds—they, too had moved into the water. "I have no visible scars," one woman said, "But I have wronged my family. Can I be forgiven?" she asked.

"The Lord will forgive you, if you truly repent and if you live the righteous life according to the law and the prophets."

More and more people waded into the water, raising their arms and praying to God, repenting their sins and pleading for forgiveness. Now Andrew and Jacob were helping with the immersions. Some who had been immersed turned and helped their brothers and sisters.

"Thank you, Lord," Joshua said. "Thank you for hearing our prayers and giving us your healing grace."

Many were now about him, laughing and crying and pulling at his arms and his clothing.

"Bless you, Joshua," they said.

"Bless the Lord," he reminded them.

"Surely the Lord has sent you," a healed man cried.

"The Messiah," said another.

The idea seemed to stun the crowd.

"Yes, it must be he."

But others in the congregation were angry at what had happened and appalled by the members of the congregation abandoning themselves to such actions and strange words.

"It's crazy," they were saying.

"He's a nobody from Nazareth," said another.

"Do the authorities know of this?" asked one of the elders.

But the words of the naysayers were swallowed up in the enthusiasm of the greater part of the congregation.

20.

BETHSAIDA

Dozens, perhaps hundreds of people were immersed that day at Chorazin. Some of the members of the congregation complained, questioning whether it was proper to do such things on the Sabbath, but their voices were lost in the general euphoria of the moment.

It was difficult for Joshua to move away from the crowd, even a few steps. He was patient and spoke to as many as he could, assuring them that the Kingdom of God was close at hand, indeed they were made in God's image and the light of his wisdom and divine holiness not only surrounded them, but was within them, each and every one. Thus the kingdom of God was within their grasp, if they would but open their hearts and minds. They had taken the first steps in repenting their sins and purifying their bodies. But, he warned them that more would soon be required of them, and they should therefore remain alert and prepared.

Many were insistent; they wanted exact and precise knowledge.

"What day, Master."

"Will the Messiah come first?"

"Are you the Messiah?"

Joshua never answered directly. Finally, Simon, exasperated by all the pressure on Joshua, pushed through the crowd. "We must go, Rabbi," he said. "We are expected."

Joshua smiled, and did not resist when Andrew, Jacob and even Judith formed a kind of protective guard and escorted him away. Still, many followed, and it was hours before the last of the crowd had fallen away and returned to Chorazin.

***

Joshua and his followers were on the road to Bethsaida.

"Why didn't you answer," Judith asked, "when they asked if you are the Messiah?"

"Such names and titles are not important. Only the word of God matters."

"But the people are expecting the Messiah and God has promised he will come," Jacob said.

"We must be patient," Joshua answered. "We've spoken only to a few people in Chorazin and Capernaum. We have to carry our message to the whole country—only then, will we be ready."

The others were silent, thinking.

"Even in Jerusalem?" Andrew asked.

Joshua laughed. "Especially in Jerusalem—that is where the message must inevitably be preached."

"They don't like Galileans there, I hear," Andrew said.

"They like Romans even less. After all, we are their brothers."

Andrew shrugged, unconvinced.

"Don't worry," Joshua said, ruffling his hair. "God will protect us."

But Simon was worrying—it hadn't even been easy protecting the Rabbi from a few hundred Jews at Chorazin. What would it be like in Jerusalem?

Jacob was more reflective than any of the others. He had always known that his brother was unique and had powers far beyond those of ordinary men, but to be able to heal the blind and the lame, that he had never expected. Then, too he had been astonished by the ecstasy that Joshua had aroused among even the "normal." Could that energy be harnessed and directed to God's will?

Joshua was wondering about the same questions. He must be careful with the office God had laid upon him. He must not act so as to injure or harm those who believed as he did. He was a shepherd and he did not want to lose any of his sheep.

***

When they reached Bethsaida, where the Jordan entered the lake from the north, they found that news of what had happened in Capernaum and Chorazin had preceded them. Throngs of people came out to meet them on the road, including many beggars and cripples, halt, lame and blind.

With all their strength and energy, the others were unable to keep the crowds away. Joshua was pushed and pulled, moved from one place to another.

Avram, a leader of the congregation offered them lodgings and they gratefully accepted. The house was large and walled from the highway, and Joshua had a few hours rest before meeting the multitudes again.

On the Sabbath, there was a quarrel in the synagogue even before the services began. Simeon ben Shabar, One of the elders was of a noble family that lived in the hinterland and had given large sums to the congregation. "The man preaches sedition," he said to the elders. "He's only a zealot in disguise. I tell you it won't be long before the Herodians and the Romans are after him."

"He speaks only of peace and peaceful conduct," said Avram. "He's been staying in my house and I've talked to him for hours. I tell you there's no harm in him."

"He's another Judas of Galilee," Simeon ben Shabar said, "and he'll come to the same end."

"Simeon is right," said another, a learned man who called himself a Pharisee, "we're asking for trouble letting some stranger talk to the congregation. Let's persuade him to move on."

"I can't believe I'm hearing this from pious Jews," Avram said. "The synagogue is open to all and to the opinions of all who believe in the One God. If a man preaches in the Lord's name, we would endanger our own souls to keep him from the house of God."

There was grumbling, but the others agreed and Joshua was allowed to speak.

Joshua sensed the split in the congregation. He could see from the faces that surrounded him, those who were open and those who were closed to his teaching. Again he chose his text from Isaiah, speaking of beating swords into plowshares and the lion lying down with the lamb. Then he saw Simeon and others smiling thinly and realized he had played into their hands. His words were too bland for this congregation—they would come away with nothing, and their own doom would be sealed.

"Woe to those who are rich and powerful and believe that the word of God does not apply to them.

"Woe to those who believe that wealth will protect them in the last days—that they will be able to buy redemption and deliverance from the Lord.

"I tell you there is no price on redemption—it is open to all, rich and poor, humble and mighty. In the end of days—on the LAST DAY, the Lord will choose those who are righteous, not those who are rich—those who have repented, not those who have built a wall of wealth to protect themselves.

"There is no protection from the justice of God. Pious words and gifts to the Temple will not be able to purchase the blessings of the Lord.

"Be not smug and self-contented, ye rich and powerful, for when the Messiah comes and the Kingdom of God is fulfilled, ye shall all be humble before the Lord and He shall reign forever."

There was a commotion along the eastern wall where the elders sat in the places of honor. Simeon ben Shabar had listened to Joshua's words with increasing anger. He had looked balefully at Avram for bringing this man under their roof. As Joshua thundered against the smug and the wealthy, Simeon had risen in his place to bring his personal condemnation on this stranger.

But even as Simeon stood up, as he raised his arm, a strange look came upon him. His face purpled and he began to gasp and wheeze. Others tried to help, but Simeon was caught by some great seizure that sent shudders through his body, even as he collapsed to the floor. The congregation pushed forward, those who had seen and those who had not.

Joshua pushed through the crowd and knelt by the side of Simeon. The man was breathing rapidly, his eyes glaring out and shudders convulsing his body. He stared at Joshua, his hatred still fixed on his face.

Joshua laid hands on his twitching body, praying aloud as he did so. Then he touched the face and the lips of Simeon, fervently invoking God's help.

The others, awed by his strength and the fervor of his words, backed away. Joshua was alone beside Simeon, circled by astonished and frightened people.

"Forgive him, Father, for the anger he showed here in your house. Forgive him for the hatred in his heart and the weakness of his spirit. Give him the strength to find your way and to repent of his sins."

As Joshua held the face of Simeon in his two hands and prayed in a strong voice, the body of Simeon gradually relaxed. His breathing slowed and the harsh look left his eyes. Then, after a moment, his eyes closed.

"He's dead!" his wife screamed.

"No," Joshua said. "He's asleep. When he awakens, he'll be well." Joshua looked to Jacob and Simon. "Carry him to his home."

They lifted Simeon, while the congregation watched, silent and fascinated, and began to carry him towards the door of the synagogue.

As they reached the door and others pushed it open, the morning sun fell on Simeon and his eyes fluttered open. He smiled at Simon. "Put me down—please," he said.

They tried to lay him on a bench, but Simeon resisted, gently, and pushed himself erect.

"Where is he?" Simeon asked in a very mild voice. "Where is the one who has saved me?"

***

The excitement that day at Bethsaida was even greater than at Capernaum and Chorazin. Much of the congregation had privately shared Simeon's reservations about the stranger, and when Simeon had been healed and then acknowledged Joshua's part in his recovery, the results were explosive.

Again, the blind and the halt clamored for Joshua's ministrations. Again he led the congregation to the lake. Joshua led the entire congregation in prayer and then, with the help of his followers and others, proceeded with immersion in the waters. Simeon was the first to be immersed and when he arose from the water, his face looked youthful and his eyes were clear. He hurried to Joshua and embraced him, wet as he was. Joshua did not retreat from his embrace or the embrace of the others who surrounded him.

"Tell me, Rabbi," what should I do?" Simeon said.

"Live righteously, give all you can unto the poor and love your God, with all your heart, all your soul and all your might."

"Done, Rabbi, it shall be done."

The members of the congregation formed circles within circles and were weaving in and out, chanting and singing psalms, praising God. Joshua watched and smiled and felt his heart expand with love of his people. The more he loved, the more love he felt.

Again, getting away was difficult. Joshua. Jacob, Judith, Simon and Andrew found themselves backed against the lake, with nowhere to go.

Then, two fishermen brought their boat close to shore. "Come aboard, Master," one of them called. "Travel with us."

"That's a good idea," Jacob said. Joshua agreed. He stepped into the boat with his followers and the fishermen swiftly poled them away from shore.

"Aren't you Johannon, the son of Zebedee?" Simon asked.

"Yes," Johannon said, "this is my brother, Jacob."

21.

RECRUITS

Johannon and Jacob, the sons of Zebedee, although several years apart, looked like twins. They were both short and wiry, with curly red hair, receding heavily and short beards. Their eyes were a lively blue and they often smiled, even when they were angry, as if the thought of a violent response was attractive to them.

They were able and energetic fishermen, but noted for their ability to drink away their profits, even before they were earned. And when they fought, which was often, they fought as a pair, back to back. They were known as the "sons of thunder," because they were lightning fast in a fight—and lightning of course, comes before the thunder.

Simon, himself a fisherman, knew most of the fishermen on the lake, at least by sight, and the sons of Zebedee by reputation. Therefore, he was reluctant to board their boat, but the press of the crowd was so great that he was afraid that otherwise, the Master would be overwhelmed.

"It's the Sabbath," a man was crying, "you mustn't sail on the Sabbath."

"The sun is down," Simon yelled. "The Sabbath is over."

"Not quite," Joshua observed mildly, but it was clear that the route of safety was over the lake, Sabbath or not.

The brothers poled out into the lake quickly, then hoisted their sail, and in a moment they were far from the crowd, still yelling and calling in the shallows.

"Where to?" Johannon Ben Zebedee smiled, and his brother Jacob echoed his smile.

"The eastern shore," Joshua said. "It will be quieter there."

The breeze caught the sail, it snapped loudly, and the trim boat turned into the wind and headed for the eastern shore, while the sky darkened all around them. Jacob, the eldest brother, handled the steering, or rather legged it, for he stood in the stern with his knee against the tiller, casually steering his boat.

"He's cocky all right," Simon muttered under his breath.

Joshua smiled, seeing Simon's hostility.

"What is it?" he asked.

Simon shook his head. He didn't want to speak openly before the brothers.

Judith skimmed a hand in the water. It was her first time on a boat and she was exhilarated. Her brother, Jacob, thought she might be frightened, but he saw the glow in her cheeks and the smile on her face. He, himself, was tight with fear at first—he was a carpenter, not a sailor, but as soon as he saw how capable the brothers were, he relaxed.

Johannon, the youngest, came up to Joshua, shyly twisting his hands.

"Saw what you did with the blind folk," he said.

"What God did," Joshua reminded him gently.

"Yuh. Right. We was...we was very...surprised. I mean...we...I don't know how to say it."

"I understand," Joshua said. "The power of the Lord is awe-inspiring."

"That's it," Johannon said.

Simon had come up, suspicious of Johannon Ben Zebedee. "What do you want?" he asked.

Johannon blinked. "Nothing—that is, we sort of felt...something when we heard the rabbi speak...we wanted to be...part of it, if you know what I mean?"

He looked anxiously at Joshua, his blue eyes blinking rapidly. Behind him, at the tiller, his brother's expression echoed his own.

"You can be part of it." Simon said. "When we reach the other shore, we'll baptize you."

Joshua covered his smile. Simon was showing real authority. Then, Simon realized what he had said. "That is, if it's all right with you, Master?"

Joshua nodded.

Simon turned and raised his voice so Jacob Ben Zebedee could also hear. "You'll have to give up your drinking."

Johannon hesitated and looked back at his brother, then, without a word, they both nodded.

"And your whoring."

They both nodded quickly.

"And your fighting."

There was a long pause. Johannon and Jacob, the sons of Zebedee, thought about that, long and hard.

"From what we seen," Johannon said, "we sort of thought the rabbi might need us to fight for him."

Simon roared. "If he needs a good fighter, he has me! Joshua is a man of peace, not war."

Simon looked at Joshua and Joshua nodded approvingly.

"Well," Johannon said, "if you ever need anyone to fight—we're here." His brother was nodding vigorously.

Joshua smiled broadly. "I'll remember that."

"You'll have to earn your keep," Simon said.

"We'll bring in the fish to feed you," Johannon said, "We're very good at that."

Now Simon was worried.

"Don't worry," Joshua said. "There will be labor enough for all."

When they reached the eastern shore, it was totally dark and Joshua said, "We'll wait until morning for the baptism."

Simon and Jacob, Joshua's brother, built a fire and the Zebedee brothers supplied fish from their boat. Judith and Andrew did the cooking. They ate together and prayed together and, led by the brothers, sang fisherman's tunes, although Simon disapproved because the songs were a bit rough. It was decided that Jacob, the son of Zebedee would be Little Jacob, to differentiate him from Jacob, Joshua's brother, who would instead be called Brother Jacob.

Then they slept together in the lee of the boat.

In the night, Joshua wakened to find Judith, hunched near the coals of the fire, laboriously writing on a small scroll. "What are you doing?" he asked.

Judith, startled, at first thought to hide the scroll that she held, then thought better of it. "Each night I recall as much as I can of what you've told the people during the day, and I write it down as you instructed me to."

"You seem to be working very hard," Joshua said, touched by her words.

"I like doing it. The words mean so much to me. When I have forgotten, I can look in the scroll and recall. It's not easy—I'm not very good at writing. The Master of the synagogue didn't think girls needed to learn such things, but mother helped me. The more I do, the better I get."

Joshua took the scroll and squinted at it in the near darkness. "Did I say that?" he asked.

"Sort of," Judith said. "I write it down as I remember it."

"You have to get some rest," Joshua said, touching her shoulder. "You mustn't sit up all night doing this."

"I'm fine," she said. "I've never been better—I want the world to know what you're saying," she burst out.

He put a finger to her lips. "You'll waken the others." He paused. "The world? I don't know. My countrymen—I hope so. If there's time." Then surprised by his own words, he amended them quickly. "The Lord will see there is time enough."

Judith smiled at him and then began writing again, slowly and painstakingly. In a moment, she had forgotten that Joshua was there. He lay down, and after a while, fell asleep.

At dawn they were awakened by voices on the water. Several boats were approaching in the pale, misty morning.

"Found 'em," a voice called.

"Told you they'd make landfall near here," another replied. The voices sounded eerie, hollow, skipping over the water.

Joshua and his followers were on their feet now, fully awake and peering into the fog. Simultaneously, several boats appeared and those aboard cheered.

"Master," "Rabbi," "Save us," "Heal us," the voices soared across the water as the boats touched land, and dozens of people, men and women, many of them cripples, spilled onto the shore.

Joshua was astonished. "I thought we would have a few quiet days," he said to Judith, noting that her eyes were red from her night's work.

Judith held on to his arm. "We'll send them off," she said.

"No," he told her. "We mustn't do that."

Joshua put on his phylacteries and his tallith and led the group in morning prayers. Then, they waded into the chilly waters, unwarmed by the still hazy sun. After Little Jacob and Johannon had voiced sincere repentence for their many sins, Joshua baptized them, praying for their souls and for Israel. They came out of the water, shaking from the cold, but exhilarated and laughing and crying, in their dedication.

"Now will you heal us," a blind man cried.

Joshua was angry. "I tell you now what I've told you before, that the Lord Almighty is your healer and I am only the instrument of his healing. Unless you believe in the Lord and have total faith in him, you cannot be healed, but if you have such faith, and are truly prepared to repent your sins, then God will bestow his blessings upon you."

The crowd was silent, hearing Joshua's powerful voice and his anger. They stood motionless and many bowed their heads. Joshua then felt sorry for them.

"Come to me, put your trust in the Lord and I will lay my hands upon you."

A man, almost a boy, hopped forward on a withered leg, his eyes bright with hope, his mouth tight with determination. As he reached Joshua, he stumbled and sprawled on the ground. Joshua reached down quickly and lifted him up. The boy smiled. "Thank you, Rabbi," he said and without thinking he put full weight on his withered leg.

Startled, he looked down. "I'm healed," he said in wonderment. He pushed down on the foot again and again. "I'm healed," he said, and then louder, "I'M HEALED."

At that moment, the sun finally burned through the mists and the heat of it struck all who stood on the beach.

Joshua looked upwards into the heavens. "Thank you, Lord, for all your blessings."

A cheer went up from the crowd and then they pressed forward. Simon and Andrew, Johannon and Little Jacob held them off as first, they repented their sins, and then Joshua immersed and healed them, one after another, while the rest sang psalms and praised God and wondered.

***

Joshua and his followers walked from town to town. The group had increased now by a number of people who insisted on following them. Joshua had not accepted them as members of his group, but neither would he turn them away. He was afraid that the larger number would be a distraction and might even arouse the opposition of the local authorities, both Herodian and Roman, but for the moment, he permitted them to follow.

In each town, on market days and on the Sabbath, Joshua preached to the people the word of God, the need for repentance and the imminence of the coming of the Messiah.

Many questioned whether he, himself was the Messiah, but he did not declare himself. Many asked him what they were supposed to do when the Messiah came and he tried to explain without causing premature reactions.

Brother Jacob was impatient. "Why don't you tell them what you want of them? Why not make it clear they are not to obey the Romans or pay their taxes, but neither are they to fight them?"

285

"The time isn't now," Joshua said. "We've only spoken to a few here in Galilee—we must speak to the nation. Only when all of Israel is ready, will our plan be effective. God doesn't want to save only a few. He plans to save us all."

"If you spoke out," Simon said, "the word would spread and the nation would rise as one man."

"Patience, Simon," Joshua said. "We must wait on the Lord.'"

22.

THE SERMON

Each night, Judith wrote down what she remembered of the day and especially what her brother had said. When doubtful, she compared her recollections with the others. It was amazing how much their memories of Joshua's words differed, but somehow, Judith managed to keep the sense of it intact. Sometimes, his words were so powerful that they rang in her ears again and again, and there was no problem being faithful to them.

The group was better organized now. The sons of Zebedee provided transportation and fished to give them food. Andrew had taken over most of the cooking.

Brother Jacob took on a few odd carpentering jobs when in town, to bring them a little money for their other needs.

Simon went into the towns ahead of the others to scout them out. If Roman or Herodian troops were there, they would bypass the town and preach elsewhere. If the town seemed to be "open" and if Simon had friends there, he would try to find a place for them to stay. If not, he would ask the people at the synagogue for help. Joshua's name and his teachings often preceded them, and there were many anxious to hear him speak. Some were willing to provide lodgings for at least part of the group.

Those without Joshua's sanction, "the wanderers," as he called them, had to find lodgings of their own, or they slept out of doors. It was summer and that was not unpleasant.

They had circled the lake, teaching, preaching and baptizing in many towns and villages and had returned to Capernaum. When they approached the synagogue on the Sabbath, they were astonished. The building was crowded and hundreds more, possibly thousands, filled the open area before the entrance.

It required the efforts of all of them to keep the crowd from crushing Joshua.

Jairus, the leader of the congregation, came out to speak to him. Jairus was a pleasant man, of vigorous middle years, with a full head of hair, still dark and a trim beard. "What will we do, Rabbi? The synagogue is already crowded and the people outside can't hear."

Joshua pointed to a grassy hilly rising east of the synagogue. "Hold your services there, and then all will hear."

"Outdoors?" Jairus asked, frowning.

"The ark of the scrolls is made of wood and can be carried. The table on the *bema* can be carried, too."

Jairus hesitated. He and the townspeople were very proud of their synagogue.

"The Lord loves the lake and the hills," Joshua said, "as much as the synagogue."

People who were standing nearby murmured in agreement. Jairus smiled suddenly and hurried into the synagogue.

Joshua called to his followers: "Simon, Andrew, Little Jacob, Brother Jacob and Johannon, go help them." They nodded and pushed their way through the crowd.

The elders and the leaders of the synagogue came first, wearing their phylacteries and prayer shawls, and then the followers of Joshua, carrying the ark and the table. The procession had a festive appearance as they walked the short distance—a clearly permitted Sabbath walk, to the top of the hill, with the people following them.

It was a beautiful summer morning, with a clear, bright sky and dazzling sun. Below the hilltop, toward the lake, stood a cluster of date palms, new and short, but thick in the trunk, with fronds whispering in the breeze.

On the lake, the breeze made little, frothy waves and on the shore, the prayer shawls riffled like banners. The people spread themselves around the hillside and settled down for the service, all breathing in the fine, clean air and enjoying this unusual outdoor service. The Sabbath clothing of the women looked especially cheerful outdoors and the gentle breeze set skirts and shawls fluttering, like the flags of God's legions.

They set the wooden ark with its covering curtain of blue velvet cloth, embroidered with gold letters, firmly on the ground, and placed the table with its covering of fine linen squarely at the center of the level area.

Then, in the open air, in the full sight of God and man, the congregation of Capernaum, swelled by thousands of curious Jews and not a few gentiles, listened to the Sabbath service.

When the time came for Joshua to teach, Jairus gestured to him. He rose and walked up the slope over the sweet smelling grass and stood before, not behind the table.

Joshua's skin had darkened during his weeks of walking and preaching, but his hair had lightened. He looked both robust and ethereal. He gazed about him at the multitude patiently waiting and he felt a great sense of love and affection for these people. Their eyes were fixed on him with hope. He could both see and feel their yearning. They trusted in him as he trusted in God and he must assure them of their place in God's plans.

Joshua did not look at the scrolls and he put aside the words he had thought of speaking, but instead, and without preparation he spoke from his heart. As he preached, his eyes on first one person, then another, one family and then another, as if he saw into their very hearts, as if he knew personally their strengths and weaknesses, their hope and despairs.

"Blessed are you who are humble in spirit, for yours is the kingdom of heaven.

"Blessed are you who mourn, for God will comfort you.

"Blessed are the gentle ones, for you will inherit the earth.

"Blessed are you who hunger for righteousness, for you shall be satisfied.

"Blessed are the merciful, for you shall have mercy.

"Blessed are the pure in heart, for you will see God.

"Blessed are the peacemakers, for you shall be called the children of God."

He glanced toward his followers, sitting near the bottom of the hill towards the lake. "Blessed are you who are persecuted for righteousness sake—rejoice and be glad, for your reward is great in heaven."

Joshua turned to address another part of his audience. "You are the salt of the earth—and you must preserve your flavor, lest you be destroyed.

"You are the light of the world." He pointed to the ark and the scrolls. "A city set on a hill cannot he hid. You do not light a lamp and then hide it under a bushel. Let your own light shine before men that they will see your good works and give glory to your Father, who is in heaven."

Once more he turned and this time he spoke to Jairus and other leaders.

"I am not here to condemn the law and the prophets. Truly, I say to you, till heaven and earth pass away, not a line, not a word, not a sign will pass from the law. He who ignores the law shall be least in the Kingdom of Heaven, but he who teaches and lives the law shall be called great.

"But the rigor of the law is not enough and surely the mouthing of pious promises unfulfilled means nothing in the eyes of God."

Some of the elders moved uncomfortably as he spoke, feeling the accusation. But already, Joshua had turned away. He raised his arms and spoke in a passionate voice to all of the audience.

"We must love the law and we must go beyond it in our love of God.

"The law says, "Thou shalt not murder," but that is only the least of what God requires. That was good enough even for the heathen. Can it be enough for us in these times of tribulation?

"No, I tell you that everyone who is angry with his brother shall be liable to judgment. He who insults his brother shall be liable to the council and he who calls another 'fool' shall be in danger of hell fire."

"Yes," he said, sensing the surprise of the congregation, "hell fire."

"When, on the festivals, you bring your gift to the altar, and there you remember you have wronged your brother—leave your gift and first be reconciled to your brother—then make your sacrifice. You must be relieved of sin before you participate in the ritual."

His eyes swept the audience again and each of them could feel the fire in Joshua's heart searching them out, sensing their sins and reminding them of their wrongdoing.

"The law says, 'Thou shalt not commit adultery,' but that is the least of what God requires. For I tell you that each of you who looks upon another lustfully has already committed adultery in his heart.

"Yes," he repeated, "in his heart. For sin is not only the outward deed— no, even more, it is the inward false spirit.

"If your right eye shows you evil, pluck it out. It is better to lose an eye than to have your whole body cast into hell. If your fingers itch to do wrong, cut them off, for it is better to have no fingers than to be cast into hell."

Joshua left the hilltop and began moving among the people. He spoke directly to them, now and then speaking to one person or another, as if knowing his or her personal sins intimately. Many cowered and covered their faces. All were silent before the force of his teaching.

"The law tells us, 'Thou shalt not swear falsely.' But I say to you, that it is the least of what God requires. Do not swear at all, either by heaven, which is the throne of God, or by earth which is His footstool.

"Don't swear by your head—by your swearing you cannot make one hair white or black. Say what you have to say simply, 'Yes,' or 'No.' Anything else comes from evil intention."

Joshua made his way back to the hilltop. "The Law demands an eye for an eye and a tooth for a tooth," but I tell you that is the least that God demands. I say, do not resist one who is evil. If any strike you on the right cheek, turn to him the other, also. If any would take your coat, give him your cloak also. If one would force you to go a mile, go with him two miles. And more than that, give freely to him who begs from you and never refuse him who would borrow from you."

Joshua could see the surprise in the faces around him, could see them look at each other in wonderment.

"Do you wonder," he said, "at this teaching? Of course, you have heard it said that you should love thy neighbor as thyself, and you believe that means you are free to hate your enemy.

"But that is not so. Your enemy is part of God's Kingdom as well. I say to you that God requires more. You must love your enemies and pray for those who persecute you. In no other way can you be sons of your Father who is in heaven, and who makes the sun shine on the good and the evil alike, who sends the blessed rain to both the just and the unjust.

"If you love only those who love you, what reward shall you have? Even the most evil of men love their wives and children and their friends. If you are kind only to those who are close to you, what more are you doing than others? Even the heathen do the same.

"No, it is not enough. The Lord God requires that you must be perfect, as your heavenly Father is perfect. Then, and then only, will you be fit to enter the Kingdom of heaven."

Joshua would have finished then, but the congregation sat in silence, tremendously moved by his words and patiently waiting for him to continue. Joshua started down the hill towards his followers.

"Please," a pretty young woman, holding the hand of her son, said to him, "we want to hear more."

He smiled and shook his head, but others took up her plea. "Please, Rabbi, speak to us."

Not all of the leaders and elders were pleased to have Joshua capture the hearts of their congregation.

"That's enough," one stern-faced man said, for he had heard words which he found to be critical of himself in Joshua's teaching, although he had not been mentioned by name.

"I agree," said another, "it *is* enough. This service outdoors was questionable, anyway."

Others, who had also heard their sins named in Joshua's sermon and were displeased, also hoped the crowd would disperse, but others, recognizing their errors, yearned to repent and to begin afresh. They looked at Joshua with new hope, although they were too chastened even to speak.

Joshua felt the struggle in the congregation between those who recognized the truth and those who denied it, and he felt compassion even for those who hated him. Overwhelmingly, he was moved by the goodness of the people and touched by the many, now on their feet, pleading with him to continue. He nodded and the crowd settled down in anticipation.

Joshua spoke directly to the stern-faced man, who had wanted to end the teaching and who still scowled at him, angry and self-righteous.

"Beware of practicing your piety before men, in order to be seen by them. The mere outward show of piety will bring no reward."

The man turned red, but Joshua had moved on until he stood before a group of wealthy men who had remained seated while others were calling for Joshua to continue. "When you give alms, sound no trumpet before you, as the hypocrites do, desiring to be praised by men, for you will have the reward you have earned. I say to you, when you give alms, don't let your left hand know what your right hand is doing. Let your alms-giving be in secret and the Father will reward you in secret."

Joshua strode on, passing by the scholars and those who prayed constantly in the synagogues. "When you pray," he told them, "be not like the hypocrites who love to pray where they may be seen by men. Go into your room and close the door. Pray to the Lord in secret and your Father will reward you—in secret."

Some nodded in agreement, while others were uncomfortable, but Joshua had left them and was speaking to the entire congregation. "When you pray, don't pile up empty phrases, like the heathen, who believe the very sound of their many words will be enough. Your Father in heaven knows your needs before you ask him. Therefore I tell you, pray simply, like this:

Our Father who art in Heaven, Hallowed be thy name. Thy Kingdom come, Thy will be done, on earth as it is in Heaven. Give us this day our daily bread, and forgive us our trespasses, as we forgive those who trespass against us. Preserve us against temptation, and deliver us from evil; For Thine is the Kingdom, The Power and the Glory, Forever...Amen."

And when he had finished, the congregation responded with a mighty "Amen" and Joshua smiled. He knew then that he had preached enough for that day and he left the hilltop and made his way towards the lake.

But the people were stirred by his words, many of them repeating to each other the prayer he had taught them, so that the words sounded again and again.

"Our Father who art in heaven,"

"Give us this day..."

"The Kingdom and the Power..."

The words ran together and over each other, and sounded in cadence and harmony, until there was a kind of chant moving through the crowd.

They were all on their feet, some angered and hurrying away, others ashamed of their sins and afraid of looking at each other, but most of them surging toward Joshua, wanting to touch him and be touched by him, to speak to him and to again hear his voice.

Simon and Andrew and the Zebedees fought their way to his side, but the crowd pressed ever closer.

"Give him room!" Simon called out in his powerful voice.

"You'll crush the rabbi!" said Little Jacob. And the crowd tried to comply, but they were too excited. Joshua found himself pushed down the hill until he reached the shore and there he stood his ground and the very force of his spirit seemed to hold the people back.

"Heal us," the sick ones pleaded, "Save us," begged the sick at heart. The urgency of their pleas touched him deeply, but he knew he could not allow the depth of their suffering to capture his own soul. He must help, but not be swept away.

Joshua gestured to those who wished to repent their sins and be immersed to enter the lake and they stepped into the shallows by the hundreds. He prayed for their souls and they clasped their hands, repented their sins and prayed with him. His followers immersed as many as they could, and others shared the duties, so that they immersed each other, while Joshua remained on the shore fervently praying for all of them.

The repentance of so many, and their choice of purity and forgiveness strengthened Joshua and he felt the spirit of God enter into him with renewed force. He called the sick to him and he healed many, while those who were well stood on the hillside and watched and rejoiced.

There was laughter and tears and many prayers and then he led them in singing psalms of liberation.

"Let's go," Judith whispered to him, her eyes shining, "it's enough."

"Yes," said Brother Jacob," you'll tire, Joshua."

Joshua shook his head. "This doesn't tire me—it makes me strong."

Thus, he waited on the shore and spoke to as many as he could, but the voices from beyond pleaded, "Speak up, Master, we can't hear you."

Joshua felt the deep hunger of the people for his words. He raised a hand to acknowledge their request and led them some distance from town to another rise of ground. He began to teach them again, as the words came to him from the Holy Spirit, continuing the sermon he had spoken before and answering the questions of the multitude.

"When you fast," he taught them, "remember what I told you about prayer. Don't put on a dismal face, like the hypocrites, but do your fasting in private so that God may see and reward you, not men.

"As you live your lives, think of your immortal souls. Why lay up treasures on earth, where moths and rust consume and thieves break in and steal. No, I tell you, lay up treasures in heaven, treasures that cannot be eaten up or stolen, for where your treasure is, there will be your heart.

"My friends, you cannot serve two masters, for you will love one and hate the other. You cannot serve both God and Greed.

"Therefore, be certain you see clearly and know what you are doing. For if your eye is sound, your whole body will be full of light, but if you hide from the truth and see only in shadow, your life will be full of darkness."

A woman who sat at his feet, got up her courage and questioned him. "We want to do right, Rabbi. How shall we live?"

He smiled. "Don't be anxious about your life. Don't worry about having enough to eat or drink, or what you wear. Isn't life more than these things?"

He pointed skyward at a flight of birds, heading across the lake. "Look at the birds of the air. They neither sow nor reap nor gather into barns, yet your heavenly Father feeds them. Are you not of greater value than they?"

He looked at a rather small young man nearing the age of adulthood, his face pimply with the juices of his youth, and he smiled. "Which of you, by worrying, can add even a finger's breadth to your height?"

He touched the head of an old man. "Which of you can add even an instant to his life?"

He spread his hands before them. "Consider the lilies of the field, how they grow. They neither toil nor spin. Yet I tell you that even Solomon in all his glory was not arrayed like one of these."

The people smiled as they regarded the wild flowers growing all about them on the hillside. Joshua's voice softened. "If God so clothes even the grain of the fields, which is alive today, but tomorrow you will cast it into the oven, will he not clothe you far better?

"Hold on to your faith and be not anxious. Even the heathen seek earthly things and God provides for all. First seek the Kingdom of God, be righteous and faithful to the Lord and the Lord will reward you with these things as well. Worry not about the morrow, for sufficient unto each day are the pangs and suffering thereof."

Once more he would have quit his teaching, but even then, with the sun sinking, they asked for more. He patiently continued, knowing he could not be certain when he would pass this way again.

"Judge not, unless you are willing to be judged yourself. Why is it that men see the speck in their brother's eye and miss the log in their own? I tell you, cleanse your own eye, purify your own self before you dare to question another.

"Cherish that which is holy—don't cast pearls before swine, lest they trample them under and turn to attack you.

"Remember that God hears all prayers. Ask, and it will be given, knock and it will open, seek and you will find. What man, if his son asks for bread would give him a stone? If you, who are not perfect, know how to give good gifts to your son, how much more will your Father in heaven give good gifts unto you—if you will but ask him with a clean and repentant heart.

"Enter by the narrow gate. Turn aside from the wide gate that leads to death and destruction. The narrow gate is the way to life, but few choose it.

"Beware of false prophets, who come to you in sheep's clothing, but are in truth, ravening wolves. They will flatter you and point out the wide gate, seeking to gain your favor. But don't believe them. You will know them by their fruits. Are grapes gathered from thorns or figs from thistles? No, only a sound tree bears sound fruit. The sick and evil tree must be cut down and cast into the fire.

"Many take the name of the Lord in vain, pretending they have followed the true way. But God knows these hypocrites and on the Last Day He will declare, 'I never knew you, depart from me, you evildoers.'

"You must build your house upon rock, not upon sand, for when the day of the Lord comes and the strong wind blows, only the house that is solidly built on the law and the prophets, on righteousness and purity, will withstand the wrath of God."

Joshua felt the affection of the people moving toward him in waves, but then he was concerned. Many were smiling, even laughing. Despite his teaching had they misunderstood the gravity of this moment? Had his message been too uplifting—were these people aware of the dangers ahead, the sacrifices that would be imposed upon them, the risk of violence and abuse? He sighed deeply and spoke again, emphasizing each word and scanning the faces of the crowd with deep concern.

"Have you heard all that I've taught you? Not just the soft words, but the hard ones? Were you listening when I told you that if you are hit on one cheek you are to turn the other cheek? That if someone takes your cloak, to offer him also your coat? That you must not only love your friends, but your enemies? Do you know what these words mean?" He paused for a moment; some were nodding, others looked confused, and still others turned and left.

Joshua glanced at Peter and Little Jacob, and they, too, seemed confused. He shook his head slightly and continued speaking. "Soon you will be called upon to put what you have learned into action. Do you wonder when the Messiah will come?" Many were nodding. "We inspire ourselves with thoughts of a great king, a warrior who will sweep our enemies away. But will the Messiah actually be a warrior? Will we arm ourselves, build walls and wait for the next assault, the next and the next? There is a better way. We must not repay violence with violence. Today is only the beginning. Let those who have ears, hear."

For a moment there was silence, then murmuring among the people. Again, some seemed to drift away, but most remained. There were few smiles, but also few frowns. Some were nodding their heads indicating they had understood. Joshua worried about those that had left.

But that was a concern for the future; today, now, he had thousands before him that must be acknowledged and—to the extent possible, perhaps, reassured.

Those who had remained were now waiting for Joshua to speak further. They had listened and been taught, they had repented and been blessed. But they were a long way from town. Some were tired and many were hungry. Before Joshua, a child began to cry, wishing to be fed, and then another.

"Are you hungry?" Joshua asked.

"Yes," many said.

"Then you must be fed."

Simon pulled at Joshua's cloak. "We're far from town," he said. "Send them back."

The pimply-faced boy whom Joshua had spoken to earlier brought out a basket. "I have two fish and five loaves of bread I brought for me and my family. We're willing to share it."

Joshua's face beamed with pleasure. He took the basket in his hands and looked toward the heavens. "Blessed art thou, O Lord, ruler of the universe, who brings forth bread from the earth and fish from the sea."

"Amen," the congregation responded

Then Joshua, holding the basket, spoke to the multitude.

"There must be others here who have something to eat and many more who have not. There must be some here who are hungry and others who are not."

He held the basket high, where all could see. "I'm going to pass this basket among you. Let those who are hungry, partake, but take only what you need, and when you have enough, pass it on. Let all the others who have food do the same. If you need it, eat from it, if you don't, pass it on to those who do."

Joshua handed the basket to a woman who sat before him. She shook her head and handed it to her husband. He, too, shook his head and passed it along.

A child took one bite from the bread and passed the basket to his sister.

Elsewhere, among the crowd, others were bringing forth food and baskets and doing the same. The food was passed from hand to hand. Some ate a bite or two; others shook their heads and passed it on, smiling as they did so.

The food passed quickly through the congregation. Some who had a crust or a morsel in their pockets or purses added it to the baskets as they moved along.

Finally, the baskets had passed through the entire throng, and were brought forward. Where Joshua had held one basket with five loaves and two fish, he now had a dozen baskets, brimming with fragments of food.

He flung his arms skyward. "Thank you, Lord for your divine mercy and goodness, for the bounty you bestow upon us."

He turned to the crowd. "Are you hungry?"

"No!" they called out in one voice.

"Are you filled?"

"Yes, yes!" they responded.

"We have seen today, a miracle. The Lord has fed us—even five thousand—with five loaves and two fish. He has shown us how we can share what we have and when we are done we will have more than we began with."

He held up one of the baskets. "Man lives not by bread alone, but by the word of God, the wisdom of the Almighty. When we share that wisdom, we can all partake of it—and when we are done we will have more than we began with—and as we share what we have been given—we will have more even than that. We must understand that a time of testing is ahead of us, that we may have to share not only bounty but pain and suffering. We can survive and prosper if we share this struggle, if we are courageous in the face of hatred and brutality.

"Remember, my brothers and my sisters, what you have learned today, and you will know all the secrets of heaven, and all the blessings of God. Take only what you need, share what you have, and the blessings of God will cascade down upon you, like manna from heaven. You will be fulfilled and you will be free."

THE MURDERED MESSIAH

BOOK 4

WAGING PEACE

1.

CORBAN

Caiaphas sat on an upholstered chair in a vast sitting room on the top story of his home. Floor to ceiling doors opened onto a broad terrace with sweeping views of Jerusalem. The chair was like a throne, and the room itself, with its high, vaulted ceiling was like a throne room. That image was not uncongenial to Caiaphas. He considered himself the ruler of his people, no matter what they thought. It was true that he had purchased his position from Valerius Gratus years before and had had to keep making "contributions" as he called them, to retain his position, but that was the despicable requirement of the Romans.

Caiaphas was serenely certain that the position of High Priest was his by birth, by right, by wealth and by wisdom. Members of his family had held the position for generations and he was surely the most able of them all.

Annas, his father-in-law, who had been High Priest himself, understood Caiaphas well. "The people should be grateful," Annas once told him, "that you are rich enough to maintain your post. Thank God it hasn't been purchased by a lesser man."

Caiaphas's eyes narrowed when Annas spoke like that. He wasn't sure whether the old man was being ironic. But Annas had a round and guileless face and his expression told Caiaphas nothing.

Despite his advanced age, Annas's skin was smooth and his color virile. Although he was fat and bald, he moved with agility and his mind was quick. Annas seldom disagreed with Caiaphas. It wasn't worth it. He was happy his daughter, Rachel, had married a rich and powerful man, but he was also aware that Caiaphas was arrogant, selfish, overbearing and insensitive. Sometimes he felt sorry for Rachel and guilty at having arranged the match, but then prudence got the better of him. The wealthy and the powerful had to do what was necessary to maintain their position. Caiaphas had strong organizational abilities, and he was personally honest. Besides, he looked like a High Priest.

"Sometimes you surprise me," Annas had said. "I think you actually believe the Roman occupation is good for Judaea."

"It is," Caiaphas answered, smiling blandly. "It brings stability to the country. If the Romans weren't here we'd have a dozen rivals for the throne—there would be wars and rebellions, revolutions and assassinations. Our country would be torn apart."

"In other words, it's better to have the Romans do the killing." Annas said. Sometimes he could hardly wait to hear what Caiaphas would tell him next.

Caiaphas frowned. "Of course—the deaths are inevitable anyway."

"Which deaths—whose deaths?"

Caiaphas sighed wearily. "Under the Romans we rule and live well."

"True," Annas said. "And if the Romans were thrown out, we might be thrown out with them."

Caiaphas shrugged. "What a price we pay to insure that our nation and its love of God both survive."

From his upholstered chair, Caiaphas could see the beautiful homes of the upper city and the great panorama of the Temple. That was his true palace, he thought, smiling inwardly. No man had a more magnificent one—and he could thank Herod for that. How difficult it was to predict from what direction great blessings would come.

Annas sat beside him, on a chair almost as high and well-upholstered. They were waiting for Nicodemus and his son, for Gamaliel and others of the Sanhedrin. It was to be an informal meeting, and Caiaphas did not relish it. Nicodemus no longer took part in the priestly courses—he had been excused for a hip ailment that disqualified him, but he was always agitating—for the people, he claimed. Nicodemus always seemed to identify with the wrong people.

A servant, bowing slavishly, announced them. Servants in Caiaphas's house had long ago learned to abase themselves if they wanted to remain in his employ. Caiaphas scorned the use of slaves. Instead, he treated free men as if they were slaves. He did not rise when his guests entered, even though Nicodemus was far older than he. Annas, however, embraced him. He liked Nicodemus and anyway, it would irritate his son-in-law.

"You look well," Annas said to the limping Nicodemus, who had to steel himself at every step.

Nicodemus smiled. "I am well," he said. "You know Nico." Even he had come to call his son by the shortened name.

Gamaliel stood a few steps away, waiting to be greeted. He was an ordinary looking man of middle years, with a high forehead and graying hair, a non-descript beard and watery eyes. He moved and talked very slowly, and one who did not know him could easily grow impatient. In fact, he was descended from the line of David, and the blessed Hillel, and his family was rich and powerful . Gamaliel was even more powerful, not because of wealth or ambition, but because of his great knowledge and wisdom and his known compassion for his people. He was a Pharisee, a devout believer in God and the law, tempered by justice and mercy and deep human feeling. If his clothes were in disarray, it was because such things were not important to him. But he knew and understood diplomacy and dignity and the prerogatives of power. He waited patiently to be called.

Caiaphas hated Gamaliel. Not because he was a Pharisee. Although Caiaphas was nominally a Sadducee, philosophical and theological issues meant nothing to him. Only power and its uses mattered. Gamaliel, who held the respect of the Sanhedrin and the people, cared nothing for power. "The man is obsessed with doing right," Caiaphas told his father-in-law, "no matter what the cost."

Caiaphas held out as long as he could. Finally, the silence was too much for him. "Welcome, Gamaliel," he said. "Please take a seat."

Servants scurried in with wooden chairs, beautifully made, but narrower and lower than the upholstered ones used by Caiaphas and his father-in-law.

Nico and Nicodemus exchanged looks at this discourtesy, but seated themselves. Gamaliel laughed, but did not sit down. Caiaphas looked at him sharply. "What amuses you, master?" Somehow he managed to say it without a capital letter.

"You wish to sit here in Solomonic splendor while the city seethes with rebellion."

"I see no rebellion," Caiaphas said smoothly.

"Following your course from this house through tunnels into the Temple, perhaps your vision is too restricted."

Annas was annoyed. "The High Priest must keep apart from the people, if he is to have their respect."

"I don't recall reading that in Holy Scripture," Gamaliel said.

Nicodemus was shifting uncomfortably. It was well known that Caiaphas and Gamaliel were spiritual opposites. This was no time for personal or philosophical quarreling.

"We came to discuss Pilate and his taking of the Corban," Nicodemus said.

"I see," Caiaphas said. "You know I am as opposed as anyone to the taking of the Temple treasury funds for the building of an aqueduct into the city. There is no precedent for it and it must be opposed."

Gamaliel could hardly believe that Caiaphas spoke so off-handedly. "It is a sacrilege," he said. "How was it done?"

"Guards from the Antonia Palace," young Nico said. "They crossed the courtyard at dawn and the minute the treasury was open, they removed vast amounts of money and jewels."

"Where were the Temple guards?" Gamaliel asked.

"I told them not to resist," Caiaphas said. "I wanted no blood shed in the Temple."

"But you told no one. We wouldn't have known if Nico hadn't reported it," said Nicodemus.

Caiaphas looked at Nico with regal disdain. "I restricted everyone to silence. Your son broke a vow."

"I made no vow, Eminence," Nico said.

"That's not important," Gamaliel broke in. "Why didn't you tell the Sanhedrin, Caiaphas?"

"I expected to work this out, quietly, with Pilate himself, before it became common knowledge."

"Well?" Nicodemus asked.

"Pilate is stubborn and uncooperative. We have exchanged several letters. He maintains he must have the right to use our funds to build an aqueduct that is for our use."

"It's not for our use," Nicodemus said. "Pilate wants another water supply to the fortress."

"It doesn't matter who is to use the water," Gamaliel said. "The Temple funds are sacred and can't be used for such a purpose."

Annas hadn't heard of this event until this very day. He watched his son-in-law and marveled. How could a man be High Priest and not erupt in outrage at such a sacrilege? Then he realized that Caiaphas was trying to avoid any sort of quarrel with Rome that might result in losing his office— no matter how vile the provocation might be. A chill went through him, as he realized how dangerous this might be for the nation.

The others sensed it, too. But nothing that Caiaphas did to appease the Romans surprised them. They had long ago realized he had few ethical standards other than the maintenance of his own power.

"We will report to the Sanhedrin this evening that action must be taken to secure the return of the Corban. If Pilate doesn't respond promptly, we'll send a delegation to Rome," said Nicodemus.

"You'll do no such thing," said Caiaphas. His serene brow was furrowed now and anger showed in his eyes. "Do you want a revolution?" he asked.

"Forgive me, Eminence," Nico said. "No matter what you told the guards, the word has spread in the city. The people are aroused and angry. If something isn't done, they may take matters into their own hands."

"You were the one who led them to Pilate when he raised the standards in the fortress," Caiaphas said. In his mouth, the words were an accusation.

"A good thing he did," Nicodemus said, supporting his son. "If the people had not been led, there would have been a bloody massacre."

"I sent Reuben to represent me," Caiaphas responded. "If the people had waited, the entire matter could have been settled quietly."

"Quietly," Gamaliel said. "That's a great word with you. What about 'honorably?'"

"'Honorably,'" Caiaphas said, "is to survive."

***

Gaius Fabricius had tried time and again to persuade Pilate to return the coins and jewels to the Temple.

"Don't be foolish," Pilate said. "If we try to assess them the cost of the aqueduct they'll try to weasel out of it. They'll cry and complain and moan to Rome and the whole matter will be delayed for more than a year. This way we'll have it built before they know it."

Gaius calmed himself, knowing that a show of anxiety would be interpreted as sympathy for the Jews. He could never allow Pilate to suspect that of him, although he constantly found himself opposing the governor's policies. However, he had learned to object only when the matter was urgent.

"Prefect, you're right of course. No people want to pay taxes and support the empire. We often have to act arbitrarily. But these are a peculiar people, as you know. To them the funds are sacred."

Pilate laughed. "Only the Jews would think money was sacred."

"Not merely money, Sire. We are talking of the Temple treasure, and by their law and even by Roman exemption that can only be used for religious purposes."

"It's a ruse, my boy, an excuse to let the would-be aristocrats hoard the treasure and divide it among their wealthy priests."

"I don't think so, but even if that were true, the people—the common people—feel it is sacred. My agents tell me there is unrest in the city, and they are planning a demonstration."

"Where?" Pilate asked. He had responded so quickly that Gaius was startled.

"Along the valley of the Cheesemakers, then around the walls of the Temple to the Antonia, and finally to this palace."

Pilate smiled and called for Septimus.

Gaius turned pale. He had believed that Septimus would be punished for his unprovoked attack on the little Galilean community, but instead Pilate had sent him off to Damascus and then, brought him back in his former position. Gaius had argued that Septimus was dangerous—that he might provoke the Jews into rebellion. But, of course, that was what attracted Pilate to him.

Gaius could not reveal his own horror and suffering over the murder of his grandchildren and the disappearance of his son, Joshua. Therefore, his complaints about Septimus sounded abstract and political rather than personal. Furthermore, Pilate relished having two subordinates who hated each other. It was unlikely they would ever combine to oppose him and their battles would be delicious to watch.

Septimus's hatred for Gaius had deepened. The man had forced him to submit to humiliation at the hands of a Jew, before his own men. That would never be forgiven. In Septimus's eyes, Gaius was the ultimate fool. He had had Septimus in his power and should have killed him. Instead, he had allowed an enemy to escape who would one day take bitter revenge.

"Tell our friend what you told me," Pilate said. When Gaius had explained about the demonstration, Septimus said, "I'll stop that before it starts."

"No," Pilate said. "I have another idea. Dress your men like civilians and have them join the crowd—get ones who look like Jews. We'll see how far the Jews will go with their moaning and complaining." Pilate stopped and smiled.

"What then, Prefect?" Septimus asked.

"When they reach this palace, fall upon them and kill them."

"Governor," Gaius was saying, "we're going to provoke a war."

"No," Pilate said, "we're going to cut it off before it begins."

2.

BAR ABBAS

Amos, the cloth merchant was having his problems with Benjamin and Josiah and other Zealot leaders.

"I tell you," Benjamin said, "if we allow the heathen to steal the Corban right out of the Temple, it's the end for the nation."

"He's right," Josiah said, "if we don't draw the line, the Romans will roll over us. Pilate is taunting us with this thing—trying to see how far he can push us."

Amos folded his arms. "Judas said, no violence in Jerusalem—not until the rising of the Messiah."

Benjamin threw up his hands. "We don't know that this man IS the Messiah—We haven't even met him."

"Go to Galilee—see for yourself," Amos said.

"Let him come here. If he's the Messiah, surely he'll come to Jerusalem."

"He'll come soon. Judas promised he would," Amos said. He hated to be arguing against taking action. He had been trying to stir up the people to resist the Romans for over twenty years. Now, Judas had urged him to keep things quiet until the proper moment.

It was getting more difficult. The people were growing restless again. Roman patrols had grown more callous in their conduct. Incidents of brutality were reported from all over the country. The harvest had been poor and that in itself led to disaffection. And there were younger men, men with even less patience than Josiah and Benjamin.

One of them sat that day in Amos's house. He was large and powerful looking, with huge arms and shoulders and swarthy skin. His hair and beard were full and untended and he was intimidating on first sight. He sat quietly, watching with narrow, unblinking eyes, listening to the older leaders, without saying a word.

His name was Gideon and his father, who had been a Zealot, himself, was called Joab. Many thought his father was particularly well-named, for although Joab had been a great general and loyal subordinate to King David, he had also been cruel and unscrupulous.

In Joab the Zealot's day, he had served the cause with fierce courage, but at times, his ferocity had awed and frightened his own supporters. He had been caught by the Romans and tortured for days before they let him die.

His son Gideon was of the same fierce cast, though larger in size and less clever than his father. His strength was legendary. Men had seen him snap a strong man's neck as if it were a twig. But mostly, he was regarded, with respect, as his father's son and that was what they called him, "Bar Abbas."

"We'll protest," Amos was saying, "but we won't be armed and we won't try to retake the Corban. We'll circle the city and go to the Herodian Palace. Pilate will only remain there until tomorrow evening. We'll have to organize in a hurry."

Bar Abbas stood up abruptly and left the house of Amos. The others were surprised and Josiah tried to follow and question him. Bar Abbas shrugged him off and stalked out of the house.

***

Young Nico stood up suddenly and hurried out onto the terrace.

"What is it?" his father asked.

"We may have waited too long," Nico said. "The protest is already under way."

The others, even Caiaphas, walked out on the terrace. Below them, in the near distance, a line of people was winding its way through the market.

Their voices drifted up over the huts and hovels of the lower city, across the walls and viaducts that separated the poorer from the wealthier districts, over the waving palms and citrons of the tended gardens, the clean swept streets and plazas of the upper city, to the polished terraces of the High Priest's palace.

"Corban," the people chanted, then walked two steps and repeated it again, "Corban." Then two more steps and "Holy," then "Holy," again.

Shopkeepers and merchants, turned to watch, then dropped their work and joined the marchers. From the Ophel, another line of men streamed down into the valley.

"Your friends," Caiaphas said to Nico scornfully. These were the younger priests who lived in near poverty on the Ophel. All of Jerusalem knew they were more radical than their elders and tended to respond to public uprisings with enthusiasm and support. Many had followed Nico to Caesarea, years earlier.

Nico, himself, remained as youthful and enthusiastic as he had ever been. Right now, he felt the urge to run from this sanctimonious place and join his brothers, but he knew he must remain.

Reuben, the Sagan, or deputy High Priest came rushing out onto the terrace. This was the man who had been sent by Caiaphas to "lead" the people to Caesarea when Pilate had posted the blasphemous standards, several years earlier. He had proved himself weak and vacillating and did not deserve the position of Sagan, powerful administrator of the Temple. Caiaphas, of course, wanted him for these very qualities. He had no mind of his own and was a thoroughly slavish follower of Caiaphas. There had been grumblings among the hierarchy when Reuben's name was proposed for Sagan, but Caiaphas had prevailed.

"Eminence," Reuben was saying, his face streaked with sweat, "the people are marching to the Governor's palace."

"We can see, Reuben," Annas said testily. "You are always amazingly well informed—after the fact."

***

The people marched through the streets of the lower city at a steady, unhurried pace. They repeated only the words "Holy" and "Corban," and said no more.

It was a market day and the city was filled with traders from Tyre and Sidon, Damascus and Antioch, Gaza and Ptolemais and a hundred other towns and cities, from Spain to Parthia, the Marches to Ethiopia.

The foreign traders watched the marching men with some annoyance because the business of buying and selling was disrupted by this activity. They did not understand what the marchers were complaining about, and even when it was explained, they were not impressed. These Jews were so passionate about their religion—who could understand them?

Some of the traders were curious enough to follow along, and see what the Jews would do. Others followed who were not traders, but the marchers were peaceful and not paying any particular attention. They were wary only of soldiers, and nowhere along their course did they see soldiers. In any case, they saw no reason to expect a violent confrontation.

***

Amos and his fellow leaders were furious. The marchers had begun without them, without authorization and without designated leaders.

"We must join them," Josiah said.

"I agree," said Benjamin.

Something made Amos hold back. "Nothing will come of it. Let them go their way. They'll soon learn they need us."

Josiah smiled. "We need them," he said.

"I believe Amos may be right," Benjamin said. "If we can't have discipline, we have nothing. Let the people learn that now, and they'll be better prepared when the real uprising comes."

Benjamin was angry. "You don't think the Corban is important. I do, and men of my group will be there. God forbid I should leave them to their own fate." He stomped out of the door. Amos and Josiah and the others continued arguing among themselves, but no one else left Amos's house.

Benjamin hurried through the streets and caught up with the marchers. Friends haled him and he was glad to find himself greeted enthusiastically.

"Where are the Roman soldiers?" he asked.

His friends shrugged. "Why look for trouble, Benjamin?"

Benjamin began to wonder if Amos had been right. But it was too late to do anything now. The marchers had swelled to thousands and their progress had an inevitable quality.

***

"I want to be with them," Nico said, arguing fiercely with his father. But old Nicodemus, bent and aged, limping with pain at every step, still held him in a firm grasp.

"You're not going. This is not the time for you to be there."

"They are my friends," Nico said. "We support each other."

Annas felt compassion for the father and son, arguing with each other.

"There are thousands already," he told Nico. They don't really need one more. Stay here and gratify your father."

Nicodemus was touched by Annas's concern. The old boy had more heart than his son-in-law.

"They're coming this way," Reuben said. "Shall I gather the guards and head them off?"

Caiaphas shook his head. "It's not us they want an audience with." He turned and walked inside, and the others, except Nico, followed him.

"Inside," Caiaphas said imperiously, "we don't need provocateurs on our terrace."

***

Gideon, known as Bar Abbas, had gone off in a different direction from the marchers. He smiled as he thought of it. The old leaders, the Amos's and Benjamins never recognized an opportunity when they saw it. They were too set in their ways to do anything really useful. When the hour came, they would sit in their houses arguing, while the Messiah passed them by.

Bar Abbas quickly mounted to the Ophel and into the house of a friend, where a group of his men were waiting. "The hour has come," he said, and they all raised their fists in a fierce salute.

***

Gaius Fabricius had tried for hours to dissuade Pilate from attacking the marchers. "They're unarmed and they intend no harm," he had said.

"They must learn that a Roman governor is not to be trifled with. I've taken their treasure for a legitimate purpose and they'll have to live with it."

"But not die with it."

Pilate gritted his teeth. "Death is their choice, not mine. If they march on the palace, I'm going to treat it as insurrection."

"Let me speak to them," Gaius said. "Perhaps I can talk them out of marching here."

Pilate smiled. "I want them to march here. I want them to learn they can't abuse the empire with impunity. These Jews are no different than Greeks or Spaniards or Gauls, and they're going to have to learn that—in their own blood if necessary."

"Sire, Tiberius Caesar has instructed us again and again to avoid violent confrontation."

"I'm not confronting anyone, deputy. Why are you attacking me?"

Pilate had turned angry and ugly. His eyes protruded from his head and his tongue flicked over his lips repeatedly; a very bad sign. His voice lisped more heavily on the sibilants; another bad sign.

"Forgive me, Sire, I meant no offense. I only want to defend you from the evil reports of your enemies."

For a moment, Pilate was placated. He was suspicious enough to believe he had enemies everywhere, so he accepted Gaius's words at face value. But only for a moment.

"Which enemies?" he asked.

***

The marchers had made their way up the great western staircase to the level of the Temple and then had swung past the High Priest's palace. They threw a few taunts at Caiaphas from below, but continued, resolutely, to the Herodian Palace. "Holy," they chanted, "Corban," and the sound of it seemed to swell as their numbers swelled.

By the time they reached the plaza in front of the palace, there were at least five thousand of them—more than the plaza could contain, so that the entering streets were crowded with marchers.

For the first time, they were confronted by Roman soldiers. An entire cohort was strung across the entrance to the palace and another cohort lined the walls and parapets. Now that the marchers had reached the palace, they were uncertain of what to do next. They had no leader and although they knew precisely what they wanted, they weren't certain how to go about it. Should they petition the governor, should they send a deputation?

They began to argue among themselves. "Give us back the Corban!" a man yelled.

"Yes, give us back the Corban!" Others took up the cry. On the parapet of the palace, a standard dipped. The marchers did not know that was a sign.

"You're shoving me!" a man yelled at one of the marchers and pushed at him.

"Get your hands off me!" yelled another.

In a moment, the soldiers in the crowd, dressed like traders, pulled their daggers and began to attack the Jews. There was great confusion. The people were so packed together, they couldn't tell what was happening; it might have been a dispute among themselves. Then, others, seeing bodies fall and blood spilled, began to scream. The screams ignited the crowd. They tried to fight against the disguised Roman soldiers, but they were intentionally weaponless and the Romans were ruthless.

The marchers tried to escape from the plaza, but the streets were clogged. People were clawing at each other, trampling each other, trying to escape the flailing daggers of the Roman soldiers.

Another sign from the parapet. "Riot! Insurrection," voices cried, and the uniformed soldiers of the cohort were sent into the plaza. Others came up from the streets, blocking exit from the plaza. There, on the flagstone ground, the slaughter was terrible.

Another sign from the parapet and the slaughter was over. Thousands lay dead and wounded in the plaza, thousands more were driven off, frightened and screaming. A few were arbitrarily held. These would be the designated ringleaders and tortured until they confessed.

***

They ran through the streets until they were close to the Antonia Palace, then they commandeered four large wagons from Syrian merchants. When the Syrians protested, they killed them. Other merchants, horrified, yelled at them.

"We're Jews," the leader yelled.

"Does that mean you can kill anyone you want to?"

"Shut up," he growled, "or you'll die, too, Jew or not."

Several of them jumped aboard the wagons and their fellows covered them with cloths. Then, they dragged the wagons to the very gate of the palace.

"Provisions," the leader yelled. "Open up!"

The soldier on duty was puzzled. He had not been told that provisions were due at the palace that day. But most of the men and all of the officers were engaged in some action elsewhere in the city. He didn't know whom to ask.

"Come on," the leader called. "Fresh meat from the Jezreel Valley. We haven't got all day."

The guard called to his fellow and the two of them came outside. They held their hands on the hilts of their swords.

They never got to raise them. Bar Abbas and his men fell upon them and killed them, before they even had a chance to call for help.

Bar Abbas's men jumped out of the wagons and ran into the palace. There were few guards and they were unprepared. The battle was fierce, but quick. All of the Romans were dead. Bar Abbas had lost two men, but that was nothing compared to his reward. The information he had gotten was good. He led his men directly to the iron gated storeroom, and there, lifting the gate, they found the Corban.

They cheered and laughed, but Bar Abbas shut them up. "No time for cheering. Drag the wagons in here."

They pushed the wagons up the ramps and lifted them up the stairs to the storeroom. Then they flung decades of years of contributions, gold and silver, precious gems and rare coins, encrusted tableware and huge vases, into the wagons.

Minutes later they had bumped the wagons down the stairs and into the streets. They were planning to distribute the treasure among a dozen houses in the lower city and they knew they must trust their countrymen not to report the passage of the wagons.

Here, on the street of the merchants, there was the risk that foreigners, traitors, or spies might betray them, but in the residential sections, they would be surrounded by friends. All they had to do was traverse this one street and their chances of safety would increase dramatically.

***

Septimus's men mopped up quickly and efficiently. But Septimus was aware he had left the Antonia short-handed and he immediately detached a century to return to the palace and then another.

"Double time!" he yelled, and they ran through the streets.

It was these soldiers who came upon Bar Abbas and his men, pulling their treasure-laden wagons along the street. Even then, they might have escaped, but one of the wagons veered, struck a wall and spilled some of its precious cargo. The centurion took one look and realized these scruffy looking creatures couldn't possibly be merchants.

"Halt!" he yelled, drew his sword and ran up.

Bar Abbas and his men turned and drew their weapons and attacked the Romans. They were outnumbered but they fought fiercely. Other Jews, in houses and stalls along the street, did what they could to help, fighting if they had weapons, throwing pots and bricks and whatever else they had at the Roman soldiers.

Caught in the narrow street, the Romans found themselves attacked on all sides. But they were trained soldiers and they kept pressing on.

Bar Abbas could see there was no hope of hiding the treasure now. In minutes, reinforcements would be upon them and then their work would be for nothing.

"The Tower!" he yelled, "Siloam tower. Drag the wagons there, we'll defend you."

He called out a dozen men who formed a rear guard, while the others pulled the wagons to the Siloam Tower, opened the gate and brought them inside.

Bar Abbas's rear guard was being cut down, one by one. They were taking Romans with them, two or three for each Jew, but it wasn't enough.

Indeed, the reinforcements came and they swung into the surrounding streets and would soon cut them off.

"Run!" Bar Abbas yelled, "Run for the tower!" His men hesitated, but he yelled again. Then he was alone in the street, swinging two swords and leaping from curb to cart to stall to street with fanatic strength and courage. He was cut in a dozen places and blood streamed from his wounds, but he yelled defiance and held them off.

For a moment, the Romans fell back, awed by the sight of this madman, swinging his swords, cutting down soldiers with blow after blow.

He sensed the pause—turned suddenly and ran. The Romans came rushing after him. A Roman bowman struck him in the shoulder with an arrow. Bar Abbas stumbled, but he ran with rage and an indomitable spirit.

Another arrow almost split the first, but still he kept his feet. His men swung open the gate of the tower, and he ran through and they slammed it behind him.

Bar Abbas couldn't stop until his men grabbed and held him. He reached over his shoulders and ripped out the arrows, spilling fresh blood that merged with the old. "Swine!" he screamed. "Roman swine!"

Then he sagged to the ground, coughing and spitting teeth and somehow, smiling.

***

The Romans quickly surrounded the tower, while Bar Abbas and his men tore up the wagons and used the wood to reinforce the gate. There was nowhere for them to go, no way to escape. They found a little food in the tower, most of it stale and a few buckets of water, all of it foul.

The Roman voices came up from the street, "Surrender, you're surrounded."

Bar Abbas's men made foul suggestions in return.

When Septimus arrived he decided to burn them out, building a huge bonfire all around the base of the tower and the wall. The flames burned mightily, but the tower was hard stone and although the heat was terrible, they simply moved up in the tower. From the ramparts they could see for miles, the gentle vineyards and pastures of Judaea. It was achingly close.

"We're defeated," one of his men said to Bar Abbas. "If we surrender, maybe they won't kill us."

Bar Abbas spat in the man's face. "Throw him out a window," he said. The others grabbed the man and would have done so, but Bar Abbas relented.

"Let him go. Anyone who feels like him is free to surrender."

The man hesitated, then shook his head. "I'll stay to the end," he said, although his knees were shaking.

***

Gaius suggested the Roman soldiers simply keep the tower surrounded. In time, the Jews inside would have to surrender.

"Bad business," Septimus said. "The people are watching. Every day they gather around the tower and watch. One day, they may attack. We have one legion outside the city and two cohorts inside. In the short run, we'd take many casualties if there was an uprising."

Pilate smiled. "I have an idea," he said.

In the morning, the sappers began their work of tunneling from the houses and streets around the Tower. It was soon evident what their intentions were, and the Jews outside managed to relay the news to Bar Abbas and his men.

"You'll destroy our own fortifications," Gaius had protested.

"They'll give up when they understand," Pilate said, "and if not we'll make the Jews rebuild the tower themselves."

After three days, the men inside could feel the work going on beneath their feet. On the fourth day, the very stones began to move ever so slightly. Bar Abbas and his men had moved to the very top of the tower.

"You'll destroy the very treasure you were trying to take," Gaius said.

"We were going to melt it down anyway," Pilate said. He told the engineers to be certain to warn him when the tower began to fall. He didn't want to miss it.

On the fifth day, the tunnels collapsed unexpectedly, killing several sappers in the ground. But the tower sank suddenly, tipped like a pitcher and began to crumble. There was no time to call Pilate.

The sound was like an earthquake, as the tower staggered and slipped, groaned and creaked, then collapsed suddenly, striking the ground with a great reverberating roar. A cloud of dust sprang up, hiding the sight, but not covering the screams of the men trapped inside.

Most were crushed to death inside. A few, maimed horribly, lay in the rubble screaming. One, Bar Abbas, lay on top of the pile, his legs and arms broken. He was unconscious but alive. Septimus had all the others killed on the spot. "As an act of "mercy," he said. Bar Abbas they dragged along the street, his broken bones scraping the stone, all the way to Pilate.

3.

DISCIPLES

When Joshua had completed his long day of teaching beside the Sea of Galilee, he was elated. For the first time, he felt he had fully expressed the feelings in his heart and explained to the people what God expected of them. He was deeply warmed by the response of the people, patient and loving and earnest for the food of the spirit. Joshua knew that, for once, he had satisfied them, for when he had finished they were content to let him go. He wasn't certain they fully understood his intentions for them, but he remained hopeful.

Trudging back to Simon's home with his closest followers, he allowed himself to feel the weariness of his long and strenuous day. It was, however, a good feeling rather than a painful one and he had no regrets. He was especially anxious to reach Simon's house. Among the crowd at the shore of the lake, Joshua had noticed a familiar figure, even though the man's face had almost been fully covered by his burnoose.

Thus, inside Simon's door, Joshua was not surprised to see Judas waiting for him.

Simon had seen him, too, and alerted Andrew, but Judith and Brother Jacob and the sons of Zebedee had never met him. "This is Judas," Joshua told them, "a friend and a patriot."

Judas acknowledged them with a brief nod. His greeting to Joshua was polite but perfunctory. "Word of your teaching has spread through Galilee," Judas said. "The people are very excited."

"Yes," Joshua said, "we're making progress. Many have repented and been baptized, although we have made some enemies."

"More than you know. I tell you, Rabbi, the time grows short."

"Time for what?" Brother Jacob asked.

Judas looked at him. "Don't they know?" Judas asked.

"They know we plan to urge the people to unite together, to oppose Roman rule, but without violence."

"And that will happen in God's time," Brother Jacob said. He hardly knew this Judas of Galilee, but the man troubled him. He was coarse and abrupt and treated Joshua not as his leader, but as an equal.

Joshua was aware of Judas's attitude, but was not bothered by his lack of deference. They were both servants of God, owing Him all honor, and each other only fair treatment. What worried him was the man's impatience.

"I tell you, Rabbi," Judas said, "we must move swiftly. Only this morning, I learned of a massacre in Jerusalem. The Romans stole the Temple treasure, the Corban, to use it to build a viaduct. The people marched peacefully to Pilate to ask for its return, but Roman soldiers, disguised in ordinary clothing, mingled with the crowd and suddenly rose up and began to slaughter them. Thousands were killed."

Joshua felt his heart contract as he listened.

"A friend of mine, an impetuous fellow named Gideon, called Bar Abbas, stole back the Corban while the others were protesting. But he and his friends were trapped in a tower. The Romans undermined the tower and killed everyone but Bar Abbas. I hate to think what the Romans have in store for him."

"Do the Romans believe the peaceful march was intended to cover the recapture of the treasure?" Joshua asked.

"You're very quick, Rabbi. Of course, that's what they'll say. But the effect on the people is worse. They will believe that peaceful action can't work—that the Romans will murder even unarmed men and women. Where will your peaceful uprising be then, Rabbi?"

Brother Jacob was appalled by what Judas said, and his pain was increased by the pain he saw on his brother's face. "It's not your fault," he said to Joshua. "You didn't tell them to march on the governor."

Joshua put his hand on Brother Jacob's shoulder. "I feel each death as if I had caused it myself—as if my failure to rouse the people soon enough is responsible for every act of brutality."

Judas was annoyed. "We're not here to assess blame, only to act usefully and promptly. Every Roman action incenses the Zealots even more. The march in Jerusalem wasn't my idea any more than yours, and the action of Bar Abbas, though well intended, only made things worse. I've tried to keep the Zealots from renewed violence while you rouse the people, but I don't know how much longer I can hold them back."

"You must, Judas. The fate of the nation depends on it."

"Every day we wait means more Jewish deaths. When will the time be?"

As he spoke there was a knock on the door. Judas leaped up as if he had been stabbed. The others paled, but Joshua was serene. "Wait in the other room, if you're concerned, Judas. I doubt that our enemies would knock so lightly."

Embarrassed, Judas sat down. Brother Jacob opened the door.

"May we come in?" The voice was warm and robust, and Simon nodded quickly and stepped aside with evident respect. It was Nathan ben Thalmai, the man Joshua had healed at the synagogue on his earlier trip to Capernaum, and his wife.

They entered humbly, nodding greetings to all and then approached Joshua, who smiled and rose and embraced both of them. "Welcome," he said. "I'm happy to see you look so well."

"He's never looked better," said Deborah, his wife, a frail bird of a woman, short and thin, with a narrow head a large beak and a quick smile.

"You've fed him well since," Joshua said.

"I watch what he eats—although he doesn't. As you can see there's a bit too much fat on him."

In earlier days, Nathan would have shown annoyance at such remarks, but now he smiled benignly. "Rabbi," he said, "We see there are guests. Should we return another time?"

"No," Joshua said. "I know that you are welcome in Simon's house"— Simon nodded—"and I am delighted to see you."

"Rabbi," Nathan said. "You—that is, God, through you, saved my life. I did not deserve it, for I was rising in anger to attack you when I myself was stricken. But, thank God, this was not held against me and I was saved. I asked you what I should do and you told me to live righteously and to give what I could to the poor.

"Deborah and I talked about nothing else for days. Then, we spoke to another landowner who wanted to acquire our farms and vineyards. We sold them immediately. Now, we would like to give all we have to you, so that you may use it to spread your message to all our people."

In the silence, Joshua felt tears come into his eyes. "God bless you for your goodness, Nathan and Deborah."

"It's nothing, really. We feel we were only caretakers of God's property and we would like to give it back to Him. Our children are grown and well off and don't need our help. But we would request one thing. We would like to walk with you through the land, Rabbi, and help you in any way we can. We are not young, but we're healthy. Both of us can read and write, and both of us know scripture. We believe we can help."

"I can cook and sew as well," Deborah said, looking anxiously at Joshua "and I'm a lot stronger than I look."

Joshua smiled at Judas. "You see, the Lord always provides. Nathan, Deborah, we welcome you with all our hearts."

***

In the morning, Judas brought Joshua and Brother Jacob to meet Simeon, a middle aged man who had been active among the Zealots, until he was wounded by the Romans. Simeon's hamstring had been cut by a sword and he could no longer be a warrior, but he was able to move with agility despite his injury.

"I heard you speak at the synagogue, Rabbi. I'd be pleased to help you."

Joshua glanced at Simeon's withered leg.

"Don't worry," he said. "I can move very well despite it, and I'm not asking to be healed. I figure the Lord wants me this way."

Joshua was startled by Simeon's words and he found them compelling enough to make him trust the man.

"Your friend, Andrew, baptized me on your last visit, so that part of the work is done. I can't say that I'm too good on scripture. I went to school as a boy, and I go to synagogue on the Sabbath. I've been to Jerusalem many times for the festivals—but aside from that, I'm no scholar."

"God doesn't want scholars," Joshua said, "He wants righteous men and women who will love him and do his will."

"I love God and I have always tried to do right," Simeon said.

"He's honest," Judas said, "and he'll work till he falls over."

Simeon laughed. "Ay," he said. "That I will, but I won't fall over easily and I get back up quick."

Joshua clapped him on the back. "Come join us."

Judas wanted to show them another man, but Joshua shook his head. He didn't want too many of Judas's followers in the inner circle of his disciples. Judas understood without being told, and once again he felt respect for the Master. Some might consider him otherworldly, but Judas found him very practical for all his virtue.

On the way back to Simon's home, they passed the Roman customs-house. Outside, at a table, sat a vigorous looking young man with wavy black hair and a full beard. His eyes were lively and he smiled easily—unusual in a tax-collector. Joshua felt drawn to him.

"You were at the lake, yesterday."

"That's right, Rabbi."

"But you didn't repent and you weren't baptized."

A cloud passed over his eyes. "I didn't think I was worthy—a tax-collector, you know what I mean."

Joshua put out his hand, the young man took it, and Joshua pulled him to his feet. "But that's the point of it," Joshua said. "None of us is worthy, but God loves us all. Let's go to the lake."

A great smile came over the young man's face. Together, Joshua and Brother Jacob, Judas, Simeon and the tax-collector hurried down to the lake.

"I think it's time for you, too, Judas."

Judas blinked and thought of clever things to say, but didn't say them. Joshua was staring into his eyes, reading the very insides of his skull. Judas closed his eyes and nodded.

Brother Jacob waded into the lake and Judas and the tax-collector followed them.

Joshua stood on the shore. Simeon stood a few feet away, respectfully waiting. "Heavenly Father," Joshua said, "we come before you again to ask your blessings. These men have sinned, but they wish to repent and they long to be forgiven. Lord give them the blessings of your love and wipe away all record of their transgressions. Let them be inscribed forever in the book of life."

As he spoke, Judas and the tax-collector were praying, each in his own words and his own way. Brother Jacob held their shoulders and firmly dipped them below the waters.

When he released them, they came up slowly, the tax-collector with a look of joy on his face, and Judas with a strange and pensive look. Joshua tried to read it, but for once the Zealot leader was a mystery to him.

"God," Joshua prayed silently, "Let Judas know your love, let him be the servant of Israel that Israel requires. Preserve him from his own doubts."

They came splashing out of the water, all smiling now.

"Mattathias," said the tax-collector, "my name is Mattathias."

"Fitting," said Judas, "The father of the Maccabees."

"We want a dove, not a hammer," Joshua said.

Mattathias looked at Joshua with surprise and pleasure. "Does that mean I can come with you?"

"That's why we stopped to talk to you."

Mattathias put his arms around Joshua and hugged him. Brother Jacob wasn't terribly happy. It was alright to save a tax-collector, but what would people think if you had one marching around with you?

"We don't care what people think," Joshua said, reading his brother perfectly as always.

"There's another fellow," Joshua said, "one who has been following us patiently all through Galilee. I've been watching him for a long time. He helps the other 'wanderers' and asks nothing for himself. He speaks excellent Greek, which will be a help in the Decapolis, and he has a Greek name, Philip."

***

They met that evening in the house of Simon. Hannah, his mother, and Ruth, his wife, bustled about, bringing food and wine. They were as anxious as the followers of Joshua because they could sense the tension in the air and they were concerned for their family.

"My friends," Joshua said, "It is now time for us to extend and expand our mission. We must meet and speak with as many people as possible in as little time as possible. We must spread the word that the hour has come—that the people must repent their sins, return to the word of God and take their stand against the Roman oppressors. But we will not be party to the violence that has devastated our people in the past. Time and again the Jews have tried to end Roman control with the sword, and every time we have been defeated, and thousands of us have been slaughtered. I do not demean the courage of those who rose up, weapons in hand, but I tell you it takes more courage to confront your enemy without weapons, in the name of peace—in the name of the Lord.

"Until now, we have dealt with the few, here in Galilee, the most familiar place to all of us. The response has been warm and moving. The people have clearly shown their love of God and their willingness to find the right way. But Galilee is only a small part of our land. We must reach the others and we must do so quickly."

He looked at his followers with affection and deep concern. "You have been chosen for your virtue and your faith, for the devotion you have shown towards God and the loyalty you have offered me.

"God demands even greater devotion and I require even greater loyalty. You will travel far and the tasks will be difficult, but with God's help, we will prevail."

"Hallelujah," said Brother Jacob, and the others echoed his word.

"Brother Jacob and Sister Judith will go to Phoenicia, to Tyre and Sidon, to speak to the people there. Mattathias will go with you. As a tax-collector, he knows many tongues and he will help you with those who do not speak Aramaic.

"Johannon and Little Jacob will go to Perea. It's a long distance, and the land is harsh, but you're young and strong and can take the hardship." They nodded cheerfully, grinning as always.

"Nathan and Deborah, you will go into Eastern Galilee, to Gaulanitis and Panaeas, as far north as Caesarea Philippi. You've been a merchant as well as a farmer, Nathan, and you know the people. Do you feel strong enough to undertake the journey?"

"Of course," Nathan said. "Deborah and I are hardy old souls."

Joshua smiled. "Philip, you and Simeon will go into the Decapolis. Your Greek will be a great help there." Both men nodded.

"Simon and Andrew, you'll remain here in Galilee, keeping up the faith among those we have already reached and such others as you can persuade. We need a base here, and this house and your family provide it."

Simon was frowning. "We would have liked to go to Phoenicia, Andrew and I," he said. "We've never been there."

"Another time, Simon. The fish in the Great Sea will wait for you."

Simon blushed, but Joshua and the others were laughing, and after a moment, he brightened considerably.

"That leaves Judas and me."

Judas sat bolt upright, surprised.

"I need you, Judas. You and I will cover the most territory, all of Judaea and such Jewish settlements as there are in eastern Samaria. We'll have to speak to all the Zealot leaders and persuade them to support us. You're the man for it. And, I'm sure you can provide horses along the route, and places to stay in the towns."

Judas was thinking, He wants me where he can keep an eye on me, but aloud, he only said, "Good, now is the time to enlist the other leaders in our cause—they must see you to truly believe."

Joshua began to pace the room. "Avoid the gentiles and the Samar-itans—now is not yet the time to involve them, and many of them will oppose us, at least in the beginning. In time they will acknowledge the wisdom of our ways. For God intends us to be a nation of priests, a holy nation, and to bring his blessings to all the peoples of the earth.

"But first you must be messengers to the lost sheep of Israel. To them you must preach that the Kingdom of Heaven is at hand, that the hour is now. They will expect miracles of you—that you will heal the sick, cleanse lepers, cast out demons, even raise the dead. You know that as mortal men you cannot do these things, except by the help of the Almighty God. If you believe in him and trust in his goodness and his mercy, his wisdom and great power, then, you will be given the power to do all things necessary to persuade the people—even such things as are called miracles by men, but only evidence the love and power of God.

"Fear not to do these things, for God will provide all that you need. Take with you neither gold, nor silver nor copper in your belts, except for the sums that Nathan has provided us. Travel lightly, without extra clothing or heavy baggage. In each town or village, you will find people who will love you and cherish your words. Among them, you'll find those who will take you in, providing food and shelter while you are there. Bless that house and bring God's peace to it.

"But if you find a house where you are unwelcome, or a town that does not want to hear your words, don't quarrel or be dismayed. Shake off the dust of that place and go on, for on the Day of Judgment it shall be more tolerable in Sodom and Gomorrah than for that place. You will tell the people that the hour is nigh—that we must give up living under the laws of the Romans, that we must oppose them in all things, yet without sword or spear. We must neither sow nor reap nor pay their taxes or customs, but if they try to force us, we will not give in.

"Then, and only then will God take our side and use his power, not ours, to relieve our oppression.

"When you teach these things, you must be careful. I am sending you out as sheep in the midst of wolves. You must be wise as a serpent and innocent as doves. What you will ask is difficult for men to do, and some will doubt. Others will hate you and betray you to the Romans. The Romans themselves will see your words as sedition, as rebellion against the state. That is why you must emphasize you are preaching peace, not war, justice not rebellion.

"If you are delivered up, worry not what to say. For in that hour it will be given to you what to speak—for it won't be you speaking, but the Spirit of your Father. Some, even those you hold dear, may turn against you. Others will claim that you come from Satan, and that I am Satan's minister.

Ignore these things. You must be brave, for if you keep your faith, you will endure to the end and you will be redeemed.

"Have no fear, for nothing is covered that will not be revealed, nothing is hidden that will not be known. What I tell you privately here in this house in the dark of night, you will proclaim publicly in the light of day. What is now whispered will be proclaimed from the housetops.

"And remember, fear not those who kill the body, but cannot touch your soul, but fear him who can destroy both body and soul in hell. Are not two sparrows sold for a penny? And yet, not one of them will fall to the ground unless your Father in heaven wills it. Even the hairs on your head are numbered. Fear not, for you are of greater value than all the sparrows, and he who acknowledges and loves the living God will stand before the Holy throne.

"You must be prepared for great sacrifices, even the loss of your own loved ones. If you seek only to preserve your life, you will surely lose it, but if you are ready for death in the name of the Almighty, your words and deeds will never die."

All of them were moved by his words, encouraged and refreshed, ready to face any adversary in God's name. Joshua could feel his strength entering them and then, enhanced further, returning and strengthening him."

"When will we take our stand?" Brother Jacob asked.

"As I told you before," Joshua said, "at the coming Passover," Joshua said. He sighed to himself, realizing that they must be taught and inspired, again and again and again.

He had read them correctly, the others, even Judas, seemed startled. Passover was almost upon them, and they had chosen to "forget" that the time for action was so close. Some felt a touch of fear, but put it aside. Judas was secretly thrilled. This was something that a man could plan for.

"Brilliant, Rabbi," Judas said. "What better time than the Feast of Liberation?"

"None better," Joshua said, "and a large part of the nation will be at the feast. We must do all we can to encourage as many as possible to be there. The Romans will find us united, overnight."

"We'll tell that to the people as we preach," Little Jacob said.

"No you won't," Joshua warned him. "That's the last thing we want to do—to alert the Romans to our intentions and the exact date of our action."

"But the people will be confused if we don't tell them when this is to happen."

"You must tell the people it will be soon, you must tell them they must be alert—ready, at all times, ready. And you must do this in words that won't arouse Romans—Herodians and Roman sympathizers—even the Sadducees and the leaders of the Temple.

"Speak in parables if you must, tell them of the bride who must be ready for the bridegroom, of the servant who must be ready for the return of his master, of the fig tree that blooms in its proper season, or the grain that must be harvested when it is ready. Let them know they must be on the watch—that the light will be lit, the signal will be sent, and the day of the Lord is coming."

"They'll understand that, Master," Simon said, "when we tell them you are the king who was promised to Israel."

"You won't tell them that, Simon, any more than you'll tell them the day we plan to act. If you do and the Romans hear of it, they'll surely arrest me as a rival to Herod, to Pilate, even to Caesar."

"And that," said Judas, "will be the end of everything."

"But, Rabbi," Nathan said, "if we don't tell them you are our leader, the people won't believe us—they must have someone they can follow."

"He's quite right," Judas said.

"Why this obsession with names and titles?" Joshua asked, but he knew they were right. "Tell the people I am the servant of God—that God has spoken to me and asked me to serve him and I have accepted."

"They'll ask for more than that," Judith said. "They wait for the Messiah, and it is only in his name they will rise."

"Very well," Joshua said. "Tell them I am the anointed one, but that I have been charged to bring peace and not war."

4.

PROPHET

They left in the morning, with fond farewells and shouts of encouragement and high hopes.

"They're good, simple people," Judas said to Joshua. "I hope they can do what you ask."

"God will guide them," Joshua said. "I have no doubt of their success."

Joshua himself lingered an extra day in Galilee so that he might travel to Nazareth and see his family. Judas was restless, but he agreed, even though he feared that one more day might make the difference.

They arrived on the eve of the Sabbath and shared the Sabbath meal with Miriam and the children. Judas was courteous to Joshua's mother, more courteous than he usually was towards others, but Miriam took an instant dislike to him. She told herself that she was being unfair, that the man's swarthy, almost ugly appearance was the true source of her dislike. But she knew it wasn't really his looks that disturbed her. There was something wrong with this man, something a bit off center, and most important, something about him that was a threat to Joshua.

Miriam spoke privately to her son, hesitantly, voicing her fears.

"I know, mother, and I understand. But you see, Judas represents that very instinct in the hearts of our people that must be dealt with—that must be overcome. In all of us there is the natural yearning to rise up and destroy those who have abused and tormented us. Our animal nature is powerful and it tells us to deal with our enemies by violently crushing them.

"Judas and his friends are good men, zealous for God, but they smart under Roman oppression and they want to grind the faces of the Romans into the dust in revenge. It is that very urge, that instinct, which has led us astray, time and again. If we follow it now, we'll be vanquished again. I must help Judas to conquer that urge and if I do so, I can persuade the entire nation. If we're split—if some say the way is peace and some war, our very division will destroy us. A house divided against itself cannot stand.

"With Judas, and those who think like him, I have the key. If I can turn it, I can open the door to the liberation of Israel."

Miriam was gratified that Joshua had taken her into his confidence, but she found his ideas, as compelling as they were, too remote for her womanly instincts to accept.

"A man like Judas can't be reasoned away, my son, no matter how persuasive your thinking. He must be watched and controlled."

Joshua smiled. "I'll remember that."

***

The next day, at Sabbath services in the synagogue of Nazareth, Joshua was given the honor of speaking. Word of his works elsewhere in Galilee had reached Nazareth and that had swelled the congregation.

As had become his custom, Joshua spoke freely, choosing his subject as he wished, not necessarily referring to the text from scripture that had been read that day.

"In the time of Noah," he began, "the Lord made us a promise. He said to Noah, 'I now establish my covenant with you and with all your descendants after you and with every living creature on earth...Never again will all life be cut off...Never again will there be a flood to destroy the earth...'

"God made this promise an everlasting covenant with all peoples and in all ages. It is a wonderful promise. It means that however great our faults or grievous our sins, God will never turn away from us, never rise up in wrath and destroy his own creation.

"Although we may be separated from God, and that separation indeed is the very meaning of sin, we will always have the opportunity to return and to be forgiven.

"When, out of all the nations, God elected the Jews and the Jews chose God, he made us a new and particular promise. He told Abraham, 'I will establish my covenant between me and you and your descendants...for an everlasting covenant...to be God to you and your descendants after you.'

"Thus God promised us that He would always be with us, no matter what our travail.

"In the days of Moses, the Lord said, 'If you will obey my voice and keep my covenant, you shall be my own possession among all peoples; for all the earth is mine, and you shall be to me a kingdom of priests and a holy nation.'

"The Lord Almighty told us then and He has told us many times since, what we must do to keep the covenant between us in force. Time and again, we have failed, but time and again we have repented and returned and God has welcomed us.

"On the side of the Lord, the covenant, the agreement never changes. The Lord holds out his salvation to us in eternity. We may lose touch, we may fall away, our lives may become lost in sin, BUT THE HAND OF THE LORD REMAINS OPEN. We have but to surrender our will to Him, to return to righteousness, to live in faith, and we will be embraced and forgiven.

"In every age, in every crisis, the circumstances may seem different to us—to require a different solution. God is compassionate; he knows we do not know, he understands we do not understand, so he offers us, time and again, a dispensation, a new way to reach him, to receive again his justice and mercy.

"In the days of Jeremiah, the Lord told the mighty prophet that the people of Judah 'have broken my covenant which I made with their fathers.' He said, 'the days are coming...when I will make a new covenant with the house of Israel and House of Judah...' Did the Lord mean a truly new covenant—a new promise from him? No, I tell you that he meant he would give us a new way to reach the holiness of the old covenant—the permanent promise which God had not and has not ever broken. God has infinite mercy. He sees our strivings, our yearnings and our weakness. He seeks not to make the world difficult for us, but pleasant and peaceful, if we will only listen.

"And yet, if we could only understand, we would know that all ways are the same way. We must turn away from false gods—not only the false gods which are carved in wood or cast in bronze, but the false gods that live within us, the false gods of wealth and pride and victory, even of family and friendship and community. We must cease to worship at these secret shrines—these inner temples of greed and jealousy, envy and self-adoration.

"There is but One God, Blessed be His Ineffable Name, forever and ever."

Before Joshua could leave the *bema*, a voice spoke out from the back of the congregation

"Why didn't you speak on the regular reading of the Sabbath?"

"I spoke on the Covenant—that is the reading of all Sabbaths."

"In this synagogue," said another. "We follow tradition. Who are you to change our tradition?"

"He's a man of God," Ezra, the leader of the congregation said. "Can't you tell?"

Joshua listened calmly. Simon, sitting in the rear of the synagogue was seething inside, but he knew that Joshua would not want him to speak.

"A man of God?" said another, speaking derisively. "Isn't he Joshua, the son of Joseph and Miriam, a carpenter and the son of a carpenter?"

"Do we insult a man because of his work?" asked Ezra, although he himself was not a supporter of Joshua's.

"No, we don't insult him, but we don't glorify him either."

"His father was descended from the Royal House of David," said Cleophas, the brother of Joseph, and therefore Joshua's uncle. He had remained aloof from Joshua and his teaching, but now, the words of some in the congregation had infuriated the old man.

"His father?" said another, standing up. "Who was his father?"

"Be careful what you say" said Simon who could no longer remain silent.

"Let him be careful—before he passes himself off as a son of the royal family."

"Miriam, too, is descended from the House of David," said a voice.

"We spoke of his father," the antagonist responded.

"Yes," said Joshua, "let us speak of the Father—the Father of all of us. Is one of us greater or less because his father is known or unknown, his father is rich or poor, a scholar or a simple farmer? Each man must stand on his own, and all men are as nothing before the Father of all of us."

"You speak with such assurance," said another man. "What right have you to tell us what to do, to call down the wrath of heaven on us?"

"He is the Messiah," Simon called out, in a loud voice.

A great shout came from the congregation, some honoring Joshua, but many shouting "No," "it can't be," "A carpenter's son," "a bastard,"

The last infuriated both Cleophas and Simon and they started through the congregation, intending to grab hold of the speaker. But Joshua was there first, shielding the man they would have attacked.

"Careful, Simon, Uncle Cleophas. Don't be offended. I'm not."

He spoke to the congregation. "Thus it has always been: A prophet is not without honor, except in his own country and his own house."

He gently turned Simon and Cleophas and led them out of the synagogue. Miriam and Ruth walked out, too, arm in arm and heads held high.

The congregation spilled into the plaza, many arguing heatedly about Joshua and the events of the morning. There were some who ran after Joshua and would have talked to him, but he shook his head and went on his way, saying nothing.

Judas caught up with him. "Are you discouraged, Rabbi?"

Joshua shook his head. "I've told them what I believe. I didn't come here to quarrel with the people, but to explain their choices to them. Those who have eyes, see, and those who have ears, listen."

5.

MEIR

That Joshua—he was a trouble maker from the time he was a child. I know because I grew up in Nazareth when we both lived there. He always thought he was better than anybody else, was always showing off. I guess he was pretty smart, that he could read scriptures and all, but so could a lot of other people, including me. I guess he was a good carpenter, too, though not as good as he thought and I wouldn't have trusted him with my work. Anyway, what does it mean to be a good carpenter? I'm a good wheelwright and that isn't going to buy me a special place in heaven.

The whole family thought they were pretty special, although I don't know why. Hannah claimed to be descended from the royal house of David, but half the Jews say that and who could prove it if they had to? The truth is that Joshua wasn't even Joseph's son. They say Miriam got involved with some Roman soldier which must be the greatest disgrace in the world. I don't know why they let people like that act pretend they're respectable citizens.

I had my share of fights with Joshua when he was little. Naturally I didn't want to beat up on him because I was so much older. Some people thought I was afraid of him but the fact is that I hate violence, even against people I can't stand, like him.

People in Nazareth thought he was a healer, that he had some mysterious powers. Now you and I know there's no such thing, and the rabbis warn us to be careful of people who claim to be magicians. They're up to no good. That sure applies to Joshua. Finally, the people in town drove him away. The got sick of all his tricks and he had to take his family to some little place on the Nir, called Beth Sholem. I tell you I wasn't sorry to see him go.

If I thought that was the end of him, I soon learned different. After what happened to his family, I heard he went further south, but then, next thing you knew, he was back here, preaching in the synagogues just like he was a real rabbi. I couldn't believe it. Here was this nobody, the bastard son of a Roman soldier and a farmer's daughter, yelling and screaming that the Kingdom of God was at hand. And people actually listened to him. I will say he was different. Blonde and blue-eyed—unusual for a Jew—but somehow more dangerous looking, and he spoke in a new kind of voice, not soft like before but very loud and powerful and it carried a long ways. I'll also say he could tell a good story, but he could also do that when he was young. Now the stories were all about God and heaven and so forth. Some people were saying he was the Messiah. I laughed out loud. God's got better judgment than that, I said. Some of them got pretty mad at me.

For a while he was kind of a local hero, had a bunch of followers that went around with him, including that fancy woman, Miriam of Magdala. What a looker. I bet he was getting some of that.

Sometimes the crowds were so big you couldn't believe it. People yelling and screaming and tearing at his clothes and those big guys he had with him, said they were fishermen, but I doubt it, and they were fighting the people off.

They said he did all kinds of cures. I never believed it. Thought it was all a game with a lot of fakers he hired to pretend he healed them. Still, folks are suckers for that sort of thing.

I heard they were talking about him all over the country, that even the High Priest was worried. That was probably a story he spread himself.

After a while though things began to change a little. The last time he preached in Nazareth, it didn't go over so well. I started whispering in the congregation: "Who does he think he is? We know his mother—God only knows who his father was." People started to laugh then and some tried to hush me. "We know his brothers and sisters and we know he's only a carpenter. Why should we listen to him?"

There was a big argument and almost a fight and Joshua got disgusted and marched out. That suited me fine.

Later I knew he went south for the Festival. I wasn't surprised the way it worked out—I always knew he was troublemaker and he'd come to a bad end.

6.

ANTIPAS

Herod Antipas was a large man, with many chins and an overlapping stomach set over very thin legs. His flesh was soft and pink and belied his Idumean ancestry. Only his narrow, slitted eyes hinted at the crafty man within.

When his father, Herod the Great, had given him Galilee and Perea, Antipas was secretly pleased. He wanted no part of Judaea, least of all of Jerusalem, with its great Temple and seething population and political disputes. He knew that Galilee was a hotbed of rebels and anarchists, holy men and brigands. But the Galileans were such individualists that he doubted they would ever combine to cause him any lasting trouble.

Herod Antipas set up his capital on the Sea of Galilee. He renamed the town Tiberias in honor of the emperor, and began building himself a city of pleasure. Like all the Herods he loved to build, and he didn't care how much of his subjects' money he used in his endeavors. Antipas made the Idumean error of building Tiberias over a cemetery, so that the Jews abhorred the place and wouldn't stay in it —but then he was not certain that was a mistake if it kept his Jewish subjects away.

Antipas was a man without ambition, who hoped only to lead a peaceful existence, enjoy himself and die in bed, but not of vile illnesses like his father. When his brother Archelaus botched the rule of Judaea and Samaria and was deposed, Antipas had no desire to add those headaches to his domain. He was delighted to have a Roman Prefect as his neighbor, even a cruel villain like Pilate. With Roman soldiers stationed nearby, Antipas always knew where to turn for help, and felt confident that no serious rebellion could ever develop.

Antipas was reluctant to deal harshly with the people, except of course, for the collection of taxes, and he was willing to ignore most problems, provided they did not threaten his rule.

Then he made the mistake of divorcing his Nabataean wife, Phasaelis, and marrying Herodias. The fact that Herodias was his niece did not seem to bother anyone—what excited them was that Herodias had been the wife of his half-brother Herod Philip .

Herodias left Philip on her own, but the separation was amicable, and Antipas's half-brother was only too delighted to be rid of her—permanently.

Antipas had wanted her as long as he could remember. She was tall and dark-haired, with flawless skin and sculptured features. A direct descendent of the Hasmonean kings, she was regal in a way that Antipas could never hope to emulate. Imagine his surprise and delight when he found that this elegant and beautiful lady was more than his equal in sexual enthusiasm. What a catch, he thought. And then the holy ones started carping on the fact of his marrying his half-brother's former wife. By convoluted reasoning, beyond Antipas's comprehension, many Jews claimed this violated the Levirate laws. Antipas hardly knew what these were and besides he had been assured by his own councilors that this was a mere technicality.

Then Johannon, the desert holy man, spoke out and the whole thing became a great scandal.

But that wasn't the worst of it. Phasaelis was the daughter of Aretas, the King of Nabataea, and although she wasn't terribly attractive with her narrow features and bony legs, she had bought him peace on the borders of Perea. Actually, Antipas had planned to discuss the divorce with Aretas, arrange a huge gift and send Phasaelis back in peace and harmony.

Unfortunately, Phasaelis, who had never complained before, even though Antipas had stayed out of her bed to avoid having an Arabian heir, caught wind of the proposed marriage to Herodias before Antipas talked to her father. She stormed out of Tiberias and returned home seething with anger, and complaining bitterly about her betrayal to her father.

Aretas had no desire to quarrel with Antipas, who was a weak and docile neighbor and no threat to the Nabateans. However, his daughter had returned home angry and his wife was furious and Antipas, slothful as always in matters of state, had missed all opportunities to patch the matter up. To keep peace in his own household, Aretas began—slowly—to prepare for war with Herod. However, even Aretas was growing irritable because Antipas, who might yet have bought his way out of the problem, had failed to do so. Partly, this was because Herodias was annoyed by Phasaelis's antics and didn't want Antipas to behave as though he had been forced to buy off Phasaelis in order to marry her.

Herodias was even more incensed by the protests of Johannon, who was behaving as if she were some kind of criminal, when she—of the

LEN LAMENSDORF

Hasmonean blood—was surely the better arbiter of right and wrong. After all, she was descended not only from kings but High Priests.

Antipas thought about all this glumly as he waited in his palace in Machaerus, where he had gone, ostensibly to prepare for war. The worst part of this dispute was not that he would have to fight, but that he had been forced to leave Tiberias in the best part of the season to camp in the desert east of the Dead Sea in a Godforsaken fortress his father had built a generation before.

Machaerus, in fact, was an elaborate institution, including a thriving town of several hundred inhabitants, established within a fortified wall protected with towers.

Within the town, long slanting ramps led to a crest on which was set a forbidding citadel with high towers at the corners. Inside the ominous walls of the citadel, Herod the Great had built an elaborate palace with huge halls and many rooms, all elegantly structured and lavishly furnished. If Machaerus was drab in comparison to Tiberias, it was still one of the most elegant establishments in the land. Only an esthete like Antipas would have felt deprived there.

"Why did I have to come here?" Herodias asked, her full, red lips pressed together in a pout.

"I'm here to defend your honor," Herod Antipas said, shifting in bed. "The least you can do is keep me company."

"It's boring here," she said, swatting at his hand which was burrowing under her breast.

Antipas sighed. "I'm doing my best to avoid fighting with Aretas. If we can settle this matter peaceably, perhaps we can be home in a month."

"A month!" she said, sitting upright suddenly and pulling the lavish sheets over her body. "You told me a week or two."

Antipas realized his error. "Teasing my dear, just teasing." He leaned close to bite her shoulder.

Herodias smiled. Antipas wasn't handsome, but then neither was her first husband. At least this one bathed often, perfumed himself and was gentle in bed. "Oh well," she thought, "why not?"

As she lowered the covering, exposing pale, perfect breasts, the door of the chamber flew open, startling both of them. It was Salome, Herodias's daughter by her first husband. She was the only one in the palace who would have dared enter the royal bedroom in such a manner.

Salome was not the equal of her mother in elegance, but she was ripe, round and lusty with dark eyes and hair and a body she loved to display. She

336

was envious of her mother, and competed with her in many ways. She did not hesitate to prance before her stepfather or to flirt with him, even while Herodias watched. Herodias was tolerant of the girl, feeling that she herself was doing more than enough to keep Antipas satisfied. She did not know that her daughter's firm, pliant sixteen year old body played a repeated role in his dreams and daydreams.

"Mother," she cried, jumping up on the bed. "I want to go to Ein Gedi with Aristobolus." Aristobolus was a young officer in Herod's army, a bright and attractive young man, whom Salome toyed with.

"Ein Gedi?" Antipas said. "It's on the other side of the sea."

"Yes," she responded, rolling on the bed, so that her thighs brushed Antipas's hand, "but they say the springs are beautiful."

"Aristobolus," Herodias said. "I don't think so." Aristobolus had been her father's name, but this man was nothing like him. She didn't feel a mere soldier was worthy of her daughter.

"But it's so boring, here," Salome said, sitting on her haunches with her bottom on Antipas's other hand.

"Yes, boring," Herodias said, "but we're having a fine dinner tonight to celebrate Antipas's birthday."

"My birthday," Antipas said, "I had forgotten." He was having trouble concentrating, with Salome's warm little bottom sliding up and back in his hand.

"The entertainment will be splendid," Herodias said.

***

Johannon, the Baptizer, sat on the stone floor in his cell, a small room in one of the towers of Machaerus. There was no window and the only light came from the torches in the corridor. The ceiling was too low for Johannon to stand up, but the room was dry and free of insects. The food was sparse but clean.

Johannon was cheerful in his captivity. He was relieved that Joshua, the Messiah, had come, and that his own service was, therefore, at an end. He hoped to see the new king firmly on the throne before he died, but considered his own continued existence of little importance. All that mattered was that God had decided that the hour for Israel's rescue had arrived and that made Johannon very happy.

He was allowed an occasional visitor, but few came. They were afraid that they, too, would be imprisoned. Once, Amos, a Zealot leader and friend of Judas, had come from Jerusalem. The meeting was brief—Amos only wanted to assure himself personally that the Baptizer was alive. "Have faith," he said, realizing as he said it that the words were unnecessary, but the Baptizer had smiled and thanked him.

Later, the Master of Qumran had sent Baruch to enquire into Johannon's case. Baruch was frightened of the task, but resigned to it. Johannon saw at once how frightened he was.

"Be brave," he whispered to Baruch. "They won't harm you. They aren't even certain they're going to harm me."

Baruch tried to calm himself. "The Master wants to know what you believe we should do about Joshua ben Joseph."

Johannon frowned. "Doesn't he realize who Joshua is?"

"He wants your assurance."

"Tell him there is no doubt—He is the Messiah of Israel."

Baruch gasped. Only now, hearing it from Johannon, did he truly understand how close he had been to the anointed one.

"The Master must bend his will to the will of God," Johannon said, knowing the Master's personal vanities. "This is no time for divisions among us."

Baruch knew the message would be difficult for the Master to accept.

"What do you hear of Joshua?" Johannon asked.

"He has been preaching in Galilee and we hear the people love him."

"Preaching?" Johannon asked. "When will he come to Jerusalem. When will he take the throne?"

Baruch shook his head. Johannon gripped his shoulders. "Go to Galilee—speak to him. Ask him when? We must know."

"I'll ask the Master for permission," Baruch said.

Johannon shook his head violently. "This is beyond the authority of the Master. The people will respond directly to the Anointed One, but they will want to prepare themselves for his coming."

It was dark when Baruch finished talking to Johannon, and he had no choice but to spend the night within the citadel, praying that, despite what the Baptizer had said, he himself would not be thrown into prison.

***

Antipas had long been fascinated with Johannon. Since he himself was curious about a man who lived by trust in some unknown god. Antipas was himself, nominally a Jew, and observed all of the holidays and most of the traditional rules. However, he also gave funds to other religions throughout his realm and in Rome, and would have prayed to a braying donkey if that would have kept the peace.

He had talked to Johannon on several occasions on the pretext of persuading the man to change his accusations, but really because he was drawn to him personally.

This evening, while Baruch was cowering in his room, praying for the dawn so that he might depart, Antipas again had himself admitted to Johannon's cell. He carried a torch, which he placed on the wall, but he carried no weapons.

"You're not afraid of me," Johannon said.

"Frankly," Antipas said, "I think you're as dangerous as a dove."

"Then why don't you set me free?"

"I'd like to, but Herodias wouldn't forgive me. Can't you stop saying all those nasty things about us?"

"Send her away and I'll commend you."

Herod Antipas sighed. "I really want to keep her, Baptizer. Have you ever seen her? She's very beautiful."

"I haven't seen her and I don't care to. Not that I am opposed to her, personally—It's your illegal marriage that bothers me."

"We've been all through that, my friend," Herod said. "Why do you care what an Idumean Tetrarch does? We're not even full-blooded Jews."

"You claim to be Jewish, full-blooded or not, and you're the ruler in these parts—at least temporarily. You have to set a good example."

"What do you mean, temporarily?"

Johannon was silent for a moment. There was no point in making additional problems for Joshua. "Everything is temporary, except the Lord."

"There's something you're not telling me," Antipas said, his eyes slitting to narrow lines.

"Make your peace with heaven, Herod, the Kingdom of God is at hand."

Johannon looked at him with such sincerity, that Antipas shuddered. "You know, Baptizer, I worry about you. Some day you're going to fall into the hands of someone who isn't as tender-hearted as I am, and then you'll lose your life."

"And gain the Kingdom of heaven," Johannon said smiling. "I'm not worried."

"I see you're not. Oh well, please remember that I tried to save you."

"It's not in your hands, Herod."

Herod shook his head. "Guards, open the door."

***

The sounds of the party rang through the stone walls of the citadel, waking Baruch who was sleeping in a tiny room near the main gates. He would have gone back to sleep, but something drew him out of the room and toward the sounds.

There was no one about and he found no obstacle as he made his way along the outside walls, up to a window that looked into a huge banquet hall. Within, the walls were festooned with draperies and smoke from torches filled the air with wispy clouds that drifted in eerie waves over the revelers. Men and women ate together at a succession of low tables, surrounded by pillows on which they reclined. At one end of the hall, twenty or more musicians made loud but not necessarily harmonious noises. Everyone, from the Tetrarch to the serving girls, had been drinking for hours and there wasn't a sober head in the house.

Baruch, living an ascetic life, had never seen nor heard such raucous revelry and he could not look away.

In the center of the floor, a dozen young girls, dressed in gauzy gowns, were dancing in wild and abandoned fashion. If there had once been a plan to their performance, it had long since been forgotten, as the drunken partyers demanded one more dance and then another. The watchers had plied the girls with wine and gradually they had stripped off almost everything they were wearing. From time to time, one would drop down on the pillows or be dragged to them by one of the guests. Then there would be laughter and pawing until the girl was able to escape.

Meanwhile, the rhythmic beat of the drums and the clash of the cymbals, kept the guests throbbing with lust and passion.

Herodias sat beside her husband, not even trying to hide her disgust at these proceedings. Antipas was coarse and had no taste and had allowed the evening to degenerate into an orgy. Even now, an officer—was it Aristobolus?—had dragged a serving girl behind a huge column and was forcing her to submit to him. No one complained. No one even noticed. Except Salome, who had been amused for a while, but now was infuriated to see that Aristobolus was getting his satisfaction elsewhere.

Antipas's attention had flitted between the almost naked dancing girls and Salome. She wore a thin and diaphanous gown, almost as transparent as the dancing girls, and during the course of the meal, she had managed to bump into her stepfather many times. He had pinched her here and there when Herodias was not looking, but that had only served to enhance his lust. He wondered if he would ever get her alone.

Herodias watched this byplay with detachment, but now she had a thought. She leaned over and whispered to her daughter. "The old fool is dying to have you. Relieve my boredom and dance for him."

"What good will that do me?" Salome said, still keeping one eye on Aristobolus, who had now finished with the serving girl and had flung her from him.

"You'll help your mother and you'll drive Aristobolus wild."

"He's already had his pleasure."

"That's what will drive him wild."

Salome smiled suddenly and stood up.

To say that Salome stood up is to denigrate a magnificent gesture. Indeed, she unwound from her cross-legged position on the pillows and rose as a serpent might rise from a basket. This simple and sensual motion immediately caught Antipas's eye. Some of his nether parts began to tingle.

Salome leaned close to the Tetrarch, so that her trim breasts swayed close to his face. She smiled, an expression he did not notice, then made her way to the dance floor. Salome wore no shoes, and she moved as if she were a forest creature, with great economy of movement, yet with all of her anatomy flowing. She walked through the line of the dancers and stood, with her back turned to Antipas.

She waited patiently. In a moment, the dancers realized she was there and scurried from the floor. The musicians were slower, but in another moment, they ceased to play. The revelers, responding to the sudden silence, looked up to see Salome, standing alone, with light from the torches outlining her body through the thin gown. They, too, grew silent.

Then, holding the moment for only a beat, Salome began to sway. Her head lolled to her breast, swaying with her body. Slowly, ever so slowly, she raised her arms and they began to sway in gentle rhythm with her body. The musicians began to play, at first just a simple beat and then with added rhythm as they found the pattern to her movements.

Slowly, ever so slowly, Salome turned, raised her head and, facing Antipas, she moved her feet for the first time. Her movements remained very slow and sensual, her arms and legs seemed to have no joints. She turned and dipped, turned and dipped, spun slowly and swayed again.

Salome moved closer to the Tetrarch. Her eyes never left him. Now she was swaying before him, the fullness of her body, firm and ripe, moving with her arms and legs, never preceding, never following, so that all of her seemed to be a pulsing fountain of fluid motion.

Salome slowly settled to the floor, never stopping her movements. She was moving more rapidly now, and the musicians followed, beating their drums and clashing their cymbals to punctuate her gestures. Now she was on her haunches before Antipas and had leaned over backward, so that her hair touched the stone. Antipas was having trouble breathing, as his eyes followed the line from between her breasts to between her legs.

Somehow she turned so that her head was close to Antipas's feet, and this time, when she arched back to the floor, her long hair escaped from its cap and cascaded to the stone. Her breasts fell free of the gauzy gown before Antipas's leering eyes.

Salome remained on the stone floor, spinning face down, then face up, writhing and twisting. Her movements pulled her totally free of her gown and she undulated, completely naked, before Antipas and his guests, who looked and leered and would have cheered except she was his stepdaughter.

Antipas forgot there was anyone else in the room, feeling only the insistent beat of the music and seeing only the sensual movements of Salome's splendid young body.

She moved closer and closer to him, then sprang suddenly into his lap and threw up her hands. The music stopped, the guests felt free to cheer and Antipas trembling with desire, felt the perspiration drenching his face.

He would have taken her there, if he could. But he remembered himself. "Tell me," he whispered hoarsely, "what do you want? Anything in my kingdom—name it."

Salome leaned across Antipas and put her ear close to the mouth of Herodias. "You little bitch," Herodias said quietly, "ask the goat for the head of Johannon, the Baptizer."

Startled, Salome slipped from Antipas's lap, but caught her balance and crouched before her mother.

Herodias nodded, her eyes fixed on Salome's eyes. "Ask him," she said. "He's made his promise."

Salome was furious. Had she danced like this only to gain the death of some stupid holy man? But her mother did not look away and her look was powerful. Salome cringed before her mother.

"Tell me, child," Antipas said, wiping his brow and trying to smile to cover the heat he felt. "What are you, two, whispering about?"

Salome retrieved her gown and wrapped it about her. She shuddered as she spoke. "Bring us the head of Johannon," she said.

7.

THE LEADERS

They rode day and night for two days. At no time did they gallop their horses for they did not want to attract attention. Judas knew the country well and was informed where Roman and Herodian troops were stationed. They gave those places a wide berth when they could, and traveled with great care when they could not.

Along the route, there were any number of safe houses, where friends provided food without question and fresh horses. Judas introduced Joshua only as his friend. This was not the time for revelations. Still, Judas saw in every case what he had seen before—the immediate response of all people to Joshua's indefinable warmth and strength, without preaching, without healing, without being told anything about him.

Joshua was deeply impressed by the network of Judas's friends and their unfailing loyalty to him. This in itself was grounds for renewed hope.

Joshua had never ridden so continuously in his life. His seat was a bit sore, and the inside of his thighs chafed, but he felt strong and enthusiastic and ready. Judas noted with pleasure that Joshua was as strong as he was, bearing the rigors of their trip with ease and grace.

They reached Bethany, on the eastern side of the Mount of Olives, in the middle of the night. At a sign from Judas, they dismounted and led their horses down a narrow cobbled street to a stone house. Two quick raps on the door and it opened and they were inside.

The owners were Eliezer, a wool merchant, and his sisters Miriam and Martha. All three were in their forties and thus close to Joshua's age. Eliezer was the nominal head of the household, a robust, cheerful man with a full head of curly brown hair, a swarthy complexion and rather hairy arms. Miriam was slender and contemplative, pale-skinned and delicate-featured with shy movements and quiet grace.

Martha was the true head of the family, robust like her brother, with the same curly brown hair and sturdy frame. She was serious, though, much more serious than her brother, who seemed almost playful by comparison. Martha thought it was her duty to keep her puckish brother and ethereal sister firmly planted in reality.

Joshua was immediately drawn to all three of them. They greeted him warmly, accepted him at face value and did all they could to make him comfortable. He felt tired for the first time since he had left Galilee, perhaps because of the task that awaited him. But Miriam cleaned his robe and Martha brought him hot food and Eliezer told him cheerful anecdotes about Bethany.

Joshua smiled in spite of himself, drawn out of his serious thoughts and his weariness by the kind attention and Eliezer's cheerful tales. Even Judas was amused, although he found Eliezer too garrulous for his taste.

"Cheer up, my brother," Eliezer said, noting Judas's frown, "the best is yet to come."

"You're right about that," Judas said, and surprised Joshua by telling Eliezer, briefly and enthusiastically, what their mission was. Eliezer's smile faded, but not entirely. When Judas was finished, he spoke to Joshua. "Thank you, Rabbi, for coming when we need you most."

Joshua was touched by the simple affirmation, by Eliezer's lack of awe and his simple faith. "I think you know, Eliezer, that it is the Lord we must thank."

Eliezer smiled. "For everything," he said. Then he left the room to help his sisters with some task.

"Don't let that smile fool you," Judas said. "Eliezer has suffered the loss of many members of his family, just as you have, and his desire to lift the Roman oppression is very deep. But he is a gentle soul, full of faith, and he has accepted his losses as the work of God, and therefore not to be questioned. But he is bright and tough and very clever at finding out what the Roman garrison is up to. He often sits on the hill opposite the Holy City, and from watching the comings and goings at the gates, and the flags draped on the Antonia Fortress, he gives us accurate data about our adversaries."

"If we think of them as adversaries, Judas, we have lost half the battle."

Judas controlled himself. "It's an old habit, Master, and hard to break."

"Those are the habits that bring death," Joshua said.

***

In the morning, they walked on foot to Jerusalem. In the pale morning light, the dew still glistened on the fields and dripped from tombs on the side of the Mount of Olives. Shepherds grazed their herds down into the Kidron Valley and those who had business in the city wound their way along the twisting, narrow roads.

The Temple floated serenely, a marble, limestone and gold ship above the pale, pink crenellations etched like formal-shaped waves on the crest of the city walls. Streaks of clouds seemed to soar from the sanctuary itself up into the heavens, like furled sails.

As Joshua described this image to Judas, the Zealot chieftain frowned. "A ship may sink, Master—but a Temple is founded on rock."

An unaccustomed tremor of fear passed through Joshua. "Then we must make certain that the ship doesn't sink," he said.

They entered north of the city by the Sheep gate and made their way slowly and patiently through the narrow streets to the house of Amos.

They gave the usual sign and were admitted quickly. The house was filled with men, perhaps two dozen of them. Judas was angry. "This is too dangerous," he said. "Every Judaean leader is here. If the Romans come, we'll have a disaster."

"No," said a hard-faced man, "THEY'LL have a disaster."

The others laughed, but Judas was not amused.

"That's what Bar Abbas thought," he said.

"We should rescue him," one of them said.

"Impossible. They've tripled the guard at the Antonia. We'd die for nothing."

"It's getting harder every day to keep the peace," Amos said. "Bar Abbas is a hothead, but the people support what he did and they love the man."

Meanwhile, they were all appraising Joshua, noting his strong face and powerful build, his height and clear eyes. His blonde hair was a surprise, but quickly overlooked. This fellow at least looked like a leader.

Amos had placed bread and wine on the tables. Joshua rose, broke the bread and blessed it, his strong voice ringing in the room. Then he blessed the wine and they shared the cup.

He surprised them by reciting the Shema, "Hear O Israel, the Lord our God, the Lord is One." They joined with him, and then said, "Blessed is His glorious Kingdom for ever and ever."

Their voices filled the house, while Judas nervously looked about, waiting for the Romans to break in.

Joshua then paraphrased the prayer that usually followed: "I know that we all love the Lord our God with all our hearts, our souls and our might.

The holy words are engraved in our hearts forever. We have taught them to our children as the Lord commanded us and we think of them constantly, wherever we may be. The words are always before our eyes, they are signs that mark the way for us—that mark every way for us."

He paused. "And yet, we are not free. We love the Lord our God, and yet we are not free.

"For hundreds of years, brave men like you have refused to bow down to idols, to bend the knee to foreign kings who desecrated our holiest places. You have won victories at great cost, at the loss of your homes and your families, and still we are not free.

"In every generation, brave men like you have risked everything for the right to worship the one God in the one, the only holy way,

"AND STILL WE ARE NOT FREE."

The words rang in their hearts. The pain of their struggle was echoed in Joshua's words.

"Shall we continue to do that which we have done before? Shall we draw our swords and battle the heathen in yet another generation? Shall we triumph—for a while? Live free lives—for a while. And then watch the hordes from all around us descend again, so that our children must fight the same battle we have fought.

"Is there no end?"

They watched him, motionless, hardly breathing, for he had voiced the fears they all held in secret.

"There is an end—I promise you there is an end, because the Lord Almighty has promised us there will be an end. That the yoke of our oppressors will be lifted from our necks, that the men and women of Israel and Judah will stand upright once more, that the holy Temple will be cleansed of all impurities and we will worship our God in peace forever.

"That is the promise—the promise repeated in the law and the prophets, the promise given by almighty God.

"But it comes at a price. The price that must be paid is that we bow down before God's word. His blessed word tells us that if we want love, we must give love. If we want peace we must give peace.

"The ways of war have failed. If we smite the heathen, he smites back and then we must smite again and again and again until we and they are all dead.

"Can this be God's will? No, no, a thousand times no. God has told us this over and over and we have stopped up our ears and refused to listen.

But no more. If we love our families, if we love our country, IF WE LOVE GOD—WE WILL DO GOD'S WILL.

"We will begin by repenting our sins, by cleansing our souls, by purifying ourselves in preparation. We will organize—yes, but not armies, we will organize our people to resist, but without violence. We will oppose the heathen, never again will we follow his laws, but we will not strike a single blow. If the heathen strikes us on one cheek, we will offer the other, but we will not retaliate.

"God tells us to love our neighbor, including the stranger within our walls. The Roman is that stranger and we will love him—hard as it may be—WE WILL LOVE HIM.

"We will not obey his laws, nor pay his taxes, nor submit our tribute, but we will love him.

"And then our God will love us as he has never loved us before. When we have submitted our will to his, given up the angry urge to strike back and kill those who would strike and kill us—when we have shown the Lord our God that He is the one, the only ruler of our lives, that even as the heathen raises his hand against us we see only the hand of God—then God will use his love and his strength to lift the oppressor's hand from off our shoulders, his yoke from around our necks, his foul laws from our people. Then God will lead the Romans away, never to return. Then we will live in peace and harmony in the land that God gave us, forever and ever."

"Amen," called Amos and several of the others, moved greatly by the passion and conviction of Joshua.

"Yes, yes," they said.

Judas's face was flushed—he too was astonished by the force of Joshua's words, the sincerity of the man and his strength that could only come from above.

But others, though moved, were not convinced.

"When, how will this be done?" asked Benjamin.

"At the Passover," Joshua said. "You will go back to your towns and villages, preparing your people in secret. At the feast, we will bring as many as possible to the city—the Romans will not be concerned, they are accustomed to huge crowds. But on the first day of the holiday, we will gather in the Temple and we will proclaim our freedom.

"I will speak to the nation, to the Romans, to all who will hear. We will invoke a new Sabbath year, a Sabbath year far greater, more widespread, more disciplined than any before in our history—a year when no

crops will be planted nor harvested, no fishing will be done, nor any hunting No buildings will be built or repaired, no animals raised or slaughtered, no taxes or tribute will be paid. We will tell the Romans there is no
profit for them in this land, and they are free to leave it—for we will not
hinder their leaving."

Judas spoke from the back of the room. "Hundreds of thousands of us
gathered at the Passover—too many even for Pilate to think of attacking—a
whole nation rising in opposition, but without striking a blow."

They watched Judas, usually the coldest of them and the most dispassionate, and saw the fervor in his eyes.

A man from Bethlehem spoke out. "But what if the Romans do attack?
Some will die."

"Are you willing to die for war, but not for peace?" Joshua asked. "Yes,
indeed, we must be prepared to die. The Romans, some Romans, may turn
to violence, and if so, we must be prepared to give our lives for the love of
the Almighty. The Lord will understand that we are as brave—no, we are
braver, than the man who dies with a sword in his hands."

"That is a hard way," another said.

"Yes, hard it is, but the only way," Joshua said.

"Are you from Bethlehem?" a man asked.

"I was born there," Joshua said. "Are you asking if I am of the house
of David?"

"Yes," the man said.

"David is dead a thousand years and you want me to trace my lineage?"
He waited while some laughed. "They say my mother is of the royal house,
but is that the question? Do you believe the Lord cannot anoint whom he
chooses?"

"Then are you the anointed one."

"In my heart, I am the anointed. In my soul, I am the anointed. The
Lord, God, has told me that I am here to save my people from death and
destruction, to lead them to redemption and freedom. These words have
come to me when I was baptized in the Jordan by Johannon, and in every
waking hour since then. Yes, I am anointed—The Lord has chosen to speak
through me and I have chosen to hear his words and give them to you.

"Now, it is time for me to anoint you." He brought forth a small vial
that he had carried with him from Galilee. "Come forward," he said.

They hesitated, but then Benjamin came forward and bent his knee
before him.

"Stand up," Joshua said, "I am not to be worshipped—only the living God is worshipped."

He sprinkled a little of the fluid from the vial on Benjamin and embraced him. "Bless you. Go and do the Lord's bidding."

Then, one after another, they came forward, and Joshua anointed them and blessed and embraced them.

There was a knock on the door. They froze where they stood, some even touching the swords in their belts, as Joshua noted. Such habits died hard. But the lookout reassured them. "It's only one man in white habit."

They admitted Baruch to the house. He was surprised to see so many there, but Amos reassured him and brought him in. Baruch was pleased to see Joshua, but then his expression darkened. "I was at Machaerus. The Master told me to report what I saw to you, Amos."

Baruch swallowed several times before he spoke. The others shifted uneasily as he tried to gain control of himself. At first his words were so soft that no one even heard him.

"Speak up," Benjamin said.

Baruch swallowed and spoke out in a cracked voice. "Johannon, the one they called the Baptizer, is dead."

The men reacted with shock and pain. Most had known and loved the Baptizer. Joshua was deeply wounded by the blow. He had hoped that Johannon would join him in his mission.

Judas held Baruch by the arm. "When? How?"

"Two days ago—Herod Antipas had him beheaded."

They rose to their feet, startled, angry and vocal. "Beheaded?" "Why?" "The bastard!" "We'll get him for that!"

Joshua watched and listened in silence as Baruch, pale and trembling, recounted the story of Salome's dance and her request for the head of the Baptizer. As he remembered Johannon's head carried into the room on a bloody platter, he felt faint, but the Zealots were angered and shouted threats and some gripped their weapons.

"Wait!" Joshua flung up his arms. "Have you forgotten already the words we spoke but a few minutes ago?"

"You see!" Amos cried. "We can't trust these people—Romans or Herodians. They're killers."

"You're being tested," Joshua said. "We're all being tested. Do you think it's only by chance we've learned this terrible thing at this time? No, the Lord God wants to know if we have the strength, the love of Him and

His word to do what He wills, no matter how hard the task, or how fierce the temptation to fall away. If we rise up in anger over the death of Johannon, we are lost and the nation is lost with us.

"You must trust the Lord and you must hear His word and do His bidding. Show God that you are truly Zealots—Zealots for the living God."

They hesitated, swayed by his words. They sheathed their swords and sat down again, watching Joshua.

"Thank you, O Lord, our God, ruler of the Universe, for giving us life and your holy word, for showing us the way of death is but temporary, but in the resurrection we shall all be with thee in thy holy kingdom."

"Amen," said the men, and then "Amen" again.

***

They left the house of Amos in small groups, so as not to arouse suspicion. Joshua went his way on a private errand, without guards, despite Judas's protests. "I'll arouse more suspicion with several men accompanying me, than alone." Judas shrugged and agreed.

Seeing that Judas remained behind, a few of the more prominent Zealot leaders stayed with him, including Amos and Benjamin.

"He IS the Messiah," Judas said firmly.

The others nodded in agreement. "We believe that," Ahaz, a leader from Caesarea said, although surely not what we expected."

"What DID you expect?" Benjamin asked.

"A warrior king, with armor and a helmet and an army."

"A child's vision," Judas said.

Ahaz only smiled. "Until now I thought it might only be a child's dream."

"It won't be easy," Benjamin said, "telling our people to put aside their arms—not after spending all these months and years slowly and painfully stealing them from the Romans."

The others laughed. They would face the same problem. Judas struggled with a thought that wormed its way inside him and that he could feel wriggling, waiting to be expressed.

"What is it, Judas?" Ahaz asked, you look like you're chewing on a live coal."

Judas smiled grimly. "I tell you this from a sincere heart. I love the man and I believe in him. Everything he says sounds right, especially when he tells it to me in that wonderful, resonant voice. At those moments. I swear I feel that I'm listening directly to the voice of God."

"It's true," Benjamin said, pulling at his beard. "I feel the same thing."

"We must follow him," Judas said, "but we don't have to burn all our bridges behind us. He didn't say we should beat our swords into plowshares—at least, not yet. Therefore, let's bury our weapons, but not forget where they are buried—in case the Lord and Joshua change their minds."

The leaders sat quietly reflecting on Judas's words.

"I don't know," Amos said. "It almost seems like betraying him."

Judas was angry. "I have no intention of betraying him, but that doesn't mean I have to act the fool. Do what you wish. I, for one, will make certain the weapons of my people are in a dry, safe place in Jerusalem."

***

Joshua had left Judas with the others, knowing full well they would discuss his plans and share their opinions of his intentions. He realized that when he spoke to men, he had the power to persuade them, to bend them to his will and he used that power reverently, with full knowledge it was God who must be served and not Joshua ben Joseph.

He also realized that when he was away from men, the spell might be broken, and if the message was not truly burned into their hearts they would fall away from it. He wanted to give them the opportunity to express and share their doubts. Then, he hoped, they would proceed with greater resolve.

He also doubted they would all have the strength to simply cast aside their weapons. They would lay them down, or hide them, but they would not destroy them. That was only natural, especially among men such as these, who had learned by bitter experience to be wary of the words of men—even of angels.

But, at least he had persuaded them that his way had merit and if they acted swiftly and in concert, the way of peace would have its fair trial. Then, when it succeeded, they would be willing to follow the words that Isaiah had brought them and turn their spears into pruning-hooks. He prayed he would have the time to help God save his people.

Joshua had another purpose in mind. He had not returned to Jerusalem since the days of the Passover he had shared with his own family and the family of Nicodemus many years before. Occasionally, a friend or family member passing through had brought kind words, but there had been no personal contact. Joshua had heard that young Nico had become a priest, following his father's example. Now, he wanted to speak to his old friends personally.

Joshua climbed the sloping cheese-makers valley until he reached the ramps leading to the upper city. Once again, he was astonished by the beauty of the wealthy section of the city and its great contrast with the neighborhoods of the poor. It was like a different universe and he wondered how people who lived like this could keep their minds on spiritual matters.

He was pleased that he remembered his way to the house of Nicodemus, but surprised by the servant who answered his knock. "No," the man said haughtily, "they don't live here any longer."

"Where do they live?" asked Joshua.

"I'm sure I don't know," the servant said. "I believe it's somewhere on the Ophel." The way he said it, the word sounded like a dung heap.

Joshua had to retrace his steps and begin again in the lower city. It took him a long time before he found anyone who knew the family. Then he was directed to one place after another, following one false lead after another.

Finally, he came upon a young priest. "Nico? Of course, he lives there." The priest pointed to a large but shabby looking structure just across the narrow street.

"Joshua!" Nico flung open his arms and literally lifted Joshua off his feet. Then, tears streaming down his face, he set him down, brushed him off and apologized.

Joshua laughed. "Why are you apologizing?"

"They say you are the Messiah?"

"Even the Messiah has friends," Joshua said, "and he needs every one of them. But tell me, why are you living here?"

"I moved to the Ophel when I began my service as a priest, not wishing to be far from my brethren and to share their life. Father felt much the same. A life of wealth and ease meant little to him, and he was tired of his hypocritical friends who claimed to love their nation, but loved money and power more. He sold our home and moved here and I was happy to join him."

Nico smiled and led Joshua into a large sitting room where his father sat, his leg elevated onto a cushion. "Joshua," he said, "after all these years." He held out his arms and Joshua embraced him.

Nicodemus held him at arms-length for a moment. "To think, the young boy who stayed at my house the year he came of age, is to be the leader of our people."

Joshua was puzzled. "How is it that you say these things? We've tried not to alarm the Romans."

Nicodemus laughed. "We think big thoughts in Judaea even though we're a small country."

"And a nation of story-tellers," Nico said.

Joshua was concerned. "If you know, then others must know, and if the word is released prematurely, our movement will be jeopardized."

"Of course," Nicodemus said, "but that is the risk you take."

"You're right. That's why we must move swiftly."

He told them briefly of his disciples spreading the word, north, east and west, of his meeting with the Zealot leaders and his plans for the Passover. They listened in silence and wonder and growing enthusiasm.

"Can we help, Joshua?" Nico asked. "What can we do?"

"You can do much. First, Nicodemus can be my eyes and ears in the Sanhedrin. I fear Caiaphas and those who think like him. I fear the rich families who believe Roman rule is in their interests. The day may come when you will learn something of value to us—forewarn us of the action of those who may be our enemies."

"Done," Nicodemus said. "There's great division on the council between those who want to cooperate and those who yearn to throw the Romans out. At the moment, the collaborators are in control, and they would do anything to save their places."

"I'll speak to you frankly, old friends," Joshua said. "There are divisions everywhere among the people, not only between rich and poor, but between zealots and collaborators, brave men and cowards. The people are confused and know not which way to turn. Every man who offers hope seems like a Messiah and many deceive and betray them.

"Even among the Zealots there are factions. Today, they all promised to follow me, to confront the Romans with peace instead of war, but the moment there was an unexpected knock on the door, they reached for their daggers. We Jews are naturally a rebellious lot, quick to anger and just as quick to forgive. But the anger may come first and then our plan will be defeated.

"Thus it is that among the Zealots, I have my concerns as to whom I can trust. Of you, two, I have no doubts. I ask if your home can be a safe house for me when I am in Jerusalem."

"Yes, of course," they both said.

"Good, there are a few men among my closest disciples, including my brother Jacob and sister Judith, whom I will tell of our arrangement, but no others. Then I will know that, in an emergency, I have a place I can use as a sanctuary."

They devised between them a few signs and some passwords and parted with deep affection and great hopes for their homeland.

8.

RULERS

Pilate spoke angrily. "I won't do it, Gaius, you can forget it."

Gaius held himself in check as always. "The High Priest's palace is quite lavish. Valerius Gratus went there when he was governor. I believe even Pompey visited it when he was in Judaea."

Pilate shook his head. "The High Priest should come to me—I am the ruler here, not he."

"The laws forbid it, Sire. Caiaphas could not remain High Priest if he came to this place."

"Unclean? Are you saying that we are unclean? That's outrageous."

"Sire, the uncleanliness has a special, religious meaning to these Jews. It's nothing personal, I can assure you."

"Let him write to me, then. I'll be damned if I want to see him, anyway."

"Prefect," Gaius said patiently. "The man is not our enemy. His desire to keep the peace, to prevent an uprising, is at least as great as ours. But he must preserve outward appearances where the people are concerned. He has no choice but to protest the massacre—"

"—Massacre? How dare you use such words, Deputy? Our troops performed a proper disciplinary action."

"Yes, I will write that in the report to the emperor, but there are some who will believe that soldiers ought not to masquerade as civilians, and peaceful protestors need not be killed."

Pilate's eyebrows rose high as he spoke and his lips moved grimly. As always, when he was angry, his lisp was more prominent, but that sibilant hiss served only to enhance the sinister quality of his speech. "Those who would say such things do not understand the Syrian Department and its dangers, and especially the insidious nature of the Jews. These people clamor about their holy books, but they understand only the whip, the cudgel and the sword."

"It may even be true that the High Priest agrees with you, but I can assure you, Sire, whatever his beliefs, his protest will only be formal and quickly served. If all Jews were like Caiaphas, this province would be easy to govern."

Pilate tilted his head and looked at Gaius quizzically. "I was beginning to think you were growing too fond of these people. I'm surprised to hear your evaluation of the High Priest."

"My loyalty is to Rome, the Emperor and to you," Gaius said, although the words almost stuck in his throat. "If Rome is to enjoy a long and peaceful hegemony over this land and you are to have a prosperous administration, it is my duty to offer you my best and most dispassionate advice. You are free to take it, or to dismiss it."

"We'll go, Gaius. Send word to Caiaphas."

***

They rode through the streets with an escort, but left it outside of the palace. Caiaphas greeted them on the first floor in an audience hall reserved for gentiles. Gaius knew this, but Pilate did not, and he was suitably impressed by the great size of the room and its lavish furnishings.

The two men, both tall and arrogant, each hating the other, met in the center of the room. They exchanged nods of the head, but no greetings. Caiaphas did not sit nor offer a seat, nor did Pilate ask for one. Each felt unspeakably defiled at being in the presence of the other.

"I did not inform the people of the removal of the Temple treasure, fearing the very protest which ensued," Caiaphas said. "I expected to resolve this peacefully between us. Unfortunately, the action was too obvious and the word spread and we both know the result.

"I have no choice, Prefect, other than to protest directly to the emperor, first of the unauthorized removal of the treasure and second of the unwarranted slaughter of the protestors."

Pilate wanted to tell him what he could do with his protest, that by law no delegation could be sent to Rome without the governor's permission. But he knew that the Jews had their own network of communication and powerful friends who had access to the emperor. If Pilate opposed sending a delegation, he would soon hear word from Rome ordering him to send such a delegation. Seething with anger, Pilate held back, waiting to hear all this arrogant Jew had to say.

"There is still time to avoid such unpleasantness, Governor. This can be done by prompt restoration of the treasure, an apology for the deaths of the citizens, and the selection of an officer who will be punished for exceeding his authority."

The Jew was crafty, Pilate thought. He was offering him a way to escape what could prove to be an embarrassment—a report to Rome that could be misunderstood at such a distance. He had few friends there, anyway, and others were always standing in line for one of these border posts. Little did they know how difficult it was for an administrator to profit in this land. The bribes were few and grudgingly given, the taxes had often to be extracted at sword's point.

But there was more at stake than that for Pilate. After the better part of a decade in this despicable place, he was ready, even eager to go home, if he could extract himself on some honorable basis. Nevertheless, he had come here hating these people and his hatred had deepened. They showed no respect for his homeland or his personal authority. They looked down upon him—these poor benighted people—looked down upon *him*, and he could not suffer that. The face of the High Priest betrayed his contempt for Pilate and the urge grew in the governor to smash the face of this rich, corrupt and arrogant man.

"There will be no return of the treasure. Those funds properly belong to Rome—required to serve you and the needs of your own people."

"The manner of their 'appropriation' is more important than the sums involved," said Caiaphas. He could see the hate welling up in this man, but he was not intimidated. He loved his place, but he would not bow to heathen swine. He would pay their price, but not bow to them. "When the treasure is returned, we can discuss the question of raising necessary funds for the aqueduct from more usual sources."

"The treasure, as you call it, will not be returned. I suggest YOU make it up from 'more usual sources.'"

Caiaphas shook his head. "Unless you do what I ask, the people will remain angry and the difficulties of governing this area will increase. I don't believe you want that—I know that I myself am entirely opposed to rebellion."

"Then stop it," Pilate hissed.

"I need your help. Will you renounce the killings and punish an officer?"

"To do so would be to admit the action was wrong in the first place."

"To do less is to permit the flames of unrest to mount higher, when a small sacrifice could dampen them."

At that moment, Pilate missed Gaius. He had insisted he meet with the Jew alone, but now he wished he had his deputy's counsel. Perhaps there was a face-saving way out of this problem, but he hated to use the alternative suggested by Caiaphas. That would be demeaning. Then he was angry at himself for even thinking of compromising with this despicable creature.

Caiaphas saw the struggle going on in Pilate. The man was so evil and yet, he was an open book. Caiaphas could read his thoughts in his eyes. Over his shoulder he saw Reuben, the Sagan of the Temple, hovering in the hallway. He also saw that Pilate might be about to explode, a result that would be dangerous for both of them.

"A moment, Governor, if you please. My own deputy stands outside—perhaps with a message of interest to both of us." He waved a hand at Reuben.

Reuben was startled. He had not expected to be noticed by the High Priest, let alone admitted to this meeting. He walked across the marble floor as if it were a narrow precipice and he was in danger of falling.

"Apologies, Eminence, I did not mean to disturb you."

"Speak up," Caiaphas said.

"We have word from Machaerus—Herod Antipas has beheaded Johannon, the one they call the Baptizer."

Both Caiaphas and Pilate almost smiled. Caiaphas nodded abruptly and Reuben scurried out of the room.

"A troublemaker," Caiaphas said, almost amiably, "a man dangerous to both of us. How fortunate that Herod has seen fit to perform this service."

Pilate looked sharply at the High Priest. Amazing, he thought, this strange Jew thinks like I do. Then, wondering if he were making a mistake, but feeling a strange kind of camaraderie with Caiaphas, he said, "Perhaps we can find a centurion to sacrifice in the name of better cooperation." He paused. "But we keep Bar Abbas."

"Of course," Caiaphas said.

The two men resisted the urge to clasp hands.

9.

ROAMING

They traveled east from Jerusalem to Jericho, then north to Archelaus, Phasaelis and Alexandrium. They turned inland and visited Arimathea, Gophna, Ephraim and Emmaus, swung south past Jerusalem to Bethlehem, Bethsura and Hebron. Then they doubled back and headed west for Emmaus, Lydda and Joppa. Afterwards, they traveled along the coast to Appollonia and Caesarea.

They rode on horseback or on carts whenever possible, but walked if necessary. Their horses, when they used them, were provided by local Zealot leaders or Essenes, and sometimes it seemed, despite their avowed differences in philosophy, that the two were interchangeable.

For the most part, they were greeted enthusiastically. The people were thirsting for a leader, a Messiah, to relieve them of their burdens. They listened to Joshua with excitement, attracted by his natural strength and presence, moved by his impassioned pleas and the evident goodness of his soul.

Along the way, they baptized thousands of men, women and children, who joyfully repented their sins and turned their faces towards a new day. Joshua, as usual, spoke in parables, preparing the people for a different kind of revolution—a war of words instead of weapons, of confrontation without armed conflict, of welcoming the enemy, not wiping him out. The word spread ahead of them, despite their attempts at secrecy. When they arrived at a town, the people would be waiting, sweeping Joshua and Judas along to the synagogue or some other central place.

Joshua had become famous for his healing as much as for his message. He was able to cure several lepers and others with ailments of the skin, using ointments and salves he had learned from Omriel, chief physician at Qumran.

Others, with defective limbs, Joshua manipulated skillfully, loosening lesions and repairing unused muscles. These skills he had also learned at

Qumran, but others had come from his own observation across many years, not the least of them from his experiences as a hard-working carpenter.

But in every case, Joshua found his ministrations useless unless the person trusted him completely and put his faith in God. For the unbeliever, Joshua's skills were of no value.

The cures he effected which impressed Judas the most, were those of troubled people, possessed by demons as they said, or otherwise in the grip of some terrible illusion or desperate fear. In such cases, ointments and salves, braces and poultices were of no avail.

It was especially in those instances, that the full force of Joshua's strength and power could be seen. It was as if he were locked in mortal combat with the forces that tormented the one possessed. Joshua brought all of his resources of love and faith and hope to bear, focusing with great intensity on the spirit of the troubled one, strengthening that spirit and enabling it to throw off the shackles that constrained and punished it.

Simon had told Judas in vivid detail how once, outside Gadara on the shores of the Sea of Galilee, Joshua and his followers had come upon a man, half-naked, wandering in a cemetery. Broken chains hung from his wrists and his eyes were haunted.

When the man turned to look at them, a local herdsman had grabbed Joshua's arm. "Be careful," he said. "When the spasms grip him, he's as strong as any three men."

"Yes," said another, "let's get out of here." He started to drive his animals, a small herd of swine down the hill.

"You keep swine," Joshua said. "That violates scripture."

The herdsman flushed. "I don't eat them myself," he said. "I sell them to the gentiles."

"That, too, is forbidden," Joshua said, frowning.

"What's it your business?" the herdsman responded. But then, the madman wandering among the gravestones, hurried towards them.

"What do you want, holy man?" the one possessed said. He spoke in a strange deep voice, with great resonance, almost as if it were the voice of another.

"I told you," the first herdsman said. "There's a demon in him—do you hear it?"

The madman screamed and the herdsmen left their animals and scrambled away, so frightened they ran a considerable distance before they stopped.

"Have you come to kill me?" the madman said, in his strange, deep voice.

"No," said Joshua, "to help relieve you from your suffering."

The madman laughed loudly, a roaring laugh that echoed among the gravestones and frightened the herdsmen and even Simon.

"Let's leave this man, Master," Simon said.

The madman rushed towards Joshua, his arms raised as if to strike him. "There's demons in me and they're going to kill you," he screamed.

Joshua stood his ground, as the madman rushed at him, and he looked steadily into the man's eyes, praying quietly.

"Dear God, save this man from the devils that possess him, help him to see thy way."

The madman, seeing that his rush had not frightened Joshua and staring straight into his eyes, was confused. He stopped a few feet in front of Joshua.

"What is your name?" Joshua asked.

"My name is Legion," said the man in his strange echoing voice, "for we are many."

"Come out then, unclean spirits," Joshua said.

"What do you want of me?" the madman roared, his eyes wild and his lips frothing.

"You have done evil," Joshua said, "and you are ashamed of that evil. The anger and hate of your deeds have summoned demons that reside within you. It is your choice, to be free of these demons, or to have them possess you for all time."

"I can't get rid of them!" he screamed.

"Yes, you can, they are the lowest and vilest part of you and the best and noblest part of you can drive them out."

The madman looked at him with a crafty smile. "Where will they go? If they linger nearby, they'll come back to haunt me, even to possess me again. They'll hide here, among the gravestones."

Joshua continued to look deep into the eyes of the madman. "They are the worst part of you, as vile as those swine grazing on the hillside. Let them leave you, let them free your soul and go into the swine. Let evil possess evil and then let evil be driven away, even as the swine are driven by the herdsmen."

"I want to believe," the man said suddenly, speaking in his own voice. I want to be free."

"Then repent your sins this moment and plead with the Lord your God for forgiveness."

"I repent," he cried. "I repent my sins. Forgive me, Lord."

"You are forgiven," Joshua said. "Your soul is free."

"Thank you, Lord," the man called out and this time his voice roared with special resonance. "I'M FREE."

The sound of his voice, booming across the hillside, startled the swine and they ran down the hill.

"I'M FREE," he called again, and this time his voice echoed off the gravestones and the hill and the swine ran even faster.

The herdsmen, frightened, began to scream at their animals and ran after them, but this frightened the swine even more, and they raced down the hillside toward the sea.

The man who had been mad, now no longer mad, watched with astonishment as the herdsmen tried desperately to pull their animals from the water.

Startled, Simon asked, "What is the meaning of this, Rabbi?"

Joshua smiled grimly. "The herdsmen represent our vilest instincts, even into herding swine, which not only violates our and their own laws but represents our basest enemies, the Romans, who indeed have legions. The poor mad fellow tried to set the herdsmen right, but instead they enslaved him, chained him time and again to the point where he could no longer resist this evil which invaded his very being. He struggled again and again to break the shackles, but failed until we happened upon him, and could, with the help of the Lord, drive his demons into the swine, with the result the faithless herdsmen received their just rewards."

Simon Peter bowed his head in astonishment.

***

Judas had seen similar deeds, time and again in Judaea and even in Samaria. In Hebron, Ishmael, the leader of the synagogue, had recognized Joshua as the Messiah and been baptized along with a crowd of many others. Then, hesitantly he told Joshua of his daughter, who was ill, perhaps dying, and asked if he could come to the house and baptize her there, so that she would at least die in peace.

Joshua felt compassion for Ishmael and readily assented. But they were surrounded by a crowd, including a woman who had been ill with bloody discharges for many years. She was afraid to ask Joshua for help, but believed that being close to him would be of benefit. Others pressed close, pushing against Joshua, and the woman, among them, touched his cloak.

"Who touched me?" Joshua asked.

Judas laughed, "Half the town of Hebron," he said.

But Joshua saw the face of the woman and read it and took her hands. "Have you been ill?" he asked, and she sighed deeply, but even then, the color was rushing back into her face. "You are not a sinner and your faith in the Lord will make you well," he said, and as he spoke she knew what he said was true and she embraced him.

Judas made a way for Joshua through the crowd, but as they hurried to the home of Ishmael, his servants came to tell him his daughter had died.

Ishmael burst into tears and almost fainted. Joshua held him up and prayed for him. "We'll go to your home, Ishmael, and pray for your daughter."

"It's too late," Ishmael said.

"We'll see," Joshua answered.

When they entered the house, the wife of Ishmael and members of the family were weeping and crying loudly. "Why do you mourn so?" Joshua asked. The mother was surprised and affronted by his words, and would have told him to leave, but Ishmael shook his head violently. "This is a holy man," he said.

Joshua said nothing, but went into the room where their daughter, a girl of twelve, lay on her bed. At the sight of this lovely child, pale and silent on the bed, Ishmael and his wife began to weep again.

"Why do you weep?" Joshua said. "The child is only sleeping."

They were astonished, and the mother was frightened, but Ishmael felt a surge of hope. Joshua knelt by the side of the bed and gently stroked the limbs and then the face of the girl. He whispered a prayer of hope and blessing, asking God to help this child.

"What is her name?" Joshua asked.

"Rebecca," the mother said.

"Rebecca," Joshua said, holding out his hands, "rise up and rejoin those who love you. Come, child, now."

Rebecca stirred on the bed and her parents gasped. The color in her face and on her limbs became rosier. Slowly her eyes blinked and opened. With a smile, she sat up suddenly, holding out her arms. Her parents rushed to her and embraced her.

"Thank you, Lord," Joshua said, "for giving us life and sustaining us in all seasons."

"Thank you, Master," Ishmael said to him.

"Thank the Lord," Joshua said, "and know that it is your faith that makes all things possible."

Time and again, as Judas watched in wonder, he saw Joshua help the sick and the wounded, the damaged and defective, the stricken and the tormented. He never ceased to be surprised, but he was always aware of Joshua's humility and intense faith, and utter rejection of any personal role in these healings, other than as the channel of the living God.

Judas saw clearly what a joy it was for Joshua to be able to help the troubled, the sick and the dying. But it worried him as well.

"I tell you," he said to Judas, "healing comes from God and it is a blessing to be able to give it in his name. But I fear the people are more touched by what they deem to be miracles, than by the word we bring. Sometimes they confuse me and the Holy One, Blessed be His name."

"Perhaps," Judas said. "But it works. You want to help our people. You have to accept them as they are. Not all are wise enough to understand the law or to judge your message. If they come to you with love and repentance in their hearts, why worry about theological questions, more suited for scribes, lawyers and Pharisees?"

"You're clever, Judas, clever enough to confound me some times. But the love of God means the love of GOD, and when it's confused with love of man it's dangerous and destructive."

Judas smiled. "Win their hearts now, Rabbi. Teach them later."

The words disturbed Joshua greatly. He strove even harder to separate himself from the message he carried and to make it clear the promise came not from him, but from God.

10.

OPPOSITION

Judas would have preferred that they speak only to the leaders of each community, preferably the Zealot leaders, and allow them to spread the word and prepare the people. But Joshua would have none of it.

"God sent me to speak to all the people, not just those who lead them. I want them to know God's message as I have understood it, not translated through the words of others."

In part, Judas was motivated by concern for his own safety. Members of his family were known agitators and revolutionaries and he was a marked man. Time and again, even as a child, he had been sought by Herodians and Romans alike whenever trouble was brewing. Even now, he was being sought in connection with various raids on Roman installations, and he had repeatedly changed his dress and appearance as much as possible to evade detection. In Judaea, he dressed like a wealthy merchant, much as it troubled him, and trimmed his beard to a Grecian shape, although that, too, irritated him.

Regardless of what he did, it was impossible to travel with Joshua and remain unnoticed. Joshua himself was striking in appearance and would do nothing to disguise himself. Word of his appearance and his message had spread through the land, carried by travelers and couriers, friends and enemies.

Then, too, many insisted on following him, so that they often traveled with a group of fifty or one hundred or more. The followers would sing and chant psalms and fortunately, the local authorities took them for harmless pilgrims. Other times, especially in towns that were predominantly Greek, the locals were unhappy with wandering Jewish holy men and would actively drive them away or warn them off.

This infuriated Judas, who would have liked to retaliate, but it saddened Joshua. He knew that this phase of his mission was to the Jews only and he turned away without recriminations in his heart.

Still, word of his actions inevitably reached the capitals of the country: Jerusalem and the priesthood, Caesarea and Pilate, Machaerus and Herod Antipas. Nowhere was it heard by the authorities with enthusiasm.

***

"My God," Antipas said, listening to his spies, "it's Johannon, the Baptizer, raised from the dead."

"Ridiculous," Herodias said. "This man has a head on his shoulders."

Antipas glowered at her. "That's not amusing, my dear. We'll both live to rue the day we slaughtered that harmless creature."

Herodias merely raised her eyebrows. Since the death of Johannon, no-one had said anything publicly about her marriage to Antipas.

***

Pilate was not impressed. "Another holy man—what of it? This accursed place is full of them. Any man who can read their foul scripture and some who can't even scribble their own names, think they are sent from some god or other. They have only to hear a clap of thunder to believe the heavens are talking to them."

"This one is different," Septimus said. "He claims to be the Messiah."

"What is this Messiah?" Pilate asked.

Gaius thought it wise to speak, to put the best face on the matter. "They believe that someday, some far distant day, their god will send a leader, a new king, who will lead them to peace and happiness."

"The deputy makes it sound like a tale for children." Septimus said.

"Well, isn't it?" Pilate asked.

"Not when the people believe it is happening, now, this very day—when they have a man they can call king—in defiance of Caesar."

"They defy nothing," Gaius said. "This man, this Messiah as you call him, preaches peace. He says you must love your enemies and when a man strikes you, you must offer him the other cheek so he may strike you again."

Pilate laughed shrilly. "Surely, Septimus, surely you don't fear fools like that?"

Septimus frowned. "These people are fanatics for their damnable religion, Prefect. One never knows when they'll boil over in rebellion."

"I know you'll be watching them carefully, Captain. And when they boil over, you'll force down the lid."

Septimus stalked grimly from the room.

"He's bored," Pilate said. "Don't we know someone who needs killing?"

***

Caiaphas sat on his throne-like chair in the upper sitting room, far enough back so that he could not be seen from the terrace, but close enough so that he could enjoy the never-ending pleasure of observing his own kingdom, the Temple.

Reuben flitted about, nervous as ever, bringing his interminable tales of objectors and protestors, rebels and brigands.

"When he was in Galilee, Eminence, it didn't seem important. There's a rebellion every week in Galilee, as you know. But usually, it drifts away, a few are imprisoned, sometimes even killed, and then there is peace for a while. But now, the man has sent his disciples into all parts of the country, and he himself has come to Judaea."

"The swords into plowshares fellow?"

"Yes, Joshua ben Joseph."

"They say his mother was raped by a Roman soldier."

Reuben's eyes narrowed. At times like these, he realized he was not the sole source of the High Priest's information. "Yes," Reuben said.

"Then he cannot be of the Royal house, and thus he cannot be a future king."

"Theology, Eminence, but in the eyes of some of the people, he IS the coming Messiah."

Caiaphas laughed. "A bastard carpenter from Nazareth? Come now."

"The people love him, and he has performed many, shall we say, miracles."

"This land is full of healers and charlatans."

"But any one of them may attract a following, and this fellow has a certain...quality to him."

Caiaphas looked at him sharply. "Don't tell me you believe some of this drivel?"

"Of course not, Eminence, but I feel it's my duty to report what I learn, especially when it may be dangerous to us. Pilate has done many things to arouse the people and he looks for reasons to abuse us. Surely, a rival king to Caesar, even an humble Galilean preacher, could be an excuse for his action."

"True, Reuben. The man is so vile, he hardly needs excuses. Keep an eye on this preacher."

***

They came at him in Caesarea. It was a difficult city for Joshua to teach in, right under the very noses of the Roman administration. Judas wanted to avoid the city altogether, but Joshua had insisted. Judas, properly concerned, remained outside the city, but that meant he was unable to help, personally.

Ahaz, the Zealot leader in the city, was alerted to Joshua's coming and he sent his own men to shadow Joshua, ready to defend him if the Romans interfered. Joshua didn't know that Ahaz's men were there, but he felt no fear. He was doing what God had directed him to do and he serenely relied on the Lord for his protection.

Joshua preached in the synagogue on the Sabbath. He spoke of the End of Days and the Last Judgment and the need of all men to be prepared. Those who listened carefully knew that he meant to alert them for an impending great event that was to come soon. When he spoke of the Exodus from Egypt and the liberation of the Jews, they also realized he was looking forward to the Passover, now only weeks away.

For some, the message was simple and direct, repent and return to God. They understood that part of what he said and responded to it. They did not understand that he was preaching revolution and perhaps it was better they did not.

After the services and the sermon, Joshua led them down to the sea and many were baptized in the swirling waters, joyfully receiving the word and cleansing and purifying themselves. Joshua smiled at the simple piety of ordinary people and his heart swelled with love for them. Soon, very soon, their day would come.

But there were others in the crowd whose aims were different. Reuben had sent a group of men from Jerusalem, all minions of the High Priest, to follow this preacher and carefully note what he said. Reuben had gone beyond his commission from Caiaphas. He had personally been exposed to Joshua and his powerful teachings and his fears were greater than the High Priest's.

"See if you can catch him in false teaching ," he told his hired hands. "Try to embarrass him or discredit him if you can. It's better to be rid of him now than have to oppose him when the mass of the people is behind him."

Demetrius, the leader of the group that Reuben had sent, and himself of a priestly family from Alexandria, looked upon this as an opportunity to ingratiate himself with the hierarchy. For the average priest, without major connections, the work was heavy and the financial rewards few. Demetrius hoped to impress his superiors and move up to a profitable position.

The previous night, in Caesarea, there had been a disturbance in the house next to the one where Demetrius and his men were staying. A tradesman named Jothan had come back from a trip unexpectedly, to find his wife in bed with a peasant farmer.

There was a struggle and the sound of it aroused Demetrius and his men. They found the adulterous farmer had beaten up Jothan and escaped, but the wife had been left behind, cowering in her nakedness.

Jothan angrily went after his wife, but Demetrius restrained him. "Calm yourself, man" he said, "let the people punish her."

Jothan was purple with anger, but he was a coward at heart, and afraid of his wife. "You're right," he said.

Demetrius stayed in the house with Jothan and his wife waiting for the new day. It was then that the plan formed in his mind.

Jothan had wanted to condemn his wife in the synagogue, but Demetrius assured him she was unclean and they should wait until the rabbi from Galilee had finished with his preaching and baptizing on the beach at Caesarea.

Then, Demetrius and his men dragged the woman forward and threw her at the feet of Joshua. He looked at the woman with compassion, saw her fear and sensed her suffering.

All around, the people of the congregation watched, curiously, knowing of Jothan's problems with his wife, of his abuse of her, of his own deeds of unfaithfulness. Joshua read this tale in the eyes of the woman and her husband, and in the responses of the townspeople.

"We found this woman," Demetrius said, "in bed with a farmer, who used her and then ran off when her husband, the righteous Jothan, arrived. The law, Rabbi, says she must be stoned to death, today, by all those assembled here. You counsel love of neighbor, and love even of your enemy, but surely you will want the law fulfilled, even though it means killing this woman."

Demetrius hid a smile. He was well satisfied with himself, feeling he had Joshua trapped. If he forsook the law, the people would be shocked, yet if he allowed the woman to be killed, the people would not trust his teachings of peace and love.

Joshua looked down at the woman, cowering in the sand on the beach. He took a stick and drew a circle around her and himself. Then, outside the circle, he wrote quickly, ten large, Hebrew letters.

Demetrius was puzzled. "We're waiting, Master, waiting for your decision."

"The law is sacred, and the law must be fulfilled," Joshua said. "The ten letters I have written are the first in each of the Ten Commandments."

He looked directly at Demetrius. "I'm pleased to learn that you are a stern believer in these commandments. But I must ask, are you personally free—totally free from transgressing them? All of them?"

Demetrius was stung, for he knew his own sins and he was silent.

Joshua's voice rang with authority. "Search your hearts, all of you. Let him who is without sin, cast the first stone."

Joshua looked straight into Demetrius's eyes, but Demetrius could not bear it and he looked down. Flushing with embarrassment, he stumbled away and his men followed him, eyes lowered.

One by one, the people of the congregation cast their eyes down and turned away. The last was Jothan, trembling with fear and anger, knowing he could not be the only one to stone his wife. He, too, hurried from the beach.

Joshua looked at the woman, who still lay face down in the sand, knowing only that the ominous shadows which had circled her had disappeared. Slowly, hesitantly, she raised her head and looked around.

Surprised, she spoke in a whisper. "No one? There's no one to condemn me?"

"Nor do I condemn you," Joshua said. "Repent now and then go and sin no more."

She stood up quickly, brushing the sand from her body, and was about to flee. "I do repent now, but I have nowhere to go, Master. If I return home, Jothan will find a way to beat or even to kill me."

Joshua waited.

"May I come with you?" she asked.

Joshua smiled in assent and she wanted to embrace him, but thought better of it.

"Thank you—Thank you for saving me."

"The word of the Lord redeemed you," Joshua said. "You must always remember that."

She nodded, smiling for the first time. "My name is Miriam and I, too, come from Galilee—from Magdala."

11.

MIRIAM OF MAGDALA

I loved him. From the first time I saw him on the beach at Caesarea, I was totally his. I had never seen a man so beautiful. His skin was flawless, prettier than a woman's and without a wrinkle or a blemish. His hair, when it was bleached by the sun, was spun gold, long and strong and with gentle waves that threw off sparks in candlelight.

His hands were strong, oh very strong. He had been a carpenter and a carpenter needs strong hands. But there were no scars or knots on his hands and the fingers were long and tapering, like a lute-player's. And the touch; the touch drove me mad.

But I couldn't show it. I wanted to. I would have made love to him in a minute if he would have asked. There were some who didn't trust me. Judas was one. He thought I was a bad influence, a wanton woman and that I might lead Joshua astray. He was right. I would have, if I could. I never stopped wanting him. At night I would dream that he had come to me and lay down beside me. I saw him smile and then he would draw the covers off my body and touch my breasts. The nipples rose then and the rest of me warmed to his caress. I threw myself around him, pressed myself to him. And then awoke. The dream repeated and repeated, but never came true.

Once, when we stayed at Eliezer's house at Bethany, when all was uproar and violence might be around the corner, I saw him sag a little and thought, "He needs me." I waited until everyone was asleep and then I crept into his room. To my surprise he was awake, and when he saw me he smiled and beckoned to me. He put an arm around me and I turned to kiss him, but he held me away. He thought that I was the one who needed comfort, that I had come to him because I was afraid. He held me for a while and spoke softly to me, reassuring me and then he sent me back to bed. That was as close to him as I ever got.

But you shouldn't believe that was all he meant to me. I never stopped seeing him as a man, but I knew what he said his mission was, and I surely believed he was the Messiah. I wanted him to succeed, to lead our people to freedom, and I would have done anything to help him, even given my life if that would have meant anything.

Simply because I admit my love for Joshua and the physical yearning that I felt, you shouldn't believe that was all there was. Anyone could see, at once, that he was the chosen of God and that he was sent to save us. My love for him was spiritual as well as physical. God knows I never forgot I was a woman, but I never forgot that Joshua was more than a mere man.

12.

THE OUTSIDERS

Judas was furious when he learned that Joshua had given Miriam of Magdala permission to travel with them. She was a beautiful woman, tall with flowing black hair, deep gray eyes and an opulent body. She would be a source of distraction among the followers—he, himself, was not unaware of her charms—and she might endanger their mission. Surely, this would give the righteous ones grounds to condemn Joshua for the kind of people he attracted.

Judas, learning from Ahaz of this disturbing new recruit, decided to chance going into Caesarea to protest. At first, he could not find Joshua. He learned that many had been baptized and accepted his message, and that he had preached successfully, time and again, but then, he had disappeared.

Ahaz's men said they had no idea where he had gone. They had asked him to let them know his plans, but he refused to be bound by such rules, and often went off by himself.

"He likes to meditate," one of them told Judas. "Goes off on a mountain top and talks to himself."

"There are no mountains here," Judas said coldly, "and you have failed in your assignment."

He stormed away and began to search the town, starting at the synagogue and speaking to several known followers. None could help him. Judas looked for a group, for it was rare that Joshua was alone, but still he could not find him. Judas was uncomfortable being in Caesarea, fearful he might be recognized and perhaps arrested. That would abort their entire mission. Yet, he had to go on. There was no mission without the Messiah.

He found himself in the gentile districts of the city, wondering why he was there. Joshua, himself, had said his mission was not to the gentiles, but Judas felt that he was being drawn inexorably.

He reached the waterfront, with its wharves and docks, piles of merchandise, hustle and bustle of traders and shippers. Some looked at him sharply and he wondered if they knew he was a Jew, but in this part of the world, there were many with features like his. It was his own awareness that made him feel uncomfortable. He ought not to be doing this on the Sabbath.

Then it was dark, and he was even more concerned. The harbor was a rough place in all towns, and if Joshua were here, God only knew what would happen to him. Judas passed inns and taverns, even brothels. Slender arms reached out and soft voices importuned him. He felt defiled by the experience, but determined to go on.

He heard a roar of laughter from a nearby tavern and looked in. There, sitting at a table, was Joshua and next to him a woman who must be Miriam of Magdala surrounded by a group of men. They all held wine cups, even Joshua, and as Judas watched, his leader, his Messiah, tipped back the cup and drank from it. For a moment, Judas was speechless. All of his hopes and dreams seemed confounded. Could this be true? Could this gentle, loving, pious man, have descended to the level of carousers in a heathen tavern?

A voice spoke behind Judas, startling him. "This is your Messiah?"

Judas turned quickly gripping the short dagger he concealed under his cloak. It was Demetrius, but Judas had not met him before and did not know him.

"Easy," the man said, holding his hands wide to show he was unarmed. "I'm not dangerous—and I'm a Jew, which I'm guessing you are, too."

"You followed me," Judas said. He was furiously disappointed that he, an experienced warrior, had allowed himself to be followed.

"No," Demetrius laughed. "I was walking along the harbor when I saw you staring in at the rabbi. I guessed you were a follower and your answer confirmed it.

"My name is Demetrius," he concluded.

Judas hesitated. This must be the man Ahaz had told him about, the one who had tried to cause trouble for Joshua at the beach.

"Judas," he said. There were many Judas's and the name would probably mean nothing to Demetrius.

"Shall we go in?" Demetrius asked.

Judas reluctantly agreed.

Joshua saw them, smiled and waved a hand. "Welcome," he said, but then he realized that both men wore pained expressions. "What is it this time?" Joshua asked Demetrius.

"You claim to be a pious Jew," Demetrius said.

"A Jew," Joshua said. "In your mouth, 'pious' sounds like a filthy epithet."

"What are you doing, eating and drinking with these people?" Demetrius's words were so contemptuous, that the people in the tavern became angry.

But Joshua spoke mildly and calmed them. "These people are my friends," he said. "Ephrem here is a tax-collector, Avram and Joachim work on the Syrian ships, the others unload cargo in the harbor. Miriam here is— my friend. Once, they all were God-fearing Jewish citizens. Somewhere, they lost their way."

Demetrius was frightened by these rough looking men, but he steeled himself and asked the questions he had been sent to ask. "Why are you teaching here—among Jews who consort with Gentiles—Jews who don't follow their own religion?"

Joshua smiled. "Shall the physician go to the house of those who are well, or those who are ill? God did not send me to the righteous—they have little need of me. I'm here to help those who have sinned and wish to repent, those who have left God and want to return. What about you—Demetrius, isn't that your name—are you ready to repent and return to God?"

Demetrius stared at him for a long moment, flushed, started to speak in anger, then clamped his mouth shut. Face purple, he stalked into the night, while those in the tavern roared with laughter.

"Hypocrite," Joshua called out, "come back and face your own sins." But Demetrius was gone.

Judas sighed. He understood now that Demetrius was an agent of the forces that opposed Joshua and another bad report would soon be sent to Jerusalem.

"Sit down," Joshua said, "you are worrying over nothing."

Judas sat down, but on the other side of the table from Miriam of Magdala. He drank his wine morosely, while Joshua preached repentance and forgiveness in a grimy, crowded tavern in the harbor of Caesarea.

***

Judas continued to argue privately with Joshua about Miriam, whom they now began to refer to as the "Magdalene."

"She's dangerous, Joshua," Judas said, "too dangerous to have around."

"Because she's beautiful?"

"That, and because of her reputation."

"Jothan has divorced her, which was his right. However, she has repented her sins and changed her ways. I believe she will live a decent life from this day forward."

"Fine, let her do so, but not in your company."

Joshua smiled. "Do you think I'll be unable to deal honorably with a lovely woman?"

Judas flushed. "It's not that. We can't afford to give your enemies any basis to discredit you."

Joshua smiled even more broadly. "They don't need to have any basis for telling their lies. They're inventive enough, whether the girl is with us or not."

But Judas was not convinced. "We'll regret this—I know it."

Joshua put a hand on Judas's shoulder. "She needs our help and our love. Miriam—the Magdalene—was a troubled woman. The first night that she came with me, she awoke in the night screaming, crying she was possessed by seven devils. I was able to calm and restore her, but she is sensitive and frightened and it may be a long time before she is strong enough to deal with the world, alone."

"Why do you spend so much time on people like her?"

"What man, having a hundred sheep, if has lost one of them, doesn't leave the ninety-nine in the wilderness and go after the one that's lost? And when he finds it, lays it on his shoulders, rejoicing. And when he returns home, tells his friends, 'Rejoice with me for I have found my sheep which was lost.' I tell you, Judas, there will be more joy in heaven over one sinner who repents than over ninety-nine righteous persons."

"Well, all I can say, Master, is keep this particular sheep off your shoulders."

Joshua laughed and Judas gave up for the moment, believing that when they left Caesarea, the Magdalene would remain behind. But Joshua called for another horse and the three of them rode off together, Judas silently cursing all the way.

***

Much of Joshua's preaching took place on the Sabbath. The crowds were larger then and their minds were on their faith, not their businesses or family affairs.

Demetrius and his friends followed Joshua from town to town, patiently waiting for him to make a move that would give them a chance to discredit him. They came at Joshua in relays, sometimes Demetrius would be the leader, sometimes another. Reuben sent fresh troops from Jerusalem, or Demetrius recruited new antagonists in each city.

With each passing day, Judas became more angry. He pleaded with Joshua for permission to give Demetrius a thrashing.

"No," Joshua said, "no and a thousand times again, No. Do you listen to my teachings? If I believe we should turn the other cheek to the Romans, how can I authorize you to attack Demetrius?"

"Because he's not a Roman, and he ought to know better."

"In time we'll convince him," Joshua said.

Judas ground his teeth.

While the Sabbath was a good time for Joshua's teaching, the presence of Demetrius, and perhaps other agents of both the priestly hierarchy and the Romans, made it necessary for him to be especially cautious. He continued to preach repentance and non-violence, but he never gave a date or a program, except by indirection.

When he said that pagan laws could not be obeyed, he was certain also to say that Jews must not wage war to get rid of the outsiders. When he preached the importance of Passover and liberation, when he shouted that the Kingdom of God was at hand, he never specifically stated that the time of the revolution would be at the coming Passover.

Repeatedly, he said, "Let those who have eyes, see and those who have ears, hear." Among the crowd, he would lock eyes with many who understood what he meant and knew that it was a call to an uprising, only weeks away.

Again and again he told the parable of the maidens who sought to be chosen by the bridegroom, of the five who kept their lamps filled and the five who didn't. How, when the bridegroom came, only the five whose lamps were filled were admitted to the feast. "Be sure your lamps are filled," Joshua said, "Watch, for you know neither the day nor the hour."

Again and again, in one form or another, he warned them they must be prepared. There would not be time to harvest a field, or plant a crop, or even to go back for a heavier coat.

As he preached in this manner, even those who did not understand the urgency sensed Joshua's love for them and the need for their repentance. The others, those who clearly foresaw the time of rebellion was coming, did all they could to be ready.

Most of the Zealot leaders in the Judaean towns were deeply moved by Joshua and accepted his teachings. Some had met him in the house of Amos and were not surprised by his strength and character and the dominating quality of his personality. Those who saw him for the first time were equally moved and thrilled that the hour had nearly come.

In every town, Judas would slip away from Joshua and his followers for a meeting with the local Zealot leaders. A few were unmoved and Judas did not argue with them, but moved on to those who saw in Joshua the promised leader.

Before they left Caesarea, Ahaz had spoken to Judas with great enthusiasm. "My people are pleased—no, they are excited by your rabbi."

"Messiah."

"Yes, of course, Messiah. They can hardly wait for the Passover."

"It's important that as many as possible come to the feast," Judas said.

"We'll leave our families behind—"

"—No," Judas said. "If the Romans see that only men in large numbers are coming to the festival, they'll grow suspicious."

Ahaz was troubled. "We don't want to risk the lives of our wives and children."

"The whole nation is at risk," Judas said. "And even the Romans will be reluctant to attack large numbers of unarmed men and their women and children."

"I suppose you're right," Ahaz said. He paused and sighed. "The people are so united, Judas. I tell you that if we were armed, we could overwhelm the Romans by force."

"I know that as well as you. Joshua knows it, too. But how long would the victory last? The Romans have unlimited manpower. In a month or a year, they'd be back with ten or even a hundred legions, if that's what they needed. Then your children would truly be in danger."

Ahaz nodded his head. It was a common occurrence. The Zealot leader, like many of them, convinced up to a point. But they had carried weapons for so long, they felt naked without them.

Judas smiled. "I still carry my dagger," he admitted. "Just a small one."

Ahaz smiled.

"Listen to me, Ahaz, have your men bring their weapons. Hide them in the carts or bury them outside the city. We'll be unarmed, ready to do what Joshua says. But if, God forbid, it doesn't work, our weapons won't be far away."

Ahaz hugged Judas. "That's my man," he said.

"Say nothing to Joshua," Judas said. "Let's not worry him."

In town after town, Judas made the same arrangement. Swearing the Zealots to nonviolence, but agreeing to let them keep their weapons where they could easily be retrieved.

13.

DRUMBEAT

One of the subjects on which Demetrius and others chose to attack Joshua was the Sabbath itself. But that was not a new problem. Once, months earlier, when Joshua had been traveling with Simon, Andrew and others in Galilee, they had gone for two days without food. After the morning Sabbath service, they passed a field where there were still ears of corn left after the harvest, in accordance with the scriptural teaching that a farmer must not pick his fields clean, but leave some for the poor.

Simon had asked if he and Andrew might pick and eat the remaining corn, and after some doubt, Joshua had agreed. They had been seen by members of the local congregation who were offended at this supposed breach of the Sabbath rules.

Joshua had considered the offense, if any, was trivial, and was astonished that anyone would create an issue over it. He told his critics, "Do you remember that when David was hungry, he ate the shewbread right out of the Temple, and that on the Sabbath?"

His critics were surprised by his example. "Do you rank your followers with King David?" they asked.

"No, and a cornfield isn't the Temple, but that shows how silly you are, finding an offense in something so trivial."

But still they criticized him and the word spread that he cared little for the Sabbath, did not take it seriously. That reputation was unfounded. Joshua had told his disciples, "I revere the Sabbath for its spiritual meaning. It is a day to rest, to be inactive, to recognize that much as we may be busy, our busyness is nothing compared to the works of the Creator. We must spend the Sabbath in study and holy service so that we fully understand how small our contribution is compared to His.

"God's universe has a heartbeat of its own and even when we are motionless, the great heart continues to beat. The sun rises and sets, the rains come and go, the winds blow and the rivers flow. That is what matters—that we recognize the greatness of God. How we do so is not important, and a thousand tiny rules will not prove to the Lord that we respect his Sabbath."

In the town of Narbata, inland on the eastern edge of the Plain of Sharon, Joshua preached in the synagogue, before a congregation made up largely of shepherds and small farmers.

Demetrius had been following Joshua silently for days, but now he saw a chance to test him again. There was a shepherd in the congregation whose hand had been injured in a fall and it had withered so that it hung from his arm almost useless.

When Joshua finished his sermon, Demetrius pushed the man forward and said, "Rabbi, is it lawful to heal on the Sabbath?"

"Don't bother the Master," the shepherd said, very embarrassed and trying to slip away.

But Joshua felt compassion for him and held his arm as he spoke to Demetrius, wearing a sad smile. "Why do you offend this man? Do you never tire of these things?"

"I ask you again, Rabbi, is it lawful to heal on this sacred day, the Sabbath?"

Joshua looked at the crippled man and then at the congregation "Which of you, if you have a sheep and it falls into a pit on the Sabbath, will not lay hands on it and lift it out? Isn't a man of greater value than a sheep?

"Yes, of course it is lawful to do good on the Sabbath."

The injured shepherd looked at Joshua with love and understanding. Joshua told him, "Hold out your hand."

With great effort the shepherd raised his hand, his eyes never leaving Joshua's, astonished that he could hold his hand this high, for he had not done so in over a year.

Joshua took the crippled hand in his own left hand, kissed the fingers and placed his right hand on the head of the shepherd and looked toward the heavens. "Bless this man, O Lord, and give him back the use of this hand, that he may better serve you."

Joshua gently let go of the shepherd's hand, but even as it dropped, the man raised it, flexed the fingers and called aloud. "I'm healed," he cried. "I can use my hand." And he did indeed use it to embrace Joshua.

The congregation was awed by this event, and many promised to repent their sins so that they might be baptized and follow Joshua. Demetrius, angered and humiliated, tried to slink out of the synagogue, prepared to send another evil report to Reuben.

Joshua called after him. "Tell your masters that Joshua ben Joseph says, they have forgotten the meaning of the ancient teachings: The Sabbath is made for man and not man for the Sabbath."

In town after town, the sick and the crippled came to him, most often on the Sabbath for that was when he preached to the largest crowds. And Joshua healed many of them, Sabbath or not, and the word was reported to Jerusalem of what he had done.

***

For the first time, Reuben's reports truly disturbed Caiaphas. He spoke to Annas who was secretly pleased to see his son-in-law rattled.

"You can't believe this Galilean nobody has such a following, eh?"

Caiaphas frowned. "The people are fickle—they follow every soothsayer, magician and charlatan who comes along."

"But this one is different."

"Yes, this one is different. There's no doubt he has great skills as a healer. Demetrius, the one Reuben sent to track him, is no fool, and Demetrius swears the man has done everything but raise the dead."

"I thought we heard he had done that, too, in Galilee." Annas didn't really believe such things, but he was enjoying watching Caiaphas fidgeting.

Caiaphas looked at him sharply, but Annas's face was bland, inquiring, interested.

"It's difficult to say," Caiaphas replied. "It seems the girl may only have swooned and her parents, agitated, thought she was dead."

Then he was angry with himself for even considering the matter. "Of course she wasn't dead. He isn't God—he's a man—a Galilean carpenter."

"And what if he could raise the dead?"

"Ridiculous," Caiaphas said, who was a Sadducee and did not believe in resurrection, even at the hands of God, let alone at the hands of a common citizen. "But the problem is that the people think he raised her—they think he is a miracle worker. Frankly, so far we haven't been able to catch him in any tricks."

He leaned forward confidentially. "Demetrius doesn't know it, but I have other men in the field--watchers watching the watchers, and none of them have been able to find a weak spot in this fellow."

"What's the harm, son?" Caiaphas did not like to be called "son" and Annas knew it. "The man preaches peace. Isn't that what we want?"

"It's a strange kind of peace he preaches. It almost sounds like war. Those who listen get the impression he is planning some action, something definitive."

Annas laughed. "How can you plan to start a peace?"

Even Caiaphas smiled. "True, isn't it? But I feel uncomfortable. I should be pleased that the Zealots have been quiet for a while. Somehow I think they're planning something, too. If they're working with this Galilean, we may be in for difficult times."

"Why haven't the Romans crucified Bar Abbas?" Annas asked.

"I don't know," Caiphas said, "but I wish it were long over. Killing Bar Abbas may provoke another outcry."

"You're worrying too much about these things, Caiaphas. In a few weeks, the carpenter will lose his following and go back to making plows."

Caiphas shook his head. "I don't know. Passover is coming and with it half the nation and a good part of the diaspora. I dread these holidays. The opportunities for mischief are multiplied."

"Why, Caiaphas, the holy days are your shining hours."

***

The reports coming in to Herod and Pilate were similar to those reaching Caiaphas. Roman and Herodian agents were tracking Joshua from town to town, carefully noting his words and sending long, largely unread reports to their masters.

Also, the agents were tracking each other. The Roman sympathizers who were on Pilate's payroll knew Demetrius, and over a period of time, he became aware of them. This was also true of Herod's people. Each group pretended to be unaware of the other, but they all knew who worked for whom and sometimes they followed the followers and lost their prey. It would have been comic except for the underlying threat.

Joshua knew about these spies, but seemed unruffled. Judas was seriously worried. "I think the number of spies is growing faster than the number of our followers," he told Joshua.

"Don't worry, we'll persuade them, too."

Judas thought he knew better, but in fact, the spies that followed Joshua for any period of time, became increasingly impressed with his healing and even with his teaching. They would not have admitted it to each other, but there was something beyond their knowledge and experience that marked this man. Still, they knew who paid their salaries and they made their reports. But what could they say? Joshua preached peace and seemed to be no threat to anyone.

The Romans had become aware that Judas was in Joshua's group, and that did worry them, because they knew his record of crimes against the state, provable and unprovable. Septimus, however, forbade them to arrest him. "One man means little. Let him lead us to the others."

But Judas was now aware that he had been identified. His own men had spied on the spies. He came to understand they had no intention of arresting him, only of finding how who his confederates might be. He became especially careful in meeting with local Zealots, making sure not to give them away.

In Caesarea, Pilate was restless. All signs indicated some plot was afoot, although he couldn't puzzle out what it might be. As the years had passed, he had come to hate this land and its people even more. He longed to do some spectacular thing—to show Rome that despite his Equestrian origins, he was capable of a higher post. If he could smell out some rebellion and crush it with great force, the reports to Rome would give him his chance.

Therefore, Pilate, too, was waiting. He did not wish to arrest a few malcontents, or kill a handful of protestors. He wanted the Jews to attempt some serious action and then he would crush it totally. With that in mind, Pilate sent secret reports to Vitellius, the Legate in Syria, indicating there was a build-up of rebels and brigands in the land, and asking for two more cohorts—Roman legionnaires, not the usual Syrian conscripts.

Similar reports had already reached Damascus, and now that the Parthians were temporarily quiet, Vitellius sent the men that Pilate requested—in centuries, rather than en masse, so that their arrival in Judaea would not arouse public notice.

***

Gaius had heard about this new prophet, this Joshua ben Joseph, with a tremor of excitement. Then, from Septimus he had learned that the man was indeed the Galilean carpenter— the man who had held Septimus's life in his hands and had not taken it. Septimus had his own spies on Joshua, hating him for not taking his life, knowing that somehow he was in the Jew's debt. But Septimus wasn't content merely to find an excuse to kill Joshua, much as that would have pleased him He was hoping to carry out some major action, himself, an action that would enable him to leave Judaea. Somehow, he felt that if he were patient, Joshua would give him the way.

Gaius was elated to learn that his son was now a revered Master of the Jews. He had kept up his own secret adherence to the Jewish religion and prayed privately whenever he could. When Joshua came to Caesarea, Gaius had disguised himself carefully and gone to hear him preach. He was astonished to see the changes in his son. Joshua had become a man of great strength and compelling power. Gaius could easily have cast aside his own life and followed him; in fact, he longed to do just that. But he knew that he could be of more use to Joshua and his movement in his present position.

He listened to Joshua preach on several occasions. Then, and only then, it dawned on him just what his son was advocating. Joshua was counseling rebellion, but not a rebellion of armed men, an uprising of an entire nation which would defy Roman rule, but without raising even a fist.

The idea staggered him. Then he was frightened, thinking others might well understand, too. But he saw they did not. They were blind to the gentle side of men. They could not believe that non-violence could ever be a powerful weapon. They were looking for warriors and weapons and all the instruments of insurrection that had been used in past history. They were not prepared for the "war" that Joshua was teaching.

14.

SAMARIA

They crossed and re-crossed Judaea and Samaria, with Joshua preaching in every major town and city and most of the minor ones. Joshua spoke in the synagogues and in private houses, in the market places and along the road. Sometimes, he would speak at length to one person while Judas tried to hurry him along, hoping for a larger audience. But Joshua's love of the people was so great, he could not allow even a single human being to be turned away.

Most of the people responded to him with great enthusiasm, but still there were some who doubted. The Sadducees were mainly based in Jerusalem: a small group of the higher priests, the nobles and the wealthy. There were very likely not more than four thousand of them in the entire country, although there were probably twenty thousand priests. Nevertheless, here and there, Joshua would come upon people at least sympathetic to the Sadducees. They scoffed at his teachings of resurrection, and doubted that he was the "Son of Man."

In their hearts they feared him, for they saw the response of the people to his teachings of universal love and felt they would lose their own positions of dominance in a more equal society. Still, they did little except disagree with him, argue against him privately and oppose him openly in the synagogues. "False prophet," they said, and hoped he would fade away.

Most of the Pharisees found much to agree with in Joshua's preaching. They believed in the resurrection and expected the Messiah. Although well-educated and often well to do, the Pharisees were usually in sympathy with the people, not remote like the Sadducees. Especially in the Temple and the synagogue they took the side of the ordinary human being and wished to soften harsh rules that stood in the way of human progress.

There were few of them in the nation, too, perhaps six or seven thousand, but they were renowned for their learning, and they tended to have important positions as lawyers and scribes. In many ways, Joshua's teachings were Pharisaical in nature. While he loved the law and the prophets, he also believes the world must move forward and that old, rigid standards must be adapted to the needs of the people. However, among the Pharisees, as amongst all human beings, those who would bend an old code tend to shape a new one in its place, often as narrow as the old. Among such people, Joshua had his enemies.

Some were scandalized by what they believed to be his views of the Sabbath. It was difficult enough in their world to get people to observe the rules of inactivity and meditation and prayer—and it seemed to them that Joshua, with his more natural and casual views, might overturn the institution altogether. Nevertheless, among the Pharisees, Joshua had many supporters and few real enemies. They were "outsiders" too, and they found a common bond with him.

Joshua's most ardent supporters were the ordinary people, the farmers, laborers and artisans. They were swept up by his message and his presence. Joshua's problem with them was not that it might be difficult to persuade them to undertake open rebellion, but rather to hold it off until the proper moment. More than once, Joshua found it prudent to limit or call off a speech, or even to leave a town, to prevent the inhabitants from sweeping him into their arms, proclaiming him king and marching on Jerusalem.

Even in Samaria, Joshua found a sympathetic audience, time and again, whether he sought it or not. These neighbors of the Judaeans whose views of scripture were more rigid even than theirs, were also among the oppressed. The Romans, even Pilate, were aware of the differences between the Jews and the Samaritans and tried to use them to keep the people in strife rather than harmony, but that did not mean they had any greater sympathy for the Samaritans. In fact, the Romans often conscripted Samaritans for services for which they would not conscript Jews and while that angered the Samaritans against the Jews, it surely did not make them love the Romans.

Once, Judas and Joshua paused to rest during the heat of the day, in a grove of Date palms near the Samaritan town of Shechem. After a few minutes, Joshua became restless and decided to walk into town.

"It's bad enough we have to pass through this territory," Judas said. "You should stay away from the people."

"I'm curious," Joshua said, "my wife and I passed through here soon after we were married."

"It's too hot, Joshua, we're supposed to be resting."

But Joshua continued into Shechem. He found it to be a shabby place, little changed from the time so many years earlier, when he and Rebecca had seen it. But Judas was right—it was hot. Joshua made his way to the field that the patriarch Jacob had given his son Joseph, and the well that was still known as Jacob's well.

When Joshua reached the well, he was dizzy from the heat, but he had no bucket to draw from it. He sat on a low stone wall nearby, trying to recover his balance. A Samaritan woman came by, hesitated when she saw a lone man, Joshua, sitting there in the midday sun, but then proceeded to draw a bucket of water.

"Please," Joshua said, "would you give me a drink?"

The woman was surprised and peered at him closely. She saw a good-looking man with blonde hair and beard and deeply tanned skin, whose eyes were weary and bloodshot. She glanced about to see if there were any others with him, but saw nothing in the baking heat.

"I'm alone," he said, "a Galilean, far from home."

"A Jew?" She was surprised when he nodded his head, then grew suspicious.

"How is it that you, a Jew, ask me for a drink?"

He smiled wanly. "I'm thirsty, and I don't believe your touch would defile me."

She smiled and handed him the bucket and he raised it to his lips, drinking so deeply that she was concerned for him.

He smiled, thanked her and wiped his mouth with the back of his hand. "Perhaps one day, I'll be able to do the same for you."

He was handsome and his voice was rich and she felt flirtatious, even in the hot sun.

"You, a Jewish man, would draw water for me?"

"The water you drew is cool and pleasant, but when you have drunk it you won't end your thirst for ever. No, you'll grow thirsty again and have to draw water again. The water I'm talking about is the stuff of life, and when you've drunk of it, you'll never grow thirsty again."

She thought he was jesting with her, and she said, "Sir, give me some of this water, so that I'll never be thirsty and never have to come to this well again." She was very close to him now and her shadow fell across his face. Joshua understood her very well.

"Go call your husband," he said, "and we can speak."

She frowned. "I have no husband," she said.

"I believe you, although I suspect you've had more than one man, and you don't live alone even today."

The Samaritan woman was startled. "You're a fortune-teller," she frowned, "or a prophet?"

"Some say so."

She was impressed. "Then tell me," she said "why do the Jews say one must pray in Jerusalem, instead of at our own temple, here on Mount Gerizim?"

"It matters not where you pray, whether here or in Jerusalem. What matters is what is in your heart, and the day is coming that all must be prepared for—the final judgment. Are you ready?"

His sincerity was so great that it overwhelmed her. She grew frightened and sat down weakly beside him on the stone wall.

"The Messiah—is he coming?"

"He is here," Joshua said. "Even now he walks the land."

She grew even more fearful. "What can I do? How can I prepare myself?"

He smiled. "Your readiness is the first step. The beginning is good."

Judas had become concerned because Joshua had not returned. He roused himself and came into town warily, having a natural distaste for the Samaritans. He was surprised to see Joshua talking to a Samaritan woman. As Judas walked up, the woman set down her water bucket, kissed Joshua's hand and ran towards the village.

"She'll bring the men," Judas said, "we must be going."

"Let's wait and see what happens," Joshua said.

"These people are of no use to us," Judas protested.

"Look," Joshua said, "the fields grow white for the harvest." He pointed to the town where many men, dressed in light-colored clothes against the sun, were following the Samaritan woman, hurrying to the well.

"I tell you there's no profit here," Judas said.

"One sows, another reaps," Joshua said.

The men came out to the well, listening to the woman, who told them the Jew was a prophet and had read her mind and might indeed be the Messiah. They doubted her, but when Joshua smiled and began to teach them, they found his words compelling.

"God is the God of all men, not only Jew or Gentile or Samaritan."

Judas sighed, realizing that Joshua would teach at length. He tried to find shade, but could not and so he sweltered.

Joshua spoke gently to the people of Shechem and his words were like cooling water and filled their hearts and they were ready to follow him.

"Wait," he said. "Your hour will come."

"Stay here with us and teach us more," they said.

He shook his head. "The Son of Man must be on his way," he said. He blessed them all and called to Judas and they went on their way.

Elsewhere in Samaria, they had similar experiences, though many were suspicious. Judas regretted this detour with the Passover being so close. But he could not persuade Joshua to give up teaching whenever and wherever he could.

***

The weather turned unseasonably cold, and it was more and more arduous to travel from town to town, more and more difficult to find a protected place to preach to the people.

But Joshua now believed they had done all they could in this phase of the mission. He was heartened that he had found supporters all through the land and encouraged that so many had repented their sins and were prepared to throw off their bondage. "Enough," he said. "We'll go back to Galilee and learn what has happened to the others. Then we can prepare for Jerusalem and the Festival."

15.

INTERVAL

The reunion in Capernaum at the house of Simon was joyous. They embraced one another with laughter and tears, each vying to tell the story of his travels.

"The people of Tyre and Sidon thought they had been forgotten," Judith said. "When Mattathias and Jacob and I preached the good news of your coming, they erupted in joy."

"The synagogues were filled," Jacob said, "not only on the Sabbath, but on every day."

"Even the Phoenicians came," Mattathias told him, "wondering what it was all about. I tell you we could have converted many, if you had wanted us to."

"The same with the people in the Decapolis," Philip said. "There was something in the air. We had only to reach a town and the people would throng to us—Jew and Gentile alike."

"We had the power," Old Nathan said. "As you healed me with the help of the Lord, I was able to heal many in Eastern Galilee. I believed and they believed and then all things were possible."

"I think it may have been my cooking," Deborah said with a twinkle in her eye, and they all laughed.

"We had a hard beginning," Little Jacob said, his brow furrowed beneath his sparse red hair. "Antipas was still in Perea and worried that killing Johannon, the Baptizer, might arouse the people

"Yes," his brother Johannon said, "there were spies and soldiers everywhere. Sometimes it seemed as if half of our congregation was in uniform."

The others laughed again, but with a note of concern.

"Still, they could see we were unarmed, had no followers and carried little baggage. We preached peace and the spies and soldiers drifted away. Some were disappointed."

Simon had waited patiently for the others to finish. He had been the closest to home and in some ways that had been the most difficult. He was dealing with many who knew him and some who had heard the message before. Joshua was anxious to hear from him.

"The people are as strong for you as ever, here in Galilee," Simon said. "Every once in a while, we would find a few backsliders, but we kept after them until they came back into the fold."

"Simon," said his younger brother Andrew, "never gave up. Some, I think, may have been impressed by the very size of him and others by his booming voice. But most of all, they knew he was strong for God, solid as a rock."

"Well then," Joshua said, "We've got a new name for you, Simon. We'll call you Cephas or Peter, if you like—solid as the rock itself."

Simon's eyes lit up. He liked the special sound of it and the affection it denoted. "Simon Peter," he said, savoring the words. "I like that."

"Tell us, Master," Simeon the Zealot said, "of your own fortune in Judaea."

Joshua gave them a brief report of his travels. They marveled at all the cities he had visited and of his luck even with the Samaritans. By the time he had completed his story, they were all glowing with enthusiasm and deepened hope.

Judas had watched and listened to these reports with detachment. He was pleased to hear the work had gone well, but he also understood that the people had never been called upon to face the kind of adversity that was coming.

"Will the people come to Jerusalem for the Festival?" he asked.

"From Galilee?" Simon Peter said. "I'm sure of it—many, many will come."

"From the east, too," said old Nathan. Deborah nodded in agreement.

"Some from Tyre and Sidon and the coast, but not as many," Judith said, "It's farther."

Judas was not impressed. "Jews come to the Passover from Rome and Alexandria, from Athens and Antioch. What is Tyre compared to that?"

Jacob was certain many would come. Philip and Simeon expected many from the ten cities—the Decapolis, and the sons of thunder, Johannon and Little Jacob, also had high expectations.

Joshua was certain that thousands would come from Judaea.

"Good," Judas said, "but only the beginning. What will you do, Master, when they are there?"

"We will be ready—hundreds of thousands of Jews in the city, eager for the Festival, many of them ready to rise, to throw off their shackles, to begin their liberation. Those who have heard will tell those who have not. By the Feast day—the first day of the holiday—all of the city will be ready."

"They must be organized," Judas said.

"It will be impossible to organize hundreds of thousands of people—especially Jews."

The others laughed, all except Judas.

Joshua said, "All of you here will have your assignments. You will spread the word to those you have met and watch over the rest. Judas, I know, will have his people well organized—they, at least, are accustomed to discipline. On the feast day, I'll go to the Temple and before all of the people, declare our liberation. I'll tell them—for all the world to hear—that we will no longer bow our heads to Roman subjugation, that we will never cooperate again, but that we will not use the weapons of war, only the weapons of peace."

"Amen," Simon Peter cried and the others echoed his cry.

"There will be no further sacrifices in the Temple, at least until the Romans have departed. As far as I am concerned, the paschal lamb is the last I will ever sacrifice, but we will pray together and sing the Hallel and march about the city. A Feast? Yes, we will have seven days of feasting and prayer, and then the people will depart to their own cities and the resistance—peaceful but strong, will begin."

They listened to him with rapt attention, imagining what he might say in the great courtyards of the Temple, imagining the joy of the people and the surprise of the Romans. They glowed with anticipation.

"What of the priests and the Sanhedrin?" Judas asked. He could see they were transported by their dreams and he wanted them to be practical.

"I'll speak to Caiaphas," Joshua said. "I'll speak to the elders. They'll follow us."

"I doubt it," Judas said.

"If not," Joshua said, "they'll have to accept responsibility for their own sins. They must face God alone—as all of us do, eventually. But of this I can assure you, we won't let the priests stop us."

They cried, "Amen!" again.

"And the Romans?" Judas asked.

"What can they do?" Joshua said. "There will be half a million of us, even with several legions, it will be too much for them."

"What if they fail to understand—if they begin to attack?"

"They won't," Joshua said. "There's no profit in it for them."

"But what if they, being only men, fall into error and decide to use their weapons to stop this thing at the beginning?"

"We shall have to face that with faith in God. The Lord does not promise us that we will follow his way without pain, without suffering, without loss. But if we believe in and trust in him, if we follow his words and his ways, we shall triumph in the end."

In the face of such unwavering faith, Judas, as always was moved. He was a tough man, a suspicious one, and he had been disappointed by others a hundred times. Still, as he looked into the eyes of Joshua ben Joseph he knew this man would not betray him, and he believed that God would not betray Joshua. The Lord would never have put such a man on earth except for His own glory, not for defeat and humiliation.

"I'll leave at once," Judas said. "To visit all the towns again as swiftly as I can, to verify who is coming and who is not, who remains on our side, and who might be trouble. We won't meet again until we're in Jerusalem for the feast."

Judas felt a surge of deep affection for all of them. They were naive, it was true, but they were loving and committed and they meant to do good. Especially, he felt a great love for Joshua, and he embraced him.

"Go with God," Joshua said, sensing the struggle within this strange man and fearing for him. "Trust me," he whispered. Then, Judas was gone into the night.

***

Gaius Fabricius hadn't slept peacefully in weeks. At first he had simply been excited to learn that his son was a holy man, a leader of the Jews. Then he had been astonished to find that Joshua was more than a mere teacher, a Rabbi or a Master, he was the anointed of God, the Messiah.

Gaius was overwhelmed. How could it be that he, an humble soldier and a Roman public servant, had fathered so great a soul? For a while, he had been so shaken that he had doubted his own paternity. Then he had felt ill, depressed, ready even to die. Only the fact that Joshua, wonderful, beautiful Joshua, was his son, made his life worth enduring. If that were to be taken from him, he didn't know how he would be able to continue to walk the earth.

But then, he had shaken off his doubts. The God of the Jews, the God he accepted and believed in, was all wise and all powerful. If He had chosen one child out of the many to grow up to be a great leader of men, why could He not choose the bastard son of a Jewish maiden and a Roman of uncertain birth? In fact, Gaius told himself, it was fitting. In a world where those of "high" birth had dishonored their own birthright—where the powerful abused the weak and betrayed the helpless, why wouldn't the Almighty turn to the poor and downtrodden for a new leader?

Reassured, he had felt a moment of serenity. But then, listening to Joshua's teachings he had understood his goals. Perhaps the ordinary Romans and Herodians didn't understand the concept of the "Son of Man," but Gaius had studied both Daniel and the books of Enoch. He knew that in the philosophy of the time, the Son of Man was a code name for the Messiah.

And he knew that the Messiah was the anointed of God and therefore a ruler on the earth. Had Joshua been the leader of an armed revolution, Gaius would have been terribly frightened. He knew that Pilate had ordered additional troops from Syria, including two full legions of Romans. And he was also aware that Pilate had put all of the surrounding legates and governors on alert against further problems in Judaea.

There were more armed men in Judaea than at any time since the actual campaigns of Pompey and Herod, and all of them were highly trained.

Gaius would have been frightened to think of the poorly armed and totally unorganized Jews fighting these machine-like soldiers, but he understood at once that Joshua planned something far more dangerous: a peaceful revolution. Did no one else see it? How could all of Judaea, all of her leaders and administrators, Herodian, Roman and otherwise be so blind?

At once the face of Pilate, sneering and cold, vicious and conniving, appeared before him. He was certain that if faced with unarmed, peaceful protestors, this man would murder them at will. That was his record until now, and this would be his opportunity to bring his administration to a final glorious conclusion. Later he would say that the protestors were armed, or he had been informed they were armed and who would prove him wrong?

Gaius had a vision, and in it, the snarling face of Pilate hovered above the dead form of Joshua, a knife in his heart. He shuddered, trembled and cried. He could not let that happen. But what could he do to prevent it?

***

Caiaphas and Reuben had reached similar conclusions. There could be no doubt that Joshua and his confederates planned to take some dramatic action at the Passover. They convened the Sanhedrin in a secret session and Reuben recounted tales of Joshua's mission.

Gamaliel was not impressed about the danger. "The man preaches peace and love—why should we be concerned?"

"He tells the people he is 'The Son of Man,'" Reuben said.

"This frightens you," Gamaliel responded. "You have studied your scripture and you are certain he means that he is the Messiah."

Reuben nodded.

"What if it's true?" Gamaliel asked.

"Ridiculous," said Caiaphas. "He's a nobody, a talkative carpenter from a small town—and don't tell me that David was a shepherd."

"You hear only what you wish to hear," said Nicodemus.

"I hear danger to the nation," said Caiaphas. "The Romans are not fools. They study conquered lands with great care. They know the Messiah is a ruler, and they are the ones who appoint the rulers. They have not appointed the nobody from Nazareth."

Ahab, a member from Galilee stood up. He was a man of means, but a rough-hewn farmer at heart. "Have you heard him, Eminence? If you had, you would not speak so lightly of him. The man is not a child—he's nearly forty years of age and I tell you with no disrespect that his knowledge of scripture is as great as your own."

"We have dozens of scribes who can quote the word from beginning to end—but to be a parrot is not to be a scholar," Caiaphas answered.

"He is no parrot, this Joshua," Ahab said. "My cousin, Nathan, and his wife Deborah, are people of means and education. Joshua saved my cousin's life and so strongly persuaded him of his wisdom, that he sold all he had and gave it to him."

"That may indicate Joshua's wisdom," Annas said, speaking for the first time, "but not the wisdom of your cousin."

Many laughed, but Ahab was angry. "You live here, you mighty ones, in your palaces and gardens, and you never even walk outside the walls. You seldom speak to the people and you never listen to them, yet you believe you know everything about your land. Strip off your arrogance, step out of your contempt, look clearly at the people, and listen well. For I tell you the days of your power and mine are numbered."

They erupted then in argument, Sadducees with Pharisees, priests with lawyers. Charges were hurled back and forth. Nicodemus tapped his fingers and watched this performance with growing despair.

Annas smiled cynically, seeing that his son-in-law had power to arouse and irritate his peers, but little to persuade them. He saw that Caiaphas was alienated not only from the people at large, but even from the Sanhedrin. Next year, when the time of re-appointment of the High Priest came again, he would see that Caiaphas was replaced. His son-in-law would hate him, but it was better for the nation.

Finally, Caiaphas regained control of the council. "Think not that I fear the Galilean preacher," he could not bear to call him by name, "but I do fear for the nation. The governor is a difficult man, and he hates us cordially. The people are aroused and they will be even more aroused at the Passover. I tell you we must be on our guard. We must be ready for some kind of demonstration, a very large one, and we must be ready for Pilate to do some unpredictable thing—something to incite them even more."

"Speak to Joshua," Annas said. "Persuade him to stay away from the city for the good of the nation."

"Impossible," Reuben said. "He has promised all of Israel that he will be there."

"You say he loves peace. Persuade him that to stay away will mean peace."

"Hopeless," Reuben said.

"Perhaps," Caiaphas said, "we can persuade the Romans to arrest him."

Ahab, infuriated, was on his feet. "For what?" he asked.

"For the very thing he claims—that he is the Messiah—who many believe will be a king, crowned by someone other than Caesar."

Gamaliel's voice rumbled through the chamber. "Do you hear yourself, High Priest? You would help the enemy of the nation to betray its savior?"

Caiaphas laughed. "You don't expect me to take him seriously."

"But that's precisely what you are doing. If not, why are we meeting, why are we quarreling? If the man is truly a nobody we are wasting our time. If he is the anointed of God, may God forgive us for our failure to give him all the love and support we are capable of."

The words of the scholar, gentle and revered, selfless and wise, affected the council greatly. There was no further discussion of a plan to obstruct Joshua.

16.

REVELATION

"I tell you, Prefect, the man is getting too close to the Jews. I don't trust him."

Pilate smiled at Septimus, who stood before his desk, his vulpine face twisted with hatred. This was an emotion that Pilate understood, one that he found it easy to deal with. "They tell me an interesting tale, Septimus. That when you performed your little mission at that town—what was it, Beth Sholem?—that Gaius Fabricius gave this Joshua a sword and told him to kill you, but he refused."

Septimus's face was now purple and the veins shown like cords in his neck. "True—a Roman offered the neck of a Roman to a Jew. Can you blame me for hating him?"

"Of course not. I'd feel exactly the same."

"Thank you, Sire. Nevertheless, I'll kill the man who told you."

Pilate laughed aloud, a skittering laugh that rang falsely through the room. "I'll not reveal the man, Septimus. But it's important for you to know you can have no secrets from me."

Septimus stared back, stolidly.

"What I don't understand is why you fear the Galilean holy man. If he refused the chance to take your life, why do you think he's a threat now?"

"I have my own spies, Sire. And they tell me the Jewish festival, the Passover, will be the time for an uprising. There will be hundreds of thousands of them here—a crowd we couldn't control even with ten legions."

"But the man preaches peace."

"He's a fool, and many of the Jews know he's a fool. They're using him for their own purposes. When he makes his call at the festival, they'll rise up in rebellion."

"Gaius Fabricius says this Joshua counsels peace, tells his followers to put aside their weapons. Surely we'll have no problem with an unarmed crowd, no matter how large."

"We'll search them as they come into the city."

"Tens of thousands of pilgrims? We'll never be able to do it."

"Yes you will, Septimus. They have no excuse for carrying weapons into the city for the festival. The law forbids it. We'll bring up additional Syrian cohorts and we'll guard every gate. We may not find everything, but we'll find most of it. And we'll be ruthless with those who do bring weapons. We'll crucify them on the spot."

Septimus was beginning to feel better. "Thank you, Sire. I'm glad we've had this talk."

But Pilate wasn't finished. A new thought had captured his imagination.

"Septimus, my friend, let me assure you that I hate these people as much as you do. But I believe they are playing into our hands. First, we'll make sure that they haven't brought new weapons into the city. Then, when this Joshua makes his appeal to the people, whatever he says, we'll treat it as a call to rebellion. We'll have armed men throughout the city, some in uniform, some among the people, disguised. The moment he speaks we'll cry treason and fall upon them."

Septimus was smiling. "Unarmed," he said. "We'll kill thousands, perhaps tens of thousands."

"Including Joshua, and perhaps the Sanhedrin for good measure. The Jews could use a set of new rulers."

Septimus laughed.

"Tell only your most trusted officers," Pilate said. "We want to catch them unprepared."

"What about Gaius Fabricius?"

"We won't share this little secret until the last possible moment. We'll give the Jews—and Gaius—a delicious surprise."

***

Gaius had left Caesarea early in the morning, pretending an errand along the coast, but immediately veering inland and heading directly for Galilee. He had expected to find Joshua in Nazareth, but he was not there. One of Joshua's brothers remembered Gaius as the one who had offered government contracts and smilingly sent him to Capernaum. "Is this a government errand?" he asked.

"In a sense," Gaius said.

It was not difficult to find Joshua in Capernaum. Everyone in town knew that he was staying at the home of a fisherman. When Gaius knocked at the door, it was opened promptly, but then the huge man who answered, peered at him suspiciously.

"What do you want?" Simon Peter asked, distrustful of the man's Roman looks and Roman clothes.

But Brother Jacob was standing in the shadows. "Welcome," he said. "I know this man," he told Simon. "He came to our shop in Nazareth. What brings you here?"

"I want to speak to Joshua. I must talk to him privately."

Simon Peter protested, but when they asked Joshua he readily agreed.

Finally, after so many years, Gaius stood before his son, alone and in private. He was no longer a young man and the trip had been a long one and now this dream of his had come true. He felt faint.

Joshua reached out and took his arms. "Sit down, my friend, you look very weary."

"Water, please, or wine if you have it."

Joshua brought him a cup of wine and Gaius sipped at it, trying to calm himself and gather his thoughts.

"My name is Gaius Fabricius I'm an official of the Roman administration, in fact I am a deputy to Pontius Pilate, the Prefect."

Joshua nodded and looked encouragingly at this man. He recalled he had seen him before, briefly, in the shop of his family and he also knew that he had seen him elsewhere, more than once, in the towns of Galilee. But there was something more to the situation, something that was going on within this man. It was obvious that he spoke with difficulty, and that he was very moved. Then it hit him: Beth Sholem.

"My sympathies, however, do not lie with Rome. I feel free to tell you this, for I know you won't betray me. Nor will I betray you. In my heart, I am a Jew. I have not been circumcised and I have not been formally converted. I don't follow your rituals. However, I have read the scriptures time and again. In fact, I have committed most of the law and the prophets and much of the writings to memory. You may test me if you wish."

Joshua shook his head.

"I'm not a scholar," Gaius said. "That's not my interest in scripture. I *am* a believer. I have put aside all the teachings of my youth, and I now believe there is but one God, and he is the God of the Hebrews."

"The God of all the world."

Gaius nodded. "Years ago, Hillel, a rabbi, told me I could accept the covenant of Noah and thereby receive my redemption. I have accepted and lived by that covenant for many years."

"Bless you," Joshua said. "The Lord has blessed you."

"No one in the Roman administration knows my feelings or my beliefs, although they are sometimes angry when I explain your side of any dispute. Nevertheless, they believe I am still loyal to the emperor. In a way, they're right, for what is best for Israel, is also best for Rome. Little will it profit Rome if she must spend thousands of lives and great treasure imposing her rule on this, small but lovely land. I could not say that to them without being accused of treason, but in my heart I know that it's true."

Joshua smiled. "We are blessed in having you for our friend."

"I knew you would understand. I've listened to your preaching and I believe I know what you are planning."

Joshua was not surprised, but he waited.

"I understand," Gaius said, "that you are the anointed one, and that you intend to proclaim your kingdom at the Passover."

"God's kingdom," Joshua said.

Gaius nodded. "I also understand that you will tell the people to oppose Roman rule, but not with violence."

"Does Pilate know this as well?"

"I'm not sure. The whole country is aware that some great event will take place at the Festival. But Pilate has confided little to me for days now. Usually that means he will do something of which I would not approve. Most often, that means he plans to use violence."

Joshua sighed. "Even though we plan no violence, ourselves?"

"Pilate is a cruel man. He loves bloodshed and hates the Jews. He would use any excuse to precipitate a slaughter."

Joshua shook his head. "There will be too many of us to kill—hundreds of thousands of Jews will be in Jerusalem, all of them unarmed."

Gaius looked into Joshua's eyes, saw the purity and the faith there. "You don't believe he would kill innocent people—even after the vicious killings weeks ago when the people protested the theft of the Corban?"

"That was terrible. That sin will be upon his soul, forever. But I don't believe that he will slaughter Jews at the Festival. Thousands will be there from other lands, some of them heathen who come merely to observe. The word will go back to Rome that Pilate has killed innocent people and that would be the end of him."

What Joshua said was true—Pilate was an angry and vicious man, but he would not want to lose his post and the emperor, Tiberius, had warned against causing insurrection. Still, Gaius felt emotions he could not express. He looked at Joshua, patient, concerned and serene, and all the love he had felt for him for all these years rose up within him. Tears sprang into his eyes, and he struggled to cover them.

Joshua began to understand that Gaius's feelings were even deeper than he had originally suspected.

"You're concerned for my people," Joshua said. "I see that, but you're more concerned for me."

Gaius could not hold back his tears and Joshua looked at him in wonder. "Why?" he asked gently.

"Because...because you...are...the Messiah."

Joshua rose and came to Gaius, who sat trembling before him, tears cascading down his face. "No," he said, "it's something else."

The touch of Joshua's hand on his shoulder was too much. Gaius reached up and grasped that hand. "Because," he said, and his voice was very thin, almost a whisper, "because you are my son."

Joshua was startled. He looked deeply into the tearful eyes of the man who sat before him, trembling, holding onto his own hand desperately.

Joshua dropped to his knees. "What are you saying?" he asked.

Gaius was shaking so hard he could barely speak, but he knew this was the moment. "Many years ago I was a centurion, and my men and I were searching the hills of Galilee for rebels."

He spoke in a near whisper, looking straight into Joshua's eyes, reliving that terrible day and once again feeling the horrible pain. The voice seemed not be his own, and as he spoke, he watched Joshua and saw that he was living that moment as Gaius recounted it.

Joshua's face twisted in suffering and tears began to seep from his eyes. As Gaius forced himself to continue, Joshua's tears began to flow and he sobbed, and as Gaius described his mother's violation, moans of pain were wrenched from him.

"Forgive me," Gaius pleaded, "forgive me." The agony he felt was so great, that if Joshua refused him he knew that he would die.

Waves, torrents of emotion, swept over Joshua. Agony over his mother's agony, and anger over the monstrous cruelty of the violence done to her, recognition that in a twisted way he owed his life to this man, remembrance of how he had been torn apart when faced with the choice of killing the soldier who had murdered his family and the time it had taken him to recover from their death, understanding more fully than ever, the brutality of Roman rule. And the need, somehow to master the hatred that he knew would destroy him—and the nation—if he gave in to it. He had never, would never, forgive that murderous soldier, but in the present circumstances, he had to muster all the generosity of soul God had given him. Joshua, trembling now himself, tried to speak, moving his lips in silence. Then, he placed both hands on Gaius's shoulders. "I forgive you, Gaius Fabricius, and God forgives you, too."

Hesitantly, he put his arms around Gaius and they clung together for a long moment.

***

Joshua had realized, even as Gaius was telling his terrible tale, that no one could actually know who the earthly father of Joshua had been. He also realized that it was useless to say this to Gaius, who was totally convinced of his parenthood. All Joshua could do was say to him that it was the Living God who was indeed the father of all, and with that Gaius agreed.

Still, in a strange way, there was a new bond between them, and Joshua of course, was truly honest in his forgiveness. For Gaius, the pain of the years could not be washed away in a second, but nevertheless he was deeply relieved to have finally confessed—and especially to Joshua.

Joshua promised to use what care he could in his mission to Jerusalem on the Festival. Gaius assured him he would use everything in his power to prevent a massacre on the day of the Feast. He also understood that nothing would keep Joshua from undertaking what he deemed to be his assignment from the Lord.

17.

VISIONS

After leaving Joshua, Judas felt serious misgivings. He had promised Joshua that the Zealots would come to the festival in great numbers, but they would not carry weapons. Nevertheless, he had told the Zealots they should bring their weapons and hide them somewhere in or very close to the city. He knew there was a deep conflict between these ideas and he felt a sense of betrayal to both sides. He hated himself for his uncertainty. Did he believe in Joshua's non-violent methods or not?

He wasn't certain. Sometimes, he would believe that Joshua could accomplish anything he chose—that he was surely God's appointed and the Lord would not fail him. But then he would remember something that Joshua had done, something terribly human and quite naive, and he would wonder whether he dared trust the fate of the nation to the beliefs, no matter how strongly held, of one frail human being.

Judas did not ride directly to the Zealot leaders as he had planned. Instead, he camped out by himself in the Galilean hills and tried to think. He wanted to clear his mind and deal dispassionately with all of the issues. He wanted to do what was right for both God and man. But he was too restless to meditate, too confused to reach a clear-cut decision. Once again, he concluded that he must protect against all eventualities. The Zealots must come unarmed, but their arms must be hidden nearby.

Again he convinced himself that in matters like this his judgment was superior to Joshua's. Hurriedly, he struck his camp and rode to Caesarea, to speak with Ahaz.

"The news is bad," Ahaz told him. "Additional legions have been called from Damascus and the Romans are conscripting more Syrians in Samaria. They'll have enough men to slaughter the pilgrims."

"That's it," Judas said. "We can't wait until the Festival. By then they'll have enough men to search everyone who enters the gates. We must bring weapons into Jerusalem NOW. By the time the people come to Jerusalem for the festival itself, we'll have weapons buried all over the city."

Ahaz's eyes sparkled. "I like you, Judas. You're always one step ahead of everybody else."

They rode all night, alerting their people and sending out messengers to the rest of the land. By morning, the carts and wagons were rolling, loaded with produce and goods hiding thousands of swords and spears. They would arrive at Jerusalem from every direction, enter the city from every gate. No single wagon would carry a great load, but each would carry some. Gradually, over the next week, they would bring enough weapons to arm thousands of Jews.

Judas rode down into Judaea, sleepless but exhilarated. He must tell Amos and Benjamin and the others to find places to hide the weapons—places within easy reach of the Temple and all of the Roman installations. This was something a man of action could relish, Judas thought. It had been hard for him, crossing and re-crossing the land with a man who used only words.

***

Now that his course was set and the Festival was only two weeks away, Joshua felt the need to reflect. It was difficult to do so in Capernaum, because the word that he had returned spread quickly and the people flocked to the city. Soon, Capernaum was filled with visitors, clamoring to see and speak to the Master, the one who was called the Son of Man.

Joshua spoke to hundreds, even thousands of people, quietly but powerfully giving them his message, healing many in body and spirit. But the clamor continued night and day, until the people of the town complained, and even Simon Peter's family began to feel put upon.

Joshua awoke suddenly in the night and sat upright. He had recalled a vision from his childhood, a vision from his first trip to Jerusalem thirty years earlier. As he sat in the house of Nicodemus, he had seen a man carefully smearing blood on the lintel of Joshua's house. The man's back had been turned and Joshua had not learned who it was. Now, he had seen that vision again and felt the same pang of pain he had felt before. But still he could not see the man's face. Joshua realized it was more important than ever for him to reflect on his situation.

He knew he couldn't find the proper atmosphere in Capernaum. With crowds dogging his every step, he could not complete his teachings to his disciples nor prepare himself for the great ordeal to come. He called to Simon Peter and his brother Jacob. "I must get away from here—at least for a few days. I want to think and to plan in quiet, away from the crowd."

"Where will you go?" Brother Jacob asked.

"North, perhaps into the hills, perhaps even to the mountains of Lebanon."

"On foot, that will take days."

"On horseback. Can you find me a horse?"

"Ezra will help," Simon Peter said. "Can we come with you? We'll be silent, we won't interfere."

Joshua smiled. "Your company will be welcome."

In the night, when the crowds had settled down, Simon Peter brought three horses to the edge of the city, near the lake. Joshua and Brother Jacob left the house quietly and found Simon.

They rode all night, through the hills of Gaulanitis, crossing the Jordan, but following it from a distance. This was the territory of Philip, Herod Antipas's brother. It was less heavily fortified than Antipas's tetrarchy, but they were still very careful, avoiding settlements when they could.

Simon Peter was concerned. What if they were stopped? What if the great plans for the Passover were destroyed by a careless act, or an ignorant Roman soldier?

Joshua had no such doubts. It was good to be riding through the clean, high air of the rising hills, to be free of the burdens of dealing with thousands of people and hundreds of details, at least for a while. He looked fondly at Simon and his brother, knowing their concern, but untroubled himself. Who knew when he would have this opportunity again? Soon the Passover would be upon them, he would make his announcement to the people, and then the true travails would begin.

On the afternoon of the second day, having by-passed Caesarea Philippi, they could see the peaks of Mount Hermon rising abruptly ahead of them. Surprisingly, they were still capped with snow and even as they watched, clouds surrounded the pinnacle and hid it from their view.

"Cold up there," Brother Jacob said, hoping they would not go up to one of the peaks. But Joshua said nothing and soon they were riding up the twisting paths. It grew colder as the horses carefully picked their way along the slopes. At the lower elevations there were shepherds, but as they rode higher, there were no sheep and the trail grew rockier.

It was almost dusk when they reached a flat, rocky shelf at the pinnacle. The temperature had dropped precipitously and Simon Peter and Brother Jacob were both trembling from the cold.

Joshua, however, was smiling, urging his horse forward, seeming not to feel the cold wind. He dismounted there and moved several paces away from his companions. Suddenly, the breeze grew sharper, blowing the clouds away and revealing the sun, which poured down on them with bright heat.

Simon Peter and Brother Jacob looked on in awe, as the bright sun flared off Joshua and his light-colored cloak. He was transfigured; he looked light, ethereal, almost transparent, as the blazing sun seemed to caress and bless him.

Joshua dropped to his knees and looked up to the heavens, clasping his hands together. "Father," he said softly, "give me your blessing. Pour into my blood the strength of your love, that I may carry out your holy words and perform the holy deeds that you have commanded me."

As he prayed, the swirling mists that had parted rose up again and surrounded him, so that he almost disappeared from the sight of his followers. The light of the sun was so bright, that the rays, reflecting off the mists almost blinded them. The wind rose again, and there was a roar in the gullies and canyons beneath them.

"Voices," Brother Jacob said. "I swear I hear voices."

"Look," Simon Peter pointed. The figure of Joshua had blended into the mists, but the swirling of the clouds was such that it seemed there were not one, but three figures on the rocky shelf, the shadows forming and reforming, as the wind howled about them. The sun broke through in flashes and the winds roared and the mists swept up and down.

"A tabernacle," Simon whispered, as the mists formed an arch over the shifting figures on the rocky shelf.

"Like Moses at Sinai," Brother Jacob said.

"I hear the voice of Elijah, calling," Simon said.

Then Joshua stepped forward out of the clouds, his face aglow. The mists swirled in the wind and floated away and the sun shone brightly on the highest peak of Mount Hermon.

"Oh, Father," Joshua said, "we thank you for your blessed word and your promise, preserved from the time of the patriarchs to the prophets and to us. Your Name is eternal and your love is eternal. Blessed is the Name of the Lord, forever and ever."

The sun was falling fast now, behind the mountain and the sky was shot through with streaks of red and pink and yellow and purple. Once again, the wind rose up and the clouds roiled in from the east.

Joshua held out his arms and his brother and Simon Peter embraced him. "My heart is so full of the love of God, that I feel dizzy," Joshua said.

And, indeed, he sagged for a moment but their embrace held him close and protected him.

"Who am I, Simon Peter?" he whispered.

"You are the anointed of God, the Son of Man."

"Yes," Joshua said, "and you and Jacob are the solid rocks on whom I depend. I tell you both the Kingdom of God is nigh, and the keys to that Kingdom are in your hands. Hold them carefully, do not lose them, for when the Son of Man is gone, you will have to be the guardians of Israel."

They were startled, frightened by his words. "What do you mean, Brother?" Jacob said.

"It's the wind and the cold," Simon Peter said, for he was afraid to hear Joshua say another word. The Festival of Passover was near and the King, Joshua, would take his throne and then there would be a thousand years of peace and happiness.

"Listen," Joshua said, "listen to what I tell you. God chooses the Messiah and the Messiah chooses God. So, too, must the people choose the Messiah. If they do not follow him, the will of God cannot be fulfilled."

"They'll follow you, Master," Simon said. "Thousands of them will rise in God's name on the Feast day."

"Have you forgotten the words of Isaiah? 'He was despised and rejected by men...He was wounded for our transgressions and he was bruised for our iniquities...They made his grave with the wicked...He poured out his soul to death.'"

"Master," Simon cried, shivering on the mountain top from a fear and a vision colder than the falling night. "Don't say this thing."

"Listen to me," Joshua said, gripping both of them by the arms. "We must do what God has chosen us to do, but we must be ready for the will of God to be fulfilled, whatever that will may be. I promise that I'll do what is demanded of me to save Israel, and you must do the same. God did not promise me a long life or an easy one. He promised me his love and salvation if I would bend my will to his. What will be is in the hands of God and it is God's wish that Israel be saved from destruction.

"But Israel must speak for Israel. If I must fall in God's war, then you must pick up God's weapon—the word, the word of God."

He held them even tighter. "Promise me, whatever happens that you won't lose your faith. You'll go on and lead the people to their redemption.

"I'm weak, Master," Simon said.

"No, you're the rock—Peter the rock and Jacob the Just—and I must know that I can rely on you."

The wind was howling now and they had to raise their voices to be "We promise, Master," they called out together, "we promise by the Living God."

***

Joshua was infused with new energy by his stay on Mount Hermon and relieved that Simon Peter and Brother Jacob had promised to persevere. He felt free now to undertake his mission. When they returned to Capernaum, he would speak in like manner to the other disciples, but Simon and Jacob had been prepared and they would help prepare the others. It was not that he anticipated failure—far from it. But he knew that whatever transpired would be God's triumph and not his own, and his humility was too great for him to predict the outcome.

For Simon Peter and Brother Jacob, the question was far different. Since the day they had committed themselves to Joshua, they had believed firmly there could be but one result: Joshua would be declared King, the Romans would leave Israel, and the Jewish people would live in peace. They had never considered the possibility of failure, least of all the prospect that anything untoward might happen to Joshua. He read to them from his little book of anticipations of the Messiah, derived from scripture, time and again, but they had heard only the glory and the success, never the doubts and the suffering. Now, he had forced them to realize it might not be that simple— that they would have a role to play no matter what the eventuality. In fact, they might be required to go forward without Joshua.

"Impossible," Simon Peter said privately to Jacob. "The people will rise, hundreds of thousands of them and Joshua will be our king."

"Of course," Jacob said. "He is too humble, too thoughtful of us. There's no way the Messiah can fail."

Yet, even though his brother had been transformed across the years, there still was a cord of shared feeling that tied Jacob to Joshua. He could sense fully his brother's sincerity and his desire to prepare the others for every eventuality.

Brother Jacob did not feel it was a prophecy; if it had been, Joshua would have said so flatly. But the risk and the danger were there and the followers, the close ones, had best prepare themselves.

Thus it was that the return trip to Capernaum was a joyous one for Joshua and a serious and frightening one for the men who accompanied him.

18.

THE GATE

"We must come," Miriam said. "All of us, your brothers and sisters, even Uncle Cleophas and the elders of the family."

"The road will be long and hard," Joshua said.

"It will be harder to remain here," Miriam said. She was no longer a young woman, but she was still very beautiful. Her graying hair set off her green eyes, still clear and luminous. Miriam's skin was the skin of a much younger woman and the glow of her deep love for life infused her entire being with an aura of serene beauty.

Joshua sighed and tried again. "The trip is dangerous and the events of the Passover will be even more so. There's no way of knowing how the Romans and Herodians will react, let alone the High Priests."

Miriam shook her head. "Knowing that, it would be impossible for us to remain here, wringing our hands and wondering what had happened."

"All right," Joshua said. Then he smiled. "Frankly, I'm glad you'll be there." They embraced happily.

***

Judas rode on top of the hayrack, handling the long reins with skill, urging the mules on with a crackling whip. He was approaching the Fountain Gate, below the walls, turning into the Hinnom Valley from the Kidron. It was a gray, overcast day, but the air was warm, and the road was clogged, as usual, with visitors to the city. In another few days, the pilgrims would begin to gather and the roads would be even busier.

He reached the gate and found it jammed. A cart coming in had banged into one leaving the city and overturned it, and the angry drivers were screaming at each other.

"Pick up your goods and let us get through!" Judas yelled.

The drivers began to yell at him. Frustrated, he realized his mistake. "All right," he said. "All right, I'll help you." He climbed down from the wagon and began to pick up scattered bolts of cloth.

A Roman patrol came up to the gate. "Let us through," the decurion yelled, pushing at the drivers.

"Watch yourself!" one of the drivers yelled. He was a younger man, excitable, and obviously not intimidated by the soldiers. Angered, the decurion and his men began kicking the merchandise out of the roadway while the drivers protested. Now they were all united in their hatred of the Romans.

Judas felt a prick of fear. This argument could lead to new problems. Deep below the hay in his wagon was a load of swords and daggers, dozens of them. Perhaps he should back away and head for another gate. But that might arouse the Roman's suspicions.

The drivers were yelling even louder at the Romans. Judas's practiced eye could see that the decurion was quickly losing patience. In a moment he would have his sword out and there would be violence.

Judas grabbed the young driver and dragged him back a few steps. "Careful, you fool," he whispered. "You're about to get a sword up your gut."

The young man snarled at Judas. "You're with them?"

"With you," Judas said. He shoved the young man roughly back. "Let's get this gate open," he yelled to the people clogging the entrance. "We've all got work to do."

He pushed at one of the carts, trying to rock it back up. A Lebanese trader began to help. The drivers of the carts watched, while others cleaned up their mess. The decurion was calming down. But then he was looking at Judas's wagon with curiosity.

"Yours?" he yelled to Judas.

"I just drive it."

"Well look at this," the decurion said. He walked directly to the wagon and began pulling at one of the slats on the side. Judas knew that if the decurion reached into the hay at that point, his hand would touch cold steel. Judas didn't know whether to strike the soldier or run.

"Slat's loose. If you don't fix it, you'll drop the whole load," he said, smiling at Judas. Then he pulled his own sword and used the hilt to hammer the slat back into place.

"Thanks," Judas said, feeling the sweat spill over his forehead.

The decurion shrugged and waved at his men. They marched around the wagon and off into the valley.

The drivers glared at Judas.

"Collaborator," the young one snarled.

Judas managed to keep from throttling him.

At the Sheep Gate and the Water Gate, the Gennath Gate and Jericho Gate, on the roads from Emmaus and Joppa, from Hebron and Beth Lechem, from east and west and north and south, the wagons of the Zealots were coming to Jerusalem, loaded with swords and daggers and spears and shields.

Ahaz of Caesarea, more enterprising than most, had even brought with him the parts of several larger weapons, launchers that could heave stones at a fortification. That would not have pleased Judas if he had known. Hand weapons were one thing, siege weapons were something else.

The men and their carts and wagons wound their way through the city. At a dozen places in the lower city, on the Akkra and the Ophel, even in the houses of a few wealthy sympathizers in the upper city and the new area of Bezetha, the weapons were carefully unloaded, usually by night, and stored. Then, the Zealots went back on the road to find more weapons and bring them back into the city. As the days passed, the stockpiles grew, until there were literally thousands of weapons hidden within the walls.

***

Septimus smiled with great satisfaction. "Two full legions are in the city, Sire, and the Jews don't even know it."

"Remarkable," Pilate said. He had decided to come to Jerusalem a week earlier than usual, to make certain that all was in readiness for the festival. Also, he had elected to stay at the Antonia Fortress, rather than Herod's palace, not in deference to Antipas, whom he could have shunted to the old Hasmonean palace, but because he wanted to have the best view possible of the great events he planned for the Jews.

"How did you manage it?" Pilate said.

"We brought the men into the city in small units, rather than marching them in maniples and we brought them in at several different gates. Some we brought in disguised as farmers or traders. We had brought their armor into the city days before. The Jews didn't even notice."

Gaius listened in silence. They had not told him their exact plans and he realized they didn't trust him. However, there was no way to avoid his knowledge of the total number of troops in the city. The Romans were a very methodical people and they reported even their clandestine operations with meticulous care. Those reports had routinely crossed the desk of the Deputy Prefect of Judaea.

The reports had not surprised him, but they did alarm him. The number of soldiers was larger than at any time he could remember, and neither Septimus nor Pilate would bring in enormous armed might, simply to display it and intimidate the Jews.

Pilate smiled at Gaius Fabricius, the same superior smile that Pilate used when he believed he was outwitting someone. "Naturally," he said, "you'll keep this information confidential."

Gaius pretended to be offended. "Of course, Sire."

"It's all been approved by the Legate," Pilate said.

"I know that, Sire. I hope the troops won't be needed."

Septimus glanced at Pilate. They hoped the troops would be needed and their desires were transparently visible on their faces.

Gaius shuddered. How could Rome survive with men like this ruling the provinces?

***

"The Romans think we're fools," Benjamin said to Amos. "They bring in huge numbers of additional men in disguise, then send them to the Antonia fortress where all we have to do is count them."

"I wonder," Amos said. "If there aren't others secreted somewhere in the city."

"We have people everywhere. This is still our city. If the Romans have additional troops they've been very clever."

"What do the lookouts tell us?" Benjamin asked.

"They've seen no new troop movements. Eliezer, on the Bethany road, says no troops have passed through there in twenty-four hours. It's the twelfth legion posted at Jericho we've been worried about."

***

For once in his life, Caiaphas betrayed deep agitation. Annas had rarely seen his son-in-law aroused, certainly had never seen him frightened. But there could be no doubt of it. Instead of posing serenely on his throne-like chair, Caiaphas was actually pacing the room.

"Calm yourself," Annas said, relishing the scene.

"I am calm," Caiaphas said, and despite his great anxiety, he forced himself to sit down, and arranging his cloak carefully, took hold of both arms of the chair. "I know we promised the Sanhedrin we wouldn't interfere with this man, but I think that was a mistake. I tell you, I foresee a great disaster at the Feast."

"Every Passover is a trial, Caiaphas, with almost half the nation in attendance, but we get past it one way or another."

"This is different," Caiaphas said. "The man definitely plans to take action at the Temple. He's going to proclaim something dangerous—probably that he's the Messiah."

"So what? We've had dozens do that before."

"The people believe in him. As soon as he proclaims he's the Messiah, they'll rise up and follow him as the new king. The Romans will say we're subverting their law and the next thing you know we'll have a bloodbath."

"I doubt it," Annas said. "The city is full of Roman soldiers. Certainly the Galilean wouldn't want to confront them."

"He doesn't know what he's doing. He doesn't realize how quickly the Jews can turn politics into violence. He thinks he can just speak out and his soft words will control the people."

Annas nodded his head. "We are an emotional lot," he said. "Well then, the moment he proclaims himself, you'll have the temple police arrest him."

"For what? No law prevents him from proclaiming he's the Messiah."

"Of course not—for creating an uproar—for endangering public safety—for breaking the laws of the Feast—something, you'll think of something—any pretext to get him out of the way."

"He keeps those Galileans around him like bodyguards. There'll be a fight."

Annas sighed. "Surely the Temple Guards can control a handful of Galilean roughnecks."

"Annas, you don't seem to understand. He has thousands of supporters—tens of thousands. Reuben and his spies have word from all over the country. They're all coming to the Festival. If we arrest him publicly; they'll start a riot—they'll overwhelm the guards."

"Then do it privately—find him before the Festival starts and hold him until it's over."

"Privately? How does one do things privately at the Passover? This Joshua Ben Joseph may be a magician, but I am not."

"I don't suppose there's any use convening the Sanhedrin again," Annas said. "Gamaliel and Nicodemus would probably persuade the others to keep hands off the Galilean."

Caiaphas nodded in agreement. "If only we could persuade the Romans that he's dangerous," he said. "That would get him off our hands and neither the Sanhedrin nor the people could blame us."

"You can't expect Pilate to help you. He's waiting for us to make a mistake."

Caiaphas threw up his hands and lapsed into a brooding silence.

"You seem to have run out of alternatives, my son," Annas said. "But think of the bright side. Perhaps this Joshua truly is the Messiah. Then all of us will receive our just deserts."

Caiaphas glared at him.

19.

PILGRIMAGE

Spring had come to the land. The cold weather had ended and the snows were fading from the peaks of Lebanon. The heaviest rains were over, although there still would be spring rains, but not with the fury of winter. The land was deep green from north to south. Citrus trees had bloomed and the fruit would soon been picked.

Now the spring flowers were blossoming, great fields of red poppies, many-hued crocuses, pale hyacinths and lilies, deep-toned roses of Sharon, pink and white Oleander. It was the month of Nisan, first month of the Hebrew Ecclesiastical Calendar. Soon it would be the Passover and the Feast of Unleavened Bread .

All over the land, people were preparing for the Festival . They were coming to Jerusalem in greater numbers than ever before. There was a new sense of hope in the nation, hope that the days of oppression were soon to end, that a new era was coming, and that Judaea and Israel would rise triumphant.

Barley, flax and wheat had been planted. Soon the early crops would be harvested. But first it was time to remember the liberation from Egypt, the era when the Jewish people had recovered their freedom and their dignity.

From Tyre and Sidon to Beersheba and Kadesh-Barnea, from Ashdod and Dor to Ramoth-Gilead and Heshbon, the people had heard the teachings of Joshua Ben Joseph and his disciples. They had learned that God was willing to forgive them for their sins, to accept their repentance and to give them new life.

Now they were going to Jerusalem on a joyous pilgrimage. Joshua, the Son of Man, would be there. He would proclaim a new day, the beginning of God's Kingdom on earth. The wicked would be punished and cast aside, the righteous would live in peace forever and ever.

Some understood that Joshua was the Messiah, the one promised by God from the days of the patriarchs. Others believed that Joshua was a prophet, and would himself announce the Messiah. In any case, the day had finally come, the day they had longed for.

There were others who were not so certain. Some had interests counter to those of the vast majority of their countrymen. They feared that a new king would take away their own power and prerogatives and they approached the Festival with trepidation. Others were simply unconvinced. Men had been proclaimed Messiahs before, the liberation of Israel had been promised many times, but had not happened. They would wait and see.

Still, for the multitudes, for the ordinary people of the land, the sense that this was the new day and that the Messiah would be revealed was the surest thing in their hearts.

Families which had never gone to Jerusalem for the Feast, others who had not been there in years, were now preparing to go. From the lands of the Diaspora, from Rome, where the emperor had decreed a special fare for Jews traveling to the Festival, from Athens and Alexandria and Antioch and Damascus and a hundred other cities, the Jews were on their way. A few in distant lands had heard whisperings of a Messiah, many had not. But in the hearts of all these pilgrims was a sense of something extraordinary about to happen and they wished to be part of it.

The caravans were on the road. Thousands upon thousands of people on foot and in carts and wagons, on donkeys and horseback and on litters, were traveling through the countryside toward the holy city. The skies were clear and blue, the land lush and in bloom, the air balmy and spirits high. They sang and laughed and prayed and spoke to each other with hope and happiness.

Joshua, his disciples, his family and their families came on foot. Many had offered him animals, even carriages, to ride, but he had refused. Although they could have followed the route through Samaria, despite the feelings of the local peoples, Joshua chose the route of the Jordan valley. It would give him a chance to review his life and to meditate on its meaning.

The waters of the Jordan were symbolic to him of life itself and the living word of God and he wanted to be close to that unending stream. He also wanted to pass by Beth Sholem and mourn his murdered wife and children one more time. The tears and the pain were gone, but the love remained and it was important for him to go into the still abandoned town and pray by himself among the crumbling ruins. Miriam and the others stayed apart, offering their own prayers. Joshua sat on the stub of a wall of his house and prayed to God for the souls of his departed and for his own soul.

Then, they were on the road again, and following the Jordan reminded him once again of the Baptizer, Johannon, calling the fallen to repent, announcing the coming of the Kingdom of God. Johannon's words and then his cruel death had lighted the flame in his own heart. He prayed for the soul of Johannon, and once more regretted the loss of this beloved friend.

But Johannon, for all his wisdom and holiness had misunderstood the end times. He was convinced that God was about to make a dramatic intervention into the world, reward good, punish evil and rule forever in peace and harmony. Johannon was correct in urging repentance and forgiveness in preparation for the beginning of God's kingdom, but he underestimated both the growing anger of the people, and the potential overwhelming violence of the leaders of the Roman Empire, and especially the governor, Pontius Pilate. Joshua feared that the people might suddenly erupt in violence, and then be cruelly massacred by the Romans. It might become a true End Time, but not of the kind the people yearned for. It was his obligation to avoid this disaster and he would do everything possible to save his people from destruction.

These thoughts obsessed Joshua as he traveled toward Jerusalem. Those following him had increased in number until there were literally a couple hundred of them attending him, trying to be close to him, asking for word of what was to come.

Near the town of Adam, he called them together. "Johannon, the Baptizer, told us over and again, that the Kingdom of God is at hand. Some listened, many did not. Others did not understand.

"I tell you, my friends that the Kingdom of God is always at hand— always within our reach and has always been within our reach.

"Some believe that the Kingdom of God is in some distant place—a paradise, far from the earth. Some believe the Kingdom of God is planned for a distant time, not for us who live today.

"All of these people are wrong. The Kingdom of God does not only surround us, it is within us. The Kingdom of God is not some future time, it is now. We are made in His image, the spark of his divinity resides in all of us. We must recognize the divine light that is both within and outside of us and bask in its beauty—allow it to illuminate our lives, our very being. We must love God, turn away from sin, follow the word and the ways of God, and we will know greater joy and peace than we have ever known before. Then, and only then, we will be free—free of fear, pain and doubt. The heathen will not be able to hurt us, the disaster that befalls our land and our home will not affect us—illness, disease and death will lose their power.

"There is the armor that warriors wear and the armor worn by the righteous. The armor of warriors will turn away swords and spears, but the armor of the righteous—the love of the living God—will turn away all pain, all fear and even death, itself.

"Believe now in the Living God, look inward to save your souls and not your substance, and the glorious Kingdom of God will begin for you, today, this instant, and will live in you forever."

His voice rang out over the throng. They were stirred by his words, moved by his passion, but not all of them understood.

"What about the Passover?" they asked. "Won't it happen then?"

"Will Joshua be king in that kingdom?" asked another.

They would have asked Joshua, but he had left them and walked into a copse of trees to be by himself.

Even Simon Peter was scratching his head. "Is this a new teaching?" he asked Brother Jacob.

Brother Jacob, who understood, shook his head. "It is the same teaching, Simon. Joshua is telling us our salvation lies within, not without."

Simon Peter wanted to ask, "Then why are we going to Jerusalem?" But he didn't ask. He decided not to think further about what Joshua had said. There was too much to do, many people to care for. He would think about it later, after the Passover, after Joshua was crowned.

***

Many families traveling to Jerusalem had brought their children. Along the roads, the parents kept them close, but when they halted for a meal or a drink of water or to camp for the night, some would be allowed to run off and play. A few found their way to Joshua, drawn by his warmth and quick smile. Even when he was teaching their elders, he would often break off and speak to the children. Occasionally, he played with them, even tossing a ball back and forth around a circle of laughing children.

Once, when he dropped a ball, they climbed all over him, almost knocking him down. Parents and some of the disciples hurried up, ready to chastise the children. But Joshua raised his hand. "Don't stop the children—let them come to me. Look into their innocent faces and there, mirrored in their eyes, you will see the Kingdom of Heaven.

"I tell you that unless you receive the Kingdom of God like these children, you will not enter into it."

Then he smiled, held out his arms and the children ran to him and he embraced them. "May the Lord bless you and keep you, from now to everlasting."

The parents, quite touched, said "Amen."

Along the way, many sought Joshua out, trying to discover what their place might be in the God's plan. Among them was a wealthy young man, Asher, son of Josiah, who had been carried on a litter all the way from Galilee. He wanted desperately to speak to Joshua, but he was shy and fearful of talking to him publicly. However, when he saw how gentle Joshua was with the children, his hopes rose, and one cool evening, mustering his courage, he approached Joshua, speaking rapidly, as if he were afraid he might be cut off.

"Good Master," he said, "what must I do to inherit eternal life?"

Joshua saw the anxiety in Asher's eyes and spoke gently, trying to calm him. "Why do you call me good, young man? None is good but God alone."

Asher took this as a rebuke and began to turn away. "Wait," Joshua said. "I will answer your question. If you wish to have eternal life, you must observe the commandments—you must not kill, or commit adultery, you must not steal or bear false witness, and of course you must honor your father and mother."

The young man looked puzzled. As he spoke, he nervously twisted a gold ring on his finger. "I have observed all these commandments, Master, since my childhood," he said. "What do I still lack?"

Joshua saw that Asher was sincere, but still troubled, and the continued twisting of the ring told him where the young man's thoughts were fixed. "If you would be perfect," Joshua said, "go and sell what you possess and give it to the poor. You will have treasure enough in heaven."

Asher looked at him startled. He realized suddenly that he had been twisting the gold ring, and he blushed deeply. He could not say another word, but cast his eyes down and hurried off.

Simon Peter, Andrew, Judith and Brother Jacob had been listening and they were surprised by Joshua's teaching. "You've driven him away," Judith said, "and I think he is a good man."

"Yes, I believe he is, but his mind is not on the Kingdom of God. I tell you, it is easier for a camel to pass through the eye of a needle than for a rich man to enter the Kingdom of Heaven."

His followers were startled, but Joshua was smiling. "I wanted to challenge the young man and astonish you, but don't think that I hate riches," Joshua said. "It's simply that great wealth is a distraction. It's difficult for a man to know whether he worships his wealth or his God."

"If it's that difficult to be saved," Andrew said, "what hope is there for us?"

Joshua smiled. "Don't worry, my friends. For men, these things seem impossible, but with the love of God, all things are possible. For you, who have loved and trusted me, and therefore loved and trusted God, my hopes are high that the almighty will reward you."

Simon Peter smiled suddenly, then hid his smile.

"What is it, Simon Peter," Joshua asked.

Simon had now blushed as red as Asher, the wealthy young man. "My mother has been nagging me," he said, "pushing me to ask you what places Andrew and I will have when you are king."

Joshua laughed. "Do you see yourself on a throne, judging the tribes of Israel?"

Simon flushed even darker and said nothing, but Joshua put his arms around his shoulders. "You have given up everything to follow me and the word of God. Having given up all, you will have all."

While they were talking, Johannon and Little Jacob, Nathan and Deborah, Simon, Mattathias and Philip had come upon them, listening to the discussion with consternation.

"Why are you bothering Joshua with such questions?" Nathan asked.

"I'm surprised at you, Simon Peter," Little Jacob said, "you're a fisherman just like us—do you expect to be a king?"

"Please, don't be angry with each other. It's natural to be concerned about the future, but quite useless. There is no way we can know what will happen—only God knows that. Nor do I believe that Simon or any of you would want to be a king, like among the gentiles, lording it over your people and ordering them to do your will.

"Whoever is to be great among you must be your servant, and whoever would be the greatest, must be like a slave to all. For the Son of Man came not to be served, but to serve.

"It is written that the first shall be last, and the last shall be first. So must it be among us. There can be no earthly king, only the king who is in heaven. Judas, our brother, and all of his family before him uttered the cry, 'No ruler but God.' And they were right. Remember this always and do not quarrel among yourselves, for that is not pleasing to the Lord."

He left them then, ashamed of their bickering, and determined not to trouble him with such matters again.

20.

TRIUMPH

When they reached Jericho, their ranks were swelled by thousands more pilgrims, many who saw Joshua for the first time, and were awed by his fine appearance and kindly eyes, his beautiful voice and his gentle ways. Some, who had not been baptized, were taken to the Jordan by the disciples and there repented and were purified. Others were thirsty for his teaching, and begged him to speak to them about the law and the prophets and the coming of the Kingdom of God.

He was weary from the road, but he could not refuse these people. He gathered them outside the walls of the city, on a little rise of ground and there he spoke of whatever came into his heart.

Many children came and sat at his feet and he felt their love and he returned it. "These are the children of God, still pure in their hearts. He who teaches children to sin—it would be better if he had a great millstone fastened around his neck and he were dropped into the great sea. The Lord is loving and patient, but those who wrong the children will suffer his undying wrath.

"Do you see these little ones? Do you see the innocence in their eyes? This is how you must be to enter the Kingdom of Heaven. You must strip away the evil things you have learned in your lives, the doubts of the Living God, the errors of your ways, the sins that you have not repented. These evil things must be washed away, not merely with the waters of the Jordan, but with the holy water of God's forgiveness. You must become again like these children, simple and pure and seeking the love of your Father. Then will God grant you his forgiveness and his everlasting love.

"If you want this forgiveness, you must be prepared to extend it to others. For the Kingdom of Heaven may be compared to a king who wished to settle accounts with his servants. One was brought to him who owed him ten thousand talents. As he could not pay, the king ordered him to be sold, along with his wife, his children and all his goods. The servant fell on his knees, imploring his lord, 'Have patience with me and in time I will pay you everything.' The king had mercy, released the servant and forgave him his debts.

"But that same servant, thereafter, came upon a fellow servant who owed him a hundred denarii, and seizing him by the throat, insisted he pay him in full. The poor man pleaded for time, promising to pay all he owed, but the servant refused and cast his fellow servant into jail until he should pay the debt.

"His fellow servants told the king and he summoned the servant before him. 'You wicked man,' he said. 'I forgave you because you asked my mercy, but you had no mercy on your fellow.' And in his anger, the king cast him into prison."

He paused and looked at the rapt faces watching him. "Remember this story, dear friends, for if you will not forgive your brother, the Living God will not forgive you."

Afterwards, many who were blind or crippled flocked to him and he prayed with them all and healed them and sent them on their way.

That night, while Joshua was sleeping, Martha, the sister of Miriam and Eliezer of Bethany, came into the camp. She was directed to the place where Joshua slept, in the open, under the stars, but as she approached, Simon and Judith stopped her.

"Please," she said, "my brother is very ill, and Joshua can save him."

"He has saved many, but he's sleeping now. Bring your brother in the morning."

"I can't," Martha said, quite upset, her voice rising. "He's in Bethany and he's too ill to travel."

"Then what can the Master do?" Judith said, feeling compassion for the woman.

"He can come to Bethany and help my brother."

"We'll be there in two days," Simon Peter said.

"That may be too late," Martha said. "My brother may die."

Joshua awakened to hear the last of what Martha was saying. He rose quickly and embraced her. She broke into tears and implored him to help her.

Joshua was deeply touched by Martha's pleas and the desire to help her was very strong. Nevertheless, he felt that he must follow the plan he had set for himself, and that it was important for him to remain on the road with the pilgrims. "I love Eliezer," he said, "but his life is in God's hands, Martha, not mine. I'll be there in two days and I'll do everything I can."

Martha's face betrayed her surprise at this rejection. She was hurt when she realized that Joshua would not leave that night, but she tried to control her feelings. "Please," she said, "come quickly." Then she left the camp and hurried back to Bethany.

In the morning, Joshua and his companions rose early. More pilgrims had come during the night and most wanted to see Joshua, to talk to him, to feel the healing touch of his hands. He spoke to many and led others to the river, where his disciples baptized them. It was difficult for him not to think of Eliezer and his sisters. He worried that he might be failing Eliezer—and God, by not hurrying to Eliezer's bedside. Joshua struggled through another day, fearful he was making a disastrous error. He tried not to betray these feeling, and to provide the pilgrims with all the knowledge and support they so deeply required. Finally, towards midday on the third day, they struck camp and headed for Jerusalem—and Bethany.

***

The road passed through barren country, but the pilgrims were in a joyful mood and their lyric voices seemed to warm the bleak landscape. Towards evening, as they approached Bethany, Martha came running towards them. She was weeping as she ran and her expression was mixed with equal parts of pain, pleading and accusation. "He's dead, my brother's dead, and you might have saved him," she said to Joshua.

He felt her pain, mixed with his own. Yes, he thought, I ought to have come here sooner. Lord help me in this sad, sad moment. Joshua tried to embrace her, but she moved away, unwilling to have him touch her. "Why didn't you come earlier?"

Joshua prayed for her silently. "I try to do what the Lord tells me," he said aloud. "I'm sorry you are suffering, but perhaps—perhaps God has other plans." He was reluctant to tell her of his own misgivings, at least not yet. Perhaps, as desperate as the situation seemed, there was still some hope.

Martha wondered at his words. "What do you mean, other plans?"

"I'll come to the house later," he said, for he had seen that as they approached Bethany, a great crowd was coming to the Mount of Olives to greet him.

Martha was even more offended, believing he was more interested in the plaudits of the crowd than in helping her brother, and without saying another word, she turned and made her way sorrowfully, through the happy crowds, to her home.

"Simon Peter," Joshua called out. "Take Andrew and go over the hill into Bethphage. You'll find a fine young colt of an ass tethered to a tree, with a man standing beside it. Tell the man you want the colt and he will ask you why. Say 'The Master needs it,' and he will untether the colt and give it to you."

Simon Peter looked at him in surprise.

"Go," Joshua said. "Now."

The brothers made their way through the boisterous crowd. From Bethany, all the way across the Mount of Olives, down into the Kidron Valley and up to walls of the City, thousands of tents were pitched, like a field of wild flowers that had sprung up overnight.

The brothers did not realize that the throngs of people were contained within a ring of bodyguards, protecting Joshua and his disciples from enemies who might try to come upon them unawares. Neither did they understand that the best places along the twisting road into the city had been staked out by Judas and his Zealot friends, to make certain that Joshua would be protected.

But Joshua knew and understood, for all of this was part of the plan that he had worked out with Judas and Nico, to make sure that everything happened as they wanted.

Simon Peter and Andrew made their way through the crowds and into the tiny square that was the center of Bethphage. They found the colt as Joshua had said and a man waiting beside it. They gave him the message Joshua had instructed them to use. He smiled, unleashed the colt and handed them the rope. It was a fine animal, pure white in color, and much larger than most. When the man had given them the lead, he turned and looked toward a shaded window in a nearby house. A hand flashed and the man nodded. Within, Nico, the son of Nicodemus smiled. All was happening as he and Joshua had discussed at the Feast of Dedication, months earlier. He was relieved that Joshua had not arrived sooner, for he had seen a Roman officer and a troop, forcing their way through the crowd, and he was afraid they might be searching for Joshua.

Nico knew the Roman officer—he had been with Pilate in the Hippodrome, years earlier, when Pilate had threatened to kill the Jews who had protested the idolatrous Roman ensigns. His name was Septimus and his evil had shown in his face.

Septimus questioned many, but Nico couldn't hear the questions. He pushed through the crowd and stood directly in the path of Septimus. The

Roman did not recognize him, but still grabbed his tunic and asked roughly, "Do you know the Galilean preacher?"

"There are many Galilean preachers," Nico said.

Septimus shoved him hard against a tree. "You know the one I mean—the blonde one who they say is your king."

"Why would a king come on the Jericho road?" Nico asked. "Wouldn't he approach from the North like King David?"

Septimus looked at him sharply, then shoved him away. "Come on!" he yelled to his men and they swung up on their horses and fought their way through the crowd, back to Jerusalem. Nico shook his head and smiled. He hadn't really lied and, besides, in a case like this, surely an exception could be made.

***

Simon and Andrew proudly brought the colt to Joshua. He smiled broadly and patted the animal on its flanks, delighted with its pure coloring and the evident power of it.

Brother Jacob, also delighted, turned to Judith. "Tell the daughter of Zion," he quoted from Zechariah,

"Behold, your king is coming to you,

humble and mounted on an ass,

on a colt, the foal of an ass."

Joshua smiled, but he said, "Zecharariah tells us, 'the Lord, God will become king over all the earth, and on that day, the Lord will be one and his name one.' He who rides the colt is only the herald for the Lord of Hosts."

The others nodded, but did not truly understand.

Meanwhile, the crowd had pressed close, and first one woman, then another and another, draped the ass with their scarves, long and beautifully made, and forming a colorful and gleaming seat for Joshua. Simon held the animal and Joshua put a hand on Andrew's shoulders and with ease, lifted himself onto its back.

Those standing nearby cheered and Joshua smiled broadly and lifted his arms in response to their voices. The sun was low in the west and the rays outlined him so that he seemed to be made of the light itself. The people began to clear a path for him and to lay their garments in the way. He would have stopped them, but they were filled with joy at the sight of Joshua and so he let them do as they pleased.

"Hosanna!" cried a gritty voice, and Joshua turned at once, knowing it was Judas. He stood on a pile of wood so that he could be seen above the crowd and his own face was glowing with happiness and hope. "Hosanna," he cried from deep within him, "Hosanna to the Son of David!"

The people took up the cry, and it went out in waves from the hill above Bethany, rippling over the Mount of Olives.

Joshua felt a surge of love for his people so great that it almost overwhelmed him and once again he raised his arms, but as he did so the love that he sent forth came back to him in huge, rolling waves, and the more he gave, the more he received. He pushed gently with his legs against the ass, and the fine animal moved slowly forward. The people cheered even more, but the animal, feeling Joshua's strength and certainty, was not troubled and picked its way confidently over the garments strewn in the way.

Ahead, the Zealots, lining the route as Judas had instructed them, had cut palm branches and they cast them, too, into the path of Joshua. Others hurried to do the same, so that Joshua's path was a river of rippling, colorful garments and green fronds. The ass stepped carefully, but with its head high, as though it was proud to follow this stream and proud to bear a king.

"Hosanna!" the voices cried.

"Blessed is he who comes in the name of the Lord!"

Pilgrims hurried up from the vast garden of tents, hearing the cries and seeing the tall man, seated proudly on the tall colt, moving serenely toward the city.

"Who is it?" they asked.

"The Messiah," said some, "Our King," said others, but Joshua did not acknowledge them.

And surely, there were many among those who saw Joshua, many who believed that this indeed was their king, this glorious and proud man, with his blonde hair streaming on the breeze, the sun gleaming on and seeming to glow through him, his hands raised in a benign gesture.

Again and again, he waved to the crowd. Again and again, their voices came to him. "Hosanna!"

"Hosanna in the highest!"

"Blessed, blessed!"

"Son of David!"

The voices rose above the tents and the people, blending into a chant, into a hymn. Musicians raised their instruments and began to play, giving forth a new song, made of old words, but with a new meaning. The chant, the song, the hymn, the love, rose in surges, as each new group of pilgrims, caught sight of Joshua and heard the voices of the others. All of the Mount of Olives and all of the Kidron was a vast garden of waving arms and scarves along the banks of the stream that Joshua followed, now red with the blood of the Temple sacrifices. Joshua shuddered .

Joshua heard the voices and yet he did not hear them. He saw the people and yet he did not see them. He rode on the colt, but did not feel it beneath him. A whole life had led him to this moment, and all the joy and pain of what had gone before seemed to be swept up and given to him again, as in a chalice from which he must drink. The sound and the sights blended together. He felt joy as never before, but yet pain, too. For this was the beginning, glorious, thrilling, but only the beginning. Still, he knew they loved him, these people of Israel, and he loved them, too, every one of them. And he would save them, of that he was certain. Whatever was required of him, whatever God wanted, that is what he would do. He was stronger now than ever before, and wiser. God had prepared him, slowly but well. God had showed him all there was to know of his people, of all people, and now it was bound up within him, like a scroll wound tightly around its core. He was the heart, the core, and the people were the scroll. He must spread the scroll and proclaim the truth and the people would be saved.

The Beautiful Gate was before him, leading into the Temple itself and to his surprise it was open. There were guards there and, seeing the crowd, they would have closed the gate. But it was too late. The people were inside, lining the way. Joshua dismounted and walked beneath the great arches. Now he was within the porticos and the people, the great sea of the people, flowed through the gate and poured into the court of the Gentiles.

Beyond, in the Temple itself, Caiaphas heard the cheers and the hosannas, the hymns and the playing of instruments. He frowned, and would have told the guards to quiet the crowd. He was prepared to give the evening prayer and the noise was unseemly.

But then, despite the huge crowd and the bleating of animals and the chirping of birds, there was sudden silence, and Joshua walked alone through the outer courts and into the court of Israel, even into the court of the Priests.

Caiaphas looked down from the platform and saw this man, tall and handsome, and walking with regal bearing, his eyes aglow and his face radiant with knowledge that Caiaphas had never had.

In the last rays of the sun, there was a feeling of sudden warmth, even as the wind ceased at sunset. But a cold wind blew through Caiaphas's heart, and he shuddered in fear as he looked upon this man, and though he had never seen him before, he knew who he was and why he was there.

21.

ELIEZER

It was gloomy when Joshua returned from Jerusalem. He had told the crowd to disperse and they had assented reluctantly. Only his disciples followed him to Bethany. He sensed that along the way, the Zealot followers of Judas were maintaining watch, but they did not show themselves. He was pleasantly tired and not at all dismayed that his return was largely unnoticed. The day had been a great triumph.

But Joshua knew that his day's work was not finished. He must return to the house of Miriam and Martha and deal with the problem of Eliezer. As he rode on the docile but splendid creature Nico had provided, he prayed with deep feeling. Seldom had he felt such confusion. Eliezer was his friend and he loved him. Yet, he had not gone to his side when Martha pleaded with him. He knew that his restraint had been required of him by God, and yet it was still unexplained.

He thought of Eliezer with his shy, lopsided smile and quick gestures, his eager words and helping hands. Surely this man did not deserve an unhappy end. Yet, the sisters had told him that Eliezer, a man his own age, had died. And he, Joshua, dear friend and God's anointed, had chosen not to be present. He felt an unusual burden of guilt.

Had God wanted to spare him the pain of Eliezer's passing? No, that could not be, for he felt the loss of Eliezer as powerfully as if he had been there.

Did God want them all—the sisters and Eliezer's friends, to know the loss, to understand that the liberation of this Passover was to be bought at a price? That some must die, so that others might live? Perhaps. That made more sense to Joshua. But still, he wasn't satisfied. The Lord knew that Joshua understood the price that must be paid, the lives that might be lost. He did not require an additional lesson.

"Tell me, Lord," Joshua prayed fervently, but in silence. "What is thy will? Why must we lose Eliezer, so beloved to us? We know he will return—that he has a good and kind and believing soul, that he is a just and righteous man who will return in the day of the resurrection. But—" He broke off his prayer, startled by the thought that struck him. Was it truly possible? He was suddenly impatient and without thinking he pressed his knees against the flanks of the ass and it broke into a trot.

Simon Peter and Andrew and the others, half-dozing even as they walked behind Joshua, were startled by the sudden clip-clop of the racing animal. They broke into a run.

***

Joshua opened the door of the house, surprising the sisters and their family. They sat huddled together, tearful and silent. When Joshua burst in upon them, his face creased with concern, they were shocked and some of them were angered.

"Where is he?" Joshua asked, his eyes searching the room.

Miriam, her eyes red, her hands twisting had risen when Joshua entered. She stared hard at him, wondering. "In the tomb," she said. "We laid him there in preparation."

"Where? Where?" He asked.

"What do you want?" a man said, a member of the family, and quite officious.

Joshua ignored him. "Where?" He asked again, but Miriam was frightened and unable to answer. Martha rose and led the way out of the house.

"This is terrible," someone was saying, but all of them followed Joshua and Martha.

She walked along the dirt street, slanting upward to where it met a rocky prominence. There, in the dark, they could make out a huge round stone rolled across the entrance to the tomb. Martha peered at Joshua, trying to make out his face in the blackness of the night. Brother Jacob and others had lit lanterns and now the light threw shifting shadows on the rock.

"Please open it," Joshua whispered. There was a note of anxiety in his voice the others had not heard before. Simon Peter and Andrew and the Zebedee brothers put their shoulders to the stone and to each other. They rocked it once and then again. Then it bumped over the niche that held it and with a great grinding sound, it rolled to the end of the trough and shuddered to a noisy halt against the jutting stone wall.

"Eliezer, my friend," Joshua whispered, "please come back to us."

There were sharp intakes of breath. Someone said, "This is not permitted." But Joshua had entered the tomb, even before Simon Peter could help him with his lantern. The sound of his sandals going down the stone steps echoed in the dark strangely and then Simon Peter, swallowing his fear, followed him inside.

The others waited silently. Then, after a minute, Joshua reappeared, carrying Eliezer in his arms, tears falling from his eyes on the face of his friend. Simon followed with his lantern, his face reflecting his confusion.

"You can't do that," someone said to Joshua, but Joshua was walking rapidly down the slanting street to the house.

"Forgive me, my friend," he was whispering. "But the Lord wanted me to enter Jerusalem this day. The Lord wants you to enter Jerusalem, too, but he knew that you must leave us and return, you must be reborn, Eliezer—reborn."

His words, strange and unworldly, carried in the darkness and even those who were offended by his actions were silenced by the strength of his feeling.

Andrew ran ahead and pushed open the door and Joshua stepped inside. He laid Eliezer on a mat on the floor before the hearth fire. Then, kneeling beside him, he called, "Water, bowls of water."

Miriam seemed unable to do anything, but Martha quickly brought him water and lengths of cloth. Joshua dipped the cloth in the bowl and gently wiped the face of Eliezer.

"Awake, Eliezer," he said. "Awake, for the Lord has need of you. Come back, Eliezer, for the Living God wants you to live."

He whispered to Eliezer and prayed and stroked his limbs and wiped his face and his body with the cool water.

"*Shema Yisroel,*" Joshua began, and as he continued, "*Adonai Elohenu--*"suddenly, there was another voice in the room, as Eliezer sat up—suddenly and unexpectedly, so that some in the house cried out and others simply cried, while Joshua and Eliezer completed the prayer together—"*Adonai Ehud!*"

"Where am I?" Eliezer asked, in a wondering voice, staring at the shroud that covered his body and all the people in the room. And then his focus came closer and he saw Joshua and smiled broadly.

"Master, thank God you've come." He threw his arms around Joshua and Joshua threw his arms around Eliezer while tears fell from his eyes.

Martha dropped to her knees and put her arms around her brother and Joshua. Miriam prayed.

Joshua was filled with wonder. The Lord had given him the power to bring back Eliezer from death itself. He had not expected anything like that. He was filled with a mixture of surprise and gratitude. And he knew that his good fortune in being able to call on the Lord in this manner demanded even greater dedication than he had felt before and a profound sense of humility.

***

The great palace of the High Priest was ablaze with light. More than a dozen members of the Sanhedrin were gathered in the vast upstairs hall. If Caiaphas had had his way, only the Sadducees, the majority party, would have been represented.

Annas had argued against it. "You'll have to inform them all eventually, why not now?"

"I want to organize and prepare them for what must be done."

"You'll anger Gamaliel and Nicodemus and some of their friends. You'll make them implacable foes. It would be better if you convened the whole Sanhedrin—at least you better make certain your opposition is represented."

Reluctantly, Caiaphas had agreed. He disliked his father-in-law intensely, but he was very powerful and often, he was quite perceptive. Caiaphas would never have admitted it, but at times he was afraid to act unless the old man supported him. He wondered if Annas suspected that. The idea made him uncomfortable.

"King," Reuben was saying, "he let them call him king."

"Did he really?" Nicodemus asked. He was surprised. Nicodemus knew much of Joshua's plans, having discussed them with him and his son at the Feast of Dedication, and he hadn't thought Joshua was prepared to make such an announcement so early.

"Someone protested, a Pharisee I think," Reuben said, clumsily trying to include the opposition in his story. 'You shouldn't let them call you king,' the man told Joshua. 'Rebuke your disciples.'

"The Galilean preacher answered, 'If I told them to be silent, the very stones in the road would cry out.'"

"Arrogant upstart," said Lael. He was a middle-aged man, a wool merchant, known for his piety but also for his hard-dealing. Lael was a long-time supporter of Caiaphas and no friend of anything he considered new or untried, least of all a Galilean pretender.

Nehemiah, a member from Galilee, had not been invited, but he was at Nicodemus's house when the summons came from Caiaphas, and he had elected to come on his own.

When Lael called Joshua an arrogant upstart, Nehemiah rose to his feet. "I've been trying to warn you for a long time. This man claims to be the Messiah and thousands believe and follow him. Personally, I see no reason to doubt his word, and I warn you again, as Gamaliel did, that if what he says is true, you are opposing not only a Galilean preacher, but the anointed of God."

Caiaphas smiled smoothly. "I have heard it said, 'Can anything good come out of Galilee?' and the answer, of course, is 'Yes,' for have we not our trusted brother, Nehemiah?" Caiaphas paused, still smiling, while Nehemiah waited, expressionless. "But I tell you," Caiaphas continued, "we need not concern ourselves about opposing the Lord. Does anyone seriously believe that the illegitimate son of an unknown Roman soldier is to be the King of Israel? The very idea is absurd."

Gamaliel had been stroking his beard thoughtfully during this exchange. When he spoke, the others turned to listen. "Some dispute your view of this man's heritage, Caiaphas." He never called him 'Eminence' as did the others. "Others, honorable men, attest that this Joshua is descended from the royal House of David on his mother's side and thus is a fitting person to be on our throne. But none of that matters. It was said by the elders that the priest is superior to the Levite, the Levite to the Israelite and the Israelite to the bastard." He paused for a moment, before he spoke again, and when he did, his voice was very mild.

"But the precedence of the priest is conditional," he said. "If the bastard is a man of learning, and the High Priest a boor, the bastard precedes the High Priest."

"Are these words directed to me?" Caiaphas, noted for his ability to contain himself, was furious. Annas masked a smile. Nehemiah was laughing.

Gamaliel's expression had not changed. "I am merely making a simple point. The ways of God are profound, mysterious and beyond our knowledge. We had no way of knowing whom he would send to be our king. It is best not to deride any man for what we conceive to be his humble beginnings, for those beginnings may mask a miracle that will overwhelm us."

There was a moment of silence and in that moment, Johannon, the son of Nicodemus, known as Nico, appeared in the doorway, pushing past a servant who had tried to prevent him from entering. He hurried to his father and whispered in his ear. A startled look crossed Nicodemus's face, a look of awe not unmixed with fear.

"What is it?" Nehemiah asked. "Is your family well?"

"The word is spreading through Jerusalem," Nicodemus said in a whisper. "There is a man in Bethany, Eliezer by name, a well-to-do gentleman. He died a few days ago, and today, many witnesses claim that Joshua raised him from the dead."

"A trick," Annas said.

"ANOTHER trick," Caiaphas said.

"How do you know that?" Nehemiah responded. "Why do you always cry fraud?"

Caiaphas voice dripped with sarcasm. "Are we to believe that this— this Galilean preacher has the power of life and death?"

"I know," Gamaliel said, "that the High Priest does not share our belief in resurrection."

"Even you," Annas said, "believe that resurrection is the gift of God, not of a mere man."

"A mere man?" Nicodemus said. "This could be the Messiah."

"Even the Messiah is only a man," Lael said.

Gamaliel waved a hand. "Are we to know the powers of the Messiah, so that we can state with certainty what he can or cannot do? The Messiah has never come until now. Our ideas of him are our own, not those of the Living God. We cannot judge the Messiah, nor can we judge his powers."

Nico spoke softly and deferentially, as he did not truly belong in this meeting of the Great Ones. "I must tell you that, whatever you believe, the people believe that Joshua has raised Eliezer from the dead. The word has spread from the tents outside the walls and into the houses within. The people are more than ever convinced that Joshua is the Messiah."

Caiaphas rose to his feet. "For once, the son of Nicodemus is right. The people, foolish and easily led, now call him 'king.' But Israel already has a ruler and that ruler is Caesar. The Galilean is guilty of sedition and the people confirm his guilt. It's only a matter of time until the Romans arrest him and kill him."

"And what will we do about that?" asked Nehemiah.

"Nothing," said Caiaphas. "It is not up to us."

"You mean," said Nicodemus, incredulously, "that we will stand by while our Messiah is murdered?"

"He is not the Messiah!" Caiaphas roared.

"He is!" shouted Nehemiah, and Nicodemus and his son joined in. Every man in the room was on his feet except Gamaliel, as they argued heatedly.

Gamaliel close his eyes and spoke quietly. For a long time, no one heard him, no one listened. But then, because of the force of his personality, they became aware of him, and the shouts died away.

His words were still very quiet, and they leaned close to listen.

"Forgive them, Lord," Gamaliel was saying, "for they seem to believe that the life of the Messiah is in their hands and not in yours."

***

Miriam, the mother of Joshua, watched the scene with a sense of wonder. Eliezer hurried from one member of his family to another, embracing them again and again, his face radiant with a perpetual smile. Now and then he danced a few steps, as if to test himself, to prove that he was really there. Whatever he did, the others laughed and cheered.

Martha labored mightily, bringing forth cakes and sweets and wine for everyone. Her response in any crisis was to be active, and when she could think of nothing else, to cook. Miriam, her sister, helped a little, but for the most part she stood in a corner, a faint smile on her face, her eyes following Eliezer's every movement.

The disciples cheerfully drank the wine and ate the cakes that Martha provided. The day had been a splendid one. They had accompanied Joshua into the very heart of Jerusalem. Usually, they were intimidated by the great city. They were ordinary men and women, accustomed to the plainer ways of Galilee. But this day, they had marched beside Joshua and heard him acclaimed. They were proud to be in his confidence, proud to have carried his message, proud to be his closest friends.

Joshua lounged on a low stool tipped against the wall. He drank sparingly of the wine and hardly touched the cakes. Now and then, Eliezer would hurry back to him and thank him again. Joshua would smile and nod and remind him God was the healer.

The others smiled shyly at Joshua, but few approached him. They, too, were grateful for Eliezer's return to life, but they were intimidated by the thought that this man—this smiling, handsome person who seemed to be a man—had been the agent of their loved one's recovery.

Miriam, Joshua's mother, could hardly take her eyes off her son. She had always been proud of him. He was so handsome, so able and so kind. She had told him time and again that he was descended from kings, but that was mostly a matter of family pride. She had never dared to dream that her son would sit upon the throne of Israel. Now, that impossible vision might soon be realized.

Miriam did not know what to think about Joshua's role in saving Eliezer. Nothing in her life had prepared her for such an event, and nothing she knew of would explain it. Joshua was her son, her flesh and blood. She could well remember his birth and every day of his childhood. She had held him in her arms, given him her breast, picked him up and comforted him when he had fallen, nursed him when he was ill. When had he ceased to be a Galilean carpenter and been transformed into this remarkable and in some ways more than human?

She prayed that God would not be offended by these questions. But meanwhile, she watched and wondered.

Joshua was there but he was not there. He was happy for Eliezer and his family, pleased to have been God's instrument in his rescue. At any earlier time he would have been distressed to learn that the story of Eliezer's miraculous recovery was spreading through the city. Not any longer. The time had come to speak in the daylight that which had been whispered in the dark. But not everything. There was still much to do, much to plan. The happy people in the room were but a faint distraction. His mind was elsewhere and it was fully occupied.

***

Reuben, the Sagan, deputy of the Temple, was shivering and trying not to show it. He had been waiting in the huge, stone anteroom of the Antonia for over an hour. It was late. The informal meeting of the Sanhedrin had broken up without reaching any conclusion. Caiaphas had been hoping to persuade them that Joshua represented a great danger to the nation and that they should act promptly. The others, to his frustration, had failed to see it. Even Annas had been equivocal.

"I see that he could cause problems, but we are a nation of holy men. Surely we can tolerate one more."

"This one is different," Caiaphas had said. "This one will cause a revolution."

But the others would not believe him.

"Now," Caiaphas had said. "We can make short work of him. Tell the governor that he preaches insurrection, and let the Romans punish him."

"I thought he preached resurrection, not insurrection," Nicodemus said and Joseph of Arimathea had agreed with him.

Caiaphas ignored them both. "Is it worth the risk?" he asked. "What if I am right?"

"If you're right," the Romans will kill him," Joseph said.

"Isn't it better that one man should die," Caiaphas asked, "then that the whole nation should suffer?"

But they recoiled from his words. "We have given up human sacrifice," Gamaliel said. "If we do not sacrifice human life to appease God, why should we do it to appease Caesar?"

Finally, the men had departed, still quarreling, while Caiaphas seethed inside. It was then that he sent Reuben to Pilate. But the hour was late and Pilate had been sleeping. At first, the guards refused to waken him. Fearfully following Caiphas's orders, Reuben insisted that his errand was important. Still, the guards temporized. They decided to rouse Gaius. He had been irritable at being awakened, but he knew that a message from the High Priest could be very telling. He dressed quickly and went downstairs, but Reuben refused to talk to anyone but Pilate.

Gaius shrugged and went off to waken the prefect, well knowing how angry his response would be.

Pilate came out of his chamber dressed in a robe, his swarthy skin unpowdered, his dark eyes flaming above the dark pouches beneath. When he heard Gaius's errand, he erupted in anger. It took great tact and diplomacy for Gaius to persuade him to see the emissary.

Pilate kept Reuben waiting for an hour, partly to re-powder his face, partly to humiliate him. When he finally entered the anteroom, his humor had not improved in the slightest. Gaius walked behind him and at a distance. It was not wise to get too close to the governor.

"Where is the High Priest?" Pilate asked.

"He waits for your answer."

"Why isn't he here?"

"He didn't want to alert others."

Pilate sniffed and glared at him. "Deliver your message."

Reuben took a deep breath and spoke in a quavering voice. Pilate was staring at him with unblinking eyes and Reuben was very nervous. "Joshua ben Joseph, a Galilean preacher, entered the city today while his supporters proclaimed him king."

Reuben paused, not knowing how much Pilate knew and awaiting his response.

"That's all?" Pilate said coldly. "Do you think our eyes are closed and our ears stuffed?"

Reuben shook his head violently. "Of course not, Eminence," (unconsciously, he had used the title applied to the High Priest).

Pilate was losing patience. "Surely, you have more to say than that."

Reuben nodded. Pilate was beginning to anger him. The man might be a Roman governor, but he could treat the emissary of the High Priest with more courtesy. "We know you are aware that by claiming to be king, this Joshua, and his supporters are committing sedition against the Roman state and the emperor."

He paused for a moment, then plunged on. "We wish you to know that we do not support the claims of this man. In fact we oppose them. The High Priest will not object if you choose to arrest him as an enemy of the state."

Pilate laughed, abruptly and without humor. His voice, lisping as always when he was angry, was pitched higher than usual. It was late and the night air was unpleasant and this fool had come on a ridiculous errand.

"Are you telling us the meaning of our own laws? Are you suggesting to us, how we should enforce them?"

"No, of course not. We are very concerned over the effect of this man on the people of Israel, here in this city on the Festival of Passover. The people are law-abiding, but sometimes they may be rather...emotional. However, they fully understand that you represent the established authority. The High Priest does not wish you to believe that the pretensions of this preacher and a few boisterous followers truly represent the position of the nation."

Once again Reuben paused and even tried to smile.

"For this you have wakened me in the middle of the night?" Pilate asked.

Reuben's voice now had a whine in it. "We regret disturbing you, Eminence (once again), but we have our duty to protect our people."

"Get out," Pilate said in cold anger, startling Reuben. "Get out of here at once. Tell your 'superior,' that we know our laws and we know our power. No Galilean preacher, not even the whole of your...nation is any threat to us. If there is sedition, we will crush it. If there are rebels, we will kill them. If there is a war, we will lay your city, your country waste."

He turned abruptly and stalked out of the room. Gaius was churning inside. He had listened to Reuben casually betraying his son, Joshua, and fear for him stabbed through his heart. Still, he could think of nothing to say to Reuben, who had surely bungled his job.

Gaius nodded to Reuben and then he, too, left the room.

Reuben hesitated, then walked slowly out of the Antonia Fortress. He was in no hurry to return to the High Priest and report on his mission.

***

Judas had watched Joshua enter the Temple, and then, in the excitement, had slipped away on errands of his own. He had memorized the location of every major arms cache within and without the city. He knew where each of the chieftains of the Zealots was stationed and where his men could be found. As soon as darkness fell, he began a swift tour of inspection, quickly making his way to section after section of the city.

It wasn't an easy task. The streets were clogged with pilgrims and the houses were filled with people. However, Judas, despite his Galilean background, knew the city well and he made his rounds with remarkable speed. In the space of several hours he had visited Ahaz and Benjamin and a dozen others. With each meeting, his enthusiasm grew. Everything was proceeding as planned. There were ten thousand Zealots within the walls and each was trained to be the leader of ten men. At a word from their chiefs, they would quickly recruit volunteers. When the time came, they were prepared to organize one hundred thousand men—for peace or for war.

Judas felt a pang of doubt. He ought not to be thinking of war—that was against the word of Joshua. But he couldn't help it. And the fact that weapons for a hundred thousand men were within the city, was a comfort to him. Even if the Romans had three full legions within the city, and that was not certain, they would be outnumbered six to one. Still, he knew that he could not tell that to Joshua.

Along the way, Judas learned a new fact that added to his optimism—the story of Joshua and Eliezer. Amazingly, it had flown from one end of the city to the other in a matter of hours. The name of Joshua was on everyone's lips.

When he slipped through the Water Gate and headed towards Bethany, Judas was in high spirits. Along the winding road that led between the tents, he inspected other Zealot stations and learned that the route was well protected. There was no chance that any substantial number of men, armed or otherwise, would surprise Joshua.

Judas smiled. The Messiah didn't know that a ring of armed and alert watchers surrounded him, from east of Bethany all the way into Jerusalem, but Judas wasn't taking any chances. The hour was near and he was ready.

When Judas reached Eliezer's house, he was accosted by two men. "Who are you?" a rough voice asked.

Judas's hand tightened on his dagger, but then a lantern was flashed suddenly in his face.

"Judas," a voice said. And then the swinging lantern revealed the face of Little Jacob, smiling in an oddly wizened way, and then Johannon his brother. The lantern was quickly covered.

"We're guarding the house," Little Jacob whispered. "My brother and me, in shifts with Mattathias and Philip."

Judas grinned in the dark. "Good," he said. "I've come to see the Master."

22.

THE PRICE

Gaius returned to his room in the Antonia after Reuben left, but he found it difficult to sleep. He was fully aware of Joshua's triumphal entry into the city and in fact, had reluctantly reported it to Pilate.

The governor had only smiled and that terrified Gaius. He realized that Joshua could be considered guilty of sedition under Roman law, and that sedition was dealt with ruthlessly in every part of the empire. It was one thing to petition the Emperor to be selected as a puppet ruler. It was something entirely different to accept the mantle without imperial approval. Joshua had not petitioned, would not petition and would not have been accepted by Rome if he had. But, of course, Pilate could not be completely certain of that. Israel had had Jewish kings before while under Roman rule. From Pilate's standpoint, the risk was very personal. If Israel had a king, it would not have a prefect, a governor. If Rome actually approved the appointment of Joshua, that would mean the end of Pilate's rule, and an ignominious end at that.

When Gaius reported to Pilate, he had expected to be ordered to arrest Joshua, and he was startled by the sly smile.

"Splendid," Pilate said, arching his eyebrows. "The dear fellow is doing precisely what we want him to."

Gaius didn't know how to respond. He didn't want to do anything that would force Pilate to act—and in a way that might result in the death of his son. The penalty for sedition was death by crucifixion. But if he said nothing, Pilate might suspect his motives.

"Forgive me, Excellency, for my ignorance; what is it we want him to do?"

Now Pilate became reticent. He no longer trusted Gaius completely, especially where Joshua and the Jews were concerned. A wrong word at the wrong time and Pilate's plans might be aborted by his self-righteous deputy.

"We're being patient, dear Gaius," Pilate said. "This is, after all, the festival, and we don't want to judge these people too harshly at such a happy time. We'll wait and see how far this man carries his royal pretensions, and we'll learn who supports him. Then we'll act accordingly."

Pilate dismissed him then and Gaius didn't know what to do. He tried pumping Septimus, but the crafty, old soldier was as secretive and sinister as ever. Gaius had hoped that in his natural bloodthirsty state, the captain would be eager to divulge his plans, but he was disappointed. Like Pilate, Septimus only grinned—horribly—and went on his way.

Reuben's appearance in the night redoubled Gaius's fears. Judging by the attitude of the High Priest, it seemed that not even the Jews would support Joshua. But then, he wondered, did the High Priest truly represent Israel, or only his own ambitions? Gaius had personally seen the people responding ecstatically to Joshua and his message. Perhaps the High Priest's fears paralleled Pilate's. He, too, might lose his position, if Joshua became king.

Unable to sleep, Gaius dressed and made his way through the dark fortress to his office. He reviewed the dispatches from Rome and those from Damascus. They were filled with the usual material, reports of Parthian war-like activity on the border, complaints about slow tax collections, requisitions of men and materials for a hundred administrative tasks. Then, a dispatch from Vitellius caught his eye. "The reassignments you requested have been approved. Act accordingly."

Gaius came fully awake for the first time. Vitellius was telling Pilate that additional troops had been mustered and sent to Judaea. When? How many? Clearly, Pilate knew and did not want anyone else to know. Gaius's sense of foreboding deepened. There would now be at least three legions deployed in and around Jerusalem, far more than at any time since the reign of Herod the Great. It was not only Joshua whose survival was at stake. The armed might of the empire now threatened all of Israel. Actions by Joshua might be used as a provocation, but the vindictive strength of the empire would crush this tiny nation and its courageous people.

Gaius could have cried with frustration. What could he do to save Israel—to save his son?

***

Joshua was unable to sleep. The entry into Jerusalem had been a wonderful event, perhaps the happiest in his life. The prospects for the future were great—within a few days he would publicly announce his mission and his call to the nation. Saving Eliezer was but one additional blessing among a host of them.

Still, he was disturbed and he knew that his concern related to Judas. There was no doubt that the Zealot leader was well-organized. He had happily told Joshua of the ten thousand Zealots in the city. Joshua was surprised and, at first, pleased. But then he had second thoughts.

"Why so many?"

"When you make your proclamation, they will help organize the joyous response."

"The people don't have to be organized—not to recognize God's word."

Judas was patient. "As you sent disciples out to all the cities, these are the disciples to the believers here assembled. Without organization, without men to lead, there may be chaos, misunderstanding, even a riot."

Everything Judas said was true. But Joshua now knew there would be ten thousand tough fighting men inside the city, men who had been waging an underground war with the Romans for years, in some cases, generations. They were easily aroused and they could be very dangerous.

Joshua sighed and tried to compose himself. The Festival was only days away, the people were gathered and he, Joshua, was prepared. As he had told his disciples, it was useless to worry about tomorrow: "Sufficient unto the day are the evils thereof."

He smiled, remembering his own words. Then he fell into a shallow, restless sleep.

***

Joshua was awake at dawn, laid on his phylacteries, said his morning prayers and prepared for the day. He was greeted by brilliant sunshine. A stiff breeze had stripped away the valley fog and the city stood out in sharp, sculptured outline. Below, on the hillsides and in the valley, the great and growing garden of Jewish pilgrims had awakened and opened with the sun.

Simon Peter, wearing fresh clothes stood waiting in the courtyard of Eliezer's house with the splendid animal that Joshua had ridden the day before.

Eliezer had been up since daybreak, perched on the hillside, once again carefully checking on the Roman troops within the city. He was anxious because he might have missed some troop movements during his illness and his "departure," but he was determined not to miss any others. He looked back toward his home and waved cheerfully to Joshua.

All of the disciples were up and ready, smiling with anticipation. Miriam, his mother, waited, too. She was free of care for the first time in months. The experience with Eliezer had reassured and refreshed her. Joshua was obviously the Lord's anointed. The fears she had so often felt for him could be put aside.

Joshua looked about at his friends and family with affection. He stretched his arms as if to include them all and shouted a powerful "Shalom Aleichem," and they responded with a resonant "Aleichem Shalom."

His expansive gaze lighted on a fig tree in the courtyard and he was startled to note that it was covered with leaves, dazzlingly green and bright, unheard of that early in the year. He stepped close because it looked as if it had already flowered and was bearing fruit.

It was not, and Joshua frowned.

"Do you see this fig tree," he said to the others. "It makes a great show of brilliant color, far ahead of its proper season. It appears to be full and rich and mature. But when we look closely we see that it bears no fruit."

He snapped off a branch, quivering with bright leaves and held it out. "You see, the fig tree is like many in this world, who put on a great show of wisdom, who wish us to believe they are mature and prepared to provide us with the nourishment we require."

His expression darkened. "But, like this fig tree, they are lying. They want to persuade us that they are ready, but they are not. They want us to believe they have something to offer, but they are all bright show and false brilliance. When we look closely, we find they bear no fruit. They are false prophets and the curse of God is upon false prophets."

He threw the branch to the ground. Then, his expression brightened and with Simon's help, he mounted the colt.

***

As they traveled into the city, the pilgrims once again responded joyously. There were more of them than the day before and in fact the crowds would continue growing until the Passover itself arrived, as the great garden of Israel blossomed in and around the holy city. Many were still wending their way along the roads, looking for a place to camp; others were raising their tents or feeding their animals. They all seemed to be aware of Joshua's arrival and they greeted him with songs and prayers and cries of

"Hosanna." Joshua smiled and waved a hand in greeting and blessed them as he passed. Small children ran alongside his donkey and he reached down and touched them and smiled.

He could not help but note that some of the men who lined his way did not join in the cries and blessings of the crowd. He sensed they were not opposed to him, but rather that they were Zealots, assigned by Judas and other leaders to guard him and his followers.

Joshua glanced at Brother Jacob and they shared a smile that told Joshua his brother was as aware of these sentinels as he was. He glanced at Judith and saw that she had seen them, too, but she did not smile.

"Is it necessary?" she asked.

Joshua shrugged. "Judas thinks so and I would not quarrel with him over a matter such as this."

Simon Peter, Andrew, the sons of Zebedee, Mattathias and Philip did not share Joshua's lack of concern. They, too, had seen the sentinels—the ones who must be Zealots. In a way, they were offended. They were stout and strong and stayed close to their master. They could defend him without help from anyone, they believed.

Joshua noted his disciples' prickly reaction, but did not smile, for he did not want to offend them, either. He called Simon to his side and said, "Simon, don't worry about the Zealots along the way. God is protecting all of us, but if I had to choose a royal guard, it would be you and the other disciples."

Simon's face, careworn for days, broke into a huge smile. He nodded vigorously and ran back along the path to share Joshua's words with the others.

The city was awake now, and the streets were clogged with pilgrims and merchants, in addition to the normal population.

Once again, Joshua turned his animal towards the Beautiful Gate. As he came close to the rosy-hued walls, he was overcome by a sense of sadness. To his own surprise, tears sprang from his eyes and he looked upon the city with a sense of despair. "Eternal peace is within your grasp," he said. "Will you see it, will you know it, or will you turn away?"

Brother Jacob saw the tears as he walked beside Joshua's mount. He reached up and took Joshua's hand.

"What is it, my brother, why are you sad?"

Joshua looked down at Jacob and gripped his hand tightly, then shook his head.

"I'm not sad, Jacob, only filled with love and the love spills out of me some times."

And then, they were crossing the stone bridge that arched over the usually dry course of the Kidron, passed between the great burnished gates and entered the outer precincts of the Court of Gentiles. A great roar of sound assaulted their ears. That day, as on all major festivals, the porticos of the temple were lined with the stalls of merchants. They provided necessary services, selling birds to those who had traveled from far off and could not bring their own offerings with them. Large animals were sold in the markets outside the Temple precincts.

Within the Court of the Gentiles, still others changed money, for it was not permitted to bring foreign coins, especially those with images of emperors and gods into the sacred parts of the temple. Thus, many who had traveled from far-off lands were obliged to exchange their foreign coins in order to make proper offerings.

But now, at this Festival of Passover, the number of merchants was greater than ever. Carts had been dragged into the courtyard, stalls had been set up randomly, under the porticos and even beyond them. Merchants and money-changers were yelling at the crowd, trying to attract business, offering special rates.

Near the Beautiful Gate, a muscular Judaean merchant of middle years was quarreling with a pilgrim from Galilee. The pilgrim was young, wide-eyed and confused.

"But you told me that the rate was eight to the shekel, and you took ten."

The merchant scowled and pushed him away. "Learn to count your money, boy; you northerners don't know what it's all about."

But the young man was insistent. "I know what I had and I know what you gave me. You cheated me."

The merchant's face turned even darker. "Get out of here, or I'll call the Temple Guards."

"Good," the boy yelled and he started to call them himself. Surprised, the merchant began to yell. "Thief, thief, he stole my money."

The little drama caught Joshua's eye and then his ear and finally his heart. As he stood in the great courtyard, taller than most men, his view taking in all of the noise and the hubbub, he was struck by a powerful sense that time and place were out of joint, that the world was not supposed to be as he now saw it, that God did not want his Temple to be like this. He had traveled to the Temple several times across the years, taken part in the purifying rites, made his sacrifices, and along the way had seen and heard the merchants in the Court of the Gentiles displaying their doves and the moneychangers calling out their rates many times. He had found it garish and irritating, but he understood that the pilgrims could not bring their sheep and other offerings from afar and that foreigners who carried offensive currency had to trade it for the Tyrian coins which were acceptable. But on this day it all seemed profoundly offensive to him. No doubt many of the pilgrims were being cheated—having traveled this far, they had little choice but to agree to the prices that were charged to them. But it was more than that. The world was about to change forever, the Messiah was in their midst, and these people were blindly going about their business as if there was nothing to think about except buying and selling.

"Stop!" he yelled at the merchant who had cheated the young Galilean pilgrim, taking the merchant's arm and spinning him about. "The lad is honest and you cheated him. Give him what you owe him."

For a moment, the merchant was overcome by the power of Joshua's presence, by the vibrant strength of his voice. A prick of conscience sliced through him. But then he looked away, consciously breaking the connection. His greed was stronger than his honor.

"They're trying to take advantage of me!" he called to the other merchants. "Help me against these strangers!"

Most of the merchants ignored him, busy with their own problems. Others frowned. A few left their stalls, aware of their own wrongs, and ready to help the merchant with his.

Anger welled up in Joshua. He threw up his arms and his voice boomed forth. "Is it not written that 'My house shall be called a house of prayer for all nations'?" His voice soared above the crowd and echoed in the porticos.

"But you, you who buy and sell and barter, you would make it a temple to trade and a den of thieves!"

The people nearby were silent, merchants and pilgrims alike, as he stood, angry and proud, righteous and powerful.

"This is the house of God, built with the work and the prayers, the blessings of the nation. Within these walls—even in this court—on this day there is room only for God and godly thoughts.

"Let the sellers of pigeons and the traders of money take themselves outside these walls, into the streets of the city."

He turned to glare at the merchant who had been cheating the youth from Galilee. "Take your cart and go into the street."

The man stared at him, motionless.

"I say, take your cart and drag it out of here."

Still the man did not move, and Joshua, impelled by deep feelings, sprang to the cart, and began to push it towards the gate. The merchant protested, but Simon Peter was there, brushing him aside and helping Joshua, shoving the cart through the vast crowd of pilgrims, hearing many protests, until the cart fairly flew through the gate, bounded down the steps and overturned, sending many pilgrims sprawling.

But Joshua was not finished. He walked rapidly along the stalls. "You," he said, "and you, get these stalls out of here."

The people were astonished by his words and they did not respond. He reached under a counter and pulled out the leg, spilling the contents onto the floor of the courtyard.

"He's right," a pilgrim said. "This is no place for business."

"Yes," said another and another.

They ran to help Joshua as he knocked over the counters and shoved the carts toward the gates. All over the vast concourse of the Court of the Gentiles, even through the huge crowd, the word spread.

"This is the house of God. The merchants must leave."

In a panic, many were striking their stalls and dragging their carts. Goods were spilled onto the floor, pigeons broke loose from their cages. Everywhere the pilgrims were yelling, telling the merchants to leave the House of God.

And striding through the midst of them, his eyes flashing, his voice booming, came Joshua. "Out!" he cried. "Out of the House of God!"

And behind him came his disciples, hurrying the merchants with righteous pleasure, tearing down the stalls and shoving the carts and hurrying the merchants along their way.

The Temple Guards, aroused by the voices and the rumble of the carts came running out into the Court of the Gentiles. But they didn't understand what was happening. All they could see were merchants in every part of the vast courtyard, tearing down their stalls, hurriedly carrying their merchandise out and through the gates.

They stood flatfooted, puzzled, unable to figure out what had happened or why. They saw Joshua, tall and powerful looking, calling in a strong voice that this was the House of God, and of course it was, and so they could find no harm in his words. But as they watched, astonished, the merchants, flowed out of the court and into the city, and the pilgrims within raised their arms high over their heads and cheered.

***

It was strangely quiet inside the Court of the Gentiles. The merchants were gone and with them the cries of the sellers, the bartering tones of the buyers, the sounds of the birds.

Pilgrims poured in, pushing past the departing merchants, and they came upon Joshua, standing in front of the Solomon's porch, with thousands of other pilgrims in a great arc radiating out from where he stood.

For a moment he stood with his eyes closed, the fine, hot Judaean sun warming his face. Then, he opened his eyes, looked at the great crowd assembled and he smiled.

"Today, together, we drove the moneychangers and the merchants out of the Temple. It was wrong for them to be here, for even though we call this the Court of the Gentiles the Temple is a place consecrated to God.

"Many of them took advantage of our pilgrims, cheated them because they had come so far and had not the means to challenge them. As we sent them away we cried aloud that this is the 'House of God.'

"What we said was true enough, but it was not all the truth. We call the Temple a holy place—and it is. We call the Holiest place within the Temple, the Holy of Holies—and it is.

"Yet when we draw aside the great curtain between the holy place and the Holy of Holies itself we find—nothing—that is, no tangible thing, no table, or ark or shrine or altar. For this, we say, is truly the House of God. And since the Lord is all powerful, all wise and yet we cannot see or touch him, we find this 'empty' room.

"There is a meaning and a purpose to this, for though we call the Temple the House of God, it is not the only house of God."

There was a deep, collective intake of breath from the crowd.

"We cannot sanctify this place or any other place, only the Almighty can sanctify it. We cannot designate a place as the House of the Lord and trap our God within it—control him, limit him, fit him within our vision. He is beyond all that we know, all that we see, all that we dream.

"Yea, though we build the Temple of cream-colored stone and gold, and adorn her with precious gems, the Temple is no more a holy place than your own homes, and in times past it has often been less holy."

The people were astonished by his words, but rapt in their attention. They were silent, the air was still, and Joshua's voice, soft but intense, remarkably carried to every corner of the Temple. On the roofs of the porticos, Roman soldiers stood unmoving, caught by the sound and the rhythm of Joshua's words, even though few of them understood the language.

The Temple Guards, too, stood listening, thinking the priests must know the money-changers had abandoned the Temple and might be angry that the guards had not protected the merchants, a portion of whose revenues accrued to the authorities, but the guards, too, were captured by Joshua.

Joshua's voice rose a notch. "There is a holier place than Israel, a holier place than your home or the Temple. And that place is within you. Your body is the Temple, and within that Temple is the spirit of the living God, granted unto you from time immemorial. That life, that spirit, which the Lord has entrusted to each of us, that is the holiest shrine, the place of greatest purity. That is the place that may be defaced, defiled or destroyed—or it may be a place of life, of holiness, of wisdom, and of good."

He smiled and raised his arms. "The prophets spoke time and again of the Kingdom of Heaven. Johannon, the beloved prophet, stood in the waters of the Jordan and proclaimed in a mighty voice that 'the Kingdom of God is at hand.'

"All of the Prophets—Johannon among them, were right. The Kingdom of God is always at hand. If we close our arms and embrace ourselves, we will hold the Temple of that kingdom within our grasp.

"There are those who would tell you that the Kingdom of God is in some future time or in some future place. There are those who would have you believe the Kingdom of God is in the sky—above the clouds or in some other higher place we cannot see.

"In a way, they are right. For the Kingdom of God is the highest place within us, if we will have it so." Then he repeated the words, softly, but still so that all could hear: "If we will have it so.

"We come to Jerusalem to celebrate the Feast of Passover, the feast of liberation. It is a beautiful tradition that we do this—that we share the joy of our Festival with each other in this beautiful place.

"But we need not have traveled a single step from our homes to celebrate our liberation. The dream, the hope, the opportunity for our liberation, travels with us, wherever we may go. Our liberation comes from within, not from without, from God, not from priest or king or earthly ruler of any kind. We spend only a matter of days or weeks here in the Temple, and though many come here, many may never be able to come, and yet they may be among the elect of Israel

"We must repent our sins, purify ourselves, dwell in the heavenly kingdom that God has provided for and within each of us. We are holy shrines, we must be purified. No priest can do it for us; no sacrifice of either man or beast will fully satisfy the Lord or have any meaning in his eyes, if we have not already repented our sins, cleaned our hearts and purified our bodies. This great Temple may stand or fall, but with it or without it, our commission will be the same: to love the Lord with all our hearts, all our souls and all our might, and to love our neighbors as ourselves. For our neighbor, too like us, was created in the image of God, so the light from above, the divinity we seek, is already within us and around us—if we will but recognize it.

"For the Lord is holy and His word is holy and his promise is to each of us. Hark ye to the word of the Lord. Praise God and all his creation. Thank the Almighty for the gifts he has given you and the greatest gift of all, the freedom to be holy, the freedom to dwell in your own Kingdom of Heaven, for this day and for everlasting."

When he had spoken, his words rang through the Court of the Gentiles, and the people listened, greatly moved, but wondering. Was he saying the Temple, the great temple within whose walls they stood, was primarily a symbol? Were the great sacrifices, daily, on the Sabbath and at the great feasts, mere tribal ritual, without meaning if they had not already cleansed their bodies and souls?

Had they yearned for freedom all these years under Roman rule when in fact true freedom was within their grasp?

But even as they wondered, and murmured among themselves, Joshua, surrounded by his disciples, strode away. And the people remained in the Temple, talking among themselves, questioning the meaning of his words, not certain whether to be frightened or inspired.

THE MURDERED MESSIAH

BOOK 5

DEATH AND TRANFIGURATION

1.

FACE TO FACE

Caiaphas was dozing in a soft, upholstered chair in his own bedroom when a servant hesitantly knocked on the door. He rested in this manner every afternoon, alone, with his heavy formal garments removed and only a light gown over his shoulders. His staff, cowed and defensive, pretended that he used those hours for private work, and no one, not even his wife, would have dared to disturb him.

Although Caiaphas had been lounging, eyes closed, half asleep, he was actually very restless. The sounds of pilgrims and merchants filled the streets and penetrated even the heavy drapes that covered the windows. In a few days he would make his expected appearance in the Temple and his very presence would awe the multitude. Unfortunately, one had to put up with these very same crowds in order to enjoy such glorious moments.

But it was not the crowds that irritated Joseph ben Caiaphas. It was the vision of Joshua ben Joseph standing before and below him in the Temple the day before. Until then, Caiaphas had had no clear picture of the man. He had imagined a coarse preacher, perhaps in the mold of of what he had heard about Johannon, the Baptizer. He had expected a curly-headed, hook-nosed, rabble-rouser, not this tall, serene and dominant figure.

As Caiaphas had glared down from his accustomed height, he had felt himself shrink and Joshua grow. He had actually felt that he was looking up, not down, into the eyes of Joshua. Even now, Caiaphas shifted uneasily remembering them. He could not describe their color, but the flash and brilliance, the compelling strength of them was unforgettable.

Caiaphas frowned and, with his eyes closed, swatted at the image with one be-ringed hand, as if it were a fly that could be driven away.

Then came the knock. His eyes opened slowly. He could not believe that anyone had the effrontery to bother him during this private hour. It must be his wife. Well, she would learn not to repeat this action. He rose with jaw clenched and faced the door.

"Enter," he said in imperious tones.

It was Mesha, an ancient graybeard and the oldest member of the High Priest's household.

"Mesha," Caiaphas was too surprised to say anything but his name.

"Apologies, Eminence, but there is someone here to see you—Joshua ben Joseph, of Nazareth."

Caiaphas tried not to show his surprise. His eyes narrowed and he studied Mesha. The old man's face said, I know this is against the rules, Eminence, and every other servant refused to disturb you, but I believe it is important and you will want to see this man.

Caiaphas almost smiled. What wisdom Mesha had, perhaps greater than many of the Sanhedrin. Clearly, his knowledge and his information extended far beyond the walls of the house. Caiaphas wondered how much this ancient fellow really knew and what he understood of the will of the people. It was a frightening thought. Perhaps the people of Jerusalem, the people of Israel, had goals that did not coincide, in fact conflicted, with those of their High Priest. Even now they might be marching towards some great event of which he was totally unaware.

"Tell him I will be down shortly," Caiaphas said. Mesha nodded slowly and closed the door.

***

Joshua waited alone in the vast Entry Hall on the ground floor of the High Priest's palace. He did not know that this room was equivalent to the Court of the Gentiles in the Temple, and that as a devout Jew he was entitled to wait in another room. Had he known, he would only have laughed.

Simon Peter, Judith, Brother Jacob and the others waited outside in the courtyard. They had wanted to come inside with Joshua, but the servants refused and Joshua had indicated he did not mind speaking to the High Priest alone.

In fact, except for an old fellow with a gray beard and a quick grin, not even Joshua would have been admitted. But Mesha—Joshua learned that was his name—had been in the Kidron Valley, visiting an old friend from Jericho, when Joshua had made his entry into the city on the first day of the week. All around him, pilgrims were saying that this handsome, light-haired fellow was the Messiah, and Mesha's heart had instinctively confirmed their judgment. Such a person could not be turned away from the High Priest's palace, not even by the High Priest himself.

Joshua had never been inside a building of any sort that was as ornate as Caiaphas's palace. The floors and walls were polished marble. The ceiling was coffered and the cedar coffers were edged with gold. Great hangings draped the windows and plush furniture lined the walls. Joshua was both affronted and amused. He wondered at whose cost these riches had been assembled and he thought of the good he could do with a fraction of the wealth displayed here.

The High Priest appeared as if by magic. Joshua had merely turned his head and when he looked back, the High Priest was standing there, resplendent in his fine tunic, with a high, gold-edged hat upon his head.

They studied each other in silence. Joshua noted the carved, strong features of Caiaphas, his regal bearing and his flint-cold eyes. Here was a man of great intelligence, accustomed to power. There was arrogance in him that was offensive, yet so much a part of his total being that it was more than a cloak, to be donned or cast aside. There was knowledge here, too, but the knowledge was worldly more than Godly, self-serving rather than generous.

This man hates me, Joshua thought, without surprise, without feeling any corresponding reaction.

Caiaphas's appraisal at close range, confirmed for him his earlier irritation. He saw at once that Joshua had no fear of him, no fear of any man. He recognized the wisdom in his eyes, the grace in his bearing, and the strength of his commitment. Caiaphas was arrogant and pretentious, but no fool. He had a great instinct for the shortcomings in his fellow man, and he was a master at using them to his own advantage, but he sensed no weakness here. That disturbed him, but he was determined to overcome this man, to put him in his place.

Each waited for the other to speak, Joshua from a deep sense of courtesy to the man, his office and his age; Caiaphas, to indicate his superiority.

Joshua smiled, a beautiful guileless smile that startled Caiaphas and nearly disarmed him. "Please be seated," he heard himself say, amazed by his own courteous words and tones.

Joshua shook his head. "On the first full day of the Passover, I will come to the Temple early in the morning, soon after the morning sacrifice. The Court of the Gentiles will be filled with our people—"

Caiaphas felt impelled to cut him off. The bearing, the authority of the man were too much for him. "—And you want me to anoint you as the King of Israel." Caiaphas forced a harsh laugh.

There was a moment of silence, while Joshua continued to look into Caiaphas's eyes, unblinking, and unmoved by the interruption.

"I plan to tell the people what God expects of them, so they will be prepared in their hearts and in their minds. A time of great trial is upon us, and the people need help in readying themselves."

Once again, Caiaphas felt the need to break the mood. His voice dripped with sarcasm.

YOU will tell them what God expects of them?" He paused. "By what authority?"

"I think you know. I don't believe you could be the High Priest of Israel and not know."

"I have heard," Caiaphas said, "that in the Temple this morning, you led the people to believe that the time for Temple sacrifices was over."

That wasn't quite correct, but Joshua said nothing.

Caiaphas's voice rose slightly. "You told them the Temple was a symbol, and that every man was his own Temple and the Kingdom of God was within him."

Still Joshua was silent, and once again his silence was as powerful an affirmation as if a clap of thunder had sounded in the room. Caiaphas was feeling his irritation grow. The interview was not proceeding as he had planned and he had no idea where it was going. He felt the need to overwhelm this Galilean preacher, but he did not know where to begin.

"I will not anoint you as King of Israel," he said with some bitterness. "No matter what you do."

"I have not asked for your anointing," Joshua said mildly. "The choice belongs to God."

"I will not accept you," Caiaphas said, "no matter how you put the matter."

"You misunderstand me," Joshua said. "The question of a king for Israel is not before us. That question, in itself, is of little importance. I am sure you agree that in the larger sense, there can be no ruler but God."

"You are a Zealot," Caiaphas said.

Joshua shook his head slowly, patiently, as if he were talking to a child.

"I have not come here to quarrel with you. I am here in the hope that we share the same vision: the peaceful liberation of Israel and that we, as all Jews, may share in that liberation. I want you to know what my intentions are, so that you may inform the Sanhedrin, if you choose, so that all men of wisdom and influence may share in this great day."

Caiaphas was totally confused. He had been certain Joshua had come to ask him to participate in his coronation and he had been ready to refuse in the most ringing terms. Joshua, it seemed to him, had evaded the issue, but he wasn't even certain of that. What did this man want? Caiaphas was too arrogant to ask a direct question. He did not realize that his right eye was twitching.

"You may continue," he said.

"Israel is not intended to live forever under the rule of another nation. That is not God's plan. Israel must be free to be a Kingdom of Priests and a Holy Nation, to witness to the world. We have been so long under Roman rule that the people have forgotten God's plan for them. It is time to reclaim that plan. It is time to repent our sins, to be cleansed and forgiven, to turn our heads and our hearts toward our chosen place.

"Those who would throw off the shackles of Rome with war and bloodshed are mistaken. That is not God's plan. We must rid ourselves of the Romans, but without war, without weapons."

Caiaphas listened with increasing incredulity, matched with a growing sense of the hypnotic quality of Joshua, the profound and holy assurance in his words, the complete sense of commitment. His envy struggled with his admiration, and both were overcome by Joshua's purity.

"We can no longer pay tribute to the Romans. We cannot pay their customs or their land or head taxes nor any other compensation. We can no longer obey their laws. We cannot feed or house them in our land, we cannot send our ships to do their errands."

"You are preaching insurrection," Caiaphas said, more in awe than in anger.

"Call it what you will. I counsel neither war nor any other form of violence. We will simply refuse to do what they demand—all of us, the entire nation of Israel."

Caiaphas was silent for a moment.

"The Romans will respond with violence," he said, finally, although he had to struggle to find the words. "They will treat this as sedition and they will slaughter the people."

"You misjudge them. The Romans are misguided, but they are not fools. It may be simple to attack one man, but not an entire people. When they see we will not cooperate, but yet we will not fight—when they realize they will have to provide a warder for every man, woman and child, they will realize it is unprofitable to be Israel's jailer. When they learn the whole nation is opposed, that no one will cooperate, they will realize the occupation is fruitless and they will leave."

For the first time Joshua smiled. "And they will leave with our blessings. We will offer them our scripture and our spiritual beliefs. We will generously give our holy word as it has been given to us, and they will have the choice to join in our belief in the one, the only God, the creator of Heaven and Earth."

Caiaphas struggled within himself. As a man of the world, wealthy, wise and experienced, he considered this was a chimera, a dream of a naive Galilean peasant. And yet, there was beauty and grandeur and great spiritual strength to it. Nor could he deny that it was in harmony with God's plan. He, who knew the scriptures as totally as he knew the feel his hand and the sound of his own voice, knew well that the Kingdom of God which Joshua preached was in accordance with the Law and the Prophets. A feeling of sympathy for Joshua struggled with his sense of his own position. Where and who would he be in such a world?

"You are a fool," Caiaphas said quietly, "to believe that you can accomplish such a thing. The people are not ready, the time is not ripe."

"The people are ready," Joshua said. "I have spoken to them in the towns and the cities, in their homes and in the streets. They are sick unto death of war and oppression, of evil and subjugation. They know that God wants more for Israel and demands more of her people. I am telling you what I intend to do and what I know the people will follow me in doing. I am asking you to share in this great mission, to join with me on the Passover and proclaim the liberation of Israel."

Caiaphas moved for the first time. He stepped close to Joshua and stared into his eyes, then turned abruptly and left the room. He had no choice. He was so shaken that he could not have spoken without a break in his voice, without giving way to tears.

2.

EVENING

"He's mad," Annas said, "clearly mad."

"Perhaps." Caiaphas was pensive, nervous and irritable.

"Perhaps? Is there a question in your mind?"

"Annas," Caiaphas said with a sigh, "you were not there, you did not hear him with your own ears."

Annas studied his son-in-law. Ever since they had first heard of this Galilean preacher, many months earlier, Caiaphas had been in a state of agitation. For some reason, he had responded to this new challenge with more energy than Annas had thought him capable of, yet with great annoyance and apparent overreaction. Annas smiled. "Don't tell me he's convinced even you?"

Caiaphas roused himself irritably. "Don't be a fool," he said, and then he was surprised he had spoken thus to his father-in-law. Whatever Caiaphas thought of the old man, he was still rich and powerful. But the words were out, and Annas didn't even raise his eyebrows. In fact, he was even more concerned than before.

"I'm not thinking of myself," Caiaphas said. "I'm worried about the people. This man may be, as you say, 'mad,' but his madness has a spiritual quality to it, and when you combine that with his imposing appearance, resonant voice and air of total assurance, well, it's not surprising to me that the people are swayed by him."

For the first time, Annas was truly frightened. Caiaphas did not realize it, but he had just spoken of Joshua with profound respect. For the moment, at least, his sneering references to the man had disappeared. Annas tapped Caiaphas on the arm, as if to bring him back to himself.

"You can't let it happen," Annas said. "You can't permit him to appear in the Temple and tell the people to stop paying taxes and stop obeying Roman law. There will be a riot, a massacre."

"Perhaps that would be best."

Annas couldn't believe his ears. He was too shocked to speak.

Caiaphas said, "Maybe that's the only way the people will realize how hopeless this is. Maybe then they'll turn on this preacher."

Annas blinked. "They won't have to—the Romans will kill him first," he said.

Caiaphas had regained some of his arrogance and self-importance. The meeting with Joshua had unnerved him and it had taken time for him to regain his balance. Now, the old Caiaphas was reasserting himself.

"That could be a blessing," Caiaphas said. "As I told the Sanhedrin, better one man should die than the whole country be subject to slaughter. Of course, they were too pious to believe me."

"I believe you, but I don't think you can stand idly by and wait for the Romans to take care of this preacher."

"I've had Reuben speak to Pilate already—I let him know we would not stand in the way if the prefect elected to arrest this man."

Once again, Annas was surprised.

Caiaphas waved a hand at him. "Don't tell me I should have informed the Sanhedrin. Events are moving too quickly. If I had to convene that debating society every time action was called for, we'd never accomplish anything."

Annas nodded in grudging agreement. He, too, had dealt with the Sanhedrin across the years of his own service as High Priest. They were a good and honest lot and the most powerful and knowledgeable men in the nation, but they were quick to argue and slow to move.

"What will you do?" Annas asked.

"I've called down Demetrius, the one who tracked him through Judaea and several other men. He'll be teaching in the Temple until the Festival, 'preparing the people,' as he says. We've got to try and force his hand, get him to say something the people will resent, or the Romans won't tolerate."

Annas was incredulous. "Isn't that a weak and prayerful program?"

Caiaphas slammed his hand down on the arm of his chair. "He is surrounded by supporters and loved by a growing number of the people. If we act directly against him, they'll turn on us, and I don't know where that might lead."

Yes, you do, Annas thought, straight to the High Priest's palace, and your neck. But even then, Annas wasn't certain. Surely there was more that Caiaphas could do if he roused himself, if he exercised all the powers of his office. It seemed to him that Caiaphas was stepping aside, as if this drama were to be played out on a basis he dared not interfere with, as if he were only a spectator and the control was in other hands. Was it possible that in his later years, Caiaphas was beginning to believe in divine judgment?

***

That night, as the night before, Judas brought additional leaders to the house of Eliezer, to meet and talk to Joshua. It was important that all be prepared for the great Passover liberation, knowing what to do and how to react, but more important than that was the need to keep their enthusiasm high, and Judas knew that Joshua's very presence was enough to impress almost anyone.

But this evening, Judas had a rude shock: Joshua recounted his meeting with the High Priest. Judas's brow furrowed and the scar line, almost hidden by his mustache turned faintly red. He tried to find the right words to respond to this news, but couldn't find them.

"I can't believe it," he muttered and looked down.

Joshua took him by the shoulders and forced him to look at him.

"What can't you believe, my friend?"

"That you would tell the High Priest precisely what you are planning to do."

"God told me I must give him the opportunity to join us. He is, after all, a Jew, and I have not been told that only some are to be saved, but that all who choose to follow God's words will be saved."

There seemed no answer to what Joshua said. What good would it do, Judas thought, to repeat to Joshua that he, himself, had been aware of the need for secrecy, the need not to reveal their plans until the proper moment? While these thoughts were passing through Judas's mind, Joshua continued to speak to him.

"He is the High Priest, and though it may be that in God's kingdom there will be no need for such an office, it is nevertheless sanctified by all that has gone before."

"It's not the office," Judas said, a bit timidly, "but the man. This is the same Caiaphas who sent legions of spies to watch and trap you."

Joshua smiled. "Legions? I think those have come only from Rome or Satan?"

Judas swallowed the thought that Caiaphas himself was Satan, but Joshua read it in his eyes and laughed.

For the rest of the evening, Judas withdrew. He introduced the leaders as they arrived and was himself introduced to those he had not known before. But his mind was working, rapidly and unhappily. Here they were, gathered for the day of liberation, hundreds of thousands, many of them armed—an overwhelming force by any measure. The opportunity would not come again soon. Was Joshua about to cast it away? He shuddered as he thought of it. He tried to convince himself that Joshua was God-sent and that God's plan would triumph. He argued with himself in thinking about the value of non-violence, the surprise element of it and the strength that it would give the Jews as against those who trusted in weapons. But his belief had dropped a notch and there seemed to be little he could do to ratchet it higher. In some pain, he sighed deeply and bowed his head. Perhaps, tomorrow, in the bright Judaean sunshine, his faith would be renewed.

***

Nicodemus, the son of Nicodemus, known to his friends as Nico, had lived at a high level of excitement for many weeks, going back to the Feast of Purim, when Joshua had told him and his father of his plans for the Passover. Nico had been unable to share his excitement with anyone. Even his father had raised a warning finger when Nico began to discuss the coming Feast.

They had done everything that Joshua had asked, hiring a house and a fine animal so as to be prepared for the entry into Jerusalem.

They had also prepared their home for the feast, leaving only the most trusted of servants on the premises and stocking food and other supplies in case Joshua would have need of the house for any purpose. They had brought in the supplies gradually, across the weeks, so that no one would notice. Of course, on the Ophel, most of the younger priests who lived there, and the common people as well, would have been sympathetic to Joshua and his cause. But there was no reason to take any chances, nor to place others at risk unnecessarily.

Try as he might, however, Nico could barely contain his enthusiasm. His fellow priests noted his nervous actions and teased him about it. He told them he was in love. In fact, it was true, his feelings for Joshua could only be characterized as deep love, spiritual of course, but love nonetheless.

The other priests had seen Nico flirting with Deborah, the youngest daughter of a local scholar and they assumed that she was the object of his affection. That started the teasing in earnest. Nico didn't mind. He had told them nothing, and he was happy to have their attention deflected from his real interests.

Ezra, one of his friends, insisted on having Nico over to his small and shabby home for dinner, where he and several others, continued to probe at Nico.

"Tell us, my boy," Ezra said in a pompous affected tone, "when shall we expect to hear word of your betrothal?"

"Perhaps it has already happened," Nico said, smiling enigmatically.

They stared at him for a moment, then burst into laughter. "Now you're teasing us," Ezra said. Too pleasantly intoxicated to feel anger, he proposed another toast to the "future bridegroom."

The young men drank too much that night, far more than they should have, considering their duties and the code of their position. Ordinarily, Nico would have remonstrated with them, but he was happy to have them following a false trail. Besides, their course would not be called until the Festival itself, when all twenty-four of the national courses of priests would be on duty.

By late evening, they were drowsily in their cups and one by one they staggered off to their own homes, usually tiny rooms in the houses of local people. Finally, only Ezra and Nico were left, and Ezra, planning a final toast, dropped his head on the table, and fell fast asleep.

Nico smiled and looked around the room. An opening, draped only with cloth, led into a tiny bedroom. Within, Nico found a mat for Ezra to rest on. He pulled it from the wall and the edge of it caught on a strip of wood nailed to a panel. The strip pulled away, and the panel popped open and fell to the floor. There was a sharp clatter of steel and ten bright, polished swords, piled behind the panel were released and fell on it.

At first, Nico was too surprised to move. Then he went back into the other room and made certain Ezra was still sleeping. The young man's deep snores reassured him. Nico hurried back into the bedroom, stacked the swords back into their niche, propped the panel and the strip of wood against the wall, hiding it and shoved the mat back to its original position.

He carried the sleeping Ezra into the bedroom and gently put him down on the mat. Then he left the house.

***

"Strange," Nicodemus said, "but then, on reflection, not so strange."

"What do you mean?" Nico asked.

"Ezra ben Avram, is the nephew of Ahaz, whom many say is a Zealot leader in Caesarea."

Nico's eyes lighted with sudden recollection. "And the cousin of Bar Abbas."

"Of course," Nicodemus said. "I had almost forgotten."

"Do you think there is a plan to free Bar Abbas?" Nico asked.

"Perhaps. Bar Abbas is a bear of a man, harsh as he is strong, but no one can deny his patriotism, and the young ones are very angry over his imprisonment."

"True," Nico said, "but Ezra, for all his bluster, is a gentle soul. I can't imagine him with a sword in his hand."

"You're probably right, but he may be storing the weapons for others."

They discussed the matter at great length, without coming to any conclusion. Finally, Nicodemus said, "Ezra is your friend. He knows you won't betray him. Why not simply ask him?"

3.

THE TRAP

Joshua awoke even before first light, weary but anxious to begin the day. There had been many meetings with various leaders the night before, but Judas had not been there. When he returned later he explained to Joshua that if Roman or Herodian spies were watching the house of Eliezer, they would have seen him repeatedly bringing men there. They might follow them and thus learn the names and locations of many Zealot leaders.

"The time for secrecy is almost over," Joshua said.

Judas was silent, believing that Joshua had compromised any hope for total secrecy by speaking to the High Priest. "We owe much to these people," he said. "They are risking their lives on your behalf."

Joshua frowned. "This is not my cause, but God's cause. They do what they do because it is the Lord's command, and they do it for their own immortal souls."

Judas would not argue. "Tonight, I'll be elsewhere. If we are being watched, I'll lead the watchers astray."

Joshua was aware of the growing doubt in Judas's mind, the whispery devil that was warping his spirit, ever so slightly. Joshua wanted to help, but he realized that he had done and said all he could. If Judas went astray now, it would be in willful violation of the word of God, and he would bear the responsibility for it on his own shoulders.

When he was gone, the Sons of Thunder came to Joshua. "Let us follow Judas, Master, just to make sure."

Joshua smiled. "You're not clever enough by half, dear brothers. Judas would sniff you out in a minute, and then he would feel betrayed. Let him go his own way. All is in the hands of the Almighty, blessed be his Holy name."

Now, awakening before dawn, Joshua wondered if he had been right in turning down the brothers. Perhaps, in their simple souls, they understood

Judas better than he did. Still, he must trust his own sense of rightness; he must follow the word as he understood it.

Joshua was pleased with the response of the people, even of the Zealot leaders. A few grumbled, some had frowned, one or two had smiled at what they deemed to be his simplicity, but the overwhelming majority had embraced his views enthusiastically. Much as they yearned to defeat the Romans on the battlefield, they understood the slaughter that would ensue. Joshua's challenge—that it took more courage not to resist, struck them powerfully. They were men of courage and they were capable of self-sacrifice. Few of them had taken up arms for reasons of self-glorification or the pursuit of power. They were God-fearing men and Joshua's pleas were persuasive.

Yet another day loomed ahead. Once again he would teach in the Temple, once again, he would spell out his message clearly and for all to hear. Thus far the Romans had not acted. Thus far, he was able to say what he pleased without being thrown in irons. His faith in God and his calling was total. Still, he was grateful that God had stood by him, and that all was proceeding as planned.

Today he would ask Nico to bring him to Gamaliel. The leader of the Pharisees was noted as a man of great wisdom and goodness of soul. He could be very helpful in bringing those of his party into the fold, and he could help thwart any contrary move of the Sanhedrin.

Joshua recalled his meeting with Caiaphas with sadness. He realized that at one moment, the man had almost broken, that he had come close to acknowledging the moral rightness of what Joshua had told him, but quickly the breach in his armor had been sealed and the goodness so nakedly exposed had been covered up. Was there more he could have done? Joshua thought not. As with Judas, he had given the man the choice. Now he must choose, God's side or his own.

As the day dawned, Joshua slowly and carefully put on his phylacteries and his prayer shawl and prayed, with deep fervor, for Judas and Caiaphas.

***

Gaius had exhausted all his sources, all his subtlety, in trying to divine Pilate's plans for the vast number of legionnaires arrayed in and around the city. He had learned nothing, but he knew that Pilate, evil and devious as ever, must intend some violent action. Surely it would take place during the purifying week before the festival, or during the festival itself, but where and how and on what day, he could not imagine. Finally, he decided it was necessary to confront the governor directly.

Early in the morning, he entered Pilate's ornate office, nervous and breathing quickly, prepared for an angry response. He was surprised to find the prefect and Septimus together, cheerfully discussing some matter, which evidently brought mutual enjoyment.

Gaius hesitated. It was not wise to discuss this matter before the Captain of the Guards.

"Come in, Gaius," Pilate said pleasantly. His face and hair were powdered as usual, but there was no hint of spleen beneath the whitish surface. He seemed genuinely at his ease.

"I don't want to disturb you, Excellency," Gaius said.

"Nonsense," Pilate said, speaking so agreeably that his lisp almost disappeared. "We want to share our plans with you."

Gaius never betrayed his shock, or at least he didn't believe he had, but the governor and the captain exchanged knowing looks.

"Oh come now, Gaius," (this was the second time he had been called by name—usually, Pilate called him by his anonymous title, "Deputy"), "we know by now you've puzzled out the meaning of Vitellius's dispatches and you are aware the city is fairly gorged with our soldiers. Surely you want to know what we have in store for your friends, the Jews?"

"They're not my friends," Gaius said, "although I confess I don't hate them as some do among us."

Septimus laughed. "I don't hate them," he said. "I despise them."

Pilate laughed and then both of them were laughing heartily. Gaius tried to keep his face expressionless. What manner of men could find such sentiments humorous?

"You're not laughing, Deputy."

"Is that an order, Sire?"

Pilate frowned at Gaius's unusually sharp response. Seeing the governor's frown, Gaius's heart sank. Had he lost an opportunity to learn Pilate's plans just because he could not be diplomatic for a little longer?

"I am of course interested," Gaius said quickly, "and I'm flattered that you are willing to share your plans with me."

Pilate smiled again.

"Four days from now, the preacher from Galilee will appear in the Temple to make his proclamation. For weeks, for months, he has craftily kept the people from proclaiming him King of Israel.

"Even in the past two days, when they welcomed him as only a ruler can be welcomed, he was careful not to say that he was their king. But, when he appears in the Temple on the first full day of the Feast, he will, perhaps with a show of reluctance, accept the call of his countrymen and tell them that he is indeed,"—Pilate's voice deepened into a sonorous parody—"the predestined King of Israel, chosen by God and anointed by his holy word."

Pilate's performance brought laughter from Septimus. Pilate bowed in playful acceptance of Septimus's approval. Then, the smile left his lips. "At that moment, guards from the Antonio will approach from all quarters and take him into custody, to be tried as a revolutionary, guilty of sedition, insurrection and high crimes against the state."

Gaius was silent. He could not protest the Governor's interpretation. If and when Joshua was proclaimed King, he would indeed be a public viola-tor of the law. But there was still one thing to be considered. He spoke as calmly as deep emotion would permit.

"Of course, Excellency. If this should occur, there is no question our law would be violated. However, the Temple will be crowded with tens of thousands of people. I fear they will react angrily to the arrest of the Gali-lean, and then there will be violence."

"Precisely," Septimus said, his face alive with a smile so evil that Gaius almost stepped back.

The governor was nodding his head. "You will be present, Gaius Fabri-cius, as the representative of the state. It is well known that you favor the Jews—don't argue with me—I've never been fooled by your protesta-tions. Even the Legate, Vitellius himself, has told me that you are sympa-thetic to them. On that day, you will stand on the balcony of the Fortress Antonio and you will attest that Joshua Ben Joseph, citizen of Israel, was proclaimed King of his people—that when the guards arrested him, peace-ably and without provocation, the populace arose in a riot and attacked the soldiers, jeopardizing their lives."

He walked rapidly to Gaius until his face was only a notch below his deputy's. "You will report that Captain Septimus, responding to the dire jeopardy of his own men, and perhaps their murder, struggled mightily to preserve the peace, but that the wild rage and uncontrolled violence of the people led to their own slaughter in their own temple."

A thin spray of spittle struck Gaius's face, as the governor lisped his angry litany. Gaius blinked but did not move. Pilate was so close that the evil in him was palpable. Gaius wanted to reach out, to take that gray, corded neck and snap it, but he knew that if he had ever been called upon to maintain his presence of mind, now was that time.

He understood now why they were telling him. They knew that he knew, but they would also use that knowledge to entrap him. The people would indeed proclaim their king and when the Roman soldiers arrested him, they would defend their king with their lives. And Gaius Fabricius, their sole friend in the Roman administration, would be forced to report that the Romans had responded as they were required to respond.

"I understand, Excellency," he said quietly

Pilate stepped back and stared at him. Gaius was wise enough to evade his eyes, to look down humbly, while Septimus laughed softly in the background.

"I think you do," Pilate said, his eyes still glaring at Gaius, who dipped his head and asked permission to be excused.

When the door had closed behind him, Pilate turned to Septimus. "This time we have him," he said.

4.

AUTHORITY

In the courtyard of Eliezer's house, the disciples were talking together excitedly when Joshua came out.

"What is it?" he asked.

Wordlessly, Judith pointed to the fig tree that Joshua had noticed the previous day. It had withered. Many of the green leaves were mottled with brown, others had fallen to the ground, and some of the branches had sagged to the earth.

Joshua frowned. "Life and death are not within my power. But there is a lesson here, nonetheless. As I said before, the fig blossomed out of season and it has died, out of season. Beware of those who urge rash and foolhardy actions, who promise what they cannot provide, for they, like the fig, will wither away without fulfilling their promises."

He looked about him at the disciples gathered in the courtyard, their eyes rapt upon him, their love and their trust surrounding and supporting him. He felt a great rush of love for them, not untouched with sadness. For a moment, he had a vision of them together, but he was not there, and he felt their anguish at the loss. They had placed so much of their lives in his hands. What would they do without him?

"You have followed me in hope and in trust and I am grateful. The Lord knows what you have done and how faithful you have been to His mission. I may not always be with you—" They began to protest, but he waved them off. "Still, you must persevere. You must remember the laws of God which have directed us to this mission, you must trust in the wisdom of the prophets who have conveyed God's word, foretelling the very path we are taking.

"Times will come of great tribulation, perhaps even of violence and death. Evil men will test you, great cataclysms will frighten you. False prophets will rise up to lure you from God's way. You must be firm, you must be strong, you must persevere. The Lord God is on your side, the

Law and the Prophets sustain and protect you. Fear not, for the Almighty is always with you, and my love is with you, too."

He embraced them one after another. Some cried and he shed tears with them. They wondered at his words, but did not question him. He was the Messiah—no harm could come to him or to them as long as they were with him. That was what they believed, and while they heard his warning, they were not prepared to acknowledge it, not on this bright, sunny day, with the glorious promise of the Passover close upon them.

***

At first, Nico accepted his father's explanation—Ezra must be hiding arms for the supporters of Bar Abbas. That was dangerous enough and Nico felt the need to talk to his friend, to warn him. But then, he was not so certain. Ezra was hardly the type to be storing weapons for the kind of rough and ruthless men who followed Bar Abbas. There must be some other reason for his actions.

Nico's fears sent him out on the Ophel early, walking the twisting streets, searching for a sign, of what he hardly knew. But he did know the Akkra, the citadel, and the Ophel. This was his home town, familiar to him as the back of his hand. He had friends in every lane, favorite inns in every section. He could hardly walk fifty paces without being haled.

Even when the area was clogged with pilgrims, he knew the patterns of the congestion. He knew what houses were available and which were too small. He knew which men were generous with their homes and which ones closed the doors to outsiders. He knew the look and the smell of every street, and he would immediately spot anything new or strange or suspicious.

But of course he had not been looking for such things, buoyed as he was by his hopes for Joshua and Israel. He had lived in a state of euphoria, noticing little besides the blue sky and his own visions of his homeland, liberated and triumphant, with his beloved friend to lead her.

Now, his attention had focused closer to the earth. He recalled scenes he had ignored a week earlier. For days on end, there had been a procession of carts, large ones, passing through the district. The men driving them were strangers and he was certain they were not traders.

Where had they gone, what had they been carrying?

Then he noticed the house of Shimon, an elderly salt merchant, who usually moved in with his son at the time of the Festival. But the shutters were open and a strange man sat sullenly in the doorway, warily watching the passersby.

On impulse, Nico approached him. The man narrowed his eyes and stood up quickly. Before Nico could speak, the man asked, "What do you want?"

"I'm looking for Shimon."

"He's staying with his son. I've rented his house for the Festival."

Nico forced a smile. "I see," he said. But he knew it was a lie. Shimon might have given his house to a pilgrim, but he would never have rented it.

Nico walked casually down the street with the eyes of the stranger burning into his back. When he had turned a corner, he broke into a run.

***

When Joshua entered the Temple that morning, the merchants were back in their places, but he ignored them. A great throng awaited him and they rushed forward and only the spirited efforts of his disciples kept the crowd from crushing him against the colonnade. They soon quieted down and Joshua spoke to them, repeating briefly his message of the day before, that the Temple was indeed a holy place, but that the Kingdom of God was always at hand, that in fact it was within them and not in some external place.

"Look not in the sky or towards the hills for your salvation, but within yourself. For there, in the peaceful eternity of your immortal soul, you will find the path to the living God.

"Once you understand that repentance, forgiveness, love and salvation are yours for the asking—that the Lord waits with his hands outstretched, ever offering redemption—that no other person has power over you. If you will but follow the way of the Lord, if you will find that inner spiritual strength and give your life to Him, no ruler no matter how powerful, not even Satan himself, will be able to afflict you.

"God does not promise that you will never face danger, that violence will never strike, that evil men will not assault you. What he does promise is that if you repent your sins, accept his word and love only Him, you will have the strength and serenity to endure any hardship and to withstand any enemy. Men fear illness, disease, poverty, violence, cataclysm and death. But you will fear none of these."

At the back of the crowd, there was a sudden sound of angry voices. "Get back," a man was saying. "We were here first."

Then the words were lost as several men pushed through the crowd. The others were angry and would have pushed them back. Simon Peter and Andrew started after them, but Joshua called out, "Wait, I know them."

It was Demetrius, the agent of the High Priest and a group of burly men, all of them Jews, but spoiling for a fight.

"They want us to quarrel with them, they want you to fight with them," Joshua said. "They are anxious to have you show the very violence that we condemn, so that they will have reason to call the Temple Guards."

Demetrius smiled. He was an engaging looking fellow, handsome and well-constructed and relaxed in manner. "Not true, Master. We are merely anxious to hear what you have to say. Your name is famous in the city— famous all over the country—we are justifiably interested in hearing your teaching."

"He's lying," Simon Peter growled. "He's followed us from one end of Judaea to the other, trying to cause trouble."

The crowd was angry now, and some began to push Demetrius towards the rear. "Get back," a man said. "You're no better than the rest of us."

Again, Joshua spoke: "Let him remain. It's better to keep your enemy where you can see him." He smiled and some in the crowd laughed.

Demetrius smiled, too. "How can I be the enemy of a man who promises me forgiveness for my sins and resurrection?"

"That's not my promise. It is the promise of the Lord, your God."

"But you defy the High Priest and all of his party, who do not believe in resurrection."

"I do not defy the High Priest—I bless God." The crowd murmured in approval.

"Tell me," Demetrius said, and it was clear he had prepared this question, "Moses wrote that if a man's brother dies and leaves a wife, but leaves no child, the man must take the wife and raise up children for his brother. There were seven brothers; the first took a wife, and when he died, left no children; and the second took her, and died, leaving no children; and the third likewise; and the seven left no children. Last of all the woman also died. In the resurrection whose wife will she be? For the seven had her as wife."

When he was finished, Demetrius folded his arms and smiled, well-satisfied with himself.

Joshua looked at him for a moment and then laughed aloud. "How long did it take you to conjure up this silly question? We are here assembled to deal with the future of the nation, with the saving of our own souls, and you bring us foolish tales of foolish people.

"But I will answer you, nonetheless. Is this how you imagine resurrection? As flesh and blood men and women, marrying and conceiving and living the same lives we live today? What would God's purpose be in such a thing? Have we not in this life the chance to marry and to have children, to eat and to sleep, to breathe the fresh air and drink clean water, to plow our fields and fish our lakes, to read our scriptures and build our Temple?

"We have but one life on this earth and one is enough. It is not man who is immortal, but mankind. It is not one soul that is immortal, but all the souls of all who have lived and died on this earth. These souls flow together, unseen and unheard, untouchable but not untouched. This is the endless stream from which we come and into which we go, the deep river that flows to us and through us.

"And as the stream of our souls flows through eternity, the dross falls away, the good and the true remain. That which came from God belongs to God, returns to God and with God, lives forever."

The pilgrims were silent, absorbing Joshua's words, nodding their heads and sharing the beauty of his thought and his wisdom. Demetrius could see that he had lost them, and he turned with head down to push his way through the crowd.

But now the attack came from another quarter. Reuben, the deputy to the High Priest had been listening quietly to Joshua, together with several other priests of similar persuasion. He was a man of rough and ordinary appearance, but within the Temple precincts he wore the impressive robes of his office, and the people made way as he, too, approached Joshua.

Joshua was not surprised. Once the High Priest had failed to agree to help his mission, Joshua had known they would not allow him to teach in the Temple, unchallenged. He did not fear them; in fact he welcomed them, for he was certain that he carried God's word and that he would triumph over them. He had not prepared himself in any special way, believing God would give him the words with which to respond.

"I've listened to you carefully, Rabbi," Reuben said. He spoke strongly although he was frightened. The crowd was large and he knew he was not loved, nor was the High Priest, but he would do what he had been told to do.

"I do not find your teaching in scripture."

"You have not looked carefully enough," Joshua responded mildly.

"You make your own interpretations."

"As others before me."

"You dispute the word of the Sanhedrin, of the High Priest, of the sages of Israel."

"I dispute the word of no man. I affirm the word of God."

Reuben was growing angry. "By what authority are you doing these things, and who gave you this authority?"

Joshua answered him: "I will ask you a question, and if you tell me the answer, I will gladly tell you by what authority I do these things. The baptism of Johannon—whence came it? From God or from men?"

Reuben was startled. His mouth opened and then closed. He turned to his fellow priests and they whispered together for a moment.

"If I say from God," Reuben whispered to them, "the Galilean will ask why didn't we believe in him, and if I say from men, the crowd will attack us—they loved Johannon."

The others nodded bleakly, and Reuben turned back to Joshua. "I will not answer," he said.

"Then," said Joshua, "neither will I tell you by what authority I do these things."

5.

NICO AND NAOMI

Ezra ben Avram was groggy. His eyes were clouded with a film that wouldn't blink away and his head ached fiercely.

"Stop shaking me," he said irritably.

"I'm not shaking you, I'm helping you wake up," Nico said.

"I don't want to wake up," said Ezra and he slumped again towards the rumpled mat.

"Oh no," Nico told him and dragged him from the tiny bedroom into the other room. He propped his friend on a bench, found a bucket of water, sighed, and splashed it over Ezra's head.

Ezra yelled and came to his feet, angrily putting out his arms to grab Nico.

"Good," Nico said, pushing him away, "welcome back to the land of the living."

Ezra slumped back on the bench, his long hair dripping water on his face, but his eyes, though still red, were wide open.

"I thought you were my friend," he said petulantly, shivering a little as the water dried on his gown.

"I am your friend and I'm afraid for you."

Suddenly, Ezra ben Avram grew alert. Involuntarily, he glanced toward the bedroom.

"Yes," Nico said, "I've seen them. The panel fell open last night when I put you to bed."

Ezra was on his feet, soggy and pale, his fingers shaking. "What have you done— who have you told?"

"Nothing—no-one. I told you, I'm your friend."

Ezra remained on his feet, confused and troubled.

"Forget it, Nico, forget everything. It's better if you don't know."

Nico took him by the shoulders and set him down forcibly on the bench.

"I know there are caches of arms like this all over the Ophel, perhaps all over Jerusalem. I know the Zealots have been bringing them in for days."

Ezra's jaw dropped open. "How did you know that?" he asked.

Nico hadn't known at all—he had merely guessed and tried his guess on his friend, but he would not tell him that.

"Do you think I am a fool, Ezra, do you think I have no eyes?"

"Perhaps others know, too." Ezra was truly frightened.

"Perhaps, but the question, Ezra, is why is the city filled with weapons before a peaceful Festival, when a leader has come out of the north, Joshua ben Joseph, who preaches not war but non-violence?"

Ezra shook his head. "Judas swore me to silence."

"It's too late, Ezra."

Ezra sighed. "To tell you the truth I took him at his word. He's an old friend of the family and a righteous man. He said it was only a precaution."

"A precaution," Nico said, "that may destroy us all."

***

Judas decided he would go during daylight. In a way it was safer. He might be highly visible, but no one would believe that he, the craftiest of men, would visit anyone close to him during the day.

Actually, he doubted that he was being followed. He had not slept for more than a few minutes at a time in many days, constantly changing his position, slipping from one part of town to another, in and out of the gates.

This past night he had changed his appearance again, shaving off his beard, trimming his curly hair down close to his head and staining his face to a deep hue. He looked like an Armenian trader, or perhaps a Greek. It didn't matter. At least he didn't look like Judas the Galilean.

He had told himself that he wouldn't go at all. The hour was near, either liberation or death would be his portion. He was convinced there was no middle ground. With that in mind, he had avoided all who meant anything to him, so that he would not softened, so that he would not cry for them, so they would not be endangered by his very presence.

Judas's children lived with the family of their mother, far away in Gaulanitis. Probably, they no longer remembered him. Surely, they could feel little affection for a father whom they had hardly seen. Judas had told the family not to speak of him, to spare the children the aching sense of loss if anything happened.

"Pretend I am dead," he had said. "Soon it will probably be true, anyway."

His brothers, Micah and Medad, were Zealots, but he had broken with them over Joshua. They could not, would not accept him as the Messiah, not unless he would clearly claim the throne and call for revolution against the Romans. They did not believe in peaceful change and they had ridiculed Judas for his faith in the Galilean preacher.

"You're a fool, Judas," Micah had said. "Your `Messiah' is too gentle to save Israel, but clever enough to lead you to your death."

"If you survive this game," Medad told him, "come look for us. We'll be in the hills, bashing the Romans as we've always done."

It was useless to quarrel with them. They were descended from generations of rebels, of warrior kings, and they could imagine no other way. Still, the parting was sad and the brothers embraced. They had a sense that, one way or another, their parting was final.

Judas missed them as he walked along the market street in the newer area known as Bezetha. His brothers were older by many years, but strong and fierce battlers. It would be good to have them at his side. But not now. They would only have deepened his doubts. He was torn, as he had been a hundred times, between the peaceful plans of Joshua and his own urge to follow the lead of his brothers and slaughter the Romans. Hardly a day passed without an inner struggle. He could not doubt the strength and wisdom of Joshua. His impact on the people was evident, everywhere he went. He gave love and received it in return. He offered strength and was strengthened in return. Judas never doubted that Joshua's mission was God's mission. He was morally certain that God had chosen Joshua for this mission and that now was the time of its fulfillment. What worried him was whether Joshua truly read his calling aright. He was after all, still a man, and therefore not perfect. He could fall into error as any man might do, anointed or otherwise.

Judas tried to reassure himself. All alternatives were covered. If Joshua proclaimed himself king and decreed peaceful and non-violent resistance, he would follow him, and the people would follow, too. If the Romans responded with violence, well then, he was prepared. Some might die, but the weapons and the warriors were available. Even Joshua would have to agree, king or not. If your people are being slaughtered, you must defend them. Would not the shepherd fight off the wolf?

For the moment he was content with his thoughts, certain he was following the proper course. Then he found he was standing in front of the house of Asher, the gold merchant. It was a large and imposing house, one of the most beautiful in the district, with high walls, a large courtyard and lovely gardens. Asher was known as a Sadducee, in fact, as one of the more conservative members of the group.

Judas stood stock still in the middle of the street. Then he realized that by doing so, he would be drawing attention to himself—and perhaps even to Asher himself. He bowed his head quickly and continued walking. For a few minutes he believed he would simply continue on his way—that he would return to the Ophel, or perhaps to Bethany, but in any case, far away from Bezetha and the house of the gold merchant.

He was beginning to perspire and his eyes grew watery and his vision blurred. He told himself that it was the heat, that he had not eaten well for days. He told himself many things to explain his agitation, but nothing changed his sense of despair. He found that he had to stop, to lean against a building, to gain his strength. But he could not do that without being noticed. Even as he thought these thoughts, an elderly man stepped over to ask how he felt. Judas pushed past the man and hurried away.

He found he was once again heading toward the house of Asher. He almost screamed in despair, but he continued walking, head down. No matter what, he would not stop at the house of the gold merchant. He would keep going in this direction until he found himself far away from this area.

Judas stood in front of the door, helpless to go on. Never had he felt so weak. He could have wept, but still he could not force his feet to move.

The door opened suddenly. Even in the dark, he could make out her face. Her surprise was total and for a moment, she could not move or speak. Judas realized that anything she did might be dangerous, and he hurried to the door, pushed inside and slammed it shut behind him.

For a long moment they stood there, motionless, staring at each other, unable to speak or move. Then, involuntarily, his eyes glanced away, towards the stairway leading to the upstairs.

"They're gone," she said. "All of them."

He groaned inside of himself, not knowing whether to be pleased or distressed.

"How are you?" he asked, stalling for time. He could see that she looked well, even beautiful. He had not seen her for over a year and he had almost forgotten the beauty of her gray eyes and the lustrous sway of her hair. Naomi, the love of his life. Naomi, for fifteen years, his suffering, ever loyal, ever devoted wife.

She stared at him without answering. She was not put off by the swarthy color he had painted his skin, or the shortness of his hair, or even the slimness of his body. She was not put off by anything, but the expression in his eyes, which was one of darkness and desperation. She had known him since childhood, loved him stalwartly and without reason, ever since. She had seen him wounded, desperately wounded, and she had nursed him when he was terribly ill. But she had never seen such suffering in his eyes.

Naomi wanted to raise her arms and reach for him, to hold him to her breast and comfort him. But she had been trained to act far differently, never to show her emotion, never to admit the pain she felt when he left, usually on a mission that might end with his death.

No, she would not reach for him. She would embrace him in her heart, as she had done all these years. She would give him up, without ever having given him up. She would love him as if he were an ordinary man, a farmer or a shopkeeper, who left on his business every day and returned for his supper every night. She would not torment either of them by crying or wailing, or complaining—or reaching out to hold him.

He saw all that in her eyes, and he loved her all the more for it. He knew that the days that lay ahead would be the most difficult in his life and that the risk of his losing his life was greater than ever. He hated himself for coming to the house of Asher the gold merchant, and creating this crisis for both of them.

"You shouldn't have opened the door," he said, trying for a light touch, smiling as he spoke. But his voice came out hoarse, and then it cracked. He was embarrassed.

And then he couldn't take it any longer. He reached for her, roughly pulled her to him, and crushed her against his chest, while tears streamed from his eyes. "I missed you," he said, thinking he spoke only to himself, but she heard him.

"I love you," he said, and he didn't care who heard him.

She felt the tremor in his body and his tears fell and merged with her own. She whispered back her love, and her lips moved, but no sound came out. Still, the breath of her words against his cheek told him all he wanted to hear.

She gathered herself and spoke to him, but he did not respond and this time she realized he hadn't heard. She took a deep breath and spoke again.

"Take me upstairs," she said.

He pulled away, shaking his head violently. This was something he couldn't bear. He had been afraid to come here, afraid to see her, for fear that the meeting would soften him, make it impossible for him to do that which he knew must be done. Even seeing her had sapped his strength, hiding her had weakened his resolution. To love her might destroy him.

Once again he shook his head, but she stepped closer and kissed him firmly on the lips. Judas moaned aloud and then swept her off her feet.

6.

GAMALIEL

Joshua remained in the Courtyard of the Gentiles teaching throughout the day. He ignored the merchants and money-changers, most of whom were those he had previously driven away, and who had become subdued as soon as he appeared. But he had made his point before, and now he was engaged in much more important work. The pilgrims came and went, hundreds replacing hundreds, thousands replacing thousands. Most were so taken with him they could have remained there for the entire day, but they realized that wasn't fair; they should share Joshua with their friends and neighbors.

Joshua noted the ebb and flow of the crowds, seeing the pilgrims from the outer boundaries of the crowd work their way to the forefront, then move away so that others could take their place. He himself was not tired. He could have preached all day without stopping.

Judith, however, was watching him carefully. From time to time, she brought him water to drink and he accepted it gratefully. Later, as the sun arched overhead, she maneuvered him under the portico and into the shade. He smiled to himself, noting her care for him. In fact, he loved the blazing sun and would have preferred to remain in it, but he didn't want to worry his sister unnecessarily.

Simon and Andrew, Johannon and Little Jacob—the sons of thunder— patrolled the edges of the crowd, watching for "troublemakers." Demetrius and his friends were gone, but they could not know when others of similar persuasion might take their place. Reuben, too, had slipped away, humiliated by his exchange with Joshua. Still, the city was large and the crowds enormous and growing with every additional day. They were outsiders, strangers from Galilee, and they couldn't tell until someone moved or spoke whether he was a friend or an enemy. Furthermore, they understood that Joshua would not want them to discourage a true pilgrim who had an honest question.

But few of the pilgrims asked questions. They were drawn by Joshua's imposing appearance and powerful voice. Then they were captured by the intensity of his preaching and the beauty of his words. This was not a man to debate, but someone to listen to. And listen they did, drinking in his words as if it were the very stuff of life.

Judith watched the faces of the pilgrims with fascination. Their eyes were fixed on Joshua and never left him. She had seen people listening to a fine speaker before, captured by his words, but even then, at times they would look away, smile at their neighbors, share their pleasure with a friend or stranger. But that was not the case with Joshua. Each listener seemed wrapped in a world of his own, a world that contained only Joshua and himself. The contact was immediate and powerful. The listener drew sustenance from Joshua, but Joshua was also strengthened by the response from the listener. Judith blushed. She realized guiltily that she was observing the crowd rather than listening to her brother. She turned her attention to him and listened as closely as any pilgrim.

***

Gamaliel had spent the day in deep meditation. He was not an imposing man. His stature was slight, his features undistinguished, his head balding and his beard thin. Only his voice was unusual, deep and resonant. It made him seem a head taller than he was.

But Gamaliel's stature was not measured by his slight frame or his powerful voice. Nor, in the long run, did it come from his heritage, descended as he was from the blessed Hillel. No, Gamaliel was a man revered for his learning, admired for his wisdom and loved for his goodness. The Pharisees were not a large party and surely not powerful in worldly terms. Few of them were wealthy and few were members of the priestly class. Some were merchants, some were farmers, many were lawyers and scribes. Their status came from their learning and their devout life.

The Sadducees avowed their belief that all of life must be sanctified, that there was no part of human existence that did not belong to God, but often their observance was perfunctory. For the Pharisees, every aspect of life was sacred and every action, every word had spiritual significance. At times this led them to excess, to investing even the most trivial actions with importance. And among them were some, a minority, for whom the show of piety was more important than reality. But then, there had always been hypocrites among every group, and there were probably fewer among the

Pharisees than any others. It was for that reason that the ordinary people looked up to them, for knowledge, for learning, for leadership.

None was more respected than Gamaliel. Like his predecessor, Hillel, he insisted on following a trade, even though he was a noted scholar. Hillel had been a woodcutter. Gamaliel was a tailor. His hands were somewhat gnarled, and the joints enlarged from heavy usage, but his fingers were still quick, and when he spoke his hands moved rapidly, as if he were sewing together his ideas just as he sewed together a cloak.

Gamaliel's knowledge was formidable, his memory prodigious. Even Caiaphas was careful what he said before him, for Gamaliel would not only understand—he would surely remember. But for all his wisdom, he remained humble. Gamaliel was more interested in knowledge than prestige, more devoted to ethics than precedence. He was often the first to note and to advance a young man with bright ideas, even one who disagreed with him. Furthermore, he had done something that was uncommon in his time. He had insisted that his three daughters be as well-educated as his three sons.

On this day, Gamaliel had waited in his house, a simple structure of modest proportions in Bezetha. He had not gone to his shop as was his usual custom, but instead had waited at home. When the knock came at the door, a servant hurried to answer, but Gamaliel waved him off, smiling. He was still smiling when he opened the door. "I have been waiting," he said.

Joshua came into the house out of the brilliant sunlight and into the shadowed room. Gamaliel had never seen him before, nor had Joshua seen Gamaliel, but the older man spontaneously held out his arms and Joshua welcomed the embrace.

They sat in the tiny garden of Gamaliel's house, a small square area paved with un-mortared stones, with a few flowers in pots and a single lemon tree offering sparse shade. Fortunately, the sun had passed the meridian and the entire area was in shadow. Because the garden was so small, it was in the sun for only a few hours each day, and although there was no breeze, the air was mild.

They sat beside each other on a stone bench, half turned toward each other.

"I did not expect a handsome Messiah," Gamaliel said, smiling.

"Did you expect the Messiah at all?" Joshua asked.

From anyone else the question might have seemed rude, but Joshua's voice was gentle and his eyes were so intense it was obvious the question was sincerely asked.

"Yes," Gamaliel said, "but not quite yet."

Joshua was silent. He did not truly require Gamaliel's approval; he would proceed as he thought best no matter what the elder thought. Still, it would be better to have Gamaliel with him than against him; better for the people, better for everyone.

"Clearly the Messiah does not need nor ask my acceptance of him," Gamaliel said, reading Joshua well, "and yet you are here."

"I have taught my disciples in every town that God chooses the Messiah, but also that the Messiah must choose God. I have also taught them that God has chosen the Jews, but also that the Jews have chosen God. That, as you know, is what distinguishes us from the heathen."

"There are some who report that you do not believe that salvation may be earned by sacrifices in the Temple."

Joshua smiled; he had been waiting for Gamaliel to raise this matter. "I quote Isaiah—"

Gamaliel gently, but firmly cut him off: "'—I do not delight in the blood of bulls, or of lambs, or of goats.'" Gamaliel smiled as he continued, "'I cannot endure iniquity and solemn assembly. Your new moons and your appointed feasts my soul hates.' But is this all the prophet teaches us?"

Joshua almost blushed, but he was not surprised that this man knew scripture at least as well as he did. He nodded. "I believe the prophet's true message lies further on, as you well know," and in humble tones he quoted, "'Wash yourselves, make yourselves clean—remove the evil of your doing from before my eyes—learn to do good—seek justice. Correct oppression— defend the fatherless, plead for the widow.' Is that not the teaching? We must cleanse and purify our hearts before we come to the Temple and perform the rituals."

Now it was Gamaliel's turn to nod. "Yes, that is it—precisely. Our sacrifices in the Temple are meaningless—almost an abomination—if we walk in the sacred precincts and pretend to participate in the offering when our hearts are impure."

Joshua leaned closer. "I have seen and spoken to people throughout the land, and those who follow me have done the same. The people of Israel are strong in their faith, fervent in their love of God. Those who would tell you otherwise, have not gone out among the people."

"That's good to hear," Gamaliel said. "The Roman occupation has been harsh and if the people have not fallen away, it is to their credit."

"Like all people in all times, they often doubt, but in the end they return to God. Only their faith has sustained them in their time of hardship."

"Only their hope in God's redemption has kept them going—their belief that the Messiah would soon relieve their suffering."

Joshua stared at Gamaliel for a moment. "In that they are mistaken. Suffering is part of the human burden. Pain cannot be avoided. Disappointment and doubt are natural conditions, leavened, of course, with love and companionship, learning and trust. But he who seeks only joy, only happiness, does not understand God. He is, in fact, a fool."

Gamaliel's eyes quickened. "Can the people bear to hear this?"

"In freedom, yes—in slavery, no. But slavery is not external, it is internal. If a man is free in his heart, he is free in the only way that matters. He can endure anything because he knows that the outside world cannot damage his soul, his very being, made in the image of God."

Gamaliel frowned. "I can't believe you would tell the people to bend the knee to the Romans?"

"Never," Joshua said. "But I will tell them to turn the other cheek."

Gamaliel waited. He did not want to lead this man—to tell him his own thoughts or impose his own ideas. He was old and wise and he knew when to listen.

Joshua was silent, himself, gathering his thoughts. He wanted his ideas to be clearly understood. "On the Passover, I will tell the people they can no longer obey Roman law, nor pay Roman taxes, nor work for Roman masters. I will tell them that such slavery is not God's will. But I will also tell them that he does not want them to wage war for their freedom. God wants them to oppose Roman rule, but without violence."

Gamaliel listened and waited. He was aware of Joshua's teachings and he knew that Joshua was being courteous in repeating them. But when Joshua, too, was silent, he responded.

"Are the people ready for this?"

"If not now, when?"

"That is always the question isn't it? Hillel was right. God's love, God's freedom is always available to man, if he will but take it."

Joshua abruptly stood up. He had heard enough to know that Gamaliel, gentle, wise Gamaliel did not, would not oppose him.

"The people," he said, "expect the Messiah to be a king."

"Are they in error?" Gamaliel asked.

"Scripture speaks of the anointed of God in royal terms, as a descendant of kings and as one who sits on a royal throne. Yet the meaning is more symbolic than literal. We must not be carried away by the image, and therefore miss reality."

Gamaliel studied Joshua for a moment, stroking his sparse beard. "To the simple as well as the wise, the symbols are important."

Joshua, pacing the tiny courtyard, turned suddenly and looked at Gamaliel. "Have the people done well with their so-called 'kings?'"

Gamaliel said, "Samuel tried to warn them: 'He will take your sons... to be his horsemen...he will appoint commanders...and some to plow his ground...and to make his chariots. He will take your daughters to be perfumers and cooks and bakers. He will take the best of your fields and vineyards and olive orchards and give it to his officers and to his servants. He will take your menservants and maidservants, and the best of your cattle, and your asses...And in that day you will cry out because of your king, whom you have chosen for yourselves; but the Lord will not answer you in that day.'

"And still," Gamaliel concluded, "the people have not learned."

"They must learn," Joshua said. "For to believe in kings is to believe in death. To believe in kings is to deny God. For, no matter what a man says, his loyalty will be divided between his king and his God. And there cannot be such division, without the death of the soul, and therefore, of the man."

"The Messiah," Gamaliel said, "isn't the Messiah different?"

"There is no ruler but God," Joshua said.

"The Messiah rules under God."

"God rules. Men including the Messiah, do God's will."

"You are afraid to be king."

Joshua's eyes flashed. "I fear only God," he said. Then he paused, and when he spoke again his voice was softer. "In truth, I fear one other thing. I fear being worshipped as God, for that would be the greatest blasphemy of all."

Gamaliel sprang to his feet and embraced Joshua. Tears, unexpected tears, sprang to his eyes. "Israel need not fear you," he said. "There can be no question that the Lord is on your side."

After a moment, he released Joshua and held him at arm's length, searching his eyes. "I pray that the people will understand you, as well as you understand the word of the Almighty."

7.

WEAPONS

Nico tried to hold back a rising feeling of panic. He wondered if he could believe the plain evidence of his senses. There was no doubt that he had seen the swords in Ezra's room and that Ezra had admitted he was hiding them for the Zealots. Further, he had seen the surly stranger at the house of Shimon and he recalled quite vividly the unusual number of carts he had seen in the lower city and on the Ophel. Still, it was possible that he misread what he had seen. Shimon could have rented his house to a stranger, and the carts might have carried merchandise for the crowds expected for this Passover.

But he couldn't get around the swords in Ezra's room. Of course, he could tell himself that these were being stored for a handful of hard-bitten Zealots, not men known to Judas, but others who had refused to go along. They could be terrorists, planning some brief uprising, or perhaps even waiting for the end of the Festival to attempt some action. In other words, they might be isolated, stubborn holdouts.

Nico wanted to believe that. He wanted to believe that the day of liberation would be as Joshua had planned it, a day of joy and dedication, but no violence.

He realized what he must do. He must tell Judas about the cache of arms and Judas would see that the men were stopped or controlled in some way. He began to smile to himself. Joshua was the Messiah, the Lord's anointed. No harm could come to him. Nothing could interfere with the glorious event.

Then, walking along the street of the cheese-makers, he saw Judas. At first, he did not recognize him. The man had cut his hair close to his head and darkened his skin and his beard was different. But there was something in his walk, purposeful, athletic and powerful, that he had not learned to hide.

There was something else about him, something Nico had not seen before. Something so unusual, that Nico had never seen it before. Judas looked happy.

Nico could not understand why that changed everything for him, but it did. His sense of serenity disappeared in the presence of Judas's almost smiling face. He was plunged suddenly into a sense of fear and foreboding, even of anger. Nico was shocked by his own feelings. Why should a happy-looking Judas derange him so?

He stepped into the street and grabbed his arm.

Judas's hand instinctively went for the short dagger hidden in the folds of his tunic. Then he recognized Nico and smiled.

"It's you," he said, realizing at once that his careful disguise was of no use with anyone who knew him. At the same time he saw the strained look on Nico's face and immediately he was alerted to danger. Instinct took over. "Not here," he said. "The house of Amos."

Judas held on to Nico's arm so tightly that Nico pulled away. Judas tried to smile to reassure him, but this time the smile did not come so easily. He felt hostility from Nico, powerful aversion or anger. He was too experienced with men not to note it and to realize it was dangerous to him. Thoughts of Naomi, lovely, caring Naomi, were entirely forgotten.

Amos opened the door into his house himself, seeing the anger on Nico's face and the concern on Judas's. Once inside, Judas stationed himself between Nico and the door. When he spoke, his mouth smiled, but his eyes did not.

"What is it?" he asked.

Nico had planned to tell him about the weapons in Ezra's house and hear Judas's plan to resolve the problem. But now, his approach was different—his feelings were different. He decided to deal with Judas just as he had with Ezra.

"Zealots have been bringing large quantities of weapons into the city. They are stored all over the Ophel and in the streets below."

Judas smiled smoothly. "Ridiculous," he said.

"There's no use lying to me, Judas. I've been to the house of Ezra and seen them, myself."

Still, Judas remained calm. "Seen what?"

"A dozen swords, hidden behind a panel."

Judas laughed. "A dozen swords? Do you think that's enough to start a revolution?" He glanced quickly at Amos, who also forced a laugh.

"Don't worry" Judas said. "I'll find out who stored the weapons and take care of the situation."

Nico stared at him. These were the words he had hoped to hear. But not any longer. He simply did not, could not, believe Judas.

"There are other weapons—some stored in the house of Shimon." He caught a flicker of a response in the eyes of Amos, but Judas showed nothing. "And that's only the beginning. Carts have been bringing weapons into the city for days."

Judas sighed deeply. "I like you, Nico, and I know that Joshua loves you."

"What has that to do with anything, Judas. Those arms must be removed from the city."

"Impossible," Judas said. "The Romans would be certain to notice large numbers of wagons leaving the city instead of entering it, unless they were empty."

Nico heard Judas's words and knew they were correct. Still, he had the sense that words were meaningless in this affair

"Then I have no choice except to tell Joshua."

"I knew you would reach that conclusion, but do you think it's wise? The knowledge would be certain to distress him."

Despite the tension in the room, Nico laughed. He sensed that his situation was a delicate one, but he was a brave man and no one was more devoted than he to the cause of Joshua.

"You should have thought of that before you brought the weapons into the city."

"I did," Judas said, wondering why he was bothering to explain himself. "But I couldn't take the chance that the Romans won't understand that Joshua's revolution is non-violent, and that they might murder thousands of defenseless people."

Nico's sense of despair was overwhelming. "You don't believe," he said, and the words came out twisted and strained and his face was creased with pain.

Judas was now growing angry. "I do believe," he said, "I believe in Almighty God and his overwhelming power. I believe that Joshua was sent by God, but I'm not certain that Joshua understands God's commission."

Angered, Nico took a step towards him. "You fool," he said. "You think you are wiser than God's anointed."

Judas saw Nico's great anger, but was not intimidated. He too, stepped forward.

Amos stepped in. "Wait a minute," he said. "It's useless for friends to quarrel."

"You're right," Judas said. "We'll have to silence him." His hand went to his tunic, to the short dagger hidden within. Nico and Amos gaped at him.

"Have you gone mad?" Amos asked. "This man is one of us."

"This man," Judas said, "is Israel's greatest enemy. If left alone, he will tell Joshua about the weapons. And then, well, I can't predict what Joshua will do, but I don't believe he'll go through with his plans. He might even want us to turn the weapons over to the Romans to show our good faith. They'll have us then, we'll have no way to protect ourselves if his plan fails."

Nico and Amos continued to stare at him. Nico's eye strayed to the door. He had no weapon, and he wondered if he could reach the door without being caught. He was perspiring now, looking back at the knife in Judas's hand, then into his eyes, cold and implacable, a man resolved on killing.

Judas was watching Amos, more concerned about the Zealot leader than the priest. The priest he could take care of.

"You must understand, Amos," Judas said. "We all want to save the nation and we've come too far to change our plans now. For all we know, even Joshua may decide that the Messiah's role is as a warrior king—even he may wish we had weapons. Surely he loves us all, doesn't want us to die."

"Let's ask him," Nico said. He looked to Amos. "It's the least we can do."

Judas shook his head fiercely. "We can't take the chance. Everything is prepared now—everything is moving perfectly. We can't let Nico talk to Joshua."

He pulled his dagger and walked firmly toward Nico.

"No," Amos said. "I can't be party to this."

Judas shoved him aside. "I'll do it," he said. But Amos pulled him away.

Nico broke for the door. Judas slashed at him, but missed, and then Nico ran towards the door again. Judas ran after him, but Nico was quicker. In desperation, Judas left his feet and threw his body at Nico.

Even as Nico's hand stretched toward the latch, Judas's hurtling body struck him from behind and knocked him to the ground. They struggled fiercely, turning over and over. But Judas was more powerful and he still held the dagger. Now he held Nico below him, twisting and squirming, one hand on Judas's wrist, trying to force the weapon away. His strength was failing.

Then Amos was on the floor next to them, his hand holding Judas's arm, pulling it back.

Judas's eyes never left Nico's face. "Let go," he whispered huskily. "I'll do it now."

Amos's face was next to Judas's. "No, Judas, it's against God's law to kill this innocent man. We'll tie him up, keep him here until after the Festival. I'll help you, Judas. But if you kill him, you'll have to kill me."

Judas's eyes flickered. He sensed that Amos was depending on him to change his mind, that's Amos's grip had loosened and that he could easily kill them both. But then the image of Naomi came into his mind, and his own grip eased.

"All right," he said. "We'll spare him."

8.

MISSING

By the time the sun was setting and Joshua was returning to the house of Eliezer, the valley of the Kidron was filled with tents as far as the eye could see. Somehow the Jews, with their sense of order, had laid out streets and ways, circling in ever large circles from the lowest point of the valley. As Joshua had seen before, the valley looked like a vast flower garden and in the breeze, the tents rippled like blossoms tossed by the wind.

To Joshua it was a good omen. Israel was neither dead nor stagnant, but rather she was a fertile garden in which the Lord's word was well planted. Along the way, the pilgrims, as usual greeted him with hosannas and blessings. They came out of their tents, expecting him, yearning to see him pass, reaching out to touch the now familiar colt or, even better, his garments, or best of all, his hands.

Joshua smiled continually all along the way, rocking easily on the back of the colt, which now had learned the path to the house of Eliezer and trod it quickly, seeking the meal of oats and hay that awaited it in the courtyard.

Joshua was pleasantly tired. Judith had been right; the sun was too hot to spend the entire day with an uncovered head, and it was a good thing that she had persuaded him to preach under the portico instead of in the blazing sun.

He was pleased, very pleased, by his meeting with Gamaliel. The man had lived up to his reputation as a sage and had proved to be a loving human being in the bargain. Joshua was not certain that Gamaliel accepted him as the Messiah, but he surely would not oppose him. In fact, Joshua believed that Gamaliel would stand up for Joshua's rights to express himself and share his message in any group, especially in the Sanhedrin. Joshua said a silent prayer of thanks for the tzadikim and sages that God had sent to earth.

Once again, he spent the evening talking to Zealot leaders and pilgrims seeking a meeting. Judas was surly and withdrawn, saying what was necessary, but showing little enthusiasm. Joshua watched him and worried. He had always known that Judas was a man who might thwart him, a man of great strength and well-loved among the Zealots. A man who could turn prayerful penitents into raging warriors with a word.

Joshua had felt his own strength feeding the Zealot leaders and felt their strength add to his own. But he had seen that despite his impact on these men, sooner or later they looked to Judas for approval. Thinking of it made Joshua feel sad. These were good men, moral men, men strong for the Lord, and yet they couldn't break away from their earthly dependence on their earthly strength. They loved God and trusted Joshua, but they were earthly men and they knew how their own right arms had saved and protected them.

This night two men, cousins from the south, sat before Joshua, listening to his teaching, obviously captured by his words. They hardly looked towards Judas at all, but Joshua felt the need to use their presence.

He leaned forward and placed a hand on each of their shoulders. "I know you are brave men," he said, "very brave, and you have learned to trust the strength of your arms in protecting yourselves and your families. For men like you it is difficult to give up this reliance on what you know, on what you see and what you can touch, to trust completely in the goodness and strength of God. Don't deny it; it's difficult to set aside your swords and trust in the word. But that is what you must do."

"We trust you, Rabboni," one of them said, "and we believe in your cause."

"I know you do," Joshua said smiling. "But when the hour of your test comes, when a Roman soldier approaches sword in hand, will your own hand itch for a weapon? Will you be able to trust God then, when your very life is at stake?"

They were silent, waiting, listening and thinking.

"It takes great courage to be a soldier—to take up your weapons and fight for your life. It takes even more courage to withstand your enemy without a weapon. To face him without fear and refuse to do what he demands, knowing that God's demands are greater, and that it is God alone who will protect you."

They smiled together, with one smile that made them seem like brothers. "We can do it," they said simultaneously, then laughed because they had spoken in unison.

"With you to lead us," Judas said, his eyes fierce. He knew that Joshua was speaking more to him than the cousins, and he was angered because in his heart he knew that Joshua was right to speak to him in these terms.

"With God to lead us," Joshua amended with a smile, gazing steadily at Judas until he flushed and looked away.

The evening wore on, as many pilgrims came to the house to see Joshua, and he would not turn them away, even though his disciples warned him that he would be too tired for the great work ahead. But there was something that troubled him.

"Have you seen Nico?" he asked. His disciples shook their heads. Joshua's eyes rested on Judas.

"I saw him earlier in the city," Judas said truthfully, "but not since."

There was something there, but Joshua could not divine what it was. He was troubled. He and Nico and old Nicodemus had worked out plans for the Festival, and those plans were very important to his mission. He wanted to speak to Nico and make certain that all was going well. He could not understand why Nico was not present, but he knew there must be an excellent reason. Nico was as trustworthy as any of his Galilean disciples, and very likely cleverer by half.

The evening wore on and still Nico did not appear. Joshua had decided to ask Judas to find him, but when he looked around the room, he saw that Judas was not there. He asked for him, and the disciples told him that Judas had gone out on some private errand.

"What is it, Master?" Simon Peter asked. He had watched Joshua all evening and had noticed that he was concerned.

"Nico promised to be here tonight, and Nico is always as good as his word. Go to the house of his father, Nicodemus, and ask him where we may find his son."

***

Simon found Nicodemus in a state of agitation.

"Have you seen my son?" asked Nicodemus. "Is he at the house of Eliezer?"

Simon shook his rough, shaggy head. "No, Joshua sent me to you to ask where he is."

Nicodemus's pale gray eyes flickered for a moment. "He must be with friends. I know that he stayed with Ezra yesterday—perhaps he's still there. Simon, my leg is still bothering me. Will you please go look for him at the house of Ezra?"

"Gladly," Simon Peter said, and set off through the streets of the city at a rapid pace. Simon was troubled. He had often felt jealous of Nico because it was so obvious that Joshua loved him, but he knew that was an unworthy feeling. In fact, he had always found Nico to be direct and honest, friendly and warm and, despite his jealousy, Simon couldn't help liking him.

Still, he felt no deep concern until he reached Ezra's lodging.

"Yes," Ezra said, standing in the doorway, blocking Simon from entering.. "I saw him earlier today, just for a few minutes, but I haven't seen him since. Is anything wrong?"

"Probably not," Simon Peter said. "Both Joshua and his father are anxious to see him. Please tell him that."

Ezra promised. For a moment, he felt the urge to tell Simon about Nico and the swords behind the wall. But it was an irrational urge and would certainly cause him trouble. He said nothing.

***

The pilgrims had left and most of the disciples had gone to sleep, even Simon Peter. Judith and Brother Jacob still lingered. It was not uncommon for them to be the last to leave Joshua, but now, as the day of liberation edged closer, they felt a special need to spend as much time with him as possible.

He smiled at them. "You're right," he said. "I need you more than ever."

He turned then and walked out into the courtyard and they followed him. It was a balmy, Mediterranean night, with a faint breeze and a sky that would have been inky black except for the canopy of blazing stars. Even the stars paled beside the huge, luminous moon that hung over the city. There were no sounds in the night. Even the wind was so gentle that the leaves moved without sound. Joshua stood next to the withered fig tree and, for a moment, pondered the fate of false prophets.

"Close," he said to his brother and sister. "The day is very close. I need you beside me, as I have never needed you before."

They listened in silence, feeling the gentle wash of his words as they passed over them, yielding themselves to him in love and returning that love with all their hearts.

He stepped close to them, held out his arms and embraced them. "The great adventure is about to begin. All before has been mere wordplay. Now the time for action approaches. I know what the Lord has sent me to do and I am prepared to do it."

He released them from his embrace, reluctantly, for he thrived on the love that they gave him. But he knew he must not depend on such feelings.

502

He paused for a moment, gathered himself and spoke again. "What I do not and cannot know is what the Lord will do."

They were surprised. Joshua had repeatedly told them that the work was God's, not his, but they had come to identify the two, to blend Joshua and God, so that they often saw no difference.

"I am not God," Joshua said gently. "That is the mistake that men make. When all goes well for them, when they feel the strongest, they believe their fate is in their own hands and they forget God. Then, when disappointment, failure, illness come, they are surprised. They find they are not in control of their own lives and they remember God. I understand those feelings, because sometimes—not very often, but sometimes—I have made the same mistake. That is why I remind myself that this is God's kingdom. God's world, time and again, not only every day, but many times a day.

"I know what I must do and I know there is no turning back. I have no fear of the outcome. It is in God's hands and I am serene on that count. But I worry for you and for the others who have followed me. I worry especially for Simon and Andrew, for Mattathias and Philip, Nathan and Rebecca, Johannon and Little Jacob. They are good and loyal and loving and they are committed to doing God's work. But they cannot separate me from the work, and I don't know whether their strength will survive me."

That was too much for Judith. She had followed him for the most part quietly, even though she had often feared for his welfare. She had kept her chronicle of his acts and his sayings with painstaking care, working at it night after night, searching her excellent memory to be certain she was recording his truth and not some version of her own. She had spoken to her mother, her brothers, the disciples, others who knew Joshua, confirming or correcting her impressions of Joshua and the events in his life. She loved no man but her brother, and in fact there was no room in her life for any other love. She could not bear to hear him talk like this. She raised a hand and put her fingers to his lips.

"You will survive us all," she said.

"Yes," Brother Jacob said, as tears gathered in his eyes, "that is as it is written."

Joshua shook his head. "The future is written only in the mind of God and never by the hand of man."

He saw they were troubled. "No," he said, "it cannot be this way. I need your strength, God needs your strength. I believe in His eternal promises, but I do not expect to walk this earth forever."

Again they began to protest and this time he brought his hands down firmly on their shoulders. "Listen," he said, "don't quarrel with me, but listen. No matter what comes, no matter what surprise the opening hand of God may reveal, you must be strong, you must persevere. If the others falter, you must urge them on, if they fall, you must lift them up. God will be with you and he will protect you. I will be with you, too, in love and in sprit for all time. Never doubt that. Know that my love will accompany you always."

9.

CAESAR

The day dawned bright and hot, as the clear night before had promised. Joshua leaped from his bed, fully refreshed by his sleep and strengthened by his talk with his brother and sister. They understood him better than anyone else and he knew he could rely on them.

When Joshua entered the Courtyard of the Gentiles, a cheer went up and Joshua's disciples struggled mightily to keep them from overwhelming him. One man brought a box for him to stand on, but Joshua would not use it. Still, he was tall enough to look over most of the crowd. How colorful they were, dressed in bright fine clothes, with dozens of nations represented. Once again he was struck by the analogy to flowers. Here again was the garden of Israel, ripe for God's blessings, yearning to be free.

He told them what he had been telling them all across the land. That the Kingdom of God was at hand. That eternity was theirs for the asking. That God offered them freedom and they had but to take it.

He saw Reuben, the Sagan, pushing his way through the crowd, with several other men, probably officers, too, all protected by Temple Guards in their characteristic uniforms, and a burly bunch at that. He had been wondering when they would come again, and he waited for them, smiling easily, his weight forward on the balls of his feet.

Some of the pilgrims protested, but Joshua shook his head, and the pilgrims fell back, allowing Reuben and his band through.

It was a hot day, and Reuben was already perspiring heavily. He hated what he was doing, hated Caiaphas for making him do it, and he hated Joshua for making it necessary. He was not, at heart, a cruel man, and he disliked having the people turn against him. But there seemed to be no choice. He dared not refuse the High Priest.

Facing Joshua once again, Reuben felt his energy sag. The man was so serene, so obviously sincere, it was difficult to oppose him, difficult to raise the righteous anger that he needed for his task. He swallowed a sigh and spoke as Caiaphas had told him to speak.

"Teacher," he said, "we know you are an honest man, and teach the ways of the Lord in truth. We also know that you are afraid of no man, and will speak boldly and honestly no matter what others may think."

The crowd murmured, surprised by this soft beginning.

Reuben waited until the people were quiet again. He wanted his question heard and understood. "Tell us, then, Rabbi, is it lawful to pay taxes to Caesar?"

Joshua smiled grimly. "You hypocrites," he said, "do you think I don't understand your meaning? Show me the money for the tax?"

Reuben was startled, and did not know how to respond. He would not touch money himself, for he was a priest and had been purified for the holiday. Nor would any of the pilgrims help. But there was a man, a gentile, who had been listening to Joshua, who brought out a Roman denarius and offered it.

Joshua, of course, would not touch it. "Show it," he told the man, "show it to the Sagan."

The man held the coin where Reuben could see it.

"Now," Joshua said. "You tell me, whose likeness and inscription is on that coin?"

Reuben swallowed hard before he spoke. "Caesar's," he said.

"Then I tell you," Joshua said. "Render unto Caesar the things that are Caesar's, and to God the things that are God's."

At these words, the pilgrims cheered Joshua. Reuben, thwarted, stared at Joshua and then the crowd. At last, feeling helpless and defeated, he gestured roughly and his companions followed him out of the courtyard, while the pilgrims laughed and mocked him.

***

The story of Joshua's confrontation with Reuben, the Sagan, spread quickly throughout the Temple and into the streets of the city. People did not agree on the meaning of what he said, but most seemed to think he had spoken very cleverly.

"I'm telling you," a pilgrim from Syria said to Ahaz, the Zealot leader, "he said it was lawful to pay taxes to Caesar."

"I can't believe it," Ahaz said, knowing as he did that Joshua had promised to tell the people to stop obeying Roman law and to cease paying Roman taxes.

"He's wrong," Amos told Ahaz. "He wouldn't touch the coin of course—it had the face of Caesar on it and the wording called him both emperor and god. No decent Jew would touch it, not even Reuben. But what he meant was, if this is your ruler and your god, why then pay taxes to him, but if you love the true God, the God of Israel, then you will give all you have only to Him."

Ahaz smiled. "I thought so," he said, and his faith, which had not lagged was only increased.

The pilgrim shrugged and went on his way.

"Nevertheless," Amos said, "he spoke wisely, saving his denunciation of the Romans for the Passover and not giving the Sadducees a chance to condemn him to the Romans, on his own words."

***

For two days, Gaius had been trying to find a way to leave the Antonia Fortress and speak to Joshua. Pilate, however, had kept him busy with many assignments, some of them make-work, and Gaius believed that Pilate and Septimus and their subordinates were keeping a close eye on him. He was afraid to leave the fortress openly and be followed. There was no way of knowing what Pilate would do then.

From time to time he would step out on the balconies that overlooked the Temple. There, below, in the blazing sun or under the porticoes, he would see Joshua, and his heart would ache with love for him and the yearning to save his life.

He decided he could not wait for evening. He knew that Joshua left the city each day after evening prayers, and he believed he was staying somewhere on the Mount of Olives. He couldn't wait for that, couldn't be certain he would find him. He would chance it and speak openly to him in Jerusalem, in the Temple if necessary. A glance out the windows told him that Joshua was still speaking under the colonnade that the Jews called Solomon's Porch. He would go there, directly, taking his chances.

Finally, at midday, Septimus left for an extended inspection of the troops in the city and Pilate retired to his chambers. Gaius decided he must take the chance, and gathering some papers, he bluntly told his secretary he had business in the city. If the man was a spy, so be it. He had to tell Joshua what he had learned.

It was difficult pushing through the dense crowds, especially since he was tall and did not look Semitic. But the people were generally affable because of the holiday, and he smiled his way closer and closer to Joshua.

Johannon and Little Jacob noticed his progress through the crowd.

"Roman?" Little Jacob asked, scratching his red beard.

Johannon nodded. His eyes were almost closed from squinting into the hot sun for several days. His pale skin had burned and peeled and his nose itched terribly where the skin had rubbed raw. But he noticed none of these discomforts. He was in the courtyard to protect the Master, and now that Simon was off somewhere, he believed that he was in charge of security.

When Gaius reached the first few rows of listeners, Johannon confronted him.

"No closer," he said, and Gaius, though he felt no fear, was impressed with the fierceness of the man's expression.

"Don't you remember me?" Gaius asked. "The Rabbi spoke to me in Galilee. I'm a friend of the family."

Johannon squinted at him suspiciously. The man did seem familiar, but he had seen so many men since Joshua's ministry began that he could not recall them all. Least of all, could one tell friends from foes and it was best to be on the safe side.

"Wait here," he said. "We'll see what the Master says."

Gaius could not keep smiling. "I have no time," he said. "My message is urgent. I must speak to him immediately."

"It's all right," Brother Jacob said. He had seen Gaius making his way through the crowd and he knew from past experience that the man was a friend.

Joshua saw them talking to Gaius and he sensed quickly the matter was important. "Forgive me friends," he said to the pilgrims, "even the teacher must have his rest. They murmured sadly as he turned away, but he waved to his disciples, and they joined him in the shadows under the portico. There were all there, except for Simon Peter, who was still searching for Nico, and Judas who never came to the Temple to listen to Joshua's preaching.

They made a protective circle around him, with Joshua and Gaius in the center. Gaius had wanted to speak to him alone, but he saw there was no choice.

"Pontius Pilate has told me his plans. The city, as you must know, is filled with Roman legions. Pilate himself decided to stay in the Antonia rather than the Hasmonean Palace so he can control what happens."

He took a deep breath and then continued. His voice was strained and his features were drawn with care. Joshua watched him with compassion, holding out a hand to touch his arm, to encourage and sustain him.

"On the Passover," Gaius went on, "when you are acclaimed the King of Israel, troops will come down from the fortress to arrest you for sedition. Pilate knows the people will not accept that action. They will defend you, and the minute they act in your defense, the troops will begin to attack the people."

The disciples listened to this man with his cracked voice and tormented features—they listened with increasing horror.

"But we intend no violence," Brother Jacob said. "They will be attacking unarmed men, women and children."

Gaius shook his head violently. "That doesn't matter to Pilate. He and Septimus, his Captain of the Guard, have been hoping for an excuse to attack the Jews. They will say they meant only to arrest your Master, but that they had to defend themselves when attacked."

"Terrible," Nathan said, while his wife nearly wept.

"They can't do that," Mattathias said. "Rome will not permit it."

"By the time Rome learns, it will be too late."

They were all protesting, expressing their doubts, their fears and their outrage. Joshua stood quietly, listening to them vent their feelings, giving them the opportunity to let out their outrage. But after a few moments, they realized he had not spoken.

"Beloved friends, I know and understand your feelings, and I, myself, am saddened to hear the plans of the Roman governor. But you are all worrying yourselves without reason. None of your fears will be realized. There will be no violence in the Temple."

He waited again until they had time to absorb what he had said. He smiled benignly, first at Gaius, then at the others. "There will be no violence," he repeated, "because I have no intention of being proclaimed 'King of Israel.'"

***

For a long time, they all stared at him. Terrible thoughts passed through their minds. Had Joshua lost his courage? Was he turning away from all he had promised? He watched them, studied their faces, and saw the doubt and fear that now marked them.

"No," Brother Jacob said, "you won't proclaim it on Passover." There was a pleading tone in his voice, a look of yearning on his face. "Because you're going to do it today. NOW!"

"Never," Joshua said quietly, watching them as they sagged under the weight of his words.

"Israel needs no ruler," he said. "She already has one, and that ruler is God Almighty."

"But the Messiah—" Brother Jacob began.

"—The Messiah is the anointed of God, and the anointed need not be a King. When has it profited Israel to have a king? Even in the days of David she was torn by factions. Solomon was called wise and great, but he spent the wealth of the nation glorifying himself. The Jews trusted the Hasmoneans, for they were priests as well as kings, and yet the nation suffered. No, dear friends, when men have a king they forget God. They bend their ways to the wishes of the ruler and not to the ways of the Almighty."

"But your way is the way of God," Judith said.

He nodded his head. "And that is why there is no need for a king. I tell you if I am proclaimed King, there are Jews who will treat me as the Romans treat their emperor. They will worship me as a god. And I am not God, but man—a man sent to do God's work. Those who worship men blaspheme God and I will not have it so. Even now there are those who confuse me with the Lord. I have seen men beg my mother to intercede with me and I have seen others dip their heads before her, as if she, too, somehow had become sacred."

Joshua spoke so loudly, that his words traveled beyond his disciples and could be heard in most of the Court of the Gentiles.

"Men must worship God, and God alone. They must obey God and God alone. Anoint a king and you create God's competitor. For men's thoughts are earthbound. They see the present advantage and not the eternal gain. NO-ONE can stand between God and man—not even the Messiah.

"God has directed me to serve the people, not to rule over them. On the Passover, I will tell the people of Israel what their choice is: God or Rome. I believe they will follow God, as they have tried to follow Him since the days of Abraham. But the choice will be theirs—and their destiny will be the one they have chosen."

10.

RUTHLESS

Pilate was annoyed to see the glowing look on Gaius's face. It was a bad sign. He had known that his plans for Judaea would upset his deputy, and he sincerely enjoyed that. He could not imagine what catastrophe had restored the man to cheerful enthusiasm.

"I confess, Excellency, that I have disobeyed your orders and spoken to the Galilean preacher."

Pilate purpled suddenly under the wash of his powder, and Septimus, who had walked into the room, stopped in his tracks.

"But I believe, Excellency that you will be pleased by what I have learned."

Pilate studied him with incredulity. The man was asking to be destroyed, physically or otherwise. It was unbelievable.

"I know you have rightfully feared a rebellion. The Jews, as you say, are very emotional and this holiday, the Passover, is a dangerous time. But I have spoken to the man, himself, and although he intends to address the people in the court of the gentiles on the first day of the festival, he has assured me that under no circumstances will he proclaim himself king— under no circumstances, will he permit others to do so.

"You see, the risk of rebellion is over. This man has the love of the people. They adore him, I think, and they will follow him in whatever he chooses. But he will not confront Caesar. He will not claim he is the ruler of the nation."

Gaius's gushing words were greeted with silence. He fully understood the governor's anger, but he knew what to say.

"It's great news isn't it? Now there's no chance that your tenure here will be marred by insurrection. There will be no bloodshed. The preacher has promised me he will counsel non-violence to all the people."

Still, Pilate said nothing. He now knew that Gaius was not merely useless to him, but an actual enemy. He would deal with that in time. Now he had better put the best face on matters. It was fruitless, nay, it was dangerous to tell this queer fellow anything more.

"Well done, Deputy," he said, with a grim smile. "You bring splendid news. Praise Caesar, I shall not have to spill blood on the festival."

Gaius nodded, smiled and came very close to bowing his way out of the chamber.

***

"Well done?" The question burst from Septimus's mouth like some obscene thing. "Praise Caesar? Can I have heard you right?"

Pilate smiled thinly. "That strange creature is in love with these peculiar people. It's difficult to believe that any Roman could nourish such disgusting affection, but clearly he does. Has he a lover—perhaps this Joshua?"

Septimus laughed. "I don't think so." But then his look hardened. "He's foiled us."

Pilate shook his head and smiled. "On the contrary, he's made it certain that we shall not fail. We were planning to let the Jews hang themselves. We would have waited for Joshua or his followers to proclaim him king. We shall no longer trust them to do our work. We'll have our own people in the temple dressed as Jews—with all those little black boxes on them if necessary. The moment Joshua appears, we will proclaim him King. The Jews will do the same—you can be sure of that. They love this fellow and no matter what he says, they will join in and cry that he is their king."

Septimus smiled as he listened. "And then," he said "we'll slaughter the lot of them."

***

Simon Peter was growing more anxious with every moment. He had learned nothing of the whereabouts of Nico. In Galilee he had hundreds of friends. One of them would surely have noticed something. But here in the capital, he was a stranger—a stranger surrounded by strangers. Too many people were in the city for the Festival for anyone to notice the movements of one solitary priest.

He was growing resentful. Perhaps the man was involved in something unsavory. Maybe he had a mistress somewhere in the city and was engaged in a drunken orgy. Simon did not really believe any of this, but he had been away from Joshua for too many hours. The others needed his strength—they would be in danger without him. At least that was what Simon wanted to believe. He half feared he would not be missed at all.

***

They had bound Nico, shoved a gag in his mouth and thrown him into the hewn-rock cellar below Amos's house. It was dark there, but fortunately clean and dry. They fed him when they remembered and let him use a bucket for his natural needs. Amos had climbed down to see him once. Amos was obviously uncomfortable about the arrangement and embarrassed over what he was doing.

"I like you," he told Nico, "and I like your father. You have to understand we don't have any choice in this." Then he looked at Nico and saw that he didn't accept a word of it.

"You should have gone directly to Joshua," Amos yelled at him. Then he looked up guiltily to where the ladder led to the first floor of his house. No one was there and no one heard.

"I don't know what I'm going to do with you," Amos said. "My family will be here for the Passover—right over your head. Don't think they'll hear you, because they won't. By tomorrow night, I'll have to tie you even better and cover your head with something. I'm sorry, but I can't afford to have anyone find you."

He started to pat Nico on the shoulder, but Nico turned away. Amos shrugged, climbed up the ladder, pulled it up after himself and closed the cellar.

Nico realized he would have to escape—and the sooner the better. The cellar had been carved into the rock of the Ophel. Nico edged around in the dark, until he felt a sharp edge of the rock. Then he backed against it and patiently sawed his ropes against the stone. For a long time nothing seemed to happen, then the rope loosened suddenly and he began to smile.

It was late that night when Amos returned again to the cellar. He was feeling guilty and he brought with him some food.

"Are you all right?" he asked, peering down at Nico, who lay on the floor, apparently asleep. When Nico didn't answer, Amos leaned down to touch his shoulder. It was then that Nico sprang up and grabbed him.

They wrestled together on the floor of the cellar, with first one man and then the other on top. Amos had left his sword on the floor above and Nico had only his bare hands, but he was desperate. If he didn't free himself now, it might be too late. Joshua would be walking into a trap. He brought his hands together and slammed them into the face of Amos. The larger man staggered back, and Nico lunged after him.

A shadow fell on them from above.

"That will be enough," Judas said. He stood above them, holding a lantern in one hand, and a sword in the other.

11.

SIMON PETER

Something was nagging at Simon Peter. He had talked again to Nicodemus and learned that he had still not seen his son. He brought the news to Joshua who had seemed stunned and had only nodded at Nicodemus's reassurance that all else was going well.

The other disciples all expressed their concern. Nico was well loved among them and they could not understand his disappearance. That is, all had expressed concern except Judas, who remained silent, which wasn't unusual, really. Judas was not a man who was quick to express his feelings. But this was one time when he surely might have helped. Judas knew the city better than any of them and he had dozens of friends in Jerusalem. Yet he had remained silent.

Simon wanted to shrug it off. It meant nothing. Judas's reaction only indicated he had other things on his mind. Besides, he had never really befriended any of the disciples. He was courteous enough, but when he thought about it, Simon realized that Judas was rather condescending towards them—as if they were too simple for him—as if he knew more than they did. Well, then, was it surprising if he showed little interest that one of them was missing? He probably thought they were so stupid they could get permanently lost in the holy city.

Except they were strangers, and Nico lived in Jerusalem. Except Nico had more friends in Jerusalem than Judas. On impulse, when Judas left the house of Eliezer that night, Simon slipped outside and followed him. It was a tricky business. Judas was a crafty one and he feared being followed. But not by the simple disciples of Joshua. Still, it wasn't easy. Judas passed through the great tent village that lay below the walls of Jerusalem. He stopped from time to time to check with his commanders. At least that was what Simon thought he was doing. At each stop he would ease into the shadows and wait, hoping that Judas would reappear again.

Fortunately, Judas did, but Simon knew that the commanders would also be concerned and that they, too, would be watching out for spies.

This wasn't an easy job for Simon Peter. First of all, he wasn't built for the job. He was too tall, too broad, and not exactly graceful. Not only that. It went against his grain. He was a forthright fellow, up front and outspoken. He didn't even try to sneak up on the fish in the Sea of Galilee, just slung out his nets and went straight after them. But now there was no choice. He made himself as small as he could and stepped as lightly as he could. He circled when he would have preferred to go straight. He petted a few dogs to keep them from barking and somehow made his stumbling way without losing sight of Judas for more than a few moments.

As they approached the city gate, Simon had an inspiration. Judas had stopped once more at a tent. Simon knew that it would be difficult to pass through the gate unnoticed and Judas would probably pay special attention at such a place. He hurried ahead and passed through the gate first, then stationed himself in the shadows some distance inside. If Judas turned now and went in some other direction, passed through some other gate, Simon Peter would lose him. He could only hope and wait.

Twenty minutes passed. Simon's spirits began to sink. He had botched it as usual. He was too dumb for this sort of thing. He had better go back to Bethany before they began to worry about him, too.

Judas walked through the gate. He veered into the shadows and waited. It was just as Simon had suspected. Judas was watching the gate to see if he had been followed. Simon permitted himself a small smile. He was not as dumb as others might think.

After several more minutes, Judas resumed his progress through the city. He actually walked right past Simon without seeing him.

Once more the game resumed. The restless Judas visited several houses, with Simon following him. Once he bumped into a water barrel, once he stepped on a cat, but each time, some other noise topped his and he was not discovered.

After an hour of this, Simon Peter had another hunch. It was not only important to know where the fish had been. It was even more urgent to know where they were going. Simon hardly knew the city, but he recalled clearly the parts of it he had seen. One of those places was the house of Amos and he knew that was not far ahead. He decided to take another chance and go there directly.

It was more than fortunate that he did. For this time, when Judas came out of the house he had visited, he doubled back and checked his path. He searched exactly where Simon had been hiding only moments earlier.

Once again Simon Peter had to wait. He squeezed himself between two low walls opposite the door of Amos's house. In a few minutes, Judas came up the street. And then, from the other direction, came Amos. He, too, had been checking the city commanders and now their rounds were complete. Amos whispered something, and Simon heard a snatch of it before Judas hushed him up. Something about a "guest."

***

When Simon Peter returned to Bethany, the sun was rising. He had remained outside the house of Amos as long as he dared. He had even approached the house, listened at windows, thought of climbing the roof, but then realized he was too large a man and would certainly be heard. When the sky lightened he reluctantly left the city. He found Joshua and the disciples and all of their families wide awake and fearfully worried.

"It's him," Eliezer cried from his watching post in the highest window in the house. "It's Simon Peter!"

They came running up the hillside towards him, almost all of them, Joshua included, calling his name and yelling all sorts of things. Tears sprang to his eyes when he saw that they had missed him, that they really loved him. He hugged them all, in great groups, while they continued to call his name and to question him.

"I tried to find Nico, but I didn't see him." He had decided not to tell them, not even Joshua, what he suspected. He had a plan, and if Nico did not appear by the hour of the Passover feast, he would put it into effect

To Joshua it was clear that Simon was not telling all that he knew, but he loved the rough fisherman dearly and since he knew there was not a dishonest bone in the man's body, he decided to respect his silence

"When you are rested, Simon Peter, take the others and go into the city. On the street of the cheese-makers, near the great steps that lead to the Temple you will see the same man who gave you the colt that I have been riding. Tell him all is well in Bethany and he will let you know if all is well in the house where we will celebrate the Passover. If it is, you are to help prepare the feast."

***

Gaius's state of relief did not last. For a few brief minutes he had told himself that the crisis was over. Joshua would not be proclaimed king and Pilate would have no reason to attack the Jews. But then his sense of euphoria faded. He cursed himself for a fool. He should never have told Pilate that Joshua didn't want to be king. He ought to have allowed that to come as a surprise. Pilate and Septimus would then have been caught without a reason or excuse for their planned brutality. Joshua would make his speech, the resistance would begin and all would be well.

Now, stupidly, he had forewarned them. In his joy at the salvation of his son, he had told all to Pilate. He had given them another day to plot something, to find some excuse to play out their cruel vengeance on the Jews.

He was even more depressed when he saw Septimus later in the day. The man should have been growling mad—he always showed his disappointments with rage. But, no, he was standing in one of the corridors of the Antonia, chatting amiably with a young woman. He laughed—and when he saw Gaius, he laughed even louder.

At that moment, Gaius wished he was that young and pretty woman, so that he might lure the ever available Septimus into bed and wheedle the plan out of him. Well, that might be impossible, but there was still time, still hope.

"Captain," he said, "if this pretty lady will allow it, will you come to my room?"

Surprised, Septimus curled his brows as he always did when faced with something he could not fathom. "In an hour, Deputy, perhaps a little longer."

The girl giggled.

***

When Septimus entered Gaius's quarters, he found the deputy sprawled on a couch, with a pitcher of wine and cups on the table beside him.

"Afternoon, Captain," Gaius slurred. He gestured vaguely. "Siddown."

Once again Septimus was surprised. "You, Deputy, drinking at this time of day? I can hardly believe it."

"No crime, is it? Good a man as any, you know."

"Of course, Deputy."

"Siddown, siddown. Try the wine. Roman you know—not that Judaean slop."

Septimus smiled and sat down. He watched Gaius curiously. The man did look like he was drunk. His eyes were red and his movements slack. Besides, the wine looked good. He poured himself a cup and took a deep drink.

"It's good," Septimus said. "Where did you get it?"

Gaius gave a conspiratorial wink. "From the gov'ner h'self. From his own cellar. Why not? He's got mor'n he needs."

This was an even greater surprise. Gaius, the pious one, had taken wine from the prefect's private stock. Septimus's eyes narrowed. He found it difficult to imagine this man guilty of any crime, petty or otherwise. But the evidence was before him. He settled back and took another sip of the wine. The girl had been good in bed and now this. It was going to be a very pleasant day.

***

Simon Peter and the others followed Joshua's directions, walking the street of the cheese-makers until they reached the steps to the Temple. There, as Joshua had said, they found the young man who had brought the colt. He smiled as they approached and when they asked the appropriate question, he turned without a word and led them through the twisting streets and onto the Ophel.

To their surprise, they found themselves before the house of Nicodemus, but when they turned to speak to the young man, he had slipped away and disappeared into the crowd.

Nathan shrugged and knocked on the door, which seemed to open just as he touched it. Nicodemus, looking old and drawn stood there, trying to smile as he welcomed them.

"Why," asked Mattathias, "weren't we told that we would celebrate the Passover at your home?"

"We planned it months ago, when Joshua was in Jerusalem the last time, and we thought it best not to say anything until the last possible moment. Surely you understand?"

They all nodded, but in fact, some of them were unhappy. They didn't know why they couldn't have been trusted with such simple information.

Nicodemus saw their uncertainty but had little sympathy for it. "Come," he said, "there is much to do before the Festival begins."

Simon Peter didn't mind helping the servants of Nicodemus carry the tables and couches into the upper room where the supper would be served.

He didn't care that Brother Jacob had been chosen to bring the lambs to the Temple for the sacrifice, nor that others were setting out plates and silver and other light work. What bothered him was that he felt certain great events were about to happen and he didn't want to be spending his time on such trivial tasks.

Then he remembered Nico. How surprised they would be when he found the priest and brought him home. How grateful both Nicodemus and Joshua would be when he returned with their son and favorite.

***

Septimus was feeling very pleased with himself. After the first bottle was finished, Gaius produced another, and it seemed to Septimus that it was even finer than the first.

Gaius, in his cups, shared with him all sorts of confidential information about the governor. To his surprise he learned that Pilate had been notorious in Spain for his unusual sexual preferences. Even more interesting, he had been involved in dubious financial dealings in Rome, and had only escaped humiliation because of his high born wife's wealth and connections.

In fact, that was why he had been sent to Judaea. It was deemed a safe place for him while the story of his peccadilloes was forgotten in the capital. But now it seemed that Pilate had been forgotten, too. His repeated requests for reassignment were ignored and his wife was thinking of leaving him. Life in the provinces didn't suit her at all.

Septimus learned all this with great relish. He had yearned to have something on the prefect, and now Gaius had provided him with a treasure house of information.

"You see," Gaius said, "the old boy powders his face and his hair but he can't powder over his record."

Septimus laughed heartily. "You're not a bad one, after all," he said. "Thought you were after my ass."

"Never," Gaius said. "You're tough, but you're good soldier."

Even drunk as he was, Septimus sensed the information had not been given him for nothing. "Whadaya want?" he asked.

"Nuthin'" Gaius said, "nuthin of value."

"Oh," Septimus said.

"Curious, thass all. Know you're not gonna let that Jew preacher get away with embarrassin' us—thass all."

Septimus sat up suddenly. "Shud a' known," he slurred. "You wanna spoil our fun."

Gaius shook his head. "Won' do a thing. Jus' wanna know."

Septimus frowned. "No," he said. "No and No again."

"Come on, tell me. I tol' you all about gov'ner."

Septimus heaved himself to his feet. "Gotta get goin,'" he said, and started for the door. He had taken only two steps when he found Gaius in front of him, standing steadily and holding his arm in a tight grip.

"Tell me," Gaius said. His voice was clear and strong.

Septimus looked at him, bleary-eyed, trying to gather his strength and get the cobwebs out of his head. "No," he said as strongly as he could.

Something cold touched his throat. Septimus had been a soldier long enough to know it was a dagger—a very sharp dagger.

"Tell me," Gaius said, "or I'll slit your throat."

Septimus believed him. His mind was very foggy but he knew he had seen this expression in Gaius's eyes before. Long ago. In Beth Sholem.

"Ah," he said, "wadzit matter. When he comes to the Temple, gonna have dozens of our men, dressed as pilgrims, cry out he's King a' the Jews. Then no matter what happens, we jump in and kill the lot of 'em."

Even now, drunk and somewhat fearful of Gaius, the idea made Septimus giggle. But the giggle had a funny sloshing sound and with a sharp intake of breath, he realized that Gaius had indeed slit his throat.

12.

PREPARATIONS

Long before sunset the people had gathered in their homes, permanent and temporary, to celebrate the Passover. The Temple sacrifices were completed— the pall of acrid smoke had blown away with the west wind—and a gentle quiet had settled over the city.

In the home of Nicodemus, all was ready. Upstairs, the largest room in the house had been set with a number of small tables and couches. Nicodemus's finest tablecloths and most elegant cutlery had been spread. Flowers, cut for the occasion, were arranged in tall vases about the room. The sun had not yet set, and the last rays entered through windows high in the wall, but screened through fine cloth to cut the heat and the glare.

The tables had been set in a random pattern, so that no-one would be unhappy with his place, but near the center of the room was a table for Joshua, his mother, Judith and Brother Jacob. Close to it was the table of Nicodemus and his family. It was a sad table, really, for Nicodemus's wife had died in the past year and his only son was missing. The sofa on which Nico would have sat was close to the couch of Joshua and that made it seem especially empty.

Everyone was dressed in white for the Festival, though the quality of their clothing ranged from Simon Peter's plain cotton to Nicodemus's fine, seamless linen. Except for some blue edging on the women's gowns, there was little additional adornment. Few of the women wore any jewelry and all were very restrained.

Miriam and Judith had prepared for the Festival with great care, wearing their finest clothes. Both looked very lovely, but Miriam especially glowed with great anticipation of the morrow. It seemed that her whole life had aimed towards this very time. Whenever she looked at her son, tall, handsome, at his ease with all men, rich or poor, wise or fools, she smiled. In the past, she might have covered that smile, in shyness or consideration, but not now. She could not hold it back.

Miriam's hair was lightly streaked with gray, but even the gray seemed luminous against the still startling black. Her skin remained clear, with almost no lines in her brow and her eyes were as bright and compelling a green as ever.

When Joshua, Judith and Jacob looked at their mother, they, too, glowed. Her radiance embraced them and enhanced their own joy at this feast of liberation. But still, when they looked at the forlorn Nicodemus, their pleasure was bated and their hearts touched.

The disciples, too, suffered for Nicodemus, but their spirits could not be entirely dampened. They had tramped the hills of Galilee and the plains of Perea, the seaports of Lebanon and the deserts of Judaea, their hearts filled with love for their Messiah and with hope for their nation. Now, within hours, all the dreams would be fulfilled.

Before the rituals had begun, Judas took Joshua aside.

"There may not be time in the morning," Judas said. "I thought I had better speak to you now. We have no plans for the proclamation tomorrow and, of course, no kingly crown. I believe, however, that many of the younger priests will gladly anoint you and I will speak to them if you wish."

For a moment, Joshua stared at him. "You don't know," he said. "I had forgotten you weren't there when I told the others. There will be no proclamation tomorrow or at any other time. Israel, having God Almighty, has no need of an earthly king. When I speak to the people tomorrow, I will tell them that. We must follow God's rule, not the rule of any man."

Judas stood stock still as if he had not heard. His expression did not change. He looked at Joshua mildly, as if he had not even spoken. Joshua waited, wondering at this strange reaction. Judas was listening to the words Joshua had spoken, hearing them again and again in his mind. He searched those words for a meaning he had perhaps missed before.

"You must tell me again, Joshua."

"I will not be proclaimed 'King' tomorrow," Joshua said patiently, "or at any other time."

"The people expect it," Judas said, controlling himself with great effort, knowing the importance of this moment.

Joshua said nothing.

"The people will demand it," Judas said. "When you stand in the Temple tomorrow, the people will call you 'King' and they will accept no other."

Joshua remained silent. It was necessary for Judas to work through this himself, completely. Now, in spite of his valiant attempts to restrain himself, Judas's voice was rising. The sound of it and the note of tension in it attracted the others, interrupted every conversation.

"It cannot be any other way, Joshua. For the people, the Messiah is a king, a king who will lead them to freedom. You cannot bring them to the well and then poison it."

"Lying to the people will poison the well," Joshua said. "To let them believe they should follow a mere man and not God is to tempt them with false idols. A king, the very idea of a king, is merely a graven image. We are forbidden to worship graven images."

"A King is not an image, he is a leader."

Joshua shook his head. He put out his arms and held Judas with both hands. "You have been my right hand, Judas. We could not have come to this moment without your wisdom, your energy and your strength. We need your help now, as never before. But you must understand that we, as mere men, have done all that we can. Now we must leave the rest in God's hands."

All of Judas's deepest fears were coming home to him. The day before the liberation, Joshua had either lost his mind or his nerve.

"Don't worry, Rabbi," Judas said, peering deeply into Joshua's eyes, "all is in readiness. We will protect you. There is no danger."

Joshua dropped his hands. "Do you think I am afraid? The Lord God is with me—I fear no one, but Him."

Judas stared at him, looking for the flicker of fear he had seen in other men's eyes. A man might claim to be brave, but something would give him away. Judas had seen many men, tried and tested them. Truly, one could never be certain about any man until he was actually on the field of battle. But that might be too late, so Judas had learned to study men carefully, before the day of battle. And he had become an excellent judge of courage.

He had watched Joshua for a long time and he thought he knew him well. Was he mistaken? Had he been fooled by this kind and loving, but tremendously impressive and powerful person?

He couldn't believe that. Everything he had ever learned told him that Joshua was unafraid. His heart sank. Joshua's disease was worse than fear—it was tragic misunderstanding. Judas almost nodded in agreement with his own words.

This time, Judas took Joshua's arms in his hands, and held them tightly. He was much shorter than Joshua, but his grip was powerful and his look intense. He wanted to burn his way into this man's brain. Here was the hope of Israel, the hope so long denied. Here was the chance of freedom, of liberation. This man held it in his hands. He could not be allowed to throw it away.

"I love you, Joshua, and I believe in you. You are the one, the only one who can save Israel. You can do it tomorrow—tomorrow as we all have planned. But you cannot do it without being proclaimed the King of Israel. There is no other way. I have followed you in everything, Joshua, no matter how much I might have disagreed, no matter what the cost. Now, you must listen to me. When the people proclaim you King tomorrow, the liberation of Israel will begin. God's glorious kingdom will be forever and ever. Tomorrow, Joshua, before the sun has set. Don't fail us, Joshua. Don't fail Israel. Don't fail God."

There was deep silence in the room. Some were offended at the way Judas held Joshua, the way he spoke to him. But many felt he was right. The people expected a king, and now they could have one. Why not? There was no fear that Joshua would abuse his calling. He could be trusted totally to deal honestly and fairly with all men. He had no personal ambitions—none.

Why not give Israel her king?

"I won't quarrel with you, Judas," Joshua said. "I know that you mean to do your best for the nation. I know you believe that having a king is Israel's answer." He shook his head. "How often in our history, no matter how noble the king, has Israel known peace? No, my friend, kings mean divisions among men, the following of rival parties, the eventual misery of war. The time has come to change all that. The time has come to bend our heads and bow our knees to the one king, the only king, Almighty God."

Judas began to tremble. His limbs shook and his lips quavered. He knew a despair and then an anger he had never known before. He pushed Joshua back a step, and then walked close to him. He spoke fiercely into his face, his own features contorted.

"You're a fool, Joshua Ben Joseph—the greatest fool Israel has ever known."

Joshua reached out again, but Judas pushed roughly past him and stalked out of the house.

"Judas," Joshua was saying. "Come back, before it's too late."

But Judas didn't listen. He slammed the door on Joshua's words.

"I'll go after him, Master," Simon Peter said.

Joshua shook his head. "He must decide for himself whether he will betray God to forward his own plans."

***

Nico felt like he was suffocating in Amos's cellar. He had been bound even more tightly than before, and Amos had thrown a sack of some kind over his head. The sack was driving him mad. He could hardly move now that Amos had trussed his feet, but by rolling over and over he came up against the rough stone wall. He screamed for help, but of course, made not a sound. Then, feeling he had no choice, he rubbed his head against the rough stone. The rubbing hurt, as the stone pierced the sacking and scraped his head. But he was feeling desperate, choking now with the sack over his head. Then the sack caught on something, probably a sharp edge of the stone. For a moment he could not move his head, then he twisted sharply and the sacking ripped across.

He could breathe. He could not see, but he could breathe. It was then that he heard the door slam above him, and the sound of two voices. Nico struggled to stand erect, sliding up the harsh wall until he was just beneath the floor.

***

"Where is your family?" Judas asked.

Amos flushed. "I didn't feel comfortable celebrating the Passover with Nico trussed up down there. I sent them to my brother's house for the Feast."

"But you're still here."

"I was just going."

"No, it's good you waited. There's been a change of plans."

Amos looked at him sharply. "It's off?"

"No, don't worry, everything will be as before. Joshua will come to the Temple in the morning and tell the people what they must do."

"Well?"

"He doesn't believe he should proclaim himself King—wait a minute don't interrupt. He feels it's against God's will for him to choose himself."

Amos seemed puzzled. "I don't understand."

"It's simple. We must go to all the leaders tonight and tell them: Tomorrow, as soon as Joshua sets foot in the Temple, the people must call him their King by acclamation."

Amos smiled. "Of course, that's as it should be."

Judas smiled and clapped him on the back. "The people will understand. They must speak with one voice. When Joshua enters the Temple, the roar must be loud enough to be heard in Rome."

Amos laughed. "Wonderful. I can hardly wait."

"And tell every man to carry a short sword under his cloak, just in case."

Amos again looked puzzled.

"A precaution," Judas said, "only a precaution. We'll probably never touch them again."

"We must get the word out at once," Amos said.

"I'll take the southern groups, you cover the ones to the north. Each man must tell one other, and he must do it in total secrecy."

"Good," Amos said, heading for the door.

"Wait," Judas said. "Tell them whatever happens, even if Joshua protests, the people must do it."

"Why would he protest?" Amos asked.

"He would be testing them—to see how strong their commitment is, to learn if they love God enough to follow His Messiah."

"He'll know how much we love God and him tomorrow."

They clasped hands and hurried out into the fast darkening city.

***

Gaius dragged the body through the fortress, praying he would not be seen. It was only a short distance to the room Septimus used when he was assigned to Jerusalem, and Gaius pulled him inside, huffing and puffing. Immediately he went back into the corridor and cleaned it of any signs of blood. Then he went back into his own quarters and cleaned them with great care.

Afterwards, he went back into the room where Septimus's body lay and propped it in bed. He ripped a gold chain from around his neck and scoured the room for valuables, turning the room upside down as he went. He would make it look as if someone, perhaps a slave, had murdered Septimus. It seemed a feeble attempt to him, but he could think of nothing better.

Then he carefully secreted the things he had stolen on his own body and stepped back into the hall. This time he passed a soldier running through the corridors on an errand. Gaius held his breath, but the soldier was so intent on his task that he never raised his head.

Gaius walked slowly through the corridors of the fortress, his heart pounding. Had he been challenged, he had no idea what he would do. Along the way, he passed the slave quarters. To his surprise, the door was open and unguarded. On impulse, he stepped inside. At the end of the room, behind a screen, he heard sounds and understood at once that the guard and one of the slaves were busy enjoying themselves. He quickly shoved the things he had taken into a pile of clothing thrown against the wall, then ran out of the room.

No one had seen him. Now he must make his decision—talk to Pilate and give him a last chance to change his mind, or go directly to Joshua and warn him.

One thing was certain, he could not tell him about Septimus. But if Septimus were found and Gaius was missing, they might link the two of them. Still, if he told Pilate and begged him to change his plans for the next day, Pilate would probably detain him, even forcibly, and then his chance to tell Joshua would be lost.

Gaius was on the edge of panic. He had not originally intended to kill Septimus, but when the man who had killed his only grandchildren had told him, smilingly, that he was going to kill his only son, he had lost control.

Now, the thought of his crime was beginning to possess him. He told himself it was justified. The future of an entire nation was at stake. Surely, a monster like Septimus ought to die in their place. But somehow he couldn't convince himself, couldn't believe he could tell Joshua and that Joshua would agree.

"I know better," he told himself. "I'm older and wiser and he'll thank me in the end."

But still there was the question of Pilate. Gaius wrung his hands in despair.

***

The Passover feast in the house of Nicodemus proved to be a less than joyous affair. Wine was drunk, prayers were offered and the age-old story was retold. Everyone tried to be cheerful, to chant the prayers strongly and sing the psalms with enthusiasm, but it didn't come out quite right. There were two empty places, the places of Nico and Judas, and the people's eyes continually returned to them.

Simon Peter was fidgeting in his place so much that Andrew pulled at his arm and asked him what the matter was. Simon frowned angrily and did not respond. It was important for him to be out of here, to go to the house of Amos as soon as possible. Finally he could bear it no longer. He rose and went directly to Joshua.

"Master, I believe I know how to bring them back."

Joshua studied him carefully. He had seen Simon's agitation and realized it was more than mere irritation at the disappearance of the two men.

"After the Feast," Brother Jacob said.

Simon shook his head violently.

"Go, then," Joshua said.

"I'll take Andrew," he said.

"Soon there'll be no one here," Nicodemus said sadly. He was fearful the Galilean fisherman might not find Nico. It was a poor Passover without him.

***

Gaius had no idea where Joshua could be found. His sense of despair was acute. What if he didn't reach him before morning in the Temple? A quiver of pain shot through him with such acuteness that he could hardly see. His vision darkened and his steps wobbled.

"Think," he told himself, "think carefully. Joshua's life is at stake." He calmed himself and tried to be logical. Joshua might be on the Mount of Olives, but he didn't know where. No, he thought, not there. This Passover was too important to spend anywhere but within the walls of Jerusalem.

Nor would Joshua be dining at some wealthy high priest's lavish table. That was not his way. That meant he would be in the lower city or on the Ophel. Hadn't he heard there were priests who supported him? They, the poorer ones, lived on the Ophel. He would take his chances and head that way.

He passed many homes and saw signs of the Feast everywhere. Through doorways and windows he heard prayers being offered to God and psalms being sung. He wanted to stop at each house and ask for Joshua, but he knew he wouldn't be trusted and no one would tell him. He made himself breathe slowly and deeply and he kept himself under control. He would find Joshua if it took all night.

13.

CLIMAX

Andrew tried to question his brother, but Simon Peter refused to say anything until they were far from the house of Nicodemus. Then and only then did Simon tell him his suspicions.

"I think Nico is being held a prisoner in the house of Amos the Zealot."

Andrew's jaw dropped open. He was too surprised to speak.

"You think I'm crazy, don't you? Well, you're going to do what I say, anyway." He hurried off down the street, and Andrew, his mouth still open, followed him, shaking his head from side to side.

It was darker now and a fresh breeze had come up, but there was still a tinge of light in the sky. From the houses of Jerusalem, they heard the familiar songs and chants, blending in the evening air to accompany them with sweet songs on their way. Here and there they saw Roman soldiers, more perhaps than at other festivals, but Simon and Andrew had no basis for comparison. Still, they knew enough to give the soldiers wide berth.

In minutes, they were before the house of Amos.

"Now what?" Andrew asked.

"Now we knock on the door and ask to be admitted."

"Then?"

"I don't know. We'll find him if we have to turn the house upside down."

"But the family—on Passover."

Simon gritted his teeth, ignoring his brother, and pounded on the door. He braced himself, ready for anything.

There was no answer. After a few moments, he knocked again. And then again. He began to grow angry.

"They know we're here. They just don't want to let us in."

"We better go speak to Joshua," Andrew said. He didn't like this business at all.

Simon grunted, then launched himself against the door, while his brother stared.

The impact was loud and dramatic. The latch sprang with a loud whine and Simon's momentum sent him flying through the opening. He crashed to the floor in the middle of the dark, silent room, while Andrew hurried in behind him. Simon leaped up immediately, ready for anything. He was astonished to see the room was unoccupied. In fact, the whole house was unoccupied, which he discovered with a few minutes search.

"Where could they be?" Andrew asked, following his brother through the dim and empty house.

Simon said nothing to his brother. He spoke only to himself. "He's here," he mumbled. "I know it."

He ran up on the roof and found nothing. He came back down, threw open cabinets and banged on walls, seeking for a secret hiding place.

Andrew was wandering about in the main room. He tapped his foot in one corner of the floor, then lifted a rug. He was just about to say that it sounded hollow, when he saw the door to the cellar.

"Look," he said.

Simon Peter spun about and stared, but only for a second. Then he ran to his brother's side and helped him pull up the heavy ring.

***

Each moment, the sky seemed to grow darker, and Gaius's heart darkened with the heavens. He dared not ask for Joshua without arousing the Jews on their holiday. And yet, without asking anyone, his chances of finding his son were very slim.

He had traversed the Ophel, praying silently, but walking erect and with no attempt to hide himself, so that Joshua might find him more easily. It seemed very silly, but he didn't know what else to do. He was certain he was in the right area, and that Joshua was not more than a few minutes away, but he didn't know where.

Once, he was stopped by a centurion who recognized him. The officer was surprised to see the Deputy Governor in this heavily Jewish quarter on the festival. Gaius told him he was on government business. The centurion saluted and went on his way. "Thank God," Gaius thought, "that our people are often so incurious."

But that did not help him find Joshua. Ahead, in the growing darkness, he saw three men running. He was frightened—they might be searching for him. But he knew he could not run without attracting more attention.

Now they were upon him. They were entering the very house where he was standing.

"Wait a minute," Gaius shouted. "Aren't you friends of Joshua?"

***

Pilate was enraged. "Murdered? Here in the Antonia under our very noses?" He was speaking to all the officers of the guard, assembled before him in his audience chamber.

A younger man, also a captain, Paulus Aemilius, stood before him, perspiring freely. It was not very warm in the room, but Pilate frightened him. He had seen the prefect before, but always serene and restrained. Now, his eyes blazed and his skin was livid. Spittle sprayed from his mouth as he spoke, dousing Paulus Aemilius, who did not dare even to blink.

"I'll have the murderer—whoever he is—flayed to pieces"

"We found him, Excellency," Paulus said is a quavering voice. "He was a slave. Septimus must have caught him stealing in his room and the slave stabbed him to death."

"Bring him here at once. I want to punish him, myself."

"I...that is, we, tortured him to gain his confession. He confessed, but then he died—from the torture."

Again, Pilate was furious. They had exceeded their authority, torturing the man without his authorization. Could no one be trusted in these accursed times? But just as the words of vituperation were about to issue from his mouth, he thought better of them. The deed was done. Septimus was dead and could not be brought back to life. The murderer—if indeed he was the murderer—a man might confess anything under Roman torture, had been punished. There was more at stake now. Tomorrow was the great day. He needed to focus on that. This captain who stood before him, this Paulus Aemilius, would have to be told his plans. He would have to take charge immediately. It was more important to prepare him than to do anything else.

"The rest of you are dismissed. Captain, you will remain." A thought hit him. "Where is my deputy?" he asked.

No one seemed to know. Pilate was not greatly concerned. Gaius Fabricius was supposed to have only an observer's rule during the great events. Idly, he thought, too bad it wasn't Gaius instead of Septimus.

***

In the house of Nicodemus, all of the guests were on their feet, laughing, crying, embracing. Nicodemus himself was so overcome, he could not loosen his grip on his son, and anyone who wanted to hug Nico had to include his father in his embrace.

Gaius had been admitted with the brothers, but he stood aside as this reunion took place. He tried to approach Joshua, but found that impossible, and then tried to catch his eye, but that was impossible, too. He decided that God had been very good, leading him to this place. There were many hours until morning and plenty of time to warn Joshua. There was nothing to worry about now. Once his son knew what was to happen, he would be able to avoid an attack by Pilate.

Finally, the celebrants had their fill of embracing Nico. They clamored to hear what had happened to him. He gathered himself, but then, aware of Gaius's presence, he hesitated.

Joshua said, "This man is our friend—feel free to speak of anything— anything in his presence." Gaius nodded. Nico began to speak, as dispassionately as he could.

"I learned from Ezra that the Zealots were storing weapons in the city. I wasn't sure how much he knew, so I confronted Judas in the house of Amos. The truth came out and Judas admitted there were tens of thousands of weapons stored all around Jerusalem."

At these words, the women cried out, and many of the men. Joshua heard the words with a sinking heart and a feeling of deep sadness. Faith, he thought, it is so difficult to have faith.

Nico went on, speaking plainly and in a level voice that belied the pain of the telling. "I told them I would tell you. They wouldn't let me leave. They bound me and covered my head and left me in the cellar of Amos." He hesitated briefly. "Judas would have killed me, rather than let me tell you, but Amos stopped him."

Nicodemus's hand went to his mouth to prevent a cry. Tears fell from his eyes without ceasing during Nico's tale.

"I don't know how they knew I was there, but Simon and Andrew broke into the house and freed me."

Simon Peter stood with his head down. He was proud of what he had done, and he knew that the others appreciated it, but he didn't really want to hear words of praise. Still, he heard Nicodemus's tearful, whispered thanks and Joshua touched his shoulder. That was praise enough.

"We'll get Judas," Mattathias said. "We'll make him answer for this."

"Yes," the others cried. "Find Judas—He'll pay for this!"

Their eyes were on Joshua and his eyes were on Nico. He knew the story was not complete.

"Just before Simon freed me, Judas and Amos were in the house together. Judas told Amos that Joshua insists on the people proclaiming him king tomorrow—"

"—It's not true!" Judith cried out. But Joshua raised his hand and Nico continued.

"He told Amos they must alert the leaders and tell their people that the moment you enter the Temple tomorrow, they are to cry out with one voice that you are the King of Israel."

"Impossible!" old Nathan cried. "Terrible!" said Philip. The sons of thunder were angrily twisting their hands. They wanted to get hold of Judas and strangle him at that very moment.

Miriam watched only her son as Nico told his story and the disciples and the family cried out in despair. She saw that his expression changed but little. Yet, she saw the pain in his eyes, the terrible pain. Others might not have noticed, but Miriam saw suffering in her son's face, as she had never seen it before.

"We'll stop them," Simon said. "You can be sure of that."

Nico went on, forcing out the words. "They say, no matter what you do, tomorrow, Joshua, they will proclaim you King. Judas told Amos that even if you say no, you are only testing the people, to see how strong their commitment is. I tell you the clamor in the Temple will be tremendous."

"We'll start now," old Simeon said. "We'll spread the word before morning."

"There isn't time," Nico said. "The Zealots are spread all over city. We'd never reach them all."

"It wouldn't matter," Gaius said, speaking for the first time. "Pilate is sending hundreds of soldiers into the Temple disguised as pilgrims. The moment you enter, they will acclaim you King."

Judith sucked in her breath and almost fainted. "The people will take up the cheer," she said, almost to herself. "They'll all call you King."

"Is that so bad?" Simon Peter asked. Would Israel be destroyed if Joshua were King?"

"You don't understand," Gaius said. "As soon as anyone—ANY-ONE—calls Joshua 'King,' Roman troops will pour into the Temple to arrest Joshua. They know very well that some people will protect him. Then, they will fall on the crowd and begin to slaughter them."

"Unarmed people?" Mattathias said, "Not even the Romans—"

"—But they are not unarmed," Nico said. "Judas and Amos are telling their men to bring short swords under their tunics."

That brought the room to silence. A deep, prolonged silence in which every eye turned to Joshua. He had been listening and not listening. From the moment both Gaius and Nico had appeared, simultaneously, he had read the signs. Everything he had heard since, had only confirmed his understanding.

"Strange isn't it," he said mildly, "that for once the Zealots and the Romans are in agreement. Both want me proclaimed the King of Israel."

No one responded. Joshua's eyes were on another image. One he had not understood fully until this day. He recalled the Passover of his childhood, when he had seen a man, a dark figure, spreading the blood of the Passover on the lintel of his home. Now, in his mind's eye, the man turned. Joshua saw that he, himself, was that man, and realized fully that he was the paschal lamb, the sacrifice of this Passover, that it was his blood which would be painted on the lintel to save the people of the House of Israel.

He felt dizzy for a moment and he wavered, then sat down. They came to him then in a rush, all of them, concerned for him, yearning to comfort him.

"Don't worry," Nicodemus said. He was the closest and he had taken Joshua's hand "You won't go to the Temple tomorrow. That way no harm can come to anyone."

"They'll come after you," Gaius said, "no one will stop Pilate now. He's thirsty for your blood."

"We'll take him away from here tonight," Simon said. "We'll hide in the hills until this blows over."

"That's it," Brother Jacob said

"Of course," said Mattathias. The others were nodding their heads and agreeing. All except Miriam and Judith. Their eyes were on Joshua and they saw that his jaw was set.

"The anointed of God does not flee before the heathen," he said in a firm, strong voice.

"It's a matter of life and death," Nicodemus said. "All of the scholars agree that even the High Priest may abandon his place to save—"

"—I am not the High Priest," Joshua said, cutting him off. "I have my mission given to me by the Almighty and I will not run away."

"But this is madness," old Nathan said. "What good will it do to sacrifice your life?"

"The Lord must know, or he would not have brought me here."

He felt his strength returning now and he stood up and held out his arms to make room for himself.

"If you go to the Temple, tomorrow," Brother Jacob said, "there will be a massacre. You and the people—thousands will die."

"There will be no massacre," Joshua said. "Only one man will die."

He stood very straight and tall, with his head held high. His eyes were clear and his face seemed to glow. As they all looked at him, they could hardly believe his courage. No one could doubt who he meant. They wanted to argue with him, but for the moment, the very power of his presence, prevented them from saying anything.

Some of them could not help looking at Miriam. She had not taken her eyes off her son since Nico had begun to tell his story. Even then, she had sensed the direction events were aiming and though her heart was heavy with pain, she knew that nothing she said or did would change matters. Long ago, she had realized that Joshua's life would be one of deep suffering. He had taken every loss a man could sustain and he had never lost his faith. She had known that his death would be early and hard. She had thought that she could have been prepared for Joshua's death. She was not.

Only Judith spoke. She, too, had expected the worst and tried her best to remain strong. She had fought off tears time and again. Now was not the time to cry. But she had to know—had to understand the reasons.

"Why?" she asked. "Why must one man die, and how will one man's death change anything?"

Joshua looked at her with compassion. He knew how she was suffering and he was grateful that she had asked the right questions.

"I have said that violence is not the way, that the Living God demands peace of us not war. I have said that we cannot voluntarily submit to Roman law, but we must not oppose the Romans with violence. I have said that if a man strikes you on one cheek, you must turn the other. It is only by that example that we can teach our lesson to the world. It is only by not resisting the greatest violence that we can prove that we are men of peace.

"Pilate and Judas have brought us to this inevitable collision. Pilate is an evil man who believes only in hatred and brutality. Judas is a good man, who believes physical strength must be opposed by physical strength, and in the end, he is more evil than Pilate, for he claims to love the word of God and yet he will not follow it.

"If I go to the Temple tomorrow, there will be war and the people of Israel will be slaughtered. Judas with all his weapons cannot oppose the armed might of the Empire.

"If I do not go to the Temple, the people will lose their faith in the ways of peace. They will believe Judas, who will tell them the Romans must be fought, must be driven from our land by force of arms. The people will fight. The people will die. THAT IS NOT THE DESTINY THAT GOD HAS CHOSEN FOR ISRAEL.

"There is only one alternative—one way to forestall the bloodshed. That is for one man to make a sacrifice for the nation."

"How?" Simon Peter asked. "How can that be done?" He was so close to tears that his usual powerful voice had become thin and raspy

"I must die at the hands of the Romans."

They all understood what that meant: Crucifixion. Miriam, who had been strong until then, began to feel a tremor in her hands and in her heart

Nicodemus was shaking his head. "If you are killed by the Romans, the people will surely rise up."

"Not if I am turned over to them by our own people—if I am condemned by the Jews."

"No Jew would do that," Nico said.

"Caiaphas," Joshua said simply. They said nothing, for they knew that what he said was true.

"If Caiaphas were to do that, they would tear him limb from limb," Brother Jacob said.

"Caiaphas," Joshua said, "and the Sanhedrin. Tonight, this very night, we must go to them and tell them what has happened. We must persuade them that I must be accused of sedition. They must turn me over to the Romans and demand my death."

Nicodemus could not restrain himself. "You are talking so calmly about your own death. You also assume the Sanhedrin will agree to what you are saying. We Jews don't behave in this fashion. We don't knowingly kill a man, even to save others. Every human life is precious—yours the most precious of all."

Joshua smiled. "I know you love me, Nicodemus, but there is no other choice. By the time the people gather in the Temple, I must be hung from the tree. The people may grieve, they may be shocked, but they won't riot. They will be stunned to learn that the one they believed was the anointed of God, their Messiah, has been roughly treated and condemned to die, that I am hanging from that accursed tree. They will believe my death proves that I was not the Messiah.

"At first, they will lose faith. They will believe either that I was a false prophet or that God has turned away from Israel. Whatever they believe, they won't fight. All men will turn away from me."

It was too much for Simon Peter. "Not I, Master. No matter what others may do, I will never turn away from you."

Joshua could not help smiling. "Even you, Simon Peter, before this day dawns, even you will have denied me."

Simon was stunned into silence. Joshua regretted hurting him, but he had to speak the truth as he knew it. His followers must be prepared for the worst.

"That is how it will be. It is hard for men to keep their faith in the face of disaster. At first, the people will feel betrayed and abandoned, but when they know the truth they will understand. They will come to realize that my death has prevented theirs. They will learn that I believed in non-violence and gave my life for it. They will know then that the word of God is true—that even the Messiah must give himself up in the name of peace, in the name of love, in the Name of the Most High.

"Pilate and Rome will be defeated. Those who believe in the kingdom of men will be defeated. God alone will triumph. God alone will rule."

Gaius was in tears listening to Joshua. He wanted to speak, to dissuade him, but he knew it was hopeless. There was something he had to say. He didn't wish to say it, but he knew he must.

"I am Pilate's deputy. If Joshua is not proclaimed king and if there is no violence by his followers, I don't see how even Pilate can order the slaughter of thousands of innocent people."

"You see," Joshua said. "We have only to send the word to Caiaphas, so that the process may begin. Who will carry that message?"

14.

THE CUP

Judith had taken all that she could bear. As Joshua looked about group, looking for someone to carry his message to Caiaphas, she hurried to her mother and threw her arms about her.

"Stop him!" she cried. "You're the only one who can do it."

Miriam held out her arms and embraced her daughter. She wanted to do exactly what Judith asked. She yearned to plead with her son not to do this thing—to leave the house at once and escape into the hills. Let the others work out their own fate. There must be an answer that would not end in Joshua's death.

She had held back the tears as long as she could. She would have wiped them away, hidden them somehow, but Judith clung to her and held her arms to her sides. She could no longer hold back the tears and she could not turn away. She looked at her son with all the love she had ever held for him revealed in her eyes. But her eyes did not plead, they only affirmed her deep affection and her pain.

Joshua could no more look away from her than if his own arms had been pinned to his sides. He knew what he was doing to her. She had suffered so much to have him, been tortured and tormented. She had loved Joseph and lost him. She had loved Rebecca, Joshua's wife and his children, and she had lost them. Now she would lose her eldest, and in fact, her most beloved child

Joshua saw it all in her eyes and the tears began to spill from his.

"The people will not forget me, mother."

He picked up a piece of unleavened bread and broke it in his hands and spoke to his followers.

"Whenever you break this bread, think of me, broken on the cross for all of us."

He lifted a cup of wine. "When you raise your cup of wine on Passover, think of me—remember my blood spilled like the blood of the paschal lamb, for the liberation of all of us.

"But don't recall my suffering or my pain. Think of the joy that I feel that God has chosen me for this purpose Remember the many who were freed, because the few—even the one—made the sacrifice for their liberation.

"This is not a sad occasion. It is the feast of liberation—the liberation of the Jews, and in time, the liberation of all men. Take up your cups and drink with me. Now, don't hesitate. Yes, that's better. Blessed art thou O Lord our God, ruler of the universe, who has sanctified the fruit of the vine. And the fruit, my dear ones, is freedom. Let us drink to the freedom that only God can give."

***

Nicodemus stood before Caiaphas in his private sitting room on the second floor of the palace. He had told his story as briefly and forcefully as he could. He had explained everything including the plans of Judas and the plotting of Pilate. He had explained, but not without emotion, that Joshua was prepared to sacrifice his life for the nation.

Caiaphas said nothing until he was finished. His expression had changed only slightly, but Nicodemus could tell that even he was moved—moved and surprised and at a loss.

"I'll tell you frankly, Nicodemus," he said in flat tones, "I never expected this. I had many ideas of what might happen tomorrow, but this...." His voice trailed off and he sat staring into the distance.

Nicodemus began to feel very nervous. He, too, was surprised. He had thought that the High Priest, the sworn enemy of the "Galilean Preacher," would be pleased to hear that the confrontation he had expected would not occur. It was over, the battle with Joshua was over.

"We must gather the Sanhedrin," Caiaphas said quietly. "Not all, but the most influential members. We must meet here tonight."

"Joshua?"

"I'll send Temple guards to bring him here. No one will interfere with them."

"He's waiting in the garden of Gethsemane, at the foot of the Mount of Olives. He didn't want you to come for him at my house, or any other house. He doesn't want to cause trouble for anyone."

For the first time, Caiaphas gave a hint of a smile. "He has never avoided 'trouble' before," he said.

***

The sky was clear except for a few puffy clouds beyond the city. The wind had died down so that the clouds hardly moved. Like sentinels they guarded the Temple. The night was unusually warm for the time of year. Typically, the Judaean hills cooled down considerably on a spring night, but not this one.

The people were not expecting to see Joshua on this Passover night and so they did not notice the straggly band that issued from the southern gate and made its way down the Kidron Valley and across, into the grove of olive trees at the foot of the mount.

Joshua had wanted to wait alone, to pray and to meditate, but his disciples insisted on coming with him. They were a sad and disconsolate group. All of their hopes and dreams had been dashed by the events of the evening.

It was difficult to believe. Only hours earlier they had dreamed of Israel's imminent liberation and the beginning of Joshua's kingdom. Some had imagined themselves in important roles. Others had no thought for personal advancement, but all of them realized that none of their expectations would be fulfilled on this Festival day.

In fact, they were lost. Their lives seemed at that moment to have little meaning. They had committed themselves—all they were and all they had, to Joshua's cause. Joshua had repeatedly told them that the cause was God's, not his, but they had easily slipped into identifying the two.

Now, Joshua would be gone. They would have no leader and perhaps, no cause.

Simon Peter, sharing such thoughts, felt guilty. How could he worry over what would happen to him and his companions when Joshua was facing death? He increased his pace until he was walking beside Joshua.

Joshua looked up and saw him and smiled. Brother Jacob and Judith on one side, Simon Peter on the other. That was as it should be.

The olive orchard was deserted at night. The press stood silent and motionless. The vinegary smell of the olives was faint and not oppressive. The trees, old and gnarled, clamped the ground firmly with roots that sank deep into Israel. They had witnessed great events, Joshua thought, and they will witness many others. As he looked, the silvery leaves fluttered in a brief gust, as if to acknowledge him and his words.

Joshua drew his mother aside. . Before he could speak, she whispered to him.

"I want to wait with you."

He shook his head. "Please, mother, no. This night is difficult enough. If I see you, if I feel your pain, I may weaken."

She studied his face in the brilliant moonlight. It was not necessary to memorize his features. They were already engraved in her heart. Yet she knew this might be the last time she would see her son alive, possibly the last time she would touch him. She took his hands and held them for a moment, then leaned forward and brushed his lips with a brief kiss. She turned quickly and took the arm of Eliezer and walked rapidly up the hill towards Bethany.

"Go with them," Joshua said to the sisters of Eliezer, Miriam and Martha. "Take care of her." The sisters nodded, embraced him quickly and hurried off.

Joshua turned to face his followers. He looked into the eyes of Nathan and Sarah. They were old but they were strong. They had known both victory and defeat. And they had each other. They would survive and their faith would not be destroyed.

Simeon, too, was old, but he had been a Zealot fighter. He knew that today's defeat bore the seeds of tomorrow's triumph. He was too determined to surrender.

He looked at Mattathias and Philip. They were men of the world, better educated than the others. He could not know which way they would turn, but their expressions were straightforward— they did not look away. He had hopes for them.

He thought of Judas and a pang of loss went through him. Judas had betrayed him. That was no surprise. He had known the risk of Judas's defection from the beginning. That was why he had kept him so close, struggled so hard to win him. Poor Judas. In his heart, he had known that Joshua was right, but his head had ruled him. He had sacrificed the word of God to the word of Judas. That was mankind's greatest struggle, Joshua thought. The battle that must often be fought and might never be fully won.

Joshua had a brief sense of failure. If only he could have strengthened Judas's faith enough. But the choice had always been Judas's and in the end he had chosen his own strength rather than God's. Judas was not the first and he would not be the last. In truth, the failure was his own.

Joshua looked into the eyes of Johannon and little Jacob. They were bewildered. They had never imagined this adventure would end with the death of Joshua. But they were very strong and very brave. They had followed Johannon, the Baptizer, and they had followed Joshua, but in fact, they had followed God. The sons of Zebedee were neither scholars nor priests, but they were sons of thunder, and the thunder was the Lord's.

Joshua said none of these things aloud, yet his disciples heard them in their hearts, and they were strengthened by his words. There were no words of farewell, only the unspoken truths which he imparted, the loving look in his eyes and the caress of his kindly touch. They understood and they tried to prepare themselves. They settled on the ground and on the rocky outcropping and they waited.

Only Simon Peter and Andrew, Brother Jacob and Judith remained standing. Simon tapped Andrew's shoulder and sent him off to rest among the trees. Whatever his brother wanted, Andrew would do for him.

"Come," Joshua said, "stay with me. I want to talk to you and I want to pray."

They followed him to where the rocks created a natural bench in a half circle, but before they sat down, Joshua felt a sudden surge of fear that staggered him. Jacob and Simon took his arms and would have helped him to sit, but he straightened himself and spoke to them.

"My soul is very sorrowful, even to death," he said, but as they reached out comforting arms, he waved them away. "I am fearful for myself, but I am more fearful for you. It is important that you understand the meaning of this day. It is important that you remain strong. You, the three of you, must lead the others. They will need your strength to survive this time.

"I know that tonight it seems that all is lost, all is ended. But this is not the end, it is only the beginning." He touched their hands, each in turn. "With the Almighty there is never an end, only a beginning. He asks this sacrifice of us, of me, so that all may be saved, that all may enter God's kingdom. You must know that, understand that, teach it to the others and to the world. God loves Israel and wants her to minister to mankind, but Israel cannot teach the world what she herself does not believe. Love of God is good, but not enough. Love of God's law is good, but not enough. Here, now, in this beloved land, we must make a new beginning. We must turn away from war and choose peace, even if some of us must die in the attempt.

"Hillel said it, 'if not now, when?' You must look upon my death as a true beginning, as a symbol for what men must do in God's cause, so that all may enjoy the blessing of God's love.

"In a little while, I will be gone and you will not see me. But you must know I will be with God—at his right hand, pleading with him on your account—as all the prophets plead with Him on your account.

"The day will come when we will meet again in God's Kingdom and I look forward to and pray for that day. But you must promise me now that you will not give up your faith, that you will serve the flock which I have gathered, and that you will minister to all the lost sheep of Israel. Promise it now."

They promised him in simple words, for he had taught them not to swear, but rather to say yes or no without embellishment.

Then, feeling his love for them spilling over, he embraced them again and said, "Leave me for a moment, for I must pray alone to my Father."

They nodded and moved off, leaving Joshua, who instead of sitting on the bench fell to his knees. He had been strong for the others, realizing that weakness on his part would destroy them. But now, in the dark and silent night with the dim glow of the city in the distance, he saw himself suspended on a wooden cross, his arms splayed out, his face contorted.

Joshua felt the pain, the agony, and he could not help allowing a sob to escape his lips. He saw the cup of wine that he had held out to his disciples, being held out to him, and the wine was truly his blood.

"Oh Lord," he prayed. "If it be possible, let this cup pass from me. But nevertheless, not my will but Thy will be done."

He waited then, as if for a sign. But there was none, or as he realized, that indeed was the sign. Therefore, he resigned himself to his fate.

Joshua continued with his prayers, asking for the peace of his soul and of all those he loved. He had seldom asked before for individual intercession, except in the case of illness or disease, but this time, he felt he could make an exception.

For a long time, perhaps for an hour, he remained on his knees, praying to God, for the good of Israel, for the liberation of mankind. Gradually, the feelings of fear and anxiety left him. He knew why he was where he was and what was required of him.

Joshua rose and looked toward his disciples. Judith was only a few feet away, watching him. But even Brother Jacob and Simon Peter had dozed off.

He smiled and whispered. "On this night, of all nights, could you not have waited for me?"

Simon Peter rose suddenly. "What, Master, what do you want?"

"Nothing," Joshua said quietly

Then he returned to his prayers. But again, the fear of his fate came upon him, and sweat broke out on his forehead, even in the cool night.

"Take this cup from me, Lord," he prayed again, then faltered and asked the same thing, yet in a softer voice. Still, there was only silence.

Joshua sighed then and whispered, again, "Thy will be done."

He remained on his knees for a little while longer, but he felt cleansed. He knew that for a moment he had given way to fear, but he did not believe his heavenly father would fault him for that. He was not expected to be perfect, but rather to strive with all his might for that which he knew to be right.

He was content that he had asked to be relieved of this terrible responsibility. It was as if that was his duty, too. Now, from God's silence, he knew that he must proceed.

For a brief moment another thought slipped through his defenses. He recalled that Abraham had been called upon to sacrifice his son, and that Isaac had been ready to submit to God's will. Then, and then only, God had provided a substitute.

Joshua smiled. "But I am the substitute," he told himself, "the substitute for all of Israel."

Refreshed and strengthened, he stood up, ready to do what he must.

"Look," Judith cried. "Temple Guards coming up the path."

They had come out of the northern gate, following a circuitous route as they tried to avoid the mass of the people camped in the Kidron Valley. They were ordinary men, a bit taller and stronger than most of their countrymen and they were fiercely dedicated to the protection of the Temple. They knew that their neighbors viewed them with some doubt, but they realized that men in their positions would always be somewhat estranged from their countrymen. They accepted that as part of the job, and sometimes felt pleased about it. They were men apart and that suited them. Still, they were surprised to have this mission, on this of all nights.

Their leader was a young captain, Joiachim. He was a slender, well-built young fellow from Hebron, better educated than most in his profession. He was pleased that Reuben, on the High Priest's orders, had selected him for this assignment. He would carry it off with skill and precision, and perhaps one day, he would be Captain of the Guard.

"Let's get out of here," Simon Peter said. The others roused themselves to follow.

Joshua raised his hand. "They are coming for me," he said. "The hour is nigh."

"Guards?" Nathan asked. "Why would the High Priest send guards."

"To show his authority," Joshua said.

Joiachim, coming upon the disciples, at the head of his men, was surprised. He had heard Joshua teach in the Temple and had been impressed with his grace and power. He had been told that Joshua would be with his disciples. Somehow, he had expected a more impressive group of people.

Joshua looked at him with a faint smile. That disconcerted him. This man was a notorious revolutionary, a powerful preacher. Yet he seemed so benign.

Joiachim had not been told how to bring in Joshua, only to do it and he decided to use his authority. "Take him," he told the men.

Two men stepped forward and started to grab Joshua roughly by the arms.

"Just a minute," Simon Peter said, advancing on them. They stepped back for a moment, frightened by his immense size and the fierce expression on his face. Both soldiers pulled their short swords. Peter, truly outraged, wrenched the sword from the hand of one soldier, shoved him aside and turned on the other.

Joiachim and his men drew their own weapons. Sarah screamed and Nathan took her arm and ran off a ways. Phillip and Mattathias also backed away, but Johannon and Little Jacob picked up their staves and advanced toward the soldiers.

Judith and Brother Jacob hurried toward Joshua, more interested in protecting him than themselves.

Joshua stepped between Simon and the other soldier. "No!" he said, his powerful voice booming in the night air. "There must be no bloodshed here! Haven't I taught you that those who live by the sword, perish by the sword? Simon Peter, give the soldier back his weapon. The rest of you, stand back."

Reluctantly, Simon handed the sword to the soldier he had taken it from, while Joshua turned to the captain. "Why have you come after me as if I were a criminal? You saw me teaching daily in the Temple, but you never raised a hand to me then. Why do you treat me with such disrespect now?"

Joiachim stared at him, flustered and embarrassed. "Put up your swords!" he yelled at his men.

"Will you come with us, Rabbi?" he asked Joshua in a mild voice.

Joshua nodded. He turned and waved once to his disciples, as if it were a casual departure, as if he would see them again very shortly. Then he strode off ahead of the soldiers, as though leading them.

"What will we do?" Andrew asked.

There was only silence. Their leader was gone.

"Judith," Brother Jacob said, "go back to the house of Eliezer and comfort our mother. Nathan, you and your wife, go with her. The rest of us will go back and wait in the house of Nicodemus. We'll let you know what we hear."

They did as Jacob suggested. He and the ones going to Nicodemus's house walked sadly together through the valley. Ahead, in the darkness, they could barely see the small band that must be the soldiers and Joshua moving in an arc beyond the tents of the people. Brother Jacob could not help thinking how sad and unremarked this passage was compared to the triumphant entry only a few days before.

15.

SANHEDRIN

They came from various parts of the city, most of them still in their Festival finery. Most were surprised at the call from Caiaphas. They had expected to spend a glorious holiday in the city, not to be called upon for some serious matter. Even those who had heard of the Galilean preacher, even those who deemed him the Messiah, and especially those who had not, did not expect any trouble at the Passover. They knew full well that the people were animated at the holiday and that any gathering as large as this, sampling the entire nation, had a possibility of mischief, but when the Festival began, they put such thoughts from their minds

A few, men like Annas and Ahab, Nicodemus and Joseph of Arimathea, had become aware of the growing tension between Joshua and the High Priest, and some knew of Joshua's plans for the next day. But even they had put off any thoughts of trouble, hoping for the best.

Caiaphas had chosen his own home for the meeting. To have met at the traditional hall in the Temple would have drawn unwanted attention from the Romans and might have brought about an interruption in their plans.

Further, Caiaphas had deliberately not called a formal meeting of the Sanhedrin, deliberately not called all of the members. He knew that what action might be taken would not, in terms of the established traditions, be fully legal. Caiaphas wanted to have the sense of the Sanhedrin, but not their formal action. He wanted to be able to have it both ways—to rely on their wishes, but to be able to deny that what they did might have the force of law.

They gathered in his great hall, most of the more important men of the nation. They were priests and scholars, landowners and merchants. Some were wealthy, some rather poor, most somewhere in between. They were all noted, in one degree or another, for their devotion to the law and to the nation. Most important of all, they were devoted to God.

Reuben counted them off as they entered. All who had been asked, came. A few were angry, but most were simply concerned. The servants, surly at being worked late into the night, had grouped chairs in a semicircle. Caiaphas had reserved for himself a seat at the pivot of the group, a somewhat richer and higher one, but that was his way.

The men whispered among themselves. "What is it?" they asked.

"Some new abomination from the emperor?"

"Is it that Galilean preacher?"

Those who knew not, made guesses. Those who knew were silent.

After a while, Caiaphas made his delayed entrance. He had waited purposely, wanting to have all of them gathered before he arrived. He did not want idle questioning and useless disagreements. They must deal with the true danger, swiftly and effectively.

At his appearance, the group fell silent. He sat down and slowly scanned their faces.

"We face the greatest crisis of our time," he said. "The Galilean preacher, Joshua Ben Joseph, has proclaimed himself the Messiah."

"Ridiculous," Nehemiah said, "this man is nothing more—"

"—We are not here to debate his claim," Caiaphas said in a loud voice, "but to discuss the consequences of that claim."

Nehemiah and other Sadducees subsided and Caiaphas went on.

"The Romans take as dim a view of him as you do," Caiaphas said to Nehemiah. "But that is not the issue. Pilate, the governor, as we well know, is not a friend of our people. Despite our attempts to accommodate ourselves to his rule, he has done all he can to provoke us, from the day he first raised the standards on the Antonia fortress until he stole the Corban, collapsed the Siloam Tower and imprisoned Bar Abbas.

"Pilate has responded at every opportunity with violence and oppression. Now he has chosen to take the claims of Joshua as an excuse for renewed oppression. We have learned that tomorrow, when the Galilean enters the Temple, spies have been sent to proclaim him King of Israel, and when that happens, soldiers will arrest Joshua as a revolutionary. Then, as the people defend the Galilean, the troops will turn upon the people and begin to slaughter them."

Many in the group cried out at these words. Some said, "Keep him from the Temple!" Others cried, "Persuade him not to claim he is the king!"

Caiaphas rose to emphasize his words. "None of this will do us any good," he said. "Joshua has told Nicodemus he has no intention of claiming the throne of Israel. But Pilate's spies will do it for him and then the slaughter will begin. We also face another crisis."

The men of the Sanhedrin remained on edge, anxious to hear what Caiaphas might have to say, even as they feared to know it.

"The city is filled with Zealots, chiefs and their soldiers. And, worst of all, these men have brought thousands of weapons into the city. They, too, are determined to proclaim this man the King of Israel. It matters not what we do, either our friends or our enemies are determined to bring bloodshed upon us."

"Stop them!" one cried. "We must talk to Pilate."

"He won't listen," Reuben said. "He's determined to have a bloodbath."

"Our own people—we'll speak to them," said Gamaliel. "Surely we can turn them away from this madness."

"They won't listen, either," said Nicodemus. "It's too late to stop these people."

"Then we must stop Joshua," Nehemiah said.

"Precisely," said Annas, who had remained silent until now, "but it won't do to merely keep him from the Temple tomorrow. Between the Zealots and the Romans, his mere non-appearance might not be enough to avoid war."

"What do we do?" asked Joseph of Arimathea. A terrible image was forming in his mind, but he had to hear the truth.

At that moment there was a commotion at the door of the courtyard and they heard the voice of the captain of guards yelling at the servants.

"Open the gates!" he called out. "We have brought the man that the High Priest sent us for."

***

Inside the Great Hall, there was a sudden silence. Even the long flickering flames of the tapers seemed frozen for an instant. All heads turned toward the doorway to the room.

The captain had intended to make a show of bringing Joshua to the house of Caiaphas, but the brief trip into the city had changed his mind. There was something about this Galilean, something unusual and powerful, mixed with a surprising grace and gentleness. It was beyond Joiachim's experience, and he was wise enough to know it.

To his surprise, he found himself pushing aside the draperies that edged the passage to the High Priest's hall and when Joshua entered the room, he was a step behind. Then, seeing the powers of the nation assembled, Joiachim lowered his head and backed out of the room.

Joshua walked slowly towards Caiaphas. The members of the Sanhedrin watched him with great interest. Many had never seen him and they, too, like almost all men, were impressed with his ease and grace and power. Some tried to recall when they had seen another man with similar presence, but they were at a loss.

The strange silence irritated Nehemiah.

"Do you realize what you've done? You've endangered the nation."

"Yes," said Eliakim, another Sadducee, "how dare you claim the throne of Israel?"

"Who is this man?" asked a third.

They argued among themselves, but Joshua said nothing.

Caiaphas also said nothing. He watched and listened to the reactions of those he could depend upon to support him. He wanted to measure their response to Joshua. It was obvious that despite their irritation, they were impressed.

Joshua seemed not to hear. He studied the members of the Sanhedrin with at least as much interest as they had studied him. How intelligent they looked, how well-to-do and wise. It was reassuring to him to see that the most important body in the nation was composed of men of years and fine appearance. He was not a man to be impressed by mere good looks, but he could see the intelligence and the character in the eyes of these men. Regardless of their angry words, even of their fear, they would act wisely, if given the chance.

"You stand there and say nothing," Eliakim said. "Defend yourself."

Still Joshua did not respond.

Gamaliel spoke quietly, so that the others had to lean forward to hear him. "Why do you attack, even before you know if there is to be a battle? Why do you speak when you have not heard?"

"He doesn't say anything," Eliakim protested. "What are we to do?"

"Hasn't God told you?" Joshua asked. "He has told me."

Then, again he was silent.

"Please," Joseph of Arimathea said, "please share God's word with us?"

Joshua smiled at him. "The Lord Almighty has told me that it is time for Israel to live up to her holy mission—to become a nation of priests and a holy nation. The Lord has told me that the time for war is past, the day of violence is over, the lion must lie down with the lamb.

"That is what God has always told us, but we have seldom listened. We have followed kings instead of prophets, soldiers instead of God.

"But that cannot go on. Israel will be destroyed if that continues and the children of Israel will be scattered over the face of the earth. That is the message I have carried from one end of the land to the other. That is the message I have found the people yearning to hear. They are sick to death of kings and priests who follow the laws of man instead of God, who enrich themselves at the people's expense."

Caiaphas slapped a hand against the arm of his chair. "We have not assembled to hear your preaching. We know of the crisis in Jerusalem and we will resolve it with your help or without."

Joshua laughed. "Even the High Priest believes that HE is the one who will solve Israel's problems, not God."

Nehemiah stood up. "Who are you to speak to the High Priest in this manner? You're nothing but a Galilean rebel."

"This man is the Messiah," Nicodemus threatened.

"You're crazy," said Eliakim. "He doesn't look like the Messiah to me."

A dark shadow crossed Joshua's face. "You think you would know the Messiah? You think he must appear in some way that would impress you. Do you believe that God has chosen his anointed to satisfy your image of him? How dare you challenge the Lord of Hosts?"

Shocked, frightened, Eliakim sat down in his chair, almost as if he had been pushed.

"I have told you who I am and why I am here, so that you will know what to do when I am gone. It will be your responsibility to carry on the work of the Lord, and it will be your failure if Israel does not survive. I tell you the love of God is forever, and the patience of God is great—but not forever. If you fail the Lord now, you will endure his wrath."

"Tell us," Joseph of Arimathea said, "what must we do?"

Joshua sighed and shook his head. "Have you not heard? Didn't you listen?"

"We heard," Gamaliel said. "I hope we have the courage to do what you ask. Only if we follow the word of God, will we be liberated from the Roman yoke."

Joshua smiled for the first time.

"What about now—on this night?" Caiaphas said. "What about the morning?"

Joshua shrugged. "In the morning, I must die."

***

Despite the protests of Brother Jacob, Nico and Simon Peter had insisted on going to the palace of Caiaphas. Captain Joiachim and his guards were still in the courtyard, waiting for further orders.

Nico had no difficulty entering the gates. He was well-known to the servants and they admitted him immediately. They did not know Simon Peter and at first did not want to let him in.

"Wait a minute," Joiachim said, "weren't you with the Galilean preacher?"

"No," said Simon Peter, "not I," for he feared they would not let him in if he admitted knowing Joshua.

Nico, who had gone ahead to the door of the house, came back. "He's with me," he said.

"You were with him, too," said the captain..

"What business is that of yours?" Nico said brusquely, staring him down and taking Simon's arm and leading him inside.

Joiachim, like all soldiers, was vulnerable to a show of authority and he decided not to interfere.

The servants wouldn't admit Nico to the palace. "I've been here many times," he said.

"The High Priest said no one is to be admitted."

Nico shrugged and turned away. He and Simon sat on a low stone wall and waited.

***

"Why can't you simply leave Jerusalem?" Joseph of Arimathea was asking. He hardly knew Joshua, but he had loved him at once and the thought of his sacrifice was too much.

"I was sent to Jerusalem," Joshua said, "I will not turn away."

"Even to save the people?" Caiaphas asked.

"That will not save the people. If the Zealots think I have abandoned them, they will resort to violence in any case."

"Even to save your life?" Nicodemus asked.

"He who would truly save his life must be willing to sacrifice it. Greater love has no man than to give up his life for his brothers."

They were silent for a moment, hearing these words and thinking about them. They were awed by his courage and his goodness. Even Nehemiah and Eliakim shifted in their seats, unnerved by this remarkable evidence of his spirituality.

"It is against the law," Joseph of Arimathea said, "to sacrifice a man, any man, to save his brothers. All lives are equally valuable in the eyes of God. We have no right to take your life and offer it as a substitute for our own."

"You are not offering it, I am," Joshua responded.

"But you want us to accept your offer and therefore cooperate in taking your life," Caiaphas said.

Joshua shook his head. "God alone can take it."

"Your piety is great," Gamaliel said, "and your goodness surpasses ours. We are humble before the gift you are prepared to offer to save your people, but it is difficult, very difficult for us to stand by and allow you to do it."

Joshua smiled. "Were there a choice, I would prefer not to do it. I love my life and I cherish every moment of it, but I know that while my flesh may be flayed and tormented, my soul will be with God. My soul they cannot kill, cannot even harm, for that belongs to the Lord."

He turned to Caiaphas. "This assembly must condemn me as a rebel, violating the rule of Rome and turn me over to Pilate for punishment. This assembly must insist that I be put to death as an enemy of the Emperor. You may say whatever else you please. You may call me a blasphemer, accuse me of violating our laws—whatever you choose. But you must insist that I am a criminal and that only my death will do."

Caiaphas had been watching Annas, who had said little during the proceedings. Annas's eyes had been fixed on Joshua. No matter what was said or by whom, his eyes never left Joshua. Caiaphas tried to concentrate on what was being said, but he was fascinated by his father-in-law's fascination.

Annas was thinking, Why is it they come from the common classes, the farmers, the shepherds, the carpenters? Why is it that while we in power are training the leaders, the true leaders are being trained so far from us that we never see them, and by forces we don't even understand? How is it that God humbles us in this way? While we are full of ourselves and our wealth and our power, some young man, some unknown person we had never even suspected of existing, comes marching into our chambers and sets our lives on edge.

He thought of Shammai, the great teacher of the Sadducees. Shammai would have had little use for this man's teachings. He was a strict follower of the written law, and opposed Hillel and his more tolerant views. Shammai scoffed at the Pharisees and their belief in resurrection. There was but one life, it was up to men to make certain it was holy. But even Shammai would have found this humble Galilean preacher formidable.

Annas still couldn't take his eyes off Joshua. What strength, what gentleness. He had seen men with years of public training shiver before the Sanhedrin, while this man was totally at his ease. Could anyone doubt that the spirit of God was within him? Annas did not, and yet, his heart was heavy. Groaning with the burden of his years and his message, he heaved himself out of his chair. Many in the chamber had kept half an eye on him, and when he stood, they became silent at once.

"This is madness," he said in a near whisper, but a whisper that carried into every corner of that ornate room. "This man stands before us and in all sincerity and undoubted good faith tells us that we must condemn him to death."

"Not us," Nicodemus said, "the Romans."

Annas did not even look at him when he replied. "Who will recall that fine line, a month from now, or a year—a hundred years? No one, I tell you, no one. It is we who condemn him to death when we give him to the Romans, for we know what they will do with him—nay, it is worse than that; we turn him over so that THEY WILL KILL HIM.

"Joshua Ben Joseph asks this tribunal to sentence him to death. We do not have such power. We sit tonight with only a portion of our membership and we are asked to do that which our own law forbids. It is impossible for us to do what this man asks, not if we love God and love the Law."

"You must," Joshua said. "There is no choice."

Annas's eyes flickered, but he did not look at Joshua. "He tells us we must do this for the people. Yet, if we asked the people, would they want us to condemn this man? We all know the answer, we have seen it every day in the Temple. They love him, they want him for their king, they do not want him dead. And if we do this vile thing, they, the people of Israel, will condemn us, they will hate us."

"They will learn to understand," Caiaphas said blandly. "In the meantime we will save their lives."

"Do you think so?" Annas asked. "When we have knowingly deprived them of their greatest hope, of the one man who champions their dreams? I tell you, it would be better to suffer the violence of revolution than to destroy men's souls."

For the first time, he looked about the room. All were staring at him, impressed by the strength of his convictions. Since the elevation of

Caiaphas to the High Priest's office, Annas had never publicly opposed his son-in-law, although many considered him the true power behind Caiaphas.

"I, for one, will have no part of this," Annas said. He walked towards the door.

Eliakim stood up, as if to follow him, but he saw that no-one else rose. He hesitated, then slowly sat down. Annas, old and weary and heartbroken, walked out of the chamber alone.

"He's right," Joseph of Arimathea said softly. "Yet, I could not follow him out of this chamber. This night is too important for such an action, but it's true that we have no jurisdiction of this matter under either our own or Roman law."

"There is God's law," Joshua said. "That is the law that we must follow; the law that sent me for this very reason. I must show the people of Israel that violence is not the path to peace, that war does not lead to God's kingdom. Within a few hours," and here his voice broke briefly, "the people will know that my life on earth has been ended so that theirs might continue—not only for the value of the flesh itself, but for the redemption of their souls, the very existence of God's people, and the future of their holy mission on this earth.

"Then, it will be up to you to lead them—to turn away from obedience to Rome and to demand obedience to God. Without weapons other than the word of God, itself."

He stood even taller, but his words were strained. "I must die, so that they may live. I must die, so that they may be free."

The men in the chamber watched him, believing his strength might be fading, that his resolution might slacken.

His words came forth stronger than ever:

"HEAR O ISRAEL, THE LORD OUR GOD. THE LORD IS ONE."

16.

PERHAPS

Baruch had not been the same after the death of Johannon, the Baptizer. He, himself, was too weak he believed, to ever challenge authority. But he could no longer accept the Essenes' teaching that they were in some ways elect and had the right to absent themselves from the everyday world.

He had first been tested by Joshua and his teachings, but had not had the courage to follow him when he left Qumran. However, after reporting Johannon's death to the Zealot leaders and seeing Joshua again, he was not able to continue with the brothers. On his return to Qumran, he told the Maskil he must leave Qumran, at least for a while. The Maskil was surprisingly understanding.

Benjamin, the Zealot, invited him to stay in his house. When Benjamin was killed in the Bar Abbas uprising, the family asked him to remain. He was there when Amos appeared with word of the plans for the next day. For the first time, he heard of the weapons stored about the city. He was too surprised to protest, but so disenchanted with the Zealots that he knew he must leave again.

As soon as Amos left the house, Baruch went out into the night. His thoughts were in disarray. It had been difficult for him to accept the regime of the Essenes, much as he admired them. It was even more difficult to leave that safe haven and re-enter the every-day world. He never quite understood the strange tie between the Zealots and the Essenes—between those who saw the world as an earthly struggle and those who saw it as purely spiritual, but somehow he had managed.

He felt abandoned again. He did not belong with those who would enforce their way with weapons. Also, he found it difficult to believe that the Joshua who had slept on his pallet would accept being called "King."

The need to speak to Joshua overwhelmed him. He knew it would be an imposition, arriving on the Passover, but he felt driven. There must be something he could depend on, some rock that would be his salvation.

He had heard that Joshua and his disciples were staying in Bethany and he set out for the town at once, walking very quickly. When he reached the foot of the Mount of Olives, he began to run.

***

The hours passed slowly. The air cooled considerably, and as it did, a fine thin fog crept into the city. It was a wispy fog, like thin shreds of cotton, and it wound itself around the people in the courtyard. The servants were surly. This was the Festival, and they had expected a full meal and a long night's rest. Instead, they were called upon to remain awake and care for their masters. It seemed they would never be allowed to sleep that night.

The Temple Guards were just as irritable. They, too, had expected a quiet evening and a good night's rest. Routinely, their officers prepared them for heavy duty at the time of the festivals, but the people were generally well behaved and problems rarely occurred. Yet, here they were, slouched about the High Priest's courtyard through a long night.

One of the servants started a fire in a brazier to warm himself against the chilly fog. The flames didn't travel far and the heat was as pale as the flame. Still, it looked cheerful and the very sight of it warmed them.

A maid, young and rather pretty, had flirted with the soldiers. But they were on duty and knew that nothing would come of it. After a while, she turned her attention to Nico and Simon Peter. The two of them had slowly edged towards the great gateway into the palace, hoping to be as close to Joshua as possible. They heard nothing, saw no one enter or leave the chamber.

They looked at each other from time to time, hoping one of them would have some good idea, but nothing occurred to either of them. The cool night and the fog combined to dampen their spirits. They wondered why they had come.

The serving girl approached Simon. He was a giant of a fellow and not too bad looking. She decided to talk to him.

"It's warmer by the fire," she said. "Why don't you come over?"

Simon shook his head. "I'll stay where I am," he said.

"You're one of them aren't you?" she asked in a friendly manner.

"What?" he said, startled.

"One of his followers—that Galilean preacher they brought over here."

The Temple Guards watched idly as the girl spoke to Simon. He was frightened, suddenly. Would they take him, too?

"Don't know what you're talking about," he mumbled.

"I can tell by your accent," the girl went on, prattling happily. "You're a Galilean."

"Is that a crime?" Nico asked, trying to distract her.

"Of course not," she said. "But he's not fooling me," she continued, looking at Simon. "I saw you in the Temple with the Rabbi."

"I tell you, I don't know the man," Simon said.

"Then why are you here?" asked the officer.

Simon was trapped.

"He's with me," Nico said. "I'm a priest."

Still, the captain stared at Simon and the girl smiled knowingly.

Simon's agitation was extreme. He felt a combination of fear and anger, anxiety and scorn.

"I tell you I don't know him!" he yelled.

Then, from the yard behind the palace, a cock crowed. Simon Peter listened in dismay. It was true, even as Joshua had predicted. He had denied him, over and again. He turned away sharply as tears sprang into his eyes. But in the darkness and fog, no one noticed.

***

Brother Jacob was struggling not to give way to despair. Joshua had been torn from him and he felt the wound, raw, bleeding and without relief. There was no way that he could oppose Joshua, even though the urge had been great to drag him away, forcefully. He sensed that Simon Peter and a few of the others might even have helped him. But he had chosen long ago never to oppose Joshua, and he would not turn away from that decision.

He would have liked to have the comfort of Miriam and Judith, but he had been instructed to remain where he was. Simon Peter and Nico had disappeared. Jacob knew they had gone to the House of the High Priest, to be as close as possible to Joshua. He would have liked to join them, but he felt his brother had had a sound reason for sending him to the house of Nicodemus.

He paced the rooms of the house. Philip and Mattathias, Johannon and Little Jacob and Simeon sat silently, hardly speaking, sometimes dozing. Perhaps he was supposed to cheer them up, but he was incapable of doing it. Had he tried, he might have broken down and cried.

Gaius Fabricius sat on a bench close to the door, as if waiting for a message. When Joshua had told Brother Jacob and the others to remain in Nicodemus's house, he assumed that included him. None of them had suffered more than he had over Joshua, and he was grateful not to be sent away. But he did not know what to do. Perhaps he should throw his lot in with the disciples, help them to spread Joshua's word.

Somehow, he felt his work with the Roman administration was not over. Perhaps they had identified him with the death of Septimus. In that case, there would be little he could do. But if they had not, he might still be useful by remaining "inside." The idea was distasteful, but a small sacrifice compared to the one Joshua was making. He calmed himself as best he could and sat patiently on the bench.

Brother Jacob came to the entrance way on one of his many trips through the house. He had hardly noticed Gaius before, but now he realized that the man was their greatest friend among the Romans. He wanted to thank him, but could not find words.

The knock on the door startled Gaius and Jacob and roused the others. They rushed to the entrance, watching with great hope as Brother Jacob yanked the door open. It was Baruch. He was surprised to see several disciples staring at him. Even in the dark, he could not miss their looks of disappointment.

"Sorry...uh, sorry...it's late...I wanted to see...Joshua."

Brother Jacob pulled him inside. Then, briefly, he told him what had happened. Baruch had a kind and facile face and his distress was evident. Jacob had not finished his story, before the tears began to slip down his face.

"I...I'm sorry," Baruch said. "I...I have loved him since he first came to Qumran." Then he blurted out, "There isn't anything I wouldn't do to save his life."

Brother Jacob's head snapped back sharply. He peered at Baruch with great intensity. Perhaps, perhaps this was why he had been sent here.

**

"I don't think it's possible," Baruch said.

"I will quote my brother," Jacob said. "'With God all things are possible.'"

"It's worth trying," Gaius said.

The others quickly agreed.

"But there's so little time, and I have none of those things here."

"Can you ride a horse?" Gaius asked.

Baruch nodded, "Not well, but I can ride."

"I'll get you a horse—"

"—I want to go with him," Brother Jacob said.

"Two horses. And then I'll go back to the Antonia."

***

The doors suddenly swung open and a servant called for the captain of the guards. After a whispered conference, he motioned to two of his men. They went inside and the doors closed behind them.

Nico and Simon Peter were on their feet now, pressing as close as they dared to the doorway. After a few minutes, it opened again, and the men of the Sanhedrin came out, walking quickly, their capes over their heads, hurrying away from the Palace of Caiaphas as quickly as they could.

Still, Nico and Simon had not seen Joshua. One after another the leaders left, hurrying down the streets to their homes, carrying with them the awful knowledge of that night. The doors closed and remained closed for several minutes. Caiaphas came out with Reuben a step behind him. Then came the captain, and with him, Joshua, his head held high, but his hands bound behind him. Last came two soldiers, their swords drawn.

Nico felt a sob catch in his throat. Simon Peter could neither move nor speak.

Joshua glanced over and saw them. He smiled suddenly, brightly. His look said, "Fear not, for I will be with you, always."

Both of them heard his words in their hearts. They would remember the look and the words for the rest of their lives.

***

The Maskil listened to Baruch and Jacob in silence.

"We will help in any way we can," he said. Then he called for Omriel.

The physician had changed little. His pink face still looked young and his eyes glowed with life. He had not minded being awakened in the middle of the night, and he was delighted to see Baruch again

"Of course," he said to their inquiry," a mixture of frankincense and myrrh is best, combined perhaps with gall. And a touch of another herb." He offered a trace of a smile, but provided no further information. "I can mix it for you very quickly. But remember, it loses its strength in the heat of the sun, so you must protect it until you use it."

"We'll be riding hard to get back. Will that affect it?"

The physician shook his head. "Probably not, but perhaps I should go with you." He looked at the Maskil, who did not even hesitate.

"Of course," he said. "Your vows would not prevent such an action, and your commission is to save lives."

"I'll hurry," he said.

17.

TRIAL

Roman sentries stopped Gaius at the gate.

"Come now," he said, feigning anger. "It's very late and I'm very tired."

"Apologies, Sire," the guard said nervously for he well knew that Gaius was highly ranked. "We are instructed to inform the governor the moment you return."

The words were frightening, but Gaius showed little emotion. "Bring me to him—and be quick about it."

The corridors of the fortress seemed especially dark and ominous to Gaius Fabricius. Their course led them past the slave quarters, locked now and heavily guarded. Gaius steadied himself and did not even look. The torches, restored several times during the night, were being allowed to gutter down. The light they shed was pale and weak, and the shadows they cast, long and frightening.

Gaius straightened his spine as he entered the anteroom.

To his surprise, the door to Pilate's chambers burst open at the same moment, and the prefect himself appeared, fully dressed and every hair in place.

"Thank the gods you're safe," Pilate said, truly startling his deputy, who had not heard a kind word in years. Pilate approached rapidly and clasped arms with Gaius in a firm greeting. "I thought that with Septimus murdered— you didn't know that—I see your surprise. Yes, I know you never loved the man, but murdered in his own quarters?"

Gaius had done his best to feign surprise, but now he was silent, waiting a signal for which way to turn.

Pilate was still speaking. "Then, when we couldn't find you—well, I didn't know what to expect."

Gaius was beginning to understand. Pilate had not been worried over the fate of his deputy, except inasmuch as it might indicate a massive plot against the Roman administration, perhaps an uprising of the slaves, an event with ample precedent.

"By the way," Pilate said, remembering himself. "Where were you?"

"I'm embarrassed to admit it, Excellency, but, you know, the calls of the flesh."

Pilate's face showed surprise, even pleasure. "You? Gaius, I would never have suspected." He laughed heartily, far more than the circumstances warranted.

Another soldier came to the threshold and hesitantly waited, fearful even to knock on the door.

"What is it?" Pilate asked irritably.

The soldier carried a note to Pilate who tore it open. His eyes widened. "The High Priest wishes to see me on a matter of greatest urgency." He threw the note to the floor. But then he said to Gaius, "I'll have to see him."

***

Pilate watched with great curiosity as the High Priest, the Sagan and a delegation of elders, entered his audience chamber. He was astonished that they would come to him at such an early hour, with the first streaks of dawn barely dabbing the sky.

He had thought of keeping them waiting, of pretending that he was still asleep, but he could not. He had looked curiously at his deputy. "Do you know what they want?" he had asked. Gaius had shaken his head.

They were leading a man, a tall blonde man with powerful shoulders and a fine, cleanly etched face. The man's hands were bound but he moved with grace and a look that seemed to announce that he was, in fact, a free man.

Pilate glanced quickly toward Gaius. He wanted to ask who this might be, but he saw that his deputy's eyes were fixed on the man. He had never seen such an expression in Gaius's face. Except that it couldn't be, he would have sworn that the look was one of love.

Even so, it was enough to disconcert him. He stared at Gaius for so long that the High Priest was almost upon him, and he had to wrench his attention back. The High Priest's clothing was purest white, with purple at the fringes and his crown was of the same white color, woven with gold. He held his head very high and looked out of cold, blue eyes with an expression of great arrogance.

But Pilate was neither angered nor intimidated. He knew that Caiaphas would not be standing before him on this festival, very early in the morning and in the Roman palace, unless he was in deep trouble.

They exchanged no greetings, measuring each other at length.

"We come on urgent business," Caiaphas said, his voice controlled but resonant, the words clear and his attitude commanding. "We who are in authority do not oppose the Roman state and we understand our responsibilities."

He paused, watching Pilate's response. The man's eyes were glittering, and his lips, usually turned down, were curved upward slightly, as if he were trying not to smile. Caiaphas paused, trying to master the surge of hatred that passed through him. The High Priest hated this task, hated the man who had forced it upon him, but knew that he held the fate of the nation in his hands. He could not allow his contempt for Pilate to interfere with his judgment.

"This man—this man we bring you in bonds, has declared himself to be the King of Israel. We have brought him before the most esteemed members of our Sanhedrin, to question him, to determine the truth of the charges brought against him.

"This man does not deny that his followers call him the King of Israel. Nor does he show any remorse for the words of his followers. We, who are responsible for the well-being of our people, cannot accept this claim. Further, we know that such a claim defies the laws of the Roman state. We understand that this is sedition.

"Knowing our duties, we would punish the man ourselves, but of course, we have no such authority. Therefore, we have brought him to you, to punish as you deem proper."

Pilate's expression changed while the High Priest was speaking. He began to realize what was happening. These Jews were offering him the Galilean as a criminal. They had arrested him themselves and were now denouncing him. It was incredible.

But, worse than incredible, it would destroy all his plans. There would be no rebellion today, no battle between Jews protecting their King and Roman legions defending their Emperor.

Impossible, it could not be. He had planned this moment for weeks. At this very moment, Paulus Aemilius was dressing soldiers as Jewish pilgrims, arming them for the assault. All over the city, Roman soldiers were moving into position, ready at a moment's notice to crush the opposition.

While Caiaphas spoke, he saw the recognition dawn on Pilate's face. He saw the eager snarl turn into doubt and then consternation. He watched the flush rise on the governor's face and his lips pull back, dog-like, angry and vicious. A chill spread through Caiaphas's bones. He suddenly felt old, very old, and the honor and glory of being High Priest seemed a great burden, as if all the sacrifices of a Passover had been heaped on his head instead of the altar.

Pilate's lips pried open and the words came forth like darts. He had to know, had to be sure. "Who is this man?" he asked.

For a moment, they all stared at him as if he were mad. But he had moved forward until he was within a few steps of the prisoner. Joshua looked at him with cool, blue eyes that hardly blinked. He showed no fear, and little concern. Pilate wondered, did he know, did he understand what they had in store for him? Impossible. He couldn't know, and remain serene.

"Who are you?" Pilate asked.

"If I told you," Joshua said in his mellow, compelling voice, "you would neither believe nor understand."

The words frightened Caiaphas. What if this man could affect Pilate as he had so many others? Perhaps he was beginning to understand and fear his fate.

"He is Joshua ben Joseph, of Galilee," Caiaphas said quickly.

Pilate would not back away. He stood where he was, biting his lower lip, staring at this handsome and compelling figure. "Tell me," he said, "are you the King of the Jews?"

"Are these your own words, or have others told them to you?"

"I?!" Pilate roared, "Do you think I am a Jew?!"

"Clearly not," Joshua said in a mild voice, and then he smiled.

The smile almost unnerved the Roman governor. How did one deal with such a man? Was he indeed a king—was he mad?

"To be the King of the Jews would be a brief honor," Pilate said. Yet he wondered why he spoke as he did. The important thing was to turn this matter around. He had to get this fellow out of here somehow, and get him back in the streets. It was important that he appear in the Temple within a few hours, so that the Jews could acclaim him and Pilate would be justified in sending in his troops.

"He looks harmless enough to me," Pilate said.

"This man has stirred up the nation," Caiaphas said. "There are threats of revolution, of civil war. Surely, the emperor does not want that."

Pilate circled Joshua, watching him with fascination. "Are you a revolutionary?" he asked.

"Some say so," Joshua said.

"What do you say?"

"I say, 'Follow the word of the Lord.'"

"Does the 'Lord' tell you to wage war on the Roman state?"

Joshua was silent. He knew what must be done, what must happen. But he would not lie for any man.

"You see?" Caiaphas said. "That is his way. He preaches one thing in one place, something else in another." Joshua stared at him. In some ways, the words of the High Priest were true. "The effect on the people is dangerous."

"I ask you again, are you the King of the Jews?"

"There is but one king, of all mankind, and that is God Almighty."

"I told you," Caiaphas said. "He denies the Emperor."

It was difficult for the others, for Nicodemus and Joseph of Arimathea, for Eliakim and even for Nehemiah to listen to this exchange between the Roman governor and the High Priest. The words were not false, but they were not true. Even those who detested Caiaphas did not want their High Priest to be embarrassed and demeaned. Even those who detested Caiaphas, hated the Roman governor even more.

Gaius listened with increasing concern. He knew what Joshua's purpose was and he could not oppose the wishes of his son. Nevertheless, deep within him, was the hope that somehow Joshua would be spared. Another thought, even more guilty, struck him. He really yearned to save the life of his son, no matter how many others might suffer. But as he looked at Joshua it seemed to him that he had read his mind, and Gaius almost cried out, "Forgive me."

Pilate said, "I find it astonishing that the High Priest of the Jews brings a condemnation against one of his own people. I never recall such an event occurring before, during the entire period of my service." He wanted to add, "in this accursed place," but he controlled himself.

"In the past," Caiaphas said smoothly, "we have administered the matters within our jurisdiction without troubling you, but in this case, the issue is too important. We felt we had no choice but to arrest the man and bring him to you. The city is full of our people and we fear unrest, even turmoil, if this man is allowed to appear before them publicly."

"Good," Pilate said. "Hold him yourselves. Keep him in your jurisdiction."

"We have no jurisdiction," Nicodemus said. He was reluctant to speak, but he sensed that the High Priest was nearing his limit at dealing with this Roman dog.

"Surely," Eliakim added, "the emperor would want you to act promptly and forcefully in this matter."

"I see," Pilate said. "You want us to imprison him, perhaps hold him until the festival is over, then return him to you."

Caiaphas hesitated. Pilate's suggestion was a sensible one. He had little love for Joshua, but he did not want to be the agent of his death. Perhaps, if he were jailed, the people would realize they had no leader and peacefully disperse. Joshua had frightened them with tales of murderous Romans and wild-eyed Zealots, but that might be an exaggeration.

Joshua had listened to this exchange with growing concern. He saw that Caiaphas was about to turn away from his commission. He realized that Pilate was about to outmaneuver him. If the Roman jailed him, that would not prevent Romans disguised as Jews from proclaiming him King and demanding his release and thus provoking violence. Nor would it keep the Zealots from trying to free him, with the same results.

"Do you fear me?" Joshua asked Pilate.

Pilate blinked. His lips trembled with anger before he spoke. "Do you know who you are speaking to? Do you realize what is in store for you? The crime you are accused of is sedition. The penalty is death—death by crucifixion."

"Do you fear me?" Joshua asked again.

Pilate turned and faced Caiaphas. "We will take this 'King' of yours and nail him to a wooden cross. We will show all of you that you cannot trifle with Rome."

Caiaphas was awed by Joshua's calm questioning of the governor. He understood that he had deliberately chosen to provoke the man who had the power of life and death over him. Joshua's courage strengthened Caiaphas.

"We understand, Prefect, that death is the penalty for the crime of which this man is accused."

"What kind of people are you, you Jews, that you condemn one of your own to certain and painful death?"

"We obey the law," Caiaphas said. He did not say which law.

Pilate paused, thinking rapidly. He yearned to crush these Jews. It would have pleased him most of all to grind the High Priest's face into the stone floor of the chamber. As for Joshua, he was irritated by his obstinacy, but on the whole, he seemed a rather mild fellow.

Pilate tried to keep his mind on the most important issue. This day might be his last opportunity to turn loose all of the Roman might against the Jews. The Syrian legate might never again give him the manpower he had assembled in Jerusalem. Opportunities must be taken when they were presented.

He turned abruptly, gestured to Gaius and, together, they left the chamber. Caiaphas was surprised, but he realized they intended to consult with each other. He glanced at Joshua, who stood erect as ever, his head held high, his eyes fixed on something, Caiaphas realized with envy, something that he himself might never see.

***

Baruch held onto the horse for dear life. The saddle was thin and he felt every pounding thrust of the horse's hooves beneath him. The trip to Qumran had been bad enough, but now his bottom and the insides of his legs were rubbed raw. They had given him reins to hold, but he felt totally lost using them. He brought his hands together and grabbed the thin edge of the saddle. Then he held on for dear life and prayed the saddle wouldn't fly off the horse.

He envied Brother Jacob who sat a horse as well as if he had ridden all his life. Even with Omriel sitting behind him on naked horseflesh and clinging to him, Jacob seemed shaped to the animal. Perhaps it would have been better, Baruch thought, if he had clung to Jacob and Omriel had ridden his horse.

They galloped through Bethany, past the house of Eliezer. Martha drawing water in the courtyard, saw them racing past, and dropped her bucket. But they neither turned nor called out and in a moment they were gone.

Below, in the Kidron Valley, they dismounted among the tents of the pilgrims, fearful that on horseback they would attract too much attention. Leaving the horses with friends, they hurried as swiftly as prudence allowed, through the twisting trail between the tents and into the city.

They prayed that Joshua was still alive.

18.

THE PLOT

"These Jews are crafty," Pilate said. "I don't trust them. This talk of obeying our laws—it doesn't sit right with me."

"The High Priest and his party have never opposed us in the past," Gaius said, "except in matters that involve their religion."

"Is there anything that doesn't?" Pilate asked.

"The High Priest is not a revolutionary."

"Then what is he doing here?"

"He seems to feel there is a problem that we share—Roman rulers and Jewish religious leaders. That if we handle it properly, it will be good for all of us."

"You mean he doesn't want this fellow to live, but he doesn't want to kill him, himself."

"Perhaps."

"Why don't they trump up some charge—surely there must be religious crimes they could accuse him of. If they want him out of the way, let them do it, themselves."

Gaius's agitation was growing. He could not understand why God had put him in this position. Let the High Priest and Pilate argue over Joshua's fate. How could he know that anything he did was right?

But, in fact, he did know. He knew that Joshua had always understood his place in the universe and that his connection with God was the closest of all. If he were truly trying to help his son, he would do what his son wanted, painful as it might be.

"I know what you want, Excellency," Gaius said, speaking to him with unaccustomed bluntness. "You want a riot, even a rebellion and you want to quash it with the full force of all the soldiers you have gathered here. You hope that if you turn this man back to the Jews, he will still appear in the Temple, or in any case that your men can arouse a rebellion by proclaiming him king. But you can't be sure of that. It always was a risk.

"If you imprison him yourself, you hope the same things will happen. Again, you can't be sure. The High Priest's people even now may be spreading the word. For all we know, the Jews may never appear in their Temple, may never even leave their houses. How then will we provoke a rebellion?"

Pilate smiled a huge and frightening smile. "I see your drift, Deputy. We must act swiftly. The man must die today, and he must die in the most terrible fashion imaginable. We must do it immediately, and spread the word promptly." His eyes glowed with anticipation. "Can you imagine what the Jews will do when they hear that their king has been cruelly killed—crucified? What an uprising we'll have then."

Gaius had long understood that Pilate was a cruel and vicious man. But only on this day, when Joshua's life was in jeopardy, did he truly understand the depth of the man's depravity. Here was a man who believed that by his own actions he would precipitate a terrible bloodbath, one that would mean the death of countless Jewish citizens and many of his own, Roman, soldiers. And yet, Pilate smiled with great anticipation.

Gaius prayed silently. "Forgive me Lord for what I am doing. Thank you Lord for having withheld from Pilate a true understanding of the Jewish people."

***

Now that he was resolved on a course of action, Pilate was determined to enjoy it. When he re-entered the Audience Chamber he was a different man, smooth, controlled and ready.

Nicodemus had longed to speak to Joshua. Perhaps he had changed his mind. That would be understandable, and surely none of them, not even Caiaphas would hold him to his promise.

Caiaphas wondered, too. But there was no possibility of speaking privately to Joshua with the room filled with soldiers.

Joshua kept his own counsel. Nothing had changed his mind. Everything he had seen confirmed his opinion of the Romans and his belief that he was treading the right path. He felt compassion for the others, forced to turn him over to the Romans, feeling that they were responsible for his impending death.

He smiled at Nicodemus. "Be of good cheer," he said. "We are doing God's work."

Pilate and Gaius Fabricius heard these words as they returned to the Audience Chamber. Gaius steadied himself, but Pilate smiled. He would break this man down, yet.

"We are holding in our prison, a man called Bar Abbas," Pilate said to Caiaphas. "Do you know him?"

There was no point in denying it. Caiaphas nodded.

"He, too, is a revolutionary," Pilate said. "Yet you have not condemned him or asked for his death."

"Would it matter?" Caiaphas said. "He is already in your hands and we assume he will meet Roman justice."

"He will be crucified."

The High priest and the others said nothing.

"How do you compare these criminals?" Pilate asked. He was staring straight at Joshua, trying to hold his eye. Joshua looked at him without fear.

"Compare them?" Nicodemus asked.

"Yes," said Pilate, "which of them do you believe is the greater criminal, Bar Abbas or this Galilean pretender."

"We have not come here to compare crimes, only to do our duty," Caiaphas said.

Pilate stroked his chin. "You may have to compare them," he said. "There is an old Roman custom of setting free a criminal at the time of great holidays."

Gaius stared at him. There was no such custom.

"I am thinking of reinstating this custom here and now." He stood very close to the High Priest. "What would you think of such a custom?"

"Forgiveness," Caiaphas said, "is part of God's law."

"Exactly," Pilate said. He yelled to one of the guards. "Bring in Bar Abbas."

"Excellency," Nicodemus began, "we are here on the matter of Joshua ben Joseph, and we believe—"

"—SILENCE!" Pilate roared.

They stood and they waited. Gaius edged close to the governor. "In capital cases," he began, but Pilate walked away. He would not listen.

They brought Bar Abbas in on a pallet. Both his legs and his back were broken, and he could not walk. He had lost weight during his imprisonment because they had fed him little. He was filthy and weak, but his eyes were fierce.

"Here is your hero," Pilate said. "The man who tried to recover your holy treasure. Surely such a man is dear to you."

They looked at Bar Abbas with compassion. In fact, to some of them, he was indeed a hero. Even Caiaphas had grudging admiration for his courage, though not for the uproar he had created.

Pilate smiled benignly, which is to say that he tried to curve his lips upward, but without success. "I offer you a choice. To honor your festival of freedom, I will set one of these men free, Bar Abbas or Joshua."

Gaius sucked in his breath involuntarily. It was a violation of Roman law. It was incredible, but in a moment, Joshua might be freed.

The Jews stared at each other in dismay. To be given the choice of human lives in this manner, was something only a pagan would do. They knew how the Romans set man against man in their stadiums, and now they were offered the same choice.

"We do not make choices in this fashion," Caiaphas said. "In our religion, each man must be judged on his own merits."

"You WILL make this choice, because I demand it. I have decided that one of these men is to be set free. Will it be this warrior, brave in deed, but a killer of men? Or will it be this mild fellow, who might be your king. Which of them shall I set free?"

"*You* must choose," Caiaphas said in a thin voice."

"No," the governor said. "If you do nothing, I will kill them both, and then your people will know that you might have saved a life and you refused."

They looked at each other then, the elders of Israel. Their face showed their agony, their despair. They could not look at the two men as if they were evaluating them. They could hardly look at each other. The moment became a minute and then several minutes and then an eternity.

When Caiaphas spoke, his voice was low and uneven. "Bar Abbas," he said.

"BAR ABBAS!" Pilate roared. "You would choose this broken killer over this gentle man? What will your own people think? I will tell them, you know, that I offered you the choice and you picked Bar Abbas."

He turned and ordered a servant to bring him a bowl of water. "You see, I wash my hands of this. The death of Joshua Ben Joseph is on your head, not mine. It is you who have killed him, not I."

He relished every moment of it, watching them twist in pain, believing he had trapped them so that they were the criminals not he, and when the people rose in righteous anger, he would be able to say that the Jews might have saved Joshua's life, but their leaders had refused the opportunity, he had given them.

"Do you know, do you truly know what you have condemned this man to?"

"We have done what we must, Prefect," Caiaphas said. "We will withdraw now."

"No, Pilate said, "you will not withdraw. You will remain here and see how it is that we prepare your king for his death. You will learn what the full measure of Roman justice means."

He nodded abruptly at an officer. "Prepare him," he said.

The officer spoke abruptly to a short, burly soldier. The soldier advanced on Joshua, and ripped his cloak from off his back. Then, he tore the rest of his clothing from him. He was stopped for a moment, by Joshua's bound hands, but he quickly tore open the bonds and ripped off the clothing the rest of the way.

Joshua stood before them, naked. His eyes blinked once or twice but he gave no other sign. Two soldiers approached and took Joshua by the arms, leading him out of the audience hall.

"Come," Pilate said, "this must not be missed."

The elders followed Pilate out of the audience hall, down the steps and into the open courtyard. They passed between rows of soldiers and in the courtyard they found themselves ringed by soldiers. Their bright, brass helmets and buckles, the clean, bright red and white of their uniforms formed a cruel backdrop.

Two soldiers forced Joshua to his knees before a stone pillar with a ring on top of it. They tied his hands to the ring, lashing the thongs very tightly.

The officer gestured to a tall, heavily muscled soldier. He was a swarthy fellow with black hair that pointed low into his forehead, and curly black hair that ran down his arms and sprang out of the collar of his tunic. His features were scarred and broken from a dozen battles, but his eyes were expressionless. He held a thick wooden stick with several thongs nailed to it. At the end of each thong, a rough pebble had been attached. He slapped the wooden stock into his other hand, until the officer nodded to him, then he walked slowly to where Joshua knelt, tied to the stone pillar. He studied Joshua's back for a moment, and measured the length of his stroke.

Pilate surveyed his guests with naked pleasure. They all looked pale, ill, tormented. Well, they would feel even worse before the day was ended.

He glanced at Gaius. The man was trembling. Pilate shook his head. This man had been a soldier. Surely he had seen men scourged before.

The soldier holding the scourge looked to Pilate. Pilate nodded. The soldier raised his arm high, reached far back and brought the scourge looping through the air. It struck Joshua's back with a dull crunching sound.

Joshua flinched from the impact. Pain shot out from the dozen stones to all the ends of his body. He opened his mouth. There was a cry of pain. But it was not Joshua. Eliakim had cried out.

The scourger drew back his weapon and struck again. Once more the dull, crunching sound, the arch of Joshua's back and the red welts that rose where the rocks struck.

The soldier was a master. He could make all of the stones strike the victim's back, and at the same time, draw the thongs across his skin. Red lines began to crisscross Joshua's back. Blood sprang from one cut and seeped from another.

Again the powerful arm drew back and the fusillade of stones arched through the air. Again and again.

Joshua prayed mightily, asking God for forgiveness for his weakness, asking God to help him endure the pain. He did not fight the blows. After the first scourge, he hardly winced. The force of the impact moved him, but he made himself a receptacle for this assault, not its resister.

Still, the blows continued and the pain mounted. After a while, he had reached the limit of the pain he could feel, and the blows did not enhance his suffering, only extended it.

Watching, Caiaphas would have been sick, had he permitted himself to be sick. Nicodemus struggled to keep from fainting. He did not believe he had the right to be unconscious when Joshua was undergoing such torment.

Gaius moved through pain and misery to a level of numbness. He struggled not to wince with each blow. He saw that Pilate was watching the event with obvious enjoyment. His eyes flickered between the victim and the watchers. Gaius would not let Pilate see his own suffering.

Joshua's back was no longer a human back. It was a tangled mass of torn flesh, twisted skin and seeping blood. Black and red tones came to dominate the whiteness of his fair skin.

Still the arm arched high and the sweeping blows continued. The thongs hissed through the air and thudded on Joshua, ten times, twenty, beyond counting.

Joshua's eyes were on a different vision. He was high on a scaffold with his father, Joseph, beside him. They were hammering on roof beams under a warm, Galilean sky. Birds sang and the scent of flowers was strong in the air. He heard the blow of his own hammer and then, rhythmically, the sound of Joseph's. He glanced for a moment toward his father, happily bent over his work and he smiled.

Pilate saw the smile and mistook it for a grimace. He was pleased. This Galilean preacher had taken his scourging with less show of pain than any he had seen.

Then it was over. The soldier saluted Pilate with his bloody scourge and marched off. Joshua still leaned on the pillar, head down, blood streaming from his back.

Pilate spoke to the soldiers. "This man you see before you has greater dignity than you might think. Roman soldiers, this man is the King of the Jews."

There was laughter from the ranks.

"We must treat this king with proper dignity. Surely he should not be exposed before us, naked."

The troops understood Pilate. They were a rough and callous lot, accustomed to brutal service. Their pleasures were rough, too, and they understood an invitation to coarse horseplay.

An officer whispered to some of the men. They laughed and ran from the courtyard.

"Isn't this enough?" Gaius whispered.

Pilate looked at him with contempt. "You will see these people for what they really are," he said.

The officer untied Joshua's hands and lifted him to a standing position. He was dizzy from the punishment he had taken and he sagged. The officer held him erect and in a few moments, he stood without help.

A soldier returned with a coarse woolen robe, torn in several places and dyed a mottled purple. He had ripped it off the back of a slave. The officer draped the robe over the torn shoulders of Joshua. Pilate laughed appreciatively.

Another man hurried up with a ring of thorns. He had twisted them together and now, with the approval of the officer, he placed it on Joshua's head.

The soldiers laughed heartily. Pilate was beside himself with enjoyment.

"See," he said to Caiaphas. "How they admire your king."

"Is not the scourging enough?" Caiaphas asked, his face very pale, but his eyes fiery. "You have tortured this man to the very limit, must you humiliate him as well?"

"But this is your king, Priest. Surely you wish to show him the proper respect. You might have freed him, but you chose not to. Now you must see the full power of the Roman state, now you will know how we treat renegade kings."

Joshua heard what was said as through a haze. The first touch of the woolen robe had been unpleasant, but now he was glad for the covering. The thorns scratched his brow, but that seemed unimportant considering the rest of his pain. He now knew the meaning of the words he had read about the Messiah. Condemned. Tormented and afflicted. And he knew that his suffering had only begun.

He felt something in his hand. One of the soldiers had cut a long reed and placed it in his hand, as a mockery of a scepter. The officer now turned him in a circle, so that all of the soldiers assembled in the courtyard could see him. They laughed and cheered.

"Forgive them, Lord," he prayed. "They are ignorant and oppressed."

Pilate had tired of the game. "Take him," he said, "and crucify him." He smiled suddenly. "Put a sign over his head—'King of the Jews.'" Pilate suppressed the urge to laugh.

He stalked out of the courtyard, leaving the elders behind him. They looked after him and then at Joshua. What were they to do?

Gaius said, "You are free to go." He was barely able to speak the words. He wanted to accompany Joshua to the place of crucifixion, but he knew he could not. He hurried after Pilate.

The soldiers left the Praetorium. The High Priest and the elders walked quickly toward the gate. The guards laughed at them as they passed through and went out into the street.

19.

TORMENT

Martha brought the story of what she had seen to her sister and brother with great trepidation.

"We must tell Miriam," Eliezer said.

"I'm afraid," said Martha. "We were told to remain here until they sent for us."

"That may be too late," said Eliezer."

"Then you tell her."

Eliezer sighed and went in to speak to Miriam.

"They saw your son Jacob and two other men ride by on horseback. They seemed to be in a great hurry."

Miriam turned away for a second to hide her response. When she turned back, her face was composed.

"I will go in to the city," she said.

"I'll go with you, said Eliezer.

Miriam planned to tell Judith, but it wasn't necessary. She had seen the horsemen cantering by, and had already decided to go to Jerusalem.

***

Nico and Simon Peter followed Joshua and the elders from the palace of the High Priest to the Antonia fortress. They waited in a shadowy corner, across from the gates. It seemed to them that the elders had gone in hours before. They were restless and agitated and filled with guilt.

"We should never have let him go," Simon said.

"We had no choice," Nico said, but he, too was desperately unhappy, convinced there must have been some alternative to the terrible one Joshua had proposed. They had not heard the proceedings of the Elders, and they had hoped that somehow, the members of the Sanhedrin would refuse to do as Joshua had asked. However, when they saw him leave the High priest's palace, hands bound, but head held high, they knew that he had prevailed.

Once again, waiting before the Antonia fortress, they had prayed that Joshua would be spared. Surely neither the Romans nor the Jews wanted outright conflict. Reason would triumph and Joshua would be spared.

Then they heard marching men. Despite their fear, they edged closer to the iron gates that fronted on the Praetorium. At first their hearts lifted as they saw Joshua marching into the courtyard.

"He's all right," Nico whispered.

Simon Peter had seen he was still bound and that the Elders looked deadly pale and he said nothing.

Joshua and the Elders passed from their sight. They heard the soldiers drawn up and the voice of someone, apparently the governor. But they could not make out his words. There was laughter from the soldiers. What could it be that was amusing them?

Then they heard the swoop of something in the air, the thud of impact and a single cry.

Nico held onto Simon to keep from fainting. They were beating him, scourging him, their beloved Joshua. The Messiah. They clung together in anger and fear and listened to the sound of the scourge landing on Joshua again and again.

Simon tried to pull away from Nico. "I'll get hold of Amos, the Zealot leader. We have to stop this."

Nico held him back. "No," he whispered. "We promised Joshua." Simon huge shoulders heaved with his sobbing.

***

Judas greeted the dawn with a sense of satisfaction. He had spoken to dozens of Zealot leaders and convinced them all they must proclaim Joshua the king and bring their weapons in the bargain. He had always known the leaders trusted him, but he had not realized how fully he held their confidence. He was not so foolish, however, as not to realize that it was Joshua whom they loved, Joshua whom they would exalt as highly as any mortal man. To these rough and hardy men, his name was like magic. In a few short weeks they had come to love him, and they identified the future of Israel with him.

Judas was convinced that this was the hour, the Messiah had indeed come. Joshua was the Messiah and as long as he lived, Israel would be free. He smiled at the thought as he returned to the house of Amos. There, starting out from the house, he saw his Zealot friend. He smiled, but then he saw the face of Amos.

"Nico is gone," Amos said.

***

The others had waited in the house of Nicodemus as long as they could bear it.

Deborah kept walking from room to room, straightening items of furniture, fussing with tablecloths, snapping at Nicodemus's servants. "Not good," she said, over and over again, "not good."

Nathan nodded every time she said it. He was old, but in his great age, he had lost his fear. What could they do to him now? It didn't matter. All that mattered was Joshua.

Mattathias and Johannon, Little Jacob and Andrew, even foggy old Simeon had not slept.

Dawn touched the windows. Across the city, cocks began to crow. The disciples in the house of Nicodemus stood up suddenly as if on a single command.

"Come," Johannon said.

***

Judas and Amos ran through the streets of the Ophel. If Nico had escaped, then Joshua must know. Judas felt a sense of relief. In his heart he had wanted to tell Joshua, to convince him there was only one way for Israel to be saved. Now, he would know. At the same time, all was planned for the proclamation. There was no way to change that now. No matter what anyone did, even Joshua, the people would proclaim him king in a voice so mighty it would echo all the way to Rome.

With each step, his spirits rose even higher. They would do this together, he and Joshua. Today would be the greatest day in all of Israel's history. Joshua would not only forgive him, he would thank him. He could see Joshua smiling, feel his embrace.

He saw the disciples running down the street towards him. He stopped and Amos stopped, too. They looked at each other, surprised and confused.

"It's him," Johannon said. He ran even faster and the others scurried to keep up. Nathan was puffing heavily, but Deborah glided along on her spider thin legs, running like a young girl.

Judas immediately saw the anger on Johannon's ruddy face. As he ran, his thin, red hair flopped up and down, and he would have seemed comical except for the fierce look in his eyes. Judas had made his entire life an exercise in readiness, but he could not imagine what might be troubling Johannon. If he had been paying more attention, he would have realized that the others were also angry, but they were running too hard to show any emotion.

With surprise, Judas realized that Johannon was not going to stop, that he was aiming directly for him. By then it was too late. Johannon had left his feet and launched himself chest high into Judas. He knocked him to the ground, then scrambled over and began to beat his fists in the face of the startled man.

Amos recovered from his surprise and tried to pull them apart, but Little Jacob pulled him away and would not let him interfere.

Johannon was a large man and powerfully built, and he was filled with righteous anger. He pummeled Judas again and again, while Judas struggled to protect himself. He could have reached his dagger, but even under attack, he could not imagine killing Johannon.

"Stop!" he cried. "Let me up! What is it? For God's sake stop!"

"You killed him!" Johannon was screaming. "You murderer, you killed him!"

Mattathias had felt the same urges as Johannon, but now he could see the situation was getting desperate. Judas's nose was bleeding and his right eye was purpling. Any second now, Judas would reach for a weapon and there would be true bloodshed. He glanced quickly at Philip, who nodded. Together, they pulled the two men apart.

"Let me go!" Johannon yelled, struggling with Mattathias, but then Andrew helped subdue him, and he could only glare at Judas with hatred in his eye.

"Easy," Mattathias said. "The Master told us that no matter what, we must love one another."

"I hate Judas!" Johannon yelled.

Judas allowed Philip to hold him. Philip was young and wiry, but he would have been no match for Judas, had Judas wanted to break free. But he was content to have the struggle interrupted. He had no quarrel with these people that he knew of.

"What is it?" Amos asked. "What are you angry about?"

"Joshua is to die," Mattathias said, his fine, strong chin, trembling a bit as he spoke. "He learned last night that both the Zealots and Romans, all dressed as Jews, planned to proclaim him king. As soon as the proclamation was made, the Romans planned to provoke a fight and the slaughter would begin."

He swallowed hard and continued. "To save Israel, to save us all, Joshua said he must die—be turned over to the Romans as a revolutionary and be crucified."

Judas would have screamed if he had the strength. He sagged into the arms of Philip. Now he understood the hatred he saw in their eyes. He had betrayed Joshua—he had indeed murdered him.

A last hope stirred him. "We can rescue him," he said. "Rally the Zealots and save Joshua from the Romans."

"You *will* have your war, Judas, won't you?" Mattathias asked. "Violence, only violence. You understand nothing else."

Every hope that Judas had ever held for himself and for Israel died in that moment. There would be no liberation now. The Messiah would be cruelly murdered and the dream would die with him.

Nathan, now that he had regained his breath, looked at Judas with a mixture of pity and contempt. "You believe it's over, don't you? I don't. We don't. The people will learn of Joshua's sacrifice and they will understand that he would do anything to avoid violence, even give his life. They will learn how brave he was, and they will know that they, too, must renounce violence. Then, we can all oppose the Romans as Joshua taught us, by turning the other cheek. That will bring in a new age of peace and tranquility and the brotherhood of man."

It was the longest speech any of them had ever heard the old man make. It was touching and it moved them all, even Judas. But he did not believe it. No, the mission was over and he was the one who had destroyed it. He had betrayed the most wonderful human being he had ever known, and with it, he had betrayed his country.

They saw that he understood and that he was defeated. They had no sorrow to spare for him, but they tried to follow the teachings of their master, to forgive even him.

Judas saw it in their eyes, the struggle not to hate him and he felt a deeper pain than even before. He wanted them to hate him.

"Hate me," he pleaded. "I deserve it."

Philip let him go, let him stand alone. He glanced at Amos, but Amos was deep in his own misery. Tears were running down his cheeks.

"I misled you," Judas said to him. "It was my fault."

Amos sobbed and did not answer.

The disciples turned from them and started down the street, this time at a slower pace.

"Where are you going?" Judas whispered.

"To Golgotha," Andrew said, "to watch the Master die."

For a moment, Judas thought he might follow them. Amos was following, and so might he. But he could not bear the thought. He stood in the middle of the street until he could no longer hear their steps, then with a wobbly gait he walked in the opposite direction.

***

The soldiers stripped off the purple robe and crown of thorns, threw his own tunic over his shoulders and led Joshua away. At the last moment, before the gates were opened, the officer directed two soldiers to pick up a wooden crosspiece, the arms of the tree on which they would hang him, and place it over Joshua's shoulders.

"Might as well do something useful, King of the Jews," he said and his men laughed.

When they placed the heavy wooden beam on his torn back, Joshua flinched and the weight of it made him sag to the stones of the courtyard.

"Up now," the centurion said, pulling at his arm, but giving him no real help.

Joshua staggered to his feet and stood, wavering for a moment. Then, he placed one foot before the other and began to walk, bent low towards the ground under the groaning weight, shifting his feet to balance his ungainly burden, his teeth set.

"That's a good fellow," the centurion said.

The gates swung open and they moved into the street. It was still early and most people had slept late, enjoying their festival and knowing nothing of Joshua's ordeal. A few early risers were in the street, and they looked at Joshua curiously and with concern. But they did not recognize him, even those who had heard him preach in the Temple would not have easily recognized this torn and bleeding figure with matted hair, carrying a filthy wooden beam across his back.

But Nico and Simon Peter, of course, knew him at once. Simon reacted with fury. He would have stepped into the street and attacked the Romans single-handed. Nico, recognizing his anger, dragged him back.

"I can't stand it," Simon said in a strangled voice.

"He can," Nico said. "Surely we can be strong enough to restrain ourselves."

Simon Peter gritted his teeth and forced his body to stop shaking. Then, when he had himself under control, he nodded to Nico and they moved out of the shadows and into the street, following the detachment of soldiers and Joshua.

The progress of the little contingent was slow. The streets were narrow and winding and uneven. Joshua staggered from the burden, trying to balance it as best he could, moving from foot to foot and almost falling.

The stripes on his back, the hard pavement under his bare feet, the heavy load on his shoulders blended together into a deep and throbbing pain that suffused his whole body. As during the scourging, he did not fight the pain, but accepted it. The burden and the suffering blended until his body was a single throbbing center. But his mind and his heart were not fixed on his back or his feet or the weight of the crosspiece. His mind and his heart were fixed on God.

He knew the scriptures—all of them, by heart. And so, as he moved with agonizing slowness through the streets of Jerusalem, it was to him a pilgrimage. But this time, he was on the way, not to celebrate a Festival, but to meet the Lord. Had he ever imagined the road would be an easy one? No, he had always known better than that. But at the end of this road, as the end of all roads, was the Lord Almighty. He was going to meet his heavenly father. Even in his pain, his eyes were shining.

At a corner, where two streets met, a young boy unintentionally brushed against Joshua. He lost his balance and the weight of the crosspiece knocked him to the pavement. Without thinking, Simon Peter ran forward and lifted the crosspiece from his fallen body. "Master," he whispered, "I'm here."

Vaguely, Joshua recognized him.

"Get out of there," the centurion said in surly tones.

Simon lifted Joshua with one strong arm and hoisted the crosspiece over his own shoulder with the other. "I'll carry it," he said.

"Perhaps we can use it for you, too," the centurion said. His men laughed, but he did not protest when Simon began to walk down the street, carrying the crosspiece and holding Joshua's arm. They made their way in this fashion through the streets of the city and out through the northwest gate.

It was clear and pleasant outside the walls. The sun had begun to rise and the air was a bit warmer. There were trees here, Acacia and Plane and the grass was green from the spring rains. Flowers, yellow anemones and purple gladioli edged the highway. A light breeze grazed them. It was, indeed a lovely spring morning.

***

Brother Jacob, Baruch and Omriel made their way carefully through the gates and into the city. They were in a state of high excitement, but they did not want it to show. Fortunately, the Roman guards showed no interest in them. Once within the walls they began to move more quickly, but still not so fast as to be noticed.

Finally, they reached the house of Nicodemus. They pounded on the door, but no one answered. They pounded again, frightened, and then after several minutes, Nicodemus appeared, looking like death itself.

"What is it?" Brother Jacob asked. "Are we too late?"

"Yes," Nicodemus said, nodding sadly. "They have condemned him to death—by crucifixion."

Omriel shuddered. "Have they crucified him yet?" he asked.

"Does it matter?" Nicodemus responded wearily.

"Yes, it matters," Brother Jacob said, and he quickly told him their plan.

"Madness," Nicodemus said, but there was a hint of life in his eyes.

"All can be fulfilled and we can still have our Messiah," Baruch said.

"We can't stay here talking," Omriel said irritably, shaking his pink round head. "Every minute counts."

"Wait a minute," Nicodemus cried. "We've had an offer from Joseph of Arimathea. He recently built a new tomb for his family in the garden near his house. He said we might bury Joshua there."

"Good," Omriel said. "But we must still hurry."

"I'll speak to Joseph at once," Nicodemus said. "I know he'll want to help." He stopped suddenly. "But how will you tell Joshua of your plans?"

"We don't plan to tell him," Brother Jacob said.

"It's only a thin, small hope anyway," Omriel said.

***

Miriam, the mother of Joshua, was not certain that she was doing the right thing. She did not see how her presence could help her son, and might in fact add to his anguish. She wondered, too, if she would have the strength to watch his ordeal without collapsing, and if he saw her, wouldn't that be worse?

But the others, her daughter Judith, the sisters Martha and Miriam, and kindly Eliezer, believed it was the compassionate thing to do. All of them feared to see what they knew they would see. In the past, they had each of them entered the city and passed the poor wretches being crucified by the Romans. It was a fairly commonplace occurrence, and the Romans always chose to perform their pagan brutality in a place where citizens were sure to see it and thus be frightened into obedience.

Miriam and the others had always averted their eyes when passing such atrocities. It had never occurred to them that they might one day see someone they loved stretched in agony on the hanging tree. Miriam prayed for the strength to do what was right and to not add to her son's affliction. She had mastered her sense of hysteria, but she had no idea what the sight of Joshua would do to her.

Judith hurried along beside her mother. She was doing all she could to harden herself for what she would see, but she was also concerned for her mother. She moved very close and took her arm. Miriam looked up. She did not smile, but it was clear she appreciated the support.

***

Judas walked through the streets of the city in a daze. Again and again he imagined himself with Joshua on the Passover. Only this time, instead of running out in anger, he told Joshua that he was right and that he would abide by his wishes. He hated himself then, for even trying to change what had happened. He could not change the past and he could not save Joshua's life. Someone, he could not remember which disciple, had told him it wouldn't have mattered—that Pilate had planned to plant spurious pilgrims who would proclaim Joshua king and provoke a fight no matter what happened.

That did not relieve his pain. Perhaps it was true, perhaps not. One way or another, Judas believed he had ensured Joshua's death. Had Joshua known? Joshua had spoken before of the suffering the Messiah must undergo. Had he realized that all would end in this fashion, that he would die on the cross?

"That doesn't excuse you," Judas told himself. "You abandoned Joshua and you abandoned God. Your faith was too small, far too small."

"You killed him," the voice within said. "There is no doubt that you killed him."

He continued through the streets, hardly seeing where he was going. Once, a man hailed him, but he turned his head and hurried on.

Judas came to the place where the Siloam Tower had stood—the tower that the Romans had undermined and collapsed to capture Bar Abbas and kill his men. The work of reconstruction had begun and a tall scaffolding had been erected. A Roman soldier stood on listless guard.

Judas put a hand on the scaffolding as if to climb it.

"You," the guard said "Get away from there."

He came running up to Judas, who shrugged, turned away, then swiftly turned back and hit the soldier a heavy blow with the hilt of the short sword he carried under his cloak.

The soldier fell to the pavement, unconscious.

Judas began to climb the scaffolding. The boards were close to each other, and it was easy work. He had begun in the shadows, but now he cleared the old wall and was in the sunlight. It felt warm and good.

He climbed higher, methodically, hand over hand. Now he could see into the Kidron Valley and across to the Mount of Olives. To the south, the aqueduct that Pilate had been building with the money from the Corban, wound out of the walls toward the Judaean hills.

At the top was a narrow platform. Judas turned and glanced toward the Temple, feeling a deep chill in his bones. Then he looked toward the upper city. Naomi would be up now, helping with the work in the house. He saw her face for a second and he kissed her lips. Then the face became Joshua's. He tried to kiss Joshua, but Joshua turned away. It was a traitor's kiss and he knew it.

Judas looked over the Kidron, green now between the city and the Mount, with the sculptured tombs below and rising up the hillside. Beneath him, the ground broke away abruptly and the rocks were visible far below.

He stepped off into space.

20.

THE FINISH

Even with his blood-blurred vision, Joshua thought he had never seen such a beautiful morning. The sun was still low in the sky but it had cleared the city walls and driven off the fog. The countryside had a fragile, dreamy look to it in the clear air and the light breeze felt pleasant on his face. Along the twisting road, he saw several crosses with men hanging from them. They were motionless and seemed unreal, but he realized they were real and that his fate was the same as theirs. He prayed for them, not knowing whether they were Romans or Greeks or Jews, vicious criminals or innocents like himself.

The soldiers had taken the crosspiece from Simon Peter and placed it back on Joshua. He sagged under the weight, but tried to stand erect, staggering a few feet. Then, suddenly, the weight was lifted off his shoulders. He stood straighter and lifted his eyes to the heavens. They grabbed him, ripped his cloak from his body. He heard someone nailing the cross piece into the post. They dragged him backwards roughly, his heels scraping on the rocky ground.

He was lying on his back, spread on the wooden tree. They lashed his arms to the crosspiece and his feet together. Joshua looked up to heaven and prayed again for Israel, for all the world and finally, for himself. It was rare for him to think of himself, but as he lay there, spread-eagled on the coarse and splintery wood, knowing what was to happen, he thought that God would understand.

Joshua turned his eyes to look at the man who was lashing his right hand to the crosspiece. He was not a man, he was only a boy, with a pale, fair skin and close-cropped brown hair. He was bug-eyed with fear—he had never done this before.

An older man, with a trim black beard and mottled skin handed him a nail and raised a hammer. "He's already tied to the wood," the boy stuttered.

"That's only to hold him steady," the older man said, guiding the boy's hand to the place on Joshua's wrist where he wanted the nail placed. "Shove it in and hold it steady," he said to the young man, who was shivering, "or I'll hit your hand."

Even as Joshua watched, the same thing was happening on the other side of him. Both hammers struck both nails at the same time.

Joshua screamed as the iron drove through his flesh and his back arched. Again and again they pounded on the nails until they penetrated the wood and held. But Joshua did not feel the additional blows as strongly. The first, simultaneous blows had knocked him briefly unconscious. He did not even know when they drove nails through his heels to hold his legs.

But then he was awake, with pain searing through his body. The ropes had been cut away. Only the nails held his arms to the crosspiece. Now they were lifting the cross.

"Up!" a soldier yelled.

"Not there," said an officer. "Balance it you fools."

They yelled and the cross lifted. Joshua felt himself rising in the air. The weight of his body sagged onto the nails that held his wrists. Even as he was lifted up, his body was dropping down, with only nails to support his upper body, and the nails through his ankles which held his feet above a peg that was part of the vertical wooden shaft.

The pain. The pain was unbelievable. He struggled to hold himself up, to try and brace on the peg so that the weight would not be on the nails tearing at his flesh. He twisted his head from side to side as he tried to balance himself, to relieve the stress and the pain.

The cross was upright. They braced it in the slot made for that purpose in the rocky ground and they knocked in wooden pegs from each side to hold it. The cross vibrated for a moment, and the sky wavered before Joshua's eyes. He did not know they had hung a sign above his head with the works "King of the Jews" scrawled roughly on it three times, in Latin, Greek and Aramaic

All had gone black more than once. But now, his vision cleared slightly. There was a film over his eyes, and tears running through it, but he could see the hills and the shadows on them, and the people gathered below.

The pain was beyond pain. It was an agony that vibrated through him without cease. There was no cycle, only unremitting agony. The stripes, the scourging were as nothing compared to this. Long strings of pain, honed to an edge like razors, stretched from his head to his toes. They quivered and sometimes touched and when they did, edge to sharp edge, the pain was even greater, and it never ceased. Except when his vision darkened and he felt faint.

Joshua struggled to lift his head from his chest. Eyes protruding, mouth open, panting, he searched the faces below. Simon Peter, Andrew and Nico. His mother. His mother and his sister. His head sagged. Then he lifted it again. His vision was swimming now. He thought he had seen Johannon and Little Jacob, Mattathias and Philip, Nathan and Deborah.

He wanted to bless them, to tell them all would be well. That the Kingdom of Heaven was at hand, where it had always been. But he could not gather the strength to speak.

He wanted to make a sign to them with his eyes, but he couldn't control them.

He wondered, where was his brother, Jacob?

***

Gaius remained with Pilate when he returned to his office. He wanted desperately to be with Joshua, but he knew that was impossible. Pilate would react very badly to his leaving. He wondered, though, what difference did it make now? If he defied Pilate, whatever he did wouldn't matter. Joshua would be dead in hours. There was nothing he could do for him.

Pilate was still very excited. "We have to spread the word," he said. "We must let the Jews know their king is being crucified. That will bring them out in the streets in protest. We'll have our chance then."

He called for Paulus Aemilius, and the young captain came running into his chambers.

"Change of plans, dear boy," Pilate said. "The 'King' won't be going to the Temple. We're crucifying him now outside the Northwest gate on the road to Caesarea."

Paulus smiled.

"That's not good news," Pilate said sharply and the officer snapped the smile off his face.

"Use the same men, dressed as pilgrims. Send them through the streets crying, 'They're killing the King of the Jews—they're crucifying him at Golgotha.' Then, when they begin their protest, fall on them, wherever they are, but the more you can gather together, the better. Once the protest starts, go through every neighborhood. I want thousands of bodies, dead not wounded."

Paulus nodded grimly and saluted.

"Wait a minute," Gaius said. "Don't have them call him 'King,' use their word: call him 'Messiah.' Say, 'They're crucifying your Messiah at Golgotha.'"

"Very good," Pilate said with a quizzical look on his face. "Sometimes, Gaius Fabricius, you surprise me."

***

At first they were misled. Someone told them a man was being crucified on the Jericho road. They hurried to the spot, only to learn it wasn't true.

They feared asking a Roman soldier but there was no choice.

"Probably out on the northwest road," the soldier told them. "Lots of men hanging out there. You going for the show?"

They could not answer, and hurried away, while the soldier chuckled.

Brother Jacob stopped them. "That soldier may have taught us something. Baruch, with your dark skin you could be a Syrian. Let's wrap you up to look like one."

"Why bother?" Omriel asked. "We have no time."

"Trust me," Jacob said. He tore off his own cloak, ripped it and made a turban that he wound, Syrian fashion on Baruch's head.

"Sorry," he said, as he tore the prayer fringes off Baruch's tunic."

"Now," he said, "that's all we have time for."

They circled the city walls until they reached the highway and then followed the slanting road to Golgotha. They passed several men hanging from crosses.

It was difficult to search each face, but it was clear that none of these was Joshua.

Then they saw Joshua's mother Miriam, Martha and the disciples and knew they had found him. It was terrible to look upon him, to see this beautiful man stripped and tortured, hanging in agony on the cross

Jacob yearned to go to his mother, to comfort her, but there was no time. "Go," he told Baruch, "do as I told you."

***

Joshua had hung on the cross for hours now. The pain had not diminished—rather it had increased. He tried to keep the weight of his body off his arms, hanging from the nails, but each time he lifted up, his strength ebbed a little further. His breathing became very labored and in fact he

could hardly catch his breath. From time to time, he felt the blackness
come, and he welcomed it. But then he would awaken to the suffering. He
could no longer see clearly. His vision was clouded and he didn't always
know where he was.

Memories raced through his brain, collided with each other, canceled
each other out and then crashed on him again. He saw his wife and his children and felt their hands reaching out to him. He saw Joseph, falling though
the sky from the scaffold, but then he was overhead again and smiling.

Joshua saw himself preaching in the synagogue at Capernaum, and
then along the lakeside in Bethsaida and Chorazin. He rode into the hills
and climbed Mount Hermon and saw the mists and heard God whisper.

He was telling the Zealots they must not fight, but must seek the ways
of peace and they were agreeing with him. He saw Judas, falling head over
heels from a height.

He held a sword in his hands and was staring at Septimus and he rescued a little girl from a stream and she held out her hands to him, smiled
and whispered, "God."

He saw children, many children. He laughed and played with them and
they followed him, reaching for his hands.

He was on a cross at Golgotha.

The words of a psalm, the twenty-second of David, passed through his
mind. His lips moved with the words.

"My God, my God, why hast thou forsaken me? Why art thou so far
from helping me, from the words of my groaning? O my God, I cry by day,
but thou dost not answer, and by night, but find no rest.

"Yet thou art holy, enthroned on the praises of Israel. In thee our fathers
trusted, they trusted and thou didst deliver them. To thee they cried and
were saved' in thee they trusted, and were not disappointed.

"But I am a worm, and no man; scorned by men, and despised by the
people. All who see me mock at me; they make mouths at me, they wag
their heads.

'He committed his cause to the Lord; let him deliver him. Let him rescue him, for he delights in him.'"

***

Baruch, his heart in his mouth swaggered up to the guards that flanked
Joshua.

"Is this the one they call the 'King of the Jews'?" he asked.

The soldier nodded.

"Doesn't look like much of a king to me," Baruch said.

The soldier was the dark-bearded one who had driven one of the nails. "They never do up there," he said and laughed. "The cross has a way of evening men out."

He laughed again, and the other soldier, the young one who had held the nail tried to smile, but he couldn't. He had kept his back to the cross ever since. He couldn't bear to look on the man it bore.

Joshua's mind was still fixed on the psalm. He had known them all, but now it was very hard to concentrate, to remember the words:

"I am poured out like water and all my bones are out of joint; my heart is like wax, it is melted within my breast; my strength is dried up like a pot-sherd, and my tongue cleaves to jaws; thou dost lay me in the dust of death.

"Yea dogs are round about me; a company of evildoers encircle me; they have pierced my hands and feet— I can count all my bones—"

"They think they're great ones, those Jews," Baruch said, hating himself for every word, but knowing what he must do.

The dark-bearded soldier grunted.

"Look at his tongue hang out," Baruch said. "Mind if I give him some Syrian wine?"

"Not a thing," the dark-bearded soldier said. "We've orders to give this dog nothing."

"That evil a fellow," said Baruch, feeling very frightened, but forcing himself to go on. It was up to him now and he couldn't back away, couldn't show his fear.

Joshua tried to clear his head, to remember the words. It seemed very important somehow to remember the words.

"But thou, O Lord, be not far off, O thou my help hasten to my aid! Deliver my soul from the sword, my life from the power of the dog! Save me from the mouth of the lion, my afflicted soul from the horns of the wild oxen.

"I will tell of thy name to my brethren; in the midst of the congregation I will praise thee. You who fear the Lord, praise him! All you sons of Jacob, glorify him, and stand in awe of him, all you sons of Israel! For he has not despised or abhorred the affliction of the afflicted; and he has not hid his face from him, but has heard when he cried to him."

"Come now," Baruch said. "I know how you feel about these people. You know we Syrians don't favor them, either. But a bit of wine for a man dying on the cross." He tapped the wineskin he held. "What's the harm in it?"

"No," the dark-bearded soldier said. "Not while I'm on duty."

"Why not?" the younger soldier burst out. "The poor devil will be dead soon. A little wine will ease the pain."

"No," the other said, stubbornly, "We have our orders and I intend to follow them."

The younger man grew angry. "Here," he said, "give it to me," and he tore the wineskin from Baruch's hands.

"No you don't!" said the other soldier and he reached for the bag. They wrestled over it and the cork fell out. The wine spilled on the ground, while Baruch and his friends watched in horror.

The younger soldier gave his fellow a fierce shove, grabbed his spear and wrapped a cloth around it, dipping it into the last of the wine.

"Here," he said, calling up to Joshua, touching the wet cloth to his lips.

"All the ends of the earth shall remember and turn to the Lord; and all the families of the nations shall worship before him. For dominion belongs to the Lord and he rules over the nations.

"Yea, to him shall all the proud of the earth bow down; before him shall bow all who go down to the dust, and he who cannot keep himself alive. Posterity shall serve him; men shall tell of the Lord to the coming generation, and proclaim his deliverance to a people yet unborn, that he has done it."

The cooling cloth touched Joshua's lips, and without thinking, he brought it into his mouth and squeezed it. The liquid cooled him. It was pleasant, very pleasant.

The pain began to recede. His vision cleared for a moment and he saw his mother and tried to tell her of his love. Then he felt the darkness covering his eyes. His head dropped slowly to his chest.

21.

EVIL NEWS

Pilate remained in his office all that morning. He had sent Paulus Aemilius into the city with instructions to instigate a riot or rebellion. He was waiting for word of the conflict, ready to impose the heaviest possible sanctions.

Pilate missed Septimus. There was a man you could depend upon when ruthless actions must be taken. It had been obvious that Septimus was a bit mad, but that was all to the good. That was precisely the quality that one required in a situation like this.

Paulus Aemilius was a different type altogether. He was tough enough and he clearly enjoyed military mayhem, but that was the very point. The young captain tended to draw the line between armed conflict in the field between two opposing armies, and the kind of civilian irregular conflict that one found in a place like the Syrian department, and especially here in Judaea.

After a while, the soldiers learned that these irregulars gave no quarter, that they would cut a soldier's throat without compunction. Roman soldiers were expected to know that, but somehow they had to learn it the hard way. Pilate hoped that Paulus was up to the task.

The hours passed without incident or report. Pilate shuffled through official documents and dictated missives to his secretary to fill the time. He kept making mistakes as his mind wandered and after a while he irritably dismissed his scribe.

That left him alone in the dark office of the Antonia. It was a service-able enough place, but built as a fortress, the windows were few and set high in the walls. It was depressing. Impatient, he marched out and onto the ramparts that overlooked the Temple. Instead of the huge crowd he had expected, only a modest number of people were gathered in the outer courtyard. They seemed subdued, quiet, talking together in small groups.

Well, perhaps these were the cowards. Others might even now be boil-ing into the streets, seeking to save their 'king.' He laughed at the picture of Joshua, beaten and bloody, draped in a rag of a robe and crowned with spiky thorns. His soldiers were a wonderfully humorous lot. Surely they had scourged any royal pretensions out of that Galilean.

Pilate scanned the distant parts of the city, but he could see no other activity. Of course, the streets were narrow and the stone houses piled next to each other. There might be a major battle somewhere and still it would be invisible.

The city seemed much too quiet.

***

Paulus Aemilius ranged through the city on horseback, seeking for indications that Pilate's plot was working. Thus far, he had seen nothing encouraging. He couldn't always identify his own men, disguised as they were, but he was surprised that the streets were so quiet. He had been in Jerusalem on this festival in the past, and by this time, the people would be up and about, many heading for the Temple, others merely chatting and laughing with their neighbors and visitors.

As he walked his horse through the street of the ironmongers, a pilgrim pulled at his leg. Paulus understood that the man was a Roman, and a quick look at his face told him it was the centurion, Gratus.

Paulus was surprised. This was a breach of security and he tried to ignore him, but Gratus stubbornly remained close.

"Curse you," he muttered fiercely under his breath. "Get away from me."

Gratus shrugged and moved off.

***

Gratus had wanted to tell the captain of his own experience. Earlier he had come into the street of the ironmongers with several men. The shops were shuttered for the holiday, but the people, many of whom lived above them, had begun to enter the street on their way to the Temple.

Gratus had run up to one burly looking man. "They're killing your Messiah!" he said.

Startled, the Jew had looked at him without responding. Other Jews, curious, had come up to listen.

"They've taken Joshua, the man from Galilee, and they're crucifying him on the hill of Golgotha."

The Jews responded with cries of compassion.

"Such a good man," one said.

"I saw him in the Temple, yesterday, so young and handsome."

A woman came running up, her face taut with concern. "Joshua? Of Nazareth?"

Gratus nodded. The woman began to cry. Some of the men gave way to tears. Others simply seemed shocked.

"Our hopes," one mumbled. Others nodded.

"Don't think of us," another man said, "think of him."

The first man, the one Gratus had approached, continued to look at him. "Impossible," he said.

"I'm telling you it's true," Gratus said. "They're nailing him to the cross at his very moment."

The Jews looked at each other and the pain was evident in their faces. The first man turned away and moved towards his own doorway.

"Aren't you going to do anything to stop them from killing your Messiah?" Gratus realized he should not have said 'your,' but it was too late.

"If they kill him," the Jew said, "he isn't the Messiah."

Several of the other Jews nodded. A few went back to their own homes. Others remained in the street, talking among themselves.

Confused, Gratus listened.

"I told you," one was saying, "he's a fine fellow, but not the Messiah."

"I don't know," the other responded. "He sounded very convincing to me. Still, it's terrible they should do this to him."

"It's a provocation," said another. "The Romans know how much this man is loved."

Gratus broke in, "we mustn't let them get away with it. Let's go now to Golgotha and protest."

"Do we know this fellow?" one of the Jews asked. The others shook their heads and studied Gratus carefully.

"*You* go," a tall, heavily bearded man said, "start your own protest."

Gratus flushed. "You'd let them kill your Messiah," he said, "without even raising a hand."

They only looked at him and he stalked off angrily down the street.

***

All over the city, the Romans soldiers disguised as pilgrims were spreading the word. Those who heard told others. The grief was great and the despair terrible. Many cried, others rent their clothes.

Zealot leaders and their men, hearing the news were shocked. Ahaz, dressed and armed, ready for any confrontation, heard the story in the street before the house where he was staying. He grabbed the pilgrim who told the story, not knowing that he was a Roman soldier.

"Where did you hear that?" Ahaz asked.

"I saw it with my own eyes," the spurious pilgrim said. "I saw them leading him in chains to the hill outside the city where they crucify criminals."

One of Ahaz's men, hearing the story said, "We better get there as fast as we can."

"I'll show you the place," said the soldier, pleased at the success of his ruse.

Ahaz put up his hand. "Think, think what this means," he said. "We must have been wrong. If this man were the Messiah the Romans could never take him and surely they couldn't kill him."

Everywhere the response was the same. Great despair that Joshua had been taken, deep compassion for him and his suffering, but at the same time, the belief that he could not be abused and violated in this manner and still be the Messiah.

Had Gaius been out in the streets, he would have been gratified that his inspired guess had worked— one couldn't tell the Jews that a man was their Messiah and at the same time that he was being killed by heathen.

The man who had told Ahaz kept trying. "Aren't you going to Golgotha, to see what has happened?"

"I'm surprised at you," Ahaz said. "A Jew should know we don't go to barbaric places to watch the suffering of our fellows. A Jew should realize the agony of the oppressed must not be increased by a gaping crowd."

The Roman soldier could not bear Ahaz's angry look any longer. He turned away and walked down the street. He had lost his taste for carrying this tale to the Jews.

Much of the city was in mourning. Even the Sadducees and the Herodians, those who had opposed Joshua, felt no pleasure at his affliction. Caiaphas had returned from his meeting with Pilate, thoroughly shaken. He was grateful that the crisis was ending. There had even been a time when he might have viewed the death of Joshua with detachment. But he had seen the man too closely, had learned of his great courage and moral strength, and he was confused that such a man would have to be sacrificed.

Some gathered in the Temple, sharing their disappointment at the failure of their hopes and despair over the future of their nation. They repeated the words they had heard from Joshua and wondered at the meaning of them, in view of his terrible fate. Was he a false prophet? Had God punished him for his evil deeds? They did not believe that, but they could not ignore his cruel end.

***

As the day wore on, Pilate's anger grew. No word, no sign of rebellion. What could be happening? He sent couriers out into the streets seeking information, and their reports were discouraging.

Paulus Aemilius, pale, anxious and weary, reluctantly faced his governor.

"There is no riot, Excellency. We've tried everything to incite the people, but with no success."

"They're plotting something," Pilate said, "those crafty Jews. Waiting till we relax our defenses, then they'll strike."

"I don't think so," Paulus said. "I've talked to many of my men. The very fact that we have crucified him, seems to make the people believe that he was not their Messiah."

"What do you mean?" Pilate asked. He did not want to believe what he was hearing.

"Some think he was a false prophet, others that he was mistaken, but almost all seem to feel he was not what they thought. They will not rise to save him."

Pilate's face turned an ugly color and his brows edged together. "They've tricked me, those crafty bastards. I thought I had them, but they've slipped out of the net again. How do you eliminate these slimy creatures?"

Paulus Aemilius stood with his head down, unable to stare into the twisted face of Pontius Pilate. He had never seen such naked evil in his life before. He had realized from the first that they had a difficult task, controlling a difficult people. He did not like the Jews, but he could not begin to hate them and wish them all dead. It was incredible to him, that anyone, especially such a high Roman official, would hold such thoughts.

***

When Joshua's eyes closed and his head sagged to his breast, Brother Jacob's heart sank. He prayed that what they had done had been successful, but Joshua looked totally lifeless.

Omriel, watching with him and the others, saw the sign he had been wait-ing for. He jogged Jacob's arm. Jacob, remembering himself, approached the Roman soldiers.

"He's dead," Brother Jacob said.

The Roman laughed. "Impossible," he said. "Only been up there a few hours."

"Look at him," Jacob said.

Both soldiers looked at Joshua.

"Just fainted," said the dark-bearded one. "Happens to all of them. Probably best, don't feel the pain that way."

"I'm a doctor," Omriel said, feeling the need to help, "I can tell you that man is dead."

"From down here?" the Roman soldier said. "I don't think so."

"We'll take down the body," Brother Jacob said. He signaled to Simon Peter and Andrew and they came hurrying up.

"Nobody touches that body," a soldier said. "Those are our orders, understand? You can take him down at sunset for some holiday of yours, but until then, he sits up on that post."

Nicodemus drew them aside. "This man will never let us have him. Someone has to persuade the Roman authorities to permit us to take him down soon, otherwise it'll be too late."

"Gaius," Nico said. "He's the one who can help us."

"Good," said his father. "We'll go to him now."

"No," said Nico, "I think we should send Joseph of Arimathea. He's got a good reputation, not known as a revolutionary, and it's his tomb we're planning to use. Coming from him it will sound quite innocent."

***

The guards, as usual, were insolent, but after a few uncomfortable min-utes, Joseph was admitted to see Gaius. He had thought he would never have to return to this foul place again, but he knew he had to do it.

Gaius was obviously despondent, but he greeted Joseph as politely as he could. The message surprised and staggered him.

"Dead?—already?"

"There is a doctor there who can verify it."

At first he had felt the pang, and then Gaius realized there was more to this than appeared on the surface. "Of course," he said. "I'll sign the order."

"What order?" Pilate asked. He had come to Gaius's office, filled with anger.

"This man, a respected citizen, has offered to bury Joshua, the Galilean. I'm giving him an order to take the body."

"The body—what are you talking about? He can't possibly be dead yet."

"But he is," Joseph said. "There's a doctor there—"

"—Jewish?" Pilate asked.

Joseph nodded. Pilate smiled grimly.

"Captain!" he yelled and almost immediately, Paulus came running into the office. Gaius wondered about that. It was his office, not the governor's, yet the captain had been outside, within earshot.

"They say the prisoner, Joshua the Galilean, is dead. Does that seem right to you?"

"For an old and weak man, yes. The younger ones usually last longer."

"I tell you," Joseph said, "this man is gone. The Sabbath is coming and he'll be taken down before that anyway. It would be easier to have the body now. My burial place is only a short distance away."

"Check the body, Captain. Make certain he's truly dead, before they take him away. I don't want any 'miracles.'"

The captain saluted smartly and hurried out of the office. Joseph of Arimathea began to follow him.

"No," Pilate said. "You wait here. And tell me, if you can, why a prominent citizen like you supports a criminal like this one?"

***

"It must be soon," Omriel said under his breath, "or there's no hope at all."

"There's nothing we can do," Nicodemus said. "Pray that Joseph can persuade the governor."

Baruch could not take his eyes off Joshua. He saw no movement, none whatever. It was strange, hoping that he would not move, and yet praying that he could be saved.

Brother Jacob had spoken to his mother, urging her to go back to Bethany. He didn't tell her or any of the others of what they planned for Joshua. It would be too cruel, if their plans failed.

"I want to be here when...when he's...taken down," Miriam said.

Jacob told her then of the plans to bring him to the new tomb in the garden of Joseph of Arimathea. That seemed to help, if only a little.

Nico said, "Wait, please at our home. It's in the city and you can remain there as long as you want."

Miriam tried to smile at him, but she could not. She wanted to tell him that she knew Joshua had always loved him, and that he was like another son to her, but the words would not come.

"I know," he said, reading her look. "For me it is the same, and for my father, too." He turned to Simon Peter. "Please go with Mother Miriam, Simon, and take Judith, Nathan and Deborah with you." The older people had waited patiently in the growing heat, but their age had begun to tell, and they were grateful at the thought of having a place to go.

But at that moment, Paulus Aemilius came riding up. He leaped off his horse and handed the reins to the younger, fair-haired soldier, standing near the cross..

Brother Jacob and the others pressed closer.

The Roman captain stalked in a circle around the cross on which the Jew hung. He had seen many dead men in his military career, and not a few of them on crosses. This one certainly looked dead. Still, he must have been weaker than he looked, or he would have lasted longer.

The prefect had warned him that this was an important task and he didn't want to fail, especially since the plot to arouse the citizens was such a failure. He had an inspired thought. If he made the right move now, he could fulfill his task and save the governor's plan, even now.

"Soldier!" he yelled to the dark-bearded fellow, "plunge your spear into his side."

The disciples heard this fearsome threat and ran to the cross, Jacob crying out, "No, don't do it—you blaspheme against God."

But the soldier, pleased to have the task, raised his spear and drove it into Joshua, on his left side, just below his heart, then yanked it out.

Blood and water sprayed from the wound, as the watchers cried out in protest and pain. Paulus's eyes flickered quickly back and forth between Joshua and his followers.

"Didn't move an inch," the soldier said, laughing.

The disciples stopped in their tracks, their pitying eyes on Joshua.

"Good God," Omriel muttered, "that would finish anyone."

The captain stood defiant, waiting for an excuse to call on his troops, but the Jews remained silent, staring at Joshua, with tears streaming down their faces.

"Cowards," the captain muttered.

Simon Peter's eyes flickered. He would have dearly loved to have it out with this one, armed or otherwise, but he held his ground, and forced himself to look down, where he could see his own tears striking the rock.

Paulus Aemilius spat on the ground contemptuously, then mounted his horse. When the horse raised its tail and defecated at the foot of the cross, he laughed.

Brother Jacob, seeing the wrath on Simon's face and fearful of what he might do, grabbed Simon's arm. "Please, Simon Peter," he said, please take my mother and sister and the others to Nico's home."

Simon was about to protest, but he saw the desperate appeal in Jacob's eyes, and he told himself, Joshua would want him to do this. He lifted his tear-stained face and nodded.

22.

RESURRECTION

At first there was the blackness, deep impenetrable. But then the blackness began to swirl and divide and streaks shot through it. But even the streaks were black, though a different black and the blackness was everywhere and the sense of spinning, spinning downward.

There was a roaring all around him and a roaring in his ears and the swirls of blackness on top of blackness seemed to be echoes of the roaring sounds that were outside him and inside him at the same time. He was hurtling downward into this spinning blackness, like a heavy stone dropped into a dark sea, like a cry in the night, echoing all about and reverberating inside the loudness within his head.

The darkness was not mere color, it was shape. It was shape and it was form and the form was drawing him down into it, so that he was part of the blackness and he felt it creeping over him and trying to penetrate him. He felt helpless for a moment, as if the blackness had the strength to push through him, to cover him, to enclose him and to swallow him up.

Even as he spun at terrible speed down into it, his head lower than his feet, his arms and legs splayed outward, he fought the blackness. It was not a struggle of his hands or his arms or any part of his body, but of his head. If he could keep himself together somehow, the blackness would not have him. Yet, he had been drawn very deep. The layers of blackness above him must be very thick. Thick but not solid, dense but not impenetrable.

The roaring now had a liquid sound, like the rush of waters and the touch of the blackness was damp and hot and unpleasant and still he was dropping through it at an alarming speed. For a moment, he felt a loss of hope, as though no matter what he did the very weight of his body would draw him farther into this terrible place.

And now he could sense he was not alone. There were others there, lost in the blackness, black as the blackness itself. They reached for him out of the darkness, and he could feel the slimy strokes of their fingers trying to catch his arms, his legs, every part of his body.

He realized that the roaring sound was their voices, their voices ebbing and flowing in terrible screams that blended with each other and throbbed against and within his head. Their screams were larger than they were, circles of unending blackness that grabbed at him with as much force as their terrible slimy fingers.

"Yes," the voices cried, over and over again. "Come down, down, down. Be one of us. Be one of us. Be one of us." It was a chant, without a melody, without rhythm or tone, a roaring, pounding chant that pulled and tore at his hair and his skin.

"Be one of us," the voices cried and moaned. And still he plunged lower, pushing away from their hands, twisting and turning to avoid their touch, drifting away and still plunging lower and lower, until he was certain that a million slithering shapes were between him and the world above.

He was tiring. The continual downward movement was making him dizzy and tired and he was losing confidence that he could ever make his way out of these terrible depths.

But within him, a small voice kept saying, "No," and "No" and "No" again. He continued to struggle, to push the hands away from him, to shut out the throbbing voices.

"No," he heard within himself and then, "No," again and then he felt his lips forming the word and he was shouting it against the roar of the voices.

"No!" he cried, "I won't go with you! I won't be one of you!"

Then "NO...NO...NO...NO...NO...NO...NO...NO," until all the NOs were a single NO and his arms were flailing strongly against the grasping hands and the slimy fingers were losing their grip on his body and he was no longer plunging downward and his head was level with his feet and he was no longer spinning.

Other hands came out of the darkness and they were not slimy but clean, not soft but strong and they were reaching for him and gently, gently urging him on. He was level and then he had turned and he was moving upward. His arms were raised over his head and his head was lifted. The darkness was shot through with colors and the colors were no longer black, but gray and dark gray and dark brown and then lighter brown and still lighter gray and streaks of umber and ochre and red and orange and yellow and pink and blue and green.

Then all of the colors blended and spun together so quickly they became one color: white.

Still the unseen hands, warm and strong, but gentle and firm, were lifting him upward. The roaring voices faded slowly, slowly and then were gone. He was moving upward very swiftly, but there was no sense of strain. He did not feel the wind rushing past. He was moving, he was being lifted up, but all was silent and pure and white.

He heard a voice and he knew it was the voice of Isaiah, and the voice began in a whisper:

"You will say in that day:

'I will give thanks to thee, O Lord for though thou wast angry with me' thy anger turned away, and thou didst comfort me.

'Behold, God is my salvation; I will trust, and will not be afraid; For the Lord God is my strength and my song, and he has become my salvation.'"

He smiled to hear the words and he nodded and his heart began to feel free again.

Then the whiteness began to define itself into shapes of white upon white and the white was so polished it became crystal and then it became a diamond and the diamond was in and around him and when it withdrew it spun at a great speed and multiplied itself into many glittering stones and the stones built upon themselves and became a palace of purest white and diamond, glittering and glittering with great walls and towers and gates.

A great flame suddenly appeared beyond the palace and as the light of the flame touched the glass and crystals and diamonds it reflected through them and broke into a million colors and tones and hues that echoed and re-echoed.

The Palace became a Temple and before the Temple a great Gate, and he was carried through that gate and within it he found yet another Temple soaring higher than the first, glittering more brightly and gleaming with brilliant shafts of blossoming light.

And the Gate to that Temple led him to another and another, until he had passed through six gates of ever increasing size into six Temples of every increasing grandeur.

Till he came to the last Gate and the last Temple, the Seventh, and the glory of the Seventh Temple outshone the glory of all the others. The flames rose higher, but they gave only warmth, not heat, only light, not pain and the glittering diamond Temple and the Flame became one.

The Temple which was a Flame and the Flame which was a Temple grew brighter and larger, expanding and glimmering and shattering and reforming and flickering and mounting step by step, neither up nor down but in every direction so that the Flame and the diamond surrounded and enclosed him and flashed in his heart and soul and they became white and perfect and a song grew out of the perfection and he could hear the words of which he was a part as they surrounded and carried him:

"O give thanks to the Lord, call on His Name, make known His deeds among the peoples! Sing to Him, sing praises to Him, tell of all His wonderful works! Glory in His holy Name; let the hearts of those who seek the Lord rejoice! Seek the Lord and His strength, seek His presence evermore! Remember the wonderful works that He has done, His miracles and the judgments He uttered, O, offspring of Abraham His servant, sons of Jacob, His chosen ones!

"He is the Lord our God; His judgments are in all the earth. He is mindful of his covenant forever, of the word that He commanded, for a thousand generations, the covenant that He made with Abraham, His sworn promise to Isaac, which He confirmed to Jacob as a statute, to Israel as an everlasting covenant...."

And even as he heard the last of the words dying faintly away and nodded his head in pleasure because he had recalled the words and sung them along with the great choir. Then, he realized that he was indeed being held. Strong hands were holding his arms and touching his shoulders. Other hands were holding to his fine, white cloak.

He looked and saw that to his right stood Joseph, his earthly father, and Ari the sage, and to his left was Rebecca, his wife and David and Sarah, his children. They all smiled at him and he embraced and kissed them, and his heart filled with the joy of their presence and the love they shared. They all cried tears of joy and the tears were diamonds that glittered and reflected the flame and the Temple.

His eyes lifted above the heads of those he loved and he saw three men, great of age and years and flowing of beard and he knew them. For they were Noah and Abraham and Moses and they looked upon him with grace and love and they nodded their heads, and he felt the approval of their blessing fall upon him as an anointing that blended with the happy tears of his loved ones and glittered with the great glow of the Flame that was the Temple.

As he looked towards the three men, they beckoned to him and he left Ari and Joseph and his wife and children and went to them.

The closer he came to them, the brighter their faces seemed and the brighter the glow of the Temple. The air sparkled with gold and silver flashes that splintered and reformed and became white streaks, and the whiteness grew within the whiteness and the faces of the men and the facade of the Temple dissolved into whiteness that was a swirling cloud.

He thought for an instant that he saw a face within the cloud, a face with fine features and a flowing white beard and an aureole of white hair, with eyes of all the colors, separate, but blended into one, and lips that were strong and full, but gentle and soft.

There was a rumble of thunder crashing on thunder and his vision shook with the power of it and the thunder was all around and within him and yet was not a part of him.

The lips parted and a great wind rushed upon him and he heard a voice whisper, "This is my son, in whom I am well pleased."

Then the voice was gone and the whiteness softened. He felt an aching loss and yet a sense of perfection and completion.

Now in the lambent whiteness he could see the faces of Noah and Abraham and Moses again, and they smiled upon him. They smiled and pointed upward, and as he looked upward he was lifted and they were lifted with him.

He found himself above the land of Israel, with the sea in the west and the great masses of the land in every other direction. Then he was over the holy city of Jerusalem, glistening in the glow of the setting sun. As he watched, the sun seemed to strike a torch at every corner of the city and the flames began to search inward. The flames rose and merged and rose higher. Men, women and children ran screaming before the flames. He wanted to reach out to them, but the hand of Moses held him back, and Abraham shook his head and Noah cried.

Soldiers in burnished bronze helmets raced through the city, slashing about as they ran, killing the people with abandon, piling the bodies into ever higher columns that smoked and burned.

The priests were slain in the court of the Temple and the flames entered through all the gates and converged on the holy of holies which burst into fire and was consumed.

The stones of the Temple melted and fell like hot tears that seared the people and the priests. The soldiers laughed and torched the people and the buildings and their flames mounted ever higher. The Temple melted together and became one huge tear that slipped over the walls and dropped into the Kidron Valley and ran into the earth and disappeared.

He cried as he watched and his tears touched the city like drops of rain that hissed where they struck the smoldering ruins.

All was gone, all was desolate, and in the ruins, the soldiers piled their swords and breastplates and spears and shields higher, ever higher and the pile rose above the walls and the bronze, melting in the fires which the soldiers themselves had set, was forged into the head of a man, with a fringe of curls and a beak of a nose with a helmet upon his head, and the soldiers bowed down and worshipped him.

Meanwhile, the rivers of flame, spilled over the walls of the city and raced through the countryside, carrying on them a laughing tide of soldiers, heavily armed, who slashed about them, killing man and woman and child and beast.

Fire and flame and sword cut through the countryside, until all of Israel was on fire, and the rivers ran with blood and the mountains seethed with smoke and brimstone showered out of the skies.

Still they flew above the highest mountains and now the tears of Noah and Moses and Abraham blended with his own and the rain that fell from their eyes no longer hissed on the earth, but flowed in streams that spilled across the land.

The streams stretched out like a thousand fingers across Israel and into Egypt and Africa, and out to the north and east and west. The streams entered the Great Sea and spread through it like green fingers in the blue. The haze over Israel parted and the rivers of pure water rippled across the curve of land and sea and sky, stretching far out. Everywhere that the streams touched, the land turned green and plants sprouted and flowers bloomed.

But now, his attention was fixed back on the land below, on Israel, for the streams that had reached out and spread from her had returned in a mighty rush of crystal waters.

And as he watched, the dry and sandy earth, still smoldering from the flames of its affliction, became green as grass sprouted through the tortured soil and debris, through the molten brass and stone. Trees unfolded from within the soil and pushed upward and flowers blossomed and grain waved on the hillsides.

The armies of the night disappeared and the people reappeared, laughing and working, smiling and planting, digging and plowing.

They cried again, Noah and Abraham and Moses and he with them, and the tears now fell as gentle rain and wherever their tears touched the earth a tree grew or a child or an ox or a house or a flower.

They smiled to see what their tears had wrought, and still they cried and still the land blossomed and flourished. On the mount of the flat place where the great bronze head had stood, a city began to form before their eyes, pure and white and gleaming in the dawning sunlight that burnished every stone.

He looked for the Temple, but he could not see it. He saw a flat and pleasant place with flowers and trees, but there was no Temple. He was perplexed, and he looked to the men who were with him and they smiled at him and tapped their chests and he understood that the Temple was within.

But then, on the horizon, far away, he saw a flicker of flame and even as he watched the flame began to circle the land and to increase.

Noah took the hand of Abraham and Abraham took the hand of Moses and Moses took the hand of Joshua. Joshua took the hand of Rebecca, his wife, who took the hand of David her son, who took the hand of Sarah his sister. Sarah took the hand of Judith, her aunt and the sister of Joshua and Judith took the hand of Jacob, her brother and Jacob took the hand of Miriam, his mother. Miriam took the hand of Joseph, her husband, and Joseph took the hand of Gaius Fabricius and Gaius took the hand of Ari the sage. Then Ari took the hand of Simon Peter and Simon Peter took the hand of Andrew, his brother. And Andrew took the hand of Nicodemus, who took the hand of Nicodemus, his son, and Nicodemus, the son, took the hand of Joseph of Arimathea. Joseph took the hand of Deborah and Deborah took the hand of Nathan, her husband. Nathan took the hand of Martha, who took the hand of Eliezer, her brother, who took the hand of Miriam, his sister. And Miriam took the hand of Philip and Philip took the hand of Mattathias and Mattathias took the hand of Miriam of Magdala, who took the hand of Simeon. And Simeon took the hand of a stranger. And the stranger took the hand of a stranger.

The line of them, holding hands, circled the land and screened the flames and then they trod on the flames and the flames became smoke and the smoke disappeared.

Joshua smiled then and they smiled in return and the glory of their smiles flowed together and the brilliance of it gradually filled all of the world and he realized that he could no longer see them, but he knew they were there, still smiling at him, still encouraging him, still promising the glory he had seen that God had presented to them all.

The glow of brightness was dazzling now, brighter than before, until he had to squint to see and yet he did not have to close his eyes and then he realized he could bear the brightness and he opened his eyes even wider.

"He's awake," Brother Jacob said, but Omriel hushed him and then there was a moment of silence as the words perched on a little shelf in Joshua's mind.

He blinked then and the great glow vanished, but he saw a flickering candle and the faces of his brother and Nico, Nicodemus and Joseph of Arimathea, Omriel and Baruch.

He smiled at them.

"Thank God," Nico said and the others echoed his words as they stared at Joshua in awe. He was pale still and his expression was different, but he had clearly seen them and he was smiling and his mouth was working.

He sat up and Omriel tried to stop him.

"No, not yet," the little doctor said, but Joshua had held out his arms to his brother and Jacob embraced him and they cried tears of happiness.

Omriel was about to warn Joshua about his wound, when Joshua winced suddenly and Jacob felt the startled movement of his body.

"Joshua!" he cried, but Joshua smiled through the pain and said, "Don't worry, it's all right."

He did not know what it was that hurt his side or why they were staring at him in such a strange way, but he knew he had returned from a long trip and he was very glad to see them.

Then he remembered. He remembered the scourging and the pain and the long walk and the nails in his wrists and the agony. He remembered it all in one blinding vision, but then it was past, lost forever, no longer to be a part of his consciousness.

He knew the truth of what had happened to him and where he had been and the joy of it was the greatest he had ever known.

"I've come back," he said in a soft voice, looking from face to face. "The Lord has brought me back."

Nico began to explain about the drug they had put on the spear they raised to his lips. Jacob told of Joseph of Arimathea and how he had begged for Joshua. Baruch was explaining about Omriel and all his drugs and ointments, of his skill and his knowledge.

Omriel was trying to get him to lie down and rest, gently probing the wound in his side.

Joshua heard them all as they tried to explain what they had done to save his life.

"Thank you," he said, smiling again, "for surely you have been the instruments of God. I tell you now that I have been dead and gone to Sheol and God has brought me back to life. God promised the resurrection of souls, and he said that to be pure of heart one must be born again and this is the proof of the power of the Lord."

He raised his arms overhead in the cramped space of the tomb and prayed to God.

They joined in his prayer for they were happy he was still with them, but they were puzzled that he believed he had been brought back to life when they were certain he had never died.

He might have been angry then, but he had returned from Sheol and he knew that he would never be angry again. "Why is it so hard for you to learn that nothing happens without the will of God, that not a sparrow falls from the sky or a flower pushes through the earth without him?

"Had the Almighty wanted my life to end forever on the cross, neither frankincense nor myrrh nor gall, nor all the art and wisdom of man would have changed it. If He gave you the skill and the means to help me on my journey, then bless Him for giving it to you as I bless Him in all things."

He saw that it was difficult for them to understand. He might have told them that he did not drink the drink that had been placed in his mouth, for he could not swallow. He had felt the cooling draught but he had not drunk it. Still, he did not want to argue with them, nor to give them proofs of God's will and God's work.

"We love God, brother," Jacob said, "and we know that what you say, hard as it is for us to comprehend, is true. It is a miracle that you are alive and we thank the Lord for that miracle."

The others nodded in agreement.

"There was no rebellion, then, no slaughter in the Temple," Joshua said. "The people have been spared."

"Yes," Nico said, wondering how Joshua could know, but never doubting that he did.

Joshua hesitated then, knowing what he had learned and wondering if they were prepared to hear it. Yet he realized that the knowledge had not been given to him to withhold, but rather to share.

"I must tell you," Joshua said, "of what I have seen."

"But not here," said Nico. "It isn't safe. Anyone may come along at any time and find that you are still alive and report it to the Romans."

The others reacted with concern.

"He shouldn't travel yet," Omriel said, still eyeing the wound.

"We can't stay here," Nico said. "If we do, all our efforts—and the Lord's—will have been in vain."

They offered Joshua a litter, but he refused. "I'll walk," he said. "Here, brother, you and Simon Peter support me."

"The wound is close to the heart," Omriel said, his pink face tightened into a prune by concern. "Even now, there may be bleeding inside and there's nothing I can do about it. If you rest and are careful, your body will have a chance to heal."

Joshua smiled and held out his arms and Brother Jacob and Simon Peter put their shoulders under them. Then, moving slowly he turned away from the tomb in the garden. Omriel followed, a few steps behind them. Joshua felt the tearing of his flesh inside, and it was pulling at him as he moved, but he wanted to feel the earth beneath his feet. It wouldn't do to ride in a litter, to treat God's work as poorly done.

Joseph showed the others how to close the tomb and they closed and sealed it. They agreed that Joseph should remain in the house in the garden and keep everyone away from the tomb.

They set out for Nicodemus's house, assuming that was the best place to meet and to plan what must be done.

"No," said Nico, "it's not safe there any longer. Too many people know we have used the house."

"I know where we must go," said Joshua.

***

The soldiers rattled the gate and yelled for entry.

Pilate, who hated the city, and especially at night, waited on horseback, at a distance where he could not be seen, while the soldiers, called out.

"Let us in, or we'll break down the gate!" an officer yelled.

A lantern appeared and carrying it an older man. Pilate hunched forward in his saddle and recognized him as Joseph of Arimathea, the man who had asked for and taken the body.

"What is it?" he was asking.

"Let us in, we come under the governor's orders."

"For what reason?" Joseph asked.

"I tell you if the gate isn't opened at once, we'll break it down and burn your property."

"The governor will hear of this," Joseph said, bringing out a great black key that he twisted in the lock.

The soldiers shoved the gate, almost knocking Joseph down and Pilate, unable to resist, spurred his horse and followed them, trampling the flowers in the garden in his haste.

"What—" Joseph cried out, but then he saw the governor and was silent.

The soldiers faced the tomb, with the great stone lodged in the trough and wedged shut.

"Open it," Pilate said.

"You despoil the dead, you violate the Sabbath," Joseph told him.

But Pilate ignored him, watching intently as the men leaned into the sealing stone, rocking it once and again, until it rocked out of the notch and rolled with a great grinding sound, away from the entrance.

The centurion, intimidated by the dark entrance of the Jewish tomb in the night, hesitated, looking towards Pilate. The governor waved at him irritably and the centurion took a lantern, dipped his head and walked into the tomb.

After a minute he reappeared, carrying some winding cloth.

"No one there," he said, relieved.

Pilate spurred his horse forward and slipped from the saddle.

Joseph ran up, a look of surprise on his face. "Impossible," he said. His heart was beating fiercely.

Pilate grabbed the lantern and went into the tomb. It smelled sweetly of the cloying spices the Jews used on their dead. The lantern made strange and fearful patterns, but there was only a pile of spices, a shroud and a few damp cloths. His eyes bulged with anger. They had done it again, these Jews. He stormed out of the tomb, handed the lantern to the centurion and grabbed Joseph of Arimathea by the edge of his cloak. He slapped him once across the face.

"Where is he?" Pilate demanded.

23.

SANCTUARY

They looked at his face with astonishment. He had been proud once, proud and imperious and his arrogance had quelled many men. He had been tall once, tall and impressive in appearance with a full head of hair and a luxuriant beard into his later years. He had been powerful once, forceful in every word and deed and he had feared no man, perhaps had feared not even God.

Now as they looked at Caiaphas, the robes, the flourishes of office still remained, but the man was very different. "It cannot be," he said, staring into the face of Joshua.

Joshua was silent, but Nico began to tell him of the drug and the spear and the doctor.

Caiaphas made an impatient, if wavering gesture, asking for silence. He knew that these were but details and that the overwhelming fact was there before him, Joshua the Galilean, pale but alive, walking on the arms of his disciples, but walking, nonetheless.

"What do you want?" he asked Joshua.

"Sanctuary," Joshua said, "a place to stay for me and for the others."

Caiaphas hesitated.

"We were not seen," Nico said, "except by your guards. If you can trust the men at the gate, you are safe."

Caiaphas was not concerned over the guards. They could be dealt with. He was trying to understand the meaning of what he saw.

"We are tired," Brother Jacob said, "Omriel, Baruch and I have not slept in two nights."

Caiaphas hardly heard him. He had begun the day as the High priest, full of his wisdom and strength and power. Then, Joshua had appeared, telling of his plan to save the nation from destruction. He had listened to the members of the Sanhedrin, watched them wrestle with the terrible choices Joshua had shown them.

He had appeared before the hated Roman governor, knowing that he was only an instrument in the hands of this Galilean preacher. It was then that he had begun to fade, that his strength had begun to fail.

It had been little satisfaction that the governor, too, was only an instrument, controlled by Joshua. He had never respected the Prefect, with his powdered hair and face, his prissy ways and his vicious soul. Still, he had been able to measure his own weakness against the weakness of the Roman Empire and he had found himself a match in helplessness.

The governor had scourged and mocked Joshua, tortured, crucified and humiliated him without in the least affecting his dignity, without weakening him or turning him away from his mission.

In the face of such strength, the High Priest had come to know his own weakness. He had returned to his palace a different man, shaken and confused, tormented and cast down.

But, at least, he had believed that the incident, if it could be called an incident, was over. The Galilean was dead and while that was a terrible fate, the nation was alive. He was still the High Priest, and with rest and patience his strength, his health, would return.

Now, that hope was shattered. Joshua stood before him.

He steadied himself and spoke. "When the people learn you are here, they will rise up and we will have the very massacre that you...tried to avoid."

"No," Joshua said. "For now we won't tell them."

"But Joshua," Nico said, "they are downcast, believing you dead. They're entitled to know."

"Even Pilate will be afraid to touch you now," Brother Jacob said.

"You mistake the man," Joshua said. "He'll say it was a trick, a sham, and he'll try to finish the deed at once. Then there will truly be a revolution."

"But whenever the people know, they will respond," Nico said. "You can't avoid it."

"Peace," Joshua said. "It is peace that we seek and peace that God wants us to have." He felt a sharp twinge in his side, and his vision blurred.

"Get him to a bed," Omriel said. Nico and Jacob carried him swiftly to a bedroom and laid him gently on a bed. Joshua wanted to protest, but he was too weak even to speak. He let them carry him and when he was on the bed, he tried to smile to reassure them, but as he did, another greater pain came, and his smile became a grimace.

Omriel pushed the others away and opened his tunic. He listened to Joshua's heart, checked his eyes and gently probed the wound.

Caiaphas watched the little doctor and he watched Joshua in his suffering. Was there no limit, he wondered, to the suffering this man would endure? Once he had wished him dead, then he had thought him dead. Now he was aware of the power of the Lord as he had never been before and he had lost his desire to best this man. He surprised himself and said a short, silent prayer for his recovery.

***

The banging on the gates below startled all of them.

Caiaphas had been dozing in a chair. Brother Jacob sat on a bench, head lolling forward, drifting off now and then. Nico was still very much awake.

Omriel, not young, but somehow tireless, continued to work with Joshua, who lost consciousness and recovered, time and again. Perspiration covered his face and his body shuddered involuntarily. Joshua tried to master the pain by ignoring it, but he blacked out, time and again. He was trying to think, trying to understand what he was to do. He knew God had brought him back for a reason and he was certain that the reason had been told to him in the wonderful visions he had had on his voyage back from Sheol.

He wanted to share these visions with the children of Israel and he had believed there would be time for that. Now, he was aware that the time might be extremely short. He must remain conscious, or he could do nothing. God wanted him alive and awake and teaching the people, as God had taught him. He had slipped off again into a stormy sleep, when the noise came that awakened them all.

Caiaphas shuddered and looked about fearfully. What now?

He dared not wait in this room to hear what the problem might be. Feeling his years as never before, he pushed out of his chair and left the room, carefully closing the door behind him.

***

Pilate. Unannounced and smelling of horses and sweat, his shiny, swarthy skin piercing the powder, his wig awry, his face contorted. But this was not the arrogant man who had scourged the Jewish pretender. This was hardly the glowering, pompous governor who had ordered brutality and murder without a flicker of compassion.

Caiaphas recognized his own descent in the descent of Pilate.

And Pilate saw his own doubts in the face of Caiaphas.

Both men struggled to muster their dignity.

"The hour is late," Caiaphas said. "It is both the Festival and the Sabbath. Why are you here?"

Only then did Pilate realize he could not ask the question. He was reluctant to admit that he had found the tomb empty, and that he feared the preacher had tricked him. That was bad enough. In fact, he feared something even worse—that the Jew had powers—supernatural powers, that he might have the strength of the gods—His God—on his side.

How could he admit that—even to himself? Surely, not to Caiaphas.

Pilate's eyes narrowed. Did this man know—this High Priest of the Jews? If he did, he was as shattered by the information as the Roman Governor.

Pilate gathered himself. "Your Messiah's body has been stolen," he said.

"Really? Who would do such a thing?"

"My question, exactly. See that the body is returned by morning."

"I have no body," Caiaphas said.

"Find it," Pilate snarled, "or there will be reprisals. We will not be trifled with."

"The High Priest of Israel does not 'steal' the bodies of the dead and does not deal with any who would do such a despicable act. You will have to find this body yourself. And when you do, I suggest that it not be abused."

Pilate was startled. This sniveling priest had somehow regained some of his dignity. He looked pale and drawn and one of his hands was shaking, but his eyes were fierce.

Pilate looked away, unable to hold his eyes on Caiaphas, then turned and stalked out of the palace.

***

Patrols of soldiers erupted from the Antonia and every other barracks in the city. They ran through the streets of Jerusalem and scattered through every quarter. The soldiers broke into houses, opened shuttered shops, and invaded the synagogues from Bezetha to the Ophel. The people, observing the Festival, many of them in despair over the death of Joshua, were shocked. The Romans were noted for their abrupt appearances and rough investigations, but never had they subjected the entire population to such harassment, and on a holiday that was the Sabbath as well.

What did they want? What were they searching for?

A man. A man with blonde hair and beard, who might have a wound in his side and might not. A man who might look like the Galilean preacher and might not. Their descriptions were not clear and their orders were not clear.

All that Paulus Aemilius and all the other Roman officers knew was that the governor was furious and that something must be done to placate him. A man—a man with a peculiar description must be found. They did not know why and they did not question it. They understood that their duty was not to question, but to obey.

They arrested a tall, aquiline featured Greek with thin hair and a scraggly beard. They brought in a short, fat, jolly blonde trader from Cyprus, and two whitish—haired male prostitutes from Civitavechhia.

Dozens of men, of every shape and size, but with blonde or white or whitish blonde hair, were haled into the Antonia, then discharged or tossed into the street, or held, for some other crime, unconnected with the mysterious crime that had so infuriated Pilate.

Gaius, watching his master, understood that Joshua might be alive somewhere in the city. He worked assiduously at his tasks, kept his face averted and prayed for his son. He could not go to the Jews he knew and ask them without jeopardizing Joshua.

Pilate had straightened his hair and powdered his face, but he was barely able to control his anger. As one suspect after another was dragged before him, his agitation grew. They had done it, these damnable Jews; they had found the way to drive him mad. Joshua was probably dead and buried, but how could he be certain? He must see the body, if he was to maintain his sanity.

***

Joshua was conscious now and coherent. The pain in his side had not abated and his breath was short. He had no doubt that Omriel was correct and that he was bleeding internally. But he could think clearly and he realized they must leave the palace.

Caiaphas was a study in frustration. "It's more dangerous for you to leave than to remain," he said. " If you're seen, the wrath of the Romans will come down not only on me but all of Jerusalem, all of Israel."

"If I am found here, it will be worse," Joshua said, pushing aside the covers and rising to his feet. He gestured to Brother Jacob and Nico and they took their places on either side of him.

"Like that? You plan to leave in those clothes. We must find a disguise for you."

Joshua would have laughed had the wound permitted. "Then they would surely find me," he said.

***

For two days, Miriam had heard nothing. Images of Joshua on the cross had tormented her sleeping and waking hours. She told herself that this was God's will, and yet the cruelty of it was difficult to understand. She tried to tell herself that she was blessed, that her son had given his life for his people and that nothing more noble could be imagined. These were but words, words that a mother might tell herself but could never believe.

More than once, in the course of Joshua's life, she had wished he would have been satisfied to be a carpenter. Each time, she had felt guilty and told herself that all would be well, and that her son, despite the risks that he took, would survive to an old age.

Miriam had been pleased with the love that others had shown Joshua. She was humbled by his lofty ambitions and by his intense determination to do the will of God. When he was acclaimed the Messiah, she felt exalted, but never proud. Such a designation was the work of God, not achieved by the merit of man. Of course, she thought, her son was handsome and brilliant and Godly and good. She was a mother. She would always be a mother.

She was proud of her other children, happy to have them to comfort and support her in this time of need. But now Miriam was worried about Jacob. He was the next oldest and a natural leader. He was needed now, but she did not know where he might be.

The other disciples were in doubt themselves, but they followed the orders they had been given and remained in the house of Nicodemus. When Miriam asked if they had any idea where Jacob might be, they shook their heads. Andrew and Johannon offered to go out and look for him, but Miriam told them not to. She could not be responsible for others being at risk, too. It wasn't fair to their mothers.

Judith busied herself with her history of Joshua and his teaching, including the memoirs shared with her by Gaius. She had never thought she would have to write of Joshua's death, certainly not as a young man, and on the cross. She had not expected this result, but she felt duty-bound to set it down just as it had happened.

It was difficult not to cry when she wrote of his suffering on the cross. She tried, but was not able to pretend that it was someone else, someone she did not know. The parchment blurred before her eyes, but she blinked away the tears and set the words down carefully, not slanting them, but equally as straight and true as all the others.

Simon Peter had not slept. He imagined that now that Joshua was dead, he would have to lead the others. He felt physically strong enough to do it, but awed by the responsibility. How could he take the place of Joshua? It was impossible.

He knew that Little Jacob would help and Mattathias was well-read in the law, and that would be useful, too. Judith was also a very strong person, but of course she was a woman and Simon wasn't certain whether she would be able to continue in the work.

He paced the floor and tried to plan, but his mind remained blank. He would think of Joshua and begin to weep. Then he would tell himself to be strong and try to organize his thoughts. Nothing, nothing occurred to him. He wished there was something he could do, something physical, something a plain honest chap could understand.

The Sabbath was over and it was the first day of the week. Miriam didn't know whether Joshua had been properly cared for in the garden tomb of Joseph of Arimathea. Perhaps they had not had time before darkness to properly prepare and wrap his body. At dawn, she was dressed and ready. Judith was ready, too, and Martha and Miriam, Miriam of Magdala and Deborah. All of the women of the house had reached the same conclusion.

The men were surprised that the women were awake and ready to leave. Simon Peter was embarrassed. He was the leader; he should have been dressed and ready. It wasn't enough to pace the floor.

"We'll come with you," Eliezer said.

"Come after us when you are ready," Miriam said. "We don't want to wait any longer."

The men hurried to say their prayers and dress and prepare themselves, but the women had been gone for several minutes before they, too, left the house.

"One of us should remain here," Andrew said, but they were frightened and no one wanted to stay alone.

***

Joshua and his followers made their way slowly through the streets of the city. Joshua could walk with fair speed if he rested on the arms of Brother Jacob and Nico. Omriel walked a few steps behind, but there was nothing about the little doctor that would draw the Romans to him. The streets were almost deserted except for the soldiers of Pilate searching for, well, a man who looked like Joshua. The Jews, once they were aware of the patrols had taken to their homes, locking their doors, closing their shutters and staying out of harm's way.

A few foreign traders, Greeks and Syrians and others, ventured out now and then, but there was never any business to be done on a festival and the rampaging Roman patrols were annoying.

Time and again, Roman soldiers passed Joshua and his little group. Their leaders were certain by now that no one who was in the street could be Jewish. They were embarrassed by having arrested countless men who were not Joshua and having their superiors scorn them for their stupidity. They were convinced that a man being sought by the Romans would be hiding somewhere, not walking slowly through the streets on the arms of his companions, with no hint of a disguise.

The soldiers hurried on, busy knocking on random doors and arousing innocent citizens, slamming people against walls and upsetting furniture, thumping a head here and there.

Joshua felt every step. Each contact with the rough pavement resonated through his legs and into the long wound below his heart. But he had suffered so much in the past few days that this additional punishment had little meaning.

He did not fear the patrols, correctly believing they would not bother someone who moved openly through the city. He was concerned that one of his own followers might see and identify him. If they did, they said nothing. They knew of the Roman search—by now everyone in the city knew of it—and there were few there who would have helped the Romans. If some of them actually saw him, they ould have been astonished in view of the reports that he had been crucified and killed, but no matter what, they would never have helped the Romans.

Joshua and the others were nearing the house of Nicodemus, near the dung gate at the southerly edge of the city, when they came upon a fracas in the street. The Romans had dragged some poor soul out of his house, and both he and his family were putting up a struggle.

Brother Jacob firmly steered their party into a side street, to avoid the struggle. Thus it was that they missed Miriam and the others who had left Nicodemus's house a minute later. The two parties passed within a few cubits of each other, separated only by a single house and a low wall.

Joshua and his companions moved back into the street, passing through the gate and out into the Hinnom valley. From there they would pass through the Kidron and up along the streets of the tented city of the Jewish pilgrims.

There again, the Jews remained inside, avoiding the Romans, who rode among the tents and ran between them, ripping them open with their swords, shoving people and animals about. There were many Zealots along the route, and they chafed at the Roman attacks, angry that they could not respond. Some had weapons, although most of the weapons were still stored within the city. Still, they realized that in these close quarters, it would be fruitless to fight the Romans, for thousands of innocent people would be slaughtered.

Some stood boldly in the flaps of their tents. Some saw Joshua. Some recognized him. He looked wan and pale and desperately ill, but he was alive. He could walk only with support and then at a slow pace, but he was alive. They recognized the danger at once, and they did nothing, simply observing his passage with torment in their minds and prayers in their hearts.

Afterwards, when he had passed and they talked to one another, they would ask, "Did you see him?" and, "Could it have been him?" and "I recognized the disciples, but how could it have been Joshua?" Both doubt and certainty would grow with the passage of time.

***

As Miriam, Simon Peter and the others approached the property of Joseph of Arimathea, they were surprised to see the gates stood wide open. Simon Peter wanted to rush in, but he deferred to Miriam and her feelings. From the gate, one could see the house that Joseph owned, but not the main expanse of the garden or the tomb.

"We should stop and speak to Joseph," Judith said and the others agreed.

The door was open. Inside the furniture had been strewn about and cupboards emptied. Lying on the floor, they found Joseph, bloodied and half-conscious. The women hurried to help him, to wash his face and help him onto a bed. He was weak and almost unable to speak.

"Romans," he said, "beat me...wanted to know...where Joshua is"

Then he fainted.

"Nathan and I will care for him," Deborah said to Miriam. "You go on."

Concern etched new lines into Miriam's face as she and Judith hurried out into the garden. Simon lumbered along, trying to think of what he might be able to do to help, but the situation was so dangerous and confusing that he had no useful idea.

The fine, spring air, the blazing sun, the smell of flowers and the soft breeze belied their fears. But then, led by Miriam and Judith, they all broke into a run. They ran along the path, turned at a small spring and found themselves facing the tomb. The great sealing stone stood open.

Hearts pounding, Miriam and Judith went inside. They saw only a man, shriveled and small. He was as surprised as they were.

"He's not here," Miriam said, "only these few cloths."

"Where is he?" Judith asked the man.

"Who?" he asked. He was an elderly fellow and his eyesight was poor. He had never seen these women before and he didn't like the tone in their voices.

"Joshua Ben Joseph—the man who was brought here before the Sabbath."

"Why look for him here?" the little old fellow said. "They raised him up and took him away yesterday?"

"Raised him up?" Judith asked. "Wasn't he...dead?"

The man chuckled. "Looked alive to me, but that's in God's hands, isn't it?"

The women clung to each other, not knowing what to think. Slowly they backed out of the tomb.

"What is it?" Simon Peter asked.

"He's not there," Judith said, her voice breaking.

Simon went into the tomb himself.

"Another one?" asked the old man. "What do you want?"

"The Master."

"In the house."

"Not Joseph, the man who was buried here."

"Nobody buried here—you can see that."

"Who are you?" Peter asked.

"Caretaker, gardener. I'm supposed to clean up this place, although I hate the work. I like plants you know, but this stuff in the tomb, well, it's not what—"

Simon backed out, not wishing to hear the chattering. "We must ask Joseph what this means," he said.

But Joseph was unconscious.

"Nathan and I will stay here and care for him," Deborah said.

"Maybe they took a different route." Johannon said. "Maybe we passed each other somehow. We must go back to the house of Nicodemus."

24.

THE RACE

With each passing hour, Pilate became angrier. The Jews had escaped his planned massacre, but he thought he had had the satisfaction of putting their "Messiah" to death. Now, that man had escaped, too. Pilate was determined to find him, to learn whether he was alive or dead.

"He will be dead," he told Gaius grimly, "if not now, then soon. I won't rest until I find him."

Gaius, of course, knew the plans of Brother Jacob and Nico and the others, but he did not know whether the plans had succeeded. Joshua's body might not be resting in the tomb in Joseph of Arimathea's garden, but that didn't prove he was alive.

"I understand, Sire," he told Pilate, "but it may be the Jews have simply removed his body and buried it somewhere else, in the very hope of frustrating...us. If so, we may never find it."

"I'll find it," Pilate said, sounding a note that Gaius had heard before. "Believe me I'll find it, if I have to torture every Jew in this benighted country to find out where it is."

It was useless to argue with a man in that state of mind. Gaius did not even protest when Pilate ordered the soldiers into the countryside, with the same vague orders— to find Joshua, the Galilean.

**

Simon Peter was restless. He hadn't seen the Master in many hours and he had the strong sense that he had been excluded from something. That pained him greatly. It had been terrible for him to wait outside the Antonia Fortress while Joshua was being tormented.

He hadn't been able to lessen his agony even slightly by helping to carry the cross. He watched the crucifixion in helpless wrath—he, a man who could have strangled both of the soldiers who flanked Joshua with his bare hands.

And then, they had turned him away from the cross with all sorts of strange looks among them and sent him off to herd the women about. He loved Miriam and adored Judith, but was that a man's proper work?

"Listen," he told Miriam. "It's not necessary for all of us to wait at the house of Nicodemus. I have a feeling something may be happening at Eliezer's house. Suppose Andrew and I go there—you have plenty of people with you—and we'll meet later?"

Miriam noted his anxiety and could think of no reason to restrain him.

"Of course," she said.

Simon Peter and Andrew struck out at a fast pace for the Mount of Olives, but it wasn't fast enough for Simon. In the city of tents, he saw a horse that a Roman soldier had carelessly tethered on his way to brutalize the Jews. Simon sighed and ripped the reins loose.

"Come on," he said to Andrew, leaping into the saddle and pulling his brother up behind him. The two fishermen rode the swaying horse at a fast canter up the hillside.

***

Joshua was surprised to find the house of Eliezer totally empty.

"Perhaps they've gone to Joseph's garden," he said, "thinking to care for my body." He smiled thinly.

"We can't go after them," Brother Jacob said.

Joshua nodded in agreement. He had hoped to rest in the house, but now he wasn't certain that was the best thing to do. Nico went out to the hilltop spot that Eliezer had used for his surveillance of the Roman troops.

"Soldiers," he called out, "moving among the tents. Hundreds of them on horseback, riding in many directions."

"We have to move on," Nico said.

"But where?" his father asked. The days had been difficult and he was feeling very tired. His damaged leg was paining him greatly, but he would not complain, knowing the pain that Joshua must be suffering.

"Qumran," Joshua said, "it's the only place we can go."

"You can't walk to Qumran," Omriel said.

Joshua knew that was true.

"We should not have left behind the horses that the Roman, Gaius, gave us, in the city."

"Too late," Nico said. "I'll go into Bethany. Perhaps we can find other animals."

"We still have the colt," Nicodemus said.

"Yes," Brother Jacob said, "Joshua can ride that."

"He mustn't travel alone," Omriel said.

Nico grabbed Baruch's arm. "Let's see what we can find."

***

Simon Peter, with Andrew clinging to him, rode the overburdened horse up the Mount. As they neared Bethphage, a Roman decurion on horseback noticed them riding laboriously up the hill. He spurred his animal and pulled alongside them, raising a hand to halt them, then pulling his sword.

"That's a Roman horse," he said, "where did you get it?"

Simon Peter sighed again, moved as if to get off the horse, reached out and grabbed the decurion's leg and threw him off his horse. Simon was quick for a big man, and Andrew was even quicker. The decurion was still trying to scramble to his feet, when Andrew grabbed his arms and Simon hit him over the head with the hilt of his own sword, knocking him unconscious.

Simon lifted his brother into the saddle, mounted the other horse and together they clattered off towards Bethany.

On the road, they saw Nico and Baruch, running.

"Brothers!" Simon Peter yelled in his great, gruff voice.

Nico and Baruch stopped, startled.

"How did you know the Master needed horses?" Nico asked.

Hearing the question, Simon Peter almost swooned.

"He's alive," he whispered, "Alive."

***

They rode across the bleak Judaean hills at a slow canter, which was all Omriel would permit lest the wound in Joshua's side burst open and he would bleed to death. The little doctor rode on one of the horses Simon and Nico had commandeered, clinging to Brother Jacob, so small a man that he seemed almost like a pack on Jacob's back.

Joshua rode alone on the colt, feeling the pounding of the hooves, but absorbing it rather than tensing his body. He was collecting his thoughts, gathering himself for the task ahead. He was elated to be alive, confirmed in his faith as never before. God had indeed rescued him from Sheol, had not allowed him to languish in death and humiliation.

I am reborn, he thought again and again. I am reborn for a purpose. God has shown me what lies ahead for Israel and it is my work to show that future to my people.

He knew, however, as he had always known, that time was limited, that the Lord had the capacity to wait forever, but did not choose to do so. Man must work out his salvation in man's time. The wound in Joshua's side, throbbing with every beat of the hooves, repeated that message, again and again.

Nico rode the other horse he and Simon had taken towards Qumran. The animal had an odd gait and Nico was having trouble keeping up.

***

In Bethany, Simon Peter was doing his best to find other animals. He knew the Romans would be in the town at any time, and the decurion, if he had survived Simon's blow, would be rabidly seeking revenge. But he felt no fear and all of his energy had returned. He had seen Joshua alive and his joy had been so great he had feared he would burst. Thank God, they had warned him of Joshua's wound or he would have killed him with an embrace.

Simon found a Syrian trader and persuaded him, half with money and half with his huge size, to "rent" him two carthorses.

Nicodemus, despite his limp was able to walk to the road where he bought two asses from a farmer and brought them back to Eliezer's house. He was delighted to see Simon Peter already there with the draft horses.

"Who will ride?" Nicodemus asked.

"I'll take the biggest horse," Simon Peter said, "and Andrew will ride behind me. We won't be able to travel fast or we'll break the old one down, but we'll get there. Keep the remaining animals here, and when the others return, Miriam and Judith can come to Qumran with Johannon and little Jacob. The rest will have to find their own way. As for you, Nicodemus, you've done enough. I see that you're limping badly. Stay here and rest."

Nicodemus listened with astonishment. The rough fisherman had spoken with courage and authority. He began to understand Joshua's love for the man.

"Done," Nicodemus said. "God's blessings travel with you."

***

Paulus Aemilius had tired of the entire matter. When Septimus was murdered and he had been promoted to Captain of the Guard, he was pleased. He knew there were officers in Jerusalem, leaders of the legions whose rank was higher than his own, but Pilate had arranged matters so that his own captain was virtual commander of the entire force.

But now there had been one failure after another. Pilate had revealed his true nature to Paulus, who was accustomed to tough commanders, but had never seen one as personally vindictive as Pilate. Nor was Paulus able to understand the reason for his implacable hatred for the Jews.

The night of the crucifixion of the Galilean, he had had an idle conversation with Gaius, a man he did not particularly approve of, because he seemed as soft as Pilate was hard. However, Gaius had many years of experience in the province, and not a few under the prefect. Paulus obliquely asked for an explanation of Pilate's hatred for the Jews. Gaius told him something about the Jewish practice of using a goat on their Day of Atonement to symbolically heap their sins on and then send that goat out into the desert to die. Paulus didn't understand; he merely shook his head.

Paulus's men brought spies and informants to him. Some were willing, for a price, to give information. Others were not so willing, but had been persuaded. In Rome, these practices would not have been approved, but out here on the borders, they seemed a way of life. One of the servants in the house of Nicodemus, after torture, had revealed that some of the followers had traveled to some place near the Salt Sea, to bring back a strange man, perhaps a magician or soothsayer. Another man, also persuaded, said he thought he heard someone in the group mention they might be going to a place called Qumran, but he didn't know if that was on the Sea of Galilee or the Salt Sea.

By then, Paulus had learned of Eliezer and the house in Bethany where Joshua had stayed during the past week. He regretted he had not had that information earlier. He also knew that Joshua had spent the night before the festival in the house of Nicodemus. That, too, would have been useful.

He was disgusted they had learned so little from torturing Joseph of Arimathea. Joshua had been taken to his property, and buried in his family tomb, but he claimed to know nothing else. Perhaps, Paulus thought, they should go back and work on him again.

How would any of this connect with a soothsayer from the Salt Sea—or some place called "Qumran?" He'd have to ask the prefect, perhaps even Gaius Fabricius, what they knew that might help solve this puzzle.

***

It was late in the day, when Miriam, Judith, Deborah and Nathan, Johannon and Little Jacob, Philip, Mattathias and Simeon, Martha, Miriam, the third Miriam and Eliezer made their way back to Bethany. Even Judith was on the edge of despair, but Miriam had managed to contain herself. No matter what else, she was certain that her son was in God's hands. If she could believe that when she saw him stretched on the cross, surely she could believe it when his body could not be found.

Her courage strengthened them all. Judith watched her mother in wonder. This woman had lived through so much suffering and yet her strength was undiminished. In fact, tragedy had honed her courage without destroying her compassion. Judith resolved to follow her mother's example.

Johannon and Little Jacob had chafed at staying with the women, at having so small a role in the great events that were happening. They wondered why they could not be with Simon Peter and Andrew, men more like themselves, for they believed the other Galilean brothers must be closer to Joshua.

Nathan and Deborah were simply exhausted and so was Simeon. They were the oldest and they had reached the limit of their physical and spiritual resources.

Philip and Mattathias had had all they could bear of the crowds of Jerusalem.

Nicodemus waited for them in the courtyard. Again and again he had thought of what he would say. He wanted to tell the truth, but he didn't want to shock any one, especially Miriam, any more than he had to. Nor did he wish to raise false hopes. He had seen Joshua's wound and he knew that even now it was bleeding within.

Nicodemus lifted himself from the bench where he sat and moved as quickly as he could to Miriam's side.

"Are you well?" he asked, scanning her face carefully, "I have much to tell you."

25.

ETERNITY

Tendrils of mist and fog danced on the surface of the sea, but did not touch the bleached and parched shore. The sun was rising over Moab and the sky was a glowing pink, uniform in tone except that it was brighter in an aureole above the place where the sun would first appear. Within the settlement, the brothers were rising, gathering for their morning prayers and ablutions.

Joshua had already put on his phylacteries and his prayer shawl and said his prayers. He rested on a large, flat rock, not far from the water's edge. Against the wishes of his family, against the remonstrations of Omriel, he had been there all night, praying and preparing himself. The night had been chill, but he had not felt it, even though he wore only a tunic and a cloak over his shoulders. The sky had been brilliant with stars and the moon, a bit past full, had flooded the plain with white, even light.

He saw them approaching from the gate of the settlement: his mother, his brother and sister, the disciples who had followed him through Galilee, Nico and Nicodemus. The Maskil had bent the rules to allow the women to stay the night within the community.

As they came closer, Joshua held out his arms and embraced first his mother and then the others, one at a time. They returned his embraces, carefully, concerned about his wounds. For Miriam it was an especially difficult moment, for he had refused to allow her to minister to him, insisting he must be alone in the night with God and his thoughts.

He gestured again and they sat down on the rough, sandy shore, in a semicircle at his feet. His heart filled at the sight of them. He had not believed he would soon see them again, and yet they were here. It was a great and glorious moment.

"Blessed art thou, O Lord, Our God, ruler of the universe, who has blessed us with family and friends and with life itself."

He stood up with difficulty and repeated the Shema, "Hear O Israel, the Lord our God, the Lord is One."

"Amen," they responded together, but softly, so that it seemed a whisper that spread from the shore of the Salt Sea over the waters and the land, above the hills and into the sky. The prayer, old and familiar, seemed to enfold and protect them.

"When it seemed that I hung on the tree," Joshua said, "I traveled far. I did not travel alone. I was carried by Noah and Abraham and Moses and they guided me through six temples, into a seventh. The trip was full of wonders, the brilliance of all I saw beyond description, and the seventh Temple was more glorious than any of the others."

Joshua told them how he had heard the voice of the Lord, rumbling in great waves and how the patriarchs had anointed him. He told them of the destruction of the city of Jerusalem, of the nation, of the slaughter of the people and the ravaging of the land.

As he spoke, his emotion was so intense that they traveled with him and they felt the suffering of the people and saw the dismembering of their country. They sighed, at first, then moaned, then cried.

"Do not cry," he said, "for that was but the beginning."

He told them of the fire spreading, but then of the tears quelling the fire and the green fingers returning, of the land blossoming forth and the people coming home, happy and prosperous and praising the Lord.

Simon Peter's heart swelled with hope as he heard these words.

"Are you telling us, Master, that we will go back to Jerusalem and rouse the people?"

Joshua looked at him for a long time without responding. He loved Simon for his simple goodness, his strength and his loyalty. He loved him for his kindness and his exuberance and his great energy.

"Simon, if I were to return to Jerusalem today, the results would be disastrous. If the Romans saw me first, they would either kill or jail me. In either case, the people would rise up, this time in anger, and there would be terrible slaughter.

"It was difficult for the people not to respond when they heard of my crucifixion. Many believed that proved I was not the anointed of God, but even they hated the Romans for inflicting such a penalty on me. If I were to return, nothing would prevent violence—greater violence than this nation has ever known."

Simon nodded and lowered his head.

"But you have told us the Temple will be destroyed and all of Israel ravaged," Nico said.

"That, indeed, will be our fate if we do not turn await from violence."

"It's too cruel," Judith said, "the people don't deserve such suffering."

"The people are not evil. They love God and God loves them. But the cycle of violence and death will continue until they learn that to have peace one cannot prepare for war. God's laws are true and cannot be avoided without paying the penalty. It is difficult to face a cruel and powerful adversary and make no effort to defend oneself, but that is the only way.

"It is the mission of the Jews to be a living example to all the world. Now it is the destiny of the Jews to be driven from their own land, to live in pain and suffering in other lands, but in their suffering to be a light unto the gentiles. They must live in peace no matter what the provocation; they must counsel reason when others propose violence. They must demonstrate, for all to see, that a man may love God, the one God, even when he is oppressed and threatened. They must teach the world, the laws that God has given to the Jews, so that they may know his wisdom and his peace and share in it.

"God has saved my life so that all may know that life and death are both in his hands. God has used me to teach a lesson to all mankind: that to save the world, one must be willing to give it up."

He had risen as he spoke, and in characteristic fashion began to pace. The pain in his side was forgotten as great energy flowed through his body

"If you hold on to the things of the world, you lose the promise of heaven. If your possessions are precious, you will lose them. If you value your body more than your soul, it will be taken from you.

"This is what I have taught from the beginning. I thought the time of teaching was over, but the Lord knew that you were not ready, and he has sent me back to prepare you.

"Beloved family, beloved friends, I will not remain with you, no matter what you believe. You must prepare yourself for the days when I will be gone. You must believe in the message that God has given me to give to you.

"You must go forth from this place to the ends of the earth, teaching first the Jews—the Lord almighty will scatter them, but they will carry God's word with them.

"You must help them to prepare, so that they will be strong enough to persevere, for I tell you that the sufferings they will endure until the world learns to understand are far greater than any you now imagine.

"The world will hate the Jews for carrying the word of God, for being the living indictment of all that is material and earthly and of no worth.

They will be abused and tormented until the day comes when the world is ready for God's word, ready to submit to God's will.

"You must teach the teachers. You must prepare them for the sufferings to come, so that those who survive will know the will of God and help the world to accept it.

"To be a Jew is not solely a matter of the blood in your veins or the place where you were born. To be a Jew is to Love God more than you love yourself and to seek God's way in all that you do. When you have learned that, you will be able to teach it to all men, whatever their birth, whatever their religion, and then the Kingdom of God will belong to all."

***

Joshua's voice had hardly stopped echoing in the clear morning, when they heard another sound, the sound of horses' hooves, pounding along the shores of the sea.

They were frightened, ready to rise and run, but Joshua raised a hand, and they settled back to the ground, their heads turned. They saw a troop of Roman horsemen at full gallop approaching them. At the head of the column rode Pontius Pilate, and just behind him, Gaius Fabricius and Paulus Aemilius.

Pilate signaled and the soldiers reined their horses to an abrupt halt and leapt from their saddles. Another signal and they drew their swords and encircled the group.

Pilate remained on horseback, moving his animal close to Joshua.

Joshua smiled serenely. "You need not fear us. We have no weapons."

It was difficult for Pilate to keep his composure. This man did not, had never, feared him. How could one triumph over a man who knew no fear? His face, already perspiring from the long ride, purpled faintly, but he steadied himself.

"What are you?" he asked, "a magician, a conjurer?"

Joshua said nothing.

"To die on the cross one day, disappear the next and then be found alive, that's quite a trick."

Still Joshua said nothing.

"I will not take insolence," Pilate said, feeling himself a bit unsteady and not wanting to be embarrassed before his troops. You will tell me what you did and how you did it."

"I did nothing," Joshua said. "God does everything."

Pilate smiled grimly. "This god of yours—can he save your life—again?"
Joshua was silent.

"What more do you want of him?" Miriam asked. Her voice was strangely strong.

Pilate looked at her sharply, a pretty woman, though not young, and unafraid.

"Who is she?" Pilate asked Gaius.

"Joshua's mother," Gaius said. He had never forgiven himself for his crime against this woman, even though Joshua had told him God was forgiving. Now, as he looked upon her once more, he remembered her as a girl, young, beautiful and brave. All the sufferings of her life had not truly changed her.

For some reason, the knowledge that Joshua stood unarmed before his mother gave Pilate strength. He dismounted from his horse.

"This strange fellow is your son? A man who rouses the crowd by promising eternity, who threatens the whole nation, this is your son?"

Miriam stared at him steadily without changing her expression.

Brother Jacob stood up. "I am her son, as well."

"And I am her daughter," Judith said, also rising.

"A family of revolutionaries, of criminals against the state. You Jews are a strange and despicable lot."

"Leave the family alone," Gaius said.

Pilate wheeled about and faced him. "You are defending these people—again?"

Gaius did not wish to make matters worse, but he had taken all he could tolerate of Pilate's posturing, of his evil deeds and vicious repression. He thought that, perhaps, he could draw the man's anger to him. Gaius no longer cared what happened to himself. He had done all he could for his son. God must know that. The future was of indifferent importance to him.

"There is no harm in this family—none in Joshua, but surely even less in them. What are we here for, Prefect? If we are going to arrest this man, let's have done with it."

Pilate realized that his deputy had been pushed beyond his limit. He liked that. He always wondered what a man would do when he was pushed beyond his limit. It was fascinating for him to see men lose control.

"I think," said Pilate, "that since the leader will not tell us how he manages his tricks, we should ask his followers." He reached forward suddenly and pulled Miriam to her feet. The others would have leaped to her defense, but the soldiers were there, the soldiers were everywhere and their swords were drawn.

"Tell us, mother," Pilate said, "about your son's magic."

"Take your hands off her," Gaius said. Even now the memories were clear. This was Septimus with his hand on Miriam's bodice, ready to tear her clothes and ravage her.

"Stand back," Pilate said, holding the neck of Miriam's dress in one hand, pulling his sword with the other.

"I tell you, let go," Gaius said, putting out his hand to grab Pilate's shoulder.

He never reached it. Pilate plunged his short sword to the hilt in Gaius's chest.

There were cries from Joshua's followers, but no one dared move. Paulus Aemilius watched in fascination. This was truly an unusual event for a Roman governor to be involved in.

Gaius stood erect for a moment, his eyes fixed on Miriam, his expression still pleading for forgiveness. Then he slipped to the ground and died.

Pilate had already forgotten Miriam. "Note that carefully, Captain," he said to Paulus Aemilius, while he, himself, continued to stare at Gaius Fabricius. "He was attacking his governor."

It was a moment of great satisfaction for Pilate. He had hated his deputy for a long time, and had the sense that somehow the man's machinations had contributed to his own failures. But somehow, he had never been able to catch him in an action that was truly damning. He had never dreamed he would have the satisfaction of plunging a sword into him.

Joshua watched Gaius die with a pang of loss. He would have suffered when any man was so cruelly slain, but he knew that Gaius thought of himself as Joshua's father, and he was aware that the man had spent a life in penance for the crime of his youth. Joshua's lips moved in a prayer of mourning.

Pilate's yanked his sword free and wiped the blood from the blade. "Tie his body on his own horse," he said.

He turned to Joshua.

"It would be tempting to take you back to Jerusalem, drag you before the crowd and see if they would rise in rebellion. I thought that might happen and somehow you thwarted me. I can never forgive you for that.

"Despite that disappointment, I, personally, found you mild and inoffensive, although I couldn't permit your elevation to 'king.' That would have interfered with my own position. I'm sure you understand. Actually, I enjoyed your punishment more for the effect on your fellows than anything else.

"However, I've learned to respect your craft and cunning. I simply can't take the chance of bringing you back to Jerusalem. Who knows what witchcraft you'd pull off this time. I'm afraid you'll have to die right here."

Pilate enjoyed the anguished responses of Joshua's followers, but he did not take his eyes off Joshua. The man neither blinked his eyes, nor looked away, nor spoke.

"Nothing to say?"

Joshua looked at him with unblinking green eyes. "May God have mercy on you," he said.

For a moment, Pilate was shaken. He did not want the mercy of whatever god this strange man adhered to. Even in the heat of the morning sun, he felt a chill. He noticed that his hand, still holding the sword was shaking and he hoped none of the Roman soldiers had seen it.

"What of you—will your god have mercy on you?"

"He loves us all, even you Pontius Pilate."

That was even more frightening.

"No," said Simon Peter. "We'll leave here, all of us, and take Joshua into Arabia, or anywhere that you say. There's no reason to kill him now."

Joshua turned to look at Simon and smiled. Then he looked at his mother, letting her know that his soul was at peace and that she should not fear for him. He would have liked to embrace her and his brother and sister; he would have loved to embrace them all. But that might be worse for them, so he did not ask it of Pilate.

"You will not plead?" Pilate asked.

Joshua did not even shake his head.

"Captain," Pilate said, "run him through."

Paulus Aemilius didn't move.

Pilate glared at him.

"I said, 'Run him through!'"

Paulus Aemilius looked calmly at Pilate, but he said nothing and he didn't touch his sword.

Once again, Pilate was shaken. If he pushed harder, there might be mutiny, here on this bleak and barren plain.

He turned swiftly and drove his sword into Joshua's chest, then pulled it out and drove it in again, then shoved Joshua to the ground.

Judith screamed once, a high piercing scream. Brother Jacob moved towards Joshua and Simon Peter followed him. The others yelled aloud and moved toward Joshua.

"Don't touch the others!" Pilate screamed, "unless they attack you."

The soldiers held back, puzzled, while Joshua's family and all of his followers rushed to him.

It was too late. Blood had crimsoned his robe, but his face was serene, untouched, the eyes closed and his mouth smooth and untroubled.

Pilate screamed, "Stand back!" He hurried to Joshua, swinging his sword to drive Joshua's family and followers away from his body. He bent down, grabbed Joshua by the tunic, and pulled him almost to a sitting position, his head falling backward.

"Do you see?" Pilate said. "He's dead, finally, totally dead!"

He stood up, letting go of Joshua's tunic so that he slumped slowly to the ground.

Pilate yelled to Paulus. "I said, 'Throw Gaius across his horse!'"

Paulus did as he was told, dragging Gaius by his legs across the ground and then lifting and slinging his body face down so that his head fell on one side of the horse and his legs on the other.

"Now," Pilate said, in a very low voice. "Throw this one over the horse as well."

Paulus hesitated, but Pilate was glaring at him, and Paulus knew he might already have defied the prefect once too often. But he did not drag Joshua as he had Gaius. He knelt, picked up Joshua and cradled him in his arms as he carried him to the horse. Pilate was steaming with anger, but Paulus ignored him and gently laid Joshua's body over the saddle. Joshua's arm rested on the body of Gaius.

Pilate mounted his horse.

"What of the others?" Paulus Aemilius asked, feeling very ill and dirty, as if he had wallowed in something sickening and impure, but trying now to be an officer, a Roman officer.

Pilate was surprised to hear Paulus speak. This one I'll deal with later, he thought, when I'm not surrounded by his men.

"We'll do nothing with them, Captain. We'll leave them to tell the story of how this charlatan, this magician, tried to outwit the Roman Empire and how he failed miserably and was killed as a common criminal. This time perhaps, they'll understand that no nation, let alone a single individual, can stand up to Rome."

He rode over to the horse that carried Gaius' and Joshua's bodies, and poked Joshua with his sword.

"You see?!" he cried again. "Dead! We're taking his body with us and we'll bury him or burn him up as we choose. You'll never know how or where. You won't be able to say, 'Look, the tomb is empty! He escaped!'"

He laughed sourly, wiped the blood off his sword on the flank of his horse.

"You're too forgetful, you Jews. You don't seem to learn. Try to remember this man and his death. Let it be a lesson to you."

No one even looked at him, and he turned away, shaking his head.

"In a few weeks, he'll be forgotten," Pilate said to his men," but we'll have to deal with the rest of those stubborn Jews all over again."

He spurred his horse into a gallop and the soldiers, mounting quickly, followed as he raced along the shore of the Sea of Salt. Paulus led the horse that carried Gaius and Joshua.

In minutes they had disappeared from sight. The cloud they raised lasted a little longer.

The Beginning

EPILOGUE

I awoke with a start, throwing my hands over my head, curling quickly into a defensive position on the floor, certain I was being attacked. But there was only silence. And darkness. Except for a narrow funnel of light where my flashlight lay. I picked up the flashlight and quickly scanned the room—just to make certain. Nobody. That is, nobody except for Leila, who lay on her back on the floor, her head propped on a pillow, her long dark air spread in a corona.

I remembered sitting cross-legged with the final section of the manuscript on my knees and the flashlight braced on a cardboard box. Apparently, I had fallen asleep and listed slowly but surely onto my side. When my knee touched the box it had knocked the flashlight to the floor and that was what awakened me.

Leila was stirring. I wanted desperately to talk to her, but she only sighed and rolled onto her side and resumed her even, regular breathing. It was a pleasant sound, not a snore. I smiled.

I looked at my watch: 3:00 AM. Precisely the time Wajeeh had awakened me in my apartment, three days earlier, seventy-two hours. A thought struck me: the Greek translation of the Hebrew bible was named the Septuagint, Greek for seventy, the number of scholars (but it might have been seventy-two) who had written the translation. So much had happened in these seventy-two hours and it might have as powerful an impact as the Septuagint.

The papers were spread all around me, some in neat piles, others scattered from the night before. I hadn't slept much in the past seventy-two hours, in my anxiety to read all of the documents Leila had provided. In fact, I knew that I had been awake at 2:AM because I had checked my watch, so that if it was now 3, I had only been asleep an hour or less.

Time after time, I had exclaimed involuntarily as I read the translations of the stolen scrolls, but Leila had refused to converse with me.

"Wait," she told me. "Wait until you're finished and then we'll talk."

We'd had a couple of might-have-been close calls, or at least they seemed like close calls. Gunfire in the street below Leila's apartment/office, stray or maybe not so stray shots hitting the paneled door. The first time, three days ago, we had heard steps on her staircase and someone had fired at the lock. Leila had fired her own weapon at the door and the intruder hurried away. Since then, we hadn't heard anyone outside the door, but there had been sporadic gunfire from the street and a couple of bullets whined through the broken windows.

Did I want to face something like that? Was I prepared to leave the apartment and brave the chaotic streets of East Jerusalem? Perhaps I should go back and reread everything, make certain I understood what I had read and placed it in proper perspective. No, that was cowardice, procrastination. The words of the scrolls were clear, their message simple, but powerful.

Leila stirred again. I was impatient, I couldn't help myself.

"Leila," I said, "I must talk to you."

Her voice was cloudy with sleep. "Too tired," she said. "In the morning."

She began to roll over on her side, but I put a hand on her shoulder. She didn't like that; she pulled away.

"Please," I said. "We may not have much time."

She slowly sat upright. The only light was the yellowish glow from my flashlight, but I didn't feel like turning on any of the lamps in the apartment. Even in the uncertain glow of the flashlight, she seemed very beautiful to me, especially with her hair loose and falling to her shoulders. Leila didn't speak; it was up to me.

"I've finished reading your manuscripts," I said.

Still, she was silent.

"It seems very well done. I can't judge the accuracy—"

"—Do you doubt me?"

"Of course not!" I said quickly, "but that doesn't mean I'm able to evaluate the subtleties of this work."

"I confirmed everything with Aaron Feldhammer."

Another surprise. Feldhammer was the leading paleographer at the Hebrew University, a man respected worldwide for his knowledge and wisdom.

I began again. "If the Israelis know—"

"—Aaron is sworn to silence. That was the condition I set before allowing him to read it."

"How long has this been going on?" I asked.

"Several months."

"The holy fathers just discovered the scrolls were missing a few days ago!" I said.

"They were first removed last spring, and replaced two weeks ago. I had to verify certain words to satisfy Aaron, and the scrolls were removed again. This time, the fathers noticed."

"I couldn't believe you had translated all of the scrolls in a few days."

"I didn't."

"What does Feldhammer think we should do?"

"He's a scholar, not a politician."

I didn't respond to that. There were many Israelis who were both scholars and politicians.

"What do you think?" I asked.

"We should reveal the work to the world. It's the truth and Jesus was reputed to have said, "The truth will set you free.""

"You understand the impact this will have," I said.

Leila shrugged. "We have no idea what the response will be," she said. "We can try to guess, to make suppositions, but the reality is not in our hands."

"It is. If we release your translation, it's bound to have an enormous effect, politically, philosophically, theologically—in every way known to man."

"So, you want to return the scrolls and tear up my work."

"I didn't say that."

Leila rose to her feet. "What are you saying? I trusted you to read this. Are you going to betray me?"

I swallowed hard. I loved her very much. I respected her very much. "I'm not equipped to make such a decision. We should speak to far wiser people."

"Who would that be?"

"The papal representative, the chief rabbi, the head of the protestant mission in Jerusalem."

"What about the Imam?"

I hesitated, then nodded.

"All religious?" she asked.

"I'm worried about the politicians."

"Everyone worries about the politicians."

There was a burst of gunfire—heavier than ever before. The remains of the windows shattered and splattered the floor with glass. A strange whine and something unseen roared past and exploded in the far wall, sending smoke and debris in every direction. I guessed it was a rocket-propelled grenade.

Footsteps—many—racing up towards the door while rifles and automatic weapons rattled and spluttered and thundered. Leila grabbed her Uzi and I picked up the handgun she had given me. We crouched behind the barrier of tables and chairs we had built after the first assault, but we both knew that this time the door was coming down.

We shared a look. There wasn't time for words or even a personal gesture, but the glance was enough for me. It told me that Leila still cared for me—how much I might never know, but it wasn't totally over, gone, finished.

With the horrendous squeal of steel on steel and the wrenching, crackling roar of splintering wood, the door came thundering down. I braced my gun in both hands and prepared to fire the entire clip—if I could do that before dying.

"Come out!" a voice roared over a loudspeaker. "No weapons, hands in the sky. Now! At once!"

We both shook our heads.

"I.D.F.!" the voice yelled again. COME OUT NOW!"

IDF—Israeli Defense Forces. Could it be?

The voice spoke in Hebrew, but that proved nothing. Still…

I glance at Leila, she nods, and we stand up simultaneously. We walk slowly towards the gaping hole where once her door had stood. I move closer to her. If this is going to be it, I want to be near her.

Deep breaths, then we step into the opening. We're immediately grabbed from both sides and thrown down just as gunfire erupts again. As I'm crashing to the landing, I see a slice of the roof on the building opposite. Two men in black shirts and black face masks firing at us. But in that split second the men explode into shattered fragments. A voice in my ear rattles, "Didn't see them. Sorry."

I'm released, allowed to sit up and look at a grinning Shmuel, the IDF sergeant with the faint lisp. I turn immediately to Leila, who is also sitting up, but not grinning. She's angry. Her words are cold, biting, when she speaks to the Israeli lieutenant who was holding her down.

"You destroyed my office."

I'm astonished at her chutzpah; so is the lieutenant.

"We saved your life."

She ignores his words, and waves through the ragged opening. "Everything. My computers, monitors, files, furniture—everything."

The lieutenant grabs her arm and pulls her to her feet. "Come on," he says, "before they attack again, and you're killed, too."

Leila looks as if she may make a stand, but it won't work. The lieutenant is physically too strong, and he is pulling her with him.

"The scrolls!" she yells.

He stops, perplexed.

I raise a hand. "We have to take the scrolls and the translations with us, now. If we leave them and they're stolen again, there'll be hell to pay for all of us."

He hardly hesitates, then yells at Shmuel, "Help them!"

***

Leila was truly furious, so furious I knew that despite everything we would never be friends again. The soldiers gathered the scrolls and translations in body bags (any symbolism there?) and we carried them with us as the patrol literally shot its way out of Arab Jerusalem. The lieutenant—his name was Aaron—took us to army headquarters, where Leila yelled so loudly, we ended up in the office of General ben Barak, the Chief of Staff. Leila didn't want him to look at the documents, but he ignored her. Under her scornful eyes, he read the opening sentences, then shot us a surprised look, and immediately returned the papers to the body bag and zipped it shut. He rose and took it with him.

"Wait a minute!" Leila said, but he didn't listen.

"They'll destroy those documents," Leila said to me. "I'm sure of it."

Those were the first words she had spoken directly to me in quite a while—actually I wasn't certainly they were directed to me. Perhaps I just happened to be in the same room.

"I doubt that, Leila," I said, happy to use her name, regardless of circumstances. "We know what's in them."

"They'll kill us, too" she said.

I wondered why she said, "too," but I admit a chill went through me.

"Why would they destroy the documents—let alone murder us?"

"The scrolls are too dangerous for them," she said. "Anything they do will have huge repercussions. Easier to destroy the scrolls—and the messengers."

I had nothing to say. I was disturbed that Leila seemed so paranoid, but the entire subject of the scrolls—the theft, the clandestine storage, the private translation, even the attacks by terrorists—had had a powerful, perhaps destructive, impact on her.

The general was gone for a long time. After a while, a soldier came in with coffee and rolls. We ignored the food. Neither one of us had any appetite. I began to wonder whether Leila might be right, but I rejected the idea. My country, my beloved Israel, my people would never be guilty of such a terrible crime.......would they?

An hour passed and then another. I put my head down in my arms on the table and closed my eyes. I didn't intend to fall sleep, but I did.

Someone shook me awake. A grim-faced soldier.

"You're coming with us," he said, and firmly pulled me erect. Another soldier was guiding Leila out the door.

"Where are we going?" I asked, struggling to come fully awake.

There was no answer. We were herded (perhaps too strong a word) out of the office, and into an odd-shaped vehicle. I guessed it was a "Zelda," an M113 armored personnel carrier—I remembered that from my own military service—and we had to scrunch down and climb into this angular steel box which traveled on full treads, not wheels. I started to protest, but I only got an extra shove for my trouble. A soldier was helping Leila, and she tried to question him.

"Where are the scrolls?" she asked.

The only answer was that the soldier physically lifted her inside. She glared at me with deeply accusing eyes, but while I probably shrank a little under her gaze, I had nothing to say. In a moment, the carrier door clanged shut, the dim interior light blinked off and the vehicle jolted and rumbled away. I thought I heard the sound of other vehicles over Zelda's rattle.

It was night, and I guessed we were in a small convoy heading north of Jerusalem, but there were many twists and turns, and after a while I wasn't sure of our direction. Ben Gurion International Airport was northwest of the city, but I couldn't understand why we would be going there. A young noncom had climbed into the carrier with us and I could barely see him in the darkness.

I asked him, "Where are we going?"

Still no answer.

I heard Leila mumble something. I believe it was in Arabic, and I think she said, "You fool!" I don't believe she was talking to the Israeli soldier.

After half an hour, the carrier shuddered to a halt, and the door was flung open. The noncom escorted us out, but he wasn't alone. At least twenty soldiers, all armed, accompanied us. They hurried us into a low, concrete structure, and once again, doors clanged shut behind us. The brightly lighted interior almost blinded us (the soldiers wore night goggles—I wondered if that made things better or worse for them), and we had to be led down a ramp into a huge elevator that was obviously carrying us lower.

A bunker. I had heard the military had built command and control bunkers scattered around our small nation, and I was pretty sure this was one of them. I was surprised at how long it took us to get wherever we were going. This bunker was pretty deep. Tall doors slid silently open and I certainly wasn't prepared for what I saw inside.

***

A high-ceilinged room with dark-wood paneled walls, a dozen large, wall-mounted monitors blinking with live exterior scenes, maps and charts, a long, oval-shaped dark-wood conference table, dark-leather upholstered upright chairs without arms. A few men in uniform—certainly high-ranking, but as is typical in the Israeli military, they wore nothing indicating their rank, and certainly no ribbons. Another dozen men and women in civilian clothing. In fact, one man wore a long white robe and a caftan, belted at the waist, a white covering with a rope-like ring wrapped about his head. His iron-gray beard fell almost to his waist and covered his face and chin to a point just below his eyes, merging with long, curling sideburns. The Imam. I knew him from photographs.

Another man also wore a long beard and curling sideburns, but he wore a plain black single-breasted suit that would have seemed ordinary except for the long scarflike cloth around his neck, ending in twisted threads that fell below the jacket—a tallith. His head covering was also black, satiny, multi-cornered and perched on the back of his head. The Chief Rabbi.

A short, rotund-bellied man with a large head and thin white hair—the prime minister, Nahum Aronin—spoke in heavily accented English, introducing everyone in the room, so swiftly that I didn't catch many of the names. One I was certain of was Bishop David Yager, the papal representative. He was a tall, ramrod stiff man in clerical black with a small red cap on his head, and a heavy gold chain around his neck. He was clean-shaven, tight-featured and expressionless. More than once he had made a public statement bitterly criticizing Israel and Israel's government. Another participant (I'd seen her photo in Haaretz) was Reverend Annalise Demarest, from the Protestant International Council of Churches, which differed from Evangelical Christian organizations in its lukewarm support for Israel. The prime minister gave my name without title (I have none), referred to Leila as Dr. Adjani, and then gestured everyone to be seated.

I sat down, trying to ignore the baleful gaze Leila cast on me. Leila remained standing, as did the Imam. This was not a cordial beginning. The prime minister ignored both of them and began speaking again.

"Every one of you has received a copy of the complete translation of the scrolls together with a summary prepared by Professor Shamir of Hebrew University."

I didn't have to look at Leila to feel the shock waves radiating from her. I wondered whether others did, as well. A few of them were obviously watching her.

"You had no right to deal with these documents in this manner," Leila said, her voice rasping with passion. I thought the Imam was nodding.

The prime minister spoke. "I have done what I believe is appropriate. The purpose of this meeting is to determine what should be done next."

Bishop Yager spoke in a clear, metallic voice with little emotion but obvious firmness. "Dr. Adjani is correct. You had no right to deal with these documents at all. Your actions are an affront to the entire Christian world."

Reverend Demarest didn't react; I figured she wasn't comfortable about being on the same side of anything with the Catholic Church.

"I regret you feel this way," the prime minister said calmly. "What do you suggest we do?"

"All copies of translations and summaries must be collected immediately, together with the forged documents that are alleged to be their source, and they must all be destroyed."

"Absurd!" Dr. Shamir cried aloud. He was a surprisingly youngish man, for all his known scholarship, trim, with a shaved head and dark-framed glasses. "The scrolls are of incomparable value and importance."

"They are forgeries," Bishop Yager said calmly, but with vast assurance.

Leila broke in. "They are authentic, legitimate and accurate. It may suit you to call them forgeries, but that is false and you are lying."

"One minute please!" The speaker was Naomi Schwartzbein, the Israeli Minister of Culture. "Your words are inappropriate, Dr. Adjani," Schwartzbein said to Leila. "I have high regard for your scholarship, but making such an accusation against the Vatican representative will not help resolve this extremely difficult situation."

"I have great respect for you, as well, Dr. Schwartzbein," Leila said. "But we must deal with the real world as it is, not as we may wish it to be. I'm sure Bishop Yager wishes the scrolls did not exist, but they do. He and his church will have to face up to that reality. As a matter of fact, the scrolls don't belong to anyone here. They are the property of the fathers and brothers at the Church of the Holy Sepulchre."

"That didn't stop you from appropriating and translating them," Dr. Schwartzbein said.

"The originals can now be returned, undamaged," Leila said. "The translations are another matter." She paused, "Where are the representatives of the other religious from the Church? Bishop Yager is only the leader of the Roman Catholics."

Bishop Yager spoke mildly. "They have each and every one designated me to speak for all of us. Does anyone here dispute my authority?"

There was a brief silence, and then the prime minister addressed the Imam.

"Imam Ali," he said. "I must ask you your opinion of this situation."

The imam spoke very quietly, so quietly many in the room had to lean forward to hear him. He spoke in a clipped British accent, and then I remembered that he had been educated at Oxford University in addition to Al-Azhar University in Cairo, Egypt. "I do not believe this is an issue for the Muslim community," he said very smoothly. "It seems to me to be a problem for the Christian and Jewish communities."

"We understand and respect your tolerance, Imam," the prime minister said, "but we believe this is a problem to be resolved by all of us. As you know, there is presently a major concerted effort to achieve peace between the Palestinians and the Israelis, with the support of the United States, the European Union, Russia and the Arab league. Anything which would exacerbate conflict between Christians and Jews might have a fatal effect on the negotiations and leave the conflict unresolved for another generation."

The Imam sat down. "You seem to be moving towards the position of the Vatican representative," he said.

For a moment I thought I saw the hint of a smile on Bishop Yager's face, but it was so fleeting I couldn't be certain.

The Chief Rabbi was drumming his fingers on the table. "Even if the scrolls are authentic in the sense that they actually date from Jesus' time"

(I noted he didn't say Yeshua) "and even if the author were actually related to him—his sister, as claimed—we have no way of knowing whether or not she was telling the truth."

"I hear many 'if's,'" Bishop Yager said. "Too many to pretend this is an accurate history. All Christians believe that Jesus was crucified by the Romans, that he was laid to rest, that he was resurrected, made many appearances to his disciples and others on earth, and was then translated to heaven. If you challenge these beliefs you are insulting and offending two billion people—many of whom will instantly become the enemies of Israel. I'm certain you've thought of that."

"That's why we're here," Dr. Schwartzbein said. "To make the best decision for everyone."

The prime minister was nodding. General ben Barak was nodding. Disturbingly, even Reverend Demarest was nodding. The imam was silent. It seemed to me that this group was about to decide to destroy the scrolls and the translations.

"Don't we care about the truth?" I asked.

"What is truth?" Bishop Yager said, doing his best imitation of Pontius Pilate.

I don't think anyone had expected me to speak, but I couldn't help myself.

"We know what isn't truth," I said. "The canonical Gospel versions of the life of Yeshua of Nazareth are unquestionably filled with falsehoods."

Many voices spoke at once, none of them agreeing with me.

"I can prove it to you," I said, "using the very words of the Gospels."

"We are not in need of a theology lesson," Bishop Yager said, "especially from an Israeli tour guide."

I laughed. "Clearly, you don't believe the truth will set you free. You're afraid it will destroy your religious beliefs. I believe otherwise. I believe it's time that Christians were told the real story, a story that reveals the true story of Yeshua's martyrdom—that makes sense of his sacrifice. If you accept the Gospel version, you believe God is a shmuck."

That brought several people to their feet, and for a moment I thought I might be physically attacked. Leila, who was still standing, suddenly spoke.

"Are you all too cowardly to listen to him?" she asked.

There was silence—a kind of tableau, everyone frozen in position, no one speaking. I took a quick breath and broke the silence.

"The Gospels tell of Yeshua's triumphal entry into Jerusalem, greeted with enthusiasm and love by the people. He teaches daily and is warmly received. He overthrows the table of the money-changers and drives them out of the temple. But then he's betrayed, tried, condemned to death, crucified in front of everyone."

"We know the history," Yager said with heavy sarcasm.

I ignored him.

"His body is taken down by Joseph of Arimathea and taken to a tomb, dressed in the Jewish manner with windings and spices. The stone blocking the tomb is rolled into place. But when they arrive—whoever they are in the particular version—Yeshua is gone. Gone. In one version or another he is seen by a few people, in another by hundreds."

I paused. "Does this make sense? Of course not. We have the stage set for the greatest moment in the history of the world. Yeshua—Jesus—has been killed, but he conquers death and returns to earth, alive! There are hundreds of thousands of Jews in Jerusalem plus many thousands of gentiles. Two legions of Roman troops or more. Pilate, the High Priest, the Sanhedrin. If Jesus appears in the Temple now, there can be no doubt that he will be greeted as a savior? Back from the dead! The hand of God!

"But no, it doesn't happen. God has stage-managed this event like no event since the drowning of Pharaoh's army in the Red Sea. But God doesn't follow through. Jesus doesn't follow through. He is seen by a few, or a few hundred. If Israel is to be saved, he should walk into the Temple to be adored, worshipped, and to convert the entire world to the worship of the one true God. It doesn't happen that way, not in the Gospels, not in Paul's letters. Or the Acts. It doesn't happen because it didn't happen. That tale——its many versions—is a trumped-up explanation for an apparent disaster, an amazing collapse of everything that Jesus has promised.

"Why—why? The scrolls Dr. Adjani translated tell us why. God is not a fool. Jesus is not a fool. He has willingly sacrificed himself so that Pilate will not have the excuse to slaughter the Jews. Jesus is indeed a martyr—the greatest in Jewish history, perhaps the greatest in world history. But the truth is buried, buried in a story that suits the church that was founded in his name, but a story that is childish compared to the actuality."

"That's enough!" the prime minister yelled. "You've made your point, but it doesn't answer our question. What shall be done with the scrolls, with the translation?"

"Destroy them all!" the Vatican representative cried out, his voice nearly a scream. He was on his feet. "We have all the scrolls and copies in this very place. Destroy them all! Immediately!"

"But we all know the story, now," ben Barak said. "It will be impossible to keep it secret."

"They won't have the scrolls," the prime minister said. "There may be quarrels and disputes and claims of every sort, but nothing to back the story up."

"You're right," Schwartzbein said.

"You're right," Yager said.

Even the imam murmured, "You're right."

Leila's voice was louder than anyone's, louder and stronger. "You're wrong!" she said. "You may destroy the originals, destroy the translations, but I have had the originals photographed and made copies of the translations. They are in safe hands. They will be released in three days—like Jesus, raised from the dead."

We all stared at her, astonished. I had never seen her more beautiful, her color high, eyes glowing, hair cascading to her shoulders as it framed her face.

"Now," she said. "Do what is right and true. Do it yourselves, or I will do it for you, but this time the story of Yeshua will not be buried or distorted. That I promise you!"

NOTES AND CITATIONS

This is not intended to be a complete footnoting of every reference and quotation in this book, but it represents the author's personal selection of citations I deem useful. References to the King James Version are designated (KJ); to the Revised Standard Version, (RSV), and the New International Version (NIV). These references are compiled from The New Layman's Parallel Bible; Grand Rapids: Zondervan 1981. There have been later translations, but I prefer the ease of use of this parallel bible. For references to the Gospel of Thomas (Thom), see Taussig, Hal. *A New New Testament* (NNT), Selected Bibliography, *infra.* Dates noted as BCE, refer to the presently accepted notation as Before the Common Era (in lieu of B.C.), and CE as Common Era (in lieu of A.D.). The word "Common" as used here is by no means derogatory and is meant to be a non-religious usage in common use. Because there is also an e-book version of *The Murdered Messiah,* flowing the book means that pagination will change, dependent on the font, etc. To avoid confusion these notes refer only to the Book and chapter in which they occur.

BOOK 1
CHAPTER 1

The leader of a cavalry unit in the Roman army of the 1st Century CE, perhaps should be known as a Decurion, rather than a Centurion, but that is not clear in the sources I have consulted.

CHAPTER 3

Judges 7:1 (KJ).
Jeremiah 31:15 (KJ.)

BOOK 2
CHAPTER 2

Amos 9:7 (NIV).
Exodus 19:6 (RSV).
Isaiah 49:6 (RSV).
Daniel 7:9-27 (RSV).

CHAPTER 4

Psalm 119 (KJ).
Ps 122 (RSV).
Ps 121 (KJ) blended with Ps's 119 and 122.

CHAPTER 5

Psalm 113 (KJ).
Exodus 13:8 (RSV)
Exodus 12:6 (RSV)
Ps 138: 7-8 (RSV).

CHAPTER 6

The story of Joshua and the teacher debating at the Temple. See: Micah 6.7
and Isaiah 1.11-26. (KJ), including material from Deut 17.1.

CHAPTER 14

Isaiah 40:31 (RSV);
Isaiah 11:6 (RSV).

CHAPTER 19

Ezekiel 24:17 (RSV).

BOOK 3
CHAPTER 2

1 Enoch 10 See Charlesworth, below and in Selected Bibliography.
Joshua 4: 19 (RSV).

CHAPTER 3

Isaiah 40.3 (RSV), as part of "Manual of Qumran" (translated in Schonfield, *The Passover Plot*, Page 25, note 7; see Selected Bibliography, *infra*).

Jeremiah 31:3 et seq. (RSV).

Jeremiah 33:14 et seq.

Ecclesiastes 3:1 (KJV).

Assumption of Moses 1:6ff

(Quoted in Allegro, *The Dead Sea Scrolls and Christian Myth* , Prometheus
Books 1984, P. 78)

Isaiah 8:16 (Also quoted in Allegro).

Jeremiah 31:3 et seq. (RSV).

Psalm 25: 19-21 (KJ).

CHAPTER 5

For sources of prayer for Qumran Community See Allegro, above, generally.

CHAPTER 6

Deuteronomy 18:15 (RSV).

Malachi: 3.1 (RSV) et seq. and Malachi: 4.1 (RSV)

References to books of Qumran, Jubilees, Enoch, The Testaments of the
Twelve Patriarchs, Psalms of Solomon, etc., see James H. Charlesworth,
The Old Testament, Pseudepigrapha, Volumes 1 & 2, Selected
Bibliography *infra*.

Sources for references to Hebrew Scripture regarding the Messiah.; a list of
quotes which comprise this portion of the chapter: Except as noted, all are
from the Revised Standard Version.

_. Malachi 3:1

_. Isaiah 11:4

_. Psalms of Solomon, 17:35; Translated *in The Old Testament Pseude-pigrapha*, Volume 2, Page 668 (Doubleday & Co., 1985) as: "He will strike the earth with the word of his mouth forever." This author has used the translation from Schonfield, *The Passover Plot*, Page 27, (Bantam, 1977). Please note, while I respect Schonfield for his work in this field, I do not believe that Jesus (Joshua) would have joined in any plot to deliberately deceive his people.

_. Psalm 2:2.

_. Isaiah 53:3

_. Psalm 118:22

_. Psalm 41:5-9

_. Zechariah 13:6-7

_. Psalm 109:2-4

_. Isaiah 50:6

_. Isaiah 53:7-9

_. Psalm 22:6-18, with emendations.

_. Psalm 69:20-21

_. Zechariah 12:10

_. Psalm 138:7-8

_. Psalm 18:4-17, with emendations.

_. Hosea 6:1-2

_. Psalm 16:8-11

_. Psalm 49:15

_. Psalm 21:1-5

CHAPTER 7

Israel as a holy nation and a nation of priests, a concept often referred to in this book, i.e. Exodus 19:6 (KJ).

CHAPTER 12

The War of the Sons of Light against the Sons of Darkness appears significantly in the Dead Sea Scrolls See: Vermes, Geza.

The Complete Dead Sea Scrolls in English. New York: Penguin 2004.

Also see: Taussig, Hal. *A New New Testament.* Boston: Houghton Mifflin Harcourt: 2013, especially, The Gospel of Thomas with several sayings, including 24 and 50. Generally, Bibliography, *infra.*

Also: Isaiah 31.1 (RSV); Matt 4.1-11 ((RSV); Isaiah 30.1 and Deuteronomy 8.3 (all: RSV with some emendations).

CHAPTER 15

This chapter includes the traditional Hebrew prayers, the *Shema, Shemoneh Esrei* (the 18, now 19 or 20, blessings), *Kedusha*, etc. also called *Amidah*, for the Hebrew word for standing (in the literal sense). It is not clear when these prayers and their sequence were formalized, although it was probably during the Second Temple period. For a simple explanation, please refer to Wikipedia: *Amidah.*

Also included are some readings from Isaiah:

_. Isaiah 11:6 (RSV).

_. Isaiah 5:20 (RSV).

_. Adapted from Isaiah 5:25 (RSV).

_. Based on Isaiah 9:6-9 (RSV), with paraphrases.

_. Adapted from Isaiah 11:1-4, (RSV).

CHAPTER 16

Luke 8:14 (RSV).

CHAPTER 19

Ps 37:8-11; blend of (KJ) and (RSV).

Jeremiah 21:9 (RSV)

Exodus: 23:4 (RSV).

Proverbs 24:17 (RSV).

CHAPTER 20

Luke 6:24 (RSV)

CHAPTER 22

Matt 5:1 et seq. (RSV); The "Beatitudes," also known as "The Sermon on the Mount," as edited by the author. Also, note that at line 9 from bottom on Page 289, Joshua teaches that his listeners are the "light of the world," which may be compared to the teachings on the light in the Gospel of Thomas.

Matt.6:1 et seq. (RSV), admonitions as to prayer, and the "The Lord's Prayer," leading into the feeding of the people, based in part on John 6:9-13 (RSV), but with significant changes and variations.

BOOK 4
CHAPTER 1

One of the lies told repeatedly about the Temple priesthood is that they stole Temple funds for their own personal gain—even that they lent money to the poor at extremely high rates. This is absurd, but it suits the centuries-old false image of Jews as greedy and rapacious money-grubbers.

CHAPTER 3

Matt. 10:1 et seq. (RSV): Joshua's instructions to the apostles for their missions.

CHAPTER 4

Mark 3:25 (RSV); the house divided speech.

Genesis 9:8-17 (NIV);

Genesis 17:9, Exodus: 19:5-6 and Jeremiah: 31: 31-34, all (RSV) relating to the covenant(s) with Israel.

Mark 6:4 (RSV); Matt.: 13:57 (RSV).

CHAPTER 6

In Matt. 14:3-11 the story of Johannon, Antipas, Herodias and Salome is told in brief.

CHAPTER 7

There are some scholars who believe, contrary to the thesis in this book, that Joshua's ministry was limited to the Galilee.

CHAPTER 10

The woman who was taken in adultery: John 8:1 et seq., described herein as Miriam of Migdal, Mary Magdala. Much current commentary, including the Gospel of Mary (See Taussig, *A New New Testament,* Selected Bibliography, *infra),* tends to treat her as a leader of the "church," but this author has a different viewpoint.

CHAPTER 12

Joshua "consorting with sinners." Mark 2:17 (RSV).

Luke 15; 1-7 (RSV); the parable of the lost sheep.

Matt. 25 :1-13 (RSV); parable of the bridesmaids and the lamps.

CHAPTER 13

Joshua and the Sabbath; the cornfield episode.

Mark 2:23, Matt. 12:10, Luke 13:14 (All KJ).

Healing on the Sabbath, Matt. 12:10; Luke 13: 14 (Both KJ); there is no rule in Judaism the prohibits healing on the Sabbath.

CHAPTER 14

The Samaritan woman and the well. John 4:1-26 (RSV).

CHAPTER 17

Matt.17:1-13 (RSV) The account of Joshua's trip to the "high mountain" with Peter and Jacob . The author believes the mountain is Hermon, although others say it is Tabor. Joshua affirms his role as Messiah and the future duties of Simon Peter and Jacob.

CHAPTER 19

For a parallel exposition on the subject of being made in the image of God and the divine light within, refer to *The Gospel of Thomas in* Taussig, Hal. *A New New Testament,* Sayings 24. 50 and 113 (Selected Bibliography, *infra).*

Joshua and children: Matt. 4:17 et seq. (KJ). Also, Matt. 19:23-26 (RSV), this is the story of the wealthy young man who wanted to know how to enter the Kingdom of God, followed by the story of the apostles asking what their rank will be in the "kingdom."

Matt. 19:23 (RSV).The rich man and the eye of the needle, a bit of humor, not much appreciated by his disciples, then or now.

CHAPTER 20

Parables of the little children, the lost sheep and the unmerciful servant: Matt. 18:1-35 (RSV).

The story of the colt for Joshua, based on Zechariah 9:9 (RSV).

CHAPTER 21

Luke 19:40 (NIV); "The stones would have cried out...."

The author has found similar lines about the wise commoner and the ignorant high priest, e.g., Horayoth 3:8, Mishna; also quoted in Vermes, *The Dead Sea Scrolls* (William Collins & World Publishing Co., Inc., P. 90, 1978).

John: 11.49-50 (KJ). Caiaphas; Better one man should die rather than the nation.

CHAPTER 22

Matt. 6:24 (KJ). Sufficient unto the day....

Matt. 21.18 et seq.; the fig tree with the author's different interpretation; See also Luke 21.29, about the generation which will not pass away. (both KJ); I do not accept the Luke text as accurate.

Matt. 21:12 (KJ); Joshua and the money-changers. Also see: Isaiah 56:7 (KJ). Some authors have referred to the money-changers as money-lenders

(Bill O'Reilly in *Killing Jesus)*, and further stated that the High Priest was lending money to poor peasants at exorbitant rates, but this is utterly false and only serves to confirm the prejudice of many that Jews are greedy.

BOOK 5
CHAPTER 1

Exodus 19:6 (KJ); Israel's future—a nation of priests and a holy nation.

CHAPTER 4

Whether or not Second Temple Jews believed in immortality of the soul is seriously disputed. Centuries later (See Maimonides, A *Guide of the Perplexed*) it had become s part of Jewish theology, but its exact derivation is uncertain.

Matt 21:18-22 (RSV). The now withered fig tree.

Mark 12:20-23 (RSV). Joshua faces foolish questioning about "seven brides for seven brothers"—well, something like that.

Mark 11:28-33 (RSV). The sources of the Baptizer and Joshua's teaching.

CHAPTER 6

Samuel 8:10-19 (RSV); Israel and its history with kings.

CHAPTER 9

The interpretation here differs strongly from the typical view that Joshua hereby approves the separation of church and state.

CHAPTER 14

Matt. 26:26 et seq. (RSV). Joshua blessing the bread and wine ("in memory of me").

This account of the "agony in the garden" omits the infamous "Judas kiss." While compelling as the stuff of legend, pointing out Joshua was totally unnecessary. He was a unique looking man and well known to the Temple guards, who almost certainly kept track of his movements.

CHAPTER 15
John 15:13 (KJ); greater love hath no man…

CHAPTERS 17-19

Joshua before Pilate. Matt. 27.11-54 and John 18:28 et seq. (RSV). In the Gospel telling, Pontius Pilate, one of the most vicious, depraved men in the Roman Empire, is presented as a thoughtful, almost kindly, man who finds no fault with Joshua and washes his hands of any complicity, forced by the priests and the people to torture and crucify this innocent man. The Gospel writers spun their tales long after Joshua's crucifixion (somewhere between 33 and 36 C.E.), and after the Roman destruction of the Temple in 70 C.E., the murder of tens of thousands of Jews, and the dispersal of many more. The gospel writers took this stance because messianic Jews and Gentiles were now the targets of Roman oppression, and they did not wish to offend their rulers.

To compound this historical felony, Matthew has a Jewish mob screaming for Joshua's blood and yelling, "His blood be upon us and our children." This absurd claim has been a major source of hatred of the Jews for almost 2000 years. And by the way, there was no Roman custom of freeing a criminal at the festival.

The torture of Jesus (Joshua), prior to his crucifixion. John 19.1 et seq.: (RSV). Also, Luke 23.34 (RSV); "For give them for they know not…"The language here is a little different and I have placed it before the crucifixion, but during the scourging.

According to Matt. 27:3-8 (RSV), Judas died by hanging. Acts 1:18-19 (RSV), states that he died by falling and "bursting," which (strangely) seems to support the author's version. See Luke 13.1-5 for a parallel reference to the Tower of Siloam.

CHAPTERS 20-22

The crucifixion: John 19:17 et seq. (RSV); including Psalm 22 (RSV) with some variations and interludes. The Gospel version of the actual crucifixion is very brief.

The Gospels contain varying accounts of the "empty tomb" and subsequent events. Luke 24 contains an extended version, which differs from Mark 16 and Matthew 28, and John 20 and 21, and each differs from the other.

CHAPTERS 23-25

Joshua's teaching on the Temple and the future role of the Jews. In John 21: 25 (RSV), the author of the gospel states: "But there are also many other things which Jesus did; were every one of them to be written, I suppose that the world itself could not contain the books that would be written." This is one of the rare predictions made by this gospel writer which has the ring of truth.

SELECTED BIBLIOGRAPHY

My favorite resource for studying Jewish and Christian Scripture is The New Layman's Parallel Bible. Grand Rapids, Michigan: Zondervan: 1981. This volume contains the King James Version, New International Version, Living Bible, and Revised Standard Version of "The Old Testament" and The New Testament, set in parallel columns across two facing pages. There have been more recent updates of each of these versions, but none set up in this fashion, and the revisions, although significant, are not essential for this book. There are, of course, dozens (perhaps hundreds) of other translations, and I have studied a few of them, but have not found reason to cite them here.

There are also hundreds, probably thousands, of books, some fiction and others non-fiction (or claiming to be non-fiction) about Jesus (Joshua) of Nazareth. No doubt many of them have merit, but they are easily found through the mechanism of modern internet search engines, so I have only considered it useful to list those which have had some impact on my thinking. Below, I provide reference to Reza Aslan's book, *Zealot*, which offers a very extensive bibliography, although I do not agree with his version of the history of Jesus/Joshua. The books which most closely support my own views are Bart Ehrman's *How Jesus Became God*, and Hugh Schonfield's, *After the Cross,* both listed below, although I surely don't hold either of these gentlemen in any way responsible for my interpretation.

Achtemeier, Paul J. (Editor) *Harper's Bible Dictionary.*
    San Francisco: Harper & Row, 1985
Allegro, John M. *The Dead Sea Scrolls and the Christian Myth.*
    Buffalo: Prometheus Books, 1984
Alter, Robert, Kermode, Frank. *The Literary Guide to the Bible.*
    Cambridge: Harvard University, 1990
Armstrong, Karen. *A History of God, The 4,000 Year Quest of Judaism,*
    Christianity and Islam. New York: Knopf, 1993
Aslan, Reza. *Zealot, The Life and Times of Jesus of Nazareth.*
    New York: Random House, 2013

Bond, Helen. *The Historical Jesus: A guide for the Perplexed.*
London: T & T Clark, 2012

Borg, Marcus J. *Convictions: How I learned What Really Mattered.*
New York: HarperCollins, 2014

Bultmann, Rudolf. *Theology of the New Testament.*
New York: Scribner, 1955

Charlesworth, James H. (Editor) *The Old Testament Pseudepigrapha,
Volume 1 Apocalyptic Literature and. Testaments*
Garden City: Doubleday, 1983

Charlesworth, James H. (Editor) *The Old Testament Pseudepigrapha,
Volume 2 Expansions of the "Old Testament" and Legends, Wisdom
(etc.)*
Garden City: Doubleday, 1985

Cross, Frank Moore. *Caananite Myth and Hebrew Epic:
Essays in the History of Religion of Israel.*
Cambridge: Harvard University, 1997

Crossan, John Dominic. *The Cross that Spoke.*
San Francisco: Harper & Row, 1988

Crossan, John Dominic. *The Historical Jesus-
The Life of a Mediterranean Jewish Peasant.*
New York: Harper Collins, 1992

Edersheim, Alfred. *The Life and Times of Jesus the Messiah*
Grand Rapids: Eerdmans: 1984

Ehrman, Bart D. *How Jesus Became God:
The Exaltation of a Jewish Preacher from Galilee.*
New York: HarperOne, 2014

Fox, Robin Lane. *Christians and Pagans.* New York; Knopf, 1989

Fredriksen, Paula. *Jesus of Nazareth, King of the Jews.*
New York: Vintage, 2012

Goodman, Martin. *Rome and Jerusalem:
The Clash of Ancient Civilizations.*
New York: Vintage, 2008

Isbouts, Jean Pierre. *The Story of Christianity.*
Washington, D.C.: National Geographic, 2014

Isbouts, Jean-Pierre. *In the Footsteps of Jesus.*
Washington, D.C.: National Geographic, 2012

Isbouts, Jean-Pierre. *The Biblical World – An Illustrated Atlas.*
Washington, D.C.: National Geographic, 2007

Josephus. *The Jewish War*. Gaalya Cornfeld, General Editor;
    Benjamin Mazar, Paul L. Maier, Contributing Editors.
    Grand Rapids: Zondervan, 1982
Josephus, *The Complete Works of Flavius Josephus*. Translated by
    William Whiston. Grand Rapids: Kregel Publications, 1984
King, Karen L. *The Secret Revelation of John*.
    Cambridge: Harvard University Press, 2008
Levine, Amy-Jill and Brettler, Marc Zvi, Editors.
    The Jewish Annotated New Testament.
    New York: Oxford University, 2011
Mack, Burton L. *The Lost Gospel: The Book of Q and Christian Origins*.
    San Francisco: Harper SanFrancisco: 1993
Mansfield, Stephen. *Killing Jesus*. Brentwood, Tennessee:
    Worthy Publishing, 2013
Meier, John P. *A Marginal Jew: Rethinking the Historical Jesus,
    Companions and Competitors*.
    New York: Doubleday, 1991
O'Reilly, Bill, Dugard, Martin. *Killing Jesus*.
    New York: Henry Holt, 2013
Packer, J.I., Tennet, Merrill C., White, William, Jr. *The Bible Almanac*.
    Nashville: Nelson, 1980
Pagels, Elaine. *Beyond Belief--The Secret Gospel of Thomas*.
    New York: Random House, 2005
Pagels, Elaine. *Revelations, Visions, Prophecy and Politics in the Book
    of Revelations*.
    New York: Viking, 2012
Parini, Jay. *Jesus – The Human Face of God*.
    Boston: Houghton Mifflin Harcourt, 2013
Patterson, J.H., Wiseman, D.J., Bimson, J.J., Kane, J.P. *New Bible Atlas*.
    Leicester: Tyndale, 1985
Pelikan, Jarolslav. *Jesus Through the Centuries*:
    His Place in the History of Culture.
    New Haven: Yale University, 1985
Prophet, Elizabeth Clarke. *The Lost Years of Jesus*.
    Malibu: Summit, 1984
Ricci, Nino. *Testament*. Boston: Houghton-Mifflin, 2003
Sanders, E. P., *Jesus and Judaism*, London: SCM, 1985
Schonfield, Hugh. *The Passover Plot*. Worcester: Element Books, 1985

Schonfield, Hugh. *The Essene Odyssey*. Element Books, 1985

Schonfield, Hugh. *After the Cross*. San Diego: A.S. Barnes, 1981

Scholem, Gershom. The Messianic Idea in Judaism.
New York: Schoken Books, 1971

Shanks, Hershel (Editor), *Ancient Israel: From Abraham to the Roman Destruction of the Temple*.
Washington, D.C.: Bible Archeology Association, 2011

Stern, David H. *Jewish New Testament Commentary*.
Clarksville: Jewish New Testament, 1992

Taussig, Hal. *A New New Testament—A Bible for the 21st Century*.
Boston: Houghton Mifflin Harcourt, 2013

Tillich, Paul. *A History of Christian Thought*.
New York: Touchstone, 1968

Vermes, Geza. *Jesus the Jew: A[n] Historical Reading of the Gospels*.
London: Collins, 1975

Vermes, Geza. *The Dead Sea Scrolls, Qumran in Perspective*
Cleveland: Harper Collins/World, 1978

Wilkins, Michael J., et al. *Jesus Under Fire: Modern Scholarship Reinvents the Historical Jesus*.
Grand Rapids: Zondervan,1996

Wills, Garry. *What Jesus Means*. New York: Penguin, 2006

Wright, N.T. *How Jesus Became God: The Forgotten Story of the Gospels*.
New York: HarperOne, 2012

For the attributions of images in this book plus links to other images and websites, please see the website: http://themurderedmessiah.com

AUTHOR'S BIOGRAPHY

Len Lamensdorf is the award-winning author of 9 novels, 3 full-length plays and one successful feature film. His novels, published by Simon & Schuster, Delacorte and SeaScape Press in the United States and translated into other languages, have won Gold and Silver Benjamin Franklin Awards, three IPPY (Independent Publisher) awards and a ForeWord Magazine Book-of-the-Year. Len's young adult *Will to Conquer* trilogy won the Children's Choice Award from the prestigious Children's Book Council and the International Reading Association. Len's adult novel, *Gino, the Countess & Chagall,* was described by Publisher's Weekly as, "a glowing tribute to the world of art through the life of a talented and charming painter who personifies a zest for life." His historical novel, *The Ballad of Billy Lee – George Washington's FavoriteSlave*, was acclaimed by Pulitzer Prize-winning historians Ron Chernow and Joseph J. Ellis, who called it, "One of the most poignant untold stories in American history." It was a finalist for ForeWord Book of the Year, as was his thriller, *The Mexican Gardener.*

Len is an honors graduate of the University of Chicago and the U. of C. Law School (editor, Law Review) and completed his post-graduate work at Harvard Law. He also studied playwriting at UCLA with Kenneth Macgowan, founder of the Provincetown Players and the original producer of Eugene O'Neill.

In another incarnation, Len was the builder (design, construction, management) of several large mall shopping centers and office buildings.

Len is married, the father of two children and grandfather of six. He lives in Westlake Village, California.

His personal website is www.lenlamensdorf.com

38181930R00400

Made in the USA
San Bernardino, CA
01 September 2016